THE DEPTFORD TRILOGY

Praise for Robertson Davies:

'Davies's skill lies in drawing together powerful themes – religion, mythology, the role of the artist, human aspirations – with tremendously vivid characters and a prose style which is invariably accessible. He's also very funny . . . he has taken the epic doorstep-sized novel out of the airport book racks and given it back to decent writing' – *Observer*

'Robertson Davies is the sort of novelist readers can hardly wait to tell their friends about . . . a reader just sighs with pleasure as he turns the pages' – *Washington Post Book World*

'Undoubtedly Canada's cleverest novelist' – *Daily Telegraph*

'A master storyteller . . . The murkier areas of the soul are the author's forte . . . energy, historical sweep, humorous understanding of moral inconveniences, sympathy for the unfulfilled' – *Listener*

'I know of no writer of modern fiction who has brought such intelligence and wit to the description of a world in which religious belief, sanctity and the devil are real and customary elements' – *Literary Review*

Robertson Davies, novelist, playwright, literary critic and essayist, was born in 1913 in Thamesville, Ontario. He was educated at Queen's University and Balliol College, Oxford. Whilst at Oxford he became interested in the theatre and from 1938 until 1940 he was a teacher and actor at the Old Vic in London; and has subsequently written a number of plays. He returned to Canada in 1940, where he was literary editor of *Saturday Review*, an arts, politics and current affairs journal, until 1942, when he became editor and later publisher of the *Peterborough Examiner*. Several of his books, including *The Diary of Samuel Marchbanks* and *The Table Talk of Samuel Marchbanks*, had their origins in an editorial column. In 1962 he was appointed Professor of English at the University of Toronto, and in 1963 was appointed the first Master of the University's Massey College. He retired in 1981 but remains Master Emeritus and Professor Emeritus. He holds honorary doctorates from many Canadian universities and has received numerous awards for his work, including the Governor-General's Award for *The Manticore* in 1973. But it is as a writer of fiction that Robertson Davies has achieved international recognition with such novels as *Mixture of Frailties*, *Leaven of Malice* (winner of the Leacock Award for Humour) and *Tempest Tost*, published in Penguin as the *Salterton Trilogy*. His latest works include *One Half of Robertson Davies*, *The Enthusiasms of Robertson Davies*, *Robertson Davies: The Well-Tempered Critic*, *The Rebel Angels* (Penguin), *High Spirits* and *What's Bred in the Bone* (Penguin), which was shortlisted for the 1986 Booker Prize.

ROBERTSON DAVIES
THE DEPTFORD TRILOGY

——

FIFTH BUSINESS
THE MANTICORE
WORLD OF WONDERS

A KING PENGUIN
PUBLISHED BY PENGUIN BOOKS

PENGUIN BOOKS
Published by the Penguin Group
Viking Penguin Inc., 40 West 23rd Street,
New York, New York 10010, U.S.A.
Penguin Books Ltd, 27 Wrights Lane, London W8 5TZ, England
Penguin Books Australia Ltd, Ringwood, Victoria, Australia
Penguin Books Canada Ltd, 2801 John Street,
Markham, Ontario, Canada L3R 1B4
Penguin Books (N.Z.) Ltd, 182–190 Wairau Road,
Auckland 10, New Zealand

Penguin Books Ltd, Registered Offices:
Harmondsworth, Middlesex, England

Fifth Business first published in Canada by The Macmillan Company
of Canada Limited 1970
First published in the United States of America by The Viking Press 1970
Published in Penguin Books 1977
Copyright © Robertson Davies, 1970

The Manticore first published in the United States of America
by The Viking Press 1972
Published in Canada by The Macmillan Company of Canada Limited 1972
Published in Penguin Books 1976
Copyright © Robertson Davies, 1972

World of Wonders first published in Canada by The Macmillan Company
of Canada Limited 1975
First published in the United States of America by The Viking Press 1976
Published in Penguin Books 1977
Copyright © Robertson Davies, 1975

Published in one volume in King Penguin as *The Deptford Trilogy* 1983

13 15 17 19 20 18 16 14 12

Copyright © Robertson Davies, 1983
All rights reserved

ISBN 0 14 00.6500 8

Printed in the United States of America
Set in Bembo

Contents

FIFTH BUSINESS

Contents

Fifth Business . . . Definition

Those roles which, being neither those of Hero nor Heroine, Confidante nor Villain, but which were none-theless essential to bring about the Recognition or the dénouement, were called the Fifth Business in drama and opera companies organized according to the old style; the player who acted these parts was often referred to as Fifth Business.

– Tho. Overskou, *Den Danske Skueplads*

1

Mrs Dempster

I

MY lifelong involvement with Mrs Dempster began at 5.58 o'clock p.m. on 27 December 1908, at which time I was ten years and seven months old.

I am able to date the occasion with complete certainty because that afternoon I had been sledding with my lifelong friend and enemy Percy Boyd Staunton, and we had quarrelled, because his fine new Christmas sled would not go as fast as my old one. Snow was never heavy in our part of the world, but this Christmas it had been plentiful enough almost to cover the tallest spears of dried grass in the fields; in such snow his sled with its tall runners and foolish steering apparatus was clumsy and apt to stick, whereas my low-slung old affair would almost have slid on grass without snow.

The afternoon had been humiliating for him, and when Percy was humiliated he was vindictive. His parents were rich, his clothes were fine, and his mittens were of skin and came from a store in the city, whereas mine were knitted by my mother; it was manifestly wrong, therefore, that his splendid sled should not go faster than mine, and when such injustice showed itself Percy became cranky. He slighted my sled, scoffed at my mittens, and at last came right out and said that his father was better than my father. Instead of hitting him, which might have started a fight that could have ended in a draw or even a defeat for me, I said, all right, then, I would go home and he could have the field to himself. This was crafty of me, for I knew it was getting on for suppertime, and one of our home rules was that nobody, under any circumstances, was to be late for a meal. So I was keeping the home rule, while at the same time leaving Percy to himself.

As I walked back to the village he followed me, shouting fresh insults. When I walked, he taunted, I staggered like an old cow; my woollen cap was absurd beyond all belief; my backside was immense and wobbled when I walked; and more of the same sort, for his invention was not lively. I said nothing, because I knew that this spited him more than any retort, and that every time he shouted at me he lost face.

Our village was so small that you came on it at once; it lacked the dignity of outskirts. I darted up our street, putting on speed, for I had looked ostentatiously at my new Christmas dollar watch (Percy had a watch but was not let wear it because it was too good) and saw that it was 5.57; just time to get indoors, wash my hands in the noisy, splashy way my parents seemed to like, and be in my place at six, my head bent for grace. Percy was by this time hopping mad, and I knew I had spoiled his supper and probably his whole evening. Then the unforeseen took over.

Walking up the street ahead of me were the Reverend Amasa Dempster and his wife; he had her arm tucked in his and was leaning towards her in the protective way he had. I was familiar with this sight, for they always took a walk at this time, after dark and when most people were at supper, because Mrs Dempster was going to have a baby, and it was not the custom in our village for pregnant women to show themselves boldly in the streets – not if they had any position to keep up, and of course the Baptist minister's wife had a position. Percy had been throwing snowballs at me, from time to time, and I had ducked them all; I had a boy's sense of when a snowball was coming, and I knew Percy. I was sure that he would try to land one last, insulting snowball between my shoulders before I ducked into our house. I stepped briskly – not running, but not dawdling – in front of the Dempsters just as Percy threw, and the snowball hit Mrs Dempster on the back of the head. She gave a cry and, clinging to her husband, slipped to the ground; he might have caught her if he had not turned at once to see who had thrown the snowball.

I had meant to dart into our house, but I was unnerved by

hearing Mrs Dempster; I had never heard an adult cry in pain before and the sound was terrible to me. Falling, she burst into nervous tears, and suddenly there she was, on the ground, with her husband kneeling beside her, holding her in his arms and speaking to her in terms of endearment that were strange and embarrassing to me; I had never heard married people – or any people – speak unashamedly loving words before. I knew that I was watching a 'scene', and my parents had always warned against scenes as very serious breaches of propriety. I stood gaping, and then Mr Dempster became conscious of me.

'Dunny,' he said – I did not know he knew my name – 'lend us your sleigh to get my wife home.'

I was contrite and guilty, for I knew that the snowball had been meant for me, but the Dempsters did not seem to think of that. He lifted his wife on my sled, which was not hard because she was a small, girlish woman, and as I pulled it towards their house he walked beside it, very awkwardly bent over her, supporting her and uttering soft endearment and encouragement, for she went on crying, like a child.

Their house was not far away – just around the corner, really – but by the time I had been there, and seen Mr Dempster take his wife inside, and found myself unwanted outside, it was a few minutes after six, and I was late for supper. But I pelted home (pausing only for a moment at the scene of the accident), washed my hands, slipped into my place at table, and made my excuse, looking straight into my mother's sternly interrogative eyes. I gave my story a slight historical bias, leaning firmly but not absurdly on my own role as the Good Samaritan. I suppressed any information or guesswork about where the snowball had come from, and to my relief my mother did not pursue that aspect of it. She was much more interested in Mrs Dempster, and when supper was over and the dishes washed she told my father she thought she would just step over to the Dempsters' and see if there was anything she could do.

On the face of it this was a curious decision of my mother's, for of course we were Presbyterians, and Mrs Dempster was the wife of the Baptist parson. Not that there was any ill-will among the denominations in our village, but it was understood that each looked after its own, unless a situation got too big, when outside help might be called in. But my mother was, in a modest way, a specialist in matters relating to pregnancy and childbirth; Dr McCausland had once paid her the great compliment of saying that 'Mrs Ramsay had her head screwed on straight'; she was ready to put this levelness of head at the service of almost anybody who needed it. And she had a tenderness, never obviously displayed, for poor, silly Mrs Dempster, who was not twenty-one yet and utterly unfit to be a preacher's wife.

So off she went, and I read my Christmas annual of the *Boy's Own Paper*, and my father read something that looked hard and had small print, and my older brother Willie read *The Cruise of the 'Cachalot'*, all of us sitting round the base-burner with our feet on the nickel guard, till half-past eight, and then we boys were sent to bed. I have never been quick to go to sleep, and I lay awake until the clock downstairs struck half-past nine, and shortly after that I heard my mother return. There was a stovepipe in our house that came from the general living-room into the upstairs hall, and it was a fine conductor of sound. I crept out into the hall – Willie slept like a bear – put my ear as near to it as the heat permitted and heard my mother say:

'I've just come back for a few things. I'll probably be all night. Get me all the baby blankets out of the trunk, and then go right down to Ruckle's and make him get you a big roll of cotton wool from the store – the finest he has – and bring it to the Dempsters'. The doctor says if it isn't a big roll to get two.'

'You don't mean it's coming now?'

'Yes. Away early. Don't wait up for me.'

But of course he did wait up for her, and it was four in the morning when she came home, self-possessed and grim, as I could tell from her voice as I heard them talking before she returned to the Dempsters' – why, I did not know. And I lay awake too, feeling guilty and strange.

That was how Paul Dempster, whose reputation is doubtless familiar to you (though that was not the name under which he gained it), came to be born early on the morning of 28 December in 1908.

In making this report to you, my dear Headmaster, I have purposely begun with the birth of Paul Dempster, because this is the cause of so much that is to follow. But why, you will ask, am I writing to you at all? Why, after a professional association of so many years, during which I have been reticent about my personal affairs, am I impelled now to offer you such a statement as this?

It is because I was deeply offended by the idiotic piece that appeared in the *College Chronicle* in the issue of midsummer 1969. It is not merely its illiteracy of tone that disgusts me (though I think the quarterly publication of a famous Canadian school ought to do better), but its presentation to the public of a portrait of myself as a typical old schoolmaster doddering into retirement with tears in his eyes and a drop hanging from his nose. But it speaks for itself, and here it is, in all its inanity:

FAREWELL TO THE CORK

A feature of 'break-up' last June was the dinner given in honour of Dunstan ('Corky') Ramsay, who was retiring after forty-five years at the school, and Assistant Head and Senior History Master for the last twenty-two. More than 168 Old Boys, including several MPs and two Cabinet Ministers, were present, and our able dietician Mrs Pierce surpassed herself in providing a truly fine spread for the occasion. 'Corky' himself was in fine form despite his years and the coronary that laid him up following the death of his lifelong friend, the late Boy Staunton, D.S.O., C.B.E., known to us all as an Old Boy and Chairman of the Board of Governors of this school. He spoke of his long years as a teacher and friend to innumerable boys, many of whom now occupy positions of influence and prominence, in firm tones that many a younger man might envy.

'Corky's' career may serve both as an example and a warning to young masters for, as he said, he came to the school in 1924 intending to stay only a few years and now he has completed his forty-fifth. During that time he has taught history, as he sees it, to countless boys, many of whom have gone on to a more scientific study of the subject in the universities of Canada, the U.S., and the U.K. Four heads of history departments in Canadian universities, former pupils of 'Corky's', were head-table guests at the dinner, and one of them, Dr E. S. Warren of the University of Toronto, paid a generous, non-critical tribute to 'The Cork,' praising his unfailing enthusiasm and referring humorously to his explanations of the borderland between history and myth.

This last subject was again slyly hinted at in the gift presented to 'Corky' at the close of the evening, which was a fine tape recorder, by means of which it is hoped he may make available some of his reminiscences of an earlier and undoubtedly less complicated era of the school's history. Tapes recording the Headmaster's fine tribute to 'Corky' were included and also one of the School Choir singing what must be 'The Cork's' favourite hymn – never more appropriate than on this occasion! – 'For all the saints, Who from their labours rest.' And so the school says, 'Good-bye and good luck, Corky! You served the school well according to your lights in your day and generation! Well done, thou good and faithful servant!'

There you have it, Headmaster, as it came from the pen of that ineffable jackass Lorne Packer, M.A. and aspirant to a Ph.D. Need I anatomize my indignation? Does it not reduce me to what Packer unquestionably believes me to be – a senile, former worthy who has stumbled through forty-five years of teaching armed only with a shallow, *Boy's Book of Battles* concept of history, and a bee in his bonnet about myth – whatever the dullard Packer imagines myth to be?

I do not complain that no reference was made to my V.C.; enough was said about that at the school in the days when such decorations were thought to add to the prestige of a teacher. However, I think something might have been said about my ten books, of which at least one has circulated in six languages and has sold over three-quarters of a million copies, and another exerts a widening influence in the realm of mythic history about which Packer attempts to be jocose. The fact that I am the only Protestant contributor to *Analecta Bollandiana*, and have been so for thirty-six years, is ignored, though Hippolyte Delehaye himself thought well of my work and said so in print. But what most galls me is the patronizing, dismissive tone of the piece – as if I had never had a life outside the classroom, had never risen to the full stature of a man, had never rejoiced or sorrowed or known love or hate, had never, in short, been anything except what lies within the comprehension of the donkey

Packer, who has known me slightly for four years. Packer, who pushes me towards oblivion with tags of Biblical quotation, the gross impertinence of which he is unable to appreciate, religious illiterate that he is! Packer and his scientific view of history! Oh God! Packer, who cannot know and could not conceive that I have been cast by Fate and my own character for the vital though never glorious role of Fifth Business! Who could not, indeed, comprehend what Fifth Business is, even if he should meet the player of that part in his own trivial life-drama!

So, as I feel my strength returning in this house among the mountains – a house that itself holds the truths behind many illusions – I am driven to explain myself to you, Headmaster, because you stand at the top of that queer school world in which I seem to have cut such a meagre figure. But what a job it is!

Look at what I wrote at the beginning of this memoir. Have I caught anything at all of that extraordinary night when Paul Dempster was born? I am pretty sure that my little sketch of Percy Boyd Staunton is accurate, but what about myself? I have always sneered at autobiographies and memoirs in which the writer appears at the beginning as a charming, knowing little fellow, possessed of insights and perceptions beyond his years, yet offering these with a false naïveté to the reader, as though to say, 'What a little wonder I was, but All Boy.' Have the writers any notion or true recollection of what a boy is?

I have, and I have reinforced it by forty-five years of teaching boys. A boy is a man in miniature, and though he may sometimes exhibit notable virtue, as well as characteristics that seem to be charming because they are childlike, he is also schemer, self-seeker, traitor, Judas, crook, and villain – in short, a man. Oh, these autobiographies in which the writer postures and simpers as a David Copperfield or a Huck Finn! False, false as harlots' oaths!

Can I write truly of my boyhood? Or will that disgusting self-love which so often attaches itself to a man's idea of his youth creep in and falsify the story? I can but try. And to begin I must give you some notion of the village in which Percy Boyd Staunton and Paul Dempster and I were born.

3

Village life has been so extensively explored by movies and television during recent years that you may shrink from hearing more about it. I shall be as brief as I can, for it is not by piling up detail that I hope to achieve my picture, but by putting the emphasis where I think it belongs.

Once it was the fashion to represent villages as places inhabited by laughable, lovable simpletons, unspotted by the worldliness of city life, though occasionally shrewd in rural concerns. Later it was the popular thing to show villages as rotten with vice, and especially such sexual vice as Krafft-Ebing might have been surprised to uncover in Vienna; incest, sodomy, bestiality, sadism, and masochism were supposed to rage behind the lace curtains and in the haylofts, while a rigid piety was professed in the streets. Our village never seemed to me to be like that. It was more varied in what it offered to the observer than people from bigger and more sophisticated places generally think, and if it had sins and follies and roughnesses, it also had much to show of virtue, dignity, and even of nobility.

It was called Deptford and lay on the Thames River about fifteen miles east of Pittstown, our county town and nearest big place. We had an official population of about five hundred, and the surrounding farms probably brought the district up to eight hundred souls. We had five churches: the Anglican, poor but believed to have some mysterious social supremacy; the Presbyterian, solvent and thought – chiefly by itself – to be intellectual; the Methodist, insolvent and fervent; the Baptist, insolvent and saved; the Roman Catholic, mysterious to most of us but clearly solvent, as it was frequently and, so we thought, quite needlessly repainted. We supported one lawyer, who was also the magistrate, and one banker in a private bank, as such things still existed at that time. We had two doctors: Dr McCausland who was reputed to be clever, and Dr Staunton, who was Percy's father and who was also clever, but in the realm of real estate – he was a great holder of mortgages and owned several farms. We had a dentist, a wretch without manual skill, whose wife underfed him, and who had positively the dirtiest professional premises I have ever seen; and a veterinarian who drank but could rise to an occasion. We had a canning factory, which operated noisily and feverishly when there was anything to can; also a sawmill and a few shops.

The village was dominated by a family called Athelstan, who had done well out of lumber early in the nineteenth century; they owned Deptford's only three-storey house, which stood by itself on the way to the cemetery; most of our houses were of wood, and some of them stood on piles, for the Thames had a trick of flooding. One of the remaining Athelstans lived across the street from us, a poor demented old woman who used from time to time to escape from her nurse-housekeeper and rush into the road, where she threw herself down, raising a cloud of dust like a hen having a dirt-bath, shouting loudly, 'Christian men, come and help me!' It usually took the housekeeper and at least one other person to pacify her; my mother often assisted in this way, but I could not do so for the old lady disliked me – I seemed to remind her of some false friend in the past. But I was interested in her madness and longed to talk with her, so I always rushed to the rescue when she made one of her breaks for liberty.

My family enjoyed a position of modest privilege, for my father was the owner and editor of the local weekly paper, *The Deptford Banner*. It was not a very prosperous enterprise, but with the job-printing plant it sustained us and we never wanted for anything. My father, as I learned later, never did a gross business of $5000 in any year that he owned it. He was not only publisher and editor, but chief mechanic and printer as well, helped by a melancholy youth called Jumper Saul and a girl called Nell Bullock. It was a good little paper, respected and hated as a proper local paper should be; the editorial comment, which my father composed directly on the typesetting machine, was read carefully every week. So we were, in a sense, the literary leaders of the community and my father had a seat on the Library Board along with the magistrate.

Our household, then, was representative of the better sort of life in the village, and we thought well of ourselves Some of this good opinion arose from being Scots; my father had come from Dumfries as a young man, but my mother's family had been three generations in Canada without having become a whit less Scots than when her grandparents left Inverness. The Scots, I believed until I was aged at least twenty-five, were the salt of the earth, for although this was never said in our household it was one of those accepted truths which do not need to be laboured. By far the majority of the Deptford people had come to Western Ontario from the south of England, so we were not surprised that they looked to us, the Ramsays, for common sense, prudence, and right opinions on virtually everything.

Cleanliness, for example. My mother was clean – oh, but she was clean! Our privy set the sanitary tone of the village. We depended on wells in Deptford, and water for all purposes was heated in a tank called a 'cistern' on the side of the kitchen range. Every house had a privy, and these ranked from dilapidated, noisome shacks to some quite smart edifices, of which our own was clearly among the best. There has been much hilarity about privies in the years since they became rarities, but they were not funny buildings, and if they were not to become disgraceful they needed a lot of care.

As well as this temple of hygiene we had a 'chemical closet' in the house, for use when someone was unwell; it was so capricious and smelly, however, that it merely added a new misery to illness and was rarely set going.

That is all that seems necessary to say about Deptford at present; any necessary additional matter will present itself as part of my narrative. We were serious people, missing nothing in our community and feeling ourselves in no way inferior to larger places. We did, however, look with pitying amusement on Bowles Corners, four miles distant and with a population of one hundred and fifty. To live in Bowles Corners, we felt, was to be rustic beyond redemption.

4

The first six months of Paul Dempster's life were perhaps the most exciting and pleasurable period of my mother's life, and unquestionably the most miserable of mine. Premature babies had a much poorer chance of surviving in 1908 than they have now, but Paul was the first challenge of this sort in my mother's experience of childbirth, and she met it with all her determination and ingenuity. She was not, I must make clear, in any sense a midwife or a trained person – simply a woman of good sense and kindness of heart who enjoyed the authority of nursing and the mystery which at that time still hung about the peculiarly feminine functions. She spent a great part of each day and not a few nights at the Dempsters' during that six months; other women helped when they could, but my mother was the acknowledged high priestess, and Dr McCausland was good enough to say that without her he could never have pulled little Paul safely up onto the shores of this world.

I learned all the gynaecological and obstetrical details as they were imparted piecemeal to my father; the difference was that he sat comfortably beside the living-room stove, opposite my mother, while I stood barefoot and in my nightshirt beside the stovepipe upstairs, guilt-ridden and sometimes nauseated as I heard things that were new and terrible to my ears.

Paul was premature by some eighty days, as well as Dr McCausland could determine. The shock of being struck by the snowball had brought Mrs Dempster to a series of hysterical crying fits, with which her husband was clumsily trying to cope when my mother arrived on the scene. Not long afterward it had become clear that she was about to bear her child, and Dr McCausland was sent for, but as he was elsewhere making a call he did not arrive until a quarter of an hour before the birth. Because the child was so small it came quickly, as the time for first children goes, and looked so wretched that the doctor and my mother were frightened, though they did not admit it to one another until some weeks afterward. It was characteristic of the time and the place that nobody thought to

23

weigh the child, though the Reverend Amasa Dempster christened it immediately, after a brief wrangle with Dr McCausland. This was by no means in accord with the belief of his faith, but he was not himself and may have been acting in response to promptings stronger than seminary training. My mother said Dempster wanted to dip the child in water, but Dr McCausland brusquely forbade it, and the distracted father had to be content with sprinkling. During the ceremony my mother held the child – now named Paul, as it was the first name that came into Dempster's head – as near the stove as she could, in the hottest towels she could provide. But Paul must have weighed something in the neighbourhood of three pounds, for that was what he still weighed ten weeks later, having gained little, so far as the eye could judge, in all that time.

My mother was not one to dwell on unsightly or macabre things, but she spoke of Paul's ugliness to my father with what was almost fascination. He was red, of course; all babies are red. But he was wrinkled like a tiny old man, and his head and his back and much of his face was covered with weedy long black hair. His proportions were a shock to my mother, for his limbs were tiny and he seemed to be all head and belly. His fingers and toes were almost without nails. His cry was like the mewing of a sick kitten. But he was alive, and something had to be done about him quickly.

Dr McCausland had never met with a baby so dismayingly premature as this, but he had read of such things, and while my mother held Paul as near the fire as was safe, he and the badly shaken father set to work to build a nest that would be as much as possible like what the infant was used to. It underwent several changes, but in the end it was an affair of jeweller's cotton and hot-water bottles – assisted at the beginning by a few hot bricks – with a tent over it into which the steam from a kettle was directed; the kettle had to be watched carefully so that it might neither boil dry nor yet boil the baby. The doctor did not know what to do about feeding the child, but he and my mother worked out a combination of a glass fountain-pen filler and a scrap of soft cotton wool, through which they pumped diluted, sweetened milk into Paul, and Paul feebly pumped it right back out again. It was not for two days that he kept any perceptible portion of the food, but his vomiting gained a very little in strength; it was then that my mother decided that he was a fighter and determined to fight with him.

Immediately after the birth the doctor and my mother were busy with the baby. Mrs Dempster was left to the care of her husband, and he did the best he knew how for her, which was to kneel and pray out loud by her bedside. Poor Amasa Dempster was the most serious of men, and his background and training had not provided him with tact; he besought God, if He must take the soul of Mary Dempster to Him, to do so with gentleness and mercy. He reminded God that little Paul had been baptized, and that therefore the soul of the infant was secure and would be best able to journey to Heaven in the company of its mother. He laboured these themes with as much eloquence as he could summon, until Dr McCausland was compelled to read the Riot Act to him, in such terms as a tight-lipped Presbyterian uses when reading the Riot Act to an emotional Baptist. This term – 'reading the Riot Act' – was my mother's; she had thoroughly approved of the doctor's performance, for she had the real Scots satisfaction in hearing somebody justifiably scolded and set to rights. 'Carrying on like that, right over the girl's bed, while she was fighting for her life, she said to my father, and I could imagine the sharp shake of the head that accompanied her speech.

I wonder now if Mrs Dempster was really fighting for her life; subsequent circumstances proved that she was stronger than anybody knew. But it was an accepted belief at that time that no woman bore a child without walking very close to the brink of death, and, for anything I know to the contrary, it may have been true at that stage of medical science. But certainly it must have seemed to poor Dempster that his wife was dying. He had hung about all through the birth; he had seen his hideous, misshapen child; he had been pushed about and bustled by the doctor and the good neighbour. He was a parson, of course, but at root he was a frightened farmer lad, and if he lost his head I cannot now blame him. He was one of those people who seem fated to be hurt and thrown aside in life, but doubtless as he knelt by Mary's bed he thought himself as important an actor in the drama as any of the others. This is one of the cruelties of the theatre of life; we all think of ourselves as stars and rarely recognize it when we are indeed mere supporting characters or even supernumeraries.

What the following months cost in disorganization of our household you can imagine. My father never complained of it, for he was devoted to my mother, considered her to be a wonderful woman, and would not have done anything to prevent her from manifesting her wonderfulness. We ate many a scratch meal so that little Paul might not miss his chance with the fountain-pen filler, and when the great day came at last when the infant retained a perceptible part of what it was given, I think my father was even more pleased than my mother.

The weeks passed, and Paul's wrinkled skin became less transparent and angry, his wide-set eyes opened and roamed about, unseeing but certainly not blind, and he kicked his feet just a little, like a real baby. Would he ever be strong? Dr McCausland could not say; he was the epitome of Scots caution. But my mother's lionlike spirit was already determined that Paul should have his chance.

It was during these weeks that I endured agony of mind that seems to me, looking back over more than sixty years, to have been extraordinary. I have had hard times since then, and have endured them with all the capability for suffering of a grown man, so I do not want to make foolish and sentimental claims for the suffering of a child. But even now I hesitate to recall some of the nights when I feared to go to sleep and prayed till I sweated that God would forgive me for my mountainous crime.

I was perfectly sure, you see, that the birth of Paul Dempster, so small, so feeble and troublesome, was my fault. If I had not been so clever, so sly, so spiteful in hopping in front of the Dempsters just as Percy Boyd Staunton threw that snowball at me from behind, Mrs Dempster would not have been struck. Did I never think that Percy was guilty? Indeed I did. But a psychological difficulty arose here. When next I met him, after that bad afternoon, we approached each other warily, as boys do after a quarrel, and he seemed disposed to talk. I did not at once speak of the birth of Paul, but I crept up on the subject

and was astonished to hear him say, 'Yes, my Pa says McCausland has his hands full with that one.'

'The baby came too soon,' said I, testing him.

'Did it?' said he, looking me straight in the eyes.

'And you know why,' I said.

'No I don't.'

'Yes you do. You threw that snowball.'

'I threw a snowball at you,' he replied, 'and I guess it gave
you a good smack.'

I could tell by the frank boldness of his tone that he was
lying. 'Do you mean to say that's what you think?' I said.

'You bet it's what I think,' said he. 'And it's what you'd
better think too, if you know what's good for you.'

We looked into each other's eyes and I knew that he was
afraid, and I knew also that he would fight, lie, do anything
rather than admit what I knew. And I didn't know what in
the world I could do about it.

So I was alone with my guilt, and it tortured me. I was a
Presbyterian child and I knew a good deal about damnation.
We had a Dante's *Inferno* among my father's books, with the
illustrations by Doré, such books were common in rural districts at that time, and probably none of us was really aware
that Dante was an R.C.; it had once been a shivery pleasure to
look at those pictures. Now I knew that they showed the reality of my situation, and what lay beyond this life for such a boy
as I. I was of the damned. Such a phrase seems to mean nothing to people nowadays, but to me it was utterly real. I pined
and wasted to some extent, and my mother was not so taken up
with the Dempsters that she failed to dose me regularly with
cod-liver oil. But though I did not really suffer much physically I suffered greatly in my mind, for a reason connected
with my time of life. I was just upon eleven, and I matured
early, so that some of the earliest changes of puberty were beginning in me.

How healthy-minded children seem to be nowadays! Or, is it
just the cant of our time to believe so? I cannot tell. But certainly in my childhood the common attitude towards matters of
sex was enough to make a hell of adolescence for any boy who
was, like myself, deeply serious and mistrustful of whatever

seemed pleasurable in life. So here I was, subject not only to the smutty, whispering speculations of the other boys I knew, and tormented by the suspicion that my parents were somehow involved in this hog-wallow of sex that had begun to bulk so large in my thoughts, but I was directly responsible for a grossly sexual act – the birth of a child. And what a child! Hideous, stricken, a caricature of a living creature! In the hot craziness of my thinking, I began to believe that I was more responsible for the birth of Paul Dempster than were his parents, and that if this were ever discovered some dreadful fate would overtake me. Part of the dreadful fate would undoubtedly be rejection by my mother. I could not bear the thought, but neither could I let it alone.

My troubles became no less when, at least four months after Paul's birth, I heard this coming up the stovepipe – cooler now, for spring was well advanced:

'I think little Paul is going to pull through. He'll be slow, the doctor says, but he'll be all right.'

'You must be pleased. It's mostly your doing.'

'Oh no! I only did what I could. But the doctor says he hopes somebody will keep an eye on Paul. His mother certainly can't.'

'She isn't coming around?'

'Doesn't appear so. It was a terrible shock for the poor little thing. And Amasa Dempster just won't believe that there's a time to talk about God and a time to trust God and keep your mouth shut. Luckily she doesn't seem to understand a lot of what he says.'

'Do you mean she's gone simple?'

'She's as quiet and friendly and sweet-natured as she ever was, poor little soul, but she just isn't all there. That snowball certainly did a terrible thing to her. Who do you suppose threw it?'

'Dempster couldn't see. I don't suppose anybody will ever know.'

'I've wondered more than once if Dunstable knows more about that than he's letting on.'

'Oh no, he knows how serious it is. If he knew anything he'd have spoken up by now.'

28

'Whoever it was, the Devil guided his hand.'

Yes, and the Devil shifted his mark. Mrs Dempster had gone simple! I crept to bed wondering if I would live through the night, and at the same time desperately afraid to die.

5

Ah, if dying were all there was to it! Hell and torment at once; but at least you know where you stand. It is living with these guilty secrets that exacts the price. Yet the more time that passed, the less I was able to accuse Percy Boyd Staunton of having thrown the snowball that sent Mrs Dempster simple. His brazen-faced refusal to accept responsibility seemed to deepen my own guilt, which had now become the guilt of concealment as well as action. However, as time passed, Mrs Dempster's simplicity did not seem to be as terrible as I had at first feared.

My mother, with her unfailing good sense, hit the nail on the head when she said that Mrs Dempster was really no different from what she had been before, except that she was more so. When Amasa Dempster had brought his little bride to our village the spring before the Christmas of Paul's untimely birth, the opinion had been strong among the women that nothing would ever make a preacher's wife out of that one.

I have already said that while our village contained much of what humanity has to show, it did not contain everything, and one of the things it conspicuously lacked was an aesthetic sense; we were all too much the descendants of hard-bitten pioneers to wish for or encourage any such thing, and we gave hard names to qualities that, in a more sophisticated society, might have had value. Mrs Dempster was not pretty – we understood prettiness and guardedly admitted it as a pleasant, if needless, thing in a woman – but she had a gentleness of expression and a delicacy of colour that was uncommon. My mother, who had strong features and stood for no nonsense from her hair, said that Mrs Dempster had a face like a pan of milk. Mrs Dempster was small and slight, and even the clothes approved for a preacher's wife did not conceal the fact that she had a girlish figure and a light step. When she was pregnant there was a bloom about her that seemed out of keeping with the seriousness of her state; it was not at all the proper thing for a pregnant woman to smile so much, and the least she could have done was to take a stronger line with those waving tendrils of hair that seemed so often to be escaping from a properly severe arrangement. She was a nice little thing, but was that soft voice ever going to dominate a difficult meeting of the Ladies' Aid? And why did she laugh so much when nobody else could see anything to laugh at?

Amasa Dempster, who had always seemed a level-headed man, for a preacher, was plain silly about his wife. His eyes were always on her, and he could be seen drawing pails of water from their outside well, for the washing, when this was fully understood to be woman's work, right up to the last month or so of a pregnancy. The way he looked at her would make you wonder if the man was soft in the head. You would think they were still courting, instead of being expected to get down to the Lord's work and earn his $550 *per annum*; this was what the Baptists paid their preacher, as well as allowing him a house, not quite enough fuel, and a ten-per-cent discount on everything bought in a Baptist-owned store – and a few other stores that 'honoured the cloth,' as the saying went. (Of course he was expected to give back an exact tenth of it to the church, to set an example.) The hope was widely expressed that Mr Dempster was not going to make a fool of his wife.

In our village hard talk was not always accompanied by hard action. My mother, who could certainly never have been accused of softness with her family or the world, went out of her way to help Mrs Dempster – I will not say, to befriend her, because friendship between such unequal characters could never have been; but she tried to 'show her the ropes,' and whatever these mysterious feminine ropes were, they certainly included many good things that my mother cooked and just happened to leave when she dropped in on the young bride, and not merely the loan, but the practical demonstration of such devices as carpet-stretchers, racks for drying lace curtains, and the art of shining windows with newspaper.

Why had Mrs Dempster's mother never prepared her for these aspects of marriage? It came out she had been brought up by an aunt, who had money and kept a hired girl, and how were you to forge a preacher's wife from such weak metal as that? When my father teased my mother about the amount of food she took the Dempsters, she became huffy and asked if she was to allow them to starve under her nose while that girl was learning the ropes? But the girl was slow, and my mother's answer to that was that in her condition she couldn't be expected to be quick.

Now it did not seem that she would ever learn the craft of housekeeping. Her recovery from Paul's birth was tardy, and while she grew strong again her husband looked after the domestic affairs, helped by neighbour women and a Baptist widow for whose occasional services he was able to eke out a very little money. As spring came Mrs Dempster was perfectly able-bodied but showed no signs of getting down to work. She did a little cleaning and some inept cooking, and laughed like a girl at her failures. She hovered over the baby, and as he changed from a raw monster to a small but recognizably Christian-looking infant she was as delighted as a little girl with a doll. She now breast-fed him – my mother and all the neighbours had to admit that she did it well – but she lacked the solemnity they expected of a nursing mother; she enjoyed the process, and sometimes when they went into the house there she was, with everything showing, even though her husband was present, just as if she hadn't the sense to pull up her clothes. I happened upon her once or twice in this condition and gaped with the greedy eyes of an adolescent boy, but she did not seem to notice. And thus the opinion grew that Mrs Dempster was simple.

There was only one thing to be done, and that was to help the Dempsters as much as possible, without approving or encouraging any tendencies that might run contrary to the right way of doing things. My mother ordered me over to the Dempsters' to chop and pile wood, sweep away snow, cut the grass, weed the vegetable patch, and generally make myself handy two or three times a week and on Saturdays if necessary. I was also to keep an eye on the baby, for my mother could not rid herself of a dread that Mrs Dempster would allow it to choke or fall out of

31

its basket or otherwise come to grief. There was no chance of such a thing happening, as I soon found, but obeying my instructions brought me much into the company of Mrs Dempster, who laughed at my concern for the baby. She did not seem to think that it could come to any harm in her keeping, and I know now that she was right, and that my watchfulness must have been intrusive and clumsy.

Caring for a baby is one thing, and the many obligations of a parson's wife are another, and for this work Mrs Dempster showed no aptitude at all. By the time a year had passed since Paul's birth her husband had become 'poor Reverend Dempster' to everybody, a man burdened with a simple-minded wife and a delicate child, and it was a general source of amazement that he could make ends meet. Certainly a man with $550 a year needed a thrifty wife, and Mrs Dempster gave away everything. There was a showdown once when she gave an ornamental vase to a woman who had taken her a few bakings of bread; the vase was part of the furnishings of the parsonage, not the personal property of the Dempsters, and the ladies of the church were up in arms at this act of feckless generosity and demanded of Amasa Dempster that he send his wife to the neighbour's house to ask for the vase back, and if this meant eating crow she would have to eat crow. But he would not humiliate his wife and went on the distasteful errand himself, which everybody agreed was weakness in him and would lead to worse things. One of my jobs, under instruction from my mother, was to watch for chalk marks on the Dempsters' verandah posts, and rub them out when I saw them; these chalk marks were put there by tramps as signals to one another that the house was good for a generous handout, and perhaps even money.

After a year or so most of the women in our village grew tired of pitying the Baptist parson and his wife and began to think that he was as simple as she. Like many ostracized people, they became more marked in their oddity. But my mother never wavered; her compassion was not of the short-term variety. Consequently, as they became, in a sense, charges of my family, my jobs for the Dempsters grew. My brother Willie did very little about them. He was two years older than I and his school-work was more demanding; further, after school hours he now went to the *Banner* printing plant to make himself useful and pick up the trade. But my mother was as watchful as ever, and my father, in whose eyes she could do nothing wrong, approved completely of all that was done.

6

Being unofficial watchdog to the Dempster family was often a nuisance to me and did nothing for my popularity. But at this time I was growing rapidly and was strong for my age, so not many of the people with whom I went to school liked to say too much to my face; but I knew that they said enough behind my back. Percy Boyd Staunton was one of these.

He had a special place in our school world. There are people who, even as boys, assume superior airs and are taken as grandees by those around them. He was as big as I, and rather fleshy; without being a fat boy he was plump. His clothes were better than ours, and he had an interesting pocket-knife, with a chain on it to fasten to his knickerbockers, and an ink-bottle you could knock over without spilling a drop; on Sundays he wore a suit with a fashionable half-belt at the back. He had once been to Toronto to the Exhibition, and altogether breathed a larger air than the rest of us.

He and I were rivals, for though I had none of his graces of person or wealth I had a sharp tongue. I was raw-boned and wore clothes that had often made an earlier appearance on Willie, but I had a turn for sarcastic remarks, which were known to our group as 'good ones.' If I was pushed too far I might 'get off a good one,' and as our community had a long memory such dour witticisms would be remembered and quoted for years.

I had a good one all ready for Percy, if ever he gave me any trouble. I had heard his mother tell my mother that when he was a dear little fellow, just learning to talk, his best version of his name, Percy Boyd, was Pidgy Boy-Boy, and she still called him that in moments of unbuttoned affection. I knew that I had but once to call him Pidgy Boy-Boy in the schoolyard and his goose would be cooked; probably suicide would be his only way out. This knowledge gave me a sense of power in reserve.

I needed it. Some of the oddity and loneliness of the Dempsters was beginning to rub off on me. Having double chores to do kept me out of many a game I would have liked to join; dodging back and forth between their house and ours with this, that, and the other thing, I was sure to meet some of my friends; Mrs Dempster often stood in the door when I was running home, waving and thanking me in a voice that seemed to me eerie and likely to bring mockery down on my head, not hers, if anybody overheard her, as they often did. I knew that some of them had nicknamed me Nursie. They did not call me that to my face, however.

My position here was worst of all. I wanted to be on good terms with the girls I knew; I suppose I wanted them to admire me and think me wonderful in some unspecified way. Enough of them were silly about Percy and sent him mash Valentines on February 14, without any names on them but with handwriting that betrayed the sender. No girl ever sent me a Valentine except Elsie Webb, known to us all as Spider Webb because of her gawky, straddling walk. I did not want Spider Webb, I wanted Leola Cruikshank, who had cork-screw curls and a great way of never meeting your eyes. But my feeling about Leola was put askew by my feeling about Mrs Dempster. Leola I wanted as a trophy of success, but Mrs Dempster was beginning to fill my whole life, and the stranger her conduct became, and the more the village pitied and dismissed her, the worse my obsession grew.

I thought I was in love with Leola, by which I meant that if I could have found her in a quiet corner, and if I had been certain that no one would ever find out, and if I could have summoned up the courage at the right moment, I would have kissed her. But, looking back on it now, I know I was in love with Mrs Dempster. Not as some boys are in love with grown-up women, adoring them from afar and enjoying a fantasy life in which the older woman figures in an idealized form, but in a painful and immediate fashion; I saw her every day, I did menial tasks in her house, and I was charged to watch her and keep her from doing foolish things. Furthermore, I felt myself tied to her by the certainty that I was responsible for her straying wits, the disorder of her marriage, and the frail body of the child who was her great delight in life. I had made her what she was, and in such circumstances I must hate her or love her. In a mode that was far too demanding for my age or experience, I loved her.

Loving her, I had to defend her, and when people said she was crazy I had to force myself to tell them that they were crazy themselves and I would knock their blocks off if they said it again. Fortunately one of the first people with whom I had such an encounter was Milo Papple, and he was not hard to deal with.

Milo was our school buffoon, the son of Myron Papple, the village barber. Barbers in more sophisticated communities are sometimes men with rich heads of hair, or men who have given a special elegance to a bald head, but Myron Papple had no such outward grace. He was a short, fat, pear-shaped man with the complexion and hair of a pig of the Chester White breed. He had but one distinction; he put five sticks of gum into his mouth every morning and chewed the wad until he closed his shop in the evening, breathing peppermint on each customer as he shaved, clipped, and talked.

Milo was his father in miniature, and admitted by us all to be a card. His repertoire of jokes was small but of timeless durability. He could belch at will, and did. He could also break wind at will, with a prolonged, whining note of complaint, and when he did so in class and then looked around with an angry face, whispering, 'Who done that?' our mirth was Chaucerian, and the teacher was reduced to making a refined face, as if she were too good for a world in which such things were possible. Even the girls – even Leola Cruikshank – thought Milo was a card.

One day I was asked if I would play ball after school. I said I had to do some work.

'Sure,' said Milo, 'Dunny's got to get right over to the bughouse and cut the grass.'

'The bughouse?' asked a few who were slow of wit.

'Yep. The Dempsters'. That's the bughouse now.'

It was now or never for me. 'Milo,' I said 'if you ever say that again I'll get a great big cork and stick it up you, and then nobody'll ever laugh at you again.' As I said this I walked menacingly towards him, and as soon as Milo backed away I knew I was the victor, for the moment. The joke about Milo

35

and the cork was frugally husbanded by our collectors of funny sayings, and he was not allowed to forget it. 'If you stuck a cork in Milo nobody would ever laugh at him again,' these unashamed gleaners of the fields of repartee would say and shout with laughter. Nobody said 'bughouse' to me for a long time, but sometimes I could see that they wanted to say it, and I knew they said it behind my back. This increased my sense of isolation – of being forced out of the world I belonged to into the strange and unchancy world of the Dempsters.

7

The passing of time brought other isolations. At thirteen I should have been learning the printing business; my father was neat-handed and swift, and Willie was following in his steps. But I was all thumbs in the shop, slow to learn the layout of the frames in which the fonts of type were distributed, clumsy at locking up a forme, messy with ink, a great spoiler of paper, and really not much good at anything but cutting reglet or reading proof, which my father never trusted to anyone but himself in any case. I never mastered the printer's trick of reading things upside down and backward, and I never properly learned how to fold a sheet. Altogether I was a nuisance in the shop, and as this humiliated me, and my father was a kindly man, he sought some other honourable work to keep me from under his feet. It had been suggested that our village library should be open a few afternoons a week so that the more responsible schoolchildren might use it, and somebody was needed to serve as under-librarian, the real librarian being busy as a teacher during the daytime and not relishing the loss of so much of her free time. I was appointed to this job, at a salary of nothing at all, the honour being deemed sufficient reward.

This suited me admirably. Three afternoons a week I opened our one-room library in the upstairs of the Town Hall and lorded it over any schoolchildren who appeared. Once I had the dizzy pleasure of finding something in the encyclopaedia for Leola Cruikshank, who had to write an essay about the equator and didn't know whether it went over the top or round the middle.

More afternoons than not, nobody appeared, or else those who came went away as soon as they found what they wanted, and I had the library to myself.

It was not much of a collection – perhaps fifteen hundred books in all, of which roughly a tenth part were for children. The annual budget was twenty-five dollars, and much of that went on subscriptions to magazines that the magistrate, who was chairman of the board, wanted to read. Acquisitions, therefore, were usually gifts from the estates of people who had died, and our local auctioneer gave us any books that he could not sell; we kept what we wanted and sent the rest to the Grenfell Mission, on the principle that savages would read anything.

The consequence was that we had some odd things, of which the oddest were kept in a locked closet off the main room. There was a medical book, with a frightful engraving of a fallen womb, and another of a varicocele, and a portrait of a man with lavish hair and whiskers but no nose, which made me a lifelong enemy of syphilis. My special treasures were *The Secrets of Stage Conjuring* by Robert-Houdin and *Modern Magic* and *Later Magic* by Professor Hoffmann; they had been banished as uninteresting – uninteresting! – and as soon as I saw them I knew that fate meant them for me. By studying them I should become a conjurer, astonish everybody, win the breathless admiration of Leola Cruikshank, and become a great power. I immediately hid them in a place where they could not fall into the hands of unworthy persons, including our librarian, and devoted myself to the study of magic.

I still look back upon those hours when I acquainted myself with the means by which a French conjurer had astonished the subjects of Louis-Napoleon as an era of Arcadian pleasure. It did not matter that everything about the book was hopelessly old-fashioned; great as the gap between me and Robert-Houdin was, I could accept his world as the real world, so far as the wonderful art of deception was concerned. When he insisted on the necessity of things that were unknown to Deptford, I assumed that it was because Deptford was a village and Paris was a great and sophisticated capital, where everybody who was anybody was mad for conjuring and wanted nothing more than to be delightfully bamboozled by an elegant, slightly sinister, but wholly charming master of the art. It did not surprise me in the least that Robert-Houdin's Emperor had sent him on a special diplomatic mission to Algiers, to destroy the power of the marabouts by showing that his magic was greater than theirs. When I read of his feat on the Shah of Turkey's yacht, when he hammered the Shah's jewelled watch to ruins in a mortar, then threw the rubbish overboard, cast a line into the sea, pulled up a fish, asked the Shah's chef to clean it, and stood by while the chef discovered the watch, quite unharmed, enclosed in a silk bag in the entrails of the fish, I felt that this was life as it ought to be lived. Conjurers were obviously fellows of the first importance and kept distinguished company. I would be one of them.

The Scottish practicality that I had imitated from my parents was not really in grain with me; I cared too little for difficulties. I admitted to myself that Deptford was unlikely to yield a conjurer's table – a gilded *guéridon*, with a cunning *servante* on the back of it for storing things one did not wish to have seen, and a *gibecière* into which coins and watches could noiselessly be dropped; I had no tailcoat, and if I had I doubt if my mother would have sewn a proper conjurer's *profonde* in the tails, for disappearing things. When Professor Hoffmann instructed me to fold back my cuffs, I knew that I had no cuffs, but did not care. I would devote myself to illusions that did not require such things. These illusions, I discovered, called for special apparatus, always described by the Professor as 'simple', which the conjurer was advised to make himself. For me, a boy who always tied his shoelaces backward and whose Sunday tie looked like a hangman's noose, such apparatus presented a problem that I had to admit, after a few tries, was insuperable. Nor could I do anything about the tricks that required 'a few substances, easily obtainable from any chemist,' because Ruckle's drugstore had never heard of any of them. But I was not defeated. I would excel in the realm which Robert-Houdin said was the truest, most classical form of conjuring: I would be a master of sleight-of-hand, a matchless *prestidigitateur*.

It was like me to begin with eggs – or, to be precise, one egg. It never occurred to me that a clay egg, of the kind used to deceive hens, would do just as well. I hooked an egg from my mother's kitchen and when the library was empty began to practise producing it from my mouth, elbow, and back of the knee; also putting it into my right ear and, after a little henlike clucking, removing it from my left. I seemed to be getting on splendidly, and when the magistrate made a sudden appearance to get the latest *Scribner's* I had a mad moment when I thought of amazing him by taking an egg out of his beard. Of course I did not dare to go so far, but the delightful thought that I could if I wanted to put me into such a fit of giggles that he looked at me speculatively. When he was gone I handled the egg with greater boldness until, disappearing it into my hip pocket, I put my thumb through it.

Ha ha. Every boy has experiences of this kind, and they are usually thought to be funny and childlike. But that egg led to a dreadful row with my mother. She had missed the egg – it never occurred to me that anybody counted eggs – and accused me of taking it. I lied. Then she caught me trying to wash out my pocket, because, in a house with no running water, washing cannot be a really private business. She exposed my lie and demanded to know what I wanted with an egg. Now, how can a boy of thirteen tell a Scotswoman widely admired for her practicality that he intends to become the world's foremost *prestidigitateur?* I took refuge in mute insolence. She stormed. She demanded to know if I thought she was made of eggs. Visited unhappily by a good one, I said that that was something she would have to decide for herself. My mother had little sense of humour. She told me that if I thought I had grown too old to be beaten she would show me I was mistaken, and from the kitchen cupboard she produced the pony whip.

It was not for ponies. In my boyhood such pretty little whips were sold at country fairs, where children bought them, and flourished them, and occasionally beat trees with them. But a few years earlier my mother had impounded such a whip that Willie had brought home, and it had been used for beatings ever since. It had been at least two years since I had had a beating, but now my mother flourished the whip, and when I laughed she struck me over the left shoulder with it.

'Don't you dare touch me,' I shouted, and that put her into such a fury as I had never known. It must have been a strange scene, for she pursued me around the kitchen, slashing me with the whip until she broke me down and I cried. She cried too, hysterically, and beat me harder, storming about my impudence, my want of respect for her, of my increasing oddity and intellectual arrogance – not that she used these words, but I do not intend to put down what she actually said – until at last her fury was spent, and she ran upstairs in tears and banged the door of her bedroom. I crept off to the woodshed, a criminal, and wondered what I should do. Become a tramp, perhaps, like the shabby, sinister fellows who came so often to our back door for a handout? Hang myself? I have been very miserable since – miserable not for an hour but for months on end – but I can still feel that hour's misery in its perfect desolation, if I am fool enough to call it up in my mind.

My father and Willie came home, and there was no supper. Naturally he sided with her, and Willie was very officious and knowing about how intolerable I had become of late, and how thrashing was too good for me. Finally it was settled that my mother would come downstairs if I would beg pardon. This I had to do on my knees, repeating a formula improvised by my father, which included a pledge that I would always love my mother, to whom I owed the great gift of life, and that I begged her – and secondarily God – to forgive me, knowing full well that I was unworthy of such clemency.

I rose from my knees cleansed and purged, and ate very little supper, as became a criminal. When it came time for me to go to bed my mother beckoned me to her, and kissed me, and whispered, 'I know I'll never have another anxious moment with my own dear laddie.'

I pondered these words before I went to sleep. How could I reconcile this motherliness with the screeching fury who had pursued me around the kitchen with a whip, flogging me until she was gorged with – what? Vengeance? What was it? Once, when I was in my thirties and reading Freud for the first time, I thought I knew. I am not so sure I know now. But what I knew then was that nobody – not even my mother – was to be trusted in a strange world that showed very little of itself on the surface.

8

Instead of sickening me of magic, this incident increased my appetite for it. It was necessary for me to gain power in some realm into which my parents – my mother particularly – could not follow me. Of course, I did not think about the matter logically; sometimes I yearned for my mother's love and hated myself for having grieved her, but quite as often I recognized that her love had a high price on it and that her idea of a good son was a pretty small potato. So I drudged away secretly at the magic.

It was card tricks now. I had no trouble getting a pack of cards, for my parents were great players of euchre, and of the several packs in the house I could spirit away the oldest for a couple of hours any afternoon, if I replaced it at the back of the drawer where it was kept, as being too good to throw away but too slick and supple to use. Having only the one pack, I could not attempt any tricks that needed two cards of the same suit and value, but I mastered a few of those chestnuts in which somebody chooses a card and the conjurer finds it after much shuffling; I even had a beauty, involving a silk thread, in which the chosen card hopped from the deck as the conjurer stood nonchalantly at a distance.

I needed an audience, to judge how well I was doing, and I found one readily in Paul Dempster. He was four, and I was fourteen, so on the pretext of looking after him for an hour or two I would take him to the library and entertain him with my tricks. He was not a bad audience, for he sat solemn and mute when he was bidden, chose cards at my command, and if I presented the deck to him with one card slightly protruding, while I held the deck tight, that was the card he invariably chose. He had his faults; he could neither read nor count, and so he did not relish the full wonder of it when I produced his card triumphantly after tremendous shufflings, but I knew that I had deceived him and told him so. In fact, my abilities as a teacher had their first airing in that little library, and as I was fond of lecturing I taught Paul more than I suspected.

Of course he wanted to play too, and it was not easy to explain that I was not playing but demonstrating a fascinating and involved science. I had to work out a system of rewards, and as he liked stories I read to him after he had watched me do my tricks.

Luckily we both liked the same book. It was a pretty volume I found in the cupboard of banished books, called *A Child's Book of Saints*. It was the work of one William Canton, and it began with a conversation between a little girl and her father, which I thought a model of elegant writing. I can quote passages from it still, for I used to read and reread them to Paul, and he, with the memory of a non-reader, could repeat them by heart. Here is one, and I am sure that though I have not read it for fifty years, I have it right:

Occasionally these legends brought us to the awful brink of religious controversies and insoluble mysteries, but, like those gentle savages who honour the water-spirits by hanging garlands from tree to tree across the river, W.V. – [W.V. was the little girl] – could always fling a bridge of flowers over our abysses. 'Our sense,' she would declare, 'is nothing to God's; and though big people have more sense than children, the sense of all the big people in the world put together would be no sense to His.' 'We are only little babies to Him; we do not understand Him at all.' Nothing seemed clearer to her than the reasonableness of one legend which taught that though God always answers our prayers, He does not always answer in the way we would like, but in some better way than we know. 'Yes,' she observed, 'He is just a dear old Father.' Anything about our Lord engrossed her imagination; and it was a frequent wish of hers that He would come again. 'Then,' – poor perplexed little mortal! whose difficulties one could not even guess at – 'we should be quite sure of things. Miss Catherine tells us from books: He would tell us from His memory. People would not be so cruel to Him now. Queen Victoria would not allow any one to crucify Him.'

There was a picture of Queen Victoria hanging in the library, and one look at her would tell you that anybody under her protection was in luck.

Thus for some months I used Paul as a model audience, and paid him off in stories about St Dorothea and St Francis, and let him look at the pretty pictures, which were by Heath Robinson.

I progressed from cards to coins, which were vastly more

difficult. For one thing, I had very few coins, and when my books of instruction said, 'Secure and palm six half-crowns,' I was stopped dead, for I had no half-crowns or anything that looked like them. I had one handsome piece – it was a brass medal that the linotype company had prepared to advertise its machines, which my father did not want – and as it was about the size of a silver dollar I practised with that. But oh, what clumsy hands I had!

I cannot guess now how many weeks I worked on the sleight-of-hand pass called The Spider. To perform this useful bit of trickery, you nip a coin between your index and little fingers, and then revolve it by drawing the two middle fingers back and forth, in front or behind it; by this means it is possible to show both sides of the hand without revealing the coin. But just try to do it! Try it with red, knuckly Scots hands, stiffened by grass-cutting and snow-shovelling, and see what skill you develop! Of course Paul wanted to know what I was doing, and, being a teacher at heart, I told him.

'Like this?' he asked, taking the coin from me and performing the pass perfectly.

I was stunned and humiliated, but, looking back on it now, I think I behaved pretty well.

'Yes, like that,' I said, and though it took me a few days to realize it, that was the moment I became Paul's instructor. He could do anything with his hands. He could shuffle cards without dropping them, which was something I could never be sure of, and he could do marvels with my big brass medal. His hands were small, so that the coin was usually visible, but it was seen to be doing something interesting; he could make it walk over the back of his hand, nipping it between the fingers with a dexterity that left me gasping.

There was no sense in envying him; he had the hands and I had not, and although there were times when I considered killing him, just to rid the world of a precocious nuisance, I could not overlook that fact. The astonishing thing was that he regarded me as his teacher because I could read and tell him what to do; the fact that he could do it did not impress him. He was grateful, and I was in a part of my life where gratitude and admiration, even from such a thing as Paul, were very welcome.

If it seems cruel to write 'such a thing as Paul,' let me explain myself. He was an odd-looking little mortal, with an unusually big head for his frail body. His clothes never seemed to fit him; many of them were reach-me-downs from Baptist families, and because his mother was so unhandy they always had holes in them and were ravelled at the edges and ill-buttoned. He had a lot of curly brown hair, because his mother kept begging Amasa Dempster to put off the terrible day when Paul would go to Myron Papple for the usual boy's scalping. His eyes seemed big in his little face, and certainly they were unusually wide apart, and looked dark because his thin skin was so white. My mother was worried about that pallor and occasionally took charge of Paul and wormed him – a humiliation children did not seem to need any more. Paul was not a village favourite, and the dislike so many people felt for his mother – dislike for the queer and persistently unfortunate – they attached to the unoffending son.

9

My own dislike was kept for Amasa Dempster. A few of his flock said that he walked very closely with God, and it made him spooky. We had family prayers at home, a respectful salute to Providence before breakfast, enough for anybody. But he was likely to drop on his knees at any time and pray with a fervour that seemed indecent. Because I was often around their house I sometimes stumbled on one of these occasions, and he would motion me to kneel with them until he was finished – which could be as much as ten or fifteen minutes later. Sometimes he mentioned me; I was the stranger within their gates, and I knew he was telling God what a good job I did on the grass and the woodpile; but he usually got in a dig at the end, when he asked God to preserve me from walking with a froward mouth, by which he meant my little jokes to coax a laugh or a smile from his wife. And he never finished without asking God for strength to bear his heavy cross, by which I knew that he meant Mrs Dempster; she knew it too.

This was the only unkindness he ever offered her. In everything else he was patient and, so far as his spirit permitted, loving. But before Paul's birth he had loved her because she was the blood of his heart; now he seemed to love her on principle. I do not think he knew that he was hinting to God to notice the meek spirit in which he bore his ill luck, but that was the impression his prayers left on my mind. He was no skilled rhetorician, and the poor man had nothing much in the way of brains, so very often what he felt came out more clearly than what he meant to say.

His quality of feeling was weighty. I suppose this is what made him acceptable to the Baptists, who valued feeling very highly – much more highly than we Presbyterians, who were scared of it and tried to swap it for intellect. I got the strength of his feeling one awful day when he said to me:

'Dunny, come with me to my study in the church. I want a word with you.'

Wondering what on earth all this solemnity was about, I tagged along with him to the Baptist church, where we went to the tiny parson's room beside the baptismal tank. The first thing he did was to drop to his knees and ask God to assist him to be just but not unkind, and then he went to work on me.

I had brought corruption into the innocent world of childhood. I had offended against one of God's little ones. I had been the agent – unknowingly, he hoped – by means of which the Evil One had trailed his black slime across a pure life.

Of course I was frightened. There were boys and girls known to me who made occasional trips to the groves of trees in the old gravel pit that lay to the west of our village and gave themselves up to exploratory pawing. One of these, a Mabel Heighington, was rumoured to have gone the limit with more than one boy. But I was not of this group; I was too scared of being found out, and also, I must say in justice to my young self, too fastidious, to want the pimply Heighington slut; I preferred my intense, solitary adoration of Leola Cruikshank to such frowzy rough-and-tumble. But all boys used to be open to accusations on matters of sex; their thoughts alone, to say nothing of half-willing, half-disgusted action, incriminated them before themselves. I thought someone must have given him my name to divert attention from the others.

45

I was wrong. After the preliminary mysterious talk it came out that he was accusing me of putting playing-cards – he called them the Devil's picture-book – into the hands of his son Paul. But worse – much worse that that – I had taught the boy to cheat with the cards, to handle them like a smoking-car gambler, and also to play deceptive tricks with money. That very morning there had been three cents' change from the baker's visit, and Paul had picked them up from the table and caused them to vanish! Of course he had restored them – utter corruption had not yet set in – and after a beating and much prayer it had all come out about the cards and what I had taught him.

This was bad enough, but worse was to follow. Papistry! I had been telling Paul stories about saints, and if I did not know that the veneration of saints was one of the vilest superstitions of the Scarlet Woman of Rome, he was going to have a word with the Presbyterian minister, the Reverend Andrew Bowyer, to make sure I found out. Under conviction of his wickedness Paul had come out with blasphemous stuff about somebody who had spent his life praying on a pillar forty feet high, and St Francis who saw a living Christ on a crucifix, and St Mary of the Angels, and more of the same kind, that had made his blood freeze to hear. Now – what was it to be? Would I take the beating I deserved from him, or was he to tell my parents and leave it to them to do their duty?

I was a boy of fifteen at this time, and I did not propose to take a beating from him, and if my parents beat me I would run away and become a tramp. So I told him he had better tell my parents.

This disconcerted him, for he had been a parson long enough to know that complaints to parents about their children were not always gratefully received. I was bold enough to say that maybe he had better do as he threatened and speak to Mr Bowyer. This was good argument, for our minister was not a man to like advice from Amasa Dempster, and though he would have given me the rough side of his tongue, he would first have eaten the evangelistic Baptist parson without salt. Poor Dempster! He had lost the fight, so he took refuge in banishing me. I was never to set foot in his house again, he said, nor to speak to any of his family, nor dare to come near his son. He would pray for me, he concluded.

I left the church in a strange state of mind, for a Deptford boy, though I learned later in life that it was common enough. I did not feel I had done wrong, though I had been a fool to forget how dead set Baptists were against cards. As for the stories about saints, they were tales of wonders, like *Arabian Nights*, and when the Reverend Andrew Bowyer bade all us Presbyterians to prepare ourselves for the Marriage Feast of the Lamb, it seemed to me that *Arabian Nights* and the *Bible* were getting pretty close – and I did not mean this in any scoffing sense. I was most hurt that Dempster had dragged down my conjuring to mere cheating and gambling; it had seemed to me to be a splendid extension of life, a creation of a world of wonder, that hurt nobody. All that dim but glittering vision I had formed of Paris, with Robert-Houdin doing marvels to delight grand people, had been dragged down by this Deptford parson, who knew nothing of such things and just hated whatever did not belong to life at the $550-a-year level. I wanted a better life than that. But I had been worsted by moral bullying, by Dempster's conviction that he was right and I was wrong, and that gave him an authority over me based on feeling rather than reason : it was my first encounter with the emotional power of popular morality.

In my bitterness I ill-wished Amasa Dempster. This was a terrible thing to do, and I knew it. In my parents' view of life, superstition was trash for ignorant people, but they had a few reservations, and one was that it was very unlucky to ill-wish anybody. The evil wish would surely rebound upon the wisher. But I ill-wished Dempster; I begged Somebody – some God who understood me – that he should be made very sorry for the way he had talked to me.

He said nothing to my parents, nor yet to Mr Bowyer. I interpreted his silence as weakness, and probably that was an important element in it. I saw him now, a few times each week, at a distance, and it seemed to me that the burdens of his life were bearing him down. He did not stoop, but he looked gaunter and crazier. Paul I saw only once, and he turned away from me and ran towards his home, crying; I was terribly sorry for him. But Mrs Dempster I saw often, for she had intensified her roaming and would spend a whole morning wandering from house to house – 'traipsing' was the word many of the women now used – offering bunches of wilted rhubarb, or some rank lettuce, or other stuff from her garden, which was so ill tended without me that nothing did well in it. But she wanted to give things away and was hurt when neighbours refused these profferings. Her face wore a sweet but woefully un-Deptford expression; it was too clear that she did not know where she was going next, and sometimes she would visit one house three times in a morning, to the annoyance of a busy woman who was washing or getting a meal for her husband and sons.

When I think of my mother now, I try to remember her as she was in her dealings with Mrs Dempster. A poor actress, she nevertheless feigned pleasure over the things that were given and always insisted that something be taken in return, usually something big and lasting. She always remembered what Mrs Dempster had brought and told her how good it had been, though usually it was only fit to be thrown away.

'The poor soul dearly loves to give,' she said to my father, 'and it would be wicked to deny her. The pity is that more people with more to give don't feel the same way.'

I avoided direct meetings with Mrs Dempster, for she would say, 'Dunstable Ramsay, you've almost grown to be a man. Why don't you come to see us any more? Paul misses you; he tells me so.'

She had forgotten, or perhaps she never knew, that her husband had warned me away. I never saw her without a pang of guilt and concern about her. But for her husband I had no pity.

10

Mrs Dempster's wanderings came to an end on Friday 24 October 1913. It was almost ten o'clock at night and I was reading by the stove, as was my father; my mother sewed – something for the Mission Circle bazaar – and Willie was at a practice of a Youth Band a local enthusiast had organized; Willie played the cornet and had his eye on the first flute, one Ada Blake. When the knock came at the door my father went, and after some quiet muttering asked the callers to come in while he put on his boots. They were Jim Warren, who was our part-time village policeman, and George and Garnet Harper, a couple of practical jokers who on this occasion looked unwontedly solemn.

'Mary Dempster's disappeared,' my father explained. 'Jim's organizing a hunt.'

'Yep, been gone since after supper,' said the policeman. 'Reverend come home at nine and she was gone. Nowheres round the town, and now we're goin' to search the pit. If she's not there we'll have to drag the river.'

'You'd better go along with your father,' said my mother to me. 'I'll get right over to Dempsters' and keep an eye on Paul, and be ready when you bring her home.'

Much was implied in that speech. In the instant my mother had acknowledged me as a man, fit to go on serious business. She had shown also that she knew that I was as concerned about the Dempsters, perhaps, as herself; there had been no questions about why I had not been going there to do the chores for the past few months. I am sure my parents knew Amasa Dempster had warned me away and had assumed that it was part of the crazy pride and self-sufficiency that had been growing on him. But if Mrs Dempster was lost at night, all daylight considerations must be set aside. There was a good deal of the pioneer left in people in those days, and they knew what was serious.

I darted off to get the flashlight; my father had recently bought a car – rather a daring thing in Deptford at that time – and a large flashlight was kept in the tool-kit on the runningboard, in case we should be benighted with a flat tire.

We made for the pit, where ten or twelve men were already assembled. I was surprised to see Mr Mahaffey, our magistrate, among them. He and the policeman were our law, and his presence meant grave public concern.

This gravel pit was of unusual importance to our village because it completely blocked any normal extension of streets or houses on our western side; thus it was a source of indignation to our village council. However, it belonged to the railway

49

company, which valued it as a source of the gravel they needed for keeping their roadbed in order, and which they excavated and hauled considerable distances up and down the track. How big it was I do not accurately know, but it was big, and prejudice made it seem bigger. It was not worked consistently and so was often undisturbed for a year or more at a time; in it there were pools, caused by seepage from the river, which it bordered, and a lot of scrub growth, sumac, sallow, Manitoba maple, and such unprofitable things, as well as goldenrod and kindred trashy weeds.

Mothers hated it because sometimes little children strayed into it and were hurt, and big children sneaked into it and met the like of Mabel Heighington. But most of all it was disliked because it was a refuge for the tramps who rode the rods of the railway. Some of these were husky young fellows; others were old men, or men who seemed old, in ragged greatcoats belted with a piece of rope or a strap, wearing hats of terrible dilapidation, and giving off a stench of feet, sweat, faeces, and urine that would have staggered a goat. They were mighty drinkers of flavouring extracts and liniments that had a heavy alcohol base. All of them were likely to appear at a back door and ask for food. In their eyes was the dazed, stunned look of people who live too much in the open air without eating properly. They were generally given food and generally feared as lawless men.

In later life I have been sometimes praised, sometimes mocked, for my way of pointing out the mythical elements that seem to me to underlie our apparently ordinary lives. Certainly that cast of mind had some of its origin in our pit, which had much the character of a Protestant Hell. I was probably the most entranced listener to a sermon the Reverend Andrew Bowyer preached about Gehenna, the hateful valley outside the walls of Jerusalem, where outcasts lived, and where their flickering fires, seen from the city walls, may have given rise to the idea of a hell of perpetual burning. He liked to make his hearers jump, now and then, and he said that our gravel pit was much the same sort of place as Gehenna. My elders thought this far-fetched, but I saw no reason then why hell should not have, so to speak, visible branch establishments throughout the earth, and I have visited quite a few of them since.

Under the direction of Jim Warren and Mr Mahaffey it was agreed that fifteen of us would scramble down into the pit and form a line, leaving twenty or thirty feet between each man, and advance from end to end. Anybody who found a clue was to give a shout. As we searched there was quite a lot of sound, for I think most of the men wanted any tramps to know we were coming and get out of the way; nobody liked the idea of coming on a tramps' bivouac – they were called 'jungles', which made them seem more terrible – unexpectedly. We had seen only two fires, at the far end of the pit, but there could be quite a group of tramps without a fire.

My father was thirty feet on my left, and a big fellow named Ed Hainey on my right, as I walked through the pit. In spite of the nearness of the men it was lonely work, and though there was a moon it was waning and the light was poor. I was afraid and did not know what I feared, which is the worst kind of fear. We might have gone a quarter of a mile when I came to a clump of sallow. I was about to skirt it when I heard a stirring inside it. I made a sound – I am sure it was not a yell – that brought my father beside me in an instant. He shot the beam of his flashlight into the scrub, and in that bleak, flat light we saw a tramp and a woman in the act of copulation. The tramp rolled over and gaped at us in terror; the woman was Mrs Dempster.

It was Hainey who gave a shout, and in no time all the men were with us, and Jim Warren was pointing a pistol at the tramp, ordering him to put his hands up. He repeated the words two or three times, and then Mrs Dempster spoke.

'You'll have to speak very loudly to him, Mr Warren,' she said, 'he's hard of hearing.'

I don't think any of us knew where to look when she spoke, pulling her skirts down but remaining on the ground. It was at that moment that the Reverend Amasa Dempster joined us; I had not noticed him when the hunt began, though he must have been there. He behaved with great dignity, leaning forward to help his wife rise with the same sort of protective love I had seen in him the night Paul was born. But he was not able to keep back his question.

'Mary, what made you do it?'

She looked him honestly in the face and gave the answer that became famous in Deptford: 'He was very civil, 'Masa. And he wanted it so badly.'

He put her arm under his and set out for home, just as if they were going for a walk. Under Mr Mahaffey's direction, Jim Warren took the tramp off to the lock-up. The rest of us dispersed without a word.

II

Dempster visited Mr Mahaffey early on Saturday and said that he would lay no charge and take part in no trial, so the magistrate took council with my father and a few other wise heads and told Jim Warren to get the tramp off the village bounds, with a warning never to be seen there again.

The real trial would come on Sunday, and everybody knew it. The buzzing and humming were intense all day Saturday, and at church on Sunday everybody who was not a Baptist was aching to know what would happen at the Baptist service. The Reverend Andrew Bowyer prayed for 'all who were distressed in spirit, and especially for a family known to us all who were in sore travail,' and something of a similar intention was said in the Anglican and Methodist churches. Only Father Regan at the Catholic church came out flat-footed and said from his pulpit that the gravel pit was a disgrace and a danger and that the railway had its nerve not to clean it up or close it up. But when we heard about that, everybody knew it was beside the point. Mrs Dempster had given her consent. That was the point. Supposing she was a little off her head, how insane had a woman to be before it came to that? Dr McCausland, appealed to on the steps of our church by some seekers after truth, said that such conduct indicated a degeneration of the brain, which was probably progressive.

We soon knew what the Baptist parson said that morning: he went into his pulpit, prayed silently for a short time, and then told his congregation that the time had come for him to resign his charge, as he had other duties that were incapable of being combined with it. He asked for their prayers, and went into his study. A prominent member of the congregation, a baker, took charge and turned the service into a meeting; the baker and a few other men were asking the parson to wait a while, but the majority was against them, especially the women. Not that any of the women spoke; they had done their speaking before church, and their husbands knew the price of peace. So at last the baker and one or two others had to go into the study and tell Amasa Dempster that his resignation was accepted. He left the church without any prospects, a crazy and disgraced wife, a delicate child, and six dollars in cash. There were several men who wanted to do something for him, but the opinion of their wives made it impossible.

There was a terrible quarrel in our household – the more terrible because I had never heard my parents disagree when they knew that Willie and I could hear them; what I heard by way of the stovepipe sometimes amounted to disagreement but never to a quarrel. My father accused my mother of wanting charity; she replied that as the mother of two boys she had standards of decency to defend. That was the meat of the quarrel, but before it had gone very far it reached a point where she said that if he was going to stand up for filthy behaviour and adultery he was a long way from the man she had married, and he was saying that he had never known she had a cruel streak. (I could have told him something about that.) This battle went on at Sunday dinner and drove Willie, who was the least demonstrative of fellows, to throw down his napkin and exclaim, 'Oh, for the love of the crows!' and leave the table. I dared not follow, and as my parents' wrath grew I was numbed with misery.

Of course my mother won. If my father had not given in he would have had to live with outraged female virtue for – perhaps the rest of his life. As things were, I do not believe that she ever gave up a suspicion that he was not as firm in his moral integrity as she had once believed. Mrs Dempster had transgressed in a realm where there could be no shades of right and wrong. And the reason she had offered for doing so –!

That was what stuck in the craws of all the good women of Deptford : Mrs Dempster had not been raped, as a decent woman would have been – no, she had yielded because a man wanted her. The subject was not one that could be freely discussed even among intimates, but it was understood without saying that if women began to yield for such reasons as that, marriage and society would not last long. Any man who spoke up for Mary Dempster probably believed in Free Love. Certainly he associated sex with pleasure, and that put him in a class with filthy thinkers like Cece Athelstan.

Cecil Athelstan – always known as Cece – was the black sheep of our ruling family. He was a fat, swag-bellied boozer who sat in a chair on the sidewalk outside the Tecumseh House bar when the weather was fine, and on the same chair inside the bar when it was not. Once a month, when he got his cheque, he went for a night or two to Detroit, across the border, and, according to his own account, he was the life and soul of the bawdy houses there. Foul-mouthed bum though he was, he had enough superiority of experience and native wit to hold a small group of loafers in awe, and his remarks, sometimes amusing, were widely quoted, even by people who disapproved of him.

Mrs Dempster's answer was a gift to a man like Cece. 'Hey!' he would shout across the street to one of his cronies, 'you feeling civil today? I feel so God-damned civil I got to get to Detroit right away – or maybe just up to You Know Who's!' Or as some respectable woman passed on the other side of the street from the hotel he would sing out, just loud enough to be heard, 'I wa-a-ant it! Hey, Cora, I want it so-o-o!' The strange thing was that the behaviour of this licensed fool made the enormity of Mrs Dempster's words greater, but did not lower the town's esteem of Cece Athelstan – probably because it could go no lower.

At school there were several boys who pestered me for descriptions, with anatomical detail, of what I had seen in the pit. I had no trouble silencing them, but of course Cece and his gang lay beyond my power. It was Cece, with some of his crowd, and the Harper boys (who ought to have known better) who organized the shivaree when the Dempsters moved. Amasa Dempster got out of the Baptist parsonage on the Tuesday after his resignation and took his wife and son to a cottage on the road to the school. The parsonage had been furnished, so they had little enough to move, but a few people who could not bear to think of them in destitution mustered furniture for the new place, without letting it be too clearly known who had done it.

(I know my father put up some of the money for this project, very much on the quiet.)

At midnight a gang with blackened faces beat pans and tooted horns outside the cottage for half an hour, and somebody threw a lighted broom on the roof, but it was a damp night and no harm was done. Cece's voice was heard half over the town, shouting, 'Come on out, Mary! We want it!' I wish I could record that Amasa Dempster came out and faced them, but he did not.

I never saw a man change so much in so short a time. He was gaunt and lonely before, but there had been fire in his eyes; in two weeks he was like a scarecrow. He had a job; George Alcott, who owned the sawmill, offered Dempster a place as a book-keeper and timekeeper at twelve dollars a week, which was not a bad wage for the work and in fact made the Dempsters slightly better off than they had been, for there was no church tithe ex-pected out of it. But it was the comedown, the disgrace, that broke Dempster. He had been a parson, which was the work dearest to his heart; now he was nothing in his own eyes, and clearly he feared the worst for his wife.

What passed between them nobody knew, but she was not seen in the village and very rarely in the little yard outside the cottage. There was a rumour that he kept her tied to a long rope inside the house, so that she could move freely through it but not get out. On Sunday mornings, her arm in his, she went to the Baptist church, and they sat in a back pew, never speaking to anyone as they came and went. She began to look very strange indeed, and if she was not mad before, people said, she was mad now.

I knew better. After a few weeks during which I was miser-able because of the village talk, I sneaked over there one day and peeped in a window. She was sitting on a chair by a table, staring at nothing, but when I tapped on the pane she looked at me and smiled in recognition. In an instant I was inside, and after a few minutes of uneasiness we were talking eagerly. She was a little strange because she had been so lonely, but she made good sense, and I had enough gumption to keep on general topics. I soon found out that she knew nothing of what was going on in the world because the Dempsters took no newspaper.

After that I went there two or three times a week, with a daily paper, or a copy of our own *Banner*, and I read things to her that I knew would interest her, and kept her up on the gossip of the town. Often Paul was with us, because he never played with other children, and I did what I could for him. It was well understood that these visits were not to be mentioned to Dempster, for I was sure he still thought me a bad influence.

I began this deceitful line of conduct – for my mother would have been furious, and I thought anybody who had seen me going there would have spread the word – hoping I could do something for Mrs Dempster, but it was not long before I found that she was doing much for me. I do not know how to express it, but she was a wise woman, and though she was only ten years older than myself, and thus about twenty-six at this time, she seemed to me to have a breadth of outlook and a clarity of vision that were strange and wonderful; I cannot remember examples that satisfactorily explain what I mean, and I recognize now that it was her lack of fear, of apprehension, of assumption that whatever happened was inevitably going to lead to some worse state of affairs, that astonished and enriched me. She had not been like this when first I knew her, after Paul's birth, but I see now that she had been tending in this direction. When she had seemed to be laughing at things her husband took very seriously, she had been laughing at the disproportion of his seriousness, and of course in Deptford it was very easy to understand such laughter as the uncomprehending gigglings of a fool.

It would be false to suggest that there was anything philosophical in her attitude. Rather, it was religious, and it was impossible to talk to her for long without being aware that she was wholly religious. I do not say 'deeply religious' because that was what people said about her husband, and apparently they meant that he imposed religion as he understood it on everything he knew or encountered. But she, tied up in a rotten little house without a friend except me, seemed to live in a world of trust that had nothing of the stricken, lifeless, unreal quality of religion about it. She knew she was in disgrace with the world, but did not feel disgraced; she knew she was jeered at, but felt no humiliation. She lived by a light that arose from within; I could not comprehend it, except that it seemed to be somewhat akin to the splendours I found in books, though not in any way bookish. It was as though she were an exile from a world that saw things her way, and though she was sorry Deptford did not understand her she was not resentful. When you got past her shyness she had quite positive opinions, but the queerest thing about her was that she had no fear.

This was the best of Mary Dempster. Of the disorder and discomfort of that cottage I shall not speak, and though little Paul was loved and cherished by his mother he was in his appearance a pitifully neglected child. So perhaps she was crazy, in part, but it was only in part; the best side of her brought comfort and assurance into my life, which badly needed it. I got so that I did not notice the rope she wore (it was actually a harness that went around her waist and shoulders, with the horse-smelling hemp rope knotted to a ring on one side, so that she could lie down if she wanted to), or the raggedness of her clothes, or the occasional spells when she was not wholly rational. I regarded her as my greatest friend, and the secret league between us as the tap-root that fed my life.

Close as we grew, however, there was never any moment when I could have asked her about the tramp. I was trying to forget the spectacle, so horrible in my visions, of what I had seen when first I happened on them – those bare buttocks and four legs so strangely opposed. But I could never forget. It was my first encounter with a particular kind of reality, which my religion, my upbringing, and the callowly romantic cast of my mind had declared obscene. Therefore there was an aspect of Mary Dempster which was outside my ken; and, being young and unwilling to recognize that there was anything I did not, or could not know, I decided that this unknown aspect must be called madness.

12

The year that followed was a busy one for me, and, except for my visits to Mrs Dempster, lonely. My school friends accused me of being a know-all, and with characteristic perversity I liked the description. By searching the dictionary I discovered that a know-all was called, among people who appreciated knowledge and culture, a polymath, and I set to work to become a polymath with the same enthusiasm that I had once laboured to be a conjurer. It was much easier work; I simply read the encyclopaedia in our village library. It was a *Chambers'*, the 1888 edition, and I was not such a fool as to think I could read it through; I read the articles that appealed to me, and when I found something particularly juicy I read everything around it that I could find. I beavered away at that encyclopaedia with a tenacity that I wish I possessed now, and if I did not become a complete polymath I certainly gained enough information to be a nuisance to everybody who knew me.

I also came to know my father much better, for after the search for Mrs Dempster in the pit he put himself out to make a friend of me. He was an intelligent man and well educated in an old-fashioned way; he had gone to Dumfries Academy as a boy, and what he knew he could marshal with a precision I have often envied; it was he and he alone who made the study of Latin anything but a penance to me, for he insisted that without Latin nobody could write clear English.

Sometimes on our Sunday walks along the railroad track we were joined by Sam West, an electrician with a mind above the limitations of his work; as a boy he had been kept hard at the *Bible*, and not only could he quote it freely, but there was not a contradiction or an absurdity in it that he did not know and relish. His detestation of religion and churches was absolute, and he scolded about them in language that owed all its bite to the *Old Testament*. He was unfailingly upright in all his dealings, to show the slaves of priestcraft and superstition that morality has nothing to do with religion, and he was an occasional attendant at all our local churches, in order to wrestle mentally with the sermon and confute it. His imitations of the parsons were finely observed, and he was very good as the Reverend Andrew Bowyer: 'O Lord, take Thou a live coal from off Thine altar and touch our lips,' he would shout, in a caricature of our minister's fine Edinburgh accent; then, with a howl of laughter, 'Wouldn't he be surprised if his prayer was answered!'

If he hoped to make an atheist of me, this was where he went wrong; I knew a metaphor when I heard one, and I liked metaphor better than reason. I have known many atheists since Sam, and they all fall down on metaphor.

At school I was a nuisance, for my father was now Chairman of our Continuation School Board, and I affected airs of near-equality with the teacher that must have galled her; I wanted to argue about everything, expand everything, and generally turn every class into a Socratic powwow instead of getting on with the curriculum. Probably I made her nervous, as a pupil full of green, fermenting information is so well able to do. I have dealt with innumerable variations of my young self in classrooms since then, and I have mentally apologized for my tiresomeness.

My contemporaries were growing up too. Leola Cruikshank was now a village beauty, and well understood to be Percy Boyd Staunton's girl. Spider Webb still thought me wonderful, and I graciously permitted her to worship me from a distance. Milo Papple had found that a gift for breaking wind was not in itself enough for social success, and he learned a few things from the travelling salesmen who were shaved by his father that gave him quite a new status. It was an era when parodies of popular songs were thought very funny, and when conversation flagged he would burst into:

> I had a dewlap,
>   A big flabby dewlap,
> And you had
>   A red, red nose.

Or perhaps:

> I dream of Jeannie
>   With the light brown hair,
> Drunk in the privy
>   In her underwear.

These fragments were always very brief, and he counted on his hearers bursting into uncontrollable laughter before they were finished. Nuisance that I was, I used to urge him to continue, for which he very properly hated me. He also had a few pleasantries about smelly feet, which went well at parties. I refused to laugh at them, for I was jealous of anybody who was funnier than I. The trouble was that my jokes tended to be so complicated that nobody laughed but Spider Webb, who obviously did not understand them.

The great event of the spring was the revelation that Percy Boyd Staunton and Mabel Heighington had been surprised in the sexual act by Mabel's mother, who had tracked them to Dr Staunton's barn and pounced. Mrs Heighington was a small, dirty, hysterical woman whose own chastity was seriously flawed; she had been a grass-widow for several years. What she said to Percy's father, whom she insisted on seeing just as he got nicely off into his after-dinner nap one day, was so often repeated by herself on the streets that I heard it more than once. If he thought because she was a poor widow her only daughter could be trampled under foot by a rich man's son and then flung aside, by Jesus she would show him different. She had her feelings, like anybody else. Was she to go to Mr Mahaffey right then and get the law to work, or was he going to ask her to sit down and talk turkey?

What turkey amounted to remained a mystery. Some said fifty dollars, and others said a hundred. Mrs Heighington never revealed the precise sum. There were those who said that twenty-five cents would have been a sufficient price for Mabel's virtue, such as it was; she consistently met the brakeman of a freight train that lay on a siding near the gravel pit for half an hour every Friday, and he enjoyed her favours on some sacks in a freight car; she had also had to do with a couple of farm-hands who worked over near the Indian Reservation. But Dr Staunton had money – reputedly lots of money – for he had built up substantial land holdings over the years and was doing very well growing tobacco and sugar-beet, which was just coming into its own as an important crop. The doctoring was a second string with him, and he kept it up chiefly for the prestige it carried. Still, he was a doctor, and when Mrs Heighington told him that if there was a baby she would expect him to do something about it, she struck a telling blow.

For our village, this amounted to scandal in high society. Mrs Staunton was elaborately pitied by some of the women; others blamed her for letting Percy have his own way too much. Some of the men thought Percy a young rip, but the Cece Athelstan crowd acclaimed him as one of themselves. Ben Cruikshank, a tough little carpenter, stopped Percy on the street and told him if he ever came near Leola again he would cripple him; Leola wore a stricken face for days, and it was known that she was pining for Percy and forgave him in spite of everything, which made me cynical about women. Some of our more profound moralists harked back to the incident of Mrs Dempster and said that if a parson's wife behaved like that, it was no wonder young ones picked up notions. Dr Staunton kept his own counsel, but it became known that he had decided to send Percy away to school, where he would not have his mother to baby him. And that, Headmaster, is how Percy came to be at Colborne College, of which in time he became a distinguished Old Boy, and Chairman of the Board of Governors.

13

The autumn of 1914 was remarkable in most places for the outbreak of the war, but in Deptford my brother Willie's illness ran it close as a subject of interest.

Willie had been ill at intervals for four years. His trouble began with an accident in the *Banner* plant when he had attempted to take some rollers from the big press – the one used for printing the newspaper – without help. Jumper Saul was absent, pitching for the local baseball team. The rollers were not extremely heavy but they were awkward, and one of them fell on Willie and knocked him down. At first it seemed that nothing would come of it except a large bruise on his back, but as time wore on Willie began to have spells of illness marked by severe internal pain. Dr McCausland could not do much for him; X-ray was unheard of in our part of the world, and the kind of exploratory operations that are so common now were virtually unknown. My parents took Willie to Pittstown a few times to see a chiropractor, but the treatments hurt Willie so much that the chiropractor refused to continue them. Until the autumn of 1914, however, Willie had come round after a few days in bed, with a light diet and a quantity of Sexton Blake stories to help him along.

This time he was really very ill – so ill that he had periods of delirium. His most dramatic symptom, however, spoken of around the village in hushed tones, was a stubborn retention of urine that added greatly to his distress. Dr McCausland sent to Toronto for a specialist – an alarming move in our village – and the specialist had very little to suggest except that immersions in warm water at four-hour intervals might help; he did not advise an operation yet, for at that time the removal of a kidney was an extremely grave matter.

As soon as the news of what the specialist had said got around we had a group of volunteers to assist with the immersions. These were bound to be troublesome, for we had no bathtub except a portable one, which could be put by the bed, and to which all the warm water had to be carried in pails. I have already said that our village had a kind heart, and practical help of this kind was what it understood best; six immersions a day were nothing, in the light of their desire to lend a hand. Even the new Presbyterian minister, the Reverend Donald Phelps (come to replace the Reverend Andrew Bowyer, retired in the spring of 1914), was a volunteer, comparative stranger though he was; more astonishing, Cece Athelstan was one of the group, and was cold sober every time he turned up. Getting Willie through this bad time became a public cause.

The baths certainly seemed to make Willie a little easier, though the swelling caused by the retention of urine grew worse. He had been in bed for more than two weeks when the Saturday of our Fall Fair came and brought special problems with it. My father had to attend; not only had he to write it up for the *Banner*, but as Chairman of our Continuation School Board he had to judge two or three contests. My mother was expected to attend, and wanted to attend, because the Ladies' Aid of our church was offering a Fowl Supper, and she was a noted organizer and pusher of fancy victuals. The men who would give Willie his six-o'clock plunge bath would arrive in plenty of time, but who was to stay with him during the afternoon? I was happy to do so; I would go to the Fair after supper, because it always seemed particularly gay and romantic as darkness fell.

From two until three I sat in Willie's room, reading, and between three and half-past I did what I could for Willie while he died. What I could do was little enough. He became restless and hot, so I put a cold towel on his head. He began to twist and moan, so I held his hands and said what I could think of that might encourage him. He ceased to hear me, and his twisting became jerking and convulsion. He cried out five or six times – not screaming, but spasmodic cries – and in a very few minutes became extremely cold. I wanted to call the doctor, but I dared not leave Willie. I put my ear to his heart: nothing. I tried to find his pulse: nothing. Certainly he was not breathing, for I hurried to fetch my mother's hand mirror and hold it over his mouth: it did not cloud. I opened one eye: it was rolled upward in his head. It came upon me that he was dead.

It is very easy to say now what I should have done. I can only record what I did do. From the catastrophe of realizing that Willie was dead – it was the psychological equivalent of a house falling inward upon itself, and I can still recall the feeling – I passed quickly into strong revolt. Willie could not be dead. It must not be. I would not have it. And, without giving a thought to calling the doctor (whom I had never really liked, though it was the family custom to respect him), I set out on the run to fetch Mrs Dempster.

Why? I don't know why. It was not a matter of reason – not a decision at all. But I can remember running through the hot autumn afternoon, and I can remember hearing the faint music of the merry-go-round as I ran. Nothing was very far away in our village, and I was at the Dempsters' cottage in not much more than three minutes. Locked. Of course. Paul's father would have taken him to the Fair. I was through the living-room window, cutting Mrs Dempster's rope, telling her what I wanted, and dragging her back through the window with me, in a muddle of action that I cannot clearly remember at all. I suppose we would have looked an odd pair, if there had been anyone to see us, running through the streets hand in hand, and I do remember that she hoisted up her skirts to run, which was a girlish thing no grown woman would ever have done if she had not caught the infection of my emotion.

What I do remember was getting back to Willie's room, which was my parents' room, given up to the sick boy because it was the most comfortable, and finding him just as I had left him, white and cold and stiff. Mrs Dempster looked at him solemnly but not sadly, then she knelt by the bed and took his hands in hers and prayed. I had no way of knowing how long she prayed, but it was less than ten minutes. I could not pray and did not kneel. I gaped – and hoped.

After a while she raised her head and called him. 'Willie,' she said in a low, infinitely kind, and indeed almost a cheerful tone. Again, 'Willie.' I hoped till I ached. She shook his hands gently, as if rousing a sleeper. 'Willie.'

Willie sighed and moved his legs a little. I fainted.

When I came round, Mrs Dempster was sitting on Willie's bed, talking quietly and cheerfully to him, and he was replying, weakly but eagerly. I dashed around, fetched a towel to bathe his face, the orange and albumen drink he was allowed in very small quantities, a fan to create a better current of air – everything there was that might help and give expression to my terrible joy. Quite soon Willie fell asleep, and Mrs Dempster and I talked in whispers. She was deeply pleased but, as I now remember it, did not seem particularly surprised by what had happened. I know I babbled like a fool.

The passing of time that afternoon was all awry, for it did not seem long to me before the men came to get Willie's six-o'clock plunge ready, so it must have been half-past five. They were astonished to find her there, but sometimes extraordinary situations impose their own tactful good manners, and nobody said anything to emphasize their first amazement. Willie insisted that she stand by him while he was being plunged, and she helped in the difficult business of drying him off, for he was tender all around his body. Therefore I suppose it must have been close to half-past six when my mother and father arrived home, and with them Amasa Dempster. I don't know what sort of scene I expected; something on Biblical lines would have appeared appropriate to me. But instead Dempster took his wife's arm in his, as I had seen him do it so often, and led her away. As she went she paused for an instant to blow a kiss to Willie. It was the first time I had ever seen anybody do such a thing, and I thought it a gesture of great beauty; to Willie's everlasting credit, he blew a kiss back again, and I

have never seen my mother's face blacker than at that moment.

When the Dempsters were gone, and the men had been
thanked, and offered food, which they refused (this was ritual,
for only the night plungers, at two and six in the morning,
thought it right to accept coffee and sandwiches), there was a
scene downstairs which was as bad, though not as prolonged,
as anything I later experienced in the war.

What did I mean by failing to send for Dr McCausland and
my parents at the first sign of danger? What under Heaven
had possessed me to turn to that woman, who was an insane
degenerate, and bring her, not only into our house but to the
very bedside of a boy who was dangerously ill? Did all this
cynical nonsense I had been talking, and the superior airs I had
been assuming, mean that I too was going off my head? How
did I come to be so thick with Mary Dempster in her present
condition? If this was what all my reading led to, it was high
time I was put to a job that would straighten the kinks out of
me.

Most of this was my mother, and she performed variations
on these themes until I was heartsick with hearing them. I
know now that a lot of her anger arose from self-reproach
because she had been absent, making a great figure of herself
in the Ladies' Aid, when duty should have kept her at Willie's
bedside. But she certainly took it out of me, and so, to a lesser
degree, did my father, who felt himself bound to back her up
but who plainly did not like it.

This would have gone on until we all dropped with exhaustion, I suppose, if Dr McCausland had not arrived; he had
been in the country and had just returned. He brought his own
sort of atmosphere, which was cold and chilly and smelled of
disinfectant, and took a good look at Willie. Then he questioned me. He catechized me thoroughly about what symptoms
Willie had shown, and how he had behaved before he died.
Because I insisted that Willie had indeed died. No pulse; no
breathing.

'But clenched hands?' said Dr McCausland. Yes, said I, but
did that mean that Willie could not have been dead? 'Obviously he was not dead,' said the doctor; 'if he had been dead

65

I would not have been talking to him a few minutes ago. I think you may safely leave it to me to say when people are dead, Dunny,' he continued, with what I am sure he meant as a kindly smile. It had been a strong convulsion, he told my parents; the tight clenching of the hands was a part of it, and an unskilled person could not be expected to detect very faint breathing, or heartbeat either. He was all reason, all reassurrance, and the next day he came early and did an operation on Willie called 'tapping'; he dug a hollow needle into his side and drew off an astonishing quantity of bloody urine. In a week Willie was up and about; in four months he had somehow lied his way into the Canadian Army; in 1916 he was one of those who disappeared forever in the mud at St Eloi.

I wonder if his hands were clenched after death? Later on I saw more men than I could count die, myself, and a surprising number of the corpses I stumbled over, or cleared out of the way, had clenched hands, though I never took the trouble to write to Dr McCausland and tell him so.

For me, Willie's recall from death is, and will always be, Mrs Dempster's second miracle.

14

The weeks following were painful and disillusioning. Among my friends I dropped from the position of polymath to that of a credulous ass who thought that a dangerous lunatic could raise the dead. I should explain that Mrs Dempster was now thought to be dangerous, not because of any violence on her part, but because fearful people were frightened that if she were to wander away again some new sexual scandal would come of it; I think they really believed that she would corrupt some innocent youth or bewitch some faithful husband by the unreason of her lust. It was widely accepted that, even if she could not help it, she was in the grip of unappeasable and indiscriminate desire. Inevitably it came out that I had been visiting her on the sly, and there was a lot of dirty joking about that, but the best joke of all was that I thought she had brought my brother back to life.

The older people took the matter more seriously. Some thought that my known habit of reading a great deal had unseated my reason, and perhaps that dreaded disease 'brain fever', supposed to attack students, was not far off. One or two friends suggested to my father that immediate removal from school, and a year or two of hard work on a farm, might cure me. Dr McCausland found a chance to have what he called 'a word' with me, the gist of which was that I might become queer if I did not attempt to balance my theoretical knowledge with the kind of common sense that could be learned from – well, for instance, from himself. He hinted that I might become like Elbert Hubbard if I continued in my present course. Elbert Hubbard was a notoriously queer American who thought that work could be a pleasure.

Our new minister, the Reverend Donald Phelps, took me on and advised me that it was blasphemous to think that anyone – even someone of unimpeachable character – could restore the dead to life. The age of miracles was past, said he, and I got the impression that he was heartily glad of it. I liked him; he meant it kindly, which McCausland certainly did not.

My father talked to me several times in a way that gave me some insight into his own character, for though he was a man of unusual courage as an editor, he was a peace-at-any-pricer at home. I would do best, he thought, to keep my own counsel and not insist on things my mother could not tolerate.

I might even have done so – if she had been content to let the subject drop. But she was so anxious to root out of my mind any fragment of belief in what I had seen, and to exact from me promises that I would never see Mrs Dempster again and furthermore would accept the village's opinion of her, that she kept alluding to it darkly, or bringing it out for full discussion, usually at meals. It was clear that she now regarded a hint of tenderness toward Mrs Dempster as disloyalty to herself, and as loyalty was the only kind of love she could bring herself to ask for, she was most passionate when she thought she was being most reasonable. I said very little during these scenes, and she quite rightly interpreted my silence as a refusal to change my mind.

She did not know how much I loved her, and how miserable it made me to defy her, but what was I to do? Deep inside myself I knew that to yield, and promise what she wanted, would be the end of anything that was any good in me; I was not her husband, who could keep his peace in the face of her furious rectitude; I was her son, with a full share of her own Highland temper and granite determination.

One day, after a particularly wretched supper, she concluded by demanding that I make a choice between her and 'that woman'. I made a third choice. I had enough money for a railway ticket, and the next day I skipped school, went to the county town, and enlisted.

This changed matters considerably. I was nearly two years under age, but I was tall and strong and a good liar, and I had no difficulty in being accepted. She wanted to go to the authorities and get me out, but my father put his foot down there. He said he would not permit me to be disgraced by having my mother drag me out of the Army. So now she was torn between a fear that I would certainly be shot dead the day after I began training, and a conviction that there was something even darker between Mrs Dempster and me than she had permitted herself to think.

As for my father, he was disgusted with me. He had a poor opinion of soldiers and as he had run some risks by being pro-Boer in 1901 he had serious doubts about the justice of any war. Feeling about the war in our village was romantic, because it touched us so little, but my father and Mr Mahaffey were better aware of what went into the making of that war and could not share the popular feeling. He urged me to reveal my true age and withdraw, but I was pig-headed and spread the news of what I had done as fast as I could.

What my elders thought I did not know or care, but I regained some of the position I had lost among my contemporaries. I loafed at school, as became a man waiting his call to more serious things. My friends seemed to think I might disappear at any hour, and whenever I met Milo Papple, which was at least once a day, he would seize my hand and declaim passionately:

> Say cuspidor,
> But not spittoon –

which was the barbershop version of a song of the day that began:

> Say *au revoir*,
> But not good-bye.

Girls took a new view of me, and to my delighted surprise Leola Cruikshank made it clear that she was mine on loan, so to speak. She still pined for Percy Boyd Staunton, but he was away at school and was a bad and irregular letter-writer, so Leola thought that a modest romance with a hero in embryo could do no harm – might even be a patriotic duty.

She was a delightful girl, pretty, full of sentimental nonsense, and clean about her person – she always smelled of fresh ironing. I saw a great deal of her, persuaded her that a few kisses did not really mean disloyalty to Percy, and paraded her up and down our main street on Saturday nights, wearing my best suit.

I had kept away from Mrs Dempster, partly from obedience and fear and partly because I could not bear to face her when so many hateful opinions about her were ringing in my ears. I knew, however, that I could not go off to war without saying good-bye, and one afternoon, with great stealth, I reached her cottage and climbed through the window for the last time. She spoke to me as if I had visited her as often as usual, and did not seem greatly surprised by the news that I had joined the Army. We had talked a great deal about the war when it first broke out, and she had laughed heartily at the news that two Deptford women who liked to dabble in spiritualism went several times a week to the cemetery to read the latest news from France to their dead mother, sitting on her grave, picnic-style When I had to leave she kissed me on both cheeks – a thing she had never done before – and said, 'There's just one thing to remember; whatever happens, it does no good to be afraid.' So I promised not to be afraid, and may even have been fool enough to think I could keep my promise.

In time my call came. I climbed on the train, proud of my pass to the camp, and waved from the window to my almost weeping mother, and my father, whose expression I could not interpret. Leola was in school, for we had agreed that it would not do for her to come to the station – too much like a formal engagement. But the night before I left she had confided that in spite of her best efforts to keep the image of Percy bright in her heart she had discovered that she really loved me, and would love me forever, and wait until I returned from the battlefields of Europe.

2

I Am Born Again

I

I shall say little about the war, because though I was in it from early 1915 until late 1917 I never found out much about it until later. Commanders and historians are the people to discuss wars; I was in the infantry, and most of the time I did not know where I was or what I was doing except that I was obeying orders and trying not to be killed in any of the variety of horrible ways open to me. Since then I have read enough to know a little of the actions in which I took part, but what the historians say throws no great light on what I remember. Because I do not want to posture in this account of myself as anything other than what I was at the time of my narrative, I shall write here only of what I knew when it happened.

When I left Deptford for the training camp. I had never been away from home alone before. I found myself among men more experienced in the world than I, and I tried not to attract attention by any kind of singular behaviour. Some of them knew I was desperately homesick and were kindly; others jeered at me and the other very young fellows. They were anxious to make men of us, by which they meant making us like themselves. Some of them were men indeed – grave, slow young farmers and artisans with apparently boundless resources of strength and courage; others were just riffraff of the kind you get in any chance collection of men. None of them had much education; none had any clear idea what the war was about, though many felt that England had been menaced and had to be defended; perhaps the most astonishing thing was that none of us had much notion of geography and thought that going to fight in

France might involve almost any kind of climate, from the Pole to the Equator. Of course some of us had some geography in school and had studied maps, but a school map is a terribly uncommunicative thing.

I was a member of the Second Canadian Division, and later we were part of the Canadian Corps, but such descriptions meant little to me; I was aware of the men directly around me and rarely had a chance to meet any others. I might as well say at once that although I was on pretty good terms with everybody I made no lasting friends. There were men who formed strong friendships, which sometimes led to acts of bravery, and there were men who were great on what they called 'pals' and talked and sang loudly about it. Those now living are still at it. But I was a lonely creature, and although I would have been very happy to have a friend I just never happened to meet one.

Probably my boredom was to blame. For I was bored as I have never been since – bored till every bone in my body was heavy with it. This was not the boredom of inactivity; an infantry trainee is kept on the hop from morning till night, and his sleep is sound. It was the boredom that comes of being cut off from everything that could make life sweet, or arouse curiosity, or enlarge the range of the senses. It was the boredom that comes of having to perform endless tasks that have no savour and acquire skills one would gladly be without. I learned to march and drill and shoot and keep myself clean according to Army standards; to make my bed and polish my boots and my buttons and to wrap lengths of dung-coloured rag around my legs in the approved way. None of it had any great reality for me, but I learned to do it all, and even to do it well.

Thus, when I went home for my leave before going abroad, I was an object of some wonderment. I was a man, in appearance. My mother was almost silenced, so far as her customary criticism went; she made a few attempts to reduce me to the status of her own dear laddie, but I was not willing to play that game. Leola Cruikshank was proud to be seen with me, and we got a little beyond the kissing stage in our last encounter. I desperately wanted to see Mrs Dempster, but it was impossible, for in my uniform I was unable to go anywhere without being noticed, and though I would have died rather than admit it, I was still too much afraid of my mother to defy her openly. Paul I saw once, but I do not think he knew me, for he stared and passed by.

So off I went on a troopship, lectured by officers who were anxious to harden us with tales of German atrocities. These Germans, I gathered, were absolute devils; not winning campaigns, but maiming children, ravishing women (never less than ten to a single victim), and insulting religion were the things they had gone to war to accomplish; they took their tone from their Kaiser, who was a comic, mad monster; they had to be shown that decency still ruled the world, and we were decency incarnate. I had by that time seen enough of Army life to think that if we were decency the Germans must be rough indeed, for a more foul-mouthed, thieving, whoring lot of toughs than some of the soldiers I met it would be hard to imagine. But I was not discontented with soldiering; I was discontented with myself, with my loneliness and boredom.

In France, though my boredom was unabated, loneliness was replaced by fear. I was, in a mute, controlled, desperate fashion, frightened for the next three years. I saw plenty of men whose fear found vent; they went mad, or they shot themselves (dead or badly enough to get out of service), or they were such nuisances to the rest of us that they were got rid of in one way or another. But I think there were many in my own case; frightened of death, of wounds, of being captured, but most frightened of admitting to fear and losing face before the others. This kind of fear is not acute, of course; it is a constant depleting companion whose presence makes everything grey. Sometimes fear could be forgotten, but never for long.

I saw a good deal of service, for I was strong, did not break down, and miraculously suffered no wounds. I had leaves, when it was possible to grant them, but for months on end I was at what was called the Front. What it was the Front of I never really knew, for there were always men who were ready to tell – God knows how accurately – where the Allied troops were disposed, and where we were in relation to the British and the French, and from what they said it seemed the Front was everywhere. But certainly we were often only a few hundred yards from the German lines and could see the enemy, in their cooking-

73

pot helmets, quite clearly. If you were such a fool as to show your head they might put a bullet through it, and we had men detailed for the same ugly work.

It seems now to have been a very odd war, for we have had another since then, which has set the standard for modernity of fighting. I saw things that now make my pupils regard me as comparable to one of Wellington's men, or perhaps Marlborough's. My war was greatly complicated by horses, for motor vehicles were useless in Flanders mud; if one was among the horses during a bombardment, as I once chanced to be, the animals were just as dangerous as the German shells. I even saw cavalry, for there were still generals who thought that if they could once get at the enemy with cavalry the machine-guns would quickly be silenced. These cavalrymen were as wondrous to me as Crusaders, but I would not have been on one of their horses for the earth. And of course I saw corpses, and grew used to their unimportant look, for a dead man without any of the panoply of death is a desperately insignificant object. Worse, I saw men who were not corpses but who would be soon and who longed for death.

It was the indignity, the ignominy, the squalor, to which war reduced a wounded man that most ate into me. Men in agony, smashed so that they will never be whole again even if they live, ought not to be something one ignores; but we learned to ignore them, and I have put my foot on many a wretched fellow and pushed him even deeper into the mud, because I had to get over him and onto some spot that we had been ordered to achieve or die in trying.

This was fighting, when at least we were doing something. But for days and weeks there was not much fighting, during which we lived in trenches, in dung-coloured mud into which dung and every filthiness had been trodden, in our dung-coloured uniforms; we were cold, badly fed, and lousy. We had no privacy whatever and began to doubt our individuality, for we seemed to melt into a mass; this was what the sergeants feared, and they did astonishing work in keeping that danger at bay, most of the time; occasionally the horrible loss of personality, the listlessness of degradation, got beyond them, and then we had to be sent to the rear to what were called rest camps; we never rested in them, but at least we could draw a full breath without the lime-and-dung stench of the latrines in it.

In spite of the terribly public quality of a soldier's life, in which I ate, slept, stood, sat, thought, voided my bowels, and felt the dread of death upon me, always among others, I found a little time for reading. But I had only one book, a *New Testament* some well-meaning body had distributed in thousands to the troops. It would never have been my choice; if it had to be the *Bible* I would have taken the *Old Testament* any day, but I would rather have had some big, meaty novels. But where could a private soldier keep such things? I have read often since those days of men who went through the war with books of all sorts, but they were officers Once or twice on leaves I got hold of a book or two in English but lost them as soon as we had to fight. Only my *Testament* could be kept in my pocket without making a big bulge, and I read it to the bone, over and over.

This gained me a disagreeable reputation as a religious fellow, a Holy Joe, and even the chaplain avoided that kind, for they were sure trouble, one way or another. My nickname was Deacon, because of my *Testament* reading. It was useless to explain that I read it not from zeal but curiosity and that long passages of it confirmed my early impression that religion and *Arabian Nights* were true in the same way. (Later I was able to say that they were both psychologically rather than literally true, and that psychological truth was really as important in its own way as historical verification; but while I was a young soldier I had no vocabulary for such argument, though I sensed the truth of it.) I think *Revelation* was my favourite book; the Gospels seemed less relevant to me then than John's visions of the beasts and the struggle of the Crowned Woman, who had the moon beneath her feet, with the great Red Dragon.

The nickname Deacon stuck to me until, in one of the rest camps, word went out that an impromptu show was being organized, and men were called on to volunteer if they would do something to amuse the troops. With a gall that now staggers me, I forced myself to offer an imitation of Charlie Chaplin, whom I had seen exactly twice in film shows for the troops behind the lines. I managed to get the right kind of hat from a Frenchman in the nearby village, I cut myself a little cane from a bush, and when the night came I put on a burnt-cork moustache and shuffled onto the platform; for twelve minutes I told the dirtiest jokes I knew, attaching them to all the officers – including the chaplain – and all the men who had some sort of public character. I now blush at what I remember of what I said, but I drew heavily on the repertoire of Milo Papple and was astonished to find myself a great hit. Even the former vaudevillian (who could sing *If You Were the Only Girl in the World and I Were the Only Boy* in a baritone-and-falsetto duet with himself) was less admired. And from that time forth I was called, not 'Deacon', but 'Charlie'.

What really astonished me was the surprise of the men that I could do such a thing. 'Jesus, the old Deacon, eh – getting off that hot one about the Major, eh? Jesus, and that riddle about Cookie, eh? Jesus!' They could hardly conceive that anybody who read the *Testament* could be other than a Holy Joe – could have another, seemingly completely opposite side to his character. I cannot remember a time when I did not take it as understood that everybody has at least two, if not twenty-two, sides to him. Their astonishment was what astonished *me*. Jesus, eh? People don't look very closely at other people, eh? Jesus!

I did not philosophize in the trenches; I endured. I even tried to make a good job of what I had to do. If I had not been so young and handicapped by lack of education – measured in school terms, for the Army did not know that I was a polymath and would not have cared – I might have been sent off for training as an officer. As it was, I eventually became a sergeant; casualties were heavy – which is the Army way of saying that men I had known and liked were exploded like bombs of guts almost under my nose – and my success in hiding my fear was enough to get me a reputation for having a cool head; so a sergeant I became, as well as a veteran of Sanctuary Wood and Vimy Ridge, before I was twenty. But I think my most surprising achievement was becoming Charlie.

2

My fighting days came to an end somewhere in the week of 5 November 1917, at that point in the Third Battle of Ypres where the Canadians were brought in to attempt to take Passchendaele. It was a Thursday or Friday; I cannot be more accurate because many of the details of that time are clouded in my mind. The battle was the most terrible of my experience; we were trying to take a village that was already a ruin, and we counted our advances in feet; the Front was a confused mess because it had rained every day for weeks and the mud was so dangerous that we dared not make a forward move without a laborious business of putting down duckboards, lifting them as we advanced, and putting them down again ahead of us; understandably this was so slow and exposed that we could not do much of it. I learned from later reading that our total advance was a little less than two miles; it might have been two hundred. The great terror was the mud. The German bombardment churned it up so that it was horribly treacherous, and if a man sank in much over his knees his chances of getting out were poor; a shell exploding nearby could cause an upheaval that overwhelmed him, and the likelihood even of recovering his body was small. I write of this now as briefly as I may, for the terror of it was so great that I would not for anything arouse it again.

One of the principal impediments to our advance was a series of German machine-gun emplacements. I suppose they were set out according to some plan, but we were not in a position to observe any plan; in the tiny area I knew about there was one of these things, and it was clear that we would get no farther forward until it was silenced. Two attempts were made at this dangerous job, with terrible loss to us. I could see how things were going, and how the list of men who might be expected to get to that machine-gun nest was dwindling, and I knew it would come to me next. I do not remember if we were asked to volunteer; such a request would have been merely formal anyhow; things had reached a point where pretence of choice

77

disappeared. Anyhow, I was one of six who were detailed to make a night raid, in one of the intervals of bombardment, to see if we could get to the machine-guns and knock them out. We were issued the small arms and other things we needed, and when the bombardment had stopped for five minutes we set out, not in a knot, of course, but spaced a few yards apart.

The men in the nest were expecting us, for we were doing exactly what their side would have done in the same situation. But we crawled forward, spread-eagled in the mud so as to spread our total weight over as wide an area as possible. It was like swimming in molasses, with the additional misery that it was molasses that stank and had dead men in it.

I was making pretty good progress when suddenly everything went wrong. Somebody – it could have been someone on our side at a distance or it could have been one of the Germans in the nest – sent up a flare; you do not see where these flares come from, because they explode in the air and light up the landscape for a considerable area. When such a thing happens and you are crawling toward an objective, as I was, the proper thing to do is to lie low, with your face down, and hope not to be seen. As I was mud from head to foot and had blackened my face before setting out, I would have been hard to see, and if seen I would have looked like a dead man. After the flare had died out I crept forward again and made a fair amount of distance, so far as I could judge; I did not know where the others were, but I assumed that like me they were making for the gun nest and waiting for a signal from our leader, a second lieutenant to do whatever we could about it. But now three flares exploded, and immediately there began a rattle of machine-gun fire. Again I laid low. But it is the nature of flares, when they are over the arc of their trajectory, to come down with a rush and a characteristic loud hiss; if you are hit by one it is a serious burn, for the last of the flare is still a large gob of fire. and between burning to death or drowning in mud the choice is trivial. Two of these spent flares were hissing in the air above me, and I had to get out of where I was as fast as I could. So I got to my feet and ran.

Now, at a time when we had counted on at least a half-an-hour's lull in the bombardment, it suddenly set up again, and to my bleak horror our own guns, from a considerable distance to the left, began to answer. This sort of thing was always a risk when we were out on small raids, but it was a risk I had never met before. As the shells began to drop I ran wildly, and how long I wallowed around in the dark I do not know, but it could have been anything between three minutes and ten. I became aware of a deafening rattle, with the rhythm of an angry, scolding voice, on my right. I looked for some sort of cover, and suddenly, in a burst of light, there it was right in front of me – an entry concealed by some trash, but unmistakably a door over which hung a curtain of muddy sacking. I pushed through it and found myself in the German machine-gun nest, with three Germans ahead of me firing busily.

I had a revolver, and I shot all three at point-blank range. They did not even see me. There is no use saying any more about it. I am not proud of it now and I did not glory in it then. War puts men in situations where these things happen.

What I wanted to do most of all was to stay where I was and get my breath and my wits before starting back to our line. But the bombardment was increasing, and I knew that if I stopped there one of our shells might drop on the position and blow me up, or the Germans, whose field telephone was already signalling right under my nose, would send some men to see what had happened, and that would be the end of me. I had to get out.

So out I crawled, into mud below and shells above, and tried to get my bearings. As both sides were now at the peak of a bombardment, it was not easy to tell which source of death I should crawl toward, and by bad luck I set out toward the German lines.

How long I crawled I do not know, for I was by this time more frightened, muddled, and desperate than ever before or since. 'Disorientation' is the word now fashionable for my condition. Quite soon I was worse than that; I was wounded, and so far as I could tell, seriously. It was shrapnel, a fragment of an exploding shell, and it hit me in the left leg, though where I cannot say; I have been in a car accident in later life, and the effect was rather like that – a sudden shock like a blow from a club;

and it was a little time before I knew that my left leg was in trouble, though I could not tell how bad it was.

Earlier I said that I had not been wounded; there were a surprising number of men who escaped the war without a wound. I had not been gassed either, though I had been twice in areas where gas was used nearby. I had dreaded a wound, for I had seen so many. What is a wounded man to do? Crawl to shelter and hope he may be found by his own people. I crawled.

Some men found that their senses were quickened by a wound; their ingenuity rose to exceptional heights under stress of danger. But I was one of the other kind. I was not so much afraid as utterly disheartened. There I was, a mud man in a confusion of noise, flashing lights, and the stink of gelignite. I wanted to quit; I had no more heart for the game. But I crawled, with the increasing realization that my left leg was no good for anything and had to be dragged, and the awful awareness that I did not know where I was going. After a few minutes I saw some jagged masonry on my right and dragged toward it. When at last I reached it I propped myself up with my back to a stone wall and gave myself up to a full, rich recognition of the danger and hopelessness of my position. For three years I had kept my nerve by stifling my intelligence, but now I let the intelligence rip and the nerve dissolve. I am sure there has been worse wretchedness, fright, and despair in the world's history, but I set up a personal record that I have never since approached.

My leg began to declare itself in a way that I can only describe in terms of sound; from a mute condition it began to murmur, then to moan and whine, then to scream. I could not see much of what was wrong because of the mud in which I was covered, but my exploring hand found a great stickiness that I knew was blood, and I could make out that my leg lay on the ground in an unnatural way. You will get tetanus, I told myself, and you will die of lockjaw. It was a Deptford belief that in this disease you bent backward until at last your head touched your heels and you had to be buried in a round coffin. I had seen some tetanus in the trenches, and nobody had needed a round coffin even if one had been available; still, in my condition, the belief was stronger than experience.

I thought of Deptford, and I thought of Mrs Dempster. Particularly of her parting words to me: 'There's just one thing to remember; whatever happens, it does no good to be afraid.' Mrs Dempster, I said aloud, was a fool. I was afraid, and I was not in a situation where doing good, or doing evil, had any relevance at all.

It was then that one of the things happened that make my life strange – one of the experiences that other people have not had or do not admit to – one of the things that makes me so resentful of Packer's estimate of me as a dim man to whom nothing important has ever happened.

I became conscious that the bombardment had ceased, and only an occasional gun was heard. But flares appeared in the sky at intervals, and one of these began to drop toward me. By its light I could see that the remnant of standing masonry in which I was lying was all that was left of a church, or perhaps a school – anyhow a building of some size – and that I lay at the foot of a ruined tower. As the hissing flame dropped I saw there about ten or twelve feet above me on an opposite wall, in a niche, a statue of the Virgin and Child. I did not know it then but I know now that it was the assembly of elements that represent the Immaculate Conception, for the little Virgin was crowned, stood on a crescent moon, which in its turn rested on a globe, and in the hand that did not hold the Child she carried a sceptre from which lilies sprang. Not knowing what it was meant to be, I thought in a flash it must be the Crowned Woman in *Revelation* – she who had the moon beneath her feet and was menaced by the Red Dragon. But what hit me worse than the blow of the shrapnel was that the face was Mrs Dempster's face.

I had lost all nerve long before. Now, as the last of the flare hissed towards me, I lost consciousness.

3

'May I have a drink of water?'

'Did you speak?'

'Yes. May I have a drink, Sister?'

'You may have a glass of champagne, if there is any. Who are you?'

'Ramsay, D., Sergeant, Second Canadian Division.'

'Well, Ramsay-Dee, it's marvellous to have you with us.'

'Where is this?'

'You'll find out. Where have *you* been?'

Ah, where *had* I been? I didn't know then and I don't know yet, but it was such a place as I had never known before. Years later, when for the first time I read Coleridge's *Kubla Khan* and came on –

> Weave a circle round him thrice,
> And close your eyes with holy dread,
> For he on honey-dew hath fed,
> And drunk the milk of Paradise

– I almost jumped out of my skin, for the words so perfectly described my state before I woke up in hospital. I had been wonderfully at ease and healingly at peace; though from time to time voices spoke to me I was under no obligation to hear what they said or to make a reply; I felt that everything was good, that my spirit was wholly my own, and that though all was strange nothing was evil. From time to time the little Madonna appeared and looked at me with friendly concern before removing herself; once or twice she spoke, but I did not know what she said and did not need to know.

But here I was, apparently in bed, and a very pretty girl in a nurse's uniform was asking me where I had been. Clearly she meant it as a joke. She thought she knew where I had been. That meant that the joke was on her, for no one, not I myself, knew that.

'Is this a base hospital?'

'Goodness, no. How do you feel, Ramsay-Dee?'

'Fine. What day is this?'

'This is the twelfth of May. I'll get you a drink.'

She disappeared, and I took a few soundings. It was not easy work. The last time I had been conscious of was November; if this was May I had been in that splendid, carefree world for quite a while. I wasn't in such a bad place now; I couldn't move my head very much, but I could see a marvellously decorated plaster ceiling, and such walls as lay in my vision were panelled in wood; there was an open window somewhere, and sweet air – no stink of mud or explosive or corpses or latrines – was blowing through it. I was clean. I wriggled appreciatively – and wished I hadn't, for several parts of me protested. But here was the girl again, and with a red-faced man in a long white coat.

He seemed greatly elated, especially when I was able to remember my Army number, and though I did not learn why at once I found out over a few days that I was by way of being a medical pet, and my recovery proved something; being merely the patient, I was never given the full details, but I believe I was written up in at least two medical papers as a psychiatric curiosity, but as I was referred to only as 'the patient' I could never identify myself for sure. The red-faced man was some sort of specialist in shell-shock cases, and I was one of his successes, though I rather think I cured myself, or the little Madonna cured me, or some agencies other than good nursing and medical observation.

Oh, I was a lucky man! Apparently the flare did hit me, and before it expired it burned off a good part of my clothes and consumed the string of my identification disks, so that when I was picked up they were lost in the mud. There had been some doubt as to whether I was dead or merely on the way to it, but I was taken back to our base, and as I stubbornly did not die I was removed eventually to a hospital in France, and as I still refused either to die or live I was shipped to England; by this time I was a fairly interesting instance of survival against all probabilities, and the red-faced doctor had claimed me for his own; I was brought to this special hospital in a fine old house in Buckinghamshire, and had lain unconscious, and likely to remain so, though the red-faced doctor stubbornly insisted that some day I would wake up and tell him something of value. So here it was May, and I was awake, and the hospital staff were delighted, and made a great pet of me.

They had other news for me, not so good. My burns had been severe, and in those days they were not so clever with burns as they are now, so that quite a lot of the skin on my chest and left side was an angry-looking mess, rather like lumpy sealing wax, and is so still, though it is a little browner now. In the bed, on the left side, was an arrangement of wire, like a bee-skip, to keep the sheets from touching the stump where my left leg had been. While my wits were off on that paradisal holiday I had been fed liquids, and so I was very thin and weak. What is more, I had a full beard, and the pretty nurse and I had a rare old time getting it off.

Let me stop calling her the pretty nurse. Her name was Diana Marfleet, and she was one of those volunteers who got a proper nursing training but never acquired the full calm of a professional nursing sister. She was the first English girl I ever saw at close range, and a fine specimen of her type, which was the fair-skinned, dark-haired, brown-eyed type. Not only was she pretty, she had charm and an easy manner and talked amusingly, for she came of that class of English person who thinks it bad manners to be factual and serious. She was twenty-four, which gave her an edge of four years over me, and it was not long before she confided to me that her fiancé, a Navy lieutenant, had been lost when the *Aboukir* was torpedoed in the very early days of the war. We were on tremendous terms in no time, for she had been nursing me since I had come to the hospital in January, and such nourishment as I had taken had been spooned and poured into me by her; she had also washed me and attended to the bedpan and the urinal, and continued to do so; a girl who can do that without being facetious or making a man feel self-conscious is no ordinary creature. Diana was a wonderful girl, and I am sure I gained strength and made physical progress at an unusual rate, to please her.

One day she appeared at my bedside with a look of great seriousness and saluted me smartly.

'What's that for?'

'Tribute of humble nursing sister to hero of Passchendaele.'

'Get away!' (This was a great expression of my father's, and I have never wholly abandoned it.)

'Fact. What do you think you've got?'

'I rather think I've got you.'

'No cheek. We've been tracing you, Sergeant Ramsay. Did you know that you were officially dead?'

'Dead! Me?'

'You. That's why your V.C. was awarded posthumously.'

'Get away!'

'Fact. You have the V.C. for, with the uttermost gallantry and disregard of all but duty, clearing out a machine-gun nest and thereby ensuring an advance of – I don't know how far but quite a bit. You were the only one of the six who didn't get back to the line, and one of the men saw you – your unmistakable size anyhow – running right towards the machine-gun nest; so it was clear enough, even though they couldn't find your body afterward. Anyway you've got it, and Dr Houneen is making sure you do get it and it isn't sent home to depress your mother.'

The other three men in the room gave a cheer – an ironic cheer. We all pretended we didn't care about decorations, but I never heard of anybody turning one down.

Diana was very sorry in a few days that she had said what she did about the medal going home to my mother, for a letter arrived from the Reverend Donald Phelps, in reply to one Dr Houneen had sent to my parents, saying that Alexander Ramsay and his wife, Fiona Dunstable Ramsay, had both died in the influenza epidemic of early 1918, though not before they had received news of my presumed death at Passchendaele.

Diana was ashamed because she thought she might have hurt my feelings. I was ashamed because I felt the loss so little.

4

It was years before I thought of the death of my parents as anything other than a relief; in my thirties I was able to see them as real people, who had done the best they could in the lives fate had given them. But as I lay in that hospital I was glad that I did not have to be my mother's own dear laddie any longer, or ever attempt to explain to her what war was, or warp my nature to suit her confident demands. I knew she had eaten my father, and I was glad I did not have to fight any longer to keep her from eating me. Oh, these good, ignorant, confident women! How one grows to hate them! I was mean-spiritedly pleased that my mother had not lived to hear of my V.C.; how she would have paraded in mock-modesty as the mother of a hero, the very womb and matrix of bravery, in consequence of my three years of degradation in the Flanders mud!

I confided none of this to Diana, of course. She was intensely curious about my war experience, and I had no trouble at all in talking to her about it. But as I gave her my confidence and she gave me her sympathy, I was well aware that we were growing very close and that some day this would have to be reckoned with. I did not care. I was happy to be living at all, and lived only for the sweetness of the moment.

She was a romantic, and as I had never met a female romantic before it was a delight to me to explore her emotions. She wanted to know all about me, and I told her as honestly as I could; but as I was barely twenty, and a romantic myself, I know now that I lied in every word I uttered – lied not in fact but in emphasis, in colour, and in intention. She was entranced by the idea of life in Canada, and I made it entrancing. I even told her about Mrs Dempster (though not that I was the cause of her distracted state) and felt let down that she did not respond very warmly. But when I told her about the little Madonna at Passchendaele and later as a visitor to my long coma, she was delighted and immediately gave it a conventionally religious significance, which, quite honestly, had never occurred to me. She returned to this theme again and again, and often I was reminded of the introduction to *A Child's Book of Saints* and little W.V., for whom those stories had been told. Personally I had come to think of little W.V. as rather a little pill, but I now reserved my judgement, for Diana was little W.V. to the life, and I was all for Diana.

Gradually it broke in upon me that Diana had marked me for her own, and I was too much flattered to see what that might mean. A lot of the nurses in that hospital were girls of good family, and though they worked very hard and did full nursing duty they had some privileges that cannot have been common. Most of them lived nearby, and they were able to go home in their time off.

When Diana returned from these off-duty jaunts she spoke about her home and her parents, and they seemed to be people unlike parents as I knew them. Her father, Canon Marfleet, was a domestic chaplain at Windsor as well as a parish clergyman; I had little notion what a domestic chaplain might be, but I assumed he jawed the Royal Family about morals, just as the parsons jawed us at home. Her mother was an Honourable, though the Canon was not, which surprised me, and she had been born a De Blaquiere, which, as Diana pronounced it D'Blackyer, I did not get straight for some time. Because of the war the Marfleets were living very simply – only two servants and a gardener three times a week – and the Canon had followed royal example and forbidden alcoholic liquors in his household for the duration, except for a glass or two of port when he felt peaky. They restricted their daily bath-water to three inches, to save fuel for Our Cause; I had never in my life known anyone who bathed every day and assumed that the hospital daily bath was some sort of curative measure that would eventually cease.

Diana was a very educative experience. As she gradually took me over she began to correct me about some of my usages, which she thought quaint – not wrong, just quaint. Fortunately, because I had a good measure of Scots in my speech, we did not have the usual haggle of Old and New World couples about pronunciations, though she was hilarious about me calling a reel of cotton a spool of thread and assured me that pants were things one wore under trousers. But she made it clear that one tore bread, instead of cutting it neatly, and buttered it only in bites, which I thought a time-wasting affectation; she also stopped me from eating like a man who might not live until his next mouthful, a childhood habit that had been exaggerated in the trenches and that still overcomes me when I am nervous. I liked it. I was grateful. Besides, she did it with humour and charm; there was not a nagging breath in her.

Of course this did not happen all at once. It was some time after I woke from my coma before I could get out of bed, and quite a while after that before I could begin experimenting with the succession of artificial legs that came before my final one. I had to learn to walk with crutches, and because so many of my muscles, especially in the left arm, were scarred or reduced to very little, this took time and hurt. Diana saw me through it all. Literally, I leaned on her, and now and then I fell on her. She was a wonderful nurse.

When it was at last possible to do so she took me home, and

I met the Canon and the Honourable. The best I can say about them is that they were worthy to be Diana's parents. The Canon was a charming man, quite unlike any clergyman I had ever known, and even at the Sunday midday meal he never talked about religion. Like a good Presbyterian, I tried once or twice to pass him a compliment on his discourse at morning service and pursue its theme, but he wanted none of that. He wanted to talk about the war, and as he was well informed and a Lloyd George supporter it was not the usual hate session in which he invited me to engage; there must have been a lot like him in England, though you would never have known it from the peace we finally made. The Honourable was a wonder, not like a mother at all. She was a witty, frivolous woman of a beauty congruous with her age – about forty-seven, I suppose – and talked as if she hadn't a brain in her head. But I was not deceived; she was what Diana would be at that age, and I liked every bit of it.

How my spirit expanded in the home of the Marfleets! To a man who had been where I had been it was glorious. I only hope I behaved myself and did not talk like a fool. But when I remember those days I remember the Canon and the Honourable and Diana and what I felt about them, but little of what I did or said.

5

The patchy quality of my recollection of this period is owing, I suppose, to the exhaustion of three years of war. I was out of it at last, and I was happy to take pleasure in security and cleanliness, without paying too close attention to what went on. Now and then it was possible to hear the guns in France; food was short but better than I had had in the trenches; the news came in ominous newspaper dispatches. Nevertheless I was happy and knew that for me, at least, the war was over. My plans were simple – to learn to walk with a crutch, and later with an artificial leg and a cane. Without being positively in love with Diana, I was beglamoured by her and flattered by her attention. I had fought my war and was resting.

We did win it at last, and there was a great hullabaloo in the hospital, and on the day after November 11, Dr Houneen got a car and drove me and another man who was fit for it, and Diana and another nurse, to London to see the fun. The rejoicing was a little too much like an infantry attack for my taste; I had not been in a crowd since I was wounded, and the noise and crush were very alarming to me. Indeed, I have never been much good at enduring noise and crush since late 1917. But I saw some of the excitement and a few things that shocked me; people, having been delivered from destruction, became horribly destructive themselves; people, having been delivered from license and riot, pawed and mauled and shouted dirty phrases in the streets. Nor am I in any position to talk; it was on the night of November 12, in a house in Eaton Square belonging to one of her De Blaquiere aunts, that I first slept with Diana, the aunt giving her assent by silence and discreet absence; to me at least there seemed something unseemly about the union of my scarred and maimed body with her unblemished beauty. Unseemly or not, it was my first experience of anything of the kind, for I had never been able to bring myself to make use of soldiers' brothels or any of the casual company that was available to men in uniform. Diana was not a novice – the fiancé who went down on the *Aboukir*, I suppose – and she initiated me most tenderly, for which I shall always be grateful. Thus we became lovers in the fullest sense, and for me the experience was an important step towards the completion of that manhood which had been thrust upon me so one-sidedly in the trenches.

The next night, because Diana had luck as well as influence, we had tickets for *Chu-Chin-Chow* at His Majesty's, and this was a great experience too, in quite a different way, for I had never seen any theatre more elaborate than a troop show. On one of my two very brief leaves in Paris I had sought out the site of Robert-Houdin's theatre, but it was no longer there. I must have been an odd young man to have supposed that it might still be in existence. But my historical sense developed later.

I see that I have been so muddle-headed as to put my sexual initiation in direct conjunction with a visit to a musical show, which suggests some lack of balance perhaps. But, looking back from my present age, the two, though very different, are not so unlike in psychological weight as you might suppose. Both were wonders, strange lands revealed to me in circumstances of great excitement. I suppose I was still in rather delicate health, mentally as well as physically.

The next great moment in my life was the reception of my Victoria Cross, from the King himself. Dr Houneen had established that I was really alive, and so the award that had been published as posthumous was repeated on one of the lists, and in due course I went to Buckingham Palace in a taxi, on a December morning, and got it. Diana was with me, for I was allowed to invite one guest, and she was the obvious choice. We were looked at with sentimental friendliness by the other people in the room, and I suppose an obviously wounded soldier, accompanied by a very pretty nurse, was about as popular a sight as the time afforded.

Most of the details are vague, but a few remain. A military band, in an adjoining room, played Gems from *The Maid of the Mountains* (it was Diana who told me), and we all stood around the walls until the King and some aides entered and took a place in the centre. When my turn came I stumped forward on my latest metal leg, making rather a noisy progress, and got myself into the right position, directly in front of the King. Somebody handed him the medal, and he pinned it on my tunic, then shook my hand and said, 'I am glad you were able to get here after all.'

I can still remember what a deep and rather gruff voice he had, and also the splendid neatness of his Navy beard. He was a good deal shorter than I, so I was looking down into his very blue, rather glittering eyes, and I thought I had better smile at the royal joke, so I did, and retreated in good order.

There was a moment, however, when the King and I were looking directly into each other's eyes, and in that instant I had a revelation that takes much longer to explain than to experience. Here am I, I reflected, being decorated as a hero, and in the eyes of everybody here I am indeed a hero; but I know that my heroic act was rather a dirty job I did when I was dreadfully frightened; I could just as easily have muddled it and been ingloriously killed. But it doesn't much matter, because people seem to need heroes; so long as I don't lose sight of the truth, it might as well be me as anyone else. And here before me stands a marvellously groomed little man who is pinning a hero's medal on me because some of his forebears were Alfred the Great, and Charles the First, and even King Arthur, for anything I know to the contrary. But I shouldn't be surprised if inside he feels as puzzled about the fate that brings him here as I. We are public icons, we two: he an icon of kingship, and I an icon of heroism, unreal yet very necessary; we have obligations above what is merely personal, and to let personal feelings obscure the obligations would be failing in one's duty.

This was clearer still afterward, at lunch at the Savoy, when the Canon and the Honourable gave us a gay time, with champagne; they all seemed to accept me as a genuine hero, and I did my best to behave decently, neither believing in it too obviously, nor yet protesting that I was just a simple chap who had done his duty when he saw it – a pose that has always disgusted me. Ever since, I have tried to think charitably of people in prominent positions of one kind or another; we cast them in roles, and it is only right to consider them as players, without trying to discredit them with knowledge of their off-stage life – unless they drag it into the middle of the stage themselves.

6

The business of getting used to myself as a hero was only part of the work I had on hand during my long stay in the hospital. When first I returned to this world – I will not say to consciousness because it seemed to me that I had been conscious on a different level during what they called my coma – I had to get used to being a man with one leg and a decidedly weakened left arm. I was not so clever at managing these handicaps as were some of the men in that hospital who had lost limbs; I have always been clumsy, and though Diana and the doctor assured me that I would soon walk as well as if I had a real leg I had no belief in it, and indeed I have never managed to walk without a limp and feel much happier with a cane. I was very weak physically, to begin with, and although I was perfectly sane I was a little light-headed for several months, and all my recollections of that period are confused by this quality of light-headedness. But I had to get used to being a hero – that is, not to believe it myself but not to be insulting to those who did so – and I also had to make up my mind about Diana.

There was an unreality about our relationship that had its roots in something more lasting than my light-headedness. I will say nothing against her, and I shall always be grateful to her for teaching me what the physical side of love was; after the squalor of the trenches her beauty and high spirits were the best medicine I got. But I could not be blind to the fact that she regarded me as her own creation. And why not ? Hadn't she fed me and washed me and lured me back into this world when I was far away? Didn't she teach me to walk, showing the greatest patience when I was most clumsy? Was she not anxious to re-train me about habits of eating and behaviour? But even as I write it down I know how clear it is that what was wrong be-tween Diana and me was that she was too much a mother to me, and as I had had one mother, and lost her, I was not in a hurry to acquire another – not even a young and beautiful one with whom I could play Oedipus to both our hearts' content. If I could manage it, I had no intention of being anybody's own dear laddie, ever again.

That decision, made at that time, has shaped my life and doubtless in some ways it has warped it, but I still think I knew what was best for me. In the long periods of rest in the hospital I thought as carefully as I could about my situation, and what emerged was this : I had made a substantial payment to society for anything society had given me or would give me in future; a leg and much of one arm are hard coin. Society had decided to regard me as a hero, and though I knew that I was no more a hero than many other men I had fought with, and less than some who had been killed doing what I could not have done, I deter-mined to let society regard me as it pleased; I would not trade on it, but I would not put it aside either. I would get a pension in due time, and my Victoria Cross carried a resounding fifty dollars a year with it; I would take these rewards and be grate-ful. But I wanted my life to be my own; I would live henceforth for my own satisfaction.

That did not include Diana. She seemed to assume that it did, and perhaps I was unfair to her in not checking her assumptions as soon as I became aware of them. But, to be frank, I liked having her in love with me; it fed my spirit, which was at a low ebb. I liked going to bed with her, and as she liked it too I thought this a fair exchange. But a life with Diana was simply not for me. As girls do, she assumed that we were drifting towards an engagement and marriage; though she never said so in plain words it was clear she thought that when I was strong enough we would go to Canada, and if I did not mistake her utterly, she had in her mind's eye a fine big wheat farm in the West, for she had the English delusion that farming was a great way to live. I knew enough about farming to be sure it was not a life for amateurs or wounded men.

Every two weeks Diana would appear, looking remote and beautiful, and hand me a letter from Leola Cruikshank. These were always difficult occasions because the letters embarrassed me; they were so barren of content, so ill-expressed, so utterly unlike the Leola, all curls and soft lips and whispers, that I remembered. How, I wondered, had I been so stupid as to get myself mixed up with such a pinhead? Diana knew the letters were from a girl, for Leola's guileless writing could not have belonged to any other section of humanity, and intuition told her that, as they were almost the only letters I received, the girl was a special one. I could not have told her how special, for I could no longer remember precisely what pledges I had made to Leola; was I engaged to her or was I not? The letters I wrote in reply, and painstakingly smuggled into the post so Diana should not see them, were as noncommittal as I had the heart to make them; I tried to write in such a way as to evoke from Leola some indication of what she believed our relationship to be, without committing myself. This meant subtlety of a kind that was far outside Leola's scope; she was no hand with the pen, and her flat little letters gave Deptford gossip (with all the spice left out) and usually ended, 'Everybody looks forward to your coming home and it will be lovely to see you again, Love, Leola.' Was this coolness or maidenly reserve? Sometimes I broke out in a sweat, wondering.

One of Leola's letters came just before Christmas, which I had leave to spend with Diana's family. The Canon had celebrated the Armistice by abandoning the no-alcohol vow and it looked like being a jolly occasion. I had learned to drink neat rum in the Army and was ready for anything. But, on Christmas Eve, Diana contrived a private talk between us and asked me straight out who the girl was who wrote to me from Canada and was I involved with her. *Involved* was her word. I had been dreading this question but had no answer ready, and I havered and floundered and became aware that Leola's name had an uncouth sound when spoken in such circumstances, and hated myself for thinking so. My whole trouble, jackass that I was, sprang from the fact that I tried to be decently loyal to Leola without hurting Diana, and the more I talked the worse mess I made of things. In no time Diana was crying, and I was doing my best to comfort her. But I managed to keep uppermost in my mind the determination I had formed not to get engaged to her, and this led me into verbal acrobatics that quickly brought on a blazing row.

Canadian soldiers had an ambiguous reputation in England at that time; we were supposed to be loyal, furious, hairy fellows who spat bullets at the enemy but ate women raw. Diana accused me of being one of these ogres, who had led her on to reveal feelings I did not reciprocate. Like a fool, I said I thought she was old enough to know what she thought. Aha, she said, that was it, was it? Because she was older than I, she was a tough old rounder who could look out for herself, was she? Not a bit tough, I countered, frank with a flat-footedness that now makes me blush, but after all she had been engaged, hadn't she? There it was again, she countered; I thought she was damaged goods; I was throwing it in her face that she had given herself to a man who had died a hero's death in the very first weeks of the war. I looked on her simply as an amusement, a pastime; she had loved me in my weakness, without knowing how essentially coarse-fibred I was. And much more to the same effect.

Of course this gave way in time to much gentler exchanges, and we savoured the sweet pleasures of making up after a fight, but it was not long before Diana wanted to know, just as someone who wished me well, how far I was committed to Leola. I didn't dare tell her that I wanted to know precisely the same thing; I was too young to be truthful about such a matter. Well then, she continued, was I in love with Leola? I was able to say with a good conscience that I was not. Then I was in love with herself after all, said Diana, making one of those feminine leaps in logic that leave men breathless. I made a long speech about never knowing what people meant when they said they were in love with someone. I loved Diana, I said; I really did. But as for 'being in love' – I babbled a good deal of nonsense that I cannot now recall and would not put down if I did.

Diana changed her tactics. I was too intellectual, she said, and analyzed matters on which feeling was the only true guide. If I loved her, she asked no more. What did the future hold for us?

I do not want to make Diana seem crafty in my record of this conversation, but I must say that she had a great gift for getting her own way. *She* had strong ideas on what the future held for us, and I had none, and I am certain she knew it. Therefore she was putting forward this question not to hear from me but to inform me. But I had my little store of craft too. I said that the war had been such a shake-up for me that I had no clear ideas about the future, and certainly had not considered asking her to marry anybody as badly crippled as I.

This proved to be a terrible mistake. Diana was so vehement about what a decent woman felt for a man who had been wounded and handicapped in the war – not to speak of a man who had been given the highest award for bravery – that I nearly lost my head and begged her to be my wife. I cannot look back on my young self in this situation without considerable shame and disgust. So far I had been able to reject this girl's love, but I was nearly captured by her flattery. Not that she meant it insincerely; there was nothing insincere about Diana. But she had been raised on a mental diet of heroism, Empire, decency, and the emotional superiority of womanhood, and she could talk about these things without a blush, as parsons talk about God. And I was only twenty.

What a night that was! We talked till three o'clock, complicating our situation with endless scruple, as young people are apt to do, and trying not to hurt each other's feelings, despite the fact that Diana wanted to get engaged to me and I was fighting desperately to prevent any such thing. But I have said before, and I repeat, Diana was really an exceptional girl, and when she saw she was not going to get her way she gave in with grace.

'All right,' she said, sitting up on the sofa and tidying her hair (for we had been very much entangled during parts of our argument, and my latest artificial leg had been giving some ominous croaks); 'if we aren't going to be married, that's that. But what *are* you going to do, Dunny? Surely you aren't going to marry that girl with a name like a hair tonic and go on editing your father's potty little paper, are you? There's more to you than that.'

I agreed that I was sure there was more to me than that, but I didn't know what it was and I needed time to find out. Furthermore, I knew that the finding out must be done alone. I did not tell Diana that there was the whole question of the little Madonna to be gone into, because I knew that with her conventional Christian background and her generous sentimentality she would begin then and there to explain it for me, and every scrap of intuition I possessed told me that her explanation would be the wrong one. But I did tell her that I was strongly conscious that my lack of formal education was the greatest handicap I had and that I felt that somehow I must get to a university; if I went back to Canada and explored all the possibilities I could probably manage it. It is not easy to put down what one says to a girl in such circumstances, but I managed to make it clear that what I most wanted was time to grow up. The war had not matured me; I was like a piece of meat that is burned on one side and raw on the other, and it was on the raw side I needed to work. I thanked her, as well as I could, for what she had done for me.

'Let me do one thing more for you,' she said. 'Let me rename you. How on earth did you ever get yourself called Dunstable?'

'My mother's maiden name,' said I. 'Lots of people in Canada get landed with their mother's maiden name as a Christian name. But what's wrong with it?'

'It's hard to say, for one thing,' said she, 'and it sounds like a cart rumbling over cobblestones for another. You'll never get anywhere in the world named Dumbledum Ramsay. Why don't you change it to Dunstan? St Dunstan was a marvellous person and very much like you – mad about learning, terribly stiff and stern and scowly, and an absolute wizard at withstanding temptation. Do you know that the Devil once came to tempt him in the form of a fascinating woman, and he caught her nose in his goldsmith's tongs and gave it a terrible twist?'

I took her nose between my fingers and gave it a twist. This was very nearly the undoing of all that I had gained, but after a while we were talking again. I liked the idea of a new name; it suggested new freedom and a new personality. So Diana got some of her father's port and poured it on my head and re named me. She was an Anglican, of course, and her light-minded attitude toward some sacred things still astonished the deep Presbyterian in me; but I had not waded through the mud-and-blood soup of Passchendaele to worry about foolish things; blasphemy in a good cause (which usually means one's own cause) is not hard to stomach. When at last we went to bed two splendid things had happened: Diana and I were friends instead of lovers, and I had an excellent new name.

Christmas Day was even better than I had foreseen. I am sure Diana's parents knew what was in the wind and were game enough not to stand in the way if we had really wanted to marry. But they were much relieved that we had decided against it. How they knew I cannot say, but parents are often less stupid than their children suppose, and I suspect the Honourable smelled it in the morning air. After all, what satisfaction would it have been to them to have their daughter marry a man in my physical state, of very different background, and four years younger than herself, in order to go off to seek a fortune in a country of which they knew nothing? So they were happy, and I was happy, and I suspect that Diana was a good deal happier than she would ever have admitted.

She had fallen in love with me because she felt she had made whatever I was out of a smashed-up and insensible hospital case; but I don't think it was long before she was just as sure as I that our marriage would never have worked. So I lost a possible wife and gained three very good friends that Christmas.

Getting back to Canada took some time because of the complication of Army necessities and my supposedly fragile state, but
early in the following May I got off the train at Deptford, was
greeted by the reeve, Orville Cave, and ceremonially driven
around the village as the chief spectacle in a procession.

This grandeur had been carefully planned beforehand, by
letter, but it was nonetheless astonishing for that. I had little
idea of what four years of war had done in creating a new
atmosphere in Deptford, for it had shown little interest in
world affairs in my schooldays. But here was our village shoe-
repair man, Moses Langirand, in what was meant to be a
French uniform, personating Marshal Foch; he had secured this
position on the best possible grounds, being the only French-
speaking Canadian for miles around, and having an immense
grey moustache. Here was a tall youth I did not know, in an
outfit that approximated that of Uncle Sam. There were two
John Bulls, owing to some misunderstanding that could not be
resolved without hurt feelings. There were Red Cross nurses in
plenty – six or seven of them. A girl celebrated in my day for
having big feet, named Katie Orchard, was swathed in bunting
and had a bandage over one eye; she was Gallant Little Belgium.
These, and other people dressed in patriotic but vague outfits,
formed a procession highly allegorical in its nature, which advanced down our main street, led by a band of seven brass
instruments and a thunderous drum. I rode after them in an
open Gray-Dort with the reeve, and following us was what
was then called a Calithumpian parade, of gaily dressed children
tormenting and insulting Myron Papple, who was identifiable
as the German Emperor by his immense, upturned false moustache. Myron hopped about and feigned madness and deprivation
very amusingly, but with such vigour that we wondered how a
fat man could keep it up for long. As ours was a small village we
toured through all the streets, and went up and down the main
street no less than three times. Even at that we had done our
uttermost by 2.45, and I had clumped down off the train at 1.30.

It was the strangest procession I had ever seen, but it was in my honour and I will not laugh at it. It was Deptford's version of a Roman Triumph, and I tried to be worthy of it, looked solemn, saluted every flag I saw that was 12-by-8 inches or over, and gave special heed to elderly citizens.

The procession completed, I was hidden in the Tecumseh House until 5.30, when I was to have a state supper at the reeve's house. When I write 'hidden' I mean it literally. My fellow townsmen felt that it would be unseemly for me to stroll about the streets, like an ordinary human being, before my apotheosis that night, so I was put in the best bedroom in our hotel, upon the door of which a Canadian Red Ensign had been tacked, and the barman, Joe Gallagher, was given strict orders to keep everyone away from me. So there I sat by my window, looking across a livery-stable yard toward St James' Presbyterian Church, occasionally reading *War and Peace* (for I was now well embarked on the big, meaty novels I had longed for at the Front), but mostly too excited to do anything but marvel at myself and wonder when I would be free to do as I pleased.

Freedom was certainly not to be mine that day. At six I supped ceremonially at the reeve's; there were so many guests that we ate on the lawn from trestle tables, consuming cold chicken and ham, potato salad and pickles in bewildering variety, and quantities of ice cream, pie, and cake. We then set the whole banquet well awash inside ourselves with hot, strong coffee. Our progress to the Athelstan Opera House was stately, as befitted the grandees of the occasion, and we arrived ten minutes before the scheduled proceedings at 7.30.

If you are surprised that so small a place should have an Opera House, I should explain that it was our principal hall of assembly, upstairs in the Athelstan Block, which was the chief business premises of our village, and built of brick instead of the more usual wood. It was a theatre, right enough, with a stage that had a surprising roller curtain, on which was handsomely painted a sort of composite view, or evocation, of all that was most romantic in Europe; it is many years since I saw it, but I clearly remember a castle on the shores of a lagoon, where gondolas appeared amid larger shipping, which seemed to be plying in and out of Naples, accommodated at the foot of snowtopped Alps. The floor of the Opera House was flat, as being more convenient for dancing, but this was compensated for by the fact that the stage sloped forward toward the footlights, at an angle which made sitting on chairs a tricky and even perilous feat. I do not know how many people it seated, but it was full on this occasion, and people stood or sat in the aisles on extra chairs, borrowed from an undertaker.

The reeve and I and the other notables climbed a back stairs and pushed our way through the scenery to the chairs that had been set for us on the stage. Beyond the curtain we heard the hum of the crowd above the orchestra of piano, violin, and trombone. A little after the appointed time – to allow for latecomers, said the reeve, but no latecomer could have squeezed in – the curtain rose (swaying menacingly inward toward us as it did so), and we were revealed, set off against a set of scenery that portrayed a dense and poisonously green forest. Our chairs were arranged in straight rows behind a table supporting two jugs of water and fully a dozen glasses, to succour the speakers in their thirst. We were a fine group : three clergymen, the magistrate, the Member of Parliament and the Member of the Legislature, the Chairman of the Continuation School Board, and seven members of the township council sat on the stage, as well as the reeve and myself. I expect we looked rather like a minstrel show. I was the only man in uniform on the stage itself, but in the front row were six others, and on the right-hand end of this group sat Percy Boyd Staunton, in a major's uniform, and at his side was Leola Cruikshank.

On the fourth finger of Leola's left hand was a large diamond ring. Diana had taught me something of these refinements and I got the message at once, as that ring flashed its signals to me during the applause that greeted our appearance. Was I stricken to the heart? Did I blench and feel that all my glory was as dross? No; I was rather pleased. There was one of my homecoming problems solved already, I reflected. Nevertheless I was a little put out and thought that Leola was a sneak not to have informed me of this development in one of her letters.

The purpose of the gathering was plainly signalled by the Union Jack that swathed the speaker's table and a painted streamer that hung above our heads in the toxic forest. 'Welcome To Our Brave Boys Back From The Front,' it shouted, in red and blue letters on a white ground. We stood solemnly at attention while the piano, violin, and trombone worked their way through *God Save the King*, *O Canada*, and, for good measure, *The Maple Leaf Forever*. But we did not then rush greedily upon the noblest splendours of the evening. We began with a patriotic concert, to hone our fervour to a finer edge.

Muriel Parkinson sang about the *Rose that Blows in No-Man's Land*, and when she shrieked (for her voice was powerful rather than sweet) that 'midst the war's great curse stood the Red Cross Nurse,' many people mopped their eyes. She then sang a song about Joan of Arc, which was a popular war number of the day, and thus a delicate compliment was paid to France, our great ally. Muriel was followed by a female child, unknown to me, who recited Pauline Johnson's poem *Canadian Born*, wearing Indian dress; it was at this point that I became aware that one of our Brave Boys, namely George Muskrat the Indian sniper, who had picked off Germans just as he used to pick off squirrels, was not present. George was not a very respectable fellow (he drank vanilla extract, which was mostly alcohol, to excess, and shouted in the streets when on a toot), and he had not been given any medals.

The female child reciter had an encore and was well into it before the applause for her first piece had quite subsided. Then, for no perceptible reason, another girl played two pieces on the piano, not very well; one was called *Chanson des Fleurs* and the other *La Jeunesse*, so perhaps they were further compliments to the French. Then a fellow with a local reputation as a wit, named Murray Tiffin, 'entertained'; he was often asked to 'entertain' at church evenings, but this was his greatest opportunity so far, and he toiled like a cart horse to divert us with riddles, jokes, and imitations, all of some local application.

'What's the bravest thing a man can do?' he demanded. 'Is it go right out to Africa and shoot a lion? No! *That's* not the bravest thing a man can do! Is it capture a German machine-gun nest single-handed?' (Great applause, during which I, the worst actor in the world, tried to feign a combination of modesty and mirth.) 'No! The bravest thing a man can do is go to the Deptford Post Office at one minute past six on a Saturday night and ask Jerry Williams for a one-cent stamp!' (Uncontrollable mirth, and much nudging and waving at the postmaster, who tried to look like a man who dearly loved a joke against his cranky self.)

Then Murray got off several other good ones, about how much cheaper it was to buy groceries in Bowles Corners than it was even to steal them from the merchants of Deptford, and similar local wit of the sort that age cannot wither nor custom stale; I warmed to Murray, for although his jokes were clean they had much of the quality that had assured my own rest-camp success as Charlie Chaplin.

When Murray had offended individually at least half the people present and delighted us all collectively, the reeve rose and began, 'But to strike a more serious note –' and went on to strike that note for at least ten minutes. We were gathered, he said, to honour those of our community who had risked their lives in defence of liberty. When he had finished, the Methodist parson told us, at some length, how meritorious it was to risk one's life in defence of liberty. Then Father Regan solemnly read out the eleven names of the men from our little part of the world who had been killed in service; Willie's was among them, and I think it was in that moment that I really understood that I would never see Willie again. The Reverend Donald Phelps prayed that we might never forget them, at some length; if God had not been attending to the war, He knew a good deal more about it, from our point of view, by the time Phelps had finished. The Member of the Legislature told us he would not detain us long and talked for forty minutes about the future and what we were going to do with it, building on the sacrifices of the past four years, particularly in the matter of improving the provincial road system. Then the Member of Parliament was let loose upon us, and he talked for three minutes more than one hour, combining patriotism with a good partisan political speech, hinting pretty strongly that although Lloyd George, Clemenceau, and Wilson were unquestionably good men, Sir Robert Borden had really pushed the war to a successful conclusion.

It was by now ten o'clock and even the thirst of a Canadian audience for oratory was almost slaked. Only the great moments that were to follow could have held them. But here it was that the reeve took his second bite at us; in order that Deptford might never forget those who had fought and returned, he said, and in order that our heroes should never lose sight of Deptford's gratitude, every one of us was to receive an engraved watch. Nor was this all. These were no ordinary watches but railway watches, warranted to tell time accurately under the most trying conditions, and probably for all eternity. We understood the merit of these watches because, as we all knew, his son Jack was a railwayman, a brakeman on the Grand Trunk, and Jack swore that these were the best watches to be had anywhere. Whereupon the watches were presented, three by the reeve himself and three by the Member of the Legislature.

As his name and glory were proclaimed, each man in the front row climbed up the steps that led to a pass-door at the side of the stage, squeezed through the green scenery, and made his way to the centre of the platform, while his relatives and townsmen cheered, stamped, and whistled. Percy Boyd Staunton was the sixth, the only officer in the group and the only man who accepted his watch with an air; he had put on his cap before coming to the stage, and he saluted the Member of the Legislature smartly, then turned and saluted the audience; it was a fine effect, and as I grinned and clapped, my stomach burned with jealousy.

I should have been generous, for I was number seven, a V.C., the only man to be given a seat on the stage, and the only man to receive his watch from the hands of our Member of Parliament. He made a speech. 'Sergeant Dunstable Ramsay,' said he, 'I acclaim you as a hero tonight –' and went on for quite a while, though I could not judge how long, because I stood before him feeling a fool and a fake as I had not done when I stood before my King. But at last he handed me the railway watch, and as I had left my hat outside I could not salute, so I had to bob my head, and then bob it at the audience, who cheered and stamped, rather longer than they had done for Percy, I believe. But my feelings were so confused that I could not enjoy it; I heartily wished to get away.

We concluded by singing *God Save the King* again in a classy version in which Muriel Parkinson was supposed to sing some parts alone and the rest of us to join in when she gave a signal; but there were a few people who droned along with her all the way, somewhat spoiling the effect. But when it was done we were free. Nobody seemed inclined to hurry away, and when I had made my way through the green scenery and down the steps by the pass-door I was surrounded by old friends and acquaintances who wanted to talk and shake my hand. I hurried through them as quickly as I could without being rude or overlooking anyone, but I had a little task to perform – a notion I had thought of during the long hour of the Member's speech, and I wanted to be sure I had a good audience. At last I reached Percy and Leola; I seized his hand and shook it vigorously, and then seized Leola in a bear-hug and kissed her resoundingly and at what Deptford would certainly have regarded as a very familiar length.

Leola had always been the kind of girl who closed her eyes when you kissed her, but I kept mine well open and I could see that her eyeballs were rolling wildly beneath her lids; Diana had taught me a thing or two about kisses, and I gave her a pretty good example of that art.

'Darling,' I shouted, not letting her go, 'you don't know how good it is to see you!'

Percy was grinning nervously. Public kissing was not so common then as it is now, and certainly not in our village. 'Dunny, Leola and I have a secret to tell you – not that it will be secret long, of course – but we want you to be the first to hear – outside our families, of course – but we're engaged.' And he sprayed his manly grin from side to side, for we were in the middle of a crowd and everybody could hear. There was a happy murmur, and a few people clapped.

I counted three, just to make sure that there was the right sort of pause, then I shook his hand again and roared, 'Well, well, the best man has won!' – and kissed Leola again, not so long or so proprietorially, but to show that there had been a contest and that I had been a near winner myself, and had shown some speed in the preliminary heats.

It was a good moment and I enjoyed it thoroughly. Percy was wearing a few medals, the admirable D.S.O. but otherwise minor things, mostly for having been at particular engagements. I have already said that I am not much of an actor, but I gave a powerful, if crude impersonation of the hero who is tremendous on the field of Mars but slighted in the courts of Venus. I am sure that there are people in Deptford to this day who remember it.

I suppose it was mean. But Percy, in his officer's smart uniform, got under my skin just as he had always done, and as for Leola, I didn't particularly want her but resented anybody else having her. I promised that this would be a frank record, so far as I can write one, and God forbid that I should pretend that there is not a generous measure of spite in my nature.

This encounter put us in one of those uneasy situations that are forced on people by fate, for to the crowd – and at that moment Deptford was the whole world – we were the master-spirits of the evening: two men, one of whom was a hero without a left leg and the other a handsome and rich young fellow, only somewhat less a hero, who had aspired to the hand of the prettiest girl in the village, and the winner had been acclaimed; we were a splendidly sentimental story made flesh, and it would have been maladroit in the extreme – a real flying in the face of Providence – if we had not stayed together so people could marvel at us and wonder about us. That was why we went to the bonfire as a threesome.

The bonfire was arranged to take place outside the combination village hall, public library, courthouse, and fire hall; it was to be a gay conclusion, an anti-masque, to the high proceedings in the Opera House. There we had been solemn, acclaiming the heroic young and listening to the wise old : here the crowd was lively and expectant; children dodged to and fro, and there was a lot of laughter about nothing in particular. But not for long. In the distance we heard a great beating on pots and pans and blowing of tin horns, and down our main street came a procession, lit by the flame of brooms dipped in oil – a ruddy, smoky light – accompanying Marshal Foch, the two John Bulls, Uncle Sam, Gallant Little Belgium, the whole gang, dragging at a rope's end Deptford's own conception of the German Emperor, fat Myron Papple, whose writhings and caperings outdid his afternoon efforts as the death aria of an opera tenor outdoes his wooing in Act One.

'Hang him!' we heard the representatives of the Allies shouting as they drew near, and the crowd around the village hall took it up. 'Hang him!' they yelled. 'Hang the Kaiser!'

Hang him they did. A rope was ready on the flagpole, and during some scrambling preparations a sharp eye would have seen Myron slip away into the darkness as an effigy was tied to the rope by the neck and hauled slowly up the pole. As it rose, one of the Red Cross nurses set fire to it with a broom torch, and by the time it reached the top the figure was burning merrily.

Then the cheers were loud, and the children hopped and scampered round the foot of the flagpole, shouting, 'Hang the Kaiser!' with growing hysteria; some of them were much too small to know what hanging was, or what a Kaiser might be, but I cannot call them innocent, for they were being as vicious as their age and experience allowed. And the people in the crowd, as I looked at them, were hardly recognizable as the earnest citizens who, not half an hour ago, had been so biddable under the spell of patriotic oratory, so responsive to *Canadian Born*, so touched by the romantic triangle of Leola, and Percy, and myself. Here they were, in this murky, fiery light, happily acquiescent in a symbolic act of cruelty and hatred. As the only person there, I suppose, who had any idea of what a really bad burn was like, I watched them with dismay that mounted towards horror, for these were my own people.

Leola's face looked very pretty as she turned it upward towards the fire, and Percy was laughing and looking about him for admiration as he shouted in his strong, manly voice, 'Hang the Kaiser!'

Myron Papple, an artist to his fingertips, had climbed into the tower of the village hall, so that his screams and entreaties might proceed as near as possible from the height of the burning figure. I could hear him long after I had crept away to my bed in the Tecumseh House. I had not wanted to stay till the end.

8

The next day was a Saturday, and I had plenty to do. Though still an object of wonder, I was now free to move about as I pleased, and my first move was to get the keys of my old home from the magistrate and make a melancholy tour through its six rooms. Everything was where I knew it should be, but all the objects looked small and dull – my mother's clock, my father's desk, with the stone on it he had brought from Dumfries and always used as a paperweight; it was now an unloved house, and want of love had withered it. I picked up a few things I wanted – particularly something that I had long kept hidden – and got out as fast as I could.

Then I went to see Ada Blake, the girl Willie had been sweet on, and had a talk with her; Ada was a fine girl, and I liked her very much, but of course the Willie she remembered was not the brother I knew. I judge they had been lovers, briefly, and that was what Willie meant to her: to me his chief significance now was that he had died twice, and that the first time Mrs Dempster had brought him back to life. I certainly had no intention of visiting Dr McCausland, to see if he had changed his opinion on that subject, though I did chat with two or three of our village elders before getting my midday dinner at the hotel.

As soon as I had gobbled my greasy stew and apple pie I crossed the street to get a haircut at Papple's. I had already observed that Milo was on the job alone; his father was presumably at home, resting up after his patriotic exertions of the day before, and it was a chance to catch up on the village news. Milo gave me a hero's welcome and settled me in one of the two chairs, under a striped sheet that smelled, in equal portions, of barber's perfumes and the essence of Deptford manhood.

'Jeez, Dunny, this is the first time I ever give you a haircut – you know that? Trimmed your Pa a coupla times after you went to the Front, but never you. Comes of being the same age, I guess, eh? But now I'm taking over more and more from the old man. His heart's not so good now; he says it's breathing up little bits of hair all his life; he says it forms a kind of a hairball in barbers, and a lot of 'em go that way. I don't believe it; un-scientific. He never got past third grade – you know that? But jeez, he certainly had 'em laughing yesterday, eh? And last night! But it told on him. Says he can feel the hairball today, just like it was one of his organs.

'You got a double crown. Did you know that? Makes it hard to give you a good cut. What you going to do with the old place? Live there, eh? Nice place to settle down if you was to get married. Your folks always kept it nice. Cece Athelstan always used to say, "The Ramsays sure are buggers for paint." But I guess you won't be marrying Leola, eh? Mind you, for them that had eyes to see, there was never an instant's doubt she was Percy's girl – never an instant's. Oh, I know you and her had some pretty close moments before you went to the war; every-body seen that and they kinda laughed. I had to laugh myself. It was just what we called war-fever – you in uniform, you see. But you got to admit she played fair. Wrote to you right up to the end. Jerry Williams used to tell us the letters come through the Post Office every second Monday like clockwork. Because she wrote you every second Sunday, you know that? But when Percy finished up at that school in Toronto in the summer of 'seventeen, he didn't hesitate for a minute – not for a minute. Into training right away, and went over as an officer, and come back a major. And a D.S.O. But you're the V.C., eh, boy? I guess you had a stroke of luck. I never got enlisted: flat feet. But you and Perse had the luck, I guess. He used to come down here as often as he could, and it was easy seen where Leola had give her heart. That's what her old lady used to say. "Leola's give her heart," she'd say. Ben Cruikshank wasn't strong on Perse to begin with, but the old lady shut him up. He's pleased now, all right. See him last night? Of course he thinks the sun rises and sets in Leola. It's hard for a father, I guess. But you were the main attraction last night, eh? Yep, you were the Kandy Kid with Gum Feet and Taffy Legs. One Taffy Leg, anyhow. But not with Leola. She's give her heart.

'Jeez the war's made a difference in this little old burg. Un-settled. You know what I mean? Lots of changes. Two fires – bad ones – and Harry Henderson sold his store. But I guess I mean changes in people. Young kids in trouble a lot. And Jerry

Cullen – you remember him? – sent to the penitentiary. His daughter squealed on him. Said he was always at her. She was just a kid, mind you. But the cream of it was, I don't think Jerry ever really knew what he done wrong. I think he thought everybody was like that. He was always kinda stupid. About that kinda thing, though, I guess the worst was young Grace Izzard – maybe you don't remember – she's always called Harelip because she's got this funny-looking lip. Well, she got to fourteen and got to guessing, I suppose, but who'd want her with a face like that? So she promises her kid brother Bobby, who's about twelve, a quarter if he'll do it to her, and he does but only if he gets ten cents first, and then, jeez, when he's finished she only gives him another nickel because she says that's all it's worth! Isn't that a corker, eh? These kids today, eh? And then –'

And then two bastards, a juicy self-induced abortion, several jiltings, an old maid gone foolish in menopause, and a goitre of such proportions as to make all previous local goitres seem like warts, which Dr McCausland was treating in Bowles Corners. The prurient, the humiliating, and the macabre were Milo's principal areas of enthusiasm, and we explored them all.

'The flu beat everything though. Spanish Influenza, they called it, but I always figured it was worked up by the Huns some ways. Jeez, this burg was like the Valley of the Shadda for weeks. Of course we felt it more than most in here; a barber always has everybody breathing on him, you see. The old man and me, we hung bags of assafoetida around our necks to give the germs a fight. But oh, people just dropped like flies. Like flies. McCausland worked twenty-four hours a day, I guess. Doc Staunton moved out to one of his farms to live and sort of gave up practice. But he'd been mostly a farmer in a big way for years. Rich man now. You remember Roy Janes and his wife, the Anglican minister? They never rested, going around to sick houses, and then both of 'em died themselves within forty-eight hours. The reeve put the town flag at half-mast that day, and everybody said he done right. And your Ma, Dunny – God, she was a wonderful woman! Never let up on nursing and taking soup and stuff around till your Dad went. You know he wouldn't go to bed? Struggled on when he was sick. Of course you could tell. Blue lips. Yeah, just as blue as huckleberries. That was the sign. We give 'em forty-eight hours after that. Your Dad kept on with his lips as blue as a Sunday suit for a day, then he just fell beside the make-up stone, and Jumper Saul got him home on a dray. Your Ma lost heart and she was gone herself before the week was out. Fine folks. Next issue of the *Banner*, Jumper Saul and Nell turned the column rules, and the front page just looked like a big death notice. God, when I saw it I just started bawling like a kid. Couldn't help myself. Do you know, in this little town of five hundred, and the district around, we lost ninety-eight, all told? But the worst was when Jumper turned the column rules. Everybody said he done right.

'You know 'Masa Dempster went? 'Course, he'd been no good for years. Not since his trouble, you remember? Sure you do! We used to see you skin over there after school and climb through the window to see her and Paul. Nobody ever thought there was any wrong going on, of course. We knew your Ma must have sent you. She couldn't do anything for the Dempsters publicly, of course, but she sent you to look after them. Everybody knew it an' honoured her for it. Do you remember how you said Mary Dempster raised Willie from the dead? God, you used to be a crazy kid, Dunny, but I guess the war knocked all that out of you ...

'Miz' Dempster? Oh no, she didn't get the flu. That kind is always spared when better folks have to go. But after 'Masa went she was a problem. No money, you see. So the reeve and Magistrate Mahaffey found out she had an aunt somewheres near Toronto. Weston, I believe it was. The aunt come and took her. The aunt had money. Husband made it in stoves, I heard.

'No, Paul didn't go with her. Funny about him. Not ten yet, but he run away. He had a kind of a tough time at school, I guess. Couldn't fight much, because he was so undersized, but kids used to get around him at recess and yell, "Hey, Paul, does your Ma wear any pants?" and stuff like that. Just fun, you know. The way kids are. But he'd get mad and fight and get hurt, and they just tormented him more to see him do it. They'd yell across the street, "Hoor yuh today, Paul?" Sly, you see, because he knew damn well they didn't mean "How are you today, Paul?" but "Your Ma's a hoor." Kind of a pun, I guess you'd call it. So when the circus was here, autumn of 'eighteen, he run away with one of the shows. Mahaffey tried to catch up with the circus, but he could never get nowheres with them. Tricky people. Funny, it was the best thing Paul ever done, in a way, because every kid wants to run away with a circus, and it made him kind of a hero after he'd gone. But Mary Dempster took it very bad and went clean off her head. Used to yell out the window at kids going to school, "Have you seen my son Paul?" It would of been sad if we hadn't of known she was crazy. And it was only two or three weeks after that 'Masa got the flu and died. He certainly had a hard row to hoe. And inside a week the aunt come, and we haven't seen hide nor hair of them since.'

By this time the haircut was finished, and Milo insisted on anointing me with every scent and tonic he had in the shop, and stifling me with talcum, as a personal tribute to my war record.

The next day was Sunday, and I made a much appreciated appearance in St James' Presbyterian Church. On Monday, after a short talk with the bank manager and the auctioneer, and a much longer and pleasanter talk with Jumper Saul and Nell, I boarded the train – there was no crowd at the station this time – and left Deptford in the flesh. It was not for a long time that I recognized that I never wholly left it in the spirit.

3

My Fool-Saint

I

In the autumn of 1919 I entered University College, in the University of Toronto, as an Honours student in history. I was not properly qualified, but five professors talked to me for an hour and decided to admit me under some special ruling invoked on behalf of a number of men who had been abroad fighting. This was the first time my boyhood stab at being a polymath did me any good; there was also the fact that it has been my luck to appear more literate than I really am, owing to a cadaverous and scowling cast of countenance and a rather pedantic Scots voice; and certainly my V.C. and general appearance of having bled for liberty did no harm. So there I was, and very pleased about it too.

I had sold the family house for $1200, and its contents, by auction, for an unexpected $600. I had even sold the *Banner*, to a job printer who thought he would like to publish a newspaper, for $750 down and a further $2750 on notes extending over four years; I was an innocent in business, and he was a deadbeat, so I never got all of it. Nevertheless, the hope of money to come was encouraging. I had quite a good pension for my disabilities, and the promise of wooden legs as I needed them, and of course my annual $50 that went with the V.C. I seemed to myself to be the lord of great means, and in a way it proved so, for when I got my B.A. after four years I was able to run to another year's work for an M.A. I had always meant to get a Ph.D. at some later time, but I became interested in a branch of scholarship in which it was not relevant.

During my long summer vacations I worked at undemanding

jobs – timekeeper on roadwork and the like – which enabled me to do a lot of reading and keep body and soul together without touching my education money, which was the way I looked on my capital.

I took very kindly to history. I chose it as my special study because during my fighting days I had become conscious that I was being used by powers over which I had no control for purposes of which I had no understanding. History, I hoped, would teach me how the world's affairs worked. It never really did so, but I became interested in it for its own sake, and at last found a branch of it that gripped whatever intelligence I had, and never relaxed its hold. At Varsity I never fell below fifth in my year in anything, and graduated first; my M.A. won me some compliments, though I thought my thesis dull. I gobbled up all the incidentals that were required to give a 'rounded' education; even zoology (an introductory course) agreed with me, and I achieved something like proficiency in French. German I learned later, in a hurry, for some special work, and with a Berlitz teacher. I was also one of the handful of really interested students in Religious Knowledge, though it was not much of a course, relying too heavily on St Paul's journeys for my taste, and avoiding any discussion of what St Paul was really journeying in aid of. But it was a pleasure to be inside and warm, instead of wallowing in mud, and I worked, I suppose rather hard, though I was not conscious of it at the time. I made no close friends and never sought popularity or office in any of the student committees, but I got on pretty well with everybody. A dull fellow, I suppose; youth was not my time to flower.

Percy Boyd Staunton, however, flowered brilliantly, and I met him fairly often; brilliant young men seem to need a dull listener, just as pretty girls need a plain friend, to set them off. Like me, he had a new name. I had enrolled in the university as Dunstan Ramsay: Percy, somewhere in his Army experience, had thrown aside that name (which had become rather a joke, like Algernon) and had lopped the 'd' off the name that remained. He was now Boy Staunton, and it suited him admirably. Just as Childe Rowland and Childe Harold were so called because they epitomized romance and gentle birth, he was Boy Staunton because he summed up in himself so much of the glory of youth in the postwar period. He gleamed, he glowed; his hair was glossier, his teeth whiter than those of common young men. He laughed a great deal, and his voice was musical. He danced often and spectacularly; he always knew the latest steps, and in those days there were new steps every month. Where his looks and style came from I never knew; certainly not from cantankerous old Doc Staunton, with his walrus moustache and sagging paunch, or from his mother, who was a charmless woman. Boy seemed to have made himself out of nothing, and he was a marvel.

He was a perfectionist, however, and not content. I remember him telling me during his first year as a law student that a girl had told him he reminded her of Richard Barthelmess, the screen star; he would rather have reminded her of John Barrymore, and he was displeased. I was quite a movie-goer myself and foolishly said I thought he was more like Wallace Reid in *The Dancin' Fool*, and was surprised by his indignation, for Reid was a handsome man. It was not until later that I discovered that he coveted a suggestion of aristocracy in his appearance and bearing, and Reid lacked it. He was at that time still casting around for an ideal upon whom he could model himself. It was not until his second year in law that he found it.

This ideal, this mould for his outward man, was no one less than Edward Albert Christian George Andrew Patrick David, the Prince of Wales. The papers were full of the Prince at that time. He was the great ambassador of the Commonwealth, but he had also the common touch; he spoke with what horrified old ladies thought a common accent, but he could charm a bird from a branch; he danced and was reputed to be a devil with the girls; he was said to quarrel with his father (my King, the man with the Navy torpedo beard) about matters of dress; he was photographed smoking a pipe with a distinctive apple-shaped bowl. He had romance and mystery, for over his puzzled brow hung the shadow of the Crown; how would such a dashing youth ever settle himself to the duties of kingship? He was gloated over by old women who wondered what princess he would marry, and gloated over by young women because he thought more of looks and charm than of royal blood. There were rumours of high old times with jolly girls when he had visited Canada in 1919. Flaming Youth, and yet, withal, a Prince, remote and fated for great things. Just the very model for Boy Staunton, who saw himself in similar terms.

In those days you could not become a lawyer by going to the university – not in our part of Canada. You must go to Osgoode Hall, where the Law Society of Upper Canada would steer you through until at last you were called to the Bar. This worried Boy, but not very much. The university, he admitted to me – I had not asked for any such admission – put a stamp on a man; but if you got that stamp first and studied law later, you would be old, a positive greybeard, before getting into the full tide of life. So far as I could see, the full tide of life had a lot to do with sugar.

Sugar was what old Doc Staunton was chiefly interested in. He had grabbed up a lot of land in the Deptford district and put it all into sugar-beets. The black, deep alluvial soil of the river flats around Deptford was good for anything, and wonderful for beets. Doc was not yet a Sugar-Beet King, but he was well on his way to it – a sort of Sticky Duke. Boy, who had more vision than his father, managed to get the old man to buy into the secondary process, the refining of the sugar from the beets, and this was proving profitable in such a surprising degree that Doc Staunton was rich in a sense far beyond Deptford's comprehension; so rich, indeed, that they forgot that he had skipped town when the flu epidemic struck. As for the present, a very rich man has something better to do than listen to old women's coughs and patch up farmers who have fallen into the chaff-cutter. Doc Staunton never formally dropped practice, and accepted the sanctity that came with wealth in the way he had accepted his prestige as a doctor – with a sour face and a combination of pomposity and grievance that was all his own. He did not move away from Deptford. He did not know of anywhere else to go, I suppose, and the life of a village Rich Man – far outstripping the Athelstans – suited him very well.

The Athelstans did not like it, and Cece got off a 'good one' that the village cherished for years. 'If Jesus died to redeem Doc Staunton,' he said, 'He made a damn poor job of it.'

So Boy Staunton knew that he too had a crown awaiting him. He did not mean to practise law, but it was a good training for business and, eventually, politics. He was going to be a very rich man – richer than his father by far – and he was getting ready.

He, like his ideal, was not on the best of terms with his father. Doc Staunton gave Boy what he regarded as a good allowance; it was not bad, but it was not ample either, and Boy needed more. So he made some shrewd short-term investments in the stock market and was thus able to live at a rate that puzzled and annoyed the old man, who waited angrily for him to get into debt. But Boy did not get into debt. Debt was for boobs, he said, and he flaunted such toys as gold cigarette cases and hand-made shoes under the old man's nose, without explaining anything.

Where Boy lived high, I lived – well, not low, but in the way congenial to myself. I thought twenty-four dollars was plenty for a ready-made suit, and four dollars a criminal price for a pair of shoes. I changed my shirt twice a week and my underwear once. I had not yet developed any expensive tastes and saw nothing wrong with a good boarding-house; it was years before I decided that there is really no such thing as a good boarding-house. Once, temporarily envious of Boy, I bought a silk shirt and paid nine dollars for it. It burned me like the shirt of Nessus, but I wore it to rags, to get my money out of it, garment of guilty luxury that it was.

Here we come to a point where I have to make an admission that will put me in a bad light, considering the story I have to tell. Boy was very good about passing on information to me about investment, and now and then I ventured two or three hundred from my small store, always with heartening results. Indeed, during my university days I laid the foundation for the modest but pleasant fortune I have now. What Boy did in thousands I did in hundreds, and without his guidance I would have been powerless, for investment was not in my line; I knew just enough to follow his advice – when to buy and when to sell, and especially when to hang on. Why he did this for me I can only explain on the grounds that he must have liked me. But it was a kind of liking, as I hope will be clear before we have finished, that was not easy to bear.

We were both young, neither yet fully come to himself, and whatever he may have felt for me, I knew that in several ways I was jealous of him. He had something to give – his advice about how to turn my few hundreds into a few thousands – and I make no apology for benefiting from the advice of a man I sneered at in my mind; I was too much a Scot to let a dollar get away from me if it came within my clutch. I am not seeking to posture as a hero in this memoir. Later, when I had something to give and could have helped him, he did not want it. You see how it was: to him the reality of life lay in external things, whereas for me the only reality was of the spirit – of the mind, as I then thought, not having understood yet what a cruel joker and mean master the intellect can be. So if you choose to see me as a false friend, exploiting a frank and talented youth, go ahead. I can but hope that before my story is all told you will see things otherwise.

We met about once every two weeks, by appointment, for our social lives never intersected. Why would they, especially after Boy bought his car, a very smart affair coloured a rich shade of auburn. He helled around to all the dancing places with men of his own stamp and the girls they liked, drinking a good deal out of flasks and making lots of noise.

I remember seeing him at a rugby game in the autumn of 1923; it was not a year since the Earl of Carnarvon had discovered the tomb of Tutankhamen, and already the gentlemen's outfitters had worked up a line of Egyptian fashions. Boy wore a gorgeous pullover of brownish-red, around which marched processions of little Egyptians, copied from the tomb pictures; he had on the baggiest of Oxford bags, smoked the apple-bowl pipe with casual style, and his demeanour was that of one of the lords of creation. A pretty girl with shingled hair and rolled stockings that allowed you to see delightful flashes of her bare knees was with him, and they were taking alternate pulls at a very large flask that contained, I am sure, something intoxicating but not positively toxic from the stock of the best bootlegger in town. He was the quintessence of the Jazz Age, a Scott Fitzgerald character. It was characteristic of Boy throughout his life that he was always the quintessence of something that somebody else had recognized and defined.

I was filled with a sour scorn that I now know was nothing but envy, but then I mistook it for philosophy. I didn't really want the clothes, I didn't really want the girl or the booze, but it scalded me to see him enjoying them, and I hobbled away grumbling to myself like Diogenes. I recognize now that my limp was always worse when I envied Boy; I suppose that without knowing it I exaggerated my disability so that people would notice and say, 'That must be a returned man.' God, youth is a terrible time! So much feeling and so little notion of how to handle it!

When we met we usually ended up talking about Leola. It had been agreed by Boy's parents and the Cruikshanks that she should wait until Boy had qualified as a lawyer before they married. There had been some suggestion from Leola that she might train as a nurse in the meanwhile, but it came to nothing because her parents thought the training would coarsen their darling – bedpans and urinals and washing naked men and all that sort of thing. So she hung around Deptford, surrounded by the haze of sanctity that was supposed to envelop an engaged girl, waiting for Boy's occasional weekend visits in the auburn car. I knew from his confidences that they went in for what the euphemism of the day called 'heavy petting' – mutual masturbation would be the bleak term for it – but that Leola had principles and they never went farther, so that in a technical, physical sense – though certainly not in spirit – she remained a virgin.

Boy, however, had acquired tastes in the Army that could not be satisfied by agonizingly prolonged and inadequately requited puffings and snortings in a parked car, but he had no clarity of mind that would ease him of guilt when he deceived Leola – as he did, with variety and regularity among the free-spirited girls he met in Toronto. He built up a gimcrack metaphysical structure to help him out of his difficulty and appealed to me to set the seal of university wisdom on it.

These gay girls, he explained, 'knew what they were doing,' and thus he had no moral responsibility towards them. Some of them were experts in what were then called French kisses or soul kisses, which the irreverent called 'swapping spits'. Though he might 'fall' for one of them for a few weeks – even go so far as to have a 'pash' for her – he was not 'in love' with her, as he was with Leola. I had made this fine philsophical distinction myself in my dealings with Diana, and it startled me to hear it from Boy's lips; noodle that I was, I had supposed this sophistry was my own invention. So long as he truly and abidingly loved none but Leola, these 'pashes' did not count, did they? Or did I think they did? Above all things he wanted to be perfectly fair to Leola, who was so sweet that she had never once asked him if he was tempted to fall for any of the girls he went dancing with in the city.

I would have given much for the strength of mind to tell him I had no opinions on such matters, but I could not resist the bittersweet, prurient pleasure of listening. I knew it gave him a pleasure that he probably did not yet acknowledge to himself, to confront me with his possession of Leola. He had wormed it out of her that she had once thought she loved me, and he assured me that all three of us now regarded this as a passing aberration – mere war-fever. I did not deny it, but neither did I like it.

I did not want her, but it annoyed me that Boy had her. I had not only learned about physical love in splendid guise from Diana; I had also acquired from her an idea of a woman as a delightful creature that walked and talked and laughed and joked and thought and understood, which quite outsoared any-thing in Leola's modest repertoire of charms. Nevertheless – egotistical dog in the manger that I was – I keenly resented the fact that she had thrown me over for Boy and had not had the courage to write and tell me so. I see now that it was beyond Leola's abilities to put anything really important on paper; however much she may have wanted to do so, she could not have found words for what she ought to have said. But at that time, with her parents holding her, as it were, in erotic escrow for Boy Staunton, I was sour about the whole business.

Why did I not find some other girl? Diana, Headmaster, Diana. I often yearned for her, but never to the point where I wrote to ask if we might not reconsider. I knew that Diana would stand in the way of the kind of life I wanted to live and that she would not be content with anything less than a full and, if possible, a controlling share in the life of any man she married. But that did not stop me, often and painfully, from wanting her.

A selfish, envious, cankered wretch, wasn't I?

2

The kind of life I wanted to live – yes, but I was not at all sure what it was. I had flashes of insight and promptings, but nothing definite. So when I was finished at the university, duly ticketed as an M.A. in history, I still wanted time to find my way, and like many a man in my case I took to schoolmastering.

Was it a dead end? Did I thereby join the ranks of those university men of promise whose promise is never fulfilled? You can answer that question as readily as I, Headmaster, and certainly the answer must be no. I took to teaching like a duck to water, and like a duck I never paid exaggerated attention to the medium in which I moved. I applied for a job at Colborne College principally because, being a private school, it did not demand that I have a provincial teacher's training certificate; I didn't want to waste another year getting that, and I didn't really think I would stay in teaching. I also liked the fact that Colborne was a boys' school; I never wanted to teach girls – don't, in fact, think they are best served by the kind of education devised by men for men.

I have been a good teacher because I have never thought much about teaching; I just worked through the curriculum and insisted on high standards. I never played favourites, never tried to be popular, never set my heart on the success of any clever boy, and took good care that I knew my stuff. I was not easily approachable, but if approached I was civil and serious to the boy who approached me. I have coached scores of boys privately for scholarships, and I have never taken a fee for it. Of course I have enjoyed all of this, and I suppose my enjoyment had its influence on the boys. As I have grown older my bias – the oddly recurrent themes of history, which are also the themes of myth – has asserted itself, and why not? But when I first stepped into a Colborne classroom, wearing the gown that we were all expected to wear then, I never thought that it would be more than forty years before I left it for good.

Simply from the school's point of view, I suppose my life has seemed odd and dry, though admittedly useful. As the years wore on I was finally acquitted of the suspicion that hangs over every bachelor schoolmaster – that he is a homosexual, either overt or frying in some smoky flame of his own devising. I have never been attracted to boys. Indeed I have never much liked boys. To me a boy is a green apple who I expect to expose to the sun of history until he becomes a red apple, a man. I know too much about boys to sentimentalize over them. I have been a boy myself, and I know what a boy is, which is to say, either a fool or an imprisoned man striving to get out.

No, teaching was my professional life, to which I gave whatever was its due. The sources from which my larger life was nourished were elsewhere, and it is to write of them that I address this memoir to you, Headmaster, hoping thereby that when I am dead at least one man will know the truth about me and do me justice.

Did I live chastely – I who have been so critical of Boy Staunton's rough-and-tumble sexual affairs? No memoir of our day is thought complete without some comment on the sex life of its subject, and therefore let me say that during my early years as a schoolmaster I found a number of women who were interesting, and sufficiently interested in me, to give me a sex life of a sort. They were the women who usually get into affairs with men who are not the marrying kind. There was Agnes Day, who yearned to take upon herself the sins of the whole world, and sacrifice her body and mind to some deserving male's cause. She soon became melancholy company. Then there was Gloria Mundy, the good-time girl, who had to be stoked with costly food, theatre tickets, and joyrides of all kinds. She cost more than her admittedly good company was worth, and she was kind enough to break up the affair herself. And of course Libby Doe, who thought sex was the one great, true, and apostolic key and cure and could not get enough of it, which I could. I played fair with all of them, I hope; the fact that I did not love them did not prevent me from liking them very much, and I never used a woman simply as an object in my life.

They all had enough of me quite quickly because my sense of humour, controlled in the classroom, was never in check in the bedroom. I was a talking lover, which most women hate.

And my physical disabilities were bothersome. The women were quick to assure me that these did not matter at all; Agnes positively regarded my ravaged body as her martyr's stake. But I could not forget my brownish-red nubbin where one leg should have been, and a left side that looked like the crackling of a roast. As well as these offences against my sense of erotic propriety, there were other, and to me sometimes hilarious, problems. What, for instance, is etiquette for the one-legged philanderer? Should he remove his prosthesis before putting on his prophylactic, or *vice versa?* I suggested to my partners that we should write to Dorothy Dix about it. They did not think that funny.

It was many years before I rediscovered love, and then it was not Love's Old Sweet Song, recalling Diana: no, I drank the reviving drop from the Cauldron of Ceridwen. Very well worth waiting for, too.

3

At the age of twenty-six I had become an M.A., and the five thousand dollars or so I had begun with had grown, under Boy's counselling, to a resounding eight, and I had lived as well as I wanted to do in the meanwhile on my pension. What Boy had I do not know, for he spoke of it mysteriously as 'a plum' (an expression out of his Prince of Wales repertoire), but he looked glossy and knew no care. When he married Leola in St James' Presbyterian Church, Deptford, I was his best man, in a hired morning suit and a top hat in which I looked like an ass. It was the most fashionable wedding in Deptford history, marred only by the conduct of some of the groom's legal friends, who whooped it up in the Tecumseh House when the dry party at Doc Staunton's was mercifully over. Leola's parents were minor figures at the wedding; very properly so, in everybody's opinion, for of course 'they were not in a position to entertain.' Neither were the Stauntons senior, if they had but known it; they were overwhelmed by the worldliness of Boy's friends, and had to comfort themselves with the knowledge that they could buy and sell all of them, and their parents too, and never feel it. It was clear to my eye that by now Boy had far surpassed his father in ambition and scope. All he needed was time.

Everybody agreed that Leola was a radiant bride: even in the awful wedding rig-out of 1924 she looked good enough to eat with a silver spoon. Her parents (no hired finery for Ben Cruikshank, but his boots had a silvery gleam produced by the kind of blacklead more commonly applied to stoves) wept with joy in the church. Up at the front, and without much to do, I could see who wept and who grinned.

The honeymoon was to be a trip to Europe, not nearly so common then as now. I was going to Europe myself, to blow a thousand out of my eight on a reward to myself for being a good boy. I had booked my passage second class – not then called Tourist – on the C.P.R. ship *Melita*; when I read the passenger list in my first hour aboard I was not pleased to find 'Mr and Mrs Boy Staunton' among the First Class. Like so many people, I regarded a wedding as a dead end and had expected to be rid of Boy and Leola for a while after it. But here they were, literally on top of me.

Well, let them find me. I did not care about distinction of classes, I told myself, but it would be interesting to find out if they did. As so often, I underestimated Boy. A note and a bottle of wine – half-bottle, to be precise – awaited me at my table at dinner, and he came down to see me three or four times during the voyage, explaining very kindly that ship's rules did not allow him to ask me to join them in First Class. Leola did not come but waved to me at the Ship's Concert, at which gifted passengers sang *Roses of Picardy*, told jokes, and watched a midshipman – they still had them to blow bugles for meals and so forth – dance a pretty good hornpipe.

Boy met everybody in First Class, of course, including the knighted passenger – a shoe manufacturer from Nottingham – but the one who most enlarged his world was the Reverend George Maldon Leadbeater, a great prophet from a fashionable New York church, who sailed from Montreal because he liked the longer North Atlantic sea voyage.

'He isn't like any other preacher you've ever met,' said Boy. 'Honestly, you'd wonder how old dugouts like Andy Bowyer and Phelps ever have the nerve to stand up in a pulpit when there are men like Leadbeater in the business. He makes Christianity make sense for the first time, so far as I'm concerned. I mean, Christ was really a very distinguished person, a Prince of the House of David, a poet and an intellectual. Of course He was a carpenter; all those Jews in Bible days could do something with their hands. But what kind of a carpenter was He? Not making cowsheds, I'll bet. Undoubtedly a designer and a manufacturer, in terms of those days. Otherwise, how did He make his connections? You know, when He was travelling around, staying with all kinds of rich and influential people as an honoured guest – obviously He wasn't just bumming his way through Palestine; He was staying with people who knew Him as a man of substance who also had a great philosophy. You know, the way those Orientals make their pile before they go in for philosophy. And look how He appreciated beauty! When that woman poured the ointment on His feet. He knew good ointment from bad, you can bet. And the Marriage at Cana – a party, and He helped the host out of a tight place when the drinks gave out, because He had probably been in the same fix Himself in His days in business and knew what social embarrassment was. And an economist! Driving the money-changers out of the Temple – why? Because they were soaking the pilgrims extortionate rates, that's why, and endangering a very necessary tourist attraction and rocking the economic boat. It was a kind of market discipline, if you want to look at it that way, and He was the only one with the brains to see it and the guts to do something about it. Leadbeater thinks that may have been at the back of the Crucifixion; the priests got their squeeze out of the Temple exchange, you can bet, and they decided they would have to get rid of this fellow who was possessed of a wider economic vision – as well as great intellectual powers in many other fields, of course.

 "Leadbeater – he wants me to call him George, and somehow I've got to get rid of this English trick I've got of calling people by their surnames – George simply loves beauty. That's what gets Leola, you know. Frankly, Dunny, as an old friend, I can tell you that Leola hasn't had much chance to grow in that home of hers. Fine people, the Cruikshanks, of course, but narrow. But she's growing fast. George has insisted on lending her this wonderful novel, *If Winter Comes* by A. S. M. Hutchinson. She's just gulping it down. But the thing that really impresses me is that George is such a good dresser. And not just for a preacher – for anybody. He's going to introduce me to his tailor in London. You have to be introduced to the good ones. He says God made beautiful and seemly things, and not to take advantage of them is to miss what God meant. Did you ever hear any preacher say anything like that? Of course he's no six-hundred-dollar-a-year Bible buster, but a man who pulls down eighty-five hundred from his pulpit alone, and doubles it with lectures and books! If Christ wasn't poor – and He certainly wasn't – George doesn't intend to be. Would you believe he carries a handful of gem-stones – semi-precious but gorgeous – in his right-hand coat pocket, *just to feel*! He'll pull them out two or three times a day, and strew them on the madder silk handkerchief he always has in his breast pocket, and let the light play on them, and you should see his face then! "Poverty and sin are not all that God hath wrought," he says with a kind of poetic smile. "Lo, these are beautiful even as His raindrops, and no less His work than the leper, the flower, or woman's smile." I wish you could get up to First Class to meet him, but it's out of the question, and I wouldn't want to ask him to come down here.'

So I never met the Reverend George Maldon Leadbeater, though I wondered if he had read the *New Testament* as often as I had. Furthermore, I had read *If Winter Comes* when it first came out; it had been the theme of an extravagant en-comium from the Right Honourable William Lyon Mackenzie King, Prime Minister of Canada; he had said it was unquestion-ably the finest novel of our time, and the booksellers had played it up. It seemed to me that Mr King's taste in literature, like Leadbeater's in religion, was evidence of a sweet tooth, and nothing more.

4

Boy and Leola left the ship at Southampton. I went on to Antwerp, because the first object of my journey was a tour of the battlefields. Unrecognizable, of course. Neat and trim in the manner of the Low Countries; trenches known to me as stinking mudholes were lined with cement, so that ladies would not dirty their shoes. Even the vast cemeteries woke no feeling in me; because they were so big I lost all sense that they contained men who, had they lived, would have been about my age. I got out as soon as I had scoured Passchendaele for some sign of the place where I had been wounded, and where I had encountered the little Madonna. Nobody I could find was of any use in suggesting where I might have been; the new town had probably buried it under streets and houses. Figures of Our Lady – yes, there were plenty of those, in churches and on buildings, but most of them were new, hideous and unrevealing. None was anything like mine. I would have known her anywhere, as of course I did, many years later.

It was thus my interest in medieval and Renaissance art – especially religious art – came about. The little Madonna was a bee in my bonnet; I wanted to see her again, and quite unreasonably (like a man I knew who lost a treasured walking-stick in the London Blitz and still looks hopefully in every curiosity shop in case it may turn up) I kept hoping to find her. The result was that I saw a great many Madonnas of every period and material and quickly came to know a fair amount about them. Indeed, I learned enough to be able to describe the one I sought as a Virgin of the Immaculate Conception, of polychromed wood, about twenty-four inches high, and most probably of Flemish or North German workmanship of the period between 1675 and 1725. If you think I put this together after I had found her, I can only assure you that you are wrong.

First my search, then a mounting enthusiasm for what I saw, led me to scores of churches through the Low Countries, France, Austria, and Italy. I had only afforded myself a few weeks, but

I sent for more money and stayed until the latest possible date in August. What are you doing here, Dunstan Ramsay? I sometimes asked myself, and when I had got past telling myself that I was feeding a splendid new enthusiasm for religious art and architecture I knew that I was rediscovering religion as well. Do not suppose I was becoming 'religious'; the Presbyterianism of my childhood effectively insulated me against any enthusiastic abandonment to faith. But I became aware that in matters of religion I was an illiterate, and illiteracy was my abhorrence. I was not such a fool or an aesthete as to suppose that all this art was for art's sake alone. It was about something, and I wanted to know what that something was.

As an historian by training, I suppose I should have begun at the beginning, wherever that was, but I hadn't time. Scenes from the Bible gave me no difficulty; I could spot Jael spiking Sisera, or Judith with the head of Holofernes, readily enough. It was the saints who baffled me. So I got to work on them as best I could, and pretty soon knew that the old fellow with the bell was Anthony Abbot, and the same old fellow with hobgoblins plaguing him was Anthony being tempted in the desert. Sebastian, that sanctified porcupine, was easy, and so was St Roche, with the dog and a bad leg. I was innocently delighted to meet St Martin, dividing his cloak, on a Swiss coin. The zest for detail that had first made me want to be a polymath stood me in good stead now, for I could remember the particular attributes and symbols of scores of saints without any trouble, and I found their legends delightful reading. I became disgustingly proud and began to whore after rare and difficult saints, not known to the Catholic faithful generally. I could read and speak French (though never without a betraying accent) and was pretty handy in Latin, so that Italian could be picked up on the run – badly, but enough. German was what I needed, and I determined to acquire it during the coming winter. I had no fear; whatever interested me I could learn, and learn quickly.

At this time it never occurred to me that the legends I picked up were quite probably about people who had once lived and had done something or other that made them popular and dear after death. What I learned merely revived and confirmed my childhood notion that religion was much nearer in spirit to the

Arabian Nights than it was to anything encouraged by St James'
Presbyterian Church. I wondered how they would regard it in
Deptford if I offered to replace the captive Dove that sat on the
topmost organ pipe with St James' own cockleshell. I was foolish
and conceited, I know, but I was also a happy goat who had
wandered into the wondrous enclosed garden of hagiology,
and I grazed greedily and contentedly. When the time came at
last for me to go home, I knew I had found a happiness that
would endure.

5

Schoolmastering kept me busy by day and part of each night. I
was an assistant housemaster, with a fine big room under the
eaves of the main building, and a wretched kennel of a bedroom,
and rights in a bathroom used by two or three other resident
masters. I taught all day, but my wooden leg mercifully spared
me from the nuisance of having to supervise sports after school.
There were exercises to mark every night, but I soon gained a
professional attitude towards these woeful explorations of the
caves of ignorance and did not let them depress me. I liked the
company of most of my colleagues, who were about equally
divided among good men who were good teachers, awful men
who were awful teachers, and the grotesques and misfits who
drift into teaching and are so often the most educative influences
a boy meets in school. If a boy can't have a good teacher, give
him a psychological cripple or an exotic failure to cope with;
don't just give him a bad, dull teacher. This is where the private
schools score over state-run schools; they can accommodate a
few cultured madmen on the staff without having to offer explanations.

The boys liked me for my wooden leg, whose thuds in the
corridor gave ample warning of my approach and allowed
smokers, loafers, and dreamers (these last two groups are not
the same) to do whatever was necessary before I arrived. I had
now taken to using a cane except when I was very much on
parade, and a swipe with my heavy stick over the behind was
preferred by all sensible boys to a tedious imposition. I may

have been the despair of educational psychologists, but I knew boys and I knew my stuff, and it quickly began to show up in examination results.

Boy Staunton was also distinguishing himself as an educator. He was educating Leola, and as I saw them pretty regularly I was able to estimate his success. He wanted to make her into the perfect wife for a rising young entrepreneur in sugar, for he was working hard and fast, and now had a foot in the world of soft drinks, candy, and confectionery.

He had managed brilliantly on a principle so simple that it deserves to be recorded : he set up a little company of his own by borrowing $5000 for four months; as he already had $5000 it was no trouble to repay the loan. Then he borrowed $10,000 and repaid with promptitude. On this principle he quickly established an excellent reputation, always paying promptly, though never prematurely, thereby robbing his creditor of expected interest. Bank managers grew to love Boy, but he soon gave up dealing with branches, and borrowed only at Head Office. He was now a favoured cherub in the heaven of finance, and he needed a wife who could help him to graduate from a cherub to a full-fledged angel, and as soon as possible to an archangel. So Leola had lessons in tennis and bridge, learned not to call her maid 'the girl' even to herself, and had no children as the time was not yet at hand. She was prettier than ever, had acquired a sufficient command of cliché to be able to talk smartly about anything Boy's friends were likely to know, and adored Boy, while fearing him a little. He was so swift, so brilliant, so handsome! I think she was always a little puzzled to find that she was really his wife.

It was in 1927 that Boy's first instance of startling good fortune arrived – one of those coincidences that it may be wiser to call synchronicities, which aid the ambitious – something that heaved him, at a stroke, into a higher sphere and maintained him there. He had kept up with his regiment and soldiered regularly; he had thoughts of politics, he told me, and a militia connection would earn a lot of votes. So when the Prince of Wales made his tour of Canada that year, who was more personable, youthful, cheerful, and in every way suited to be one of His Highness's aides-de-camp than Boy Staunton? And not simply for the royal appearance in Toronto, but for the duration of the tour, from sea to sea?

I saw little of this grandeur, except when the Prince paid a visit to the school, for as it has royal patronage he was obliged to do so. We masters all turned out in our gowns and hoods, and sweating members of the Rifle Corps strutted, and yelled, and swooned from the heat, and the slight descendant of King Arthur and King Alfred and Charles the Second did the gracious. I was presented, with my V.C. pinned to the silk of my gown, but my recollection is not of the youthful Prince, but of Boy, who was quite the most gorgeous figure there that day. An Old Boy of the school, and an *aide* to the Prince – it was a great day for him, and the Headmaster of that day doted upon him to a degree that might have seemed a little overdone to a critical eye.

Leola was there too, for though of course she did not go with Boy on the tour, she was expected to turn up now and then at various points across Canada, just as though she happened to be there by chance. She had learned to curtsy very prettily – not easy in the skirts of the period – and eat without seeming to chew, and do other courtier-like things required by Boy. I am sure that for her the Prince was nothing more than an excuse for Boy's brilliant appearances. Never have I seen a woman so absorbed in her love for a man, and I was happy for her and heartily wished her well.

After the Prince had gone home the Stauntons settled down again to be, in a modest manner befitting their youth, social leaders. Boy had a lot of new social usages and took to wearing spats to business. For him and for Leola their Jazz Age period was over; now they were serious, responsible Young Marrieds.

Within a year their first child was born and was conservatively, but significantly, christened Edward David. In due time – how *could* H.R.H. have known? – a christening mug came from Mappin and Webb, with the three feathers and *Ich dien* on it. David used it until he graduated to a cup and saucer, after which it stood on the drawing-room table, with matches in it, quite casually.

6

Doc Staunton and his wife never visited Boy and Leola, on what I suppose must be called religious grounds. When they came to Toronto, which was rarely, they asked the young Stauntons to their hotel – the cheap and conservative Carls-Rite – for a meal, but declined to set foot in a house where drink was consumed, contrary to the law of the land and against God's manifest will. Another stone that stuck in their crop was that Boy and Leola had left the Presbyterian church and become Anglicans.

In a movement that reached its climax in 1924, the Prestbyterians and Methodists had consummated a *mysterium coniunctionis* that resulted in the United Church of Canada, with a doctrine (soother than the creamy curd) in which the harshness of Presbyterianism and the hick piety of Methodism had little part. A few brass-bowelled Presbyterians and some truly zealous Methodists held out, but a majority regarded this union as a great victory for Christ's Kingdom on earth. Unfortunately it also involved some haggling between the rich Presbyterians and the poor Methodists, which roused the mocking spirit of the rest of the country; the Catholics in particular had some Irish jokes about the biggest land-and-property-grab in Canadian history.

During this uproar a few sensitive souls fled to the embrace of Anglicanism; the envious and disaffected said they did it because the Anglican Church was in some way more high-toned than the evangelical faiths, and thus they were improving their social standing. At that time every Canadian had to adhere, nominally, to some church; the officials of the Census utterly refused to accept such terms as 'agnostic' or 'none' for inclusion in the column marked 'Religion', and flattering statistics were compiled on the basis of Census reports that gave a false idea of the forces all the principal faiths could command. Boy and Leola had moved quietly into a fashionable Anglican church where the rector, Canon Arthur Woodiwiss, was so broad-minded he did not even insist that they be confirmed. David was confirmed, though, when his time came, and so was

Caroline, who appeared a well-planned two years after him.

My preoccupation with saints was such that I could not keep it out of my conversation, and Boy was concerned for me. 'Watch that you don't get queer, Dunny,' he would say, sometimes; and, 'Arthur Woodiwiss says that saints are all right for Catholics, who have so many ignorant people to deal with, but we've evolved far beyond all that.'

As a result I sneaked even more saints into my conversation, to irritate him. He had begun to irritate rather easily, and be pompous. He urged me to get out of schoolmastering (while praising it as a fine profession) and make something of myself. 'If you don't hurry up and let life know what you want, life will damned soon show you what you'll get,' he said one day. But I was not sure I wanted to issue orders to life; I rather liked the Greek notion of allowing Chance to take a formative hand in my affairs. It was in the autumn of 1928 that Chance did so, and lured me from a broad highway to a narrower path.

Our Headmaster of that day – your predecessor but one – was enthusiastic for what he called 'bringing the world to the school and the school to the world,' and every Wednesday morning we had a special speaker at Prayers, who told us about what he did in the world. Sir Archibald Flower told us about rebuilding the Shakespeare Memorial Theatre at Stratford-on-Avon and got a dollar from nearly every boy to help do it; Father Jellicoe talked about clearing London slums, and that cost most of us a dollar too. But ordinarily our speakers were Canadians, and one morning the Headmaster swept in – he wore a silk gown, well suited to sweeping – with Mr Joel Surgeoner in tow.

Surgeoner was already pretty well known, though I had not seen him before. He was the head of the Lifeline Mission in Toronto, where he laboured to do something for destitute and defeated people, and for the sailors on the boats that plied the Great Lakes – at that time a very tough and neglected group. He spoke to the school briefly and well, for though it was plain that he was a man of little education he had a compelling quality of sincerity about him, even though I suspected him of being a pious liar.

He told us, quietly and in the simplest language, that he had

133

to run his Mission by begging, and that sometimes begging yielded nothing; when this happened he prayed for help, and had never been refused what he needed; the blankets, or more often the food, would appear somehow, often late in the day, and more often than not, left on the steps of the Mission by anonymous donors. Now, pompous young ass that I was, I was quite prepared to believe that St John Bosco could pull off this trick when he appealed to Heaven on behalf of his boys; I was even persuaded that it might have happened a few times to Dr Barnardo, of whom the story was also told. But I was far too much a Canadian, deeply if unconsciously convinced of the inferiority of my own country and its people, to think it could happen in Toronto, to a man I could see. I suppose I had a sneer on my face.

Surgeoner's back was to me, but suddenly he turned and addressed me. 'I can see that you do not believe me, sir,' he said, 'but I am speaking the truth, and if you will come down to the Lifeline some night I will show you clothes and blankets and food that God has inspired charitable men and women to give us to do His work among His forgotten children.' This had an electrical effect; a few boys laughed, the Headmaster gave me a glance that singed my eyebrows, and Surgeoner's concluding remarks were greeted with a roar of applause. But I had no time to waste in being humiliated, for when Surgeoner looked me in the face I knew him at once for the tramp I had last seen in the pit at Deptford.

I lost no time; I was at the Lifeline Mission that very night. It was on the ground floor of a warehouse down by the lakefront. Everything about it was poor; the lower parts of the windows were painted over with green paint, and the lettering on them — 'Lifeline Mission, Come In' — was an amateur job. Inside, the electric light was scanty and eked out by a couple of coal-oil lamps on the table at the front; on benches made of reclaimed wood sat eight or ten people, of whom four or five were bums, and the rest poor but respectable supporters of Surgeoner. A service was in progress.

Surgeoner was praying; he needed a variety of things, the only one of which I can remember was a new kettle for soup, and he suggested to God that the woodpile was getting low.

When he had, so to speak, put in his order, he began to speak
to us, gently and unassumingly as he had done at the school
that morning and I was able to observe now that he had a
hearing-aid in his left ear – one of the clumsy affairs then in
use – and that a cord ran down into his collar and appeared to
join a bulge in the front of his shirt, obviously a receiving apparatus. But his voice was pleasant and well controlled; nothing
like the ungoverned quack of many deaf people.

He saw me, of course, and nodded gravely. I expected that he
would try to involve me in his service, probably to score off
me as an educated infidel and mocker, but he did not. Instead
he told, very simply, of his experience with a lake sailor who was
a notable blasphemer, a man whose every remark carried an
insult to God's Name. Surgeoner had been powerless to change
him and had left him in defeat. One day Surgeoner had talked
with an old woman, desperately poor but rich in the Spirit of
Christ, who had at parting pressed into his hand a cent, the
only coin she had to give. Surgeoner bought a tract with the
cent and carried it absent-mindedly in his pocket for several
weeks, until by chance he met the blasphemer again. On impulse he pressed the tract upon the blasphemer, who of course
received it with an oath. Surgeoner thought no more of the
matter until, two months later, he met the blasphemer again,
this time a man transfigured. He had read the tract, he had
accepted Christ, and he had begun life anew.

I fully expected that it would prove that the old woman was
the blasphemer's aged mother and that the two had been re-
united in love, but Surgeoner did not go so far. Was this the
self-denying chastity of the literary artist, I wondered, or had
he not thought of such a dénouement yet? When the meeting
had concluded with a dismal rendition of the revival hymn –

> Throw out the Life Line,
> Throw out the Life Line,
>   Someone is drifting away.
> Throw out the Life Line,
> Throw out the Life Line,
>   Someone is sinking today

– sung with the dispirited drag of the unaccompanied, untal-
ented religious, the little group drifted away – the bums to the

sleeping quarters next door and the respectable to their homes – and I was alone with Joel Surgeoner.

'Well, sir, I knew you would come, but I didn't expect you so soon,' said he and gestured me into a kitchen chair by the table. He frugally turned off the electricity, and we sat in the light of the lamps.

'You promised to show me what prayer had brought,' I said.

'You see it around you,' he replied, and then, seeing surprise on my face at the wretchedness of the Mission, he led me to a door into the next room – it was in fact a double door running on a track, of the kind you see in old warehouses – and slid it back. In the gloom leaking down through an overhead skylight I saw a poor dormitory in which about fifty men were lying on cots. 'Prayer brings me these, and prayer and hard work and steady begging provide for them, Mr Ramsay.' I suppose he had learned my name at the school.

'I spoke to our Bursar tonight,' I said 'and your talk this morning will bring you a cheque for five hundred and forty-three dollars; from six hundred boys and a staff of about thirty, that's not bad. What will you do with it?'

'Winter is coming; it will buy a lot of warm underclothes.' He closed the sliding door, and we sat down again in what seemed to be the chapel, common room, and business office of the Mission. 'That cheque will probably be a week getting here, and our needs are daily – hourly. Here is the collection from our little meeting tonight.' He showed me thirteen cents on a cracked saucer.

I decided it was time to go at him. 'Thirteen cents for a thirteen-cent talk,' I said. 'Did you expect them to believe that cock-and-bull story about the cursing sailor and the widow's mite? Don't you underestimate them?'

He was not disconcerted. 'I expect them to believe the spirit of the story,' he said, 'and I know from experience what kind of story they like. You educated people, you have a craze for what you call truth, by which you mean police-court facts. These people get their noses rubbed in such facts all day and every day, and they don't want to hear them from me.'

'So you provide romance,' I said.

'I provide something that strengthens faith, Mr Ramsay, as

well as I can. I am not a gifted speaker or a man of education, and often my stories come out thin and old, and I suppose unbelievable to a man like you. These people don't hold me on oath, and they aren't stupid either. They know my poor try at a parable from hard fact. And I won't deceive you : there is something about this kind of work and the kind of lives these people live that knocks the hard edge off fact. If you think I'm a liar – and you do – you should hear some of the confessions that come out in this place on a big night. Awful whoppers, that just pop into the heads of people who have found joy in faith but haven't got past wanting to be important in the world. So they blow up their sins like balloons. Better people than them want to seem worse than they are. We come to God in little steps, not in a leap, and that love of police-court truth you think so much of comes very late on the way, if it comes at all. What is truth? as Pilate asked; I've never pretended that I could have told him. I'm just glad when a boozer sobers up, or a man stops beating his woman, or a crooked lad tries to go straight. If it makes him boast a bit, that's not the worst harm it can do. You unbelieving people apply cruel, hard standards to us who believe.'

'What makes you think I'm an unbeliever?' I said. 'And what made you turn on me this morning, in front of the whole school?'

'I admit it was a trick,' he said. 'When you are talking like that it's always a good job near the end to turn on somebody and accuse them of disbelieving. Sometimes you see somebody laughing, but that isn't needful. Best of all is to turn on somebody behind you, if you can. Make it look as if you had eyes in the back of your head, see? There's a certain amount of artfulness about it, of course, but a greater end has been served, and nobody has been really hurt.'

'That's a thoroughly crooked-minded attitude,' said I.

'Perhaps it is. But you're not the first man I've used like that, and I promise you won't be the last. God has to be served, and I must use the means I know. If I'm not false to God – and I try very hard not to be – I don't worry too much about the occasional stranger.'

'I am not quite so much a stranger as you think,' said I. Then

137

I told him that I had recognized him. I don't know what I expected him to do – deny it, I suppose. But he was perfectly cool.

'I don't remember you, of course,' he said. 'I don't remember anybody from that night except the woman herself. It was her that turned me to God.'

'When you raped her?'

'I didn't rape her, Mr Ramsay; you heard her say so herself. Not that I wouldn't have done, the state of mind I was in. I was at the end of my rope. I was a tramp, you see. Any idea what it means to be a tramp? They're lost men; not many people understand them. Do you know, I've heard and read such nonsense about how they just can't stand the chains of civilization, and have to breathe the air of freedom, and a lot of them are educated men with a wonderful philosophy, and they laugh at the hard workers and farmers they beg off of – well, it's all a lot of cock, as they'd put it. They're madmen and criminals and degenerates mostly, and tramping makes them worse. It's the open-air life does it to them. Oh, I know the open air is a great thing, when you have food and shelter to go back to, but when you haven't it drives you mad; starvation and oxygen is a crazy mixture for anybody that isn't born to it, like a savage. These fellows aren't savages. Weaklings, mostly, but vicious.

'I got among them a very common way. Know-it-all lad; quarrelled with my old dad, who was hard and mean-religious; ran away, picked up odd jobs, then began to pinch stuff, and got on the drink. Know what a tramp drinks? Shoe-blacking sometimes, strained through a hunk of bread; drives you crazy. Or he gets a few prunes and lets them stand in the sun in a can till they ferment; that's the stuff gives you the black pukes, taken on a stomach with nothing in it but maybe some raw vegetables you've pulled in a field. Like those sugar-beets around Deptford; fermented for a while, they'd eat a hole in a copper pot.

'And sex too. Funny how fierce it gets when the body is ill fed and ill used. Tramps are sodomites mostly. I was a young fellow, and it's the young ones and the real old ones that get used, because they can't fight as well. It's not kid-glove stuff, like that Englishman went to prison for; it's enough to kill you, you'd think, when a gang of tramps set on a young fellow. But it doesn't, you know. That's how I lost my hearing, most of it; I resisted a gang, and they beat me over the ears with my own boots till I couldn't resist any more. Do you know what they say? "Lots o' booze and buggery," they say. That's their life. Mine too, till the great mercy of that woman. I know now that God is just as near them as He is to you and me at this instant, but they defy Him, poor souls.

'That night we last met, I was crazy. I'd tumbled off the freight in that jungle by Deptford, and found a fire and seven fellows around it, and they had a stew – somebody'd got a rabbit and it was in a pail over a fire with some carrots. Ever eat that? It's awful, but I wanted some, and after a lot of nastiness they said I could have some after they'd had what they wanted of me. My manhood just couldn't stand it, and I left them. They laughed and said I'd be back when I got good and hungry.

'Then I met this woman, wandering by herself. I knew she was a town woman. Women tramps are very rare; too much sense, I guess. She was clean and looked like an angel to me, but I threatened her and asked her for money. She hadn't any; then I grabbed her. She wasn't much afraid and asked what I wanted. I told her, in tramp's language, and I could see she didn't understand, but when I started to push her down and grab at her clothes she said, "Why are you so rough?" and then I started to cry. She held my head to her breast and talked nicely to me, and I cried worse, but the strange thing is I still wanted her. As if only that would put me right, you see? That's what I said to her. And do you know what she said? She said, "You may if you promise not to be rough." So I did, and that was when you people came hunting her.

'When I look back now I wonder that it wasn't all over with me that moment. But it wasn't. No, it was glory come into my life. It was as if I had gone right down into Hell and through the worst of the fire, and come on a clear, pure pool where I could wash and be clean. I was locked in by my deafness, so I didn't know much of what was said, but I could see it was a terrible situation for her, and there was nothing I could do.

'They turned me loose next morning, and I ran out of that town laughing and shouting like the man who was delivered from devils by Our Lord. As I had been, you see? He worked through that woman, and she is a blessed saint, for what she did for me – I mean it as I say it – was a miracle. Where is she now?'

How did I know? Mrs Dempster was often in my mind, but whenever I thought of her I put the thought aside with a sick heart, as part of a past that was utterly done. I had tried to get Deptford out of my head, just as Boy had done, and for the same reason; I wanted a new life. What Surgeoner told me made it clear that any new life must include Deptford. There was to be no release by muffling up the past.

We talked for some time, and I liked him more and more. When at last I left I laid a ten-dollar bill on the table.

'Thank you, Mr Ramsay,' said he. 'This will get us the soup kettle we need, and a load of wood as well. Do you see now how prayers are answered?'

7

Back to Deptford, therefore, at the first chance, pretending I wanted to consult Mr Mahaffey about the deadbeat who had bought the *Banner* from me and was still in debt for more than half of the price. The magistrate counselled patience. But I got what I wanted, which was the address of the aunt who had taken Mrs Dempster after the death of her husband. She was not, as Milo Papple thought, a widow, but an old maid, a Miss Bertha Shanklin, and she lived in Weston. He gave me the address, without asking why I wanted it.

'A bad business, that was,' he said. 'She seemed a nice little person. Then – a madwoman! Struck by a snowball. I don't suppose you have any idea who threw it, have you? No, I didn't imagine you did, or you would have said so earlier. There was guilt, you know; undoubtedly there was guilt. I don't know quite what could have been done about it, but look at the consequences! McCausland says definitely she became a moral idiot – no sense at all of right and wrong – and the result was that terrible business in the pit. I remember that you were there. And the ruin of her husband's life. Then the lad running away when he was really no more than a baby. I've never seen such grief as hers when she finally realized he had gone. McCausland had to give her very heavy morphia before Miss Shanklin could remove her. Yes, there was guilt, whether any kind of charge could have been laid or not. Guilt, and somebody bears it to this day!'

The old man's vehemence, and the way he kept looking at me over and under and around his small, very dirty spectacles, left no doubt that he thought I knew more than I admitted, and might very well be the guilty party myself. But I saw no sense in telling him anything; I still had a grudge against Boy for what he had done, but I remembered too that if I had not been so sly Mrs Dempster would not have been hit. I was anxious to regard the whole thing as an accident, past care and past grief.

Nevertheless this conversation reheated my strong sense of guilt and responsibility about Paul; the war and my adult life had banked down that fire but not quenched it. The consequence was that I did something very foolish. I paid a visit to Father Regan, who was still the Catholic priest in Deptford.

I had never spoken to him, but I wanted somebody I could talk to confidentially, and I had the Protestant notion that priests are very close-mouthed and see more than they say. Later in life I got over that idea, but at this moment I wanted somebody who was in Deptford but not wholly of it, and he seemed to be my man. So within fifteen minutes of leaving the magistrate I was in the priest's house, snuffing up the smell of soap, and sitting in one of those particularly uncomfortable chairs that find refuge in priests' parlours all over the globe.

He thought, quite rightly, that I had come fishing for something, and was very suspicious, but when he found out what it was he laughed aloud, with the creaky, short laugh of a man whose life does not afford many jokes.

'A saint, do you say? Well now, that's a pretty tall order. I couldn't help you at all. Finding saints isn't any part of my job. Nor can I say what's a miracle and what isn't. But I don't imagine the bishop would have much to say to your grounds; it'd be his job to think of such things, if anybody did. A tramp reformed. I've reformed a tramp or two myself; they get spells of repentance, like most people. This fella you tell me of, now, seems to be as extreme in his zeal as he was in his sin. I never like that. And this business of raising your brother from his deathbed, as you describe it, was pretty widely talked about when it happened. Dr McCausland says he never died at all, and I suppose he'd know. A few minutes with no signs of life. Well, that's hardly Lazarus, now, is it? And your own experience when you were wounded — man, you were out of your head. I have to say it plainly. You'd better put this whole foolish notion away and forget it.

'You were always an imaginative young fella. It was said of you when you were a lad, and it seems you haven't changed. You have to watch that kinda thing, you know. Now, you tell me you're very interested in saints. Awright, I'm not fishing for converts, but if that's the way it is you'd better take a good look at the religion saints come from. And when you've looked, I'll betcha a dollar you'll draw back like a man from a flame. You clever, imaginative fellas often want to flirt with Mother Church, but she's no flirty lady, I'm telling you. You like the romance, but you can't bear the yoke.

'You're hypnotized by this idea that three miracles makes a saint, and you think you've got three miracles for a poor woman who is far astray in her wits and don't know right from wrong. Aw, go on!

'Look, Mr Ramsay, I'll tell it to you as plain as it comes: there's a lot of very good people in the world, and a lot of queer things happen that we don't see the explanation of, but there's only one Church that undertakes to cut right down to the bone and say what's a miracle and what isn't and who's a saint and who isn't, and you, and this poor soul you speak of, are outside it. You can't set up some kind of a bootleg saint, so take my advice and cut it out. Be content with the facts you have, or think you have, and don't push anything too far — or you might get a little bit strange yourself.

'I'm trying to be kind, you know, for I admired your parents. Fine people, and your father was a fair-minded man to every faith. But there are spiritual dangers you Protestants don't even seem to know exist, and this monkeying with difficult, sacred things is a sure way to get yourself into a real old mess. Well I recall, when I was a seminarian, how we were warned one day about a creature called a fool-saint.

142

'Ever hear of a fool-saint? I thought not. As a matter of fact, it's a Jewish idea, and the Jews are no fools, y'know. A fool-saint is somebody who seems to be full of holiness and loves everybody and does every good act he can, but because he's a fool it all comes to nothing – to worse than nothing, because it is virtue tainted with madness, and you can't tell where it'll end up. Did you know that Prudence was named as one of the Virtues? There's the trouble with your fool-saint, y'see – no Prudence. Nothing but a lotta bad luck'll rub off on you from one of them. Did you know bad luck could be catching? There's a theological name for it, but I misremember it right now.

'Yes, I know a lot of the saints have done strange things, but I don't recall any of 'em traipsing through the streets with a basketful o' wilted lettuce and wormy spuds, or bringing scandal on their town by shameless goings-on. No, no; the poor soul is a fool-saint if she's anything, and I'd strongly advise you to keep clear of her.'

So, back to Toronto with a flea in my ear, and advice from Father Regan so obviously good and kind that I had either to take it or else hate Regan for giving it. Knowing by now what a high-stomached fellow I was, you can guess which I did. Within a week I was at Weston, talking with my fool-saint once again.

8

She was now forty but looked younger. An unremarkable woman really, except for great sweetness of expression; her dress was simple, and I suppose the aunt chose it, for it was a good deal longer than the fashion of the time and had a home-made air. She had no recollection of me, to begin with, but when I spoke of Paul I roused painful associations, and the aunt had to intervene, and take her away.

The aunt had not wanted to let me in the house, and as I thought this might be so I presented myself at the door without warning. Miss Bertha Shanklin was very small, of an un-guessable age, and had gentle, countrified manners. Her house was pretty and suggested an old-fashioned sort of cultivation;

much was ugly in the style of fifty years before, but nothing was trashy; there were a few mosaic boxes, and a couple of muddy oil paintings of the Italian Campagna with classical ruins and picturesque peasants, which suggested that somebody had been to Italy. Miss Shanklin let me talk with Mrs Dempster for ten minutes or so, before she took her away. I stayed where I was, though decency suggested that it was time for me to go.

'I am sure you mean this visit kindly, Mr Ramsay,' she said when she returned, 'but you can see for yourself that my niece is not up to receiving callers. There's not a particle of sense in reminding her of the days past – it frets her and does no good. So I'll say good-afternoon, and thank you for calling.'

I talked as well as I could about why I had come, and of my concern for her niece, to whom I owed a great debt. I said nothing of saints; that was not Miss Shanklin's line. But I talked about childhood kindness, and my mother's concern for Mary Dempster, and my sense of guilt that I had not sought her before. This brought about a certain melting.

'That's real kind of you. I know some terrible things went on in Deptford, and it's good to know not everybody has forgotten poor Mary. I suppose I can say to you that I always thought the whole affair was a mistake. Amasa Dempster was a good man, I suppose, but Mary had been used to an easier life – not silly-easy, you understand me, but at least some of the good things. I won't pretend I was friendly towards the match, and I guess I have to bear some of the blame. They didn't exactly run away, but it hurt me the way they managed things, as if there wasn't a soul in the world but themselves. I could have made it easier for her, but Amasa was so proud and even a little mite hateful about Mary having any money of her own that I just said, All right, they can paddle their own canoe. It cost me a good deal to do that. I never saw Paul, you know, and I'd certainly have done anything in the world for him if I could have got things straight with his father. But I guess a little bit of money made me proud, and religion made him proud, and then it was too late. I love her so much, you see. She's all the family I've got. Love can make you do some mean actions when you think it has been snubbed. I was mean, I grant you. But I'm trying to do what I can now, when I guess it's too late.'

Miss Shanklin wept, not aloud or passionately, but to the point of having to wipe her eyes and depart for the kitchen to ask for some tea. By the time this tea was brought – by the 'hired girl', whose softening influence on Mary Dempster had been so deplored by the matrons of Amasa Dempster's congregation – Miss Shanklin and I were on quite good terms.

'I love to hear you say that Mary was so good and sweet, even after that terrible accident – it was an accident, wasn't it? A blow on the head? From a fall or something? – and that you thought of her even when you were away at the war. I always had such hopes for her. Not just to keep her with me, of course, but – well, I know she loved Amasa Dempster, and love is supposed to excuse anything. But I am sure there would have been other men, and she could hardly have been worse off with one of them, now could she? Life with Amasa seems to have been so dark and wintry and hopeless. Mary used to be so full of hope – before she married.

'Now she remembers so little, and it's better so, because when she does remember she thinks of Paul. I don't even let myself speculate on what would happen to a little fellow like that, running away with show folks. As like as not he's dead long since, and better so, I suppose. But of course she thinks of him as a little boy still. She has no idea of time, you see. When she thinks of him, it's awful to hear her cry and carry on. And I can't get rid of the feeling that if I had just had a little more real sand and horse sense, things would have been very different.

'I'd meant to tell you not to come again, ever, but I won't. Come and see Mary, but promise you'll get to know her again, as a new friend. She hasn't any idea of the past, except for horrible mixed-up memories of being tied up, and Paul disappearing, and Amasa – she always remembers him with a blue mouth, like a rotten hole in his face – telling God he forgave her for ruining his life. Amasa died praying, did you know?'

9

It was the following May, in the fated year 1929, that I had a call from Boy – in itself an unusual thing, but even more unusual in its message.

'Dunny, don't be in too much of a rush, but you oughtn't to lose more than a couple of weeks in getting rid of some of your things.' And he named half-a-dozen stocks he knew I had, because he had himself advised me to buy them.

'But they're mounting every week,' I said.

'That's right,' said he; 'now sell 'em, and get hold of some good hard stuff. I'll see that you get another good block of Alpha.'

So that is what I did, and it is to Boy's advice I owe a reputation I acquired in the school as a very shrewd businessman. Just about every master, like some millions of other people on this continent, had money in the market, and most of them had invested on margin and were cleaned out before Christmas. But I found myself pleasantly well off when the worst of the crash came, because Boy Staunton regarded me as in certain respects a responsibility.

My mind was not on money at the time, however, for I was waiting impatiently for the end of term so that I could take ship and set out on a great hunt, starting in England and making my way across France, Portugal, Switzerland, Austria, and at last to Czechoslovakia. This was the first of my annual journeys, broken only by the 1939-45 war, saint-hunting, saint-identifying, and saint-describing; journeys that led to my book *A Hundred Saints for Travellers*, still in print in six languages and a lively seller, to say nothing of my nine other books, and my occasional articles. This time I was after big game, a saint never satisfactorily described and occurring in a variety of forms, whose secret I hoped to discover.

There is a saint for just about every human situation, and I was on the track of a curious specimen whose intercession was sought by girls who wanted to get rid of disagreeable suitors. Her home ground, so to speak, was Portugal, and she was reputed to have been the daughter of a Portuguese king, himself a pagan, who had betrothed her to the King of Sicily; but she was a Christian and had made a vow of virginity, and when she prayed for assistance in keeping it, she miraculously grew a heavy beard; the Sicilian king refused to have her, and her angry father caused her to be crucified.

It was my purpose to visit every shrine of this odd saint, compare all versions of the legend, establish or demolish the authenticity of a prayer reputedly addressed to her and authorized by a Bishop of Rouen in the sixteenth century, and generally to poke my nose into anything that would shed light on her mystery. Her case abounded with the difficulties that people of my temperament love. She was commonly called Wilgefortis, supposed to be derived from Virgo-Fortis, but she was also honoured under the names of Liberata, Kummernis, Ontkommena, Livrade, and in England — she once had a shrine in St Paul's — as Uncumber. The usual fate for Wilgefortis, among the more conservative hagiologists, was dismissal as an ignorant peasant misunderstanding of one of the many paintings of the Holy Face of Lucca, in which a long-haired and bearded figure in a long robe hangs from a cross; it is, of course, Christ, reputedly painted by St Luke himself; but many copies of it might well be pictures of a bearded lady.

I, however, had one or two new ideas about Uncumber, which I wanted to test. The first was that her legend might be a persistence of the hermaphrodite figure of the Great Mother, which was long worshipped in Cyprus and Carthage. Many a useful and popular wonder-working figure had been pinched from the pagans by Christians in early days, and some not so early. My other bit of information came from two physicians at the State University of New York, Dr Moses and Dr Lloyd, who had published some findings about abnormal growth of hair in unusually emotional women; they instanced a number of cases of beard-growing in girls who had been crossed in love; furthermore, two English doctors attested to a thick beard grown by a girl whose engagement had been brutally terminated. Anything here for Uncumber? I was on my way to Europe to find out.

So I jaunted cheerfully about the Continent on my apparently mad mission, hunting up Uncumber in remote villages as well as in such easy and pleasant places as Beauvais and Wissant, and once positively identifying an image that was said to be Uncumber (Wilgeforte, she was locally called, and the priest was rather ashamed of her) as Galla, the patroness of widows, who is also sometimes represented with a beard. It was not until August that I arrived in the Tyrol, searching for a shrine that was in a village about thirty-five miles northwest of Innsbruck.

It was about the size of Deptford, and its three inns did not expect many visitors from North America; this was still before the winter sports enthusiasm opened up every Tyrolean village and forced something like modern sanitation on every inn and guest-house. I settled in at the inevitable Red Horse and looked about me.

I was not the only stranger in the village.

A tent and some faded banners in the market-place announced the presence of *Le grand Cirque forain de St Vite*. I was certainly not the man to neglect a circus dedicated to St Vitus, patron of travelling showmen, and still invoked in country places against chorea and palsy and indeed anything that made the body shake. The banners showed neither the cock nor the dog that the name of St Vitus would have suggested, but they promised a Human Frog. *Le plus grand des Tyroliens*, *Le Solitaire des forêts* and – luck for me – *La Femme à barbe.* I determined to see this bearded lady, and if possible to find out if she had been violently crossed in love.

As a circus it was a pitiable affair. Everything about it stank of defeat and misery. There was no planned performance; now and then, when a sufficient crowd had assembled, a pair of gloomy acrobats did some tumbling and walked a slack wire. The Human Frog sat down on his own head, but with the air of one who took no pleasure in it. The Wild Man roared and chewed perfunctorily on a piece of raw meat to which a little fur still clung; the lecturer hinted darkly that we ought to keep our dogs indoors that night, but nobody seemed afraid. When not on view the Wild Man sat quietly, and from the motion of his jaws I judged that he was solacing himself with a quid of chewing tobacco.

There was an achondroplasic dwarf who danced on broken bottles; his bare feet were dirty, and from repeated dancing the glass had lost its sharpness. Their great turn was a wretched fellow – *Rinaldo the Heteradelphian* – who removed his robe

148

and showed us that below his breast grew a pitiful wobbling lump that the eye of faith, assisted by the lecturer's description, might accept as a pair of small buttocks and what could have been two little legs without feet – an imperfect twin. The bearded lady sat and knitted; her low-cut gown, revealing the foot-hills of enormous breasts, dispelled any idea that she was a fake. It was upon her that I fixed my attention, for the Heteradelphian and the frowst of Tyrolean *lederhosen* were trying, even for one used to a roomful of schoolboys.

I had had enough of *Le grand Cirque forain de St Vite* and was about to leave when a young man leapt up on the platform beside *Le Solitaire des forêts* and began, rapidly and elegantly, to do tricks with cards. It was Paul Dempster.

I had acquiesced for some time in the opinion put forward by Mr Mahaffey and Miss Shanklin that Paul must be dead, or certainly lost forever. Seeing him now, however, I felt no disbelief and no uncertainty. I had last seen Paul in 1915, when he was seven; fourteen years later many men would have been unrecognizably changed, from child to man, but I knew him in an instant. After all, he had been my pupil in the art of manipulating cards and coins, and I had watched him very closely as he demonstrated his superiority to my clumsy self. His face had changed from child to man, but his hands and his style of using them were not to be mistaken.

He gave his patter in French, dropping occasionally into German with an Austrian accent. He was very good – excellent, indeed, but too good for his audience. Those among them who were card-players plainly belonged to the class who play very slow games at the inns they frequent, laying down each card as if it weighed a pound and shuffling with deliberation. His rapid passes and brilliant manipulations dazzled without enlightening them. So it was when he began to work with coins. 'Secure and palm six half-crowns' – the daunting phrase came to my mind again as Paul did precisely that with the big Austrian pieces, plucking them from the beards of grown men or seeming to milk them from the noses of children, or nipping them up with long fingers from the bodices of giggling girls. It was the simplest but also the most difficult kind of conjuring because it depended on the most delicate manual skill; he brought an elegance to it that was as good as anything I had ever seen, for my old enthusiasm had led me to see a conjurer whenever I could.

When he wanted a watch to smash I offered mine, to get his eye, but he ignored it in favour of a large silver turnip handed up by a Tyrolean of some substance. Do what I could, he would not look at me, though I was a conspicuous figure as the only man in the audience not in local dress. When he had beaten the watch to pieces, made the pieces disappear, and invited a large countrywoman to return the watch from her knitting-bag, the performance was over, and the Tyroleans moved heavily towards the door of the tent.

I lingered, and addressed him in English. He replied in French, and when I changed to French he turned at once to German. I was not to be beaten. What passed between us took quite a long time and was slow and uneasy, but in the end he admitted that he was Paul Dempster – or had been so many years before. He had been Faustus Legrand for more years than the ten during which he answered to his earlier name. I spoke of his mother; told him that I had seen her not long before I came abroad. He did not answer.

Little by little, however, I got on better terms with him, principally because the other members of the troupe were curious to know what such a stranger as I wanted with one of them, and crowded around with frank curiosity. I let them know that I was from the village of Paul's birth, and with some of the cunning I had learned when trying to get priests and sacristans to talk about local shrines and the doings of saints, I let it be known that I would consider it an honour to provide the friends of Faustus Legrand with a drink – probably more than one drink.

This eased up the atmosphere at once, and the Bearded Lady, who seemed to be the social leader of Le grand Cirque forain de St Vite, organized a party in a very few minutes and closed the tent to business. They all, except Le Solitaire des forêts (who had the eyes of a dope-taker), were very fond of drink, and soon we were accommodated with a couple of bottles of that potato spirit sophisticated with brown sugar that goes by the name of Rhum in Austria, but which is not to be confused with rum. I set to work, on this foundation, to make myself popular.

It is not hard to be popular with any group, whether composed of the most conventional Canadians or of Central European freaks, if one is prepared to talk to people about themselves. In an hour I had heard about the Heteradelphian's daughter, who sang in a light opera chorus in Vienna, and about his wife, who had unaccountably wearied of his multiple attractions. The dwarf, who was shy and not very bright, took to me because I saw that he had his fair share of the Rhum. The Human Frog was a German and very cranky about war reparations, and I assured him that everybody in Canada thought they were a crying shame. I was not playing false with these poor people; they were off duty and wanted to be regarded as human beings, and I was quite ready to oblige. I became personal only with the Bearded Lady, to whom I spoke of my search for the truth about Uncumber; she was entranced by the story of the saint and insisted that I repeat it for all to hear; she took it as a tribute to Bearded Ladies in general, and began seriously to discuss having a new banner painted, in which she would advertise herself as Mme Wilgeforte, and be depicted crucified, gazing sternly at the departing figure of a pagan fiancé. Indeed, this was my best card, for the strangeness of my quest seemed to qualify me as a freak myself and make me more than ever one of the family.

When we needed more Rhum I contrived that Paul should go for it; I judged that the time had come when his colleagues would talk to me about him. And so it was.

'He stays with us only because of Le Solitaire,' said the Bearded Lady. 'I will not conceal from you, Monsieur, that Le Solitaire is not a well man, nor could he travel alone. Faustus very properly acknowledges a debt of gratitude, for before Le Solitaire became so incapable that he was forced to adopt the undemanding role of *un solitaire*, he had his own show of which Faustus was a part, and Faustus regards Le Solitaire as his father in art, if you understand the professional expression. I think it was Le Solitaire who brought him home from America.'

It was a very merry evening, and before it was over I had danced with the Bearded Lady to music provided by the dwarf, who whistled a polka and drummed with his feet; the sight of a wooden-legged man dancing seemed hilariously funny to the artistes of the one-eyed little circus as the Rhum got to them. When we broke up I had a short private conversation with Paul.

'May I tell your mother that I have seen you?'

'I cannot prevent it, Monsieur Ramsay, but I see no point in it.'

'Grief at losing you has made her very unwell.'

'As I mean to remain lost I do not see what good it would do to tell her about me.'

'I am sorry you have so little feeling for her.'

'She is part of a past that cannot be recovered or changed by anything I can do now. My father always told me it was my birth that robbed her of her sanity. So as a child I had to carry the weight of my mother's madness as something that was my own doing. And I had to bear the cruelty of people who thought her kind of madness was funny – a dirty joke. So far as I am concerned, it is over, and if she dies mad, who will not say that she is better dead?'

So next morning I went on my journey in search of the truth about Uncumber, after I had made the necessary arrangements for more money. Because somebody at *Le grand Cirque forain de St Vite* had stolen my pocket-book, and everything pointed to Paul.

4

Gyges and King Candaules

I

BOY STAUNTON made a great deal of money during the Depression because he dealt extensively in solaces. When a man is down on his luck he seems to consume all he can get of coffee and doughnuts. The sugar in the coffee was Boy's sugar, and the doughnuts were his doughnuts. When an overdriven woman without money to give her children a decent meal must give them something bulky, sweet, and interesting to stop their crying, she probably gives them a soft drink; it was Boy's soft drink. When a welfare agency wants to take the harsh look of bare necessity off a handout basket, it puts in a bag of candies for the children; they were Boy's candies. Behind tons of cheap confectionery, sweets, snacks, nibbles, biscuits, and simple cooking sugar, and the accompanying oceans of fizzy, sweet water, disguised with chemical versions of every known fruit flavour, stood Boy Staunton, though not many people knew it. He was the president and managing director of Alpha Corporation, a much-respected company that made nothing itself but controlled all the other companies that did.

He was busy and he was adventurous. When he first went into the bread business, because a large company was in difficulties and could be bought at a rock-bottom price, I asked him why he did not try beer as well.

'I may do that when the economy is steadier,' he said, 'but at present I feel I should do everything I can to see that people have necessities.' And we both took reflective pulls at the excellent whiskies-and-soda he had provided.

Boy's new bread company made quite a public stir with their

advertisements declaring that they would hold the price of bread steady. And they did so, though the loaves seemed to be a bit puffier and gassier than they had been before. We ate them at school, so I was able to judge.

There was filial piety, as well as altruism, in Boy's decision. Old Doc Staunton's annoyance at being outsmarted by his son had given way to his cupidity, and the old man was a large holder in Alpha. To have associated him with beer would have made trouble, and Boy never looked for trouble.

'Alpha concentrates on necessities,' Boy liked to say. 'In times like these, people need cheap, nourishing food. If a family can't buy meat, our vitaminized biscuits are still within their reach.' So much so, indeed, that Boy was fast becoming one of the truly rich, by which I mean one of those men whose personal income, though large, is a trifling part of the huge, mystical body of wealth that stands behind them and cannot be counted, only estimated.

A few cranky politicians of the most radical party tried to estimate it in order to show that, in some way, the very existence of Boy was intolerable in a country where people were in want. But, like so many idealists, they did not understand money, and after a meeting where they had lambasted Boy and others like him and threatened to confiscate their wealth at the first opportunity, they would adjourn to cheap restaurants, where they drank his sugar, and ate his sugar, and smoked cigarettes which, had they known it, benefited some other monster they sought to destroy.

I used to hear him abused by some of the junior masters at the school. They were Englishmen or Canadians who had studied in England, and they were full of the wisdom of the London School of Economics and the doctrine of *The New Statesman*, copies of which used to limp into the Common Room about a month after publication. I have never been sure of my own political opinions (historical studies and my fondness for myth and legend have always blunted my political partisanship), but it amused me to hear these poor fellows, working for terrible salaries, denouncing Boy and a handful of others as 'ca-*pittle*-ists'; they always stressed the middle syllables, this being a fashionable pronunciation of the period, and one that seemed to make rich men especially contemptible. I never raised my voice in protest, and none of my colleagues ever knew that I was personally acquainted with the ca-pittle-ist whose good looks, elegant style of life, and somewhat gross success made their own hard fortune and their leather-elbowed jackets and world-weary flannel trousers seem pitiful. This was not disloyalty; rather, it seemed to me that the Boy they hated and did not know was unrelated to the Boy I saw about once a fortnight and often more frequently.

I owed this position to the fact that I was the only person to whom he could talk frankly about Leola. She was trying hard, but she could not keep pace with Boy's social advancement. He was a genius – that is to say, a man who does superlatively and without obvious effort something that most people cannot do by the uttermost exertion of their abilities. He was a genius at making money, and that is as uncommon as great achievement in the arts. The simplicity of his concepts and the masterly way in which they were carried through made jealous people say he was lucky and people like my schoolmaster colleagues say he was a crook; but he made his own luck, and no breath of financial scandal ever came near him.

His ambitions did not rest in finance alone; he had built firmly on his association with the Prince of Wales, and though in hard fact it did not amount to more than the reception of a monogrammed Christmas card once a year it bulked substantially, though never quite to the point of absurdity, in his conversation. 'He isn't joining them at Sandringham this year,' he would say as Christmas drew near; 'pretty stuffy, I suppose.' And somehow this suggested that he had some inside information – perhaps a personal letter – though everybody who read the newspapers knew as much. All Boy's friends had to be pretty spry at knowing who 'he' was, or they ceased to be friends. In a less glossily successful young man this would have been laughable, but the people Boy knew were not the kind of people who laughed at several million dollars. It was after David's birth it became clear that Leola was lagging in the upward climb.

A woman can go just so far on the capital of being a pretty girl. Leola, like Boy and myself, was now past youth; he was two months younger than I, though I looked older than thirty-two and he somewhat less. Leola was not a full year younger than we, and her girlishness was not well suited to her age or her position. She had toiled at the lessons in bridge, mah-jongg, golf, and tennis; she had plodded through the Books-of-the-Month, breaking down badly in *Kristin Lavransdatter*; she had listened with mystification to gramophone records of *Le Sacre du Printemps* and with the wrong kind of enjoyment to Ravel's *Bolero*; but nothing made any impression on her, and bewilderment and a sense of failure had begun to possess her. She had lost heart in the fight to become the sort of sophisticated, cultivated, fashionably alert woman Boy wanted for a wife. She loved shopping, but her clothes were wrong; she had a passion for pretty things and leaned towards the frilly at a time when fashion demanded clean lines and a general air of knowingness in women's clothes. If Boy let her shop alone she always came back with what he called 'another god-damned Mary Pickford rig-out,' and if he took her shopping in Paris the sessions often ended in tears, because he sided with the clever shopwomen against his indecisive wife, who always forgot her painfully acquired French as soon as she was confronted with a living French creature. Nor did she speak English as became the wife of one who had once hobnobbed with a Prince and might do so again. If she positively *had* to use hick expressions, I once heard Boy tell her, she might at least say 'For Heaven's sake,' and not 'For Heaven sakes.' And 'supper' was a meal one ate after the theatre, *not* the meal they ate every night at half-past seven. Nor could she learn when to refer to herself as 'one', or remember not to say 'between you and I.'

In the early years of their marriage Leola sometimes resented this sort of talk and made spirited replies; she did not see why she should become stuck-up, and talk as she had never talked before, and behave in ways that were unnatural to her. When this happened Boy would give her what he called 'the silent treatment'; he said nothing, but Leola's inner ear was so tuned to the silence that she was aware of the answers to all her impertinences and blasphemies: it was *not* stuck-up to behave in a way that accorded with your position in the world, and the speech of Deptford was *not* the speech of the world to which they now belonged; as for unnatural behaviour, natural behaviour was the sort of thing they hired a nurse to root out of young David – eating with both hands and peeing on the floor; let us have no silly talk about being natural. Of course Boy was right, and of course Leola gave in and tried to be the woman he wanted.

It was so easy for him! He never forgot anything that was of use to him, and his own manners and speech became more polished all the time. Not that he lost a hint of his virility or youthfulness, but they sat on him as if he were one of those marvellous English actors – Clive Brook, for instance – who was manly and gentlemanly at once, in a way Canadians as a whole could never manage.

This situation did not come about suddenly; it was a growth of six years of their marriage, during which Boy had changed a great deal and Leola hardly at all. Even being a mother did nothing for her; she seemed to relax when she had performed her biological trick instead of taking a firmer hold on life.

I never intervened when Leola was having a rough time; rows between them seemed to be single affairs, and it was only when I looked backward that I could see that they were sharp outbreaks in a continuous campaign. To be honest, I must say also that I did not want to shoulder the burdens of a peacemaker; Boy never let it be forgotten that he had, as he supposed, taken Leola from me; he was very jocose about it, and sometimes allowed himself a tiny, roguish hint that it might have been better for us all if things had gone the other way. The fact was that I no longer had any feeling for Leola save pity. If I spoke up for her I might find myself her champion, and a man who champions any woman against her husband had better be sure he means business.

I did not mean business, or anything at all. I went to the Stauntons' often, because they asked me and because Boy's brilliant operations fascinated me. I enjoyed my role as Friend of the Family, though I was unlike the smart, rich, determinedly youthful people who were their 'set.' It was some time before I tumbled to the fact that Boy needed me as someone in whose presence he could think aloud, and that a lot of his thinking was about the inadequacy of the wife he had chosen to share his high destiny.

Personally I never thought Leola did badly; she offset some of the too glossy perfection of Boy. But his idea of a wife for himself would have had the beauty and demeanour of Lady Diana Manners coupled with the wit of Margot Asquith. He let me know that he had been led into his marriage by love, and love alone; though he did not say so it was clear he owed Cupid a grudge.

Only twice did I get into any sort of wrangle with them about their own affairs. The first was early in their marriage, about 1926 I think, when Boy discovered Dr Emile Coué; the doctor had been very much in the public eye since 1920, but Canada caught up with him just about the time his vogue was expiring.

You remember Dr Coué and his great success with auto-suggestion? It had the simplicity and answer-to-everything quality that Boy, for all his shrewdness, could never resist. If you fell asleep murmuring, 'Every day in every way, I am get-ting better and better,' wondrous things came of it. The plugged colon ceased to trouble, the fretful womb to ache; indigestion yielded to inner peace; twitches and trembles disappeared; skin irritations vanished overnight; stutterers became fluent; the fail-ing memory improved; stinking breath became as the zephyr of May; and dandruff but a hateful memory. Best of all it pro-vided 'moral energy', and Boy Staunton was a great believer in energy of all kinds.

He wanted Leola to acquire moral energy, after which social grace, wit, and an air of easy breeding would surely follow. She obediently repeated the formula as often as she could, every night for six weeks, but nothing much seemed to be happening.

'You're just not trying, Leo,' he said one night when I was dining with them. 'You've simply got to try harder.'

'Perhaps she's trying too hard,' I said.

'Don't be absurd, Dunny. There's no such thing as trying too hard, whatever you're doing.'

'Yes there is. Have you never heard of the Law of Reversed Effort? The harder you try, the more likely you are to miss the mark.'

'I never heard such nonsense. Who says that?'

'A lot of wise people have said it, and the latest is your Dr

Coué. Don't clench your teeth and push for success, he says, or everything will work against you. Psychological fact.'

'Bunk! He doesn't say it in my book.'

'But, Boy, you never study anything properly. That miserable little pamphlet you have just gives you a farcical smattering of Couéism. You should read Baudouin's *Suggestion and Auto-Suggestion* and get things right.'

'How many pages?'

'I don't count pages. It's a good-sized book.'

'I haven't got time for big books. I have to have the nub of things. If effort is all wrong, why does Coué work for me? I put lots of effort into it.'

'I don't suppose it does work for you. You don't need it. Every day in every way you do get better and better, in whatever sense you understand the word 'better', because that's the kind of person you are. You've got ingrained success.'

'Well, bring your book over and explain it to Leo. Make her read it, and you help her to understand it.'

Which I did, but it was of no use. Poor Leola did not get better and better because she had no idea of what betterness was. She couldn't conceive what Boy wanted her to be. I don't think I have ever met such a stupid, nice woman. So Dr Coué failed for her, as he did for many others, for which I lay no blame on him. His system was really a form of secularized, self-seeking prayer, without the human dignity that even the most modest prayer evokes. And like all attempts to command success for the chronically unsuccessful, it petered out.

The second time I came between Boy and Leola was much more serious. It happened late in 1927, after the famous Royal Tour. Boy gave me a number of reels of film and asked me to develop them for him. This was reasonable enough, because in my saint-hunting expeditions I used a camera often and had gained some skill; at the school, as I could not supervise sports, I was in charge of the Camera Club and taught boys how to use the dark room. I was always ready to do a favour for Boy to whose advice I owed my solvency, and when he said that he did not want to confide these films to a commercial developer I assumed they were pictures of the Tour and probably some of them were of the Prince.

So it was, except for two reels that were amateurish but pretentious 'art studies' of Leola, lying on cushions, peeping through veils, sitting at her make-up table, kneeling in front of an open fire, wagging her finger at a Teddy Bear, choosing a chocolate from a large ribboned box – every sentimental posture approved by the taste of the day for 'cutie' photographs, and in every one of them she was stark naked. If she had been an experienced model and Boy a clever photographer, they would have been the kind of thing that appeared in the more daring magazines. But their combined inexperience had produced embarrassing snapshots of the sort hundreds of couples take but have the sense to keep to themselves.

I do not know why this made me so angry. Was I so inconsiderable, so much the palace eunuch, that I did not matter? Or was this a way of letting me know what I had missed when Boy won Leola? Or was it a signal that if I wanted to take Leola off his hands Boy would make no objection? He had let me know that Leola had conventional ideas and that his own adventurous appetite was growing tired of her meat-and-potatoes approach to sex. Whatever it was, I was very angry and considered destroying the film. But – I must be honest – I examined the pictures with care, and I suppose with some measure of gloating, and this made me angrier still.

My solution was typical of me. I developed all the pictures as carefully as I could, enlarged the best ones (all those of Leola), returned them without a word, and waited to see what would happen.

Next time I dined with them all the pictures were brought out, and Boy went through them slowly, telling me exactly what H.R.H. had said as each one was taken. At last we came to the ones of Leola.

'Oh, don't show those!'

'Why not?'

'Because.'

'Dunny's seen them before, you know. He developed them, I expect he kept a set for himself.'

'No,' I said, 'as a matter of fact I didn't.'

'The more fool you. You'll never see pictures of a prettier girl.'

'Boy, please put them away or I'll have to go upstairs. I don't want Dunny to see them while I'm here.'

'Leo, I never thought you were such a little prude.'

'Boy, it isn't nice.'

'Nice, nice, nice! Of course it isn't *nice*! Only fools worry about what's *nice*. Now sit here by me, and Dunny on the other side, and be proud of what a stunner you are.'

So Leola, sensing a row from the edge in his voice, sat between us while Boy showed the pictures, telling me what lens apertures he had used, and how he had arranged the lights, and how he had achieved certain 'values' which, in fact, made Leola's rose-leaf bottom look like sharkskin and her nipples glare when they should have blushed. He seemed to enjoy Leola's discomfiture thoroughly; it was educational for her to learn that her beauty had public as well as private significance. He recalled Margot Asquith's account of receiving callers in her bath though – he was always a careless reader – he did not remember the circumstances correctly.

As we drew near the end of the show he turned to me and said with a grin, 'I hope you don't find it too hot in here, old man?'

As a matter of fact I did find it hot. All the anger I had felt when developing the pictures had returned. But I said I was quite comfortable.

'Oh. I just thought you might find the situation a bit unusual, as Leo does.'

'Unusual but not unprecedented. Call it historical – even mythological.'

'How's that?'

'It's happened before, you know. Do you remember the story of Gyges and King Candaules?'

'Never heard of them.'

'I thought not. Well, Candaules was a king of Lydia a long time ago, and he was so proud of his wife's beauty that he insisted his friend Gyges should see her naked.'

'Generous chap. What happened?'

'There are two versions. One is that the Queen took a fancy to Gyges and together they pushed Candaules off his throne.'

'Really? Not much chance of that here, is there, Leo? You'd find my throne a bit too big, Dunny.'

'The other is that Gyges killed Candaules.'

'I don't suppose you'll do that, Dunny.'

I didn't suppose so myself. But I think I stirred some uxorious fire in Boy, for nine months later I did some careful counting, and I am virtually certain that it was on that night little David was begotten. Boy was certainly a complex creature, and I am sure he loved Leola. What he thought of me I still do not know. That Leola loved him with all her unreflecting heart there would be no possible doubt. Nothing he could do would change that.

2

Every fortnight during the school term I made the journey to Weston on Saturday morning and had lunch with Miss Bertha Shanklin and Mrs Dempster. It took less than half an hour on a local train, so I could leave after the Saturday morning study period for boarders, which I supervised, and be back in town by three o'clock. To have stayed longer, Miss Shanklin let me know, would have been fatiguing for poor Mary. She really meant, for herself; like many people who have charge of an invalid, she projected her own feelings on her patient, speaking for Mrs Dempster as a priest might interpret a dull-witted god. But she was gentle and kind, and I particularly liked the way she provided her niece with pretty, fresh dresses and kept her hair clean and neat; in the Deptford days I had become used to seeing her in dirty disorder as she paced her room on the restraining rope.

At these meals Mrs Dempster rarely spoke, and although it was clear that she recognized me as a regular visitor, nothing to suggest any memory of Deptford ever passed between us. I played fair with Miss Shanklin and appeared in the guise of a new friend; a welcome one, for they saw few men, and most women, even the most determined spinsters, like a little masculine society.

The only other man to visit that house at any time when I

was there was Miss Shanklin's lawyer, Orpheus Wettenhall. I never discovered anything about him that would explain why his parents gave him such a pretentious Christian name; perhaps it ran in the family. He invited me to call him Orph, which was what everybody called him, he said. He was an undersized, laughing man with a big walrus moustache and silver-rimmed glasses.

Orph was quite the most dedicated sportsman I have ever known. During every portion of the year when it was legal to shoot or hook any living creature, he was at it; in off-seasons he shot groundhogs and vermin beneath the notice of the law. When the trout season began, his line was in the water one minute after midnight; when deer might be shot, he lived as did Robin Hood. Like all dedicated hunters, he had to get rid of the stuff he killed; his wife 'kicked over the traces' at game more than four or five times a week. He used to turn up at Miss Shanklin's now and then, opening the front door without ceremony and shouting, 'Bert! I've brought you a pretty!'; then he would appear an instant later with something wet or bloody, which the hired girl bore away, while Miss Shanklin gave a nicely judged performance of delight at his goodness and horror at the sight of something the intrepid Orph had slain with his own hands.

He was a gallant little particle, and I liked him because he was so cheerful and considerate towards Miss Shanklin and Mrs Dempster. He often urged me to join him in slaughter, but I pled my wooden leg as an excuse for keeping out of the woods. I had had all the shooting I wanted in the war.

I began my visits in the autumn of 1928 and was faithful in them till February 1932, when Miss Shanklin took pneumonia and died. I did not know of it until I received a letter from Wettenhall, bidding me to the funeral and adding that we must have a talk afterward.

It was one of those wretched February funerals, and I was glad to get away from the graveyard into Wettenhall's hot little office. He was in a black suit, the only time I ever saw him in other than sporting clothes.

'Let's cut the cackle, Ramsay,' he said, pouring us each a hearty drink of rye, in glasses with other people's lipmarks on the rims. 'It's as simple as this: you're named as Bert's executor. Everything goes to Mary Dempster except some small legacies – one to me, the old sweetheart, for taking good care of her affairs – and a handful of others. You are to have five thousand a year, on a condition. That condition is that you get yourself appointed Mary Dempster's guardian and undertake to look after her and administer her money for her as long as she lives. I'm to see that the Public Guardian is satisfied. After Mary's death everything goes to you. When all debts and taxes are paid, Bert ought to cut up at – certainly not less than a quarter of a million, maybe three hundred thousand. You're allowed to reject the responsibility, and the legacy as well, if you don't want to be bothered. You'll want a couple of days to think it over.'

I agreed, though I knew already that I would accept. I said some conventional but perfectly sincere things about how much I had liked Miss Shanklin and how I would miss her.

'You and me both,' said Orph. 'I loved Bert – in a perfectly decent way, of course – and damned if I know how things will be without her.'

He handed me a copy of the will, and I went back to town. I did not go to see Mrs Dempster, who had not, of course, been to the funeral. I would attend to that when I had made some other arrangements.

The next day I made inquiries as to how I could be appointed the guardian of Mary Dempster and found that it was not a very complicated process but would take time. I experienced a remarkable rising of my spirits, which I can only attribute to the relief of guilt. As a child I had felt oppressively responsible for her, but I had thought all that was dissipated in the war. Was not a leg full and fair payment for an evil action? This was primitive thinking, and I had no trouble dismissing it – so it seemed. But the guilt had only been thrust away, or thrust down out of sight, for here it was again, in full strength, clamouring to be atoned. now that the opportunity offered itself.

Another element insisted on attention though I tried to put it from me: if Mrs Dempster was a saint, henceforth she would be *my* saint. Was she a saint? Rome, which alone of human agencies undertook to say who was a saint and who was not, insisted on three well-attested miracles. Hers were the reclamation of Surgeoner by an act of charity that was certainly heroic in terms of the *mores* of Deptford; the raising of Willie from the dead; and her miraculous appearance to me when I was at the uttermost end of my endurance at Passchendaele.

Now I should be able to see what a saint was really like and perhaps make a study of one without all the apparatus of Rome, which I had no power to invoke. The idea possessed me that it might lie in my power to make a serious contribution to the psychology of religion, and perhaps to carry the work of William James a step further. I don't think I was a very good teacher on the day when all of this was racing through my head.

I was a worse teacher two days later, when the police called me to say that Orpheus Wettenhall had shot himself and that they wanted to talk to me.

It was a very hush-hush affair. People talk boldly about suicide, and man's right to choose his own time of death, when it is not near them. For most of us, when it draws close, suicide is a word of fear, and never more so than in small, closely knit communities. The police and the coroner and everybody else implicated took every precaution that the truth about Orph should not leak out. And so, of course, the truth did leak out, and it was a very simple and old story.

Orph was a family lawyer of the old school; he looked after a number of estates for farmers and people like Miss Shanklin, who had not learned about new ways of doing business. Orph's word was as good as his bond, so it would have been unfriendly to ask for his bond. He had been paying his clients a good unadventurous return on their money for years, but he had been investing that same money in the stock market for big returns, which he kept. When the crash came he was unprepared, and since 1929 he had been paying out quite a lot of his own money (if it may be called that) to keep his affairs on an even keel. The death of Bertha Shanklin had made it impossible to go on.

So the story given to the public was that Orph, who had handled guns all his life, had been cleaning a cocked and loaded shotgun and had unaccountably got the end of the barrel into his mouth, which had so much astonished him that he inadvertently trod on the trigger and blew the top of his head off. Accidental death, as clearly as any coroner ever saw it.

Perhaps a few people believed it, until a day or two later when it was known what a mess his affairs were in, and a handful of old men and women were to be met wandering in the streets, unable to believe their ill-fortune.

Nobody had time or pity for these minor characters in the drama; all public compassion was for Orph Wettenhall. What agonies of mind must he not have endured before taking his life! Was it not significant that he had launched himself into the hereafter apparently gazing upward at the large stuffed head of a moose he had shot a good forty years before! Who would have the heart to take his place on the deerhunt next autumn? When had there been his like for deftness and speed in skinning a buck? But of his ability in skinning a client little was said, except that he had obviously meant to restore the missing funds as soon as he could.

It was not positively so stated, but the consensus seemed to be that Bertha Shanklin had shown poor taste in dying so soon and thus embarrassing the local Nimrod. 'There, but for the grace of God, go I,' said several citizens; like most people who quote this ambiguous saying, they had never given a moment's thought to its implications. As for Mary Dempster, I never heard her name mentioned. Thus I learned two lessons: that popularity and good character are not related, and that compassion dulls the mind faster than brandy.

All the cash I could find in Miss Shanklin's house amounted to twenty-one dollars; of her bank account, into which Wettenhall had made quarterly payments, everything but about two hundred dollars had been spent on her final illness and burial. So I began then and there to maintain Mrs Dempster, and never ceased to do so until her death in 1959. What else could I do?

As executor I was able to sell the house and the furniture, but they realized less than four thousand dollars; the Depression was no time for auctions. In the course of time I was duly appointed the guardian of Mary Dempster. But what was I to do with her? I investigated the matter of private hospitals and found that to keep her in one would beggar me. All masters at Colborne had been invited to take a cut in salary to help in keeping the school afloat, and we did so; there were many boys whose parents either could not pay their fees or did not pay them till much later, and it was not in the school's character to throw them out. My investments were better than those of a great many people, but even Alpha was not paying much; Boy said it would not look well at such a time, and so there were stock splits instead, and a good deal of money was 'ploughed back' for future advantage. I was not too badly off for a single man, but I had no funds to maintain an expensive invalid. So much against my will I got Mrs Dempster into a public hospital for the insane, in Toronto, where I could keep an eye on her.

It was a dark day for both of us when I took her there. The staff were good and kind but they were far too few, and the building was an old horror. It was about eighty years old and had been designed for the era when the first thing that was done with an insane patient was to put him to bed. with a view to keeping him there, safe and out of the way, till he recovered or died. Consequently the hospital had few and inadequate common rooms. and the patients sat in the corridors, or wandered up and down the corridors, or lay on their beds. The architecture was of the sort that looks better on the outside than on the inside; the building had a dome and a great number of barred windows and looked like a run-down palace.

Inside the ceilings were high, the light was bad, and in spite of the windows the ventilation was capricious. The place reeked of disinfectant, but the predominating smell was that unmistakable stench of despair that is so often to be found in jails, courtrooms. and madhouses.

She had a bed in one of the long wards. and I left her standing beside it, with a kindly nurse who was explaining what she should do with the contents of her suitcase. But already her face looked as I remembered it in her worst days in Deptford. I dared not look back. and I felt meaner than I have ever felt in my life. But what was I to do?

3

Aside from my teaching, my observation of Boy's unwitting destruction of Leola, and my new and complete responsibility for Mrs Dempster, this was the most demanding period of my life, for it was during this time I became involved with the Bollandists and found my way into the mainstream of the work that has given me endless delight and a limited, specialized reputation.

I have spent a good deal of time in my life explaining who the Bollandists are, and although you, Headmaster, are assumed by the school to know everything, perhaps I had better remind you that they are a group of Jesuits whose special task is to record all available information about saints in their great *Acta Sanctorum*, upon which they have been at work (with breaks for civil or religious uproar) since John van Bolland began in 1643; they have been pegging away with comparatively few interruptions since 1837; proceeding from the festal days of the Saints beginning in January, they have now filled sixty-nine volumes and reached the month of November.

In addition to this immense and necessarily slow task, they have published since 1882 a yearly collection of material of interest to their work but not within the scope of the *Acta*, called *Analecta Bollandiana*; it is scholarly modesty of a high order to call this 'Bollandist Gleanings', for it is of the greatest importance and interest, historically as well as hagiographically.

As a student of history myself, I have always found it revealing to see who gets to be a saint in any period; some ages like wonder-workers, and some prefer gifted organizers whose attention to business produces apparent miracles. In the last few years good old saints whom even Protestants love have been losing ground to lesser figures whose fortune it was to be black or yellow or red-skinned – a kind of saintly representation by population. My Bollandist friends are the first to admit that there is more politics to the making of a saint than the innocently devout might think likely.

It was quite beyond my income to own a set of the *Acta*, but I consulted it frequently – sometimes two or three times a week – at the University Library. However, I did, by luck, get a chance to buy a run of the *Analecta*, and though it cost me a fortune by Depression reckoning, I could not let it go, and its bulk and foreign-looking binding have surprised many visitors to my study in the school.

Boys grow bug-eyed when they find that I actually read in French, German, and Latin, but it is good for them to find that these languages have an existence outside the classroom; some of my colleagues look at my books with amusement, and a few solemn asses have spread the rumour that I am 'going over to Rome'; old Eagles (long before your time) thought it his duty to warn me against the Scarlet Woman and demanded rhetorically how I could possibly 'swallow the Pope.' Since then millions have swallowed Hitler and Mussolini, Stalin and Mao, and we have swallowed some democratic leaders who had to be gagged down without relish. Swallowing the Pope seems a trifle in comparison. But to return to 1932, there I was, a subscriber and greedy reader of the *Analecta*, and busy learning Greek (not the Greek of Homer but the queer Greek of medieval monkish recorders) so as to miss nothing.

It was then that the bold idea struck me of sending my notes on Uncumber to the editor of *Acta*, the great Hippolyte Delehaye; at worst he would ignore them or return them with formal thanks. I had the Protestant idea that Catholics always spat in your eye if they could, and of course Jesuits – crafty and trained to duplicity as they were – might pinch my stuff and arrange to have me blown up with a bomb, to conceal their guilt. Anyhow I would try.

It was little more than a month before this came in the mail :

Cher Monsieur Ramsay,
Your notes on the Wilgefortis-Kummernis figure have been read with interest by some of us here, and although the information is not wholly new, the interpretation and synthesis is of such a quality that we seek your consent to its publication in the next *Analecta*. Will you be so good as to write to me at your earliest convenience, as time presses. If you ever visit Bruxelles, will you

give us the pleasure of making your acquaintance? It is always a great satisfaction to meet a serious hagiographer, and particularly one who, like yourself, engages in the work not professionally but as a labour of love.

Avec mes souhaits sincères,
Hippolyte Delehaye S.J.

Société des Bollandistes
24 Boulevard Saint-Michel
Bruxelles

Few things in my life have given me so much delight as this letter; I have it still. I had schooled myself since the war-days never to speak of my enthusiasms; when other people did not share them, which was usual, I was hurt and my pleasure diminished; why was I always excited about things other people did not care about? But I could not hold in. I boasted a little in the Common Room that I had received an acceptance from *Analecta*; my colleagues looked uncomprehendingly, like cows at a passing train, and went on talking about Brebner's extraordinary hole-in-one the day before.

I spoke of it to Boy when next I saw him; all he could get through his head was that I had written my contribution in French. To be fair, I did not tell him the story of Uncumber and her miraculous beard; he was no audience for such psychological-mythological gossip, which appealed only to the simple or the truly sophisticated. Boy was neither, but he had an eye for quality, and it was after this I began to be asked to dinner more often with the Stauntons' smart friends and not as a lone guest. Sometimes I heard Boy speaking of me to the bankers and brokers as 'very able chap – speaks several languages fluently and writes for a lot of European publications – a bit of an eccentric, of course, but an old friend.'

I think his friends thought I wrote about 'current affairs', and quite often they asked me how I thought the Depression was going to pan out. On these occasions I looked wise and said I thought it was moving towards its conclusion but we might not have seen the worst of it – an answer that contained just the mixture of hope and gloom financial people find reassuring. I thought they were a terrible pack of fatheads, but I was also aware that they must be good at something because they were so rich. I would not have had their cast of mind in order to get their money, however, much as I liked money.

They were a strange lot, these moneyed, influential friends of Boy's, but they were obviously interesting to each other. They talked a lot of what they called 'politics', though there was not much plan or policy in it, and they were worried about the average man, or as they usually called him 'the ordinary fellow'. This ordinary fellow had two great faults: he could not think straight and he wanted to reap where he had not sown. I never saw much evidence of straight thinking among these ca-pittle-ists, but I came to the conclusion that they were reaping where they had sown, and that what they had sown was not, as they believed, hard work and great personal sacrifice but talent – a rather rare talent, a talent that nobody, even its possessors, likes to recognize as a talent and therefore not available to everybody who cares to sweat for it – the talent for manipulating money.

How happy they might have been if they had recognized and gloried in their talent, confronting the world as gifted egotists, comparable to painters, musicians, or sculptors! But that was not their style. They insisted on degrading their talent to the level of mere acquired knowledge and industry. They wanted to be thought of as wise in the ways of the world and astute in politics; they wanted to demonstrate in themselves what the ordinary fellow might be if he would learn to think straight and be content to reap only where he had sown. They and their wives (women who looked like parrots or bulldogs, most of them) were so humourless and, except when they were drunk, so cross that I thought the ordinary fellow was lucky not to be like them.

It seemed to me they knew less about the ordinary fellow than I did, for I had fought in the war as an ordinary fellow myself, and most of these men had been officers. I had seen the ordinary fellow's heroism and also his villainy, his tenderness and also his unthinking cruelty, but I had never seen in him much capacity to devise or carry out a coherent, thoughtful, long-range plan; he was just as much the victim of his emotions as were these rich wiseacres. Where shall wisdom be found, and where is the place of understanding? Not among

Boy Staunton's ca-pittle-ists, nor among the penniless scheme-spinners in the school Common Room, nor yet at the Socialist-Communist meetings in the city, which were sometimes broken up by the police. I seemed to be the only person I knew without a plan that would put the world on its feet and wipe the tear from every eye. No wonder I felt like a stranger in my own land.

No wonder I sought some place where I could be at home, and until my first visit to the Collège de Saint-Michel, in Brussels, I was so innocent as to think it might be among the Bollandists. I passed several weeks there very happily, for they at once made me free of the hall for foreign students, and as I grew to know some of the Jesuits who directed the place I was taken even more into their good graces and had the run of their magnificent library. More than one hundred and fifty thousand books about saints! It seemed a paradise.

Yet often, usually at about three o'clock in the afternoon when the air grew heavy, and scholars at nearby desks were dozing over their notes, I would think: Dunstan Ramsay, what on earth are you doing here, and where do you think this is leading? You are now thirty-four, without wife or child, and no better plan than your own whim; you teach boys who, very properly, regard you as a signpost on the road they are to follow, and like a signpost they pass you by without a thought; your one human responsibility is a madwoman about whom you cherish a maggoty-headed delusion; and here you are, puzzling over records of lives as strange as fairy tales, written by people with no sense of history, and yet you cannot rid yourself of the notion that you are well occupied. Why don't you go to Harvard and get yourself a Ph.D., and try for a job in a university, and be intellectually respectable? Wake up, man! You are dreaming your life away!

Then I would go on trying to discover how Mary Magdalene had been accepted as the same Mary who was the sister of Martha and Lazarus, and if this pair of sisters, one representing the housewifely woman and the other the sensual woman, had any real counterparts in pagan belief, and sometimes — O, idler and jackass! — if their rich father was anywhere described as being like the rich men I met at Boy Staunton's dinner parties.

If he were, who would be surprised if his daughter went to the bad?

Despite these afternoon misgivings and self-reproaches I clung to my notion, ill defined though it was, that a serious study of any important body of human knowledge, or theory, or belief, if undertaken with a critical but not a cruel mind, would in the end yield some secret, some valuable permanent insight, into the nature of life and the true end of man. My path was certainly an odd one for a Deptford lad, raised as a Protestant, but fate had pushed me in this direction so firmly that to resist would be dangerous defiance. For I was, as you have already guessed, a collaborator with Destiny, not one who put a pistol to its head and demanded particular treasures. The only thing for me to do was to keep on keeping on, to have faith in my whim, and remember that for me, as for the saints, illumination when it came would probably come from some unexpected source.

The Jesuits of the Société des Bollandistes were not so numerous that I did not, in time, get on speaking terms with most of them, and a very agreeable, courteous group they were. I now realize that, although I thought I had purged my mind of nonsense about Jesuits, some dregs of mistrust remained. I thought, for instance, that they were going to be preternaturally subtle and that in conversation I would have to be very careful – about what, I did not know. Certainly if they possessed any extraordinary gifts of subtlety they did not waste them on me. I suspected too that they would smell the black Protestant blood in my veins, and I would never gain their trust. On the contrary, my Protestantism made me a curiosity and something of a pet. It was still a time when the use of index cards for making notes was not universal, and they were curious about mine; most of them made notes on scraps of paper, which they kept in order with a virtuosity that astonished me. But though they used me well in every way, I knew that I would always be a guest in this courteous, out-of-the-world domain, and I quickly discovered that the Society of Jesus discouraged its members from being on terms of intimacy with anyone, including other Jesuits. I was used to living without intimate friends, but I had a sneaking hope that here, among men whose preoccupation I shared, things might be different.

All the more reason to be flattered, therefore, when, at the conclusion of one of the two or three conversations I had with Père Delehaye, the principal editor of the *Analecta*, he said, 'Our journal, as you will have observed, publishes material provided by the Bollandists and their friends; I hope you will correspond with us often, and come here when you can, for certainly we think of you now as one of our friends.'

This was by way of leave-taking, for I was setting off the next day for Vienna, and I was travelling with an elderly Bollandist, Padre Ignacio Blazon.

Padre Blazon was the only oddity I had met at the Collège de Saint-Michel. He more than made up for the placidly unremarkable appearance and behaviour of the others, and I think they may have been a little ashamed of him. He was so obviously, indeed theatrically, a priest, which is contrary to Jesuit custom. He wore his soutane all the time indoors, and sometimes even in the streets, which was not regarded with favour. His battered black hat suggested that it might have begun long ago as part of Don Basilio's costume in *The Barber of Seville*, and had lost caste and shape since then. He wore a velvet skullcap, now green with whitened seams, indoors, and under his hat when outdoors. Most of the priests smoked, moderately, but he took snuff immoderately, from a large horn box. His spectacles were mended with dirty string. His hair needed, not cutting, but mowing. His nose was large, red, and bulbous. He had few teeth, so that his chaps were caved in. He was, indeed, so farcical in appearance that no theatre director with a scrap of taste would have permitted him on the stage in such a make-up. Yet here he was, a reality, shuffling about the Bollandist library, humming to himself, snuffing noisily, and peeping over people's shoulders to see what they were doing.

He was tolerated, I soon found out, for his great learning and for what was believed to be his great age. He spoke English eloquently, with little trace of foreign accent, and he jumped from language to language with a virtuosity that astonished everybody and obviously delighted himself. When I first noticed him he was chatting happily to an Irish monk in Erse, heedless of discreet shushings and murmurs of '*Tacete*' from the librarian on duty. When he first noticed me he tried to flummox me by addressing me in Latin, but I was equal to that dodge, and after a few commonplaces we changed to English. It was not long before I discovered that one of his enthusiasms was food, and after that we dined together often.

'I am one of Nature's guests,' he said, 'and if you will take care of the bill I shall be happy to recompense you with information about the saints you will certainly not find in our library. If, on the contrary, you insist that I should take my turn as host, I shall expect you to divert me – and I am not an easy man to amuse, Monsieur Ramezay. As a host I am exigent, rebarbative, unaccommodating. As a guest – ah, quite another set of false teeth, I assure you.'

So I was always host, and we visited several of the good restaurants in Brussels. Padre Blazon was more than true to his word.

'You Protestants, if you think of saints at all, regard them with quite the wrong sort of veneration,' he said to me at our first dinner. 'I think you must be deceived by our cheap religious statuary. All those pink and blue dolls, you know, are for people who think them beautiful. St Dominic, so pretty and pink-cheeked, with his lily, is a peasant woman's idea of a good man – the precise contrary of the man she is married to, who stinks of sweat and punches her in the breast and puts his cold feet on her backside in the winter nights. But St Dominic himself – and this is a Jesuit speaking, Ramezay – was no confectionary doll. Do you know that before he was born his mother dreamed she would give birth to a dog with a lighted torch in its mouth? And that was what he was – fierce and persistent in carrying the flame of faith. But show the peasant woman a dog with a torch and she will not care for it; she wants a St Dominic who can see the beautiful soul in her, and that would be a man without passions or desires – a sort of high-minded eunuch.

'But she is too much herself to want that all the time. She would not take it in exchange for her smelly man. She gives her saints another life, and some very strange concerns, that we Bollandists have to know about but do not advertise. St Joseph, now – what is his sphere of patronage, Ramezay?'

'Carpenters, the dying, the family, married couples, and people looking for houses.'

'Yes, and in Naples, of confectioners; don't ask me why. But what else? Come now, put your mind to it. What made Joseph famous?'

'The earthly father of Christ?'

'Oho, you nice Protestant boy! Joseph is history's most celebrated cuckold. Did not God usurp Joseph's function, reputedly by impregnating his wife through her ear? Do not nasty little seminarians still refer to a woman's *sine qua non* as *auricula* – the ear? And is not Joseph known throughout Italy as Tio Pepe – Uncle Joe – and invoked by husbands who are getting worried? St Joseph hears more prayers about cuckoldry than he does about house-hunting or confectionery, I can assure you. Indeed, in the underworld hagiology of which I promised to tell you, it is whispered that the Virgin herself, who was born to Joachim and Anna through God's personal intervention, was a divine daughter as well as a divine mate; the Greeks could hardly improve on that, could they? And popular legend has it that Mary's parents were very rich, which makes an oddity of the Church's respect for poverty but is quite in keeping with the general respect for money. And do you know the scandal that makes it necessary to keep apart the statues of Mary and those of St John –'

Padre Blazon was almost shouting by this time, and I had to hush him. People in the restaurant were staring, and one or two ladies of devout appearance were heaving their bosoms indignantly. He swept the room with the wild eyes of a conspirator in a melodrama and dropped his voice to a hiss. Fragments of food, ejected from his mouth by this jet, flew about the table.

'But all this terrible talk about the saints is not disrespect, Ramezay. Far from it! It is faith! It is love! It takes the saint to the heart by supplying the other side of his character that history or legend has suppressed – that he may very well have suppressed himself in his struggle toward sainthood. The saint triumphs over sin. Yes, but most of us cannot do that, and because we love the saint and want him to be more like ourselves, we attribute some imperfection to him. Not always sexual, of course. Thomas Aquinas was monstrously fat; St Jerome had a terrible temper. This gives comfort to fat men, and cross men. Mankind cannot endure perfection; it stifles him. He demands that even the saints should cast a shadow. If they, these holy ones who have lived so greatly but who still carry their shadows with them, can approach God, well then, there is hope for the worst of us.

'Sometimes I wonder why so few saints were also wise. Some were, of course, but more were down-right pig-headed. Often I wonder if God does not value wisdom as much as heroic virtue. But wisdom is rather unspectacular; it does not flash in the sky. Most people like spectacle. One cannot blame them. But for oneself – ah, no thank you.'

It was with this learned chatterbox that I set out to travel from Brussels to Vienna. I was early at the station, as he had commanded, and found him already in sole possession of a carriage. He beckoned me inside and went on with his task, which was to read aloud from his breviary, keeping the window open the while, so that passers-by would hear him.

'Give me a hand with a Paternoster,' he said and began to roar the Lord's Prayer in Latin as loud as he could. I joined in, equally loud, and we followed with a few rousing Aves and Agnus Deis. By dint of this pious uproar we kept the carriage for ourselves. People would come to the door, decide that they could not stand such company, and pass on, muttering.

'Strange how reluctant travellers are to join in devotions that might – who can say? – avert some terrible accident,' said Blazon, winking solemnly at me as the guard's whistle blew, the engine peeped, and we drew out of the station. He spread a large handkerchief over his lap and put the big snuffbox in the middle of it, skimmed his dreadful hat into the luggage rack to join a bundle held together by a shawl strap, and composed himself for conversation.

'You have brought the refreshment basket?' said he. I had, and I had not stinted. 'It might be provident to take some of that brandy immediately,' he said. 'I know this journey, and sometimes the motion of the train can be very distressing.' So at half-past nine in the morning we began on the brandy, and soon Padre Blazon was launched into one of those monologues, delivered at the top of his voice, which he preferred to more even-handed conversation. I shall boil it down.

'I have not forgotten your questions about the woman you

keep in the madhouse, Ramezay. I have said nothing on that subject during our last few dinners, but it has not been absent from my mind, you may be assured. Invariably I come back to the same answer: why do you worry? What good would it do you if I told you she is indeed a saint? I cannot make saints, nor can the Pope. We can only recognize saints when the plainest evidence shows them to be saintly. If you think her a saint, she is a saint to you. What more do you ask? That is what we call the reality of the soul; you are foolish to demand the agreement of the world as well. She is a Protestant. What does it matter? To be a Protestant is halfway to being an atheist, of course, and your innumerable sects have not recognized any saints of their own since the Reformation, so-called. But it would be less than Christian to suppose that heroic virtue may not assert itself among Protestants. Trust your own judgement. That it what you Protestants made such a dreadful fuss to assert your right to do.'

'But it is the miracles that concern me. What you say takes no account of the miracles.'

'Oh, miracles! They happen everywhere. They are conditional. If I take a photograph of you, it is a compliment and perhaps rather a bore. If I go into the South African jungle and take a photograph of a primitive, he probably thinks it a miracle and he may be afraid I have stolen a part of his soul. If I take a picture of a dog and show it to him, he does not even know what he looks like, so he is not impressed; he is lost in a collective of dogginess. Miracles are things people cannot explain. Your artificial leg would have been a miracle in the Middle Ages – probably a Devil's miracle. Miracles depend much on time, and place, and what we know and do not know. I am going to Vienna now to work on the Catalogue of Greek Manuscripts in what used to be the Emperor's Library. I shall be drowned in miracles, for those simple Greek monks liked nothing better and saw them everywhere. I tell you frankly, I shall be sick of miracles before I am taken off that job. Life itself it too great a miracle for us to make so much fuss about potty little reversals of what we pompously assume to be the natural order.

'Look at me, Ramezay. I am something of a miracle myself. My parents were simple Spanish people living a few leagues from Pamplona. They had seven daughters – think of it, Ramezay, seven! My poor mother was beside herself at the disgrace. So she vowed solemnly, in church, that if she might bear a son, she would give him to the service of God. She made her vow in a Jesuit church, so it was natural enough that she should add that she would make him a Jesuit. Within a year – behold, little Ignacio, so named after the saintly founder of the Society of Jesus. To a geneticist, I suppose it is not breathtaking that after seven daughters a woman should have a son, but to my mother it was a miracle. The neighbours said – you know how the neighbours always say – "Wait, the trouble is to come; he will be a wild one, this Ignacio; the jail gapes for these sanctified children." Was it so? Not a bit! I seemed to be a Jesuit from the womb – studious, obedient, intelligent, and chaste. Behold me, Ramezay, a virgin at the age of seventy-six! Of how many can that be said? Girls laid themselves out to tempt me; they were incited to seduce me by my sisters, who had only ordinary chastity and thought mine distasteful. I will not say I was not flattered by these temptations. But always I would say, "God did not give us this jewel of chastity to be trampled in the dirt, my dear Dolores (or Maria or whoever it was); pray for an honourable and loving marriage, and put me from your mind." Oh, how they hated that! One girl hit me with a big stone; you see the mark here still, just where my hair used to begin. This was a real miracle, for every morning I had unmistakable assurance that I could have been a great lover – you understand me? – but I loved my vocation more.

'I loved it so much that when the time came for me to enter the Jesuits my examiners were mistrustful. I was too good to be true. My mother's vow, my own abstentions – it worried them. They raked around, trying to discover some streak of unredeemed nature in me – some shadow, as we were saying a while ago – but I had none. Do you know, Ramezay, it stood in my way as much as if I had been a stiff-necked recalcitrant and troublemaker? Yes, my novitiate was very rough, and when I had got through that and was a formed scholastic, every dirty job was put in my way, to see if I would break. It was a full seventeen years before I was allowed to take my four final vows and become a professed member of the Society. And then – well,

179

you see what I am now. I am a pretty useful person, I think, and I have done good work for the Bollandists, but nobody would say I was the flower of the Jesuits. If ever I was a miracle, it is done with now. My shadow manifested itself quite late in life.

'You know that Jesuit training is based on a rigorous reform of the self and achievement of self-knowledge. By the time a man comes to the final vows, anything emotional or fanciful in his piety is supposed to have been rooted out. I think I achieved that, so far as my superiors could discover, but after I was forty I began to have notions and ask questions that should not have come to me. Men have this climacteric, you know, like women. Doctors deny it, but I have met some very menopausal persons in their profession. But my ideas – about Christ, for instance. He will come again, will He? Frankly I doubt if He has ever been very far away. But suppose He comes again, presumably everybody expects He will come to pull the chestnuts out of the fire for them. What will they say if he comes blighting the vine, flogging the money-changers out of the temple one day and hob-nobbing with the rich the next, just as He did before? He had a terrible temper, you know, undoubtedly inherited from His Father. Will He come as a Westerner – let us say, as an Irishman or a Texan – because the stronghold of Christianity is in the West? He certainly won't be a Jew again, or the fat will be in the fire. The Arabs would laugh their heads off if Israel produced an embarrassing Pretender. Will He settle the disagreement between Catholic and Protestant? All these questions seem frivollous, like the questions of a child. But did He not say we are to be as children?

'My own idea is that when He comes again it will be to continue his ministry as an old man. I am an old man and my life has been spent as a soldier of Christ, and I tell you that the older I grow the less Christ's teaching says to me. I am sometimes very conscious that I am following the path of a leader who died when He was less than half as old as I am now. I see and feel things He never saw or felt. I know things He seems never to have known. Everybody wants a Christ for himself and those who think like him. Very well, am I at fault for wanting a Christ who will show me how to be an old man? All Christ's teaching is put forward with the dogmatism, the certainty, and the strength of youth : I need something that takes account of the accretion of experience, the sense of paradox and ambiguity that comes with years! I think after forty we should recognize Christ politely but turn for our comfort and guidance to God the Father, who knows the good and evil of life, and to the Holy Ghost, who possesses a wisdom beyond that of the incarnated Christ. After all, we worship a Trinity, of which Christ is but one Person. I think when He comes again it will be to declare the unity of the life of the flesh and the life of the spirit. And then perhaps we shall make some sense of this life of marvels, cruel circumstances, obscenities, and commonplaces. Who can tell? – we might even make it bearable for everybody.

'I have not forgotten your crazy saint. I think you are a fool to fret that she was knocked on the head because of an act of yours. Perhaps that was what she was for, Ramezay. She saved you on the battlefield, you say. But did she not also save you when she took the blow that was meant for you?

'I do not suggest that you should fail in your duty toward her; if she has no friend but you, care for her by all means. But stop trying to be God, making it up to her that you are sane and she is mad. Turn your mind to the real problem; who is she? Oh, I don't mean her police identification or what her name was before she was married. I mean, who is she in your personal world? What figure is she in your personal mythology? If she appeared to save you on the battlefield, as you say, it has just as much to do with you as it has with her – much more probably. Lots of men have visions of their mothers in time of danger. Why not you? Why was it this woman?

'Who is she? That is what you must discover, Ramezay, and you must find your answer in psychological truth, not in objective truth. You will not find out quickly, I am sure. And while you are searching, get on with your own life and accept the possibility that it may be purchased at the price of hers and that this may be God's plan for you and her.

'You think that dreadful? For her, poor sacrifice, and for you who must accept the sacrifice? Listen, Ramezay, have you heard what Einstein says? – Einstein, the great scientist, not some Jesuit like old Blazon. He says, "God is subtle, but He is not cruel." There is some sound Jewish wisdom for your muddled Protestant mind. Try to understand the subtlety, and stop whimpering about the cruelty. Maybe God wants you for something special. Maybe so much that you are worth a woman's sanity.

'I can see what is in your sour Scotch eye. You think I speak thus because of this excellent picnic you have provided. "Old Blazon is talking from the inspiration of roast chicken and salad, and plums and confectioneries, and a whole bottle of Beaune, ignited by a few brandies," I hear you thinking. "Therefore he urges me to think well of myself instead of despising myself like a good Protestant." Nonsense, Ramezay. I am quite a wise old bird, but I am no desert hermit who can only prophesy when his guts are knotted with hunger. I am deep in the old man's puzzle, trying to link the wisdom of the body with the wisdom of the spirit until the two are one. At my age you cannot divide spirit from body without anguish and destruction, from which you will speak nothing but crazy lies!

'You are still young enough to think that torment of the spirit is a splendid thing, a sign of a superior nature. But you are no longer a young man; you are a youngish middle-aged man, and it is time you found out that these spiritual athletics do not lead to wisdom. Forgive yourself for being a human creature, Ramezay. That is the beginning of wisdom; that is part of what is meant by the fear of God; and for you it is the only way to save your sanity. Begin now, or you will end up with your saint in the madhouse.'

Saying which, Padre Blazon spread his handkerchief over his face and went to sleep, leaving me to think.

4

It was all very well for Blazon to give me advice, and to follow it up during the years that followed with occasional postcards (usually of the rowdier Renaissance masters – he liked fat nudes) on which would be written in purple ink some such message as, 'How do you fare in the Great Battle? Who is she? I pray for you. I.B., S.J.' These caused great curiosity in the school, where one rarely got a postcard before two or three other people had read it. But even if I had been better at taking advice than I am, my path would have been strewn with difficulties.

My visits to Mrs Dempster weighed on me. She was not a troublesome patient at the hospital, but she became very dull; the occasional lightening of the spirit that had shown itself when she lived with Bertha Shanklin never came now. My weekly visits were the high spots of her life; she was always waiting for me on Saturday afternoon with her hat on. I knew what the hat meant; she hoped that this time I would take her away. This was the hope of many of the patients, and when the presiding physician made his appearance there were scenes in which women clutched at his sleeves and even – I could not have believed it if I had not seen it – fell on their knees and tried to kiss his hands, for all those who had some freedom of movement knew that the power to dismiss them lay with him. A few of the younger ones tried to make a sexual association of it, and their cries were, 'Aw, Doc, you know I'm your girl, Doc; you're gonna let me go this time, aren't you, Doc? You know you like me best.' I couldn't have stood it, but he did. The sexual fetor in the place was hateful to me. Of course, I was known as 'Mary's fella,' and they assured her that every visit was sure to bring deliverance. I took her chocolates because they were something she could give the others, most of whom did not have regular visitors.

Let me say again that I was not bitter against the hospital; it was a big place in a big city, obliged to take all who were brought to it. But an hour among these friendless, distracted people was all I could bear. Many of them became known to me, and I got into the custom of telling them stories; as the stories of the saints were the bulk of my store, I told many of those, avoiding anything too miraculous or disquieting, and especially – after one bad experience – anything about wonderful deliverances from prison or bondage of any sort. They liked to be talked to, and when I was talking to a group I was at least not struggling to make conversation with Mrs Dempster alone, and seeing the unvoiced expectancy in her eyes.

Those visits rubbed deep into me the knowledge that though reason may be injured, feeling lives intensely in the insane. I know my visits gave her pleasure, in spite of the weekly disappointment about not being taken elsewhere; after all, I was her special visitor, looked on by the others as an amusing fellow with a fund of tales to tell, and I gave her a certain status. I am ashamed to say how much it cost me in resolution; some Saturdays I had to flog myself to the hospital, cursing what seemed to be a life sentence.

I should have been objective. I should have regarded it as my 'good work'. But my association with Mrs Dempster made that impossible. It was as though I were visiting a part of my own soul that was condemned to live in hell.

Are you wondering: Why didn't he go to Boy Staunton and ask for money to put Mrs Dempster in a better place, on the grounds that she was a Deptford woman in need, if not because of Staunton's part in making her what she was? There is no simple reply. Staunton did not like to be reminded of Deptford except as a joke. Also, Boy had a way of dominating anything with which he was associated; if I got help from him – which was not certain, for he always insisted that one of the first requirements for success was the ability to say 'no' – he would have established himself as Mrs Dempster's patron and saviour and I would have been demoted to his agent. My own motives were not clear or pure: I was determined that if I could not take care of Mrs Dempster, nobody else should do it. She was mine.

Do you ask: If he couldn't afford to put the woman in a private hospital, or get her into a private patients' section of a government hospital, how did he pay for those jaunts abroad every summer? He seems not to have stinted himself there. True, but in my servitude to Mrs Dempster I was not wholly lost to my own needs and concerns. I was absorbed in my enthusiasm for the world of the saints, and ambitious to distinguish myself in explaining them to other people. And I had to have some rest, some refreshment of the spirit.

My diary tells me that I visited Mrs Dempster forty Saturdays every year and at Easter, Christmas, and on her birthday in addition. If that does not seem much to you, try it, and judge then. She was always downcast when I announced that I was off on my summer travels, but I hardened myself and promised her plenty of postcards, for she liked the pictures, and the receipt of mail gave her status among the patients. Did I do all that I could? It seemed so to me, and certainly it was not my intention to join my saint in the madhouse, as Blazon had threatened, by making myself a mere appendage to her sickness.

My life was absorbing as well. I was now a senior master in the school, and a very busy man. I had completed my first book, *A Hundred Saints for Travellers*, and it was selling nicely in five languages, though mostly in English, for Europeans do not travel as Britishers and Americans do. It was written simply and objectively, telling readers how to identify the most common saints they saw in pictures and statuary, and why these saints were popular. I avoided the Catholic gush and the Protestant smirk. I was collecting material for my next book, a much bigger piece of work, to be called *The Saints: A Study in History and Popular Mythology*, in which I wanted to explore first of all why people needed saints, and then how much their need had to do with the saintly attainments of a wide range of extraordinary and gifted people. This was biting off a very large chunk indeed, and I was not sure I could chew it, but I meant to try. I was keeping up my association with the Bollandists too, and writing for *Analecta* and also for the Royal Historical Society whenever I had anything to say.

I had become even more caught up in the life of the Stauntons. Boy liked to have me around much as he liked to have valuable pictures and handsome rugs; I gave the right tone to the place. By that I mean that it put him in a position of advantage with his friends to have someone often in his house who was from a different world, and when he introduced me as a Writer I could hear the capital letter. Of course he had other writers, and painters, musicians, and actors as well, but I was the fixture in the collection, and the least troublesome.

If this sounds like a sneering requital for the hundredweights of excellent food and the pailfuls of good drink I consumed under his roof, let me say that I paid my way: I was the man who could be called at the last minute to come to dinner when somebody else failed, and I was the man who would talk to the dullest woman in the room, and I was the man who disseminated an air of culture at the most Philistine assemblage of sugar-boilers and wholesale bakers without making the other guests feel cheap. Having me in the dining-room was almost the equivalent of having a Raeburn on the walls; I was classy, I was heavily varnished, and I offended nobody.

Why did I accept a place that I now describe in such terms? Because I was tirelessly curious to see how Boy was getting on, to begin with. Because I really liked him, in spite of his affectations and pomposities. Because if I did not go there, where else would I meet such a variety of people? Because I was always grateful to Boy for his financial advice, which was carrying me nicely through the Depression, and which would in time make it possible for me to do better for Mrs Dempster and to arrange a broader life for myself. My motives, like those of most people, were mingled.

If his social life interested me, his private life fascinated me. I have never known anyone in whose life sex played such a dominating part. He didn't think so. He once told me that he thought this fellow Freud must be a madman, bringing everything down to sex the way he did. I attempted no defence of Freud; by this time I was myself much concerned with that old fantastical duke of dark corners, C. G. Jung, but I had read a great deal of Freud and remembered his injunction against arguing in favour of psychoanalysis with those who clearly hated it.

Sex was so much of the very grain of Boy's life that he noticed it no more than the air he breathed. Little David must be manly in all things; I remember a noisy row he had with Leola when she allowed the child to have a Highlander doll; did she want to make his son a sissy? The doll was put in the garbage pail before the weeping eyes of David, who liked to take it to bed (he was six at the time), and then he was rewarded with a fine practical steam-engine, which drove a circular saw that would really cut a matchstick in two. At eight he was given boxing gloves and had to try to punch his father on the nose as Boy knelt before him.

With little Caroline, Boy was humorously gallant. 'How's my little sweetheart tonight?' he would say as he kissed her small hand. When she had been brought in by the nurse, to be shown off to a roomful of guests, Boy always followed them

186

into the hall, to tell Caroline that she had been by far the prettiest girl in the room. Not surprisingly, David was a confused lad, pitifully anxious to please, and Caroline was spoiled rotten.

Leola was never told that she was the prettiest woman in the room. Boy's usual attitude toward her was one of chivalrous patience, with a discernible undertone of exasperation. She loved him abjectly, but she was the one person on whom he spent none of his sexual force – except in the negative form of bullying. I tried to stand up for Leola as much as I could, but as she was utterly unable to stand up for herself I had to be careful. If I was angry with Boy, as sometimes happened, she took his side. She lived her life solely in relation to him; if he thought poorly of her, it did not matter what I might say to defend her. He must be right.

Of course it was not always as black-and-white as this. I remember very well when first she discovered that he was having affairs with other women. She did so by the classic mishap of finding a revealing note in his pocket – the Stauntons rarely escaped cliché in any of the essential matters of life.

I knew of his philandering, of course, for Boy could not keep anything to himself and used to justify his conduct to me late at night, when we had both had plenty of his whisky. 'A man with my physical needs can't be tied down to one woman – especially not a woman who doesn't see sex as a partnership – who doesn't give anything, who just lies there like a damned sandbag,' he would say, making agonized faces so that I would know how tortured he was.

He was explicit about his sexual needs; he had to have intercourse often, and it had to be all sorts of things – intense, passionate, cruel, witty, challenging – and he had to have it with a Real Woman. It all sounded very exhausting and strangely like a sharp workout with the punching bag; I was glad I was not so demandingly endowed. So there were two or three women in Montreal – not whores, mind you, but women of sophistication and spirit, who demanded their independence even though they were married – whom he visited as often as he could. He had business associations in Montreal and it was easy.

The mention of business reminds me of another phase of Boy's sexuality of which he was certainly unconscious, but which I saw at work on several occasions. It was what I thought of as Corporation Homosexuality. He was always on the look-out for promising young men who could be advanced in his service. They must be keen apostles of sugar, or doughnuts, or pop, or whatever it might be, but they must also be 'clean-cut'. Whenever he discovered one of these, Boy would 'take him up' – ask him to luncheon at his club, to dinner at his home, and to private chats in his office. He would explain the mystique of business to the young man and push him ahead as fast as possible in the corporation, sometimes to the chagrin of older men who were not clean-cut but merely capable and efficient.

After a few months of such an association disillusion would come. The clean-cut young man, being ambitious and no more given to gratitude than ambitious people usually are, would assume that all of this was no more than his due and would cease to be as eagerly receptive and admiring as he had been at the beginning of the affair, and might even display a mind of his own. Boy was dismayed to find that these protégés thought him lucky to have such gifted associates as themselves.

Some went so far as to marry on the strength of their new-found hopes, and Boy always asked them to bring their brides to dinner at his house. Afterward he would demand of me why a clean-cut young fellow with everything in his favour would wreck his chances by marrying a girl who was obviously a dumb cluck and would simply hold him back from real success in the corporation? One way or another, Boy was disappointed in most of these clean-cut young men; of those who survived this peril he wearied in the natural course of things, and they became well placed but not influential in his empire.

I do not suggest that Boy ever recognized these young men as anything but business associates; but they were business associates with an overtone of Jove's cup-bearer that I, at least, could not ignore. Corporation Ganymedes, they did not know their role and thus were disappointments.

Leola's awakening came at the fated Christmas of 1936. It had been an emotionally exhausting year for Boy. The old King, George V, had died in January, and in memory of that glance that had once passed between us I wore a black tie for a week. But Boy was in high feather, for 'he' would at last mount the Throne; they had not met for nine years, but Boy was as faithful to his hero as ever. He reported every bit of gossip that came his way; there would be great changes, a Throne more meaningful than ever before, a wholesale ousting of stupid old men, a glorious upsurge of youth around the new King, and of course a gayer Court – the gayest, probably, since that of Charles the Second. And a gay Court, to Boy, meant an exaltation of the punching-bag attitude to sex. If he had ever read any of those psychologists who assert that a crowned and anointed King is the symbolic phallus of his people, Boy would have agreed whole-heartedly.

As everyone knows, it was not long before the news took a contrary turn. On the North American continent we got it sooner than the people of England, for our papers did not have to be so tactful. The young King – he was forty-two, but to people like Boy he seemed very young – was having trouble with the old men, and the old men with him. Stanley Baldwin, who had been with him on that visit to Canada in 1927 and whom Boy had revered as a statesman with a strong literary bent, became a personal enemy of Boy's, and he spoke of the Archbishop of Canterbury in terms that even Woodiwiss – now an archdeacon – found it hard to overlook.

When the crisis came, there was some extravagant talk of forming a group of 'King's Men' who would, in an unspecified way, rally to the side of their hero and put his chosen lady beside him on the Throne. Boy was determined to be a King's Man; everybody who considered himself a gentleman, and a man who understood the demanding nature of love, must necessarily feel as he did. He lectured me about it every time we met; as a historian I was very sorry for the King but could see no clear or good way out of the mess. I believe Boy even sent a few telegrams of encouragement, but I never heard of any answers. When the black month of November came I began to fear for his reason; he read everything, heard every radio report, and snatched at every scrap of gossip. I was not with him when he heard the sad broadcast of Abdication on 11 December, but I looked in at his house that evening and found him, for the only time in his life, to my knowledge, very drunk and alternating between tears and dreadful tirades against all the repressive forces that worked against true love and the expression of a man's real self.

Christmas was a dark day at the Stauntons'. Leola had had to buy all the presents for the children, and Boy found fault with most of them. The fat janitor from the Alpha offices appeared in a hired suit to play Santa Claus, and Boy told him, in front of the children, not to make a jackass of himself but to get on with his job and get out. He would not open his own gifts from Leola and the children. By the time I had made my visit to Mrs Dempster at the hospital, and turned up for midday Christmas dinner, Leola was in tears. David was huddled up in a corner with a book he was not reading, and Caroline was rampaging through the house demanding attention for a doll she had broken. I joked with David, mended the doll so that it was crippled but in one piece, and tried to be decent to Leola. Boy told me that if I had to behave like one of the bloody saints I was always yapping about, he wished I would do it somewhere else. I unwisely told him to take his Abdication like a man, and he became silently hateful and soured the food in our stomachs. He announced that he was going for a walk, and he was going alone.

Leola, grieved for him, went to fetch his overcoat and happened on the note from one of the great-spirited women in Montreal while looking for his gloves in a pocket. She was crouching on the stairs, sobbing dreadfully, when he went out into the hall, and he took in the meaning of her desolation at a glance.

'There's no reason to carry on like that,' he said, picking up the fallen coat and putting it on. 'Your situation is perfectly secure. But if you think I intend to be tied down to this sort of thing' – and he gestured towards the drawing-room, which was, I must say, a dismal, toy-littered waste of wealthy, frumpish domesticity – 'you can think again.' And off he went, leaving Leola howling.

I wish I did not have to say howling, but Leola was not beautiful in her grief. The nurse was off duty for the day, but I managed to shoo the children upstairs to their own quarters and spent a hard hour quieting her. I wish I could say I comforted her, but only one man could have done that, and he was trudging through the snow, deep in some egotistical hell of his own. At last I persuaded her to sleep, or at least to lie down, and wait to see what would happen. Nothing was ever quite so bad as it looked, I assured her. I did not really believe it, but I intended to have a word with Boy.

She went to her room, and when I thought a sufficient time had passed I went up to see how things were getting on. She had washed her face and tidied her hair and was in bed in one of the expensive nightdresses Boy liked.

'Will you be all right if I go now?'

'Kiss me, Dunny. No, not like that. That's just a peck. You used to like to kiss me.'

Whether she knew it or not, this was an invitation that might lead to much more. Was the story of Gyges and Candaules to have the ending in which Gyges takes his friend's wife? No; upon the whole I thought not. But I leaned over and kissed her a little less formally.

'That's no good. Kiss me *really*.'

So I did, and if my artificial leg had not given an ominous croak as I knelt on the bed I might have gone on, doubtless to cuckold Boy Staunton, which he certainly deserved. But I recovered myself and stood up and said, 'You must sleep now. I'll look in later tonight and we'll talk with Boy.'

'You don't love me!' she wailed.

I hurried out the door as she burst into tears again.

Of course I didn't love her. Why would I? It had been at least ten years since I had thought of her with anything but pity. I had made my bed and I intended to lie on it, and there was no room for Leola in it. On my last few visits abroad I had spent a weekend with Diana and her husband at their delightful country house near Canterbury and had enjoyed myself greatly. I had survived my boyish love for Diana, and I certainly had survived anything I ever felt for Leola. I was not to be a victim of her self-pity. The emotional upheaval caused by her disappointment about Boy's unfaithfulness had sharpened her sexual appetite; that was all. I do not suppose Boy had slept with her since the beginning of the trouble that led to the Abdication. I was not going to be the victim of somebody else's faulty chronology. I went for a walk myself, had another Christmas dinner – it was impossible to avoid heavy food on that day – and arrived back at the school at about nine o'clock, intending to do some reading.

Instead I was greeted by a message from the furnace man, who was the only person left on duty that day. I was to call the Stauntons' number at once. It was an emergency.

I called, and the children's nurse spoke. She had come back from her holiday, found the housemaid and the cook and butler still out, and had looked in on Mrs Staunton to say goodnight. Had found her in a very bad way. Did not like to explain over the phone. Yes, had called the doctor but it was Christmas night and an hour had gone by and he still had not come. Would I come at once? Yes, it was *very* serious.

The nurse was becoming a little hysterical, and I hurried to obey. But on Christmas night it is not simple to get taxis, and altogether it was half an hour before I ran upstairs to Leola's bedroom and found her in bed, white as the sheets, with her wrists bound up in gauze, and the nurse near to fits.

'Look at this,' she said, gasping, and pushed me towards the bathroom.

The bath seemed to be full of blood. Apparently Leola had cut her wrists and laid herself down to die in the high Roman fashion, in a warm bath. But she was not a good anatomist and had made a gory but not a fatal job of it.

The doctor came not long after, rather drunk but fairly capable. The nurse had done all that was immediately necessary, so he re-dressed the wrists, gave Leola an injection of something, and said he would call again on Boxing Day.

'I sent for you at once because of this,' said the nurse as soon as the doctor had gone. She handed me a letter with my name on the envelope. It read:

Dearest Dunny:
  This is the end. Boy does not love me and you don't either so it is best for me to go. Think of me sometimes. I always loved you.

Love,
Leola

Fool, fool, fool! Thinking only of herself and putting me in an intolerable position with such a note. If she had died, how would it have sounded at an inquest? As it was, I am sure the nurse read it, for it was not sealed. I was furious with Leola, poor idiot. No note for Boy. No, just a note for me, which would have made me look like a monster if she had not made a mess of this, as of so much else.

However, as she began to pull around I could not reproach her, though I was very careful not to mention the note. Nor did she. It was never spoken of between us.

Boy could not be found. His business address in Montreal knew nothing of him, and he did not return until after New Year's Day, by which time Leola was on the mend, though feeble. What passed between them I do not know and was never told, but from that time onward they seemed to rub along without open disagreement, though Leola faded rapidly and looked more than her years. Indeed, the pretty face that had once ensnared both Boy and me became pudgy and empty. Leola had joined the great company of the walking wounded in the battle of life.

The people who seemed to suffer most from this incident were the children. The nurse, controlled and efficient in emergency, had broken down in the nursery and hinted broadly that Mummy had almost died. This, taken with the quarrel earlier in the day, was enough to put them on edge for a long time; David was increasingly quiet and mousy, but Caroline became a screamer and thrower of tantrums.

David told me many years later that he hated Christmas more than any other day in the calendar.

5

Liesl

I

LET me pass as quickly as possible over the years of the Second World War – or World War Too, as the name my pupils give it always sounds in my ears; it is as if they were asserting firmly that the World War I remember so vividly was not the only, or the biggest, outburst of mass lunacy in our century. But I cannot leave it out altogether, if only because of the increase in stature it brought to Boy Staunton. His growth as an industrialist with, figuratively speaking, his finger in hundreds of millions of pies, not to speak of other popular goodies, made him a man of might in the national economy, and when the war demanded that the ablest men in the country be pressed into the national service, who but he was the obvious candidate for the post of Minister of Food in a coalition Cabinet?

He was very good in the job. He knew how to get things done, and he certainly knew what the great mass of people like to eat. He put the full resources of his Alpha Corporation, and all the subsidiary companies it controlled, to the job of feeding Canada, feeding its armed services, and feeding Britain so far as the submarine war would permit. He was tireless in promoting research that would produce new concentrates – chiefly from fruits – that would keep fighting men, and the children in a bombed country, going when bulkier eatables were not to be had. If the average height of the people of the British Isles is rather greater today than it was in 1939, much of the credit must go to Boy Staunton. He was one of the few men not a professional scientist who really knew what a vitamin was and where it could be found and put to work cheaply.

Of course he had to spend most of his time in Ottawa. He saw little of Leola or his children during the war years, except on flying visits during which lost intimacies could not be recaptured, not even with his adored Caroline.

I saw him from time to time because he was by now a member of our Board of Governors, and also because David was a boarder in the school. David could have lived at home, but Boy wanted him to have the experience of a community life and of being disciplined by men. So the boy spent the years from his tenth to his eighteenth birthday at Colborne, and when he got into the Upper School, at about twelve, he came under my eye almost every day.

Indeed it was my duty in 1942 to tell this unhappy boy that his mother had died. Poor Leola had become more and more listless since the outbreak of war; as Boy grew in importance and his remarkable abilities became increasingly manifest, she faded. She was not one of those politicians' wives who lets it be known that her husband's competence is kept up to the mark by the support and understanding she gives him. Nor was she of the other strain, who tell the newspapers and the women's clubs that though their husbands may be men of mark to the world, they are sorry wretches at home. Leola had no public life and wanted none.

She had completely given up any pretence at golf or bridge or any of the other pastimes in which she had attained to mediocrity in her younger days; she no longer read fashionable books or anything at all. Whenever I went to see her she was knitting things for the Red Cross – vast inner stockings for sea-boots and the like – which she seemed to do automatically while her mind was elsewhere. I asked her to dinner a few times, and it was heavy work, though not so heavy as having dinner at the Stauntons' house. With Boy away and both the children in school, that richly furnished barrack became more and more lifeless, and the servants were demoralized, looking after one undemanding woman who was afraid of them.

When Leola fell ill of pneumonia I informed Boy and did all the obvious things and did not worry. But that was before the drugs for dealing with pneumonia were as effective as they now are, and after the worst of it was over a considerable period of convalescence was needed. As it was difficult to travel to any warmer climate, and as there was nobody to go with Leola, she had to spend it at home. Although I cannot vouch for this, I have always thought it suspicious that Leola opened her windows one afternoon, when the nurse had closed them, and took a chill, and was dead in less than a week.

Boy was in England, arranging something or other connected with his Ministry and duty and the difficulty of transatlantic flights in wartime kept him there. He asked me, by cable, to do what had to be done, so I arranged the funeral, which was easy, and told the people who had to be told, which was not. Caroline made a loud fuss and I left her with some capable schoolmistress who bore the weight of that. But David astonished me.

'Poor Mum,' he said, 'I guess she's better off, really.'

Now what was I to make of that, from a boy of fourteen? And what was I to do with him? I could not send him home, and I had no home of my own except my study and bedroom in the school, so I put him there and made sure one of the matrons looked in every hour or so to see that he was not utterly desolate and had anything it was in the school's power to give him. Fortunately he slept a lot, and at night I sent him to the infirmary, where he could have a room of his own.

I kept him by me at the funeral, for both the older Stauntons were now dead, and the Cruikshanks were so desolated themselves that they could only hold hands and weep. Association with the Cruikshanks had not been encouraged by Boy, so David was not really well known to them.

It was one of those wretched late autumn funerals, and though it did not actually rain everything was wet and miserable. There were not a great many present, for all the Stauntons' friends were important people, and it seemed that all the important people were so busy fighting the war in one way or another that they could not come. But there were mountains of costly flowers, looking particularly foolish under a November sky.

One unexpected figure was at the graveside. Older, fatter, and unwontedly quiet though he was, I knew Milo Papple in an instant. As Woodiwiss read the committal, I found myself thinking that his own father had died at least twelve years before, and I had written to Milo at that time. But the Kaiser (whom Myron Papple had impersonated so uproariously at the hanging-in-effigy after the Great War) had lived, presumably untroubled by the hatred of Deptford and places like it, until 1941; had lived at Doorn, sawing wood and wondering what world madness had dethroned him, for twenty-three years after his fall. I pondered on the longevity of dethroned monarchs when I should have been taking farewell of Leola. But I well knew that I had taken leave of her, so far as any real feeling went, that Christmas afternoon when she had appealed to me for comfort and I had run away. Everything since had been a matter of duty.

Milo and I shook hands as we left the cemetery. 'Poor Leola,' he said in a choked voice. 'It's the end of a great romance. You know we always thought her and Perse was the handsomest pair that ever got married in Deptford. And I know why you never got married. It must be tough on you to see her go, Dunny.'

My shame was that it was not tough at all. What was tough was to go with David back to that awful, empty house and talk to him until the servants gave us a poor dinner; then take him back to school and tell him I thought it better that he should go to his own room, as he must some time resume his ordinary life, and the sooner the better.

Boy was always fussing that David would not be a real man. He seemed a very real man to me through all this bad time. I could not have seen as much of him as I did if I had not been temporary Headmaster. When the war began our Head had rushed off to throw himself upon the foe from the midst of the Army's education program; he stepped in front of a truck one night in the blackout, and the school mourned him as a hero. When he left, the Governors had to get a Headmaster in a hurry, but the war made good men so scarce that they appointed me, *pro tem*, without any increase in salary, as we must all shoulder our burdens without thought of self. It was taxing, thankless work, and I hated all the administrative side of it. But I bent to the task and did what I could until 1947, when I had a difficult conversation with Boy, who was now a C.B.E. (for his war work) and the Chairman of our Board of Governors.

'Dunny, you've done a superb job during the whole of the war, and long beyond. But it was fun, wasn't it?'

'No, not fun. Damned hard slogging. Endless trouble getting and keeping staff. Managing with our old men and some young ones who weren't fit for service – or teaching, if it comes to that. Problems with 'war-guest' boys who were homesick or hated Canada, or thought they could slack because they weren't in England. Problems with the inevitable hysteria of the school when the news was bad, and the worse hysteria when it was good. The fag of keeping up nearly all my own teaching and doing the administration as well. Not fun, Boy.'

'None of us had an easy war, Dunny. And I must say you look well on it. The question is, what are we to do now?'

'You're the Chairman of the Board. You tell me.'

'You don't want to go on being Head, do you?'

'That depends on the conditions. It might be much pleasanter now. I've been able to get a pretty good staff during the last eighteen months, and I suppose money will be more plentiful now the Board can think about it again.'

'But you've just said you hated being Head.'

'In wartime – who wouldn't? But, as I say, things are improving. I might get to like it very much.'

'Look, old man, let's not make a long business of this. The Board appreciates everything you've done. They want to give you a testimonial dinner. They want to tell you in front of the whole school how greatly indebted they are to you. But they want a younger Headmaster.'

'How young? You know my age. I'm not quite fifty, like yourself. How young does a Headmaster have to be nowadays?'

'It isn't entirely that. You're making this awfully tough for me. You're unmarried. A Headmaster needs a wife.'

'When I needed a wife, I found that you needed her even more.'

'That's hitting below the belt. Anyhow, Leo wouldn't have – never mind. You have no wife.'

'Perhaps I could find one in a hurry. Miss Gostling, at our sister school, Bishop Cairncross's, has been giving me the glad eye in an academic way for two or three years.'

'Be serious. It's not just the wife. Dunny, we have to face it. You're queer.'

'The Sin of Sodom, you mean? If you knew boys as I do, you would not suggest anything so grotesque. If Oscar Wilde had pleaded insanity, he would have walked out of court a free man.'

'No, no, no! I don't mean kid-simple, I mean *queer* – strange, funny, not like other people.'

'Ah, that's very interesting. How am I queer? Do you remember poor old Iremonger who had a silver plate in his head and used to climb the waterpipes in his room and address his class from the ceiling? Now he was queer. Or that unfortunate alcoholic Bateson who used to throw a wet boxing glove at inattentive boys and then retrieve it on a string? I always thought they added something to the school – gave boys a knowledge of the great world that state schools dare not imitate. Surely you do not think I am queer in any comparable way?'

'You are a fine teacher. Everybody knows it. You are a great scholarship-getter, which is quite another thing. You have a reputation as an author. But there it is.'

'There is what?'

'It's this saint business of yours. Of course your books are splendid. But if you were a father, would you want to send your son to a school headed by a man who was an authority on saints? Even more, would you do it if you were a mother? Women hate anything that's uncanny about a man if they think of entrusting a son to him. Religion in the school is one thing; there is a well-understood place for religion in education. But not this misty world of wonder-workers and holy wizards and juiceless women. Saints aren't in the picture at all. Now I'm an old friend, but I am also Chairman of the Board, and I tell you it won't do.'

'Are you kicking me out?'

'Certainly not. Don't be extreme. You surely understand that you are a tremendous addition to the school as a master – well-known writer on a difficult subject, translated into foreign languages, amusingly eccentric, and all that – but you would be a disaster as a peacetime Headmaster.'

'Eccentric? Me!'

'Yes, you. Good God, don't you think the way you rootle in

your ear with your little finger delights the boys? And the way you waggle your eyebrows – great wild things like moustaches, I dont know why you don't trim them – and those terrible Harris tweed suits you wear and never have pressed. And that disgusting trick of blowing your nose and looking into your handkerchief as if you expected to prophesy something from the mess. You look ten years older than your age. The day of comic eccentrics as Heads has gone. Parents nowadays want somebody more like themselves.'

'A Headmaster created in their own image, eh? Well, you obviously have somebody virtually hired or you wouldn't be in such a rush to get rid of me. Who is it?'

(Boy named you, Headmaster. I had never heard of you then, so there can be no malice in reporting this conversation.)

We haggled a little more, and I made Boy squirm a bit, for I felt I had been shabbily used. But at last I said, 'Very well, I'll stay on as chief of history and Assistant Head. I don't want your testimonial dinner, but I should like you, as Chairman, to address the school and make it very clear that I have not been demoted as soon as you could get somebody their parents like better. It will be a lie, but I want my face saved. Say the demands of my writing made me suggest this decision and I pledge my full support to the new man. And I want six months' leave of absence, on full pay, before I return to work.'

'Agreed. You're a good sport, Dunny. Where will you go for your six months?'

'I have long wanted to visit the great shrines of Latin America. I shall begin in Mexico, with the Shrine of the Virgin of Guadalupe.'

'There you go, you see! You go right on with the one thing that really stood between you and a Headmaster's job.'

'Certainly. You don't expect me to pay attention to the opinion of numskulls like you and your Board and the parents of a few hundred cretinous boys, do you?'

So there I was, a few months later, sitting in a corner of the huge nineteenth-century Byzantine basilica at Guadalupe, watching the seemingly endless crowd of men and women, old and young, as it shuffled forward on its knees to get as near as possible to the miraculous picture of the Virgin.

The picture was a surprise to me. Whether it was because I had some ignorant preconception about the tawdriness of everything Mexican, or the extravagantly Latin nature of the legend, I had expected something artistically offensive. I was by now in a modest way a connoisseur in holy pictures, ranging from catacombs and the blackened and glaring Holy Face at Lucca to the softest Raphaels and Murillos. But here was a picture reputedly from no mortal hand – not even that of St Luke – that had appeared miraculously on the inside of a peasant's cloak.

In 1531 the Virgin had appeared several times on this spot to Juan Diego and bidden him to tell Bishop Zumárraga that a shrine in her honour should be built here; when Zumárraga very naturally asked for some further evidence of Juan Diego's authority, the Virgin filled the peasant's cloak with roses though it was December; and when he opened his cloak before the Bishop, not only were the roses there, but also, on the inner side of it, this painting, before which the Bishop fell on his knees in wonderment.

As unobtrusively as possible (for I try hard not to be objectionable when visiting shrines) I examined the picture through a powerful little pocket telescope. Certainly it was painted on cloth of a very coarse weave, with a seam up the middle of it that deviated from the straight just enough to avoid the Virgin's face. The picture was in the mode of the Immaculate Conception; the Virgin, a peasant girl of about fifteen, stood on a crescent moon. The painting was skilled, and the face beautiful, if you dismiss from your mind the whorish mask that modern cosmetics have substituted for beauty and think of the human face. Why was the right eye almost closed, as though swollen? Very odd in a holy picture. But the colours were fine, and the gold, though lavish, was not barbarically splashed on. Spain might be proud of such a picture. And the proportions – the width would go about three and a half times into the length – were those of a *tilma* such as I had seen peasants wearing outside the city. A very remarkable picture indeed.

The picture was not my chief concern, however. My eyes were on the kneeling petitioners, whose faces had the beauty virtually every face reveals in the presence of the goddess of mercy, the Holy Mother, the figure of divine compassion. Very different, these, from the squinnying, lip-biting, calculating faces of the art lovers one sees looking at Madonnas in galleries. These petitioners had no conception of art; to them a picture was a symbol of something else, and very readily the symbol became the reality. They were untouched by modern education, but their government was striving with might and main to procure this inestimable benefit for them; anticlericalism and American bustle would soon free them from belief in miracles and holy likenesses. But where, I ask myself, will mercy and divine compassion come from then? Or are such things necessary to people who are well fed and know the wonders that lie concealed in an atom? I don't regret economic and educational advance; I just wonder how much we shall have to pay for it, and in what coin.

Day after day I sat in the basilica for a few hours and wondered. The sacristans and nuns who gave out little prints of the miraculous picture grew accustomed to me; they thought I must be a member of that tiny and eccentric group, the devout rich, or perhaps I was writing an article for a tourist magazine. I put something in every out-thrust box and was left alone. But I am neither rich nor conventionally devout, and what I was writing, slowly, painstakingly, and with so many revisions that the final version was not even in sight, was a sort of prologue to a discussion of the nature of faith. Why do people all over the world, and at all times, want marvels that defy all verifiable facts? And are the marvels brought into being by their desire, or is their desire an assurance rising from some deep knowledge, not to be directly experienced and questioned, that the marvellous is indeed an aspect of the real?

Philosophers have tackled this question, of course, and answered it in ways highly satisfactory to themselves; but I never knew a philosopher's answer to make much difference to anyone not in the trade. I was trying to get at the subject without wearing either the pink spectacles of faith or the green spectacles of science. All I had managed by the time I found myself sitting in the basilica of Guadalupe was a certainty that faith was a psychological reality, and that where it was not invited to fasten itself on things unseen, it invaded and raised bloody hell with things seen. Or in other words, the irrational will have its say, perhaps because 'irrational' is the wrong word for it.

Such speculation cannot fill the whole of one's day. I used to rise early and go to the shrine in the morning. After luncheon I followed the local custom and slept. I explored the city until dinner. After dinner, what? I could not sit in the public rooms in my hotel for they were uncomfortable after the Spanish fashion. The writing-room was dominated by a large painting of the Last Supper, a more than usually gloomy depiction of that gloomiest of parties; apparently nobody had been able to touch a bite, and a whole lamb, looking uncomfortably alive though flayed, lay on a platter in the middle of the table with its eyes fixed reproachfully on Judas.

I tried the theatre and found myself sitting through a drama that I identified as Sardou's *Frou Frou*, heavily Hispanicized and given a further Mexican flavour. It was slow going. I went to one or two films, American pieces with Spanish sound tracks. With relief I discovered from a morning paper that a magician might be seen at the Teatro Chueca, and I booked a seat through my hotel.

Enthusiasm for magic had never wholly died in me, and I had seen the best illusionists of my time – Thurston, Goldin, Blackstone, the remarkable German who called himself Kalanag, and Harry Houdini, not long before his death. But the name of the man who was to perform in Mexico was unknown to me; the advertisement announced that Magnus Eisengrim would astonish Mexico City after having triumphantly toured South America. I assumed that he was a German who thought it impolitic to appear in the States at present.

Very soon after the curtain rose I knew that this was a magic entertainment unlike any I had ever seen. In the twentieth century stage magicians have always been great jokers; even Houdini grinned like a film star through most of his show. They kept up a run of patter designed to assure the audience that they were not to be taken seriously as wonder-workers; they were entertainers and mighty clever fellows, but their magic was all in fun. Even when they included a little hypnotism – as Blackstone did so deftly – nobody was given any cause for alarm.

Not so Magnus Eisengrim. He did not wear ordinary evening clothes, but a beautiful dress coat with a velvet collar, and silk knee breeches. He began his show by appearing in the middle of the stage out of nowhere; he plucked a wand from the air and, wrapping himself in a black cloak, suddenly became transparent; members of his company – girls dressed in fanciful costumes – seemed to walk through him; then, after another flourish of the cloak, he was present in the flesh again, and four of the girls were sufficiently ghostly for him to pass his wand through them. I began to enjoy myself; this was the old Pepper's Ghost illusion, familiar enough in principle but newly worked up into an excellent mystery. And nobody on the stage cracked a smile.

Eisengrim now introduced himself to us. He spoke in elegant Spanish, and it was clear at once that he did not present himself as a funny-man but as one who offered an entertainment of mystery and beauty, with perhaps a hint of terror as well. Certainly his appearance and surroundings were not those of the usual stage magician; he was not tall, but his bearing was so impressive that his smallness was unimportant. He had beautiful eyes and an expression of dignity, but the most impressive thing about him was his voice; it was much bigger than one would expect from a small man, and of unusual range and beauty of tone. He received us as honoured guests and promised us an evening of such visions and illusions as had nourished the imagination of mankind for two thousand years – and a few trifles for amusement as well.

This was a novelty – a poetic magician who took himself seriously. It was certainly not the role in which I had expected to re-encounter Paul Dempster. But this was Paul, without a doubt, so self-assured, so polished, so utterly unlike the circus conjurer with the moustache and beard and shabby clothes whom I had met in *Le grand Cirque forain de St Vite* more than fifteen years before, that it was some time before I could be sure it was he. How had he come by this new self, and where had he acquired this tasteful, beautiful entertainment?

It was so elegantly presented that I doubt if anyone in the Teatro Chueca but myself realized how old it was in essence. Paul did not do a single new trick; they were all classics from the past, well known to people who were interested in the history of this curious minor art and craft.

He invited members of the audience to have a drink with him before he began his serious work, and poured red and white wine, brandy, tequila, whisky, milk, and water from a single bottle; a very old trick, but the air of graceful hospitality with which he did it was enough to make it new. He borrowed a dozen handkerchiefs – mine among them – and burned them in a glass vessel; then from the ashes he produced eleven handkerchiefs, washed and ironed; when the twelfth donor showed some uneasiness, Eisengrim directed him to look towards the ceiling, from which his handkerchief fluttered down into his hands. He borrowed a lady's handbag, and from it produced a package that swelled and grew until he revealed a girl under the covering; he caused this girl to rise in the air, float out over the orchestra pit, return to the table, and, when covered, to dwindle once again to a package, which, when returned to the lady's purse, proved to be a box of bonbons. All old tricks. All beautifully done. And all offered without any of the facetiousness that usually makes magic shows so restless and tawdry.

The second part of his entertainment began with hypnotism. From perhaps fifty people who volunteered to be subjects he chose twenty and seated them in a half-circle on the stage. Then, one by one, he induced them to do the things all hypnotists rely on – row boats, eat invisible meals, behave as guests at a party, listen to music, and all the rest of it – but he had one idea that was new to me; he told a serious-looking man of middle age that he had just been awarded the Nobel Prize and asked him to make a speech of acceptance. The man did so, with such dignity and eloquence that the audience applauded vigorously. I have seen displays of hypnotism in which people were made to look foolish, to show the dominance of the hypnotist; there was nothing of that here, and all of the twenty left the stage with dignity unimpaired, and indeed with a heightened sense of importance.

Then Eisengrim showed us some escapes, from ropes and straps bound on him by men from the audience who fancied themselves as artists in bondage. He was tied up and put into a trunk, which was pulled on a rope up into the ceiling of the theatre; after thirty seconds Eisengrim walked down the centre aisle to the stage, brought the trunk to ground, and revealed that it contained an absurd effigy of himself.

His culminating escape was a variation of one Houdini originated and made famous. Eisengrim, wearing only a pair of bathing trunks, was handcuffed and pushed upside down into a metal container like a milk can, and the top of the milk can was fastened shut with padlocks, some of which members of the audience had brought with them; the milk can was lowered into a tank of water, with glass windows in it so that the audience could see the interior clearly; curtains were drawn around the tank and its contents, and the audience sat in silence to await events. Two men were asked to time the escape; and if more than three minutes elapsed, they were to order the theatre fireman who was in attendance to break open the milk can without delay.

The three minutes passed. The fireman was given the word and made a very clumsy business of getting the can out of the tank and opening the padlocks. But when he had done so the milk can was empty, and the fireman was Eisengrim. It was the nearest thing to comedy the evening provided.

The third and last part of the entertainment was serious almost to the point of solemnity, but it had an erotic savour that was unlike anything I had ever seen in a magic show, where children make up a considerable part of the audience. *The Dream of Midas* was a prolonged illusion in which Eisengrim, assisted by a pretty girl, produced extraordinary sums of money in silver dollars from the air, from the pockets, ears, noses, and hats of people in the audience, and threw them all into a large copper pot; the chink of the coins seemed never to stop. Possessed by unappeasable greed, he turned the girl into gold, and was horrified by what he had done. He tapped her with a hammer; he chipped off a hand and passed it through the audience; he struck the image in the face. Then, in an ecstasy of renunciation, he broke his magician's wand. Immediately the copper pot was empty, and when we turned our attention to the girl she was flesh again, but one hand was missing and blood was running from her lip. This spice of cruelty seemed to please the audience very much.

His last illusion was called *The Vision of Dr Faustus*, and the program assured us that in this scene, and this alone, the beautiful Faustina would appear before us. Reduced to its fundamentals, it was the familiar illusion in which the magician makes a girl appear in two widely separated cabinets without seeming to pass between them. But as Eisengrim did it, the conflict was between Sacred and Profane Love for the soul of Faust: on one side of the stage would appear the beautiful Faustina as Gretchen, working at her spinning wheel and modestly clothed; as Faust approached her she disappeared, and on the other side of the stage in an arbour of flowers appeared Venus, wearing as near to nothing at all as the Mexican sense of modesty would permit. It was plain enough that Gretchen and Venus were the same girl, but she had gifts as an actress and conveyed unmistakably the message that beauty of spirit and lively sensuality might inhabit one body, an idea that was received with delight by the audience. At last Faust, driven to distraction by the difficulties of choice, killed himself, and Mephistopheles appeared in flames to drag him down to Hell. As he vanished, in the middle of the stage but about eight feet above the floor and supported apparently on nothing at all, appeared the beautiful Faustina once more, as, one presumes, the Eternal Feminine, radiating compassion while showing a satisfactory amount of leg. The culminating moment came when Mephistopheles threw aside his robe and showed that, whoever may have been thrust down into Hell, this was certainly Eisengrim the Great.

The audience took very kindly to the show, and the applause for the finale was long and enthusiastic. An usher prevented me from going through the pass-door to the stage, so I went to the stage door and asked to see Señor Eisengrim. He was not to be seen, said the doorman. Orders were strict that no one was to be admitted. I offered a visiting card, for although these things have almost gone out of use in North America they still possess a certain amount of authority in Europe, and I always carry a few. But it was no use.

I was not pleased and was about to go away in a huff when a voice said, 'Are you Mr Dunstan Ramsay?'

The person who was speaking to me from the last step of the stairs that led up into the theatre was probably a woman but she wore man's dress, had short hair, and was certainly the ugliest human creature I had ever seen. Not that she was misshapen; she was tall, straight, and obviously very strong, but she had big hands and feet, a huge, jutting jaw, and a heaviness of bone over the eyes that seemed to confine them to small, very deep caverns. However, her voice was beautiful and her utterance was an educated speech of some foreign flavour.

'Eisengrim will be very pleased to see you. He noticed you in the audience. Follow me, if you please.'

The backstage arrangements were not extensive, and the corridor into which she led me was noisy with the sound of a quarrel in a language unfamiliar to me – probably Portuguese. My guide knocked and entered at once with me behind her, and we were upon the quarrellers. They were Eisengrim, stripped to the waist, rubbing paint off his face with a dirty towel, and the beautiful Faustina, who was naked as the dawn, and lovely as the breeze, and madder than a wet hen; she also was removing her stage paint, which seemed to cover most of her body; she snatched up a wrapper and pulled it around her, and extruded whatever part she happened to be cleaning as we talked.

'She says she must have more pink light in the last tableau,' said Eisengrim to my guide in German. 'I've told her it will kill my red Mephisto spot, but you know how pig-headed she is.'

'Not now,' said the ugly woman. 'Mr Dunstan Ramsay, your old friend Magnus Eisengrim, and the beautiful Faustina.'

The beautiful Faustina gave me an unnervingly brilliant smile and extended a very greasy hand that had just been wiping paint off her upper thigh. I may be a Canadian of Scots descent, and I may have first seen the light in Deptford, but I am not to be disconcerted by Latin American showgirls, so I kissed it with what I think was a good deal of elegance. Then I shook hands with Eisengrim, who was smiling in a fashion that was not really friendly.

'It has been a long time, Mr Dunstable Ramsay,' he said in Spanish. I think he meant to put me at a disadvantage, but I am pretty handy in Spanish, and we continued the conversation in that language.

'It has been over thirty years, unless you count our meeting in *Le grande Cirque forain de St Vite*,' said I. 'How are *Le Solitaire des forêts* and my friend the Bearded Lady?'

'Le Solitaire died very shortly after we met,' said he. 'I have not seen the others since before the war.'

We made a little more conversation, so stilted and uneasy that I decided to leave; obviously Eisengrim did not want me there. But when I took my leave the ugly woman said, 'We hope very much that you can lunch with us tomorrow?'

'Liesl, are you sure you know what you are doing?' said Eisengrim in German, and very rapidly

But I am pretty handy in German, too. So when the ugly woman replied, 'Yes, I am perfectly sure and so are you, so say no more about it,' I got it all and said in German, 'It would be a very great pleasure, if I am not an intruder.'

'How can a so old friend possibly be an intruder?' said Eisengrim in English, and thenceforth he never spoke any other language to me, though his idiom was creaky. 'You know, Liesl, that Mr Ramsay was my very first teacher in magic?' He was all honey now. And as I was leaving he leaned forward and whispered, 'That temporary loan, you remember – nothing would have induced me to accept it if *Le Solitaire* had not been in very great need – you must permit me to repay it at once.' And he tapped me lightly on the spot where, in an inside pocket, I carry my cash.

That night when I was making my usual prudent Canadian-Scots count, I found that several bills had found their way into

my wallet, slightly but not embarrassingly exceeding the sum
that had disappeared from it when last I met Paul. I began to
think better of Eisengrim. I appreciate scrupulosity in money
matters.

3

Thus I became a member of Magnus Eisengrim's entourage, and
never made my tour of the shrines of South America. It was all
settled at the luncheon after our first meeting. Eisengrim was
there, and the hideous Liesl, but the beautiful Faustina did not
come. When I asked after her Eisengrim said, 'She is not yet
ready to be seen in public places.' Well, thought I, if he can
appear in a good restaurant with a monster, why not with the
most beautiful woman I have ever seen? Before we had finished
a long luncheon, I knew why.

Liesl became less ugly after an hour or two. Her clothes were
like a man's in that she wore a jacket and trousers, but her shirt
was soft and her beautiful scarf was drawn through a ring. If I
had been in her place I should not have worn men's patent-
leather dancing shoes – size eleven at least – but otherwise she
was discreet. Her short hair was smartly arranged, and she even
wore a little colour on her lips. Nothing could mitigate the
extreme, the deformed ugliness of her face, but she was graceful, she had a charming voice, and gave evidence of a keen intelligence held in check, so that Eisengrim might dominate the
conversation.

'You see what we are doing,' he said. 'We are building up
a magic show of unique quality, and we want it to be in the
best possible condition before we set out on a world tour. It is
rough still – oh, very kind of you to say so, but it is rough in
comparison with what we want to make it. We want the uttermost accomplishment, combined with the sort of charm and romantic flourish that usually goes with ballet – European ballet,
not the athletic American stuff. You know that nowadays the
theatre has almost abandoned charm; actors want to be sweaty
and real, playwrights want to scratch their scabs in public. Very
well; it is in the mood of the times. But there is always another

mood, one precisely contrary to what seems to be the fashion. Nowadays this concealed longing is for romance and marvels. Well, that is what we think we can offer, but it is not done with the back bent and a cringing smile; it must be offered with authority. We are working very hard for authority. You remarked that we did not smile much in the performance; no jokes really. A smile in such a show is half a cringe. Look at the magicians who appear in night clubs; they are so anxious to be loved, to have everybody think "What a funny fellow," instead of "What a brilliant fellow, what a mysterious fellow." That is the disease of all entertainment: love me, pet me, pat my head. That is not what we want.'

'What do you want? To be feared?'

'To be wondered at. This is not egotism. People want to marvel at something, and the whole spirit of our time is not to let them do it. They will pay to do it, if you make it good and marvellous for them. Didn't anybody learn anything from the war? Hitler said, "Marvel at me, wonder at me, I can do what others can't," – and they fell over themselves to do it. What we offer is innocent – just an entertainment in which a hungry part of the spirit is fed. But it won't work if we let ourselves be pawed and patronized and petted by the people who have marvelled. Hence our plan.'

'What is your plan?'

'That the show must keep its character all the time. I must not be seen off the stage except under circumstances that carry some *cachet*; I must never do tricks outside the theatre. When people meet me I must be always the distinguished gentleman conferring a distinction; not a nice fellow, just like the rest of the boys. The girls must have it in their contract that they do not accept invitations unless we approve, appear anywhere except in clothes we approve, get into any messes with boy friends, or seem to be anything but ladies. Not easy, you see. Faustina herself is a problem; she has not yet learned about clothes, and she eats like a lioness.'

'You'll have to pay heavily to make people live like that.'

'Of course. So the company must be pretty small and the pay tempting. We shall find the people.'

'Excuse me, but you keep saying *we* will do this and *we* will do that. Is this a royal *we*? If so, you may be getting into psychological trouble.'

'No, no. When I speak of *we* I mean Liesl and myself. I am the magician. She is the autocrat of the company, as you shall discover.'

'And why is Liesl the autocrat of the company?'

'That also you shall discover.'

'I'm not at all sure of that. What do you want me for? My abilities as a magician are even less than when you were my audience in the Deptford Free Library.'

'Never mind. Liesl wants you.'

I looked at Liesl, who was smiling as charmingly as her dreadfully enlarged jaw would permit, and said, 'She cannot possibly know anything about me.'

'You underestimate yourself, Ramsay,' she said. 'Are you not the writer of *A Hundred Saints for Travellers*? And *Forgotten Saints of the Tyrol*? And *Celtic Saints of Britain and Europe*? When Eisengrim mentioned last night that he had seen you in the audience and that you had insisted on lending your handkerchief, I wanted to meet you at once. I am obliged to you for much information, but far more for many happy hours reading your delightful prose. A distinguished hagiographer does not often come our way.'

There is more than one kind of magic. This speech had the effect of revealing to me that Liesl was not nearly so ugly as I had thought, and was indeed a woman of captivating intellect and charm, cruelly imprisoned in a deformed body. I know flattery when I hear it; but I do not often hear it. Furthermore, there is good flattery and bad; this was from the best cask. And what sort of woman was this who knew so odd a word as 'hagiographer' in a language not her own? Nobody who was not a Bollandist had ever called me that before, yet it was a title I would not have exchanged to be called Lord of the Isles. Delightful prose! I must know more of this.

Many people when they are flattered seek immediately to show themselves very hard-headed, to conceal the fact that they have taken the bait. I am one of them.

'Your plan sounds woefully uneconomic to me,' I said. 'Travelling shows in our time are money-losers unless they play to capacity audiences and have strong backing. You are planning an entertainment of rare quality. What makes you think it can survive? Certainly I have no advice to give you that can be of help there.'

'That is not what we ask of you,' said Liesl. 'We shall look for advice about finance from financiers. From you we want the benefit of your taste, and a particular kind of unusual assistance. For which, of course, we expect to pay.'

In other words, no amateurish interference or inquisitiveness about the money. But what could this unusual assistance be?

'Every magician has an autobiography, which is sold in the theatre and elsewhere,' she continued. 'Most of them are dreadful things, and all of them are the work of another hand – do you say ghost-written? We want one that will be congruous with the entertainment we offer. It must be very good, yet popular, persuasive, and written with style. And that is where you come in, dear Ramsay.'

With an air that in another woman would have been flatteringly coquettish, she laid a huge hand over one of mine and engulfed it.

'If you want me to write it over my own name it is out of the question.'

'Not at all. It is important that it appear to be an autobiography. We ask you to be the ghost. And in case such a proposal is insulting to such a very good writer, we offer a substantial fee. Three thousand five hundred dollars is not bad; I have made inquiries.'

'Not good either. Give me that and a half-share in the royalties and I might consider it.'

'That's the old, grasping Ramsay blood!' said Eisengrim and laughed the first real laugh I had heard from him.

'Well, consider what you ask. The book would have to be fiction. I presume you don't think the world will swallow a courtier of polished manner if he is shown to be the son of a Baptist parson in rural Canada –'

'You never told me your father was a parson,' said Liesl. 'What a lot we have in common! Several of my father's family are parsons.'

'The autobiography, like the personality, will have to be hand-made,' said I, 'and as you have been telling me all through lunch, distinguished works of imagination are not simply thrown together.'

'But you will not be hard on us,' said Liesl. 'You see, not any writer will do. But you, who have written so persuasively about the saints – slipping under the guard of the sceptic with a candour that is brilliantly disingenuous, treating marvels with the seriousness of fact – you are just the man for us. We can pay, and we will pay, though we cannot pay a foolish price. But I think that you are too much an old friend of magic to say no.'

In spite of her marred face her smile was so winning that I could not say no. This looked like an adventure, and, at fifty, adventures do not come every day.

4

At fifty, should adventures come at all? Certainly that was what I was asking myself a month later. I was heartily sick of Magnus Eisengrim and his troupe, and I hated Liselotte Vitzlipützli, which was the absurd name of his monstrous business partner. But I could not break the grip that their vitality, their single-mindedness, and the beautiful mystery of their work had fastened on my loneliness.

For the first few days it was flattering to my spirit to sit in the stalls in the empty theatre with Liesl while Eisengrim rehearsed. Not a day passed that he did not go through a searching examination of several of his illusions, touching up one moment, or subduing another, and always refining that subtle technique of misdirecting the attention of his audience, which is the beginning and end of the conjurer's art.

To me it was deeply satisfying to watch him, for he was a master of all those sleights that had seemed so splendid, and so impossible, in my boyhood. 'Secure and palm six half-crowns.' He could do it with either hand. His professional dress coat almost brought tears to my eyes, such a marvel was it of loading-pockets, *pochettes* and *profondes*; when it was filled and ready for his appearance in *The Dream of Midas* it weighed twelve pounds, but it fitted him without a bulge.

My opinion was sought, and given, about the program. It was on my advice that the second part of his entertainment was reshaped. I suggested that he cut out the escape act entirely; it was not suitable to an illusionist, for it was essentially a physical trick and not a feat of magic. There was no romance about being stuck in a milk can and getting out again. This gave Liesl a chance to press for the inclusion of *The Brazen Head of Friar Bacon* and I supported her strongly; it was right for the character of the show they were building. But Eisengrim the Great had never heard of Friar Bacon, and like so many people who have not heard of something, he could not believe that anybody but a few eccentrics would have done so.

'It is unmistakably your thing,' I said. 'You can tell them about the great priest-magician and his Brazen Head that foretold the future and knew the past; I'll write the speech for you. It doesn't matter whether people have heard of Bacon or not. Many of them haven't heard of Dr Faustus, but they like your conclusion.'

'Oh, every educated person has heard of Faust,' said Eisengrim with something like pomposity. 'He's in a very famous opera.' He had no notion that Faust was also in one of the world's greatest plays.

He had virtually no education, though he could speak several languages, and one of the things Liesl had to teach him, as tactfully as possible, was not to talk out of his depth. I thought that much of his extraordinarily impressive personality arose from his ignorance – or, rather, from his lack of a headful of shallow information that would have enabled him to hold his own in a commonplace way among commonplace people. As a schoolmaster of twenty years' experience I had no use for smatterers. What he knew, he knew as well as anybody on earth; it gave him confidence, and sometimes a naïve egotism that was hard to believe.

We worked very hard on the Brazen Head, which was no more than a very good thought-reading act dressed in a new guise. The Brazen Head was 'levitated' by Eisengrim and floated in the middle of the stage, apparently without wires or supports; then the girls moved through the audience, collecting objects that were sealed in envelopes by their lenders. Eisengrim received these envelopes on a tray on the stage and asked the Head to describe the objects and identify their owners; the Head did so, giving the row and seat number for each; only then did Eisengrim touch them. Next, the Head gave messages to three members of the audience, chosen apparently at random, relating to their personal affairs. It was a first-rate illusion, and I think the script I wrote for it, which was plain and literate, and free of any of the pompous rhetoric so dear to conjurers, had a substantial part in creating its air of mystery.

Rehearsal was difficult because much depended on the girls who collected the objects; they had to use their heads, and their heads were not the best-developed part of them. The random messages were simple but dangerous, for they relied on the work of the company manager, a pickpocket of rare gifts; but he had an air of transparent honesty and geniality, and as he mingled with the audience when it entered the theatre, shaking hands and pressing through the crowd as if on his way somewhere else to do something very important, nobody suspected him. Sometimes he found invaluable letters in the coats of distinguished visitors when he took these to his office to spare such grandees the nuisance of lining up at the *garderobe*. But in the case of ladies or men of no special importance it was straight 'dipping', and potentially dangerous. He enjoyed it; it put him in mind of the good old days before he got into trouble and left London for Rio.

Because of a message the Brazen Head gave a beautiful lady in the very first audience before which it was shown, a duel was fought the next day between a well-known Mexican lawyer and a dentist who fancied himself as a Don Juan. Nothing could have been better publicity, and all sorts of people offered large sums to be permitted to consult the Brazen Head privately. Eisengrim, who had a perfectionist's capacity for worry, was fearful that such revelations would keep people out of the theatre, but Liesl was confident and exultant; she said they would come to hear what was said about other people, and they did.

Liesl's job was to speak for the Brazen Head, because she was the only member of the company capable of rapidly interpreting a letter or an engagement book, and composing a message that was spicy without being positively libellous. She was a woman of formidable intelligence and intuition: she had a turn for improvising and phrasing ambiguous but startling messages that would have done credit to the Oracle at Delphi.

The Brazen Head was such a success that there was some thought of putting it at the end of the show, as the 'topper', but I opposed this; the foundation of the show was romance, and *The Vision of Dr Faustus* had it. But the Head was our best effort in sheer mystery.

I cannot refrain from boasting that it was I who provided the idea for one of the illusions that made Eisengrim the most celebrated magician in the world. Variety theatres everywhere abounded with magicians who could saw a woman in two; it was my suggestion that Eisengrim should offer to saw a member of the audience in two.

His skill as a hypnotist made it possible. When we had worked out the details and put the illusion on the stage, he would first perform the commonplace illusion, sawing one of his showgirls into two sections with a circular saw and displaying her with her head smiling from one end of a box while her feet kicked from the other – but with a hiatus of three feet between the two parts of the box. Then he would offer to do the same thing with a volunteer from the audience. The volunteer would be 'lightly anaesthetized' by hypnosis, ostensibly so that he would not wriggle and perhaps injure himself, after which he would be put in a new box, and Eisengrim would saw him in two with a large and fearsome lumberman's saw. The volunteer was shown to be divided but able to kick his feet and answer questions about the delightfully airy feeling in his middle. Rejoined, the volunteer would leave the stage decidedly dazed, but marvelling at himself and pleased with the applause.

The high point of this illusion was when two assistants held a large mirror so that the volunteer could see for himself that he had been sawn in two. We substituted this illusion for the rather ordinary hypnotic stuff that had been in the show when first I saw it.

Working on these illusions was delightful but destructive of my character. I was aware that I was recapturing the best of my childhood; my imagination had never known such glorious freedom; but as well as liberty and wonder I was regaining the untruthfulness, the lack of scruple, and the absorbing egotism of a child. I heard myself talking boastfully, lying shamelessly. I blushed but could not control myself. I had never, so far as I can tell, been absorbed completely into the character of a Head-master – a figure of authority, of scholarship, of probity – but I was an historian, a hagiographer, a bachelor of unstained character, a winner of the Victoria Cross, the author of several admired books, a man whose course of life was set and the bounds of whose success were defined. Yet here I was, in Mexico City, not simply attached to but subsumed in a magic show. The day I found myself slapping one of the showgirls on the bottom and winking when she made her ritual protest, I knew that something was terribly wrong with Dunstan Ramsay.

Two things that were wrong I could easily identify: I had become a dangerously indiscreet talker, and I was in love with the beautiful Faustina.

I cannot say which dismayed me the more. Almost from the earliest days of my childhood I had been close-mouthed; I never passed on gossip if I could help it, though I had no objection to hearing it; I never betrayed a confidence, preferring the costive pleasure of being a repository of secrets. Much of my intimacy with Boy Staunton rested on the fact that he could be sure I would never repeat anything I was told in confidence, and extremely little that was not so regarded. My pleasure depended on what I knew, not on what I could tell. Yet here I was, chattering like a magpie, telling things that had never before passed my lips, and to Liesl, who did not look to me like a respecter of confidences.

We talked in the afternoons, while she was working on the properties and machinery of the illusions in the tiny theatre workshop under the stage. I soon found out why Liesl dominated the company. First, she was the backer, and the finance of the whole thing rested either on her money or money she had guaranteed. She was a Swiss, and the company buzz was that she came of a family that owned one of the big watch firms. Second, she was a brilliant mechanic; her huge hands did wonders with involved springs, releases and displacements, escapements and levers, however tiny they might be. She was a good artificer too; she made the Brazen Head out of some light plastic so that it was an arresting object; nothing in Eisengrim's show was tawdry or untouched by her exacting taste. But unlike many good craftsmen, she could see beyond what she was making to its effect when in use.

Sometimes she lectured me on the beauty of mechanics. 'There are about a dozen basic principles,' she would say, 'and if they cannot be made to do everything, they can be made to create magic – if you know what you want. Some magicians try to use what they call modern techniques – rays and radar and whatnot. But every boy understands those things. Not many people really understand clockwork because they carry it on their wrists in full sight and never think about it.'

She insisted on talking to me about the autobiography of Eisengrim I was preparing. I had never been used to talking to anyone about a work in progress – had indeed a superstitious feeling that such talk harmed the book by robbing it of energy that should go into the writing. But Liesl always wanted to know how it was getting on, and what line I meant to take, and what splendid lies I was concocting to turn Paul Dempster into a northern wizard.

We had agreed in general terms that he was to be a child of the Baltic vastnesses, reared perhaps by gnomelike Lapps after the death of his explorer parents, who were probably Russians of high birth. No, better not Russians; probably Swedes or Danes who had lived long in Finland; Russians caused too much trouble at borders, and Paul still kept his Canadian passport. Or should his parents perish in the Canadian vastnesses? Anyhow, he had to be a child of the steppes, who had assumed his wolfname in tribute to the savage animals whose midnight howls had been his earliest lullaby, and to avoid revealing his distinguished family name. I had worked on the lives of several northern saints, and I had a store of this highly coloured material at my fingers' ends.

As we discussed these fictions, it was not surprising that Liesl should want to know the facts. In spite of her appearance, and the mistrust of her I felt deep within me, she was a woman who could draw out confidences, and I heard myself rattling on about Deptford, and the Dempsters, and Paul's premature birth, though I did not tell all I knew of that; I even told her about the sad business in the pit, and what came of it, and how Paul ran away; to my dismay I found that I had told her about Willie, about Surgeoner, and even about the Little Madonna. I lay awake the whole night after this last piece of blethering, and got her alone as soon as I could the next day, and begged her not to tell anyone.

'No, Ramsay, I won't promise anything of the sort,' said she. 'You are too old a man to believe in secrets. There is really no such thing as a secret; everybody likes to tell, and everybody does tell. Oh, there are men like priests and lawyers and doctors who are supposed not to tell what they know, but they do – usually they do. If they don't they grow very queer indeed; they pay a high price for their secrecy. You have paid such a price, and you look like a man full of secrets – grim-mouthed and buttoned-up and hard-eyed and cruel, because you are cruel to yourself. It has done you good to tell what you know; you look much more human already. A little shaky this morning because you are so unused to being without the pressure of all your secrets, but you will feel better quite soon.'

I renewed my appeal again that afternoon, but she would give no promise, and I don't think I would have believed her if she had done so; I was irrationally obsessed with an ideal of secrecy that I had carried for fifty years, only to betray it now.

'If a temperamental secret-keeper like you cannot hold in what he knows about Eisengrim, how can you expect it of anyone you despise as you despise me?' she said. 'Oh yes, you do despise me. You despise almost everybody except Paul's mother. No wonder she seems like a saint to you; you have made her carry the affection you should have spread among fifty people. Do not look at me with that tragic face. You should thank me. At fifty years old you should be glad to know something of yourself. That horrid village and your hateful Scots family made you a moral monster. Well, it is not too late for you to enjoy a few years of almost normal humanity.

'Do not try to work on me by making sad faces, Ramsay.

221

You are a dear fellow, but a fool. Now, tell me how you are going to get the infant Magnus Eisengrim out of that dreadful Canada and into a country where big spiritual adventures are possible?'

If the breakdown of character that made me a chatterbox was hard to bear, it was a triviality beside the tortures of my love for the beautiful Faustina.

It was a disease, and I knew it was a disease. I could see plainly everything that made her an impossible person for me to love. She was at least thirty years younger than I, to begin, and she had nothing that I would have recognized as a brain in her head. She was a monster of vanity, venomously jealous of the other girls in the show, and sulky whenever she was not being admired. She rebelled against the company rule that she might not accept invitations from men who had seen her on the stage, but she delighted in having them surge forward when she left the stage door, to press flowers, sweets, and gifts of all kinds on her as she stepped into a hired limousine with Eisengrim. There was one wild-eyed student boy who thrust a poem into her hand, which, as it was writing, I suppose she took for a bill and handed back to him. My heart bled for the poor simpleton. She was an animal.

But I loved her! I hung about the theatre to see her come and go. I lurked in the wings – to which I had been given the entrée, for large screens were set up to protect the illusions from stage hands who were not members of the company – to watch her very rapid changes from Gretchen to Venus and back again, because there was an instant when, in spite of the skilled work of two dressers, she was almost naked. She knew it, and some nights she threw me a smile of complicity and on others she looked offended. She could not resist admiration from anyone, and although I was something of a mystery to most of the company, she knew that I had a voice that was listened to in high places.

There were whole nights when I lay awake from one o'clock till morning, calling up her image before my imagination. On such nights I would suffer, again and again, the worst horror of the lover : I would find myself unable to summon up the adored one's face and – I write it hardly expecting to be believed ex-

cept by someone who has suffered this abjection of adoration –
I would shake at the blasphemy of having thus mislaid her
likeness. I plagued myself with fruitless questions: would the
promise of a life's servitude be enough to make her stoop to
me? And then – for common sense never wholly left me – I
would think of the beautiful Faustina talking to curious, gaping
boys at Colborne College, or meeting the other masters' wives
at one of their stupefying tea parties, and something like a
laugh would shake me. For I was so bound to my life in Canada,
you see, that I always thought of Faustina in terms of marriage
and the continuance of my work.

My work! As if she could have understood what education
was, or why anyone would give a life to it! When I wrestled
with the problem of how it could be explained to her I was
further shaken because, for the first time in my life, I began to
wonder if education could be quite the splendid vocation I had,
as a professional, come to think it. How could I lay my accom-
plishments at her beautiful feet when she was incapable of
knowing what they were? Somebody – I suppose it was Liesl
– told her I knew a lot about saints, and this made a kind of
sense to her.

One happy day, meeting me in the corridor of the theatre
after I had been watching her transformations in *The Vision of
Dr Faustus*, she said, 'Good evening, St Ramsay.'

'St Dunstan,' said I.

'I do not know St Dunstan. Was he a bad old saint who
peeps, eh? O-o-h, shame on you, St Dunstan!' She made a very
lewd motion with her hips and darted into the dressing-room
she shared with Eisengrim.

I was in a melting ecstasy of delight and despair. She had
spoken to me! She knew I watched her and probably guessed
that I loved her and longed for her. That bump, or grind, or
whatever they called it, made it very clear that – yes, but to
call me St Dunstan! What about that? And 'bad old saint' –
she thought me old. So I was. I was fifty, and in the chronology
of a Peruvian girl who was probably more than half Indian,
that was very old. But she had spoken, and she had shown
awareness of my passion for her, and –

I muddled on and on, most of that night, attributing subtleties to Faustina that were certainly absurd but that I could not fight down.

Officially she was Eisengrim's mistress, but they were always quarrelling, for he was exquisitely neat and she made a devastation of their dressing-room. Further, it was clear enough to me that his compelling love affair was with himself; his mind was always on his public personality, and on the illusions over which he fussed psychologically quite as much as Liesl did mechanically. I had seen a good deal of egotism in my life, and I knew that it starved love for anyone else and sometimes burned it out completely. Had it not been so with Boy and Leola? Still, Eisengrim and the beautiful Faustina shared quarters at the hotel. I knew it, because I had left my own place and moved into the even more Spanish establishment that housed the superior members of the company. They shared a room, but did it mean anything?

I found out the day after she called me St Dunstan. I was in the theatre about five o'clock in the afternoon and chanced to go down the corridor on which the star's dressing-room lay. The door was open, and I saw Faustina naked – she was always changing her clothes – in the arms of Liesl, who held her close and kissed her passionately; she had her left arm around Faustina, and her right hand was concealed from me, but the movement of Faustina's hips and her dreamy murmurs made it clear, even to my unaccustomed eyes, what their embrace was.

I have never known such a collapse of the spirit even in the worst of the war. And this time there was no Little Madonna to offer me courage or ease me into oblivion.

5

'Well, dear Ramsay, you are looking a little pale.'

It was Liesl who spoke. I had answered a tap on my door at about one o'clock in the morning, and there she stood in pyjamas and dressing-gown, smiling her ugly smile.

'What do you want?'

'To talk. I love to talk with you, and you are a man who needs talk. Neither of us is sleeping; therefore we shall talk.'

In she came, and as the little room offered only one uncompromising straight-backed chair, she sat down on the bed.

'Come and sit by me. If I were an English lady, or somebody's mother, I suppose I should begin by saying, "Now what is the matter?" – but that is just rhetoric. The matter is that you saw me and Faustina this afternoon. Oh yes, I saw you in the looking-glass. So?'

I said nothing.

'You are just like a little boy, Ramsay. Or no, I am forgetting that only silly men like to be told they are like little boys. Very well, you are like a man of fifty whose bottled-up feelings have burst their bottle and splashed glass and acid everywhere. That is why I called you a little boy, for which I apologize; but you have no art of dealing with such a situation as a man of fifty, so you are thrown back to being like a little boy. Well, I am sorry for you. Not very much, but some.'

'Don't patronize me, Liesl.'

'That is an English word I have never really understood.'

'Don't bully me, then. Don't know best. Don't be the sophisticated European, the magic-show gypsy, the wonderfully intuitive woman, belittling the feelings of a poor brute who doesn't know any better than to think in terms of decency and honour and not taking advantage of people who may not know what they're doing.'

'You mean Faustina? Ramsay, she is a wonderful creature, but in a way you don't begin to grasp. She isn't one of your North American girls, half B.A. and half B.F. and half good decent spud – that's three halves, but never mind. She is of the earth, and her body is her shop and her temple, and whatever her body tells her is all of the law and the prophets. You can't understand such a person, but there are more of them in the world than of the women who are tangled up in honour and decency and the other very masculine things you admire so much. Faustina is a great work of the Creator. She has nothing of what you call brains; she doesn't need them for her destiny. Don't glare at me because I speak of her destiny. It is to be glorious for a few years: not to outlive some dull husband and live on his money till she is eighty, going to lectures and comparing the attractions of winter tours that offer the romance of the Caribbean.'

'You talk as if you thought you were God.'

'I beg your pardon. That is your privilege, you pseudo-cynical old pussy-cat, watching life from the sidelines and knowing where all the players go wrong. Life is a spectator sport to you. Now you have taken a tumble and found yourself in the middle of the fight, and you are whimpering because it is rough.'

'Liesl, I am too tired and sick to wrangle. But let me tell you this, and you may laugh as loud and as long as you please, and babble it to everybody you know because that is your professed way of dealing with confidences: I loved Faustina.'

'But you don't love her now because of what you saw this afternoon! Oh, knight! Oh, saint! You loved her but you never gave her a gift, or paid her a compliment, or asked her to eat with you, or tried to give her what Faustina understands as love – a sweet physical convulsion shared with an interesting partner.'

'Liesl, I am fifty, and I have a wooden leg and only part of one arm. Is that interesting for Faustina?'

'Yes, anything is for Faustina. You don't know her, but far worse you don't know yourself. You are not so very bad, Ramsay.'

'Thank you.'

'Oooh, what dignity! Is that a way to accept a compliment from a lady? I tell him he is not so very bad, and he ruffles up like an old maid and makes a sour face. I must do better; you are a fascinating old fellow. How's that?'

'If you have said what you came to say, I should like to go to bed now.'

'Yes, I see you have taken off your wooden leg and stood it in the corner. Well, I should like to go to bed now too. Shall we go to bed together?'

I looked at her with astonishment. She seemed to mean it.

'Well, do not look as if it were out of the question. You are fifty and not all there: I am as grotesque a woman as you are likely to meet. Wouldn't it have an unusual savour?'

I rose and began to hop to the door. Over the years I have

become a good hopper. But Liesl caught me by the tail of my pyjama coat and pulled me back on the bed.

'Oh, you want it to be like Venus and Adonis! I am to drag you into my arms and crush out your boyish modesty. Good!'

She was much stronger than I would have supposed, and she had no silly notions about fighting fair. I was dragged back to the bed, hopping, and pulled into her arms. I can only describe her body as rubbery, so supple yet muscular was it. Her huge, laughing face with its terrible jaw was close to my own, and her monkeylike mouth was thrust out for a kiss. I had not fought for years – not since my war, in fact – but I had to fight now for – well, for what? In my genteel encounters with Agnes Day, and Gloria Mundy, and Libbie Doe, now so far in the past, I had always been the aggressor, insofar as there was any aggression in those slack-twisted amours. I certainly was not going to be ravished by a Swiss gargoyle. I gave a mighty heave and got a handful of her pyjama coat and a good grip on her hair and threw her on the floor.

She landed with a crash that almost brought down plaster. Up she bounced like a ball, and with a grab she caught up my wooden leg and hit me such a crack over my single shin that I roared and cursed. But when next she brought it down – I had never considered it as a weapon, and it was terrible with springs and rivets – I had a pillow ready and wrenched it from her.

By this time someone downstairs was pounding on his ceiling and protesting in Spanish, but I was not to be quieted. I hopped towards Liesl, waggling the leg with such angry menace that she made the mistake of retreating, and I had her in a corner. I dropped the leg and punched her with a ferocity that I should be ashamed to recall; still, as she was punching back and had enormous fists, it was a fair enough fight. But she began to be afraid, for I had a good Highland temper and it was higher than I have ever known. Tears of pain or fright were running from her deep-set eyes. and blood was dribbling from a cut lip. After a few more smart cuffs. keeping my legless side propped against the wall, I began to edge her towards the door. She grasped the handle behind her, but as she turned it I got a good hold on the bedhead with one hand, and seized her nose between the fingers of the other, and gave it such a twist that I thought I heard something crack. She shrieked, managed to tug the door open, and thundered down the passage.

I sank back on the bed. I was worn out, I was puffing, but I felt fine. I felt better than I had done for three weeks. I thought of Faustina. Good old Faustina! Had I trounced Liesl to avenge her? No, I decided that I had not. A great cloud seemed to have lifted from my spirit, and though it was too soon to be sure, I thought that perhaps my reason, such as it was, had begun to climb back into the saddle and that with care I might soon be myself again.

I had eaten no dinner in my misery, and I discovered I was hungry. I had no food, but I had a flask of whisky in my brief-case. I found it and lay back on the bed, taking a generous swig. The room was a battlefield, but I would tidy it in the morning. Liesl's dressing-gown and a few rags from her pyjamas lay about, and I left them where they were. Honourable trophies.

There came a tap on the door.

'What is it?' I called out in English.

'Señor,' hissed a protesting voice, 'zis honeymoon – oh, very well, very well for you, señor, but please to remember there are zose below who are not so young, if you please, señor!'

I apologized elaborately in Spanish, and the owner of the voice shuffled back down the passage. Honeymoon! How strangely people interpret sound!

In a few minutes there was another tap, even gentler. I called out, 'Who is it?' – in Spanish this time.

The voice was Liesl's voice. 'You will be so kind as to allow me to recover my key,' it said thickly and very formally.

I opened the door, and there she stood, barefooted and holding what was left of her pyjama coat over her bosom.

'Of course, señora,' said I, bowing as gracefully as a one-legged man can do and gesturing to her to come in. Why I closed the door after her I do not know. We glared at each other.

'You are much stronger than you look,' said she.

'So are you,' said I. Then I smiled a little. A victor's smile, I

228

suppose; the kind of smile I smile at boys whom I have frightened out of their wits. She picked up the dressing-gown, taking
care not to turn her back on me.

'May I offer you a drink,' said I, holding out the flask. She
took it and raised it to her lips, but the whisky stung a cut in
her mouth and she winced sharply. That took all the lingering
spite out of me. 'Sit down,' I said, 'and I'll put something on
those bruises.'

She sat down on the bed, and not to make a long tale of it, I
washed her cuts and put a cold-water compress on her nose,
which had swollen astonishingly, and in about five minutes we
were sitting up in the bed with the pillows behind us, taking
turn and turn about at the flask.

'How do you feel now?' said I.

'Much better. And you? How is your shin?'

'I feel better than I have felt in a very long time.'

'Good. That is what I came to make you feel.'

'Indeed? I thought you came to seduce me. That seems to
be your hobby. Anybody and anything. Do you often get beaten
up?'

'What a fool you are! It was only a way of trying to tell you
something.'

'Not that you love me, I hope. I have believed some strange
things in my time, but that would test me pretty severely.'

'No. I wanted to tell you that you are human, like other
people.'

'Have I denied it?'

'Listen, Ramsay, for the past three weeks you have been
telling me the story of your life, with great emotional detail,
and certainly it sounds as if you did not think you were human.
You make yourself responsible for other people's troubles. It is
your hobby. You take on the care of a poor madwoman you
knew as a boy. You put up with subtle insult and being taken
for granted by a boyhood friend – this big sugar-man who is
such a power in your part of the world. You are a friend to this
woman – Leola, what a name! – who gave you your *congé*
when she wanted to marry Mr Sugar. And you are secret and
stiff-rumped about it all, and never admit it is damned good of
you. That is not very human. You are a decent chap to every-

body, except one special somebody, and that is Dunstan Ramsay. How can you be really good to anybody if you are not good to yourself?'

'I wasn't brought up to blow a trumpet if I happened to do something for somebody.'

'Upbringing, so? Calvinism? I am a Swiss, Ramsay, and I know Calvinism as well as you do. It is a cruel way of life, even if you forget the religion and call it ethics or decent behaviour or something else that pushes God out of it.

'But even Calvinism can be endured, if you will make some compromise with yourself. But you – there is a whole great piece of your life that is unlived, denied, set aside. That is why at fifty you can't bear it any longer and fly all to pieces and pour out your heart to the first really intelligent woman you have met – me, that's to say – and get into a schoolboy yearning for a girl who is as far from you as if she lived on the moon. This is the revenge of the unlived life, Ramsay. Suddenly it makes a fool of you.

'You should take a look at this side of your life you have not lived. Now don't wriggle and snuffle and try to protest. I don't mean you should have secret drunken weeks and a widow in a lacy flat who expects you every Thursday, like some suburban ruffian. You are a lot more than that. But every man has a devil, and a man of unusual quality, like yourself, Ramsay, has an unusual devil. You must get to know your personal devil. You must even get to know his father, the Old Devil. Oh, this Christianity! Even when people swear they don't believe in it, the fifteen hundred years of Christianity that has made our world is in their bones, and they want to show they can be Christians without Christ. Those are the worst; they have the cruelty of doctrine without the poetic grace of myth.

'Why don't you shake hands with your devil, Ramsay, and change this foolish life of yours? Why don't you, just for once, do something inexplicable, irrational, at the devil's bidding, and just for the hell of it? You would be a different man.

'What I am saying is not for everybody, of course. Only for the twice-born. One always knows the twice-born. They often go so far as to take new names. Did you not say that English girl renamed you? And who was Magnus Eisengrim? And me – do you know what my name really means, Liselotte Vitzlipützli? It sounds so funny, but one day you will stumble on its real meaning. Here you are, twice-born, and nearer your death than your birth, and you have still to make a real life.

'Who are you? Where do you fit into poetry and myth? Do you know who I think you are, Ramsay? I think you are Fifth Business.

'You don't know what that is? Well, in opera in a permanent company of the kind we keep up in Europe you must have a prima donna – always a soprano, always the heroine, often a fool; and a tenor who always plays the lover to her; and then you must have a contralto, who is a rival to the soprano, or a sorceress or something; and a basso, who is the villain or the rival or whatever threatens the tenor.

'So far, so good. But you cannot make a plot work without another man, and he is usually a baritone, and he is called in the profession Fifth Business, because he is the odd man out, the person who has no opposite of the other sex. And you must have Fifth Business because he is the one who knows the secret of the hero's birth, or comes to the assistance of the heroine when she thinks all is lost, or keeps the hermitess in her cell, or may even be the cause of somebody's death if that is part of the plot. The prima donna and the tenor, the contralto and the basso, get all the best music and do all the spectacular things, but you cannot manage the plot without Fifth Business! It is not spectacular, but it is a good line of work, I can tell you, and those who play it sometimes have a career that outlasts the golden voices. Are you Fifth Business? You had better find out.'

This is not a verbatim report, Headmaster; I said a good deal myself, and I have tidied Liesl's English, and boiled down what she said. But we talked till a clock somewhere struck four, and then fell happily asleep, but not without having achieved the purpose for which Liesl had first of all invaded my room.

With such a gargoyle! And yet never have I known such deep delight or such an aftermath of healing tenderness!

Next morning, tied to my door handle, was a bunch of flowers and a message in elegant Spanish :

Forgive my ill manners of last night. Love conquers all and youth must be served. May you know a hundred years of happy nights. Your Neighbour in the Chamber Below.

6

The Soirée of Illusions

I

THE autobiography of Magnus Eisengrim was a great pleasure
to write, for I was under no obligation to be historically correct
or to weigh evidence. I let myself go and invented just such a
book about a magician as I would have wanted to read if I had
been a member of his public; it was full of romance and marvels,
with a quiet but sufficient undertone of eroticism and sadism,
and it sold like hot-cakes.

Liesl and I had imagined it would sell reasonably well in the
lobbies of theatres where the show was appearing, but it did
well in book stores and, in a paper-back edition that soon followed, it was a steady seller in cigar stores and other places
where they offer lively, sensational reading. People who had
never done an hour's concentrated work in their lives loved to
read how the young Magnus would rehearse his card and coin
sleights for fourteen hours at a stretch, until his body was
drenched in nervous sweat, and he could take no nourishment
but a huge glass of cream laced with brandy. People whose own
love-lives were pitched entirely in the key of C were enchanted
to know that at the time when he was devoting himself entirely to the study of hypnotism, his every glance was so super-
charged that lovely women forced themselves upon him, poor
moths driven to immolate themselves in his flame.

I wrote about the hidden workshop in a Tyrolean castle where
he devised his illusions, and dropped hints that girls had sometimes been terribly injured in some device that was not quite
perfect; of course Eisengrim paid to have them put right again;
I made him something of a monster but not too much of a

monster. I also made his age a matter of conjecture. It was a lively piece of work, and all I regretted was that I had not made a harder bargain for my share of the profit. As it was, it brought me a pleasant annual addition to my income and does so still.

I wrote it in a quiet place in the Adirondacks to which I went a few days after my nocturnal encounter with Liesl. Eisengrim's engagement at the Teatro Chueca was drawing to an end, and the show was to visit a few Central American cities before going to Europe, where a long tour was hoped for. I gave the beautiful Faustina a handsome and fairly expensive necklace as a parting present, and she gave me a kiss, which she and I both regarded as a fair exchange. I gave Eisengrim a really expensive set of studs and links for his evening dress, which staggered him, for he was a miser and could not conceive of anybody giving anything away. But I had talked earnestly with him and wrung from him a promise to contribute to the maintenance of Mrs Dempster; he did not want to do it, swore that he owed her nothing and had indeed been driven from home by her bad reputation. I pointed out to him, however, that if this had not been the case, he would not have become the Great Eisengrim but would probably be a Baptist parson in rural Canada. This was false argument and hurt his vanity, but it helped me gain my point. Liesl helped too. She insisted that Eisengrim sign a banker's order for a sum to be paid to me monthly; she knew that if he had to send me cheques he would forget very soon. The studs and links were something to soothe his wounded avarice. I gave nothing to Liesl; by this time she and I were strong friends and took from each other something that could find no requital in presents.

That money from Eisengrim was not entirely necessary, but I was glad to get it. Within a month of the end of the war I had been able to transfer Mrs Dempster from the public wards of that hateful city asylum to a much better hospital near a small town, where she could have the status of a private patient, enjoying company if she wanted it and gaining the advantages of better air and extensive grounds. I was able to work this through a friend who had some influence; the asylum doctors agreed that she would be better in such a place. and that she was unfit for liberty even if there had been anywhere for her to go. It meant a substantial monthly cost, and though my fortunes had increased to the point where I could afford it, my personal expenditures had to be curtailed, and I was wondering how often in future I would be able to travel in Europe. I would have thought myself false to her, and to the memory of Bertha Shanklin, if I had not made this change in her circumstances, but it meant a pinch, considering that I was trying to build up a fund for my retirement as well. My position was a common one; I wanted to do the right thing but could not help regretting the damnable expense.

So, as I say, I was glad to get a regular sum from Eisengrim, which amounted to about a third of what was needed, and my sense of relief led me into a stupid error of judgement. When first I visited Mrs Dempster after returning from my six months' absence I told her I had found Paul.

Her condition at this time was much improved, and the forlorn and bemused look she had worn for so many years had given place to something that was almost like the sweet and sometimes humorously perceptive expression I remembered from the days when she lived at the end of a rope in Deptford. Her hair was white, but her face was not lined and her figure was slight. I was very pleased by the improvement. But she was still in a condition to which the psychiatrists gave a variety of scientific names but which had been called 'simple' in Deptford. She could look after herself, talked helpfully and amusingly to other patients, and was of use in taking some of the people who were more confused than herself for walks. But she had no ordered notion of the world about her, and in particular she had no sense of time. Amasa Dempster she sometimes recalled as if he were somebody in a book she had once read inattentively; she knew me as the only constant factor in her life, but I came and went, and now if I were absent for six months it was not greatly different in her mind from the space between my weekly visits. The compulsion to visit her regularly was all my own and sprang from a sense of duty rather than from any feeling that she missed me. Paul, however, held a very different place in her confused world, as I soon discovered.

Paul, to her, was still a child, a lost boy – lost a distance of time ago that was both great and small – and to be recovered just as

235

he had run away. Not that she really thought he had run away; surely he had been enticed, by evil people who knew what a great treasure he was; they had stolen him to be cruel, to rob a mother of her child and a child of his mother. Of such malignity she could form no clear picture, but sometimes she spoke of gypsies; gypsies have carried the burden of the irrational dreads of stay-at-homes for many hundreds of years. I had written a passage in my life of Eisengrim in which he spent some of his youth among gypsies, and as I listened to Mrs Dempster now I was ashamed of it.

If I knew where Paul was, why had I not brought him? What had I done to recover him? Had he been ill used? How could I tell her that I had news of Paul if I havered and temporized and would neither bring her child to her or take her to him?

In vain I told her that Paul was now over forty, that he travelled much, that he had a demanding career in which he was not his own master, that he would surely visit Canada at some time not now very far in the future. I said that he sent his love – which was a lie, for he had never said anything of the kind – and that he wanted to provide her with comfort and security. She was so excited, and so unlike herself, that I was shaken and even said that Paul was maintaining her in the hospital, which God knows was untrue, and proved to be another mistake.

To say that a child was keeping her in a hospital was the most ridiculous thing she had ever heard. So that was it? The hospital was an elaborately disguised prison where she was held to keep her from her son! She knew well enough who was her jailer. I was the man. Dunstan Ramsay, who pretended to be a friend, was a snake-in-the-grass, an enemy, an undoubted agent of those dark forces who had torn Paul from her.

She rushed at me and tried to scratch my eyes. I was at a great disadvantage, for I was alarmed and unnerved by the storm I had caused, and also my reverence for Mrs Dempster was so great that I could not bear to be rough with her. Fortunately – though it scared the wits out of me at the moment – she began to scream, and a nurse came on the run, and between us we soon had her powerless. But what followed was a half-hour of confusion, during which I explained to a doctor what the trouble was, and Mrs Dempster was put to bed under what they called light restraint – straps – with an injection of something to quiet her .

When I called the hospital the next day the report was a bad one. It grew worse during the week, and in time I had to face the fact that I seemed to have turned Mrs Dempster from a woman who was simple and nothing worse, into a woman who knew there was a plot to deprive her of her little son, and that I was its agent. She was under restraint now, and it was inadvisable that I should visit her. But I did go once, driven by guilt, and though I did not see her, her window was pointed out to me, and it was in the wing where the windows are barred.

2

Thus I lost, for a time, one of the fixed stars in my universe, and as I had brought about this great change in Mrs Dempster's condition by my own stupidity I felt much depressed by it. But I suffered another loss – or at least a marked change – when Boy Staunton married for the second time, and I did not meet with the approval of his wife.

During the war Boy acquired a taste for what he believed to be politics. He had been elected in easy circumstances, for he was a Conservative, and in their plan for a coalition Cabinet the Liberals had not nominated anybody to oppose him. But in the years when he had great power he forgot that he had been elected by acclamation and came somehow to think of himself as a politician – no, a statesman – with a formidable following among the voters. He had all the delusions of the political amateur, and after the war was over he insisted that he detected an undertone, which grew in some parts of the country to a positive clamour, that he should become leader of the Conservative party as fast as possible and deliver the people of Canada from their ignominious thralldom to the Liberals. He had another delusion of the political novice: he was going to apply 'sound business principles' to government and thereby give it a fine new gloss.

So he attempted to become Conservative leader, but as he

237

was a newcomer he had no chance of doing so. It seemed to me that everything about Boy was wrong for politics : he was very rich and could not understand that very rich men are not loved by the majority; he was handsome, and handsome men are not popular in politics, even with women; he had no political friends and could not understand why they were necessary.

In spite of his handicaps he was elected once, when a by-election opened a Parliamentary seat traditionally Conservative. The voters remembered his services during the war and gave him a majority of less than a thousand. But he made a number of silly speeches in the Commons, which caused a few newspapers to say that he was an authoritarian; then he abused the newspapers in the Commons, and they made him smart for it. Boy had no idea what a mark he presented to jealous or temperamentally derisive people. However, he gained some supporters, and among them was Denyse Hornick.

She was a power in the world of women. She had been in the W.R.N.S. during the war and had risen from the ranks to be a lieutenant commander and a very capable one. After the war she had established a small travel agency and made it a big one. She liked what Boy stood for in politics, and after a few meetings she liked Boy personally. I must not read into her actions motives of which I can have no knowledge, but it looked to me as if she decided that she would marry him and make him think it was his own idea.

Boy had always been fond of the sexual pleasure women could give him, but I doubt if he ever knew much about women as people, and certainly a determined and clever woman like Denyse was something outside his experience. He was drawn to her at first because she was prominent in two or three groups that worked for a larger feminine influence in public affairs, and thus could influence a large number of votes. Soon he discovered that she understood his political ideas better than anybody else, and he paid her a compliment typical of himself by assuring everybody that she had a masculine mind.

The by-election gave him a couple of years in Parliament before a general election came along to test his real strength. By that time any public gratitude for what he had done as a war organizer had been forgotten, the Conservative party found him an embarrassment because he was apt to criticize the party leader in public, the Liberals naturally wanted to defeat him, and the newspapers were out to get him. It was a dreadful campaign on his part, for he lost his head, bullied his electors when he should have wooed them, and got into a wrangle with a large newspaper, which he threatened to sue for libel. He was defeated on election day so decisively that it was obviously a personal rather than a political rejection.

He made an unforgettable appearance on television as soon as his defeat had been conceded. 'How do you feel about the result in your riding, Mr Staunton?' asked the interviewer, expecting something crisp, but not what he got. 'I feel exactly like Lazarus,' said Boy, 'licked by the dogs!'

The whole country laughed about it, and the newspaper he thought had libelled him read him a pompous little editorial lecture about the nature of democracy. But there were those who were faithful, and Denyse was at the top of that list.

In the course of time the press tired of baiting him, and there were a few editorials regretting that so much obvious ability was not being used for the public good. But it was no use. Boy was through with politics and turned back to sugar, and everything sugar could be made to do, with new resolve.

Denyse had other ambitions for him, and she was a wilier politician than he. She thought he would make a very fine Lieutenant-Governor of the Province of Ontario and set to work to see that he got it.

Necessarily it was a long campaign. The Lieutenant-Governorship was in the gift of the Crown, which meant in effect that the holder of the office was named by the Dominion Cabinet. A Lieutenant-Governor had only recently been appointed, and as he was in excellent health it would be five years and possibly longer before Boy would have a chance. On his side was one strong point; it cost a lot of money to be Lieutenant-Governor, for the duties were ample and the stipend was not, so candidates for the post were never many. But a Liberal Government at Ottawa would not be likely to appoint a former Conservative parliamentarian to such a post, so there would have to be a change of government if Boy were to have a chance. It was a plan full of risks and contingencies, and if it were to succeed it would be through careful diplomacy and a substantial amount of luck. It was characteristic of Denyse that she decided to get busy with the diplomacy at once, so as to be ready for the luck if it came.

Boy thought the idea a brilliant one. He had never lost his taste for matters connected with the Crown; he had no doubt of his ability to fill a ceremonial post with distinction, and even to give it larger dimensions. He had everything the office needed with one exception. A Lieutenant-Governor must have a wife.

It was here that Denyse's masculinity of mind showed itself with the greatest clarity. Boy told me exactly what she said when first the matter came up between them. 'I can't help you there,' she said; 'you're on your own so far as that goes.' And then she went straight on to discuss the rationale of the Lieu-tenant-Governor's office – those privileges which made it a safeguard against any tyrannous act on the part of a packed legislature. It was by no means a purely ceremonial post, she said, but an agency through which the Crown exercised its traditional function of safeguarding the Constitution against politicians who forgot that they had been elected to serve the people and not to exploit them. She had informed herself thoroughly on the subject and knew the powers and limitations of a Lieutenant-Governor as well as any constitutional lawyer.

Boy had been aware for some time that Denyse was attractive; now he saw that she was lovable. Her intelligent, cool, unswerving devotion to his interests had impressed him from very early in their association, but her masculinity of mind had kept him at a distance. Now he became aware that this poor girl had sacrificed so much of her feminine self in order to gain success in the business world, and to advance the cause of women who lacked her clarity of vision and common sense, that she had almost forgotten that she was a woman, and a damned attractive one.

When love strikes the successful middle-aged they bring a weight of personality and a resolution to it that makes the romances of the young seem timid and bungling. They are not troubled by doubt; they know what they want and they go after it. Boy decided he wanted Denyse.

Denyse was not so easily achieved. Boy told me all about his wooing. Matters between us were still as they had been for thirty years, and the only difference was that Liesl had taught me that his confidences were not wrung from him against his will but gushed like oil from a well, and that I as Fifth Business was his logical confidant. Denyse at first refused to hear his professions of love. Her reasons were two : her business was her creation and demanded the best of her, and as a friend of Boy's she did not want him to imperil a fine career by an attachment that contained dangers.

What dangers ? he demanded. Well, she confided, rather unwillingly, there had been Hornick. She had married him very early in the war, when she was twenty; it had been a brief and disagreeable marriage, which she had terminated by a divorce. Could a representative of the Crown have a wife who was a divorcee?

Boy swept this aside. Queen Victoria was dead. Even King George was dead. Everybody recognized the necessity and humanity of divorce nowadays, and Denyse's splendid campaigns for liberalizing the divorce laws had put her in a special category. But Denyse had more to confess.

There had been other men. She was a woman of normal physical needs – she admitted it without shame – and there had been one or two other attachments.

Poor kid, said Boy, she was still a victim of the ridiculous Double Standard. He told Denyse about his dreadful mistake with Leola, and how it had driven him – positively driven him – to seek outside marriage qualities of understanding and physical response that were not to be found at home. She understood this perfectly, but he had to argue for a long time to get her to see that the same common-sense view applied to herself. It was in such things as this, Boy told me with a fatuous smile, that Denyse's masculinity of mind failed her. He had to be pretty stern with her to make her understand that what was sauce for the gander was certainly sauce for the goose. Indeed, he called her Little Goose for a few days but gave it up because of the ribald connotation of the word.

Then – he smiled sadly when he explained the absurdity of this to me – there was her final objection, which was that people might imagine she married him for his money and the position he could give her. She was a small-town girl, and though she had gained a certain degree of know-how through her experience of life (I am not positive but I think she even went so far as to say that she was a graduate of the School of Hard Knocks), she doubted if she was up to being Mrs Boy Staunton, and just possibly the Lieutenant-Governor's lady. Suppose – just suppose for a moment – that she were called upon to entertain Royalty! No, Denyse Hornick knew her strengths and her weaknesses and she loved Boy far too well ever to expose him to embarrassment on her account.

Yes, she loved him. Had always done so. Understood the fiery and impatient spirit that could not endure the popularity-contest side of modern politics. Thought of him – didn't want to seem highbrow, but she did do a little serious reading – as a Canadian Coriolanus. 'You common cry of curs, whose breath I hate.' She could imagine him saying it to those sons-of-bitches who had turned on him at the last election. Yearned towards him in her heart as a really great man who was too proud to shake hands and kiss babies to persuade a lot of riffraff to let him do what he was so obviously born to do.

Thus the masculinity of mind that had made Denyse Hornick a success in her world was swept aside, and the tender, loving woman beneath was discovered and awakened by Boy Staunton. They were married after appropriate preparations.

As a wedding it was neither a religious ceremony nor a merry-making. It is best described as A Function. Everybody of importance in Boy's world was there, and by clever work on Denyse's part quite a few Cabinet Ministers from Ottawa were present and the Prime Minister sent a telegram composed by the most eloquent of his secretaries. Bishop Woodiwiss married them, being assured that Denyse had not been the offending party in her divorce; he demurred even then, but Boy persuaded him, saying to me afterward that diocesan care and rumours of the death of God were eroding the Bishop's intellect. The bride wore a ring of unusual size; the best man was a bank president; the very best champagne flowed like the very best champagne under the care of a very good caterer (which is to say, not more than three glasses to a guest unless they made a fuss). There was little jollity but no bitterness except from David.

'Do we kiss the bride?' a middle-aged guest asked him.

'Why not?' said he. 'She's been kissed oftener than a police-court Bible and by much the same class of people.'

The guest hurried away and told somebody that David was thinking of his mother.

I do not think this was so. Neither David nor Caroline liked Denyse, and they hated and resented her daughter, Lorene.

Not much attention had been paid to Lorene during the courtship, but she was an element to be reckoned with. She was the fruit of the unsatisfactory marriage with Hornick, who may, perhaps, have had the pox, and at this time she was thirteen. Adolescence was well advanced in Lorene, and she had large, hard breasts that popped out so close under her chin that she seemed to have no neck. Her body was heavy and short, and her physical coordination was so poor that she tended to knock things off tables that were quite a distance from her. She had bad vision and wore thick spectacles. She already gave rich promise of superfluous hair and sweated under the least stress. Her laugh was loud and frequent, and when she let it loose, spittle ran down her chin, which she sucked back with a blush. Unkind people said she was a half-wit, but that was untrue; she went to a special boarding-school where her teachers had put her in the Opportunity Class, as being more suited to her powers than the undemanding academic curriculum, and she was learning to cook and sew quite nicely.

At her mother's wedding Lorene was in tearing high spirits. Champagne dissolved her few inhibitions, and she banged and thumped her way among the guests, wet-chinned and elated. 'I'm just the luckiest kid in the world today,' she whooped. 'I've got a wonderful new Daddy, my Daddy-Boy – he says I can call him Daddy-Boy. Look at the bracelet he gave me!'

In the goodness of her innocent heart Lorene tried to be friendly with David and Caroline. After all, were they not one family now? Poor Lorene did not know how many strange gradations of relationship the word 'family' can imply. Caroline, who had never had a pleasant disposition, was extremely rude to her. David got drunk and laughed and made disrespectful remarks in an undertone when Boy made his speech in response to the toast to the bride.

Rarely is there a wedding without its clown. Lorene was the clown at Boy's second marriage, but it was not until she fell down – champagne or unaccustomed high heels, or both – that I took her into an anteroom and let her tell me all about her dog, who was marvellously clever. In time she fell asleep, and two waiters carried her out to the car.

3

Denyse had the normal dislike of a woman for the friends her husband has made before he married her, but I felt she was more than usually severe in my case. She possessed intelligence, conventional good looks, and unusual quality as an intriguer and politician, but she was a woman whose life and interests were entirely external. It was not that she was indifferent to the things of the spirit; she sensed their existence and declared herself their enemy. She had made it clear that she consented to a church wedding only because it was expected of a man in Boy's position; she condemned the church rite because it put women at a disadvantage. All her moral and ethical energy, which was abundant, was directed towards social reform. Easier divorce, equal pay for equal work as between men and women, no discrimination between the sexes in employment – these were her causes, and in promoting them she was no comic-strip feminist termagant, but reasonable, logical, and untiring.

Boy often assured me that underneath this public personality of hers there was a shy, lovable kid, pitifully anxious for affection and the tenderness of sex, but Denyse did not choose to show this aspect of herself to me. She had a fair measure of intuition, and she sensed that I regarded women as something other than fellow-citizens who had been given an economic raw deal because of a few unimportant biological differences. She may even have guessed that I held women in high esteem for qualities she had chosen to discourage in herself. But certainly she did not want me around the Staunton house, and if I dropped in, as had been my habit for thirty years, she picked a delicate quarrel with me, usually about religion. Like many people who are ignorant of religious matters, she attributed absurd beliefs to those who were concerned with them. She had found out about my interest in saints; after all, my books were not easy to overlook if one was in the travel business. The whole notion of saints was repugnant to her, and in her eyes I was on a level with people who believed in teacup reading or Social Credit. So, although I was asked to dinner now and then, when the other guests were people who had to be worked off for some tiresome reason, I was no longer an intimate of the household.

Boy tried to smooth things over by occasionally asking me to lunch at his club. He was more important than ever, for as well as his financial interests, which were now huge, he was a public figure, prominent in many philanthropic causes, and even a few artistic ones, as these became fashionable.

I sensed that this was wearing on him. He hated committees, but they were unavoidable even when he bossed them. He hated inefficiency, but a certain amount of democratic inefficiency had to be endured. He hated unfortunate people, but, after all, these are one's raw material if one sets up shop as a philanthropist. He was still handsome and magnetic, but I sensed grimness and disillusion when he was at his ease, as he was with me. He had embraced Denyse's rationalism – that was what she called it – fervently, and one day at the York Club, following the publication and varied reviews of my big book on the psychology of myth and legend, he denounced me petulantly for what he called my triviality of mind and my encouragement of superstition.

He had not read the book and I was sharp with him. He pulled in his horns a little and said, as the best he could do in the way of apology, that he could not stand such stuff because he was an atheist.

'I'm not surprised,' said I. 'You created a God in your own image, and when you found out he was no good you abolished him. It's a quite common form of psychological suicide.'

I had only meant to give him blow for blow, but to my surprise he crumpled up.

'Don't nag me, Dunny,' he said. 'I feel rotten. I've done just about everything I've ever planned to do, and everybody thinks I'm a success. And of course I have Denyse now to keep me up to the mark, which is lucky – damned lucky, and don't imagine I don't feel it. But sometimes I wish I could get into a car and drive away from the whole damned thing.'

'A truly mythological wish,' I said. 'I'll save you the trouble of reading my book to find out what it means: you want to pass into oblivion with your armour on, like King Arthur, but modern medical science is too clever to allow it. You must grow old, Boy; you'll have to find out what age means, and how to be old. A dear old friend of mine once told me he wanted a God who would teach him how to grow old. I expect he found what he wanted. You must do the same, or be wretched. Whom the gods hate they keep forever young.'

He looked at me almost with hatred. 'That's the most lunatic defeatist nonsense I've ever heard in my life,' he said. But before we drank our coffee he was quite genial again.

Although I had been rather rough I was worried about him. As a boy he had been something of a bully, a boaster, and certainly a bad loser. As he grew up he had learned to dissemble these characteristics, and to anyone who knew him less well than I it might have appeared that he had conquered them. But I have never thought that traits that are strong in childhood disappear; they may go underground or they may be transmuted into something else, but they do not vanish; very often they make a vigorous appearance after the meridian of life has been passed. It is this, and not senility, that is the real second childhood. I could see this pattern in myself; my boyhood trick of getting off 'good ones' that went far beyond any necessary self-defence and were likely to wound, had come back to me in my fifties. I was going to be a sharp-tongued old man as I had been a sharp-tongued boy. And Boy Staunton had reached a point in life where he no longer tried to conceal his naked wish to dominate everybody and was angry and ugly when things went against him.

As we neared our sixties the cloaks we had wrapped about our essential selves were wearing thin.

4

Mrs Dempster died the year after Boy's second marriage. It
came as a surprise to me, for I had a notion that the insane
lived long and had made preparations in my will for her maintenance if I should die before her. Her health had been unimpaired by the long and wretched stay in the city asylum, and she
had been more robust and cheerful after her move to the country,
but I think my foolish talk about Paul broke her. After that
well-meant piece of stupidity she was never 'simple' again.
There were drugs to keep her artificially passive, but I mistrusted
them (perhaps ignorantly) and asked that so far as possible she
be spared the ignominy of being stunned into good conduct.
This made her harder to care for and cost more money. So she
spent some of her time in fits of rage against me as the evil
genius of her life, but much more in a state of grief and desolation.

It wore her out. I could not talk to her, but sometimes I
looked at her through a little spy-hole in her door, and she grew
frailer and less like herself as the months passed. She developed
physical ailments – slight diabetes, a kidney weakening, and
some malfunctioning of the heart – which were not thought to
be very serious and were controlled in various ways; the doctors
assured me, with the professional cheeriness of their kind, that
she was good for another ten years. But I did not think so, for
I was born in Deptford, where we were very acute in detecting
when someone was 'breaking up', and I knew that was what
was happening to her.

Nevertheless it was a surprise when I was called by the hospital authorities to say she had had a serious heart seizure and
might have another within a few hours. I had known very little
of life without Mrs Dempster, and despite my folk wisdom
about 'breaking up' I had not really faced the fact that I might
lose her. It gave me a clutching around my own heart that
scared me, but I made my way to the hospital as quickly as I
could, though it was some hours after the telephone call when I
arrived.

She was in the infirmary now, and unconscious. The outlook was bad, and I sat down to wait – presumably for her death. But after perhaps two hours a nurse appeared and said she was asking for me. As it was now some years since she had seen me without great distress of mind I was doubtful about answering the call but I was assured it would be all right, and I went to her bedside.

She looked very pale and drawn, but when I took her hand she opened her eyes and looked at me for quite a long time. When she spoke her speech was slack and hardly audible.

'Are you Dunstable Ramsay?' she said.

I assured her. Another long silence.

'I thought he was a boy,' said she and closed her eyes again.

I sat by her bed for quite a long time but she did not speak. I thought she might say something about Paul. I sat for perhaps an hour, and then to my astonishment the hand I held gave a little tug, the least possible squeeze. It was the last message I had from Mrs Dempster. Soon afterward her breathing became noisy and the nurses beckoned me away. In half an hour they came to tell me she was dead.

It was a very bad night for me. I kept up a kind of dismal stoicism until I went to bed, and then I wept. I had not done such a thing since my mother had beaten me so many years before – no, not even in the worst of the war – and it frightened and hurt me. When at last I fell asleep I dreamed frightening dreams, in some of which my mother figured in terrible forms. They became so intolerable that I sat up and tried to read but could not keep my mind on the page; instead I was plagued by fantasies of desolation and wretchedness so awful that I might as well not have been sixty years old, a terror to boys, and a scholar of modest repute, for they crushed me as if I were the feeblest of children. It was a terrible invasion of the spirit, and when at last the rising bell rang in the school I was so shaken I cut myself shaving, vomited my breakfast half an hour after I had eaten it, and in my first class spoke so disgracefully to a stupid boy that I called him back afterward and apologized. I must have looked stricken, for my colleagues were unusually considerate towards me, and my classes were uneasy.

I think they thought I was very ill, and I suppose I was, but not of anything I knew how to cure.

I had arranged for Mrs Dempster's body to be sent to Toronto, as I wanted it to be cremated. An undertaker had it in his care, and the day after her death I went to see him.

'Dempster,' he said. 'Yes, just step into Room C.'

There she was, not looking very much like herself, for the embalmer had been generous with the rouge. Nor can I say that she looked younger, or at peace, which are the two conventional comments. She just looked like a small, elderly woman, ready for burial. I knelt, and the undertaker left the room. I prayed for the repose of the soul of Mary Dempster, somewhere and somehow unspecified, under the benevolence of some power unidentified but deeply felt. It was the sort of prayer that supported all the arguments of Denyse Staunton against religion, but I was in the grip of an impulsion that it would have been spiritual suicide to deny. And then I begged forgiveness for myself because, though I had done what I imagined was my best, I had not been loving enough, or wise enough, or generous enough in my dealings with her.

Then I did an odd thing that I almost fear to record, Headmaster, for it may lead you to dismiss me as a fool or a madman or both. I had once been fully persuaded that Mary Dempster was a saint, and even of late years I had not really changed my mind. There were the three miracles, after all; miracles to me, if to no one else. Saints, according to tradition, give off a sweet odour when they are dead; in many instances it has been likened to the scent of violets. So I bent over the head of Mary Dempster and sniffed for this true odour of sanctity. But all I could smell was a perfume, good enough in itself, that had obviously come out of a bottle.

The undertaker returned, bringing a cross with him; seeing me kneel, he had assumed that the funeral would be of the sort that required one. He came upon me sniffing.

'Chanel Number Five,' he whispered, 'we always use it when nothing is supplied by the relatives. And perhaps you have noticed that we have padded your mother's bosom just a little; she had lost something there, during the last illness, and when the figure is reclining it gives a rather wasted effect.'

He was a decent man, working at a much-abused but necessary job, so I made no comment except to say that she was not my mother.

'I'm so sorry. Your aunt?' said he, desperate to please and be comforting but not intimate.

'No, neither mother nor aunt,' I said, and as I could not use so bleak and inadequate a word as 'friend' to name what Mary Dempster had been to me, I left him guessing.

The following day I sat quite alone in the crematory chapel as Mary Dempster's body went through the doors into the flames. After all, who else remembered her?

5

She died in March. The following summer I went to Europe and visited the Bollandists, hoping they would pay me a few compliments on my big book. I am not ashamed of this; who knew better than they if I had done well or ill, and whose esteem is sweeter than that of an expert in one's own line? I was not disappointed; they were generous and welcoming as always. And I picked up one piece of information that pleased me greatly: Padre Blazon was still alive, though very old, in a hospital in Vienna.

I had not meant to go to Vienna, though I was going to Salzburg for the Festival, but I had not heard from Blazon for years and could not resist him. There he was, in a hospital directed by the Blue Nuns, propped up on pillows, looking older but not greatly changed except that his few teeth were gone; he even wore the deplorable velvet skullcap rakishly askew over his wild white hair.

He knew me at once. 'Ramezay!' he crowed as I approached. 'I thought you must be dead! How old you look! Why, you must be all kinds of ages! What years? Come now, don't be coy! What years?'

'Just over the threshold of sixty-one,' I said.

'Aha, a patriarch! You look even more though. Do you know how old I am? No, you don't, and I am not going to tell. If the

Sisters find out they think I am senile. They wash me too much now; if they knew how old I am they would flay me with their terrible brushes – flay me like St Bartholomew. But I will tell you this much – I shall not see one hundred again! How much over that I tell nobody, but it will be discovered when I am dead. I may die any time. I may die as we are talking. Then I shall be sure to have the last word, eh? Sit down. You look tired!

'You have written a fine book! Not that I have read it all, but one of the nuns read some of it to me. I made her stop because her English accent was so vile she desecrated your elegant prose, and she mispronounced all the names. A real murderer! How ignorant these women are! Assassins of the spoken word! For a punishment I made her read a lot of *Le Juif errant* to me. Her French is very chaste, but the book nearly burned her tongue – so very anticlerical, you know. And what it says about the Jesuits! What evil magicians, what serpents! If we were one scruple as clever as Eugène Sue thought we should be masters of the world today. Poor soul, she could not understand why I wanted to hear it or why I laughed so much. Then I told her it was on the Index, and now she thinks I am an ogre disguised as an old Jesuit. Well, well, it passes the time. How is your fool-saint?'

'My what?'

'Don't shout; my hearing is perfectly good. Your fool-saint, your madwoman who dominates your life. I thought we might get something about her in your book but not a word. I know. I read the index first; I always do. All kinds of saints, heroes, and legends but no fool-saint. Why?'

'I was surprised to hear you call her that because I haven't heard that particular expression for thirty years. The last man to use it about Mary Dempster was an Irishman.' And I told him of my conversation with Father Regan so long ago.

'Ah, Ramezay, you are a rash man. Imagine asking a village priest a question like that! But he must have been a fellow of some quality. Not all the Irish are idiots; they have a lot of Spanish blood, you know. That he should know about fool-saints is very odd. But do you know that one is to be canonized quite soon? Bertilla Boscardin, who did wonders – truly wonders – during the First World War with hospital patients; many

251

miracles of healing and heroic courage during air-raids. Still, she was not quite a classic fool-saint; she was active and they are more usually passive – great lovers of God, with that special perception that St Bonaventura spoke of as beyond the power of even the wisest scholar.'

'Father Regan assured me that fool-saints are dangerous. The Jews warn against them particularly because they are holy meddlers and bring ill-luck.'

'Well, so they do, sometimes, when they are more fool than saint; we all bring ill-luck to others, you know, often without in the least recognizing it. But when I talk of a fool-saint I do not mean just some lolloping idiot who babbles of God instead of talking filth as they usually do. Remind me about this Mary Dempster.'

So I did remind him, and when I had finished he said he would think about the matter. He was growing weary, and a nun signalled to me that it was time to leave.

'He is a very dear and good old man,' she told me. 'but he does so love to tease us. If you want to give him a treat, bring him some of that very special Viennese chocolate; he finds the hospital diet a great trial. His stomach is a marvel. Oh, that I might have such a stomach, and I am not even half his massive age!'

So next day I appeared with a lot of chocolate, most of which I gave to the nun to be rationed to him; I did not want him to gorge himself to death before my eyes. But the box I gave him was one of those pretty affairs with a little pair of tongs for picking out the piece one wants.

'Aha, St Dunstan and his tongs!' he whispered. 'Keep your voice down, St Dunstan, or all these others will want some of my chocolate, and it probably would not be wholesome for them. Oh, you saintly man! I suppose a bottle of really good wine could not be got past the nuns? They dole out a thimble-ful of some terrible belly-vengeance they buy very cheap, on their infrequent feast days.

'Well, I have been thinking about your fool-saint, and what I conclude is this : she would never have got past the Bollandists, but she must have been an extraordinary person, a great lover of God, and trusting greatly in His love for her. As for the miracles, you and I have looked too deeply into miracles to dogmatize; you believe in them, and your belief has coloured your life with beauty and goodness; too much scientizing will not help you. It seems far more important to me that her life was lived heroically; she endured a hard fate, did the best she could, and kept it up until at last her madness was too powerful for her. Heroism in God's cause is the mark of the saint, Ramezay, not conjuring tricks. So on All Saints' Day I do not think you will do anything but good by honouring the name of Mary Dempster in your prayers. By your own admission you have enjoyed many of the good things of life because she suffered a fate that might have been yours. Though a boy's head is hard, Ramezay, hard − as you, being a schoolmaster, must surely know. You might just have had a nasty knock. Nobody can say for sure. But your life has been illuminated by your fool-saint, and how many can say so much?'

We talked a little further of friends we shared in Brussels, and then suddenly he said, 'Have you met the Devil yet?'

'Yes,' I replied, 'I met Him in Mexico City. He was disguised as a woman − an extremely ugly woman but unquestionably a woman.'

'Unquestionably?'

'Not a shadow of a doubt possible.'

'Really, Ramezay, you astonish me. You are a much more remarkable fellow than one might suppose, if you will forgive me for saying so. The Devil certainly changed His sex to tempt St Anthony the Great, but for a Canadian schoolmaster! Well, well, one must not be an snob in spiritual things. From your certainty I gather the Devil tempted you with success?'

'The Devil proved to be a very good fellow. He suggested that a little compromise would not hurt me. He even suggested that an acquaintance with Him might improve my character.'

'I find no fault with that. The Devil knows corners of us all of which Christ Himself is ignorant. Indeed, I am sure Christ learned a great deal that was salutary about Himself when He met the Devil in the wilderness. Of course, that was a meeting of brothers; people forget too readily that Satan is Christ's elder brother and has certain advantages in argument that pertain to a senior. On the whole, we treat the Devil shamefully, and the worse we treat Him the more He laughs at us. But tell me about your encounter.'

I did so, and he listened with a great show of prudery at the dirty bits; he sniggered behind his hand, rolling his eyes up until only the whites could be seen; he snorted with laughter; when I described Liesl and the beautiful Faustina in the dressing-room he covered his face with his hands but peeped wickedly between his fingers. It was a virtuoso display of clerical-Spanish modesty. But when I described how I had wrung Liesl's nose until the bone cracked he kicked his counterpane and guffawed until a nun hurried to his bedside, only to be repelled with full-arm gestures and hissing.

'Oho, Ramezay, no wonder you write so well of myth and legend! It was St Dunstan seizing the Devil's snout in his tongs, a thousand years after his time. Well done, well done! You met the Devil as an equal, not cringing or frightened or begging for a trashy favour. That is the heroic life, Ramezay. You are fit to be the Devil's friend, without any fear of losing yourself to Him!'

On the third day I took farewell of him. I had managed to arrange for some chocolate to be procured when he needed more, and as a great favour the nuns took six bottles of a good wine into their care to be rationed to him as seemed best.

'Good-bye,' he cried cheerfully. 'We shall probably not meet again, Ramezay. You are beginning to look a little shaky.'

'I have not yet found a God to teach me how to be old,' I said. 'Have you?'

'Shhh, not so loud. The nuns must not know in what a spiritual state I am. Yes, yes, I have found Him, and He is the very best of company. Very calm, very quiet, but gloriously alive: we *do*, but He *is*. Not in the least a proselytizer or a careerist, like His sons.' And he went off into a fit of giggles.

I left him soon after this, and as I looked back from the door for a last wave, he was laughing and pinching his big copper nose with the tiny chocolate tongs. 'God go with you, St Dunstan,' he called.

He was much in my mind as I tasted the pleasures of Salzburg, and particularly so after my first visit to the special display called *Schöne Madonnen*, in the exhibition rooms in the Cathedral. For here, at last, and after having abandoned hope and forgotten my search, I found the Little Madonna I had seen during my bad night at Passchendaele. There she was, among these images of the Holy Mother in all her aspects, collected as examples of the wood and stone carver's art, and drawn from churches, museums, and private collections all over Europe.

There she was, quite unmistakable, from the charming crown that she wore with such an air to her foot set on the crescent moon. Beneath this moon was what I had not seen in the harsh light of the flare – the globe of the earth itself, with a serpent encircling it, and an apple in the mouth of the serpent. She had lost her sceptre, but not the Divine Child, a fat, reserved little person who looked out at the world from beneath half-closed eyelids. But the face of the Madonna – was it truly the face of Mary Dempster? No, it was not, though the hair was very like; Mary Dempster, whose face my mother had described as being like a pan of milk, had never been so beautiful in feature, but the expression was undeniably hers – an expression of mercy and love, tempered with perception and penetration.

I visited her every day during my week in Salzburg. She belonged, so the catalogue told me, to a famous private collection and was considered a good, though late, example of the Immaculate Conception aspect of the Madonna figure. It had not been considered worthy of an illustration in the catalogue, so when my week was up I never saw it again. Photography in the exhibition was forbidden. But I needed no picture. She was mine forever.

6

The mysterious death of Boy Staunton was a nine days' wonder, and people who delight in unsolved crimes – for they were certain it must have been a crime – still talk of it. You recall most of the details, Headmaster, I am sure : at about four o'clock on the morning of Monday, November 4, 1968, his Cadillac convertible was recovered from the waters of Toronto harbour, into which it had been driven at a speed great enough to carry it, as it sank, about twenty feet from the concrete pier. His body was in the driver's seat, the hands gripping the wheel so tightly that it was very difficult for the police to remove him from the car. The windows and the roof were closed, so that some time must have elapsed between driving over the edge and the filling of the car with water. But the most curious fact of all was that in Boy's mouth the police found a stone – an ordinary piece of pinkish granite about the size of a small egg – which could not possibly have been where it was unless he himself, or someone unknown, had put it there.

The newspapers published columns about it, as was reasonable, for it was local news of the first order. Was it murder? But who would murder a well-known philanthropist, a man whose great gifts as an organizer had been of incalculable value to the nation during the war years? Now that Boy was dead, he was a hero to the press. Was it suicide? Why would the President of the Alpha Corporation, a man notably youthful in appearance and outlook, and one of the two or three richest men in Canada, want to kill himself? His home-life was of model character; he and his wife (the former Denyse Hornick, a figure of note in her own right as an advocate of economic and legal reform on behalf of women) had worked very closely in a score of philanthropic and cultural projects. Besides, the newspapers thought it now proper to reveal, his appointment by the Crown to the office of Lieutenant-Governor of Ontario was to have been announced within a few days. Was a man with Boy Staunton's high concept of service likely to have killed himself under such circumstances?

Tributes from distinguished citizens were many. There was a heartfelt one from Joel Surgeoner, within a few hundred yards of whose Lifeline Mission the death occurred – a Mission that the dead man had supported most generously. You wrote one yourself, Headmaster, in which you said that he had finely exemplified the school's unremitting insistence that much is demanded of those to whom much has been given.

His wife was glowingly described, though there was little mention of 'a former marriage, which ended with the death of the first Mrs Staunton, nee Leola Crookshanks, in 1942.' In the list of the bereaved, Lorene took precedence over David (now forty, a barrister and a drunk) and Caroline (now Mrs Beeston Bastable and mother of one daughter, also Caroline).

The funeral was not quite a state funeral, though Denyse tried to manage one; she wanted a flag on the coffin and she wanted soldiers, but it was not to be. However, many flags were at half-staff, and she did achieve a very fine turnout of important people, and others who were important because they represented somebody too important to come personally. It was agreed by everyone that Bishop Woodiwiss paid a noble tribute to Boy, whom he had known from youth, though it was a pity poor Woodiwiss mumbled so now.

The reception after the funeral was in the great tradition of such affairs, and the new house Denyse had made Boy build in the most desirable of the suburbs was filled even to its great capacity. Denyse was wonderfully self-possessed and ran everything perfectly. Or almost perfectly; there was one thing in which she did not succeed.

She approached me after she had finished receiving the mourners – if that is the right way to describe the group who were now getting down so merrily to the Scotch and rye – and, 'Of course you'll write the official life,' said she.

'What official life?' I asked, startled and clumsy.

'What official life do you suppose?' she said, giving me a look that told me very plainly to brace up and not be a fool.

'Oh, is there to be one?' I asked. I was not trying to be troublesome; I was genuinely unnerved, and with good cause.

'Yes, there is to be one,' she said, and icicles hung from every word. 'As you knew Boy from childhood, there will be a good deal for you to fill in before we come to the part where I can direct you.'

'But how is it official?' I asked, wallowing in wonderment. 'I mean, what makes it official? Does the government want it or something?'

'The government has had no time to think about it,' she said, 'but I want it, and I shall do whatever needs to be done about the government. What I want to know now is whether you are going to write it or not.' She spoke like a mother who is saying 'Are you going to do what I tell you or not?' to a bad child. It was not so much an inquiry as a flick of the whip.

'Well, I'll want to think it over,' I said.

'Do that. Frankly, my first choice was Eric Roop – I thought it wanted a poet's touch – but he can't do it, though considering how many grants Boy wangled for him I don't know why. But Boy did even more for you. You'll find it a change from those saints you're so fond of.' She left me angrily.

Of course I did not write it. The heart attack I had a few days later gave me an excellent excuse for keeping free of anything I didn't want to do. And how could I have written a life of Boy that would have satisfied me and yet saved me from murder at the hands of Denyse? And how could I, trained as a historian to suppress nothing, and with the Bollandist tradition of looking firmly at the shadow as well as the light, have written a life of Boy without telling all that I have told you, Headmaster, and all I know about the way he died? And even then, would it have been the truth? I learned something about the variability of truth as quite rational people see it from Boy himself, within an hour of his death.

You will not see this memoir until after my own death, and you will surely keep what you know to yourself. After all, you cannot prove anything against anyone. Nor was Boy's manner of death really surprising to anyone who knows what you now know about his life.

It was like this.

7

Magnus Eisengrim did not bring his famous display of illusions to Canada until 1968. His fame was now so great that he had once had his picture on the cover of *Time* as the greatest magician in history. The *Autobiography* sold quite well here, though nobody knew that its subject (or its author) was a native. It was at the end of October he came to Toronto for two weeks.

Naturally I saw a good deal of him and his company. The beautiful Faustina had been replaced by another girl, no less beautiful, who bore the same name. Liesl, now in early middle age and possessed of a simian distinction of appearance, was as near to me as before, and I spent all the time I could spare with her. She and Blazon were the only people I have ever met with whom one resumed a conversation exactly where it had been discontinued, whether yesterday or six years earlier. It was through her intercession – perhaps it would be more truthful to call it a command – that I was able to get Eisengrim to come to the school on the Sunday night in the middle of his fortnight's engagement, to talk to the boarders about hypnotism; schoolmasters are without conscience in exacting such favours.

He was a huge success, of course, for though he had not wanted to come he was not a man to scamp anything he had undertaken. He paid the boys the compliment of treating them seriously, explaining what hypnotism really was and what its limitations were. He emphasized the fact that nobody can be made to do anything under hypnotism that is contrary to his wishes, though of course people have wishes that they are unwilling to acknowledge, even to themselves. I remember that this concept gave trouble to several of the boys, and Eisengrim explained it in terms, and with a clarity, that suggested to me that he was a much better-informed man than I had supposed. The idea of the hypnotist as an all-powerful demon, like Svengali, who could make anybody do anything, he pooh-poohed; but he did tell some amusing stories about odd and embarrassing facets of people's personalities that had made their appearance under hypnotism.

Of course the boys clamoured for a demonstration, but he refused to break his rule of never hypnotizing anyone under twenty-one without written consent from their parents. (He did not add that young people and children are difficult hypnotic subjects because of the variability of their power of concentration.) However, he did hypnotize me, and made me do enough strange things to delight the boys without robbing me of my professional dignity. He made me compose an extemporary poem, which is something I had never done before in my life, but apparently it was not bad.

His talk lasted for about an hour, and as we were walking down the main corridor of the classroom building Boy Staunton came out of the side door of your study, Headmaster. I introduced them, and Boy was delighted.

'I saw your show last Thursday,' he said. 'It was my stepdaughter's birthday, and we were celebrating. As a matter of fact, you gave her a box of sweets.'

'I remember perfectly,' said Eisengrim. 'Your party was sitting in C21-25. Your stepdaughter wears strong spectacles and has a characteristic laugh.'

'Yes, poor Lorene. I'm afraid she became a bit hysterical; we had to leave after you sawed a man in two. But, may I ask you a very special favour? – how did your Brazen Head know what was implied in the message it gave to Ruth Tillman? That has caused some extraordinary gossip.'

'No, Mr Staunton, I cannot tell you that. But perhaps you will tell me how you know what was said to Mrs Tillman, who sat in F32 on Friday night, if your party came to the theatre on Thursday?'

'Mightn't I have heard it from friends?'

'You might, but you did not. You came back to see my exhibition on Friday night because you had missed some of it by reason of your daughter's over-excitement. I can only assume my exhibition offered something you wanted. A great compliment. I appreciated it, I assure you. Indeed, I appreciated it so much that the Head decided not to name you and tell the audience that your appointment as Lieutenant-Governor would be announced on Monday. I am sure you understand how much renunciation there is in refusing such a scoop. It would have brought me wonderful publicity, but it would have embarrassed you, and the Head and I decided not to do that.'

'But you can't possibly have known! I hadn't had the letter myself more than a couple of hours before going to the theatre. I had it with me as a matter of fact.'

'Very true, and you have it now; inside right-hand breast pocket. Don't worry, I haven't picked your pocket. But when you lean forward, however slightly, the tip of a long envelope made of thick creamy paper can just be seen; only governments use such ostentatious envelopes, and when a man so elegantly dressed as you are bulges his jacket with one of them, it is probably – you see? There is an elementary lesson in magic for you. Work on it for twenty years and you may comprehend the Brazen Head.'

This took Boy down a peg; the good-humoured, youthful chuckle he gave was his first step to get himself on top of the conversation again. 'As a matter of fact,' he said, 'I've just been showing it to the Headmaster; because, of course, I'll have to resign as Chairman of the Board of Governors. And I was just coming to talk to you about it, Dunny.'

'Come along then,' I said. 'We were going to have a drink.'

I was conscious already that Boy was up to one of his special displays of charm. He had put his foot wrong with Eisengrim by asking him to reveal the secret of an illusion; it was unlike him to be so gauche, but I suppose the excitement about his new appointment blew up his ego a little beyond what he could manage. It seemed to me that I could already see the plumed, cocked hat of a Lieutenant-Governor on his head.

Eisengrim had been sharp enough with him to arouse hostility, and Boy loved to defeat hostility by turning the other cheek – which is by no means a purely Christian ploy, as Boy had shown me countless times. Eisengrim further topped him by the little bit of observation about the letter, which had made Boy look like a child who is so besotted by a new toy that it cannot let the toy out of its grasp. Boy wanted a chance to right the balance, which of course meant making him master of the situation.

It was clear to me that one of those sympathies, or antipathies, or at any rate unusual states of feeling, had arisen between these two which sometimes lead to falling in love, or to sudden warm friendships, or to lasting and rancorous enmities, but which are always extraordinary. I wanted to see what would happen, and my appetite was given the special zest of knowing who Eisengrim really was, which Boy did not, and perhaps would never learn.

It was like Boy to seek to ingratiate himself with the new friend by treating the old friend with genial contempt. When the three of us had made our way to my room at the end of the top-floor corridor – my old room, which I have always refused to leave for more comfortable quarters in the newer buildings – he kicked the door open and entered first, turning on the lights and touring the room as he said, 'Still the same old rat's nest. What are you going to do when you have to move? How will you ever find room anywhere else for all this junk? Look at those books! I'll bet you don't use some of them once a year.'

It was true that several of the big volumes were spread about, and I had to take some of them out of an armchair for Eisengrim, so I was a little humbled.

But Eisengrim spoke. 'I like it very much,' said he. 'I so seldom get to my home, and I have to live in hotel rooms for weeks and months on end. Next spring I go on a world tour; that will mean something like five years of hotels. This room speaks of peace and a mind at work. I wish it were mine.'

'I wouldn't say old Dunny's mind was at work,' said Boy. 'I wish all I had to do was teach the same lessons every year for forty years.'

'You are forgetting his many and excellent books, are you not?' said Eisengrim.

Boy understood that he was not going to get what he wanted, which cannot have been anything more than a complicity with an interesting stranger, by running me down, so he took another tack. 'You mustn't misunderstand if I am disrespectful towards the great scholar. We're very old friends. We come from the same little village. In fact I think we might say that all the brains of Deptford – past, present, and doubtless to come – are in this room right now.'

For the first time in Boy's company, Eisengrim laughed. 'Might I be included in such a distinguished group?' he asked.

Boy was pleased to have gained a laugh. 'Sorry, birth in Deptford is an absolute requirement.'

'Oh, I have that already. It was about my achievements in the world that I had doubt.'

'I've looked through your *Autobiography* – Lorene asked me to buy a copy for her. I thought you were born somewhere in the far north of Sweden.'

'That was Magnus Eisengrim; my earlier self was born in Deptford. If the *Autobiography* seems to be a little high in colour you must blame Ramsay. He wrote it.'

'Dunny! You never told me that!'

'It never seemed relevant,' said I. I was amazed that Paul would tell him such a thing, but I could see that he, like Boy, was prepared to play some high cards in this game of topping each other.

'I don't remember anybody in the least like you in Deptford. What did you say your real name was?'

'My real name is Magnus Eisengrim; that is who I am and that is how the world knows me. But before I found out who I was, I was called Paul Dempster, and I remember you very well. I always thought of you as the Rich Young Ruler.'

'And are you and Dunny old friends?'

'Yes, very old friends. He was my first teacher of magic. He also taught me a little about saints, but it was the magic that lingered. His speciality as a conjurer was eggs – the Swami of the Omelette. He was my only teacher till I ran away with a circus.'

'Did you? You know I wanted to do that. I suppose it is part of every boy's dream.'

'Then boys are lucky that it remains a dream. I should not have said a circus; it was a very humble carnival show. I was entranced by Willard the Wizard; he was so much more skilful than Ramsay. He was quite clever with cards and a very neat pickpocket. I begged him to take me, and was such an ignorant little boy – perhaps I might even call myself innocent, though it is a word I don't like – that I was in ecstasy when he consented. But I soon found out that Willard had two weaknesses – boys and morphia. The morphia had already made him careless or he would never have run the terrible risk of stealing a boy. But when I had well and truly found out what travelling with Willard meant, he had me in slavery; he told me that if anybody ever found out what we did together I would certainly be hanged, but he would get off because he knew all the judges everywhere. So I was chained to Willard by fear; I was his thing and his creature, and I learned conjuring as a reward. One always learns one's mystery at the price of one's innocence, though my case was spectacular. But the astonishing thing is that I grew to like Willard, especially as morphia incapacitated him for his hobby and ruined him as a conjurer. It was then he became a Wild Man.'

'Then he was *Le Solitaire des forêts*?' I asked.

'That was even later. His first decline was from conjurer to Wild Man – essentially a geek.'

'Geek?' said Boy.

'That is what carnival people call them. They are not an advertised attraction, but word that a geek is in a back tent is passed around quietly, and money is taken without any sale of tickets. Otherwise the Humane Societies make themselves a nuisance. The geek is represented as somebody who simply has to have raw flesh, and especially blood. After the spieler has lectured terrifyingly on the psychology and physiology of the geek, the geek is given a live chicken; he growls and rolls his eyes, then he gnaws through its neck until the head is off, and he drinks the spouting blood. Not a nice life, and very hard on the teeth, but if it is the only way to keep yourself in morphia, you'd rather geek than have the horrors. But geeking costs money; you need a live chicken every time, and even the oldest, toughest birds cost something. Before Willard got too sick even to geek, he was geeking with worms and gartersnakes when I could catch them for him. The rubes loved it; Willard was something even the most disgusting brute could despise.

'There was trouble with the police, at last, and I thought we would do better abroad. We had been over there quite a time, Ramsay, before you you I met in the Tyrol, and by then Willard was in very poor health, and *Le Solitaire des forêts* was all he could manage. I doubt if he even knew where he was. So that is what running away with a circus was like, Mr Staunton.'

'Why didn't you leave him when he was down to geeking?'

'Shall I answer you honestly? Very well, then; it was loyalty. Yes, loyalty to Willard, though not to his geeking or his nasty ways with boys. I suppose it was loyalty to his dreadful, inescapable human need. Many people feel these irrational responsibilities and cannot crush them. Like Ramsay's loyalty to my mother, for instance. I am sure it was an impediment to him, and certainly it must have been a heavy expense, but he did not fail her. I suppose he loved her. I might have done so if I had ever known her. But, you see, the person I knew was a woman unlike anybody else's mother, who was called "hoor" by people like you, Mr Staunton.'

'I really don't remember,' said Boy. 'Are you sure?'

'Quite sure. I have never been able to forget what she was or what people called her. Because, you see, it was my birth that made her like that. My father thought it his duty to tell me, so that I could do whatever was possible to make it up to her. My birth was what robbed her of her sanity; that sometimes happened, you know, and I suppose it happens still. I was too young for the kind of guilt my father wanted me to feel; he had an extraordinary belief in guilt as an educative force. I couldn't stand it. I cannot feel guilt now. But I can call up in an instant what it felt like to be the child of a woman everybody jeered at and thought a dirty joke – including you, the Rich Young Ruler. But I am sure your accent is much more elegant now. A Lieutenant-Governor who said "hoor" would not reflect credit on the Crown, would he?'

Boy had plenty of experience in being baited by hostile people, and he did not show by a quiver how strange this was to him. He prepared to get the attack into his own hands.

'I forget what you said your name was.'

Eisengrim continued to smile, so I said, 'He's Paul Dempster.'

This time it was my turn for surprise. 'Who may Paul Dempster be?' asked Boy.

'Do you mean to say you don't remember the Dempsters? In Deptford? The Reverend Amasa Dempster?'

'No. I don't remember what is of no use to me, and I haven't been in Deptford since my father died. That's twenty-six years.'

'You have no recollection of Mrs Dempster?'

'None at all. Why should I?'

I could hardly believe he spoke the truth, but as we talked on I had to accept it as a fact that he had so far edited his memory of his early days that the incident of the snowball had quite vanished from his mind. But had not Paul edited his memories so that only pain and cruelty remained? I began to wonder what I had erased from my own recollection.

We had drinks and were sitting as much at ease as men can amid so many strong currents of feeling. Boy made another attempt to turn the conversation into a realm where he could dominate.

'How did you come to choose your professional name? I know magicians like to have extraordinary names, but yours sounds a little alarming. Don't you find that a disadvantage?'

'No. And I did not choose it. My patron gave it to me.' He turned his head towards me, and I knew that the patron was Liesl. 'It comes from one of the great northern beast fables, and it means Wolf. Far from being a disadvantage, people like it. People like to be in awe of something, you know. And my magic show is not ordinary. It provokes awe, which is why it is a success. It has something of the quality of Ramsay's saints, though my miracles have a spice of the Devil about them – again my patron's idea. That is where you make your mistake. You have always wanted to be loved; nobody responds quite as we would wish, and people are suspicious of a public figure who wants to be loved. I have been wiser than you. I chose a Wolf's name. You have chosen forever to be a Boy. Was it because your mother used to call you Pidgy Boy-Boy, even when you were old enough to call my mother "hoor"?'

'How in God's name did you know that? Nobody in the world now living knows that!'

'Oh yes, two people know it – myself and Ramsay. He told me, many years ago, under an oath of secrecy.'

'I never did any such thing!' I shouted, outraged. Yet, even as I shouted, a doubt assailed me.

'But you did, or how would I know? You told me that to comfort me once, when the Rich Young Ruler and some of his gang had been shouting at my mother. We all forget many of the things we do, especially when they do not fit into the character we have chosen for ourselves. You see yourself as the man of many confidences, Ramsay. It would not do for you to remember a time when you told a secret. Dunstan Ramsay – when did you cease to be Dunstable?'

'A girl renamed me when I had at last broken with my mother. Liesl said it made me one of the twice-born. Had you thought that we are all three of the company of the twice-born? We have all rejected our beginnings and become something our parents could not have foreseen.'

'I can't imagine your parents foreseeing that you would become a theorizer about myth and legend,' said Eisengrim. 'Hard people – I remember them clearly. Hard people – especially your mother.'

'Wrong,' said I. And I told him how my mother had worked and schemed and devised a nest to keep him alive, and exulted when he decided to live. 'She said you were a fighter, and she liked that.'

Now it was his turn to be disconcerted. 'Do you mind if I have one of your cigars?' he said.

266

I do not smoke cigars, but the box he took from a shelf on the other side of the room might easily be mistaken for a humidor – rather a fine one. But as he took it down and rather superciliously blew dust from it his face changed.

He brought it over and laid it on the low table around which our chairs were grouped. 'What's this?' he asked.

'It is what it says it is,' said I.

The engraving on the silver plaque on the lid of the box was beautiful and clear, for I had chosen the script with care:

> *Requiescat in pace*
> MARY DEMPSTER
> 1888–1959
> Here is the patience
> and faith of the saints.

We looked at it for some time. Boy was first to speak.

'Why would you keep a thing like that with you?'

'A form of piety. A sense of guilt unexpiated. Indolence. I have always been meaning to put them in some proper place, but I haven't found it yet.'

'Guilt?' said Eisengrim.

Here it was. Either I spoke now or I kept silence forever. Dunstan Ramsay counselled against revelation, but Fifth Business would not hear.

'Yes, guilt. Staunton and I robbed your mother of her sanity.' And I told them the story of the snowball.

'Too bad,' said Boy. 'But if I may say so, Dunny, I think you've let the thing build up into something it never was. You unmarried men are terrible fretters. I threw the snowball – at least you say so, and for argument's sake let that go – and you dodged it. It precipitated something which was probably going to happen anyhow. The difference between us is that you've brooded over it and I've forgotten it. We've both done far more important things since. I'm sorry if I was offensive to your mother, Dempster. But you know what boys are. Brutes, because they don't know any better. But they grow up to be men.'

'Very important men. Men whom the Crown delighteth to honour,' said Eisengrim with an unpleasant laugh.

'Yes. If you expect me to be diffident about that, you're wrong.'

'Men who retain something of the brutish boy, even,' said I.
'I don't think I understand you.'

Fifth Business insisted on being heard again. 'Would this jog your memory?' I asked, handing him my old paperweight.

'Why should it? An ordinary bit of stone. You've used it to hold down some of the stuff on your desk for years. I've seen it a hundred times. It doesn't remind me of anything but you.'

'It is the stone you put in the snowball you threw at Mrs Dempster,' I said. 'I've kept it because I couldn't part with it. I swear I never meant to tell you what it was. But, Boy, for God's sake, get to know something about yourself. The stone-in-the-snowball has been characteristic of too much you've done for you to forget it forever!'

'What I've done! Listen, Dunny, one thing I've done is to make you pretty well-off for a man in your position. I've treated you like a brother. Given you tips nobody else got, let me tell you. And that's where your nice little nest-egg came from. Your retirement fund you used to whine about.'

I hadn't thought I whined, but perhaps I did. 'Need we go on with this moral bookkeeping?' I said. 'I'm simply trying to recover something of the totality of your life. Don't you want to possess it as a whole – the bad with the good? I told you once you'd made a God of yourself, and the insufficiency of it forced you to become an atheist. It's time you tried to be a human being. Then maybe something bigger than yourself will come up on your horizon.'

You're trying to get me. You want to humiliate me in front of this man here; you seem to have been in cahoots with him for years, though you never mentioned him or his miserable mother to me – your best friend, and your patron and protector against your own incompetence! Well, let him hear this, as we're dealing in ugly truths: you've always hated me because I took Leola from you. And I did! It wasn't because you lost a leg and were ugly. It was because she loved me better.'

This got me on the raw, and Dunstable Ramsay's old inability to resist a cruel speech when one occurred to him came uppermost. 'My observation has been that we get the women we deserve, King Candaules,' I said, 'and those who eat jam before breakfast are cloyed before bedtime.'

'Gentlemen,' said Eisengrim, 'deeply interesting though this is, Sunday nights are the only nights when I can get to bed before midnight. So I shall leave you.'

Boy was all courtesy at once. 'I'm going too. Let me give you a lift,' said he. Of course; he wanted to blackguard me to Eisengrim in the car.

'Thank you, Mr Staunton,' said Eisengrim. 'What Ramsay has told us puts you in my debt – for eighty days in Paradise, if for nothing in this life. We shall call it quits if you will drive me to my hotel.'

I lifted the casket that contained Mary Dempster's ashes. 'Do you want to take this with you, Paul?'

'No thanks, Ramsay. I have everything I need.'

It seemed an odd remark, but in the emotional stress of the situation I paid no heed to it. Indeed, it was not until after the news of Boy's death reached me next morning that I noticed my paperweight was gone.

8

Because of the way he died, the consequent police investigations, and the delays brought about by Denyse s determination to make the most of the nearly official funeral, Boy was not buried until Thursday. The Saturday evening following I went to see Eisengrim's *Soirée of Illusions*, as he now called it, at its last performance, and though I spent much of the evening behind the scenes with Liesl, I went into the front of the house during *The Brazen Head of Friar Bacon*. Or rather, I hid myself behind the curtains of an upper box so that I could look down into the auditorium of our beautiful old Royal Alexandra Theatre and watch the audience.

Everything went smoothly during the collecting and restoration of borrowed objects, and the faces I saw below me were the usual studies in pleasure, astonishment, and – always the most interesting – the eagerness to be deceived mingled with resentment of deception. But when the Head was about to utter its three messages to people in the audience and Eisengrim had said what was to come, somebody in the top balcony shouted out, 'Who killed Boy Staunton?'

There was murmuring in the audience and a hiss or two, but silence fell as the Head glowed from within, its lips parted, and its voice – Liesl's voice, slightly foreign and impossible to identify as man's or woman's – spoke.

'He was killed by the usual cabal: by himself, first of all; by the woman he knew; by the woman he did not know; by the man who granted his inmost wish; and by the inevitable fifth, who was keeper of his conscience and keeper of the stone.'

I believe there was an uproar. Certainly Denyse made a great to-do when she heard of it. Of course she thought 'the woman he knew' must be herself. The police were hounded by her and some of her influential friends, but that was after Eisengrim and his *Soirée of Illusions* had removed by air to Copenhagen, and the police had to make it clear that they really could not investigate impalpable offences, however annoying they might be. But I knew nothing about it, because it was there, in that box, that I had my seizure and was rushed to the hospital, as I was afterward told, by a foreign lady.

When I was well enough to read letters I found one – a post-card, to my horror – that read:

Deeply sorry about your illness which was my fault as much as most such things are anybody's fault. But I could not resist my temptation as I beg you not to resist this one: come to Switzerland and join the Basso and the Brazen Head. We shall have some high old times before The Five make an end of us all.

Love,
L.V.

And that, Headmaster, is all I have to tell you.

Sankt Gallen
1970

270

THE MANTICORE

Contents

1

Why I Went to Zürich

I

WHEN did you decide you should come to Zürich, Mr Staunton?

'When I heard myself shouting in the theatre.'

'You decided at that moment?'

'I think so. Of course I put myself through the usual examination afterward to be quite sure. But I could say that the decision was made as soon as I heard my own voice shouting.'

'The usual examination? Could you tell me a little more about that, please.'

'Certainly. I mean the sort of examination one always makes to determine the nature of anyone's conduct, his degree of responsibility, and all that. It was perfectly clear. I was no longer in command of my actions. Something had to be done, and I must do it before others had to do it on my behalf.'

'Please tell me again about this incident when you shouted. With a little more detail, please.'

'It was the day before yesterday, that is to say November ninth, at about ten forty five p.m. in the Royal Alexandra Theatre in Toronto, which is my home. I was sitting in a bad seat in the top gallery. That in itself was unusual. The performance was something rather grandiosely called *The Soirée of Illusions* – a magic show, given by a conjuror called Magnus Eisengrim. He is well known, I understand, to people who like that kind of thing. He had an act which he called *The Brazen Head of Friar Bacon*. A large head that looked like brass, but was made of some almost transparent material, seemed to float in the middle of the stage; you couldn't see how it was done – wires of some sort, I suppose. The Head gave what purported to be advice to people in the audience. That was what infuriated me. It was imprudent, silly stuff hinting at scandal – adulteries, little bits of gossip, silly, spicy rubbish – and I felt irritation growing in me that people should be concerned about such trash. It was an unwarranted invasion of privacy, you understand, by this conjuror fellow whose confident assumption of superiority – just a charlatan, you know, seeming to patronize serious people! I knew I was fidgeting in my seat, but it wasn't until I heard my own voice that I realized I was standing up, shouting at the stage.'

'And you shouted –?'

'Well, what would you expect me to shout? I shouted, as loud as I could – and that's very loud, because I have some experience of shouting – I shouted, "Who killed Boy Staunton?" And then all hell broke loose!'

'There was a furore in the theatre?'

'Yes. A man standing in a box gave a cry and fell down. A lot of people were murmuring and some stood up to see who had shouted. But they quieted down immediately the Brazen Head began to speak.'

'What did it say?'

'There are several opinions. The broadcast news reported that the Head suggested he had been killed by a gang. All I heard was something about "the woman he knew – the woman he did not know," which, of course, could only mean my stepmother. But I was getting away as fast as I could. It is a very steep climb up to the doors in that balcony, and I was in a state of excitement and shame at what I had done, so I didn't really hear well. I wanted to get out before I was recognized.'

'Because you are Boy Staunton?'

'No, no, no; Boy Staunton was my father.'

'And was he killed?'

'Of course he was killed! Didn't you read about it? It wasn't just some local murder where a miser in a slum is killed for a few hundred dollars. My father was a very important man. It's no exaggeration to say it was international news.'

'I see. I am very sorry not to have known. Now, shall we go over some of your story again?'

And we did. It was long, and often painful for me, but he was an intelligent examiner, and at times I was conscious of being an unsatisfactory witness, assuming he knew things I hadn't told him, or that he couldn't know. I was ashamed of saying 'of course' so often, as if I were offering direct evidence instead of stuff that was at best presumptive – something I would never tolerate in a witness myself. I was embarrassed to be such a fool in a situation that I had told myself and other people countless times I would never submit to – talking to a psychiatrist, ostensibly seeking help, but without any confidence that he could give it. I have never believed these people can do anything for an intelligent man he can't do for himself. I have known many people who leaned on psychiatrists, and every one of them was a leaner by nature, who would have leaned on a priest if he had lived in an age of faith, or leaned on a teacup-reader or an astrologer if he had not had enough money to afford the higher hokum. But here I was, and there was nothing to do now but go through with it.

It had its amusing side. I had not known what to expect, but I rather thought I would be put on a couch and asked about sex, which would have been a waste of time, as I have no sex to tell about. But here, in the office of the Director of the Jung Institute, 27 Gemeindestrasse, Zürich, there was no couch – nothing but a desk and two chairs and a lamp or two and some pictures of a generally Oriental appearance. And Dr Tschudi. And Dr Tschudi's big Alsatian, whose stare of polite, watchful curiosity was uncannily like the doctor's own.

'Your bodyguard?' I had said when I entered the room.

'Ha ha,' laughed Dr Tschudi in a manner I came to be

277

well acquainted with in Switzerland; it is the manner which acknowledges politely that a joke has been made, without in any way encouraging further jokiness. But I received the impression – I am rather good at receiving impressions – that the doctor met some queer customers in that very Swiss little room, and the dog might be useful as more than a companion.

The atmosphere of the whole Jung Institute, so far as I saw it, puzzled me. It was one of those tall Zürich houses with a look that is neither domestic nor professional, but has a smack of both. I had had to ring the bell several times to be admitted through the door, the leaded glass of which made it impossible to see if anyone was coming; the secretary who let me in looked like a doctor herself, and had no eager public-relations grin; to reach Dr Tschudi I had to climb a tall flight of stairs, which echoed and suggested my sister's old school. I was not prepared for any of this; I think I expected something that would combine the feeling of a clinic with the spookiness of a madhouse in a bad film. But this was – well, it was Swiss. Very Swiss, for though there was nothing of the cuckoo-clock, or the bank, or milk chocolate about it, it had a sort of domesticity shorn of coziness, a matter-of-factness within which one could not be quite sure of its facts, that put me at a disadvantage. And though when visiting a psychiatrist I had expected to lose something of my professional privilege of always being at an advantage, I could not be expected to like it when I encountered it.

I was an hour with the Director, and a few important things emerged. First, that he thought I might benefit by some exploratory sessions with an analyst. Second, that the analyst would not be himself, but someone he would recommend who was free to accept another patient at this time and to whom he would send a report; third, that before that I must undergo a thorough physical examination to make sure that analysis, rather than some physical treatment, was appropriate for me. Dr Tschudi rose and shook me by the hand. I offered also to shake the paw of the Alsatian, but it scorned my jocosity, and the Director's smile was wintry.

I found myself once again in Gemeindestrasse, feeling a fool. Next morning, at my hotel, I received a note giving directions as to where my medical examination would take place. I was also instructed to call at ten o'clock in the morning, three days hence, on Dr J. von Haller, who would be expecting me.

2

The clinic was thorough beyond anything I had ever experienced. As well as the familiar humiliations – hanging about half-naked in the company of half-naked strangers, urinating in bottles and handing them warm and steamy to very young nurses, coughing at the behest of a physician who was prodding at the back of my scrotum, answering intimate questions while the same physician thrust a long finger up my rectum and tried to catch my prostate in some irregularity, trudging up and down a set of steps while the physician counted; gasping, puffing, gagging, sticking out my tongue, rolling my eyes, and doing all the other silly tricks which reveal so much to the doctor while making the patient feel a fool – I underwent a few things that were new to me. Quite a lot of blood was taken from me at various points – much more than the usual tiny bit removed from the ear lobe. I drank a glass of a chocolate-flavoured mixture and was then, every hour for six hours, stood on my head on a movable X-ray table to which I had been strapped, as pictures were taken to see how the mess was getting through my tripes. A variety of wires was attached to me whose purpose I could only guess, but as my chair was whirled and tilted I suppose it had something to do with my nervous system, sense of balance, hearing, and all that. Countless questions, too, about how long my grandparents and parents had lived, and of what they had died. When I gave the cause of my father's death as 'Murder' the clinician blinked slightly, and I was glad to have disturbed his Swiss phlegm, even for an instant. I had not been feeling well when I came to Zürich, and after two days of medical rough-house I was tired and dispirited and in a mood to go – not home, most certainly not – somewhere else. But I thought I ought to see Dr J. von Haller at least once, if only for the pleasure of a good row with him.

Why was I so hostile toward a course of action I had undertaken of my own will? There was no single answer to that. As I told the Director, I made the decision on a basis of reason, and I would stick with it. Netty had always told me that when something unpleasant must be done – medicine taken, an apology made for bad behaviour, owning up to something that would bring a beating from my father – I had to be 'a little soldier.' Little soldiers, I understood, never hesitated; they did what was right without question. So I must be a little soldier and visit Dr J. von Haller at least once.

Ah, but did little soldiers ever have to go to the psychiatrist? They visited the dentist often, and many a time I had shouldered my little invisible musket and marched off in that direction. Was this so very different? Yes, it was.

I could understand the use of a dentist. He could grind and dig and refill, and now and then he could yank. But what could psychiatrists do? Those I had seen in court contradicted each other, threw up clouds of dust, talked a jargon which, in cross-examination, I could usually discredit. I never used them as witnesses if I could avoid it. Still, there was a widespread belief in their usefulness in cases like mine. I had to do whatever seemed best, whether I personally approved or not. To stay in Toronto and go mad simply would not do.

Why had I come to Zürich? The Director accepted it as perfectly in order for me to do so, but what did he know about my situation? Nothing would have got me to a psychiatrist in Toronto; such treatment is always supposed to be confidential, but everybody seems to know who is going regularly to certain doctors, and everybody is ready to give

a guess at the reason. It is generally assumed to be homosexuality. I could have gone to New York, but everyone who
did so seemed to be with a Freudian, and I was not impressed
by what happened to them. Of course, it need not have been
the Freudians' fault, for as I said, these people were leaners,
and I don't suppose Freud himself could have done much
with them. Nothing will make an empty bag stand up, as
my grandfather often said. Of the Jungians I knew nothing,
except that the Freudians disliked them, and one of my
acquaintances who was in a Freudian analysis had once said
something snide about people who went to Zürich to –

> hear sermons
> From mystical Germans
> Who preach from ten till four.

But with a perversity that often overtakes me when I have
a personal decision to make, I had decided to give it a try.
The Jungians had two negative recommendations: the Freudians hated them, and Zürich was a long way from Toronto.

3

It was a sharp jolt to find that Dr J. von Haller was a
woman. I have nothing against women; it had simply never
occurred to me that I might talk about the very intimate
things that had brought me to Zürich with one of them.
During the physical examination two of the physicians I
encountered were women and I felt no qualm. They were
as welcome to peep into my inside as any man that ever
lived. My mind, however, was a different matter. Would a
woman – could a woman – understand what was wrong?
There used to be a widespread idea that women are very
sensitive. My experience of them as clients, witnesses, and
professional opponents had dispelled any illusions I might
have had of that kind. Some women are sensitive, doubtless,
but I have met with nothing to persuade me that they are,

on the whole, more likely to be sensitive than men. I thought I needed delicate handling. Was Dr J. von Haller up to the work? I had never heard of a woman psychiatrist except as someone dealing with children. My troubles were decidedly not those of a child.

Here I was, however, and there was she in a situation that seemed more social than professional. I was in what appeared to be her sitting-room, and the arrangement of chairs was so unprofessional that it was I who sat in the shadow, while the full light from the window fell on her face. There was no couch.

Dr von Haller looked younger than I; about thirty-eight, I judged, for though her expression was youthful there was a little gray in her hair. Fine face; rather big features but not coarse. Excellent nose, aquiline if one wished to be complimentary but verging on the hooky if not. Large mouth and nice teeth, white but not American-white. Beautiful eyes, brown to go with her hair. Pleasant, low voice and a not quite perfect command of colloquial English. Slight accent. Clothes unremarkable, neither fashionable nor dowdy, in the manner Caroline calls 'classic.' Altogether a person to inspire confidence. But then, so am I, and I know all the professional tricks of how that is done. Keep quiet and let the client do all the talking; don't make suggestions – let the client unburden himself; watch him for revealing fidgets. She was doing all these things, but so was I. The result was a very stilted conversation, for a while.

'And it was the murder of your father that decided you to come here for treatment?'

'Doesn't it seem enough?'

'The death of his father is always a critical moment in a man's life, but usually he has time to make psychological preparation for it. The father grows old, relinquishes his claims on life, is manifestly preparing for death. A violent death is certainly a severe shock. But then, you knew your father must die sometime, didn't you?'

'I suppose so. I don't remember ever thinking about it.'

'How old was he?'

Seventy.'

'Hardly a premature death. The psalmist's span.'

'But this was murder.'

'Who murdered him?'

'I don't know. Nobody knows. He was driven, or drove himself, off a dock in Toronto harbour. When his car was raised he was found clutching the steering-wheel so tightly that they had to pry his hands from it. His eyes were wide open, and there was a stone in his mouth.'

'A stone?'

'Yes. This stone.'

I held it out to her, lying on the silk handkerchief in which I carried it. Exhibit A in the case of the murder of Boy Staunton: a piece of Canadian pink granite about the size and shape of a hen's egg.

She examined it carefully. Then, slowly, she pushed it into her own mouth, and looked solemnly at me. Or was it solemnly? Was there a glint in her eye? I don't know. I was far too startled by what she had done to tell. Then she took it out, wiped it very carefully on her handkerchief, and gave it back.

'Yes; it could be done,' she said.

'You're a cool customer,' said I.

'Yes. This is a very cool profession, Mr Staunton. Tell me, did no one suggest that your father might have committed suicide?'

'Certainly not. Utterly unlike him. Anyhow, why does your mind turn immediately to that? I told you he was murdered.'

'But no evidence of murder was found.'

'How do you know?'

'I had Dr Tschudi's report about you, and I asked the librarian at our *Neue Zürcher Zeitung* to check their archive. They did report your father's death, you know; he had connections with several Swiss banks. The report was necessarily discreet and brief, but it seemed that suicide was the generally accepted explanation.'

'He was murdered.'

'Tschudi's report suggests you think your stepmother had something to do with it.'

'Yes, yes; but not directly. She destroyed him. She made him unhappy and unlike himself. I never suggested she drove him off the dock. She murdered him psychologically –'

'Really? I had the impression you didn't think much of psychology, Mr Staunton.'

'Psychology plays a great part in my profession. I am rather a well-known criminal lawyer – or have you checked that, too? I have to know something about the way people function. Without a pretty shrewd psychological sense I couldn't do what I do, which is to worm things out of people they don't want to tell. That's your job, too, isn't it?'

'No. My job is to listen to people say things they very badly want to tell but are afraid nobody else will understand. You use psychology as an offensive weapon in the interest of justice. I use it as a cure. So keen a lawyer as yourself will appreciate the difference. You have shown you do. You think your stepmother murdered your father psychologically, but you don't think that would be enough to drive him to suicide. Well – I have known of such things. But if she was not the real murderer, who do you think it might have been?'

'Whoever put the stone in his mouth.'

'Oh, come, Mr Staunton, nobody could put that stone in a man's mouth against his will without breaking his teeth and creating great evidence of violence. I have tried it. Have you? No, I thought you hadn't. Your father must have put it there himself.'

'Why?'

'Perhaps somebody told him to do it. Somebody he could not or did not wish to disobey.'

'Ridiculous. Nobody could make Father do anything he didn't want to do.'

'Perhaps he wanted to do this. Perhaps he wanted to die. People do, you know.'

'He loved life. He was the most vital person I have ever known.'

'Even after your stepmother had murdered him psychologically?'

I was losing ground. This was humiliating. I am a fine cross-examiner and yet here I was, caught off balance time and again by this woman doctor. Well, the remedy lay in my own hands.

'I don't think this line of discussion profitable, or likely to lead to anything that could help me,' I said. 'If you will be good enough to tell me your fee for the consultation, we shall close it now.'

'As you wish,' said Dr von Haller. 'But I should tell you that many people do not like the first consultation and want to run away. But they come back. You are a man of more than ordinary intelligence. Wouldn't it simplify things if you skipped the preliminary flight and continued? I am sure you are much too reasonable to have expected this kind of treatment to be painless. It is always difficult in the beginning for everyone, and especially people of your general type.'

'So you have typed me already?'

'I beg your pardon; it would be impertinent to pretend anything of the kind. I meant only that intelligent people of wealth, who are used to having their own way, are often hostile and prickly at the beginning of analytical treatment.'

'So you suggest that I bite the bullet and go on.'

'Go on, certainly. But let us have no bullet-biting. I think you have bitten too many bullets recently. Suppose we proceed a little more gently.'

'Do you consider it gentle to imply that my father killed himself when I tell you he was murdered?'

'I was telling you only what was most discreetly implied in the news report. I am sure you have heard the implication before. And I know how unwelcome such an implication usually is. But let us change our ground. Do you dream much?'

'Ah, so we have reached dreams already? No, I don't dream much. Or perhaps I should say that I don't pay much attention to the dreams I have.'

'Have you had any dreams lately? Since you decided to come to Zürich? Since you arrived?'

Should I tell her? Well, this was costing me money. I might as well have the full show, whatever it might be.

'Yes. I had a dream last night.'

'So?'

'Quite a vivid dream, for me. Usually my dreams are just scraps – fragmentary things that don't linger. This was of quite a different order.'

'Was it in colour?'

'Yes. As a matter of fact, it was full of colour.'

'And what was the general tone of the dream? I mean, did you enjoy it? Was it pleasant?'

'Pleasant. Yes, I would say it was pleasant.'

'Tell me what you dreamed.'

'I was in a building that was familiar, though it was nowhere known to me. But it was somehow associated with me, and I was somebody of importance there. Perhaps I should say I was surrounded by a building, because it was like a college – like some of the colleges at Oxford – and I was hurrying through the quadrangle because I was leaving by the back gate. As I went under the arch of the gate two men on duty there – porters, or policemen, functionaries and guardians of some kind – saluted me and smiled as if they knew me, and I waved to them. Then I was in a street. Not a Canadian street. Much more like a street in some pretty town in England or in Europe; you know, with trees on either side and very pleasant buildings like houses, though there seemed to be one or two shops, and a bus with people on it passed by me. But I was hurrying because I was going somewhere, and I turned quickly to the left and walked out into the country. I was on a road, with the town behind me, and I seemed to be walking beside a field in which I could see excavations going on, and I knew that some ruins were being turned up. I went through the field to the little makeshift hut that was the centre of the archaeological work – because I knew that was what it was – and went in the door. The hut was very different inside from what I had expected, because as I said it looked like a temporary shelter for tools and plans and things of that kind, but inside it was Gothic; the ceiling was low, but beautifully groined in stone, and the whole affair was a stone structure. There were a couple of young men in there, commonplace-looking fellows in their twenties, I would say, who were talking at the top of what I knew was a circular staircase that led down into the earth. I wanted to go down, and I asked these fellows to let me pass, but they wouldn't listen, and though they didn't speak to me and kept on talking to one another, I could tell that they thought I was simply a nosey intruder, and had no right to go down, and probably didn't want to go down in any serious way. So I left the hut, and walked to the road, and turned back towards the town, when I met a woman. She was a strange person, like a gypsy, but not a dressed-up showy gypsy; she wore old-fashioned, ragged clothes that seemed to have been faded by sun and rain, and she had on a wide-brimmed, battered black velvet hat with some gaudy feathers in it. She seemed to have something important to say to me, and kept pestering me, but I couldn't understand anything she said. She spoke in a foreign language; Romany, I presumed. She wasn't begging, but she wanted something, all the same. I thought, "Well, well; every country gets the foreigners it deserves" – which is a stupid remark, when you analyse it. But I had a sense that time was running short, so I hurried back to town, turned sharp to the right, this time, and almost ran into the college gate. One of the guardians called to me, "You can just make it, sir. You won't be fined this time." And next thing I knew I was sitting at the head of a table in my barrister's robes, presiding over a meeting. And that was it.'

'A very good dream. Perhaps you are a better dreamer than you think.'

'Are you going to tell me that it means something?'

'All dreams mean something.'

'For Joseph and Pharaoh, or Pilate's wife, perhaps. You will have to work very hard to convince me that they mean anything here and now.'

'I am sure I shall have to work hard. But just for the moment, tell me without thinking too carefully about it if you recognized any of the people in your dream.'

'Nobody.'

'Do you think they might be people you have not yet seen? Or had not seen yesterday?'

'Doctor von Haller, you are the only person I have seen whom I did not know yesterday.'

'I thought that might be so. Could I have been anybody in your dream?'

'You are going too fast for me. Are you suggesting that I could have dreamed of you before I knew you?'

'That would certainly seem absurd, wouldn't it? Still – I asked if I could have been anybody in your dream?'

'There was nobody in the dream who could possibly have been you. Unless you are hinting that you were the incomprehensible gypsy. And you won't get me to swallow that.'

'I am sure nobody could get a very able lawyer like you to swallow anything that was ridiculous, Mr Staunton. But it is odd, don't you think, that you should dream of meeting a female figure of a sort quite outside your experience, who was trying to tell you something important that you couldn't understand, and didn't want to understand, because you were so eager to get back to your enclosed, pleasant surroundings, and your barrister's robes, and presiding over something?'

'Doctor von Haller, I have no wish to be rude, but I think you are spinning an ingenious interpretation out of nothing. You must know that until I came here today I had no idea that J. von Haller was a woman. So even if I had dreamed of coming to an analyst in this very fanciful way, I couldn't have got that fact right, could I?'

'It is not a fact, except insofar as all coincidences are facts. You met a woman in your dream, and I am a woman. But not necessarily that woman. I assure you it is nothing uncommon for a new patient to have an important and revealing dream before treatment begins – before he has met his doctor. We always ask, just in case. But an anticipatory dream containing an unknown fact is a rarity. Still, we need not pursue it now. There will be time for that later.'

'Will there be any later? If I understand the dream, I cannot make head or tail of the gypsy woman with the incomprehensible conversation, and go back to my familiar world. What do you deduce from that?'

'Dreams do not foretell the future. They reveal states of mind in which the future may be implicit. Your state of mind at present is very much that of a man who wants no conversation with incomprehensible women. But your state of mind may change. Don't you think so?'

'I really don't know. Frankly, it seems to me that this meeting has been a dogfight, a grappling for advantage. Would the treatment go on like this?'

'For a time, perhaps. But it could not achieve anything on that level. Now – our hour is nearly over, so I must cut some corners and speak frankly. If I am to help you, you will have to speak to me from your best self, honestly and with trust ; if you continue to speak always from your inferior, suspicious self, trying to catch me out in some charlatanism, I shall not be able to do anything for you, and in a few sessions you will break off your treatment. Perhaps that is what you want to do now. We have one minute, Mr Staunton. Shall I see you at our next appointment, or not? Please do not think I shall be offended if you decide not to continue, for there are many patients who wish to see me, and if you knew them they would assure you that I am no charlatan, but a serious experienced doctor. Which is it to be?'

I have always hated being put on the spot. I was very angry. But as I reached for my hat, I saw that my hand was shaking, and she saw it, too. Something had to be done about that tremor.

'I shall come at the appointed time,' I said.

'Good. Five minutes before your hour, if you please. I keep a very close schedule.'

And there I was, out in the street, furious with myself, and Dr von Haller. But in a quiet corner of my mind I was not displeased that I should be seeing her again.

4

Two days passed before my next appointment, during which I changed my mind several times, but when the hour came, I was there. I had chewed over everything that had been said and had thought of a number of good things that I would have said myself if I had thought of them at the proper time. The fact that the doctor was a woman had put me out more than I cared to admit. I have my own reasons for not liking to be instructed by a woman, and by no means all of them are associated with that intolerable old afreet Netty Quelch, who has ridden me with whip and spur for as long as I can remember. Nor did I like the dream-interpretation game, which contradicted every rule of evidence known to me ; the discovery of truth is one of the principal functions of the law, to which I have given the best that is in me ; is truth to be found in the vapours of dreams? Nor had I liked the doctor's brusque manner of telling me to make up my mind, not to waste her time, and to be punctual. I had been made to feel like a stupid witness, which is as ridiculous an estimate of my character as anybody could contrive. But I would not retreat before Dr Johanna von Haller without at least one return engagement, and perhaps more than that.

A directory had told me her name was Johanna. Beyond that, and that she was a Prof. Dr med. und spezialarzt für Psychiatrie, I could find out nothing about her.

Ah well, there was the tremor of my hand. No sense in making a lot of that. Nerves, and no wonder. But was it not because of my nerves I had come to Zürich?

This time we did not meet in the sitting-room but in Dr von Haller's study, which was rather dark and filled with books, and a few pieces of modern statuary that looked pretty good, though I could not examine them closely. Also, there was a piece of old stained glass suspended in the window, which was fine in itself, but displeased me because it seemed affected. Prominent on the desk was a signed photograph of Dr Jung himself. Dr von Haller did not sit behind the desk, but in a chair near my own; I knew this trick, which is supposed to inspire confidence because it sets aside the natural barrier – the desk of the professional person. I had my eye on the doctor this time, and did not mean to let her get away with anything.

She was all smiles.

'No dogfight this time, I hope, Mr Staunton?'

'I hope not. But it is entirely up to you.'

'Entirely? Very well. Before we go further, the report has come from the clinic. You seem to be in depleted general health and a little – nervous, shall we say? What used to be called neurasthenic. And some neuritic pain. Rather underweight. Occasional marked tremor of the hands.'

'Recently, yes. I have been under great stress.'

'Never before?'

'Now and then, when my professional work was heavy.'

'How much have you had to drink this morning?'

'A good sharp snort for breakfast, and another before coming here.'

'Is that usual?'

'It is what I usually take on a day when I am to appear in court.'

'Do you regard this as appearing in court?'

'Certainly not. But as I have already told you several times, I have been under heavy stress, and that is my way of coping with stress. Doubtless you think it a bad way. I think otherwise.'

'I am sure you know all the objections to excessive use of alcohol?'

'I could give you an excellent temperance lecture right now. Indeed, I am a firm believer in temperance for the kind of people who benefit from temperance. I am not one of them. Temperance is a middle-class virtue, and it is not my fate. On the contrary, I am rich and in our time wealth takes a man out of the middle class, unless he made all the money himself. I am the third generation of money in my family. To be rich is to be a special kind of person. Are you rich?'

'By no means.'

'Quick to deny it, I observe. Yet you seem to live in a good professional style, which would be riches to most people in the world. Well – I *am* rich, though not so rich as people imagine. If you are rich you have to discover your own truths and make a great many of your own rules. The middle-class ethic will not serve you, and if you devote yourself to it, it will trip you up and make a fool of you.'

'What do you mean by rich?'

'I mean good hard coin, Doctor. I don't mean the riches of the mind or the wealth of the spirit, or any of that pompous crap. I mean money. Specifically, I count a man rich if he has an annual income of over a hundred thousand dollars *before* taxes. If he has that he has plenty of other evidences of wealth, as well. I have considerably more than a hundred thousand a year, and I make much of it by being at the top of my profession, which is the law. I am what used to be called "an eminent advocate." And if being rich and being an eminent advocate also requires a drink before breakfast, I am prepared to pay the price. But to assure you that I am not wholly unmindful of my grandparents, who hated liquor as the prime work of the Devil, I always have my first drink of the day with a raw egg in it. That is my breakfast.'

'How much in a day?'

'Call it a bottle, more or less. More at present, because as I keep telling you, I have been under stress.'

'What made you think you needed an analyst, instead of a cure for alcoholics?'

'Because I do not think of myself as an alcoholic. To be an alcoholic is a middle-class predicament. My reputation in the country where I live is such that I would cut an absurd figure in Alcoholics Anonymous; if a couple of the brethren came to minister to me, they would be afraid of me; anyhow I don't go on the rampage or pass out or make a notable jackass of myself – I just drink a good deal and talk rather frankly. If I were to go out with another A.A. to cope with some fellow who was on the bottle, the sight of me would terrify him ; he would think he had done something dreadful in his cups, and that I was his lawyer and the police were coming with the wagon. Nor would I be any good in group therapy ; I took a look at that, once ; I am not an intellectual snob, Doctor – at least, that is my story at present – but group therapy is too chummy for me. I lack the confessional spirit ; I prefer to encourage it in others, preferably when they are in the witness-box. No, I am not an alcoholic, for alcoholism is not my disease, but my symptom.'

'Then what do you call your disease ?'

'If I knew, I would tell you. Instead, I hope you can tell me.'

'Such a definition might not help us much at present. Let us call it stress following your father's death. Shall we begin talking about that ?'

'Don't we start with childhood ? Don't you want to hear about my toilet-training ?'

'I want to hear about your trouble now. Suppose we begin with the moment you heard of your father's death.'

'It was about three o'clock in the morning on November 4 last. I was wakened by my housekeeper, who said the police wanted to talk to me on the telephone. It was an inspector I knew who said I should come to the dock area at once as there had been an accident involving my father's car. He didn't want to say much, and I didn't want to say anything that would arouse the interest of my housekeeper, who was hovering to hear whatever she could, so I called a taxi and went to the docks. Everything there seemed to be in confusion, but in fact it was all as orderly as the situation permitted. There was a diver in a frog-man outfit, who had been down to the car first ; the Fire Department had brought a crane mounted on a truck, which was raising the car ; there were police cars and a truck with floodlights. I found the inspector, and he said it was my father's car for a certainty and there was a body at the wheel. So far as they could determine, the car had been driven off the end of a pier at a speed of about forty miles an hour ; it had carried on some distance after getting into the water. A watchman put in an alarm as soon as he heard the splash, but by the time the police arrived it was difficult to find exactly where it was, and then all the diving, and getting the crane, and putting a chain on the front part of the frame, had taken over two hours, so that they had seen the licence plate only a matter of minutes before I was called; it was a car the police knew well. My father had a low, distinctive licence number.

'It was one of those wretched situations when you hope that something isn't true which common sense tells you is a certainty. Nobody else drove that car except my father. At last they got it on the pier, filthy and dripping. A couple of firemen opened the doors as slowly as the weight of water inside would allow, because the police didn't want anything washed out that might be of evidence. But it was quickly emptied, and there he sat, at the wheel.

'I think what shocked me most was the terrible dishevelment of his body. He was always such an elegant man. He was covered with mud and oil and harbour filth, but his eyes were wide open, and he was gripping the wheel. The firemen tried to get him out, and it was then we found that his grip was so tight nothing ordinary would dislodge it. Probably you know what emergencies are like; things are done that nobody would think of under ordinary circumstances; finally they got him free of the wheel, but his hands had been terribly distorted and afterwards we found that most of the fingers had been broken in doing it. I didn't blame the firemen; they did what had to be done. They laid him on a tarpaulin and then everybody held back, and I knew they were waiting for me to do something. I knelt beside him and wiped his face with a handkerchief, and it was then we saw that there was something amiss about his mouth. The police surgeon came to help me, and when my father's jaws were pried open we found the stone I showed you. The stone you tried yourself because you doubted what I told you.'

'I am sorry if I shocked you. But patients come with such strange stories. Go on, please.'

'I know police procedure. They were as kind as possible, but they had to take the body to the morgue, make reports, and do all the routine things that follow the most bizarre accidents. They strained a point by letting me get away with the stone, though it was material evidence; they knew I would not withhold it if it should be necessary, I suppose. Even as it was, some reporter saw me do it, or tricked the doctor into an admission, and the stone played a big part in the news. But they all had work to do, and so had I, but I had nobody to help me with my work.

'So I did what had to be done. I went at once to my father's house and wakened Denyse (that's my stepmother) and told what had happened. I don't know what I expected. Hysterics, I suppose. But she took it with an icy self-control for which I was grateful, because if she had broken down I think I would have had some sort of collapse myself. But she was extremely wilful. "I must go to him," she said. I knew the police would be making their examination and tried to persuade her to wait till morning. Not a chance. Go she would, and at once. I didn't want her to drive, and it is years since I have driven a car myself, so that meant rousing the chauffeur and giving some sort of partial explanation to him. Oh, for the good old days – if there ever were such days – when you could tell servants to do something without offering a lot of reasons and explanations! But at last we were at the central police station, and in the morgue, and then we had another hold-up because the police, out of sheer decency, wouldn't let her see the body until the doctor had finished and some not very efficient cleaning-up had been done. As a result, when she saw him he looked like a drunk who has been dragged in out of the rain. Then she did break down, and that was appalling for me, because you might as well know now that I heartily dislike the woman, and having to hold her and soothe her and speak comfort to her was torture, and it was then I began to taste the full horror of

295

what had happened. The police doctor and everybody else who might have given me a hand were too respectful to intrude; wealth again, Dr von Haller – even your grief takes on a special quality, and nobody quite likes to dry your golden tears. After a while I took her home, and called Netty to come and look after her.

'Netty is my housekeeper. My old nurse, really, and she has kept my apartment for me since my father's second marriage. Netty doesn't like my stepmother either, but she seemed the logical person to call, because she has unshakable character and authority.

'Or rather, that is what I thought. But when Netty got over to my father's house and I told her what had happened, she flew right off the handle. That is her own expression for being utterly unstrung, "flying right off the handle." She whooped and bellowed and made awful feminine roaring noises until I was extremely frightened. But I had to hold her and comfort her. I still don't know what ailed her. Of course my father was a very big figure in her life – as he was in the life of anybody who knew him well – but she was no kin, you know. The upshot of it was that very soon my stepmother was attending to Netty, instead of the other way round, and as the chauffeur had roused all the other servants there was a spooky gathering of half-clad people in the drawing-room, staring and wondering as Netty made a holy show of herself. I got somebody to call my sister, Caroline, and quite soon afterward she and Beesty Bastable appeared, and I have never been so glad to see them in my life.

'Caroline was terribly shocked, but she behaved well. Rather a cold woman, but not a fool. And Beesty Bastable – her husband – is one of those puffing, goggle-eyed, fattish fellows who don't seem worth their keep, but who have sometimes a surprising touch with people. It was he, really, who got the servants busy making hot drinks – and got Netty to stop moaning, and kept Caroline and my stepmother from having a fight about nothing at all, or really because Caroline started in much too soon assuming that proprietorial attitude people take toward the recently bereaved, and my stepmother didn't like being told to go and lie down in her own house.

'I was grateful to Beesty because when things were sorted out he said, "Now for one good drink, and then nothing until we've had some sleep, what?" Beesty says "what?" a great deal, as a lot of Old Ontario people with money tend to do. I think it's an Edwardian affectation and they haven't found out yet that it's out of fashion. But Beesty kept me from drinking too much then, and he stuck to me like a burr for hours afterward, I suppose for the same reason. Anyhow, I went home at last to my apartment, which was blessedly free of Netty, and though I didn't sleep and Beesty very tactfully kept me away from the decanters, I did get a bath, and had two hours of quiet before Beesty stuck his head into my room at eight o'clock and said he'd fried some eggs. I didn't think I wanted fried eggs; I wanted an egg whipped up in brandy, but it was astonishing how good the fried eggs tasted. Don't you think it's rather humbling how hungry calamity makes one?

'As we ate, Beesty told me what had to be done. Odd, perhaps, because he's only a stockbroker and my father and I had always tended to write him off as a fool, though decent enough. But his family is prominent, and he'd managed quite a few funerals and knew the ropes. He even knew of a good undertaker. I wouldn't have known where to look for one. I mean, who's ever met an undertaker? It's like what people say about dead donkeys: who's ever seen one? He got on the telephone and arranged with his favourite undertaker to collect the body whenever the police were ready to release it. Then he said we must talk with Denyse to arrange details of the burial. He seemed to think she wouldn't want to see us until late in the morning, but when he called she was on the line at once and said she would see us at nine o'clock and not to be late because she had a lot to do.

'That was exactly like Denyse, whom as I told you I have never liked because of this very spirit she showed when Beesty called. Denyse is all business, and nobody can help her or do anything for her without being made a subordinate: she must always be the boss. Certainly she bossed my father far more than he knew, and he was not a man to subject himself to anybody. But women are like that. Aren't they?'

'Some women, certainly.'

'In my experience, women are either bosses or leaners.'

'Isn't that your experience of men, too?'

'Perhaps. But I can talk to men. I can't talk to my stepmother. From nine o'clock till ten, Denyse talked to us, and would probably have talked longer if the hairdresser had not been coming. She knew she would have to see a lot of people, and it was necessary for her hair to be dressed as she would have no opportunity later.

'And what she said! My hair almost stood on end. Denyse hadn't slept either: she had been planning. And I think this is the point, Doctor, when you will admit that I have cause to be nervous. I've told you my father was a very important man. Not just rich. Not just a philanthropist. He had been in politics, and during the greater part of the Second World War he had been our Minister of Food, and an extraordinarily able one. Then he had left active politics. It was the old story, not unlike Churchill's; the public hate a really capable man except when they can't get along without him. The decisive, red-tape-cutting qualities that made my father necessary in war got him into trouble with the little men as soon as the war was over and they hounded him out of public life. But he was too big to be ignored and his public service entitled him to recognition, and he was to be the next Lieutenant-Governor of our Province. Do you know what a Lieutenant-Governor is?'

'Some sort of ceremonial personage, I suppose.'

'Yes: a representative of the Crown in a Canadian province.'

'A high honour?'

'Yes, but there are ten of them. My father might suitably have been Governor-General, which is top of the heap.'

'Ah yes; very grand, I see.'

'Silly people smile at these ceremonial offices because they don't understand them. You can't have a parliamentary system without these official figures who represent the state, the Crown, the whole body of government, as well as the elected fellows who represent their voters.

'He had not taken office. But he had received the official notice of his appointment from the Secretary of State, and the Queen's charge would have come at the proper time, which would have been in about a month. But Denyse wanted him to be given a state funeral, as if he were already in office.

'Well! As a lawyer, I knew that was absurd. There was a perfectly valid Lieutenant-Governor at the time we were discussing this crazy scheme. There was no way in the world my father could be given an official funeral. But that was what she wanted – soldiers in dress uniform, a cushion with his D.S.O. and his C.B.E. on it, a firing-party, a flag on the coffin, as many officials and politicians as could be mustered. I was flabbergasted. But whatever I said, she simply replied, "I know what was owing to Boy even if you don't."

'We had a blazing row. Things were said that had poor Beesty white with misery, and he kept mumbling, "Oh come on, Denyse, come on, Davey; let's try to get along" – which was idiotic, but poor Beesty has no vocabulary suitable to large situations. Denyse dropped any pretence of liking me and let it rip. I was a cheap mouthpiece for crooks of the worst kind, I was a known drunk, I had always resented my father's superiority and tried to thwart him whenever I could, I had said inexcusable things about her and spied on her, but on this one occasion, by the living God, I would toe the line or she would expose me to unimaginable humiliations and disgraces. I said she had made a fool of my father since first she met him, reduced his stature before the public with her ridiculous, ignorant pretensions and stupidities, and wanted to turn his funeral into a circus in which she would ride the biggest elephant. It was plain speaking for a while, I can tell you. It was only when Beesty was near to tears – and I don't mean that metaphorically; he was sucking air noisily and mopping his eyes – and when Caroline turned up that

299

we became a little quieter. Caroline has a scornful manner that exacts good behaviour from the humbler creation, even Denyse.

'So in the end Beesty and I were given our orders to go to the undertaker and choose a splendid coffin. Bronze would be the thing, she thought, because it would be possible to engrave directly upon it.

'"Engrave what?" I asked. I will say for her that she had the grace to colour a little under her skilful make-up. "The Staunton arms," she said. "But there aren't any –" I began, when Beesty pulled me away. "Let her have it," he whispered. "But it's crooked," I shouted. "It's pretentious and absurd and crooked." Caroline helped him to bustle me out of the room. "Davey, you do it and shut up," she said, and when I protested, "Carol, you know as well as I do that it's illegal," she said, "Oh, *legal!*" with terrible feminine scorn.'

5

At my next appointment, feeling rather like Scheherazade unfolding one of her never-ending, telescopic tales to King Schahriar, I took up where I had left off. Dr von Haller had said nothing during my account of my father's death and what followed, except to check a point here and there, and she made no notes, which surprised me. Did she truly hold all the varied stories told by her patients in her head, and change from one to another every hour? Well, I did no less with the tales my clients told me.

We exchanged a few words of greeting, and I continued.

'After we had finished with the undertaker, Beesty and I had a great many details to attend to, some of them legal and some arising from the arrangement of funeral detail. I had to get in touch with Bishop Woodiwiss, who had known my father for over forty years, and listen to his well-meant condolences and go over the whole funeral routine. I went to the Diocesan House, and was a little surprised, I can't really say why, that it was so businesslike, with secretaries drinking coffee, and air-conditioning and all the atmosphere of business premises. I think I had expected crucifixes on the walls and heavy carpets. There was one door that said "Diocesan Chancellery: Mortgages" that really astonished me. But the Bishop knew how to do funerals, and there wasn't really much to it. There were technicalities: our parish church was St Simon's, but Denyse wanted a cathedral ceremony, as more in keeping with her notions of grandeur, and as well as the Bishop's, the Dean's consent had to be sought. Woodiwiss said he would take care of that. I still don't know why I was so touchy about the good man's words of comfort; after all, he had known my father before I was born, and had christened and confirmed me, and he had his rights both as a friend and a priest. But I felt very personally about the whole matter –'

'Possessively, would you say?'

'I suppose so. Certainly I was angry that Denyse was determined to take over and have everything her own way, especially when it was such a foolish, showy way. I was still furious about that matter of engraving the coffin with heraldic doodads that weren't ours, and couldn't ever be so, and which my father had rejected himself, after a lot of heart-searching. I want that to be perfectly clear to you; I have no quarrel with heraldry, and people who legitimately posess it can use it as they like, but the Staunton arms weren't ours. Do you want to know why?'

'Later, I think. We'll come to it. Go on now about the funeral.'

'Very well. Beesty took over the job of seeing the people from the papers, but it was snatched from him by Denyse, who had prepared a handout with biographical details. Silly, of course, because the papers had that already. But she achieved one thing by it that made me furious: the only mention of my mother in the whole obituary was a reference to "an earlier marriage to Leola Crookshanks, who died in 1942." Her name was Cruikshank, *not* Crookshanks, and she had been my father's wife since 1924 and the mother of his children, and a dear, sad, unhappy woman. Denyse knew that perfectly well, and nothing will convince me that the mistake wasn't the result of spite. And of course she dragged in a reference to her own wretched daughter, Lorene, who has nothing to do with the Staunton family – nothing at all.

'When was the funeral to be? That was the great question. I was for getting it over as quickly as possible, but the police did not release the body until late on Monday – and *that* took some arranging, I can assure you. Denyse wanted as much time as possible to arrange her semi-state funeral and assemble all the grandees she could bully, so it was decided to have it on Thursday.

'Where was he to be buried? Certainly not in Deptford, where he was born, though his parents had providently bought a six-holer in the cemetery there years ago, and were themselves the only occupants. But Deptford wouldn't do for Denyse, so a grave had to be bought in Toronto.

'Have you ever bought a grave? It's not unlike buying a house. First of all they show you the poor part of the cemetery, and you look at all the foreign tombstones with photographs imbedded in them under plastic covers, and the inscriptions in strange languages and queer alphabets, and burnt-out candles lying on the grass, and your heart sinks. You wonder, can this be death? How sordid! Because you aren't your best self, you know; you're a stinking snob; funerals bring out that sort of thing dreadfully. You've told yourself for years that it doesn't matter what happens to a corpse, and when cocktail parties become drunken-serious you've said that the Jews have the right idea, and the quickest, cheapest funeral is the best and philosophically the most decent. But when you get into the cemetery, it's quite different. And the cemetery people know it. So you move out of the working-class and ethnic district into the area of suburban confines, but the gravestones are really rather close together and the inscriptions are in bad prose, and you almost expect to see jocular inscriptions like "Take-It-Easy" and "Dunroamin" on the stones along with "Till the Day Breaks" and "In the Everlasting Arms." Then things begin to brighten; bigger plots, no crowding, an altogether classier type of headstone and – best of all – the names of families you know. On the Resurrection Morn, after all, one doesn't want to jostle up to the Throne with a pack of strangers. And that's where the deal is settled.

'Did you know, by the way, that somebody has to own a grave? Somebody, that is, other than the occupant. I own my father's grave. A strange thought.'

'Who owns your mother's grave? And why was your father not buried near her?'

'I own her grave, because I inherited it as part of my father's estate. The only bit of real estate he left me, as a matter of fact. And because she died during the war, when my father was abroad, the funeral had to be arranged by a family friend, and he just bought one grave. A good one, but single. She lies in the same desirable area as my father, but not near. As in life.

'By Tuesday night the undertakers had finished their work, and the coffin was back in his house, at the end of the drawing-room, and we were all invited in to take a look. Difficult business, of course, because an undertaker – or at any rate his embalmer – is an artist of a kind, and when someone has died by violence it's a challenge to see how well they can make him look. I must say in justice they had done well by Father, for though it would be stupid to say he looked like himself, he didn't look as though he had been drowned. But you know how it is; an extremely vital, mercurial man, who has always had a play of expression and even of colour, doesn't look like himself with a mat complexion and that inflexible calm they produce for these occasions. I have had to see a lot of people in their coffins, and they always look to me as if they were under a malign enchantment and could hear what was said and would speak if the enchantment could be broken. But there it was, and somebody had to say a kind word or two to the undertakers, and it was Beesty who did it. I was always being amazed at the things he could do in this situation, because my father and I had never thought he could do anything except manage his damned bond business. The rest of us looked with formal

303

solemnity, just as a few years before we had gathered to look at Caroline's wedding cake with formal pleasure ; on both occasions we were doing it chiefly to give satisfaction to the people who had created the exhibit.

'That night people began to call. Paying their respects is the old-fashioned phrase for it. Beesty and Caroline and I hung around in the drawing-room and chatted with the visitors in subdued voices. "So good of you to come. . . . Yes, a very great shock. . . . It's extremely kind of you to say so. . . ." Lots of that sort of thing. Top people from my father's business, the Alpha Corporation, doing the polite. Lesser people from the Alpha Corporation, seeing that everybody who came signed a book ; a secretary specially detailed to keep track of telegrams and cables, and another to keep a list of the flowers.

'Oh, the flowers! Or, as just about everybody insisted on calling them, the "floral tributes." Being November, the florists were pretty well down to chrysanthemums, and there were forests of them. But of course the really rich had to express their regret with roses because they were particularly expensive at the time. The rich are always up against it, you see ; they have to send the best, however much they may hate the costly flower of the moment, or somebody is sure to say they've been cheap. Denyse had heard somewhere of a coffin being covered with a blanket of roses, and she wanted one as her own special offering. It was Caroline who persuaded her to hold herself down to a decent bunch of white flowers. Or really, persuaded isn't the word ; Caroline told me she was finally driven to saying, "Are you trying to make us look like the Medici?" and that did it, because Denyse had never heard any good spoken of the Medici.

'This grisly business went on all day Wednesday. I was on duty in the morning, and received and made myself pleasant to the Mayor, the Chief of Police, the Fire Chief, a man from the Hydro-Electric Power Commission, and quite a crowd of dignitaries of one sort and another. There was a representative of the Bar Association, which called to mind the almost forgotten fact that my father's professional training had been as a lawyer; I knew this man quite well because he was a frequent associate of my own, but the others were people I knew only by name or from their pictures in the newspapers. There were bank presidents, naturally.

'Denyse, of course, did none of the receiving. It wouldn't have suited the role for which she had cast herself. Officially, she was too desolated to be on view, and only special people were taken to an upstairs room where she held state. I don't quarrel with that. Funerals are among the few ceremonial occasions left to us, and we assume our roles almost without thinking. I was the Only Son, who was bearing up splendidly, but who was also known not to be, and to have no expectation of ever being, the man his father was. Beesty was That Decent Fellow Bastable, who was doing everything he could under difficult circumstances. Caroline was the Only Daughter, stricken with grief, but of course not so catastrophically stricken as Denyse, who was the Widow and assumed to be prostrate under her affliction. Well – all right. That's the pattern, and we break patterns at our peril. After all, they become patterns because they conform to realities. I have been in favour of ceremonial and patterns all my life, and I have no desire to break the funeral pattern. But there was too much real feeling behind the pattern for me to be anything other than wretchedly overwrought, and the edicts Denyse issued from her chamber of affliction were the worst things I had to bear.

'Her edict that at all costs I was to be kept sober, for instance. Beesty was very good about that. Not hatefully tactful, you know, but he said plainly that I had to do a great many things that needed a level head and I'd better not drink much. He knew that for me not drinking much meant drinking what would be a good deal for him, but he gave me credit for some common sense. And Caroline was the same. "Denyse is determined that you're going to get your paws in the sauce and disgrace us all. So for God's sake spite her and don't," was the way she put it. Even Netty, after her first frightful outburst, behaved very well and didn't try to watch over me for my own good, though she lurked a good deal. Consequently, though I drank pretty steadily, I kept within my own appointed bounds. But I hated Denyse for her edict.

'Nor was that her only edict. On Wednesday, before lunch, she called Beesty to her and told him to get me to look over my father's will that afternoon, and see her after I had done so. This was unwarrantable interference. I knew I was my father's principal executor, and I knew, being a lawyer, what had to be done. But it isn't considered quite the thing to get down to business with the will before the funeral is over. There's nothing against it, particularly if there is suspicion of anything that might prove troublesome in the will, but in my father's case that was out of the question. I didn't know what was in the will, but I was certain it was all in perfect order. I thought Denyse was rushing things in an unseemly way.

'I suppose if you are to do anything for me, Doctor, I must be as frank as possible. I didn't want to look at the will until it became absolutely necessary. There have been difficulties about wills in our family. My father had a shock when he read his own father's will, and he had spoken to me about it more than once. And relations between my father and myself had been strained since his marriage to Denyse. I thought there might be a nasty surprise for me in the will. So I put my foot down and said nothing could be done until Thursday afternoon.

'I don't know why I went to my father's house so early on Thursday, except that I woke with an itching feeling that there was a great deal to be settled, and I would find out what it was when I was on the spot. And I wanted to take farewell of my father. You understand? During the last forty-eight hours it had been impossible to be alone in the room with his body, and I thought if I were early I could certainly manage it. So I went to the drawing-room as softly as possible, not to attract attention, and found the doors shut. It was half past seven, so there was nothing unusual about that.

'But from inside there were sounds of a man's voice and

a woman's voice, apparently quarrelling, and I heard scuffling and thudding. I opened the door, and there was Denyse at the coffin, holding up my father's body by the shoulders, while a strange man appeared to be punching and slapping its face. You know what people say in books – "I was thunderstruck . . . my senses reeled."'

'Yes. It is a perfectly accurate description of the sensation. It is caused by a temporary failure of circulation to the head. Go on.'

'I shouted something. Denyse dropped the body, and the man jumped backward as if he thought I might kill him. I knew him then. He was a friend of Denyse's, a dentist; I had met him once or twice and thought him a fool.

'The body had no face. It was entirely covered in some shiny pinkish material, so thickly that it was egglike in its featurelessness. It was this covering they were trying to remove.

'I didn't have to ask for an explanation. They were unnerved and altogether too anxious to talk. It was a story of unexampled idiocy.

'This dentist, like so many of Denyse's friends, was a dabbler in the arts. He had a tight, ill-developed little talent as a sculptor, and he had done a few heads of Chairmen of the Faculty of Dentistry at the University, and that sort of thing. Denyse had been visited by one of her dreadful inspirations, that this fellow should take a death-mask of my father, which could later be used as the basis for a bust or perhaps kept for itself. But he had never done a corpse before, and it is quite a different business from doing a living man. So, instead of using plaster, which is the proper thing if you know how to work it, he had the lunatic idea of trying some plastic mess used in his profession for taking moulds, because he thought he could get a greater amount of detail, and quicker. But the plastic wasn't for this sort of work, and he couldn't get it off!

'They were panic-stricken, as they had every right to be. The room was full of feeling. Do you know what I mean? The atmosphere was so alive with unusual currents that I swear I could feel them pressing on me, making my ears ring. Don't say it was all the whisky I had been drinking. I was far the most self-possessed of us three. I swear that all the tension seemed to emanate from the corpse, which was in an unseemly state of dishevelment, with coat and shirt off, hair awry, and half-tumbled out of that great expensive coffin.

'What should I have done? I have gone over that moment a thousand times since. Should I have seized the poker and killed the dentist, and forced Denyse's face down on that dreadful plastic head and throttled her, and then screamed for the world to come and look at the last scene of some sub-Shakespearean tragedy? What in fact I did was to order them both out of the room, lock it, telephone the undertakers to come at once, and then go into the downstairs men's room and vomit and gag and retch until I was on the floor with my head hanging into the toilet bowl, in a classic Skid Row mess.

'The undertakers came. They were angry, as they had every right to be, but they were fairly civil. If a mask was wanted, they asked, why had they not been told? They knew how to do it. But what did I expect of them now? I had pulled myself together, though I knew I looked like a drunken wreck, and I had to do whatever talking was done. Denyse was upstairs, having divorced herself in that wonderful feminine way from the consequences of her actions, and I am told the dentist left town for a week.

'It was a very bad situation. I heard one of the undertakers ask the butler if he could borrow a hammer, and I knew the worst. After a while I had my brief time beside my father's coffin; the undertakers did not spare me that. The face was very bad, some teeth had been broken; no eyebrows or lashes, and a good deal of the front hair was gone. Much worse than when he lay on the dock, covered in oil and filth, with that stone in his mouth.

'So of course we had what is called a closed-coffin funeral. I know they are common here, but in North America it is still usual to have the corpse on display until just before the burial service begins. I sometimes wonder if it is a hold-over from pioneer days, to assure everybody that there has been no foul play. That was certainly not the case this time. We had had foul play. I didn't explain to Caroline and Beesty; simply said Denyse had decided she wanted it that way. I know Caroline smelled a rat, but I told her nothing because she might have done something dreadful to Denyse.

'There we all were, in the cathedral, with Denyse in the seat of the chief mourner, of course, and looking so smooth a louse would have slipped off her, as Grandfather Staunton used to say. And he would certainly have said I looked like the Wreck of the Hesperus; it was one of his few literary allusions.

'There was the coffin, so rich, so bronzey, so obviously the sarcophagus of somebody of the first rank. Right above where that pitifully misused face lay hidden was the engraving of the Staunton arms: Argent two chevrons sable within a bordure engrailed of the same. Crest, a fox statant proper. Motto, *En Dieu ma foy*.

'Bishop Woodiwiss might have been in on the imposture, so richly did he embroider the *En Dieu ma foy* theme. I have to give it to the old boy; he can't have seen that engraving until the body arrived at the cathedral door, but he seized on the motto and squeezed it like a bartender squeezing a lemon. It was the measure of our dear brother gone, he said, that the motto of his ancient family should have been this simple assertion of faith in Divine Power and Divine Grace, and that never, in all the years he had known Boy Staunton, had he heard him mention it. No: deeds, not words, was Boy Staunton's mode of life. A man of action; a man of great affairs; a man loving and tender in his personal life, open-handed and perceptive in his multitudinous public benefactions, and the author of countless unknown acts of simple generosity. But no jewel of great price could be concealed forever, and here we saw, at last, the mainspring of Boy Staunton's great and – yes, he would say it, he would use the word, knowing that we would understand it in its true sense – his beautiful life. *En Dieu ma foy*. Let us all carry that last word from a great man away with us, and feel that truly, in this hour of mourning and desolation, we had found an imperishable truth. *En Dieu ma foy.*

'Without too much wriggling, I was able to look about me. The congregation was taking it with that stuporous receptivity which is common to Canadians awash in oratory. The man from the Prime Minister's department, sitting beside the almost identical man from the Secretary of State's department ; the people from the provincial government ; the civic officials; the Headmaster of Colborne School; the phalanx of rich business associates : not one of them looked as if he were about to leap up and shout, "It's a God-damned lie; his life-long motto wasn't *En Dieu ma foy* but *En moi-même ma foy* and that was his tragedy." I don't suppose they knew. I don't suppose that even if they knew, they cared. Few of them could have explained the difference between the two faiths.

'My eye fell on one man who could have done it. Old Dunstan Ramsay, my father's lifelong friend and my old schoolmaster, was there, not in one of the best seats – Denyse can't stand him – but near a stained-glass window through which a patch of ruby light fell on his handsome ravaged old mug, and he looked like a devil hot from hell. He didn't know I was looking, and at one point, when Woodiwiss was saying *En Dieu ma foy* for the sixth or seventh time, he grinned and made that snapping motion with his mouth that some people have who wear ill-fitting false teeth.

'Is this hour nearly finished, by the way? I feel wretched.'

'I am sure you do. Have you told anyone else about the death-mask?'

'Nobody.'

'That was very good of you.'

'Did I hear you correctly? I thought you analysts never expressed opinions.'

'You will hear me express many opinions as we get deeper in. It is the Freudians who are so reserved. You have your schedule of appointments? No doubts about coming next time?'

'None.'

Back again, after two days' respite. No: respite is not the word. I did not dread my appointment with Dr von Haller, as one might dread a painful or depleting treatment of the physical kind. But my nature is a retentive, secretive one, and all this revelation went against the grain. At the same time, it was an enormous relief. But after all, what was there in it? Was it anything more than Confession, as Father Knopwood had explained it when I was confirmed? Penitence, Pardon, and Peace? Was I paying Dr von Haller thirty dollars an hour for something the Church gave away, with Salvation thrown in for good measure? I had tried Confession in my very young days. Father Knopwood had not insisted that I kneel in a little box, while he listened behind a screen ; he had modern ways, and he sat behind me, just out of sight, while I strove to describe my boyish sins. Of course I knelt while he gave me Absolution. But I had always left the two or three sessions when I tried that feeling a fool. Nevertheless, despite our eventual quarrel, I wouldn't knock Knopwood now, even to myself ; he had been a good friend to me at a difficult time in my life – one of the succession of difficult times in my life – and if I had not been able to continue in his way, others had. Dr von Haller now – had it something to do with her being a woman? Whatever it was, I looked forward to my next hour with her in a state of mind I could not clarify, but which was not wholly disagreeable.

'Let me see ; we had finished your father's funeral. Or had we finished? Does anything else occur to you that you think significant?'

'No. After the Bishop's sermon, or eulogy or whatever it was, everything seemed to be much what one might have expected. He had so irrevocably transposed the whole thing into a key of fantasy, with his rhapsodizing on that irrelevant motto, that I went through the business at the cemetery without any real feeling, except wonderment. Then perhaps of the funeral people a hundred and seventy trooped back to the house for a final drink – a lot of drinking seems to go on at funerals – and stayed for a fork lunch, and when that was over I knew that all my time of grace had run out and I must get on with the job of the will.

'Beesty would have been glad to help me, I know, and Denyse was aching to see it, but she wasn't in a position to bargain with me after the horrors of the morning. So I picked up copies for everybody concerned from my father's solicitors, who were well known to me, and took them to my own office for a careful inspection. I knew I would be cross-examined by several people, and I wanted to have all the facts at my finger-tips before any family discussion.

'It was almost an anti-climax. There was nothing in the will I had not foreseen, in outline if not in detail. There was a great deal about his business interests, which were extensive, but as they boiled down to shares in a single controlling firm called Alpha Corporation it was easy, and his lawyers and the Alpha lawyers would navigate their way through all of that. There were no extensive personal or charity bequests, because he left the greatest part of his Alpha holdings to the Castor Foundation.

'That's a family affair, a charitable foundation that makes grants to a variety of good, or apparently good, causes. Such things are extremely popular with rich families in North America. Ours had a peculiar history, but it isn't important just now. Briefly, Grandfather Staunton set it up as a fund to assist temperance movements. But he left some loose ends, and he couldn't resist some fancy wording about "assisting the public weal," so when father took it over he gently eased all the preachers off the board and put a lot more money into it. Consequence: we now support the arts and the social sciences, in all their lunatic profusion. The name is odd. Means "beaver" of course, and so it has Canadian relevance; but it also means a special type of sugar – do you know the expression castor-sugar, the kind that goes in shakers? – and my father's money was made in part from sugar. He began in sugar. The name was suggested years ago as a joke by my father's friend Dunstan Ramsay ; but Father liked it, and used it when he created the Foundation. Or, rather, when he changed it from the peculiar thing it was when Grandfather Staunton left it.

'This large bequest to Castor ensured the continuance of all his charities and patronages. I was pleased, but not surprised, that he had given a strong hint in the will that he expected me to succeed him as Chairman of Castor. I already had a place on its Board. It's a very small Board – as small as the law will permit. So by this single act he had made me a man of importance in the world of benefactions, which is one of the very few remaining worlds where the rich are allowed to say what shall be done with the bulk of their money.

'But there was a flick of the whip for me in the latter part of the will, where the personal bequests were detailed.

'I told you that I am a rich man. I should say that I have a good deal of money, caused, if not intended, by a bequest from my grandfather, and I make a large income as a lawyer. But compared with my father I am inconsiderable – just "well-to-do," which was the phrase he used to dismiss people who were well above the poverty line but cut no figure in the important world of money. First-class surgeons and top lawyers and some architects were well-to-do, but they manipulated nothing and generated nothing in the world where my father trod like a king.

'So I wasn't looking for my bequest as something that would greatly change my way of life or deliver me from care. No, I wanted to know what my father had done about me in his will because I knew it would be the measure of what he thought of me as a man, and as his son. He obviously thought I could handle money, or he wouldn't have tipped me for the chairmanship of Castor. But what part of his money – and you must understand money meant his esteem and his love – did he think I was worth?

'Denyse was left very well off, but she got no capital – just a walloping good income for life or – this was Father speak-

313

ing again – so long as she remained his widow. I am sure he thought he was protecting her against fortune-hunters; but he was also keeping fortune-hunters from getting their hands on anything that was, or had been, his.

'Then there was a bundle for "my dear daughter, Caroline" which was to be hers outright and without conditions – because Beesty could have choked on a fishbone at his club any day and Caroline remarried at once and Father wouldn't have batted an eye.

'Then there was a really large capital sum in trust "for my dear grandchildren, Caroline Elizabeth and Boyd Staunton Bastable, portions to be allotted *per stirpes* to any legitimate children of my son Edward David Staunton from the day of their birth." There it was, you see.'

'Your father was disappointed that you had no children?'

'Certainly that is how he would have expected it to be interpreted. But didn't you notice that I was simply his son, when all the others were his dear this and dear that? Very significant, in something carefully prepared by Father. It would be nearer the truth to say he was angry because I wouldn't marry – wouldn't have anything to do with women at all.'

'I see. And why is that?'

'It's a very long and complicated story.'

'Yes. It usually is.'

'I'm not a homosexual, if that's what you are suggesting.'

'I am not suggesting that. If there were easy and quick answers, psychiatry would not be very hard work.'

'My father was extremely fond of women.'

'Are you fond of women?'

'I have a very high regard for women.'

'That is not what I asked.'

'I like them well enough.'

'Well enough for what?'

'To get along pleasantly with them. I know a lot of women.'

'Have you any women friends?'

'Well – in a way. They aren't usually interested in the things I like to talk about.'

'I see. Have you ever been in love?'

'In love? Oh, certainly.'

'Deeply in love?'

'Yes.'

'Have you had sexual intercourse with women?'

'With a woman.'

'When last?'

'It would be – let me think for a moment – December 26, 1945.'

'A very lawyer-like answer. But – nearly twenty-three years ago. How old were you?'

'Seventeen.'

'Was it with the person with whom you were deeply in love?'

'No, no ; certainly not !'

'With a prostitute?'

'Certainly not.'

'We seem to be approaching a painful area. Your answers are very brief, and not up to your usual standard of phrasing.'

'I am answering all your questions, I think.'

'Yes, but your very full flow of explanation and detail has dried up. And our hour is drying up, as well. So there is just time to tell you that next day we should take another course. Until now we have been clearing the ground, so to speak. I have been trying to discover what kind of man you are, and I hope you have been discovering something of what I am, as well. We are not really launched on analysis, because I have said little and really have not helped you at all. If we are to go on – and the time is very close when you must make that decision – we shall have to go deeper, and if that works, we shall then go deeper still, but we shall not continue in this extemporaneous way. Just before you go, do you think that by leaving you nothing in his will except this possibility of money for your children, your father was punishing you – that in his own terms he was telling you he didn't love you?'

'Yes.'

'And you care whether he loved you or not?'

'Must it be called love?'

'It was your own word.'

'It's a very emotional term. I cared whether he thought I was a worthy person – a man – a proper person to be his son.'

'Isn't that love?'

'Love between father and son isn't something that comes into society nowadays. I mean, the estimate a man makes of his son is in masculine terms. This business of love between father and son sounds like something in the Bible.'

'The patterns of human feeling do not change as much as many people suppose. King David's estimate of his rebellious son Absalom was certainly in masculine terms. But I suppose you recall David's lament when Absalom was slain?'

'I have been called Absalom before, and it isn't a comparison I like.'

'Very well. There is no point in straining an historical comparison. But do you think your father might have meant something more than scoring a final blow in the contest between you when he arranged his will as he did?'

'He was an extremely direct man in most things, but in personal relationships he was subtle. He knew the will would be studied by many people and that they would know he had left me obligations suitable to a lawyer but nothing that recognized me as his child. Many of these people would know also that he had had great hopes of me at one time, and had named me after his hero, who had been Prince of Wales when I was born, and that therefore something had gone wrong and I had been a disappointment. It was a way of driving a wedge between me and Caroline, and it was a way of giving Denyse a stick to beat me with. We had had some scenes about this marriage and woman business, and I would never give in and I would never say why. But he knew why. And this was his last word on the subject: spite

316

me if you dare; live a barren man and a eunuch; but don't think of yourself as my son. That's what it meant.'

'How much does it mean to you to think of yourself as his son?'

'The alternative doesn't greatly attract me.'

'What alternative is that?'

'To think that I am Dunstan Ramsay's son.'

'The friend? The man who was grinning at the funeral?'

'Yes. It has been hinted. By Netty. And Netty might just have known what she was talking about.'

'I see. Well, we shall certainly have much to talk about when next we meet. But now I must ask you to give way to my next patient.'

I never saw these next patients or the ones who had been with the doctor before me because her room had two doors, one from the waiting-room but the other giving directly into the corridor. I was glad of this arrangement, for as I left I must have looked very queer. What had I been saying?

7

'Let me see; we had reached Friday in your bad week, had we not? Tell me about Friday.'

'At ten o'clock, the beginning of the banking day, George Inglebright and I had to meet two men from the Treasury Department in the vault of the bank to go through my father's safety-deposit box. When somebody dies, you know, all his accounts are frozen and all his money goes into a kind of limbo until the tax people have had a full accounting of it. It's a queer situation because all of a sudden what has been secret becomes public business, and people you've never seen before outrank you in places where you have thought yourself important. Inglebright had warned me to be very quiet with the tax men. He's a senior man in my father's firm of lawyers, and of course he knows the ropes, but it was new to me.

'The tax men were unremarkable fellows, but I found it embarrassing to be locked up in one of the bank's little cubbyholes with them while we counted what was in the safety-deposit box. Not that I counted; I watched. They warned me not to touch anything, which annoyed me because it suggested I might snatch a bundle of brightly coloured stock certificates and make a run for it. What was in the box was purely personal, not related to Alpha or any of the companies my father controlled. It wasn't as personal as I feared, however; I've heard stories of safety-deposit boxes with locks of hair, and baby shoes, and women's garters, and God knows what in them. But there was nothing of that sort. Only shares and bonds amounting to a very large amount, which the tax men counted and inventoried carefully.

'One of the things that bothered me was that these men, obviously not paid much, were cataloguing what was in itself a considerable fortune: what did they think? Were they envious? Did they hate me? Were they glorying in their authority? Were they conscious of putting down the mighty from their seat and exalting the humble and meek? They looked crusty and non-committal, but what was going on in their heads?

'It took most of the morning and I had nothing whatever to do but watch, which I found exhausting because of the reflections it provoked. It was the kind of situation that leads one to trite philosophizing: here is what remains of a very large part of a life's effort – that kind of thing. Now and then I thought about the chairmanship of Castor, and a phrase I hadn't heard since my law-student days came into my head and wouldn't be driven out. *Damnosa hereditas*; a ruinous inheritance. It's a phrase from Roman Law; comes in Gaius's *Institutes*, and means exactly what it says. Castor could very well be that to me because it is big already, and with what will come into it from my father's estate it will be a very large charitable foundation even by American standards, and being the head of it will devour time and energy and could very well be the end of the kind of career I have tried to make for myself. *Damnosa hereditas*. Did he

mean it that way? Probably not. One must assume the best.
Still –

'I gave George lunch, then marched off like a little soldier
to talk to Denyse and Caroline about the will They had had
a chance to go over their own copies, and Beesty had explained most of it, but he isn't a lawyer and they had a lot
of points they wanted clarified. And of course there was a
row, because I think Denyse had expected some capital, and
in fairness I must say that she was within her rights to do so.
What really burned her, I think, was that there was nothing
for her daughter Lorene, though what she had been left for
herself would have been more than enough to take care of
all that. Lorene is soft in the head, you see, though Denyse
pretends otherwise, and she will have to be looked after all
her life. Although Lorene's name was never mentioned, I
could sense her presence; she had called my father Daddy-
Boy, and Daddy-Boy hadn't lived up to expectation.

'Caroline is above fussing about inheritances. She is really
a very fine person, in her frosty way. But naturally she was
pleased to have been taken care of so handsomely, and
Beesty was openly delighted. After all, with the trust money
and Caroline's personal fortune and what would come from
himself and his side of the family, his kids were in the way
of being rich even by my father's demanding standards. Both
Caroline and Beesty saw how I had been dealt with, but they
were too tactful to say anything about it in front of Denyse.

'Not so Denyse herself. "This was Boy's last chance to get
you back on the rails, David," said she, "and for his sake I
hope it works."

' "What particular rails are you talking about?" I said. I
knew well enough, but I wanted to hear what she would
say. And I will admit I led her on to put her foot in it because I wanted a chance to dislike her even more than I did
already.

' "To be utterly frank, dear, he wanted you to be married,
and to have a family, and to cut down on your drinking. He
knew what a balancing effect a wife and children have on a
man of great talents. And of course everybody knows that

you have great talents – potentially." Denyse was not one to shrink from a challenge.

'"So he has left me the toughest job in the family bundle, and some money for children I haven't got," I said. "Do you happen to know if he had anybody in mind that he wanted me to marry? I'd like to be sure of everything that is expected of me."

'Beesty was wearing his toad-under-the-harrow expression, and Caroline's eyes were fierce. "If you two are going to fight, I'm going home," she said.

'"There will be no fighting," said Denyse. "This is not the time or the place. David asked a straight question and I gave him a straight answer – as I have always done. And straight answers are something David doesn't like except in court, where he can ask the questions that will give him the answers he wants. Boy was very proud of David's success, so far as it went. But he wanted something from his only son that goes beyond a somewhat notorious reputation in the criminal courts. He wanted the continuance of the Staunton name. He would have thought it pretentious to talk of such a thing, but you know as well as I do that he wanted to establish a line."

'Ah, that line. My father had not been nearly so reticent about mentioning it as Denyse pretended. She has never understood what real reticence is. But I was sick of the fight already. I quickly tire of quarrelling with Denyse. Perhaps, as she says, I only like quarrelling in court. In court there are rules. Denyse makes up her rules as she goes along. As I must say women tend to do. So the talk shifted, not very easily, to other things.

'Denyse had two fine new bees in her bonnet. The death-mask idea had failed, and she knew I would not tell the others, so as far as she was concerned it had perished as though it had never been. She does not dwell on her failures.

'What she wanted now was a monument for my father, and she had decided that a large piece of sculpture by Henry Moore would be just the thing. Not to be given to the Art

Gallery or the City, of course. To be put up in the cemetery. I hope that gives you the measure of Denyse. No sense of congruity; no sense of humour; no modesty. Just ostentation and gall working under the governance of a fashionable, belligerent, unappeasable ambition.

'Her second great plan was for a monument of another kind; she announced with satisfaction that my father's biography was to be written by Dunstan Ramsay. She had wanted Eric Roop to do it – Roop was one of her protégés and as a poet he was comparable to her dentist friend as a sculptor – but Roop had promised himself a fallow year if he could get a grant to see him through it. I knew this already, because Roop's fallow years were as familiar to Castor as Pharaoh's seven lean kine, and his demand that we stake him to another had been circulated to the Board, and I had seen it. The Ramsay plan had merit. Dunstan Ramsay was not only a schoolmaster but an author who had enjoyed a substantial success in a queer field: he wrote about saints – popular books for tourists, and at least one heavy-weight work that had brought him a reputation in the places where such things count.

'Furthermore, he wrote well. I knew because he had been my history master at school; he insisted on essays in what he called the Plain Style; it was, he said, much harder to get away with nonsense in the Plain Style than in a looser manner. In my legal work I had found this to be true and useful. But – what would we look like if a life of Boy Staunton appeared over the name of a man notable as a student of the lives of saints? There would be jokes, and one or two of them occurred to me immediately.

'On the other hand, Ramsay had known my father from boyhood. Had he agreed? Denyse said he had wavered a little when she put it to him, but she would see that he made up his mind. After all, his own little estate – which was supposed to be far beyond what a teacher and author could aspire to – was built on the advice my father had given him over the years. Ramsay had a nice little block of Alpha. The time had come for him to pay up in his own coin. And

Denyse would work with him and see that the job was properly done and Ramsay's ironies kept under control.

'Neither Caroline nor I was very fond of Ramsay, who had been a sharp-tongued nuisance in our lives, and we were amused to think of a collaboration between him and our stepmother. So we made no demur, but determined to spike the Henry Moore plan.

'Caroline and Beesty got away as soon as they could, but I had to wait and hear Denyse talk about the letters of condolence she had been receiving in bulk. She graded them ; some were Official, from public figures, and subdivided into Warm and Formal ; some were from personal friends, and these she classified as Moving and Just Ordinary ; and there were many from Admirers, and the best of these were graded Touching. Denyse has an orderly mind.

'We did not talk about a dozen or so hateful letters of abuse that had come unsigned. Nor did we say much about the newspaper pieces, some of which had been grudging and covertly offensive. We were both habituated to the Canadian spirit, to which generous appreciation is so alien.

'It had been a wearing afternoon, and I had completed all my immediate tasks, so I thought I would permit myself a few drinks after dinner. I dined at my club and had the few drinks, but to my surprise they did nothing to dull my wretchedness. I am not a man who is cheered by drink. I don't sing or make jokes or chase girls, nor do I stagger and speak thickly ; I become remote – possibly somewhat glassy-eyed. But I do manage to blunt the edge of that heavy axe that seems always to be chopping away at the roots of my being. That night it was not so. I went home and began to drink seriously. Still the axe went right on with its destructive work. At last I went to bed and slept wretchedly.

'It is foolish to call it sleep. It was a long, miserable reverie, relieved by short spells of unconsciousness. I had a weeping fit, which frightened me because I haven't cried for thirty years ; Netty and my father had no use for boys who cried. It was frightening because it was part of the destruction of my mind that was going on ; I was being broken down to a very primitive level, and absurd kinds of feeling and crude, inexplicable emotions had taken charge of me.

'Imagine a man of forty crying because his father hadn't loved him! Particularly when it wasn't true, because he obviously had loved me, and I know I worried him dreadfully. I even sank so low that I wanted my mother, though I knew that if that poor woman could have come to me at that very time, she wouldn't have known what to say or do. She never really knew what was going on, poor soul. But I wanted something, and my mother was the nearest identification I could find for it. And this blubbering booby was Mr David Staunton, Q.C., who had a dark reputation because the criminal world thought so highly of him, and who played up to the role, and who secretly fancied himself as a magician of the courtroom. But in the interest of justice, mind you; always in the constant and perpetual wish that everyone shall have his due.

'Next morning the axe was making great headway, and I began with the bottle at breakfast, to Netty's indignation and dismay. She didn't say anything, because once before when she had interfered I had given her a few sharp cuffs, which she afterward exaggerated into "beating her up." Netty hasn't seen some of the beatings-up I have observed in court or she wouldn't talk so loosely. She has never mastered the Plain Style. Of course I had been regretful for having struck her, and apologized in the Plain Style, but she understood afterward that she was not to interfere.

'So she locked herself in her room that Saturday morning, taking care to do it when I was near enough to hear what she was doing; she even pushed the bed against the door. I knew what she was up to; she wanted to be able to say to Caroline, "When he's like that I just have to barricade myself in, because if he flew off the handle like he did that time, the Dear knows what could happen to me." Netty liked to tell Caroline and Beesty that nobody knew what she went through. They had a pretty shrewd notion that most of what she went through was in her own hot imagination.

'I went back to my club for luncheon on Saturday, and

although the barman was as slow as he could be when I wanted him, and absent from the bar as much as he could manage, I got through quite a lot of Scotch before I settled down to having a few drinks before dinner. A member I knew called Femister came in and I heard the barman mutter something to him about "tying on a bun" and I knew he meant me.

'A bun! These people know nothing. When I bend to the work it is no trivial bun, but a whole baking of double loaves I tie on. Only this time nothing much seemed to be happening, except for a generalized remoteness of things, and the axe was chopping away as resolutely as ever. Femister is a good fellow, and he sat down by me and chatted. I chatted right back, clearly and coherently, though perhaps a little fancifully. He suggested we have dinner together, and I agreed. He ate a substantial club dinner, and I messed my food around on my plate and tried to take my mind off its smell, which I found oppressive. Femister was kindly, but my courteous *non sequiturs* were just as discouraging as I meant them to be, and after dinner it was clear that he had had all the Good Samaritan business he could stand.

'"I've got an appointment now," he said. "What are you going to do? You certainly don't want to spend the evening all alone here, do you? Why don't you go to the theatre? Have you seen this chap at the Royal Alec? Marvellous! Magnus Eisengrim his name is, though it sounds unlikely, doesn't it? The show is terrific! I've never seen such a conjuror. And all the fortune-telling and answering questions and all that. Terrific! It would take you right out of yourself."

'"I can't imagine anywhere I'd rather be," I said slowly and deliberately. "I'll go. Thank you very much for suggesting it. Now you run along, or you'll miss your appointment."

'Off he went, grateful to have done something for me and to have escaped without trouble. He wasn't telling me anything I didn't already know. I had been to Eisengrim's *Soirée of Illusions* the week before, with my father and Denyse and Lorene, whose birthday it was. I was sucked into it at the last minute, and had not liked the show at all, though I could see that it was skilful. But I detested Magnus Eisengrim.

'Shall I tell you why? Because he was making fools of us all, and so cleverly that most of us liked it; he was a con man of a special kind, exploiting just that element in human credulity that most arouses me – I mean the *desire* to be deceived. You know that maddening situation that lies behind so many criminal cases, where somebody is so besotted by somebody else that he lays himself open to all kinds of cheating and ill-usage, and sometimes to murder? It isn't love, usually; it's a kind of abject surrender, an abdication of common sense. I am a victim of it, now and then, when feeble clients decide that I am a wonder-worker and can do miracles in court. I imagine you get it, as an analyst, when people think you can unweave the folly of a lifetime. It's a powerful force in life, yet so far as I know it hasn't even a name –'

'Excuse me – yes, it has a name. We call it projection.'

'Oh. I've never heard that. Well, whatever it is, it was going full steam ahead in that theatre, where Eisengrim was fooling about twelve hundred people, and they were delighted to be fooled and begging for more. I was disgusted, and most of all with the nonsense of the Brazen Head.

'It was second to the last illusion on his program. I never saw the show to the end. I believe it was some sexy piece of nonsense vaguely involving Dr Faustus. But *The Brazen Head of Friar Bacon* was what had caused the most talk. It began in darkness, and slowly the light came up inside a big human head that floated in the middle of the stage, so that it glowed. It spoke, in a rather foreign voice. "Time is," it said, and there was a tremble of violins; "Time was," it said, and there was a chord of horns; "Time's past," it said, and there was a very quiet ruffle of drums, and the lights came up just enough for us to see Eisengrim – he wore evening clothes, but with knee-breeches, as if he were at Court – who told us the legend of the Head that could tell all things.

'He invited the audience to lend him objects, which his assistants sealed in envelopes and carried to the stage, where he mixed them up in a big glass bowl. He held up each envelope as he chose it by chance, and the Head identified the owner of the hidden object by the number of the seat in which he was sitting. Very clever, but it made me sick, because people were so delighted with what was, after all, just a very clever piece of co-operation by the magician's troupe.

'Then came the part the audience had been waiting for and that caused so much sensation through the city. Eisengrim said the Head would give personal advice to three people in the audience. This had always been sensational, and the night I was there with my father's theatre party the Head had said something that brought the house down, to a woman who was involved in a difficult legal case; it enraged me because it was virtually contempt of court – a naked interference in something that was private and under the most serious consideration our society provides. I had talked a great deal about it afterward, and Denyse had told me not to be a spoil-sport, and my father had suggested that I was ruining Lorene's party – because of course this sort of nonsense was just the kind of thing a fool like Lorene would think marvellous.

'So you see I wasn't in the best mood for the *Soirée of Illusions*, but some perversity compelled me to go, and I bought a seat in the top gallery, where I assumed nobody would know me. A lot of people had been going to this show two and even three times, and I didn't want anybody to say I had been among their number.

'The program was the same but the flatness I had expected in a show I had seen before was notably missing, and that annoyed me. I didn't want Eisengrim to be as good as he was. I thought him dangerous and I grudged him the admiration the audience plainly felt for him. The show was very clever; I must admit that. It had real mystery, and beautiful girls very cleverly and tastefully displayed, and there was a quality of fantasy about it that I have never seen in any other magician's performance, and very rarely in the theatre.

'Have you ever seen the Habima Players do *The Dybbuk?*

326

I did, long ago, and this had something of that quality about it, as if you were looking into a stranger and more splendid world than the one you know – almost a solemn joy. But I had not lost my grievance, and the better *The Soirée of Illusions* was, the more I wanted to wreck it.

'I suppose the drink was getting to me more than I knew, and I muttered two or three times until people shushed me. When *The Brazen Head of Friar Bacon* came, and the borrowed objects had been identified, and Eisengrim was promising his answers to secret questions, I suddenly heard myself shouting, "Who killed Boy Staunton?" and I found I was on my feet, and there was a sensation in the theatre. People were staring at me. There was a crash in one of the boxes, and I had the impression that someone had fallen and knocked over some chairs. The Head began to glow, and I heard the foreign voice saying something that seemed to begin, "He was killed by a gang . . ." then something about "the woman he knew . . . the woman he did not know," but really I can't be sure what I heard because I was dashing up the steps of the balcony as hard as I could go – they are very steep – and then pelting down two flights of stairs, though I don't think anybody was chasing me. I rushed into the street, jumped into one of the taxis that had begun to collect at the door, and got back to my apartment, very much shaken.

'But it was as I was leaving the theatre in such a sweat that the absolute certainty came over me that I had to do something about myself. That is why I am here.'

'Yes, I see. I don't think there can be any doubt that it was a wise decision. But in the letter from Dr Tschudi he said something about your having put yourself through what you called "the usual examination." What did you mean?'

'Ah – well. I'm a lawyer, as you know.'

'Yes. Was it some sort of legal examination, then?'

'I am a thorough man. I think you might say a whole-hearted man. I believe in the law.'

'And so – ?'

'You know what the law is, I suppose? The procedures of law are much discussed, and people know about lawyers and courts and prisons and punishment and all that sort of thing, but that is just the apparatus through which the law works. And it works in the cause of justice. Now, justice is the constant and perpetual wish to render to everyone his due. Every law student has to learn that. A surprising number of them seem to forget it, but I have not forgotten it.'

'Yes, I see. But what is "the usual examination"?'

'Oh, it's just a rather personal thing.'

'Of course, but clearly it is an important personal thing. I should like to hear about it.'

'It is hard to describe.'

'Is it so complex, then?'

'I wouldn't say it was complex, but I find it rather embarrassing.'

'Why?'

'To someone else it would probably seem to be a kind of game.'

'A game you play by yourself?'

'You might call it that, but it misrepresents what I do and the consequences of what I do.'

'Then you must be sure I do not misunderstand. Is this game a kind of fantasy?'

'No, no ; it is very serious.'

'All real fantasy is serious. Only faked fantasy is not serious. That is why it is so wrong to impose faked fantasy on children. I shall not laugh at your fantasy. I promise. Now – please tell me what "the usual examination" is.'

'Very well, then. It's a way I have of looking at what I have done, or might do, to see what it is worth. I imagine a court, you see, all perfectly real and correct in every detail. I am the Judge, on the Bench. And I am the prosecuting lawyer, who presents whatever it is in the worst possible light – but within the rules of pleading. That means I may not express a purely personal opinion about the rights or wrongs of the case. But I am also the defence lawyer, and I put the best case I can for whatever is under examination – but again I mayn't be personal and load the pleading. I can even call myself into the witness-box and examine and cross-examine myself. And in the end Mr Justice Staunton must make up his mind and give a decision. And there is no appeal from that decision.'

'I see. A very complete fantasy.'

'I suppose you must call it that. But I assure you it is extremely serious to me. This case I am telling you about took several hours. I was charged with creating a disturbance in a public place while under the influence of liquor, and there were grave special circumstances – creating a scandal that would seriously embarrass the Staunton family, for one.'

'Surely that is a moral rather than a legal matter?'

'Not entirely. And anyhow, the law is, among other things, a codification of a very large part of public morality. It expresses the moral opinion of society on a great number of subjects. And in Mr Justice Staunton's court, morality carries great weight. It's obvious.'

'Truly? What makes it obvious?'

'Oh, just a difference in the Royal Arms.'

'The Royal Arms?'

'Yes. Over the judge's head, where they are always displayed.'

'And what is the difference? . . . Another of your pauses, Mr Staunton. This must mean a great deal to you. Please describe the difference.'

'It's nothing very much. Only that the animals are complete.'

'The animals?'

'The supporters, they are called. The Lion and the Unicorn.'

'And are they sometimes incomplete?'

'Almost always in Canada. They are shown without their privy parts. To be heraldically correct they should have distinct, rather saucy pizzles. But in Canada we geld everything, if we can, and dozens of times I have sat in court and looked at those pitifully deprived animals and thought how they exemplified our attitude toward justice. Everything that spoke of passion – and when you talk of passion you talk of morality in one way or another – was ruled out of order or disguised as something else. Only Reason was welcome. But in Mr Justice Staunton's court the Lion and the Unicorn are complete, because morality and passion get their due there.'

'I see. Well, how did the case go?'

'It hung, in the end, on the McNaghten Rule.'

'You must tell me what that is.'

'It is a formula for determining responsibility. It takes its name from a nineteenth-century murderer called McNaghten whose defence was insanity. He said he did it when he was not himself. This was the defence put forward for Staunton. The prosecution kept hammering away at Staunton to find out whether, when he shouted in the theatre, he fully understood the nature and quality of his act, and if he did, did he know it was wrong? The defence lawyer – Mr David Staunton, a very eminent Q.C. – urged every possible extenuating circumstance: that the prisoner Staunton had been under severe stress for several days; that he had lost his father in a most grievous fashion, and that he had undergone severe psychological harassment because of that loss; that unusual responsibilities and burdens had been placed upon him; that his last hope of regaining the trust and approval of his late father had been crushed. But the prosecutor – Mr David Staunton, Q.C., on behalf of the Crown – would not recognize any of that as exculpatory, and in the end he put the question that defence had been dreading all along. "If a policeman had been standing at your elbow, would you have acted as you did? If a policeman had been in the seat next to you, would you have shouted your scandalous question at the stage?" And of course the prisoner Staunton broke down and wept and had to say, "No," and then, to all intents, the case was over. The Judge – Mr Justice Staunton, known for his fairness but also for his sternness – didn't even leave the Bench. He found the prisoner Staunton guilty, and the sentence was that he should seek psychiatric help at once.'

'Then what did you do?'

'It was seven o'clock on Sunday morning. I called the airport, booked a passage to Zürich, and twenty-four hours later

I was here. Three hours after arrival I was sitting in Dr Tschudi's office.'

'Was the prisoner Staunton very much depressed by the outcome of the case?'

'It could hardly have been worse for him, because he has a very poor opinion of psychiatry.'

'But he yielded?'

'Doctor von Haller, if a wounded soldier in the eighteenth century had been told he must have a battlefield amputation, he would know that his chances of recovery were slim, but he would have no choice. It would be: die of gangrene or die of the surgeon's knife. My choice in this instance was to go mad unattended or to go mad under the best obtainable auspices.'

'Very frank. We are getting on much better already. You have begun to insult me. I think I may be able to do something for you, Prisoner Staunton.'

'Do you thrive on insult?'

'No. I mean only that you have begun to feel enough about me to want to strike some fire out of me. That is not bad, that comparison between eighteenth-century battlefield surgery and modern psychiatry; this sort of curative work is still fairly young and in the way it is sometimes practised it can be brutal. But there were recoveries, even from eighteenth-century surgery, and as you point out, the alternative was an ugly one.

'Now let us get down to work. The decisions must be entirely yours. What do you expect of me? A cure for your drunkenness? You have told me that it is not your disease, but your symptom; symptoms cannot be cured – only alleviated. Illnesses can be cured when we know what they are and if circumstances are favourable. Then the symptoms abate. You have an illness. You have talked of nothing else. It seems very complicated, but all descriptions of symptoms are complicated. What did you expect when you came to Zürich?'

'I expected nothing at all. I have told you that I have seen many psychiatrists in court, and they are not impressive.'

'That's nonsense. You wouldn't have come if you hadn't had some hope, however reluctant you were to admit it. If we are to achieve anything you must give up the luxury of easy despair. You are too old for that, though in certain ways you seem young for your age. You are forty. That is a critical age. Between thirty-five and forty-five everybody has to turn a corner in his life, or smash into a brick wall. If you are ever going to gain a measure of maturity, now is the time. And I must ask you not to judge psychiatrists on what you see in court. Legal evidence and psychological evidence are quite different things, and when you are on your native ground in court, with your gown on and everything going your way, you can make anybody look stupid, and you do –'

'And I suppose the converse is that when you have a law-yer in your consulting-room, and you are the doctor, you can make him look stupid and you do ?'

'It is not my profession to make anyone look stupid. If we are to do any good here, we must be on terms that are much better than that ; our relationship must go far beyond merely professional wrangling for trivial advantages.'

'Do you mean that we must be friends ?'

'Not at all. We must be on doctor-and-patient terms, with respect on both sides. You are free to dispute and argue any-thing I say if you must, but we shall not go far if you play the defence lawyer every minute of our time. If we go on, we shall be all kinds of things to each other, and I shall pro-bably be your stepmother and your sister and your house-keeper and all sorts of people in the attitude you take toward me before we are through. But if your chief concern is to maintain your image of yourself as the brilliant, drunken counsel with a well-founded grudge against life, we shall take twice as long to do our work because that will have to be changed before anything else can be done. It will cost you much more money, and I don't think you like wasting money.'

'True. But how did you know ?'

'Call it a trade secret. No, that won't do. We must not deal with one another in that vein. Just recognize that I have had

332

rich patients before, and some of them are great counters of their pennies. . . . Would you like a few days to consider what you are going to do?'

'No. I've already decided. I want to go ahead with the treatment.'

'Why?'

'But surely you know why.'

'Yes, but I must find out if you know why.'

'You agree with me that the drinking business is a symptom, and not my disease?'

'Let us not speak of disease. A disease in your case would be a psychosis, which is what you fear and what of course is always possible. Though the rich are rarely mad. Did you know that? They may be neurotic and frequently they are. Psychotic rarely. Let us say that you are in an unsatisfactory state of mind and you want to get out of it. Will that do?'

'It seems a little mild, for what has been happening to me.'

'You mean, like your Netty, nobody knows what you are going through? I assure you that very large numbers of people go through much worse things.'

'Aha, I see where we are going. This is to destroy my sense of uniqueness. I've had lots of that in life, I assure you.'

'No, no. We do not work on the reductive plan, we of the Zürich School. Nobody wants to bring your life's troubles down to having been slapped because you did not do your business on the pot. Even though that might be quite important, it is not the mainspring of a life. You are certainly unique. Everyone is unique. Nobody has ever suffered quite like you before because nobody has ever been you before. But we are members of the human race, as well, and our unique quality has limits. Now – about treatment. There are a few simple things to begin with. You had better leave your hotel and take rooms somewhere. There are quite good pensions where you can be quiet, and that is important. You must have quiet and retirement, because you will have to do a good deal of work yourself between appointments with me, and you will find that tiring.'

'I hate pensions. The food is usually awful.'

'Yes, but they have no bars, and they are not pleased if guests drink very much in their rooms. It would be best if it were inconvenient, but not impossible, for you to drink very much. I think you should try to ration yourself. Don't stop. Just take it gently. Our Swiss wines are very nice.'

'Oh God! Don't talk about *nice* wine.'

'As you please. But be prudent. Much of your present attitude toward things comes from the exacerbations of heavy drinking. You say it doesn't affect you, but of course it does.'

'I know people who drink just as much as I do and are none the worse.'

'Yes. Everybody knows such people. But you are not one of them. After all, you would not be in that chair if you were.'

'If we are not going to talk about my toilet-training, what is the process of your treatment? Bullying and lectures?'

'If necessary. But it isn't usually necessary, and when it is, that is only a small part of the treatment.'

'Then what are you going to do?'

'I am not going to *do* anything to you. I am going to try to help you in the process of becoming yourself.'

'My best self, I expected you to say. A good little boy.'

'Your real self may not be a good little boy. It would be very fortunate if that were so. Your real self may be something very disagreeable and unpleasant. This is not a game we are playing, Mr Staunton. It can be dangerous. Part of my work is to see the dangers as they come and help you to get through them. But if the dangers are inescapable and possibly destructive, don't think I can help you fly over them. There will be lions in the way. I cannot pull their teeth or tell them to make paddy-paws; I can only give you some useful tips about lion-taming.'

'Now you're trying to scare me.'

'I am warning you.'

'What do we do to get to the lions?'

'We can start almost anywhere. But from what you have

told me I think we would be best to stick to the usual course and begin at the beginning.'

'Childhood recollections?'

'Yes, and recollections of your life up to now. Important things. Formative experiences. People who have meant much to you, whether good or bad.'

'That sounds like the Freudians.'

'We have no quarrel with the Freudians, but we do not put the same stress on sexual matters as they do. Sex is very important, but if it were the single most important thing in life it would all be much simpler, and I doubt if mankind would have worked so hard to live far beyond the age when sex is the greatest joy. It is a popular delusion, you know, that people who live very close to nature are great ones for sex. Not a bit. You live with primitives – I did it for three years, when I was younger and very interested in anthropology – and you find out the truth. People wander around naked and nobody cares – not even an erection or a wiggle of the hips. That is because their society does not give them the brandy of Romance, which is the great drug of our world. When sex is on the program they sometimes have to work themselves up with dances and ceremonies to get into the mood for it, and then of course they are very active. But their important daily concern is with food. You know, you can go for a lifetime without sex and come to no special harm. Hundreds of people do so. But you go for a day without food and the matter becomes imperative. In our society food is just a start for our craving. We want all kinds of things – money, a big place in the world, objects of beauty, learning, sainthood, oh, a very long list. So here in Zürich we try to give proper attention to these other things, as well.

'We generally begin with what we call *anamnesis*. Are you a classicist? Do you know any Greek? We look at your history, and meet some people there whom you may know or perhaps you don't, but who are portions of yourself. We take a look at what you remember, and at some things you thought you had forgotten. As that goes on we find we are going much deeper. And when that is satisfactorily explored, we decide whether to go deeper still, to that part of you which is beyond the unique, to the common heritage of mankind.'

'How long does it take?'

'It varies. Sometimes long, sometimes surprisingly short, especially if you decide not to go beyond the personal realm. And though of course I give advice about that, the decision, like all the decisions in this sort of work, must be your own.'

'So I should begin getting a few recollections together? I don't want to be North American about this, but I haven't unlimited time. I mean, three years or anything of that sort is out of the question. I'm the executor of my father's will. I can do quite a lot from here by telephone or by post but I can't be away forever. And there is the problem of Castor to be faced.'

'I have always understood that it takes about three years to settle an estate. In civilized countries, that is ; there are countries here in Europe where it can go on for ten if there is enough money to pay the costs. Does it impress you as interesting that to settle a dead man's affairs takes about the same length of time as settling a life's complications in a man of forty? Still, I see your difficulty. And that makes me wonder if a scheme I have been considering for you might not be worth a trial.'

'What are you thinking of?'

'We do many things to start the stream of recollection flowing in a patient, and to bring forth and give clues to what is important for him. Some patients draw pictures, or paint, or model things in clay. There have even been patients who have danced and devised ceremonies that seemed relevant to their situation. It must be whatever is most congenial to the nature of the analysand.'

'Analysand? Am I an analysand?'

'Horrid word, isn't it? I promise I shall never call you that. We shall stick to the Plain Style, shall we, in what we say to one another?'

'Ramsay always insisted that there was nothing that could not be expressed in the Plain Style if you knew what you were talking about. Everything else was Baroque Style, which he said was not for most people, or Jargon, which was the Devil's work.'

'Very good. Though you must be patient, because English is not my cradle-tongue, and my work creates a lot of Jargon. But about you, and what you may do; I think you might create something, but not pictures or models. You are a lawyer, and you seem to be a great man for words: what would you say to writing a brief of your case?'

'I've digested hundreds of briefs in my time.'

'Yes, and some of them were for cases pleaded before Mr Justice Staunton.'

'This would be for the case pleaded in the court of Mr Justice von Haller.'

'No, no; Mr Justice Staunton still. You cannot get away from him, you know.'

'I haven't often pleaded very successfully for the defendant Staunton in that court. The victories have usually gone to the prosecution. Are you sure we need to do it this way?'

'I think there is good reason to try. It is the heroic way, and you have found it without help from anyone else. That suggests that heroic measures appeal to you, and that you are not really afraid of them.'

'But that was just a game.'

'You played it with great seriousness. And it is not such an uncommon game. Do you know Ibsen's poem –

> To live is to battle with trolls
>   in the vaults of heart and brain.
> To write: that is to sit
>   in judgement over one's self.

I suggest that you make a beginning. Let it be a brief for the defence; you will inevitably prepare a brief for the prosecution as you do so, for that is the kind of court you are to appear in – the court of self-judgement. And Mr Justice Staunton will hear all, and render judgement, perhaps more often than is usual.'

'I see. And what are you in all this?'

'Oh, I am several things; an interested spectator, for one, and for another, I shall be a figure that appears only in military courts, called Prisoner's Friend. And I shall be an authority on precedents, and germane judgements, and I shall keep both the prosecutor and the defence counsel in check. I shall be custodian of that constant and perpetual wish to render to everyone his due. And if Mr Justice Staunton should doze, as judges sometimes do –'

'Not Mr Justice Staunton. He slumbers not, nor sleeps.'

'We shall see if he is as implacable as you suppose. Even Mr Justice Staunton might learn something. A judge is not supposed to be an enemy of the prisoner, and I think Mr Justice Staunton sounds a little too eighteenth century in his outlook to be really good at his work. Perhaps we can lure him into modern times, and get him to see the law in a modern light. . . . And now – until Monday, isn't it?'

2

David Against the Trolls

(*This is my Zürich Notebook, containing notes and sum-
maries used by me in presenting my case to Dr von
Haller; also memoranda of her opinions and interpretations as I made them after my hours with her. Without
being a verbatim report, this is the essence of what
passed between us.*)

I

IT is not easy to be the son of a very rich man.

This could stand as an epigraph for the whole case, for and
against myself, as I shall offer it. Living in the midst of great
wealth without being in any direct sense the possessor of it
has coloured every aspect of my life and determined the
form of all my experience.

Since I entered school at the age of seven I have been
aware that one of the inescapable needs of civilized man –
the need for money – showed itself in my life in a way that
was different from the experience of all but a very few of
my acquaintances. I knew the need for money. Simple
people seem to think that if a family has money, every member dips what he wants out of some ever-replenished bag
that hangs, perhaps, by the front door. Not so. I knew the
need for money, as I shall demonstrate, with special acute-

ness because although as a boy I was known to be the son of a very rich man, I had in fact a smaller allowance than was usual in my school. I knew that my carefulness about buying snacks or a ticket to the movies was a source of amusement and some contempt among the other boys. They thought I was mean. But I knew that I was supposed to be learning to manage money wisely, and that this was a part of the great campaign to make a man of me. The other boys could usually get an extra dollar or two from their fathers, and were virtually certain to be able to raise as much again from their mothers; to them their allowance was a basic rather than an aggregate income. Their parents were good-natured and didn't seem to care whether, at the age of nine or ten, they could manage money or not. But with my dollar a week, of which ten cents was earmarked for Sunday-morning church, and much of which might be gobbled up by a sudden need for a pair of leather skate-laces or something of that sort, I had to be prudent.

My father had read somewhere that the Rockefeller family preserved and refined the financial genius of the Primal Rockefeller by giving their children tiny allowances with which they had learned, through stark necessity, to do financial miracles. It may have been fine for the Rockefellers, but it was no good for me. My sister Caroline usually had lots of money because she was under no necessity to become a man and had to have money always about her for unexplained reasons connected with protecting her virtue. Consequently I was always in debt to Caroline, and because she domineered over me about it I was always caught up in some new method of scrimping or cheese-paring. When I was no more than eight a boy at school told my friends that Staunton was so mean he would skin a louse for the hide and tallow. I was ashamed and hurt; I was not a mini-miser: I was simply, in terms of my situation, poor. I knew it; I hated it; I could not escape from it.

I am not asking for pity. That would be absurd. I lived among the trappings of wealth. Our chauffeur dropped me at school every morning from a limousine that was an object of wonder to car-minded little boys. I was not one of them ; to me a car was, and still is, anything that – mysteriously and rather alarmingly – goes. In the evening, after games, he picked me up again, and as Netty was usually with him, ready to engulf me, it was impossible for me to offer car-fanciers a ride. At home we lived in what I now realize was luxury, and certainly in most ways it was less troublesome than real poverty, which I have since had some opportunities to examine. I was enviable, and if I had the power to cast curses, I should rank the curse of being enviable very high. It has extensive ramifications and subtle refinements. As people assured me from time to time, I had everything. If there was anything I wanted, I could get it by asking my father for it and convincing him that I really needed it and was not merely yielding to a childish whim. This was said to be a very simple matter, but in my experience it might have been simple for Cicero on one of his great days. My father would listen carefully, concealing his amusement as well as he could, and in the end he would knuckle my head affectionately and say: 'Davey, I'll give you a piece of advice that will last you all your life: never buy anything unless you really need it ; things you just *want* are usually junk.'

I am sure he was right, and I have always wished I could live according to his advice. I have never managed it. Nor did he, as I gradually became aware, but somehow that was different. I needed to be made into a man, and he was fully and splendidly and obviously a man. Everybody knew it.

Lapped as I was in every comfort, and fortunate above other boys, how could I have thought I needed money?

What I did need, and very badly, was character. Manhood. The ability to stand on my own feet. My father left me in no doubt about these things, and as my father loved me very much there could be no question that he was right. Love, in a parent, carries with it extraordinary privileges and unquestionable insight. This was one of the things which was taken for granted in our family, and so it did not need to be said.

Was I then a poor little rich boy, wistful for the pleasures

available to my humble friends, the sons of doctors and lawyers and architects, most of whom could not have passed
even the hundred-thousand-a-year test? Not at all. Children
do not question their destiny. Indeed, children do not live
their lives; their lives, on the contrary, live them. I did not
imagine myself to be the happiest of mortals because no such
concept as happiness ever entered my head, though sometimes I was happy almost to the point of bursting. I was told
I was fortunate. Indeed, Netty insisted that I thank God for
it every night, on my knees. I believed it, but I wondered
why I was thanking God when it was so obviously my father
who was the giver of all good things. I considered myself
and my family to be the norm of human existence, by which
all other lives were to be measured. I knew I had troubles
because I was short of pocket-money, but this was trivial
compared with the greater trouble of not being sure I would
ever be a man, and able to stand on my own two feet, and
be worthy of my father's love and trust. I was told that
everything that happened to me was for my good, and by
what possible standard of judgement would I have reached
a dissenting opinion?

So you must not imagine I have come here to whine and
look for revenge on the dead; this retrospective spiting and
birching of parents is one of the things that gets psychoanalysis a bad name. As a lawyer I know there is a statute of
limitations on personal and spiritual wrongs as well as on
legal ones, and that there is no court in the world that can
provide a rescript on past griefs. But if some thoughtful consideration of my past can throw useful light on my present, I
have the past neatly tucked away and can produce it on
demand.

DR VON HALLER: Yes, I think that would be best. You
have got into the swing, and done all the proper lawyer-like
things. So now let us get on.

MYSELF: What do you mean, exactly, 'the proper lawyer-like things'?

DR VON HALLER: Expressing the highest regard for the

person you are going to destroy. Declaring that you have no real feeling in the matter and are quite objective. Suggesting that something is cool and dry which by its nature is hot and steamy. Very good. Continue, please.

MYSELF: If you don't believe what I say, what is the point of continuing? I have said I am not here to blacken my father; I don't know what else I can do to convince you that I speak sincerely.

DR VON HALLER: Very plainly you must go on, and convince me that way. But I am not here to help you preserve the *status quo*, and leave all your personal relationships exactly as you believe them to be now. Remember, among other things, I am Prisoner's Friend. You know what a friend is, I suppose?

MYSELF: Frankly, I'm not sure that I do.

DR VON HALLER: Well – let us hope you will find out. About your early childhood –?

I was born on September 2, 1928, and christened Edward David because my father had been an aide-de-camp – and a friend, really – of the Prince of Wales during his 1927 tour of Canada. My father sometimes jokingly spoke of the Prince as my godfather, though he was nothing of the kind. My real godfathers were a club friend of Father's named Dorris and a stockbroker named Taylor, who moved out of our part of the world not long after my christening; I have no recollection of either of them. I think they had just been roped in to fill a gap, and Father had dropped them both by the time I was ready to take notice. But the Prince sent me a mug with his cipher on it, and I used to drink my milk from it; I still have it, and Netty keeps it polished.

I had a number of childhood diseases during my first two years, and became what is called 'delicate.' This made it hard to keep nurses, because I needed a lot of attention, and children's nurses are scarce in Canada and consequently don't have to stay in demanding places. I had English and Scots nurses to begin with, I believe, and later I used to hear stories of the splendid outfits they wore, which were the wonder of the part of Toronto where we lived. But none of them stuck, and it was my Grandmother Staunton who said that what I needed was not one of those stuck-up Dolly Vardens but a good sensible girl with her head screwed on straight who would do what she was told. That was how Netty Quelch turned up. Netty has been with us ever since.

Because I was delicate, life in the country was thought good for me, and for all of my early years I spent long summers with my grandparents in Deptford, the little village where they lived. My upbringing was a good deal dominated by my grandparents at that time because neither of my parents could stand Deptford, though they had both been born there, and referred to it between themselves as 'that hole.' So every May I was shipped off to Deptford, and stayed till the end of September, and my memories of it are happy. I suppose unless you are unlucky, anywhere you spend your summers as a child is an Arcadia forever. My grandmother couldn't bear the English nurses, and in my second year she told my mother to send her the baby and she would find a local girl to care for me. Indeed, she had such a girl in mind.

Grandmother was a placid, sweet woman whose great adoration was my father, her only son. She had been 'a daughter of the parsonage,' and in my scale of values as a child this was fully equivalent to being a friend of the Prince of Wales. I remember that when I was quite small – four or five – I used to pass the time before I went to sleep thinking what a fine thing it would be if the Prince and Grandmother Staunton could meet ; they would certainly have some fine talks about me, and I could imagine the Prince deferring to Grandmother on most matters because of her superior age and experience of the world, although of course as a man he would have some pretty interesting things to say ; it was likely that he would want me to take charge of Deptford and run it for him. Grandmother was not an active person; she liked sitting, and when she moved she was deliberate. Indeed, she was fat, though I quickly learned that 'fat' was a rude word, to be thought but not spoken of older people. It was the job of the good sensible girl to be active, and Netty Quelch was furiously active.

Netty was one of Grandmother's good works. Her parents, Abel and Hannah Quelch, had been farmers, and were wiped out by one of those fires caused by an overheated stove which were such a common disaster in rural Ontario. They were good, decent folk, and had come as young people from the Isle of Man. Henrietta and her younger brother, Maitland, were left orphans and a responsibility of the neighbours because there was no orphanage nearby, and anyhow an orphanage was a place of last resort. A nearby farmer and his wife added them to their own six children and brought them up. And now Netty was sixteen and was to be launched on the world. Level-headed. A demon for work. Deserving. Just what Grandmother Staunton wanted.

I have never known the world without Netty, so her personal characteristics seemed to me for a long time to be ordained and not matters on which likes or dislikes had any bearing. She was, and is now, below medium height, so spare that all her tendons, strings, and muscles show when they are at work, noisy and clumsy as small people sometimes are, and of boundless overheated energy. Indeed, the impression you get from Netty is that there is a very hot fire burning inside her. Her skin is dry, her breath is hot and strong and suggests combustion, though it is not foul. She is hot to the touch, but not moist. Her complexion is a reddish-brown, as though scorched, and her hair is a dark, dry-red – not carroty but a withered auburn. Her responses are quick, and her gaze is a parched glare. Of course I am used to her, but people who meet her for the first time are sometimes alarmed and mistake the intensity of her personality for some furious, pent-up criticism of themselves. Caroline and Beesty call her the Demon Queen. She is now my housekeeper, and considers herself my keeper.

Netty regards work as the natural state of man. Not to be doing something is, to her, to be either seriously unwell or bone idle, which ranks well below crime. I do not suppose it ever occurred to her when she took on the job of being my nurse that she was to have any time to herself or let me out of her sight, and that was how she functioned. I ate, prayed, defecated, and even slept in the closest proximity with her. Only when she was doing nursery laundry, which was every morning after breakfast, could I escape her. She had a cot in my room, and sometimes when I was restless she took me into her bed to soothe me, which she did by stroking my spine. She could be gentle with a child, but oh – how hot she was! I lay beside her and fried, and when I opened my eyes hers were always open, goggling hotly at me, reflecting whatever light might be in the room.

She had been very helpful to her foster-parents, and they were good people who had done their best for her. She always speaks of them with affection and respect. There had been some babies after she joined the family, and Netty had learned all the elementary arts of child-raising. It was my grandmother who finished her education in that realm, and my grandmother who gave her what I suppose must be called post-doctoral instruction.

Grandfather Staunton was a physician by profession, though when I knew him his chief occupation was his business, which was raising sugar-beets on a large scale and manufacturing them into raw sugar. He was an awesome figure, tall, broad, and fat, with a big stomach that had got away from him, so that when he sat down it rested on his thighs, almost like some familiar creature he was coddling. He looked, in fact, not unlike J. P. Morgan, and like Morgan he had a big strawberry nose. I know he liked me, but it was not his way to show affection, though on a few occasions he called me 'boykin,' an endearment nobody else used. He had great resources of dissatisfaction and disapproval, but he never vented them on me. However, so much of his conversation with my grandmother was rancorous about the government, or Deptford, or his employees, or his handful of remaining patients, that I felt him to be dangerous and never took liberties.

Netty held him in great awe because he was rich, and a doctor, and looked on life as a serious, desperate struggle. As

I grew older, I found out more about him by snooping in his office. He had qualified as a physician in 1887, but before that he had done some work, under the old Upper Canada medical-apprentice system, with a Dr Gamsby, who had been the first doctor in Deptford. He had retained all Doc Gamsby's professional equipment, for he was never a man to get rid of anything, and it lay in neglect and disorder in a couple of glass-fronted cases in his office, a fearful museum of rusty knives, hooks, probes, speculums, and even a wooden stethoscope like a little flageolet. And Doc Gamsby's books! When I could give Netty the slip – and she never thought of looking for me in Grandfather's consulting-room, which was holy ground to her – I would very quietly lift one out of the shelves and gloat over engravings of people swathed in elaborate bandages, or hiked up in slings for 'luxations,' or being cauterized, or – this was an eye-popper – being reamed out for fistula. There were pictures of amputations of all kinds, with large things like pincers for cutting off breasts, diggers for getting at polyps in the nose, and fierce saws for bone. Grandfather did not know I looked at his books, but once, when he met me in the hall outside his room, he beckoned me in and took something out of Doc Gamsby's cabinet.

'Look at this, David,' he said. 'Any idea what that might be?'

It was a flat metal plate about six inches by three, and perhaps three-quarters of an inch thick, and at one end of it was a round button.

'That's for rheumatism,' he said. 'People with rheumatism always tell the doctor they can't move. Seized right up so they can't budge. Now this thing here, Davey, is called a scarifier. Suppose a man has a bad back. Nothing helps him. Well, in the old days, they'd hold this thing here right tight up against where he was stiff, and then they'd press this button –'

Here he pressed the button, and from the surface of the metal plate leapt twelve tiny knife-points, perhaps an eighth of an inch long.

'Then he'd budge,' said Grandfather, and laughed.

His laugh was one I have never heard in anyone else ; he did not blow laughter out, he sucked it in, with a noise that sounded like snuk-snuk, snuk-snuk, snuk.

He put the scarifier away and took out a cigar and hooked the spittoon toward him with his foot, and I knew I was dismissed, having had my first practical lesson in medicine.

What he taught Netty was the craft of dealing with constipation. He had been trained in an era when this was a great and widespread evil, and in rural districts it was, as he himself said with unconscious humour, a corker. Farm people understandably dreaded their draughty privies in winter and cultivated their powers of retention to a point where, in my grandfather's opinion, they were inviting every human ill. During his more active days as a doctor he had warred against constipation, and he kept up the campaign at home. Was I delicate ? Obviously I was full of poisons, and he knew what to do. On Friday nights I was given cascara sagrada, which rounded up the poisons as I slept, and on Saturday morning, before breakfast, I was given a glass of Epsom salts to drive them forth. On Sunday morning, therefore, I was ready for church as pure as the man from whom Paul drove forth the evil spirits. But I suppose I became habituated to these terrible weekly aids, and nothing happened in between. Was Doc Staunton beaten? He was not. I was a candidate for Dr Tyrrell's Domestic Internal Bath.

This nasty device had been invented by some field-marshal in the war against auto-intoxication, and it was supposed to bring all the healing miracle of Spa or Aix-les-Bains to its possessor. It was a rubber bag of a disagreeable gray colour, on the upper side of which was fixed a hollow spike of some hard, black composition. It was filled with warm water until it was fat and ugly ; I was impaled on the spike, which had been greased with Vaseline ; a control stopcock was turned, and my bodily weight was supposed to force the water up inside me to seek out the offending substances. I was not quite heavy enough, so Netty helped by pushing downward on my shoulders. As I was dismayingly invaded below, her breath, like scorching beef, blew in my face Oh, Calvary!

Grandfather had made a refinement of his own on the great invention of Dr Tyrrell; he added slippery elm bark to the warm water, as he had a high opinion of its healing and purgative properties.

I hated all of this, and most of all the critical moment when I was lifted off the greasy spike and carried as fast as Netty could go to the seat of ease. I felt like an overfilled leather bottle, and was in dread lest I should spill. But I was a child, and my wise elders, led by all-knowing Grandfather Staunton, who was a doctor and could see right through you, had decreed this misery as necessary. Did Grandfather Staunton ever resort to the Domestic Internal Bath himself? I once asked timidly. He looked me in the eye and said solemnly that there had been a time when, he was convinced, he owed his life to its efficacy. There was no answer to that except the humblest acquiescence.

Was I therefore a spiritless child? I don't think so. But I seem to have been born with an unusual regard for authority and the power of reason, and I was too small to know how readily these qualities can be brought to the service of the wildest nonsense and cruelty.

Any comment?

DR VON HALLER: Are you constipated now?

MYSELF: No. Not when I eat.

DR VON HALLER: All of this is still only part of the childhood scene. We usually remember painful and humiliating things. But are they all of what we remember? What pleasant recollections of childhood have you? Would you say that on the whole you were happy?

MYSELF: I don't know about 'on the whole.' Sensations in childhood are so intense I can't pretend to recall their duration. When I was happy I was warmly, brimmingly happy, and when I was unhappy I was in hell.

DR VON HALLER: What is the earliest recollection you can honestly vouch for?

MYSELF: Oh, that's easy. I was standing in my grandmother's garden, in warm sunlight, looking into a deep red peony. As I recall it, I wasn't much taller than the peony. It was a moment of very great – perhaps I shouldn't say happiness, because it was really an intense absorption. The whole world, the whole of life, and I myself, became a warm, rich peony-red.

DR VON HALLER: Have you ever tried to recapture that feeling?

MYSELF: Never.

DR VON HALLER: Well, shall we go on with your childhood?

MYSELF: Aren't you even interested in Netty and the Domestic Internal Bath? Nothing about homosexuality yet?

DR VON HALLER: Have you ever subsequently felt drawn toward the passive role in sodomy?

MYSELF: Good God, no!

DR VON HALLER: We shall keep everything in mind. But we need more material. Onward, please. What other happy recollections?

Church-going. It meant dressing up, which I liked. I was an observant child, so the difference between Toronto church and Deptford church kept me happy every Sunday. My parents were Anglicans, and I knew this was a sore touch with my grandparents, who belonged to the United Church of Canada, which was a sort of amalgam of Presbyterians and Methodists, and Congregationalists, too, wherever there happened to be any. Its spirit was evangelical and my grandmother, who was the child of the late Reverend Ira Boyd, a hell-fire Methodist, was evangelical; she had family prayers every morning, and Netty and I and the hired girl all had to be there; Grandfather wasn't able to make it very often, but the general feeling was that he didn't need it because of being a doctor. She read a chapter of the Bible every day of her life. And this was the 'thirties, mind you, not the reign of Queen Victoria. So I was put in the way of thinking a lot about God, and wondering what God thought about me.

350

As with the Prince of Wales, I suspected that He thought rather well of me.

As for church, I liked to compare the two rituals to which I was exposed. The Uniteds didn't think they were ritualists, but that was not how it looked to me. I acquired some virtuosity in ritual. In the Anglican church I walked in smiling, bent my right knee just the proper amount – my father's amount – before going into the pew, and then knelt on the hassock, gazing with unnaturally wide-open eyes at the Cross on the altar. In the United Church, I put on a meek face, sat forward in my pew, and leaned downward, with my hand shielding my eyes, and inhaled the queer smell of the hymn-books in the rack in front of me. In the Anglican church I nodded my head, as if to say 'Quite so,' or (in the slang of the day) 'Hot spit!' whenever Jesus was named in a hymn. But in the United Church if Jesus turned up I sang the name very low, and in the secret voice I used when talking to my grandmother about what my bowels were doing. And of course I was aware that the United minister wore a black robe, a great contrast to Canon Woodiwiss's splendid and various vestments, and that Communion at Deptford meant that everybody got a little dose of something in his pew, and there was no walking about and traffic control by the sidesmen, as at St Simon Zelotes. It was a constant, delightful study, and I appreciated all its refinements. This won me a reputation outside the family as a pious child, and I think I was held up to lesser boys as an example. Imagine it – rich *and* pious! I suppose I bodied forth some ideal for a lot of people, as the plaster statues of the Infant Samuel at Prayer used to do in the nineteenth century.

Sunday was always a great day. Dressing up, my hobby of ritual study, and a full week to go before another assault on my uncooperative colon! But there were wonderful weekdays, too.

Sometimes my grandfather took me and Netty to what was called 'the farm' but was really his huge sugar-beet plantation and the big mill at the centre of it. The country around

Deptford is very flat, alluvial soil. So flat, indeed, that often Netty took me to the railway station, which she elegantly called 'the deepo' just before noon, so that I could have the thrill of seeing a plume of smoke rising far down the track as the approaching train left Darnley, seven miles away. As we drove along the road Grandfather would sometimes say, 'Davey, I own everything on both sides of this road for as far as you can see. Did you know that?' And I always pretended I didn't know it and was amazed, because that was what he wanted. A mile or more before we reached the mill its sweet smell was apparent, and when we drew nearer we could hear its queer noise. It was an oddly inefficient noise – a rattly, clattering noise – because the machinery used for chopping the beets and pressing them and boiling down their sweetness was all huge and powerful, rather than subtle. Grandfather would take me through the mill, and explain all the processes, and get the important man who managed the gauge on the boiler to show me how that worked and how he tested the boiling every few minutes to see that its texture was right.

Best of all was a tiny railway, like a toy, that pulled little carloads of beets from distant fields, puffing and occasionally tooting in a deeply satisfying way as it bustled along. My grandfather owned a railway! And – oh, joy beyond all telling! – he would sometimes tell the engine-driver, whose name was Elmo Pickard, to take me on one of his jaunts into the fields, riding in the little engine! Whether Grandfather wanted to give me a rest, or whether he simply thought women had no place near engines, I don't know, but he never allowed Netty to go with me, and she sat at the mill, fretting that I would get dirty, for the two hours it took to make a round trip. The little engine burned wood, and the wood was covered in a fine layer of atomized sugar syrup, like everything else near the mill, so its combustion was dirty and deliciously smelly.

Elmo and I chuffed and rattled through the fields, flat as Holland, which seemed to be filled with dwarves, for most of the workers were Belgian immigrants who worked on their knees with sawed-off hoes. Elmo scorned them and had only a vague notion where they came from. 'Not a bad fella, fer an Eye-talian!' was the best he would say of the big hulking Flemings, who talked (Elmo said they 'jabbered') in a language that was in itself like the fibrous crunching of chopped beets. But there were English-speaking foremen here and there on the line, and from their conversation with Elmo I learned much that would not have done for Netty's ears. When we had filled all the trucks, we hurtled back to the mill, doing ten miles an hour at the very least, and I was allowed to pull the whistle to tell the mill, and the frantic Netty, that we were approaching.

There were other expeditions. Once or twice every summer Grandmother would say, 'Do you want to go see the people down by the crick today?' I knew from her tone that no great enthusiasm would be welcome. The people down by the crick were my other grandparents, my mother's people, the Cruikshanks.

The Cruikshanks were poor. That was really all that was wrong with them. Ben Cruikshank was a self-employed carpenter, a small dour Scot, whose conversation was full of references to himself as 'independent' and 'self-respecting' and 'owing nothing to no man.' I realize now that he was talking at me, justifying himself for daring to be a grandfather without any money. I think the Cruikshanks were frightened of me because I was such a glossy little article and full of politeness which had a strong edge of sauce. Netty held them cheap ; mere orphan though she was herself, she carried a commission from the great Doc Staunton. Well do I remember the day when my Cruikshank grandmother, who was making jam, offered me some of the frothy barm to eat as she skimmed it from the pot. 'Davey isn't let eat off an iron spoon,' said Netty, and I saw tears in the inferior grandmother's eyes as she meekly found a spoon of some whiter metal (certainly not silver) for her pernickety grandson. She must have mentioned it to Ben, because later in the day he took me into his workshop and showed me his tools and all the things they could do, while talking in a strain I did not

353

understand, and often in a kind of English I could not easily follow. I know now that he was quoting Burns.

> The rank is but the guinea stamp;
> The man's the gowd for a' that –

he said, and in strange words I could not follow I neverthe-less knew he was getting at Grandfather Staunton –

> Ye see yon birkie, ca'd a lord
>   Wha struts and stares, and a' that:
> Tho' thousands worship at his word,
>   He's but a coof for a' that,
> For a' that, and a' that,
>   His riband, star and a' that,
> The man of independent mind
>   He looks and laughs at a' that.

But I was a child, and I suppose I was a hateful child, for I snickered at the repetitions of 'for a' that' and the Lowland speech because I was on Grandfather Staunton's side. And in justice I suppose it must be said that poor Ben overdid it; he was as self-assertive in his humility as the Stauntons were in their pride, and both came to the same thing; nobody had any real charity or desire to understand himself or me. He just wanted to be on top, to be best, and I was a prize to be won rather than a fellow-creature to be respected.

God, I've seen the gross self-assertion of the rich in its most sickening forms, but I swear the orgulous self-esteem of the deserving poor is every bit as bad! Still, I wish I could apologize to Ben and his wife now. I behaved very, very badly, and it's no good saying that I was only a child. So far as I understood, and with the weapons I had at hand, I hurt them and behaved badly toward them. The people down by the crick . . .

(*Here I found I was weeping and could not go on.*)

It was at this point Dr von Haller moved into a realm that was new in our relationship. She talked quite a long time about the Shadow, that side of oneself to which so many real but rarely admitted parts of one's personality must be assigned. My bad behaviour toward the Cruikshanks was certainly a reality, however much my Staunton grandparents might have allowed it to grow. If I had been a more loving child, I would not have behaved so. Lovingness had not been greatly encouraged in me; but had it shown itself as present for encouragement? Slowly, as we talked, a new concept of Staunton-as-Son-of-a-Bitch emerged, and for a few days he gave me the shivers. But there he was. He had to be faced, not only in this, but in a thousand instances, for if he were not understood, none of his good qualities could be redeemed.

Had he good qualities? Certainly. Was he not unusually observant, for a child, of social differences and other people's moods? At a time when so many children move through life without much awareness of anything but themselves and their wants, did he not see beyond, to what other people were and wanted? This was not just infant Machiavellianism; it was sensitivity.

I had never thought of myself as sensitive. Touchy, certainly, and resentful of slights. But were all the slights unreal? And were my antennae always used for negative purposes? Well, perhaps not. Sensitivity worked both in sunlight and shadow.

MYSELF: And I presume the notion is to make the sensitivity always work in a positive way.

DR VON HALLER: If you manage that, you will be a very uncommon person. We are not working to banish your Shadow, you see, but only to understand it, and thereby to work a little more closely with it. To banish your Shadow would be of no psychological service to you. Can you imagine a man without a Shadow? Do you know Chamisso's story of Peter Schlemihl? No? He sold his shadow to the Devil, and he was miserable ever after. No, no; your Shadow is one of the things that keeps you in balance. But you must recognize him, you know, your Shadow. He is not such a terrible fellow if you know him. He is not lovable; he is quite ugly. But accepting this ugly creature is needful if you are really looking for psychological wholeness. When we

355

were talking earlier I said I thought you saw yourself to some extent in the role of Sydney Carton, the gifted, misunderstood, drunken lawyer. These literary figures, you know, provide us with an excellent shorthand for talking about aspects of ourselves, and we all encompass several of them. You are aware of Sydney; now we are getting to know Mr Hyde. Only he isn't Dr Jekyll's gaudy monster, who trampled a child; he is just a proud little boy who hurt some humble people, and knew it and enjoyed it. You are the successor to that little boy. Shall we have some more about him?

Very well. I could pity the boy, but that would be a falsification because the boy never pitied himself. I was a little princeling in Deptford, and I liked it very much. Netty stood between me and everyone else. I didn't play with the other boys in the village because they weren't clean. Probably they did not wash often enough under their foreskins. Netty was very strong on that. I was bathed every day, and I dreaded Netty's assault, the culmination of the bath, when I stood up and she stripped back my foreskin and washed under it with soap. It tickled and it stang and I somehow felt it to be ignominious, but she never tired of saying, 'If you're not clean under there, you're not clean anyplace; you let yourself get dirty under there, and you'll get an awful disease. I've seen it thousands of times.' Not being clean in this special sense was as bad as spitting. I was not allowed to spit, which was a great deprivation in a village filled with accomplished spitters. But it was possible, Netty warned, to spit your brains out. Indeed, I remember seeing an old man in the village named Cece Athelstan, who was quite a well-known character; he had the staggering, high-stepping gait of a man well advanced in syphilis, but Netty assured me that he was certainly a victim of unchecked spitting.

My greatest moment as the young princeling of Deptford was certainly when I appeared as the Groom in a Tom Thumb Wedding at the United Church.

It was in late August, when I was eight years old, and it

was an adjunct of the Fall Fair. This was a great Deptford occasion, and in addition to all the agricultural exhibits, the Indians from the nearby reservation offered handiwork for sale – fans, bead-work, sweet-grass boxes, carved walking-canes, and so forth – and there was a little collection of carnival games, including one called Hit the Nigger in the Eye! where, for twenty-five cents, you could throw three baseballs at a black man who stuck his head through a canvas and defied you to hit him. My grandfather bought three balls for me, and I threw one short, one wide, and one right over the canvas, to the noisy derision of some low boys who were watching and at whom the black man – obviously a subversive type – kept winking as I made a fool of myself. But I pitied their ignorance and despised them, because I knew that when night fell I would be the star of the Fair.

A Tom Thumb Wedding is a mock nuptial ceremony in which all the participants are children, and the delight of it is its miniature quality. The Ladies' Aid of the United Church had arranged one of these things to take place in the tent where, during the day, they had served meals to the fair-goers, and it was intended to offer a refined alternative to the coarse pleasures of the carnival shows. At half-past seven everything was ready. Quite a large audience was assembled, consisting chiefly of ladies who were congratulating themselves on having minds above sword-swallowing and the pickled foetuses of two-headed babies. The tent was hot, and the light from the red, white, and blue bulbs was wavering and rather sickly. At the appropriate moment the boy who played the part of the minister and my best man and I stepped forward to await the Bride.

This was a little girl who had been given the part for her virtue in Sunday School rather than for outward attractions, and although her name was Myrtle she was known to her contemporaries as Toad Wilson. A melodeon played the Wedding Chorus from *Lohengrin* and Toad, supported by six other little girls, walked toward us as slowly as she could, producing an effect rather of reluctance than ceremony.

Toad was dressed fit to kill in a wedding outfit over which

her mother and nobody knows how many others had laboured for weeks ; her figure was bunchy, but she lacked nothing in satin and lace, and was oppressed by her wreath and veil. She should have been the centre of attention, but my grandmother and Netty had taken care of that.

I was a figure of extraordinary elegance, for my grandmother had kept old Mrs Clements, the local dressmaker, busy for a month. I wore black satin trousers, a tail-coat made of velvet, and a sash, or cummerbund, of red silk. With a satin shirt and a large flowing red bow tie I was a rich, if rather droopy, sight. Everybody agreed that a silk hat was what was wanted to crown my finery, but of course there was none of the right size; however, in one of the local stores, my grandmother had unearthed a bowler hat of a type fashionable perhaps in 1900, for it had a narrow flat brim and a very high crown, as if it might have been made for a man with a pointed skull. It fitted, when plenty of cotton wool had been pressed under the inner band. I wore this until the Bride approached, at which moment I swept it off and held it over my heart. This was my own idea, and I think it shows some histrionic flair, because it kept Toad from unfairly monopolizing everybody's attention.

The ceremony was intended to be funny, and the parson was the clown of the evening. He had many things to say that were in a script some member of the Ladies' Aid must have kept since the heyday of Josh Billings – because these Tom Thumb Weddings were already old-fashioned in the 'thirties. 'Do you, Myrtle, promise to get up early and serve a hot breakfast every day in the week?' was one of his great lines, and Toad piped up solemnly, 'I do.' And I recall that I had to promise not to chew tobacco in the house, or use my wife's best scissors to cut stovepipe wire.

All, however, led up to the culminating moment when I kissed the Bride. This had been carefully rehearsed, and it was meant to bring down the house, for I was to be so pressing, and kiss the Bride so often, that the parson, after feigning horror, had to part us. Sure-fire comedy, for it had just that spice of sanctified lewdness that the Ladies' Aid loved, the innocence of children giving it a special savour. But here again I had an improvement; I disliked being laughed at as a child, and I felt that being kissed by me was a serious matter and far too good for such a pie-face as Toad Wilson. I had been to the movies a few times, as a great treat, and had seen kissers of international renown at work. So I went along with the foolish ideas of the Ladies' Aid at rehearsals, but when the great moment arrived at the performance, I threw my hat to one side, knelt gracefully, and lifted Toad's unready paw to my lips. Then I rose, seized her around her nail-keg waist, and pressed a long and burning kiss upon her mouth, bending her backward at the same time as much as her thicky-thumpy body would allow. This, I thought, would show Deptford what romance could be in the hands of a master.

The effect was all I could have hoped. There were oohs and ahs, some of delight, some of disapproval. As Toad and I walked down the aisle to wheezy Mendelssohn it was I, and not the Bride, who held all eyes. Best of all, I heard one woman murmur, with implications that I did not then understand, 'That young one is Boy Staunton's son, all right.' Toad showed a tendency to shine up to me afterward, when we were having ice-cream and cake at the Ladies' Aid expense, but I was cold. When I have squeezed my orange, I throw it away ; that was my attitude at the time.

Netty was not pleased. 'I suppose you thought you were pretty smart, carrying on like that,' was her comment as I was going to bed, and this led to high words and tears. My grandmother thought I was overwrought by public performance, but my chief sensation was disappointment because nobody seemed to understand how remarkable I truly was.

(It was not easy work, this dredging up what could be recovered of my childish past and displaying it before another person. Quite a different thing from realizing, as everybody does, that at some far-off time they have not behaved well.

359

It was at this period that I had a dream, or a vision between waking and sleeping one night, that I was once again on that pier, and was wiping filth and oil from the face of a drowned figure; but as I worked I saw that it was not my father, but a child who lay there, and that the child was myself.)

2

Dreaming had become a common experience for me, though I had never been a great dreamer. Dr von Haller asked me to recover some dreams from childhood, and although I was doubtful, I found that I could do so. There was my dream from my sixth year that I saw Jesus in the sky, floating upward as in pictures of the Ascension; within His mantle, and it seemed to me part of His very figure, was a globe of the world, which He engulfed as though protecting it and displaying it to me, as I stood in the middle of the road down below. Had this been a dream, or a day-time vision? I could never satisfactorily decide, but it was brilliantly clear. And of course there was my recurrent dream, so often experienced, always in a somewhat different form but always the same in the quality of dread and terror that it brought. In this dream I was in a castle or fortress, closed against the outer world, and I was the keeper of a treasure – or sometimes it seemed to be a god or idol – the nature of which I never knew though its value was great in my mind. An Enemy was threatening it from without; this Enemy would run from window to window, looking for a way in, and I would pant from room to room to thwart it and keep it at bay. This dream had been attributed by Netty to my reading of a book called *The Little Lame Prince*, in which a lonely boy lived in a tower, and the book was arbitrarily forbidden; Netty liked to forbid books and always mistrusted them. But I knew perfectly well that I had had the dream long before I read the book and continued to have it long after the book had lost colour in my mind. The intensity of the dream and its sense of threat were of quite a different order from any book I knew.

Dr von Haller and I worked for some time on this dream, trying to recover associations that would throw light on it. Although it seems plain enough to me now, it took several days for me to recognize that the tower was my life, and the treasure was what made it precious and worth defending against the Enemy. But who was this Enemy? Here we had quite a struggle because I insisted that the Enemy was external, whereas Dr von Haller kept leading me back to some point at which I had to admit that the Enemy might be some portion of myself – some inadmissible entity in David which did not accept every circumstance of his life at face value, and which, if it beheld the treasure or the idol, might not agree about its superlative value. But at last, when I had swallowed that and admitted with some reluctance that it might be true, I was anxious to consider what the treasure might be, and it was here that the doctor showed reluctance. Better to wait, she said, and perhaps the answer would emerge of itself.

DR VON HALLER: We do not want to use your grandfather's severe methods for getting at harmful things, do we? We must not press you down upon the hateful, invading spike. Let it alone, allow Nature to have her curative way, and all will be well.

MYSELF: I'm not afraid, you know. I'm willing to go straight ahead and get it over.

DR VON HALLER: You have had quite enough of being a little soldier for the moment. Please accept my assurance that patience will bring better results here than force.

MYSELF: I don't want to go on stressing this, but I am not a stupid person. Haven't I been quick to accept – as an hypothesis anyhow – your ideas about dream interpretation?

DR VON HALLER: Indeed, yes. But accepting an hypothesis is not facing psychological truth. We are not building up an intellectual system; we are attempting to recapture some forgotten things and arousing almost forgotten feelings in the hope that we may throw new light on them, but even more new light on the present. Remember what I have said so many times ; this is not simply rummaging in the trash-heap of the past for its own sake. It is your present situation and your future that concern us. All of what we are talking about is gone and unchangeable ; if it had no importance we could dismiss it. But it has importance, if we are to heal the present and ensure the future.

MYSELF: But you are holding me back. I am ready to accept all of what you say ; I am ready and anxious to go ahead. I learn quickly. I am not stupid.

DR VON HALLER: Excuse me, please. You *are* stupid. You can think and you can learn. You do these things like an educated modern man. But you cannot feel, except like a primitive. Your plight is quite a common one, especially in our day when thinking and learning have been given such absurd prominence, and we have thought and learned our way into world-wide messes. We must educate your feeling and persuade you to experience it like a man and not like a maimed, dull child. So you are not to gobble up your analysis greedily, and then say, 'Aha, I understand that!' because understanding is not the point. Feeling is the point. Under-standing and experiencing are not interchangeable. Any theologian understands martyrdom, but only the martyr ex-periences the fire.

I was not prepared to accept this, and we set off on a long discussion which it would be useless to record in detail, but it hung on the Platonic notion that man apprehends the world about him in four main ways. Here I thought I was at a considerable advantage, because I had studied *The Republic* pretty thoroughly in my Oxford days and had the Oxford man's idea that Plato had been an Oxford man before his time. Yes, I recalled Plato's theory of our fourfold means of apprehension, and could name them: Reason, Understand-ing, Opinion, and Conjecture. But Dr von Haller, who had not been to Oxford, wanted to call them Thinking, Feeling, Sensation, and Intuition, and seemed to have some conviction that it was not possible for a rational man to make his choice or establish his priorities among these four, plumping naturally for Reason. We were born with a predisposition toward one of the four, and had to work from what we were given.

She did say – and I was pleased about this – that Thinking (which I preferred to call Reason) was the leading function in my character. She also thought I was not badly endowed with Sensation, which made me an accurate observer and not to be confused about matters of physical detail. She thought I might be visited from time to time by Intuition, and I knew better than she how true that was, for I have always had a certain ability to see through a brick wall at need and have treasured Jowett's rendering of Plato's word for that ; he called it 'perception of shadows'. But Dr von Haller gave me low marks for Feeling, because whenever I was confronted with a situation that demanded a careful weighing of values, rather than an accurate formulation of relevant ideas, I flew off the handle, as Netty would put it. 'After all, it was because your feelings became unbearable that you decided to come to Zürich,' said she.

MYSELF: But I told you ; that was a rational decision, arrived at somewhat fancifully but nevertheless on the basis of a strict examination of the evidence, in Mr Justice Staunton's court. I did everything in my power to keep Feeling out of the matter.

DR VON HALLER: Precisely. But have you never heard that if you drive Nature out of the door with a pitchfork, she will creep around and climb in at the window? Feeling does that with you.

MYSELF: But wasn't the decision a right one? Am I not here? What more could Feeling have achieved than was brought about by Reason?

DR VON HALLER: I cannot say, because we are talking about you, and not about some hypothetical person. So we must stick to what you are and what you have done. Feeling types have their own problems ; they often think very badly, and it gets them into special messes of their own. But you should recognize this, Mr Justice Staunton : your decision to come here was a cry for help, however carefully you may have disguised it as a decision based on reason or a sentence imposed on yourself by your intellect.

MYSELF: So I am to dethrone my Intellect and set Emotion in its place. Is that it?

DR VON HALLER: There it is, you see! When your unsophisticated Feeling is aroused you talk like that. I wonder what woman inside you talks that way? Your mother, perhaps? Netty? We shall find out. No, you are not asked to set your Intellect aside, but to find out where it can serve you and where it betrays you. And to offer a little nourishment and polish to that poor Caliban who governs your Feeling at present.

(Of course it took much longer and demanded far more talk than what I have put down in these notes, and there were moments when I was angry enough to abandon the whole thing, pay off Dr von Haller, and go out on a monumental toot. I have never been fond of swallowing myself, and one of my faults in the courtroom is that I cannot hide my chagrin and sense of humiliation when a judge decides against me. However, my hatred of losing has played a big part in making me win. So at last we went on.)

If Deptford was my Arcadia, Toronto was a place of no such comfort. We lived in an old, fashionable part of the city, in a big house in which the servants outnumbered the family. There were four Stauntons, but the houseman (who was now and then sufficiently good at his job to be called a butler), the cook, the parlourmaid, the laundry maid, the chauffeur, and of course Netty were the majority and dominated. Not that anybody wanted it that way, but my poor mother had no gift of dealing with them that could prevent it.

People who have no servants often have a quaint notion that it would be delightful to have people always around to

364

do one's bidding. Perhaps so, though I have never known a house where that happened, and certainly our household was not a characteristic one. Servants came and went, sometimes bewilderingly. Housemen drank or seduced the women-servants; cooks stole or had terrible tempers; laundry maids ruined expensive clothes or put crooked creases in the front of my father's trousers; housemaids would do no upstairs work and hadn't enough to do downstairs; the chauffeur was absent when he was wanted or borrowed the cars for joy-riding. The only fixed and abiding star in our household firmament was Netty, and she tattled on all the others and grew in course of time to want the absolute control of a housekeeper, and so was always in a complicated war with the butler. Some servants were foreign and talked among themselves in languages that Netty assumed must conceal dishonest intentions; some were English and Netty knew they were patronizing her. Children always live closer to the servants than their elders, and Caroline and I never knew where we stood with anybody, and sometimes found ourselves hostages in dark, below-stairs intrigues.

The reason, of course, was that my poor mother, who had never had a servant in her life before her marriage (unless you count Grandmother Cruikshank, who seemed to fear her daughter and defer to her and I suppose had always done so) had no notion how to manage such a household. She was naturally kind, and somewhat fearful, and haunted by dread that she would not come up to the standards the servants expected. She courted their favour, asked their opinions, and I suppose it must be said that she was more familiar with them than was prudent. If the housemaid were near her own age she would invite her views on dress; my father knew this, and disapproved, and sometimes said Mother dressed like a housemaid on her day out. Mother knew nothing about the kind of food professional cooks prepare, and let them have their head, so that Father complained that the same few dishes appeared in a pattern. Mother did not like being driven by a chauffeur, so she had a car of her own which she drove, and the chauffeur had not enough to do. She did not insist that the servants speak of my sister and myself as Miss Caroline and Mr David, which was what my father wanted. I suppose there must have been good servants somewhere – other people seemed to find them, and keep them – but we never found any except Netty, and Netty was a nuisance.

There were two major things wrong with Netty. She was in love with my father, and she had known my mother before her marriage and subsequent wealth. It was not until my mother's death that I recognized this, but Caroline was quick to spot it, and it was she who opened my eyes. Netty loved Father abjectly and wordlessly. I doubt if it ever entered her head that her love might be requited in any lasting way – certainly not in any physical way. All she wanted was an occasional good word, or one of his wonderful smiles. As for my mother, I think if Netty had ever clarified her thoughts she would have recognized my mother as a beautiful toy, but without real substance or importance as a wife, and it was not in Netty's nature to recognize any justice in the position my mother had achieved because of her beauty. She had been aware of Mother as the most beautiful girl in Deptford – no, better than that, for Mother was the most beautiful woman I have ever seen – but she had known Mother as the daughter of the people down by the crick. And beauty excepted, what set somebody from down by the crick above Netty herself?

My mother could not have known anything of the spirit that drove my father on and sometimes made him behave in a way that very few people – perhaps nobody but myself – understood. People saw only his present success ; they knew nothing of his great dreams and his discontentment with things as they were. He was rich, certainly, and he had made his money by his own efforts. Grandfather Staunton was quite content to be the local rich man in Deptford, and his ventures in beet sugar had been shrewd. But it was my father who saw that the trifling million and a half pounds of beet sugar produced every year in Canada was nothing compared to what might be done by a man who moved boldly but intelligently into the importation and refining of cane sugar.

People eat about a hundred pounds of sugar a year in one form or another. Father supplied eighty-five pounds of it. And certainly it was Father who saw that much of what had been thought of as waste from the refining process could be used as mineral supplement to poultry and stock foods. So it was not very long before Father was heavily involved in all kinds of bakeries and candy-making and soft drinks and scientifically prepared animal foods, which were managed from a single central agency called the Alpha Corporation. But to look on that as the guiding element in his life was to misunderstand him completely.

His deepest ambition was to be somebody remarkable, to live a fully realized life, to leave nothing undone that came within the range of his desires. He hated people who slouched and slummocked through life, getting nowhere and being nothing. He used to quote a line from a Browning poem he had studied at school about 'the unlit lamp and the ungirt loin.' His lamp was always blazing and his loins were girded as tight as they could be. I suppose that according to the rigmarole about types to which Dr von Haller was introducing me (and which I was inclined to take with a pinch of salt) he would be called a Sensation man, because his sense of the real, the actual and tangible, was so strong. But he was sometimes mistaken about people, and I am much afraid he was mistaken about my mother.

She was a great beauty, but not in the classical style. Hers was the sort of beauty people admired so much in the 'twenties, when girls were supposed to have boyish figures and marvellous big eyes and pretty pouting mouths and above all a great air of vitality. Mother could have been a success in the movies. Or perhaps not, because although she had the looks she was not in the least a performer. I think Father saw in her something that wasn't really there. He thought that a girl with such stunning looks couldn't be just a Deptford girl; I think he supposed that her association with the people down by the crick was not one of parents-and-child, but a fairy-tale arrangement where a princess has been confided to the care of simple cottage folk. It was just

367

a matter of lots of fine clothes and lots of dancing and travelling abroad and unlimited lessons at tennis and bridge, and the princess would stand revealed as what she truly was.

Poor Mother! I always feel guilty about her because I should have loved her more and supported her more than I did, but I was under my father's spell, and I understand now that I sensed his disappointment, and anyone who disappointed him could not have my love. I took all his ambitions and desires for my own and had as much as I could do to endure the fact which became so plain as I grew older, that I was a disappointment myself.

During my work with Dr von Haller I was astonished when one night Felix came to me in a dream. Felix had been my great comfort and solace when I was about four years old, but I had forgotten him.

Felix was a large stuffed bear. He had come to me at a very bitter time, when I had disappointed my father by playing with a doll. Not a girl doll, but a doll dressed like a Highlander that somebody had given me – I cannot recall who it was because I tore all details of the affair out of my mind. It made no difference to Father that it was a soldier doll; what he saw was that I had wrapped it up in a doll's blanket belonging to Caroline and taken it to bed. He smashed the doll against the wall and demanded of Netty in a terrible voice if she was bringing his son up to be a sissy, and if that were so, what further plans had she? Dresses, perhaps? Was she encouraging me to urinate sitting down, so that I could use the ladies' room in hotels when I grew up? I was desolate, and Netty was stricken but tearless, and it was a dreadful bedtime which took unlimited cocoa to alleviate. Only my mother stood up for me, but all she could say was, 'Boy, don't be so *silly!*' and this merely succeeded in drawing his anger on herself.

However, she must have made some compromise with him, for next day she brought Felix to me and said he was a very strong, brave bear for a very strong, brave boy, and we would have lots of daring adventures together. Felix was large, as nursery bears go, and a rich golden-brown, to begin with, and he had an expression of thoughtful determination. He had been made in France, and that was how he came to be named Felix ; my mother thought of all the French names for boys that she knew, which were Jules and Felix, and Jules was rejected as not being so fully masculine as we desired and not fitting the character of this brave bear. So Felix he was, and he was the first of a large brotherhood of bears which I took to bed every night. There was a time when there were nine bears of various sizes in my bed, and not much room left for me.

My father knew about the bears, or at least about Felix, but he raised no objection, and from one or two remarks he let drop I know why. He had been impressed by what he had heard of Winnie-the-Pooh, and he felt that a bear was a proper toy for an upper-class little English boy ; he had a great admiration for whatever was English and upper class. So Felix and I led an untroubled life together even after I had begun to go to school.

My father's admiration for whatever was English was one aspect of the ambiguous relationship between Canada and England. I suppose unkind people would say it was evidence of a colonial quality of mind, but I think it was the form taken by his romanticism. There was something terribly stuffy about Canada in my boyhood – a want of daring and great dimension, a second-handedness in cultural matters, a frowsy old-woman quality – that got on his nerves. You could make money, certainly, and he was doing that as fast as he could. But living the kind of life he wanted was very difficult and in many respects impossible. Father knew what was wrong. It was the Prime Minister.

The Right Honourable William Lyon Mackenzie King was undoubtedly an odd man, but subsequent study has led me to the conclusion that he was a political genius of an extraordinary order. To Father, however, he was the embodiment of several hateful qualities; Mr King's mistrust of England and his desire for greater autonomy for Canada seemed to my father simply a perverse preferring of a lesser to a greater thing; Mr King's conjuror-like ability to do something distracting with his right hand while preparing the denouement of his trick unobtrusively with his left hand had not the dash and flair my father thought he saw in British statesmanship; but the astonishing disparity between Mr King's public and his personal character was what really made my father boil.

'He talks about reason and necessity on the platform, while all the time he is living by superstition and the worst kind of voodoo,' he would roar. 'Do you realize that man never calls an election without getting a fortune-teller in Kingston to name a lucky day? Do you realize that he goes in for automatic writing? And decides important things – nationally important things – by opening his Bible and stabbing at a verse with a paper-knife, while his eyes are shut? And that he sits with the portrait of his mother and communes – *communes* for God's sake! – with her spirit and gets her advice? Am I being taxed almost out of business because of something that has been said by Mackenzie King's mother's ghost? And this is the man who postures as a national leader!'

He was talking to his old friend Dunstan Ramsay, and I was not supposed to be listening. But I remember Ramsay saying, 'You'd better face it, Boy; Mackenzie King rules Canada because he himself is the embodiment of Canada – cold and cautious on the outside, dowdy and pussy in every overt action, but inside a mass of intuition and dark intimations. King is Destiny's child. He will probably always do the right thing for the wrong reasons.'

That was certainly not the way to reconcile Father to Mackenzie King.

Especially was this so when, around 1936, things began to go wrong in England in a way that touched my father nearly.

3

I never really understood Father's relationship with the Prince of Wales, because I had included the Prince as a very special and powerful character in my childish daydreams, and the truth and the fantasy were impossible to disentangle. But children hear far more than people think, and understand much, if not everything. So it began to be clear to me in the autumn of 1936 that the Prince was being harassed by some evil men, whose general character was like that of Mackenzie King. It had to do with a lady the Prince loved, and these bad men – a Prime Minister and an Archbishop – wanted to thwart them both. Father talked a great deal – not to me, but within my hearing – about what every decent man ought to do to show who was boss, and what principles were to prevail. He lectured my mother on this theme with an intensity I could not understand but which seemed to oppress her. It was as if he could think of nothing else. And when the actual Abdication came about he ordered the flag on the Alpha building to fly at half-staff, and was utterly miserable. Of course, we were miserable with him, because it seemed to Caroline and me that terrible misfortune had overtaken our household and the world, and that nothing could ever be right again.

Christmas of that year brought one of the great upheavals that influenced my life. My father and mother had some sort of dreadful quarrel, and he left the house ; as it proved, he did not come back for several days. Dunstan Ramsay, the family friend I have mentioned so often, was there, and he was as kind to Caroline and me as he knew how to be – but he had no touch with children and when our father was angry and in pain we wanted nothing to do with any other man – and he seemed to be very kind and affectionate toward Mother. Netty was out for the day, but Ramsay sent us children up to our own quarters, saying he would look in later; we went, but kept in close touch with what was going on downstairs. Ramsay talked for a long time to our weeping mother; we could hear his deep voice and her sobs. At last she went to her bedroom, and after some rather confused discussion, Carol and I thought we would go along and see her; we didn't know what we would do when we were with her, but we desperately wanted to be with somebody loving and comforting, and we had always counted on her for that. But if she were crying? This was terrible, and we were not sure we could face it. On the other hand we couldn't possibly stay away. We were lonely and frightened. So we crept silently into the passage, and were tip-toeing toward her door when it opened and Ramsay came out, and his face was as we had never seen it before, because he was grinning, but he was also quite clearly angry. He had an alarming face for children, all eyebrows and big nose and lantern jaws, and although he was genial toward us we were always a little frightened by him.

But far worse than this we heard Mother's voice, strange with grief, crying, 'You don't love me!' It was in no tone we had ever heard from her before, and we were terribly alarmed. Ramsay did not see us, because we were some distance away, and when he had thumped downstairs – he has a wooden leg from the First Great War – we scuttled back to our nursery in misery.

What was wrong? Caroline was only six and all she could think of was that Ramsay was hateful not to love Mother and make her cry. But I was eight – a thinking eight – and I had all kinds of emotions I could not understand. Why should Ramsay love Mother? That was what Father did. What was Ramsay doing in Mother's room? I had seen movies and knew that men did not go to bedrooms just to make conversation; something special went on there, though I had no clear idea what it was. And Mother so wretched when Father had inexplicably gone away! Bad things were going on in the world; wicked men were interfering between people who loved each other; what mischief might Ramsay be making between my parents? Did this in some way connect with the misfortunes of the Prince? I thought about it till I had a headache, and I was cross with Caroline, who was not inclined to put up with that from me and made a terrible fuss.

At last Netty came home. She had been spending Christmas with her brother Maitland and his fiancée's family, and she was loaded down with things they had given her. But when she wanted to show them to us we would have none of it. Mother was crying and had gone to bed, and Mr Ramsay had been in her room, and she had called those strange words after him in that strange voice. Netty became very grave and went to Mother's room, Caroline and I close on her heels. Mother was not in her bed. The bathroom door was slightly ajar, and Netty tapped on it. No answer. Netty peeped around the door. And shrieked. Then she turned at once and drove us from the room with instructions to go to the nursery and not dare to budge out of it till she came.

She came at last, and though she was not inclined to yield to our demands to see our mother she must have seen that it was the only way to keep us from further hysteria, so we were allowed to go to her room and very quietly creep up to the bed and kiss her. Mother was apparently asleep, pale as we had never seen her, and her arms lay stiffly on the counterpane, wrapped in bandages. She roused herself enough to smile faintly at us, but Netty forbade any talk and quickly led us away.

But out of the corner of my eye, in an instant as I passed, I saw the horror in the bathroom, and what seemed to be a tub filled with blood. I did not cry out, but cold terror seized me, and it was quite a long time before I could tell Caroline. Not, indeed, until Mother was dying.

Children do not give way to emotional stresses as adults do; they do not sit and mope or go to bed. We went back to the nursery and Caroline played with a doll, wrapping and unwrapping its wrists with a handkerchief and murmuring comfort; I held a book I was not able to read. We were trying to cling to normality; we were even trying to get some advantage out of being up much later than was proper. So we knew that Dunstan Ramsay came back and thumped up the stairs to the room he had left four hours ago, and a doctor came, and Netty did a great deal of running about. Then the doctor came to see us and suggested that we each have some warm milk with a few drops of rum in it to make us sleep. Netty was horrified by the suggestion of rum, so we had crushed aspirin, and at last we slept.

And that was the Christmas of the Abdication for us.

After that, home was never really a secure place. Mother was not the same, and we supposed it was because of whatever happened on Christmas night. The vitality of the 'twenties girl never returned, and her looks changed. I shall never say that she was anything but beautiful, but she had always seemed to have even more energy than her children, which is one of the great fascinations in adults, and after that terrible night she had it no longer, and Netty kept telling us not to tire her.

I see now that this milestone in our family history meant a great advance in power for Netty, because she was the only person who knew what had happened. She had a secret, and a secret is an invaluable adjunct of power.

Her power was not exercised for her own direct advantage. I am sure that all of Netty's world and range of ambition was confined to what went on in our house. Later, when I was studying history, I saw a great deal of the feudal age in terms of Netty. She was loyal to the household and never betrayed it to any outside power. But within the household she was not to be thought of as a paid servant who could be discharged with two weeks' notice, nor do I think it ever crossed her mind that she was free to leave on the same terms. She was somebody. She was Netty. And because of who she was and what she felt, she was free to express opinions and take independent lines that lay far outside the compass of a servant in the ordinary sense. My father once told me that in all the years of their association Netty never asked him for a raise in pay; she assumed that he would give her what was fair and that in emergency she could call upon him with complete certainty of her right to do so. I recall years later some friend of Caroline's questioning the strange relationship between Don Giovanni and Leporello in the opera ; if Leporello didn't like the way the Don lived, why didn't he leave him? 'Because he was a Netty,' said Caroline, and although the friend, who was very much of this age, didn't understand, it seemed to me to be an entirely satisfactory answer. 'Though he slay me, yet will I trust in him,' expressed half of Netty's attitude toward the Staunton family ; the remainder was to be found in the rest of that verse – 'but I will maintain mine own ways before him.' Netty knew about Deptford ; she knew about the people down by the crick ; she knew what happened on Abdication Christmas. But it was not for lesser folk to know these things.

Did all of this make Netty dear to us? No, it made her a holy terror. People who prate about loyal old servants rarely know the hard-won coin of the spirit in which their real wages are paid. Netty's terrible silences about things that were foremost in our minds oppressed Caroline and me and were a great part of what seemed to us to be the darkness that was falling over our home.

DR VON HALLER: Did you never ask Netty what happened on Christmas night?

MYSELF: I cannot recall whether I did, but Caroline asked the next day and got Netty's maddening answer, 'Ask no questions and you'll be told no lies.' When Caroline insisted, 'But I want to know,' there came another predictable answer, 'Then Want will have to be your master.'

DR VON HALLER: And you never asked your mother?

MYSELF: How could we? You know how it is with children ; they know there are forbidden areas, charged with intense feeling. They don't know that most of them are concerned with sex, but they suspect something in the world that would open up terrifying things and threaten their ideas about their parents ; half of them wants to know, and half dreads to know.

DR VON HALLER: Did you know nothing of sex, then?

MYSELF: Odds and ends. There was Netty's insistence about washing 'under there', which conveyed something special. And in Grandfather Staunton's office I had found a curious students' aid called Philips' Popular Manikin, which was a cardboard man who opened up to show his insides, and who had very discreet privy parts like my own. There was also a Popular Manikin (Female) who was partly flayed so that her breasts could only be guessed at, but who had a kind of imperforate bald triangle where the gentleman had ornaments. From some neat spy-work when Caroline was being dressed I knew that Philips had not told the whole story, and as soon as I went to school I was deluged with fanciful and disgusting information, none of which threw much light on anything and which I never dreamed of associating with my mother. I don't think I was as curious about sex as most boys. I wanted to keep things – meaning the state of my own knowledge – pretty much as it was. I suppose I had an intuition that more knowledge would mean greater complications.

DR VON HALLER: Were you happy at school?

It was a good school, and on the whole I liked it there. Happiness was not associated with it because my real life was with my home and family. I was not bad at lessons and managed well enough at games not to be in trouble, though I never excelled. Until I was twelve I went to the preparatory part of the school by the day, but when I was twelve Father decided I should be a boarder and come home only at weekends. That was in 1940, and the war was getting into its stride, and he had to be away a great deal and thought I ought to have masculine influences in my life that Netty certainly could not have provided and my fading mother didn't know about.

Father became very important during the war because one of our jobs in Canada was to provide as much food as we could for Britain. Getting it there was a Navy job, but providing as much as possible of the right things was a big task of organization and expert management, and that was Father's great line. Quite soon he was asked to take on the Ministry of Food, and after warm assurances from the hated Prime Minister that he could have things his own way, Father decided that Mr King had great executive abilities and that anyhow personal differences had to be set aside in an emergency. So he was away for months at a time, in Ottawa and often abroad, and home became a very feminine place.

I see now that one of the effects of this was to make Dunstan Ramsay a much bigger figure in my life. He was the chief history master at my school, Colborne College, and because he was a bachelor and lived a queer kind of inward life, he was one of the masters who was resident in the school and supervised the boarders. Indeed he was Acting Headmaster for most of the war years, because the real Headmaster had gone into the Army Education Service. But he still taught a good many classes, and he always taught history to the boys who were fresh from the Prep, because he wanted them to get a good grounding in what history was ; he caught up with them afterward when they were in the top classes and gave them a final polishing and pushed them for university scholarships. So I saw Ramsay nearly every day.

Like so many good schoolmasters, he was an oddity, and the boys liked him and dreaded him and jeered at him. His nickname was Old Buggerlugs, because he had a trick of jabbing his little finger into his ear and rooting with it, as if he were scratching his brain. The other masters called him Corky because of his artificial leg, and they thought we did so too, but it was Buggerlugs when the boys were by themselves.

The bee in his bonnet was that history and myth are two aspects of a kind of grand pattern in human destiny : history is the mass of observable or recorded fact, but myth is the abstract or essence of it. He used to dredge up extraordinary myths that none of us had ever heard of and demonstrate –

in a fascinating way, I must admit – how they contained some truth that was applicable to widely divergent historical situations.

He had another bee, too, and it was this one that made him a somewhat suspect figure to a lot of parents and consequently to their sons – for the school always had a substantial anti-Ramsay party among the boys. This was his interest in saints. The study of history, he said, was in part a study of the myths and legends that mankind has woven around extraordinary figures like Alexander the Great or Julius Caesar or Charlemagne or Napoleon; they were mortal men, and when the fact could be checked against the legend it was wonderful to see what hero-worshippers had attributed to them. He used to show us a popular nineteenth-century picture of Napoleon during the retreat from Moscow, slumped tragically in his sleigh, defeat and a sense of romantic doom written on his face and on those of the officers about him: then he would read us Stendhal's account of the retreat, recording how chirpy Napoleon was and how he would look out of the windows of his travelling carriage – no open sleigh for him, you can bet – saying, 'Wouldn't those people be amazed if they knew who was so near to them!' Napoleon was one of Ramsay's star turns. He would show us the famous picture of Napoleon on Elba, in full uniform, sitting on a rock and brooding on past greatness. Then he would read us reports of daily life on Elba, when the chief concern was the condition of the great exile's pylorus, and the best possible news was a bulletin posted by his doctors, saying, 'This morning, at 11.22 a.m., the Emperor passed a well-formed stool.'

But why, Ramsay would ask, do we confine our study to great political and military figures to whom the generality of mankind has attributed extraordinary, almost superhuman qualities, and leave out the whole world of saints, to whom mankind has attributed phenomenal virtue? It is trivial to say that power, or even vice, are more interesting than virtue, and people say so only when they have not troubled to take a look at virtue and see how amazing, and sometimes inhuman and unlikable, it really is. The saints also belong among the heroes, and the spirit of Ignatius Loyola is not so far from the spirit of Napoleon as uninformed people suppose.

Ramsay was by way of being an authority on saints, and had written some books about them, though I have not seen them. You can imagine what an uncomfortable figure he could be in a school that admitted boys of every creed and kind but which was essentially devoted to a modernized version of a nineteenth-century Protestant attitude toward life. And of course our parents were embarrassed by real concern about spiritual things and suspicious of anybody who treated the spirit as an ever-present reality, as Ramsay did. He loved to make us uncomfortable intellectually and goad us on to find contradictions or illogicalities in what he said. 'But logic is like cricket,' he would warn, 'it is admirable so long as you are playing according to the rules. But what happens to your game of cricket when somebody suddenly decides to bowl with a football or bat with a hockeystick? Because that is what is continually happening in life.'

The war was a field-day for Ramsay as an historian. The legends that clustered around Hitler and Mussolini were victuals and drink to him. 'The Führer is inspired by voices – as was St Joan: Il Duce feels no pain in the dentist's chair – neither did St Appollonia of Tyana when her teeth were wrenched out by infidels. These are the attributes of the great; and I say attributes advisedly, because it is we who attribute these supernormal qualities to them. Only after his death did it leak out that Napoleon was afraid of cats.'

I liked Ramsay, then. He worked us hard, but he was endlessly diverting and made some pretty good jokes in class. They were repeated around the school as Buggerlugs' Nifties.

My feelings about him underwent a wretched change when my mother died.

4

That was in the late autumn of 1942, when I was in my fifteenth year. She had had pneumonia, and was recovering, but I don't think she had much will to live. Whatever it was, she was convalescent and was supposed to rest every afternoon. The doctor had given instructions that she was on no account to take a chill, but she hated heavy coverings and always lay on her bed under a light rug. One day there was a driving storm, turning toward snow, and her bedroom windows were open, although they certainly should have been shut. We assumed that she had opened them herself. A chill, and in a few days she was dead.

Ramsay called me to his room at school and told me. He was kind in the right way. Didn't commiserate too much, or say anything that would break me down. But he kept me close to him during the next two or three days, and arranged the funeral because Father had to be in London and had cabled to ask him to do it. The funeral was terrible. Caroline didn't come because it was still thought by Netty and the Headmistress of her school that girls didn't go to funerals, so I went with Ramsay. There was a small group, but the people from down by the crick were there, and I tried to talk to them ; of course they hardly knew me and what could anybody say ? Both my Staunton grandparents were dead, so I suppose if there was a Chief Mourner – the undertakers asked who it was and Ramsay dealt with that tactfully – I was the one. My only feeling was a kind of desolated relief, because without ever quite forming the thought in my mind, I knew my mother had not been happy for some years, and I supposed it was because she felt she had failed Father in some way.

I recall saying to Ramsay that I thought perhaps Mother was better off, because she had been so miserable of late ; I meant it as an attempt at grown-up conversation, but he looked queer when he heard it.

Much more significant to me than my mother's actual

death and funeral – for, as I have said, she seemed to be taking farewell of us for quite a long time – was the family dinner on the Saturday night following. Caroline had been at home all week, under Netty's care, and I went home from school for the week-end. There was a perceptible lightening of spirits, and an odd atmosphere, for Father was away and Caroline and I were free of the house as we had never been. What I would have done about this I don't know ; I suppose I should have swanked about a little and perhaps drunk a glass of beer to show my emancipation. But Caroline had different ideas.

She was always the daring one. When she was eight and I was ten she had cut one of Father's cigars in two and dared me to a smoke-down; we were to light up and puff away while soaring and descending rhythmically on the see-saw in the garden. She won. She had a reputation at her school, Bishop Cairncross's, as a practical joker, and had once captured a beetle and painted it gaily before offering it to the nature mistress for identification. The nature mistress, who was up to that one, got off the traditional remark in such circumstances. 'This is known as the *nonsensicus impudens*, or Impudent Humbug, Caroline,' she had said, and gained great face among her pupils as a wit. But when Mother died, Caroline was twelve, and in that queer time between childhood and nubile girlhood, when some girls seem to be wise without experience, and perhaps more clear-headed than they will be again until after their menopause. She took a high line with me on this particular Saturday and said I was to make myself especially tidy for dinner.

Sherry beforehand! We had never been allowed that before, but Caroline had it set out in the drawing-room, and Netty was taken unaware and did not get her objection in until we had glasses. Netty took none herself ; she was fiercely T.T. But Caroline had asked her to dine with us, and Netty must have been shaken by that, because it had never occurred to her that she would do otherwise. She had put on some ceremonial garments instead of her nurse's uniform, and Caroline was in her best and had even put on a dab of lipstick. But this was merely a soft prelude to what was to follow.

There were three places at table and it was clear enough that I was to have Father's chair, but when Netty was guided by Caroline to the other chair of state – my mother's – I wondered what was up. Netty demurred, but Caroline insisted that she take this seat of honour, while she herself sat at my right. It did not occur to me that Caroline was pulling Netty's teeth; she was exalting her as a guest, only to cast her down as a figure of authority. Netty was confused, and missed her cue when the houseman brought in wine and poured a drop for me to approve; she barely recovered in time to turn her own glass upside down. We had had wine before; on great occasions my father gave us wine diluted with water, which he said was the right way to introduce children to one of the great pleasures of life; but undiluted wine, and me giving the nod of approval to the houseman, and glasses refilled under Netty's popping eyes – this was a new and heady experience.

Heady indeed, because the wine, following the sherry, was strong within me, and I knew my voice was becoming loud and assertive and that I was nodding agreement to things that needed no assent.

Not Caroline. She hardly touched her wine – the sneak! – but she was very busy guiding the conversation. We all missed Mother dreadfully, but we had to bear up and go on with life. That was what Mother would have wanted. She had been such a gay person; the last thing she would wish would be prolonged mourning. That is, she had been gay until five or six years ago. What had happened? Did Netty know? Mother had trusted Netty so, and of course she knew things that we were not thought old enough to know – certainly not when we had been quite small children, really. But that was long ago. We were older now.

Netty was not to be drawn.

Daddy was away so much. He couldn't avoid it, really, and the country needed him. Mummy must have felt the loneliness. Odd that she seemed to see so little of her friends during the last two or three years. The house had been gloomy. Netty must have felt it. Nobody came, really, except Dunstan Ramsay. But he was a very old friend, wasn't he? Hadn't Daddy and Mummy known him since before they were married?

Netty was a little more forthcoming. Yes, Mr Ramsay had been a Deptford boy. Much older than Netty, of course, but she heard a few things about him as she grew up. Always a queer one.

Oh? Queer in what way? We had always remembered him coming to the house, so perhaps we didn't notice the queerness. Daddy always said he was deep and clever.

I felt that as host I should get into this conversation – which was really more like a monologue by Caroline, punctuated with occasional grunts from Netty. So I told a few stories about Ramsay as a schoolmaster, and confided that his nick-name was Buggerlugs.

Netty said I should be ashamed to use a word like that in front of my sister.

Caroline put on a face of modesty, and then said she thought Mr Ramsay was handsome in a kind of scary way, like Mr Rochester in *Jane Eyre*, and she had always wondered why he never married.

Maybe he couldn't get the girl he wanted, said Netty.

Really? Caroline had never thought of that. Did Netty know any more? It sounded romantic.

Netty said it had seemed romantic to some people who had nothing better to do than fret about it.

Oh, Netty, don't tease! Who was it?

Netty underwent some sort of struggle, and then said if anybody had wanted to know they had only to use their eyes.

Caroline thought it must all have been terribly romantic when Daddy was young and just back from the war, and Mummy so lovely, and Daddy so handsome – as he still was, didn't Netty think so?

The handsomest man she had ever seen, said Netty, with vehemence.

Had Netty ever seen him in those days?

Well, said Netty, she had been too young to pay much heed to such things when the war ended. After all, she wasn't exactly Methuselah. But when Boy Staunton married Leola Cruikshank in 1924 she had been ten, and everybody knew it was a great love-match, and they were the handsomest pair Deptford had ever seen or was ever likely to see. Nobody had eyes for anyone but the bride, and she guessed Ramsay was like all the rest. After all, he had been Father's best man.

Here Caroline pounced. Did Netty mean Mr Ramsay had been in love with Mother?

Netty was torn between her natural discretion and the equally natural desire to tell what she knew. Well, there had been those that said as much.

So that was why he was always around our house! And why he had taken so much care of Mother when Father had to be away on war business. He was heart-broken but faithful. Caroline had never heard of anything so romantic. She thought Mr Ramsay was sweet.

This word affected Netty and me in different ways. Old Buggerlugs sweet! I laughed much louder and longer than I would have done if I had not had two glasses of Burgundy. But Netty snorted with disdain, and there was that in her burning eyes that showed what she thought of such sweetness.

'Oh, but you'd never admit any man was attractive except Daddy,' said Caroline. She even leaned over and put her hand on Netty's wrist.

What did Caroline mean by that, she demanded.

'It sticks out a mile. You adore him.'

Netty said she hoped she knew her place. It was a simple remark, but extremely old-fashioned for 1942, and if ever I have seen a woman ruffled and shaken, it was Netty as she said it.

Caroline let things simmer down. Of course everybody

adored Daddy. It was inescapable. He was so handsome, and attractive, and clever, and wonderful in every way that no woman could resist him. Didn't Netty think so?

Netty guessed that was about the size of it.

Later Caroline brought up another theme. Wasn't it extraordinary that Mother had taken that chill, when everybody knew it was the worst possible thing for her? How could those windows have been open on such a miserable day?

Netty thought nobody would ever know.

Did Netty mean Mother had opened them herself, asked Caroline, all innocence. But – she laid down her knife and fork – that would be suicide! And suicide was a mortal sin! Everybody at Bishop Cairncross's – yes, and at St Simon Zelotes, where we went to church – was certain of that. If Mother had committed a mortal sin, were we to think that now –? That would be horrible! I swear that Caroline's eyes filled with tears.

Netty was rattled. No, of course she meant nothing of the kind. Anyway that about mortal sins was just Anglican guff and she had never held with it. Never.

But then, how did Mother's windows come to be open?

Somebody must have opened them by mistake, said Netty. We'd never know. There was no sense going on about it. But her baby girl wasn't to think about awful things like suicide.

Caroline said she couldn't bear it, because it wasn't just Anglican guff, and everybody knew suicides went straight to Hell. And to think of Mummy –!

Netty never wept, that I know of. But there was, on very rare occasions, a look of distress on her face which in another woman would have been accompanied by tears. This was such a time.

Caroline leapt up and ran to Netty and buried her face in her shoulder. Netty took her out of the room and I was left amid the ruins of the feast. I thought another glass of Burgundy would be just the thing at that moment, but the butler had removed it, and I had not quite the brass to ring the bell, so I took another apple from the dessert plate and ate it reflectively all by myself. I could not make head or tail of

what had been going on. When the apple was finished, I
went to the drawing-room and sat down to listen to a hockey-
game on the radio. But I soon fell asleep on the sofa.

When I woke, the game was over and some dreary war
news was being broadcast. I had a headache. As I went upstairs I saw a light under Caroline's door, and went in. She
was in pyjamas, carefully painting her toe-nails red.

'You'd better not let Netty catch you at that.'

'Thank you for your invaluable, unsought advice. Netty is
no longer a problem in my life.'

'What have you two been hatching up?'

'We have been reaching an understanding. Netty doesn't
fully comprehend it yet, but I do.'

'What about?'

'Dope! Weren't you listening at dinner? No, you weren't,
of course. You were too busy stuffing your face and guzzling
booze to know what was happening.'

'I saw everything that happened. What didn't I see? Don't
pretend to be so smart.'

'Netty opened up and made a few damaging admissions.
That's what happened.'

'I didn't hear any damaging admissions. What are you
talking about?'

'If you didn't hear it was because you were drinking too
much. Booze will be your downfall. Many a good man has
gone to hell by the booze route, as Grandfather used to say.
Didn't you hear Netty admit that she loves Father?'

'What? She never said that!'

'Not in so many words. But it was plain enough.'

'Well! She certainly has a crust!'

'For loving Father? How refreshingly innocent you are!
One of these days, if you remind me, I'll give you my little
talk about the relation of the sexes. It's a lot more complicated than your low schoolboy mind can comprehend.'

'Oh, shut up! I'm older than you are. I know things you've
never even heard of.'

'You probably mean about fairies. Old stuff, my poor
boy!'

'Carol, I'm going to have to swat you.'

'Putting me to silence by brute strength? Okay, Tarzan. Then you'll never hear the rest – which is also the best.'

'What?'

'Do you acknowledge me as the superior mind?'

'No. What do you know that makes you so superior?'

'Just the shameful secret of your birth, that's all.'

'What!'

'I have every reason to believe that you are the son of Dunstan Ramsay.'

'Me!'

'You. Now I take a good look, in the light of my new information, you are quite a bit like him.'

'I am not! Listen, Carol, you just explain what you've said or I'll kill you!'

'Lay a finger on me, dear brother, and I'll clam up and leave you forever in torturing doubt.'

'Is that what Netty said?'

'Not in so many words. But you know my methods, Watson. Apply them. Now, attend very carefully. Daddy took Mummy away from Dunstan Ramsay and married her. Dunstan Ramsay went right on visiting this house as Trusted Friend. If you read more widely and intelligently you would know the role that Trusted Friend plays in all these affairs. Cast your mind back six years, to that awful Christmas. A quarrel. Daddy sweeps out in a rage. Ramsay remains. We are sent upstairs. Later we see Ramsay leave Mummy's bedroom, where she is in her nightie. We hear her call out, "You don't love me." A few hours later, Mummy tries to kill herself. You remember all that blood, that you couldn't keep your mouth shut about. Daddy isn't around home nearly so much after that, but Ramsay keeps coming. The obvious – the only – conclusion is that Daddy discovered Ramsay was Mummy's lover and couldn't bear it.'

'Carol, you turd! You utter, vile, maggoty, stinking turd! How can you say that about Mother?'

'I don't enjoy saying it, fathead. But Mummy was a very beautiful, attractive woman. Being rather in that line myself

387

I understand the situation, and her feelings, as you never will. I know how passion drives people on. And I accept it. To know all is to forgive all.'

'You'll never get me to believe it.'

'Don't, then. I can't help what you believe. But if you don't believe that you certainly won't believe what came of it.'

'What?'

'What's the good of my telling you, if you don't want to hear?'

'You've got to tell me. You can't just tell me part. I'm a member of this family too, you know. Come on. If you don't I'll get hold of Father next time he's home and tell him what you just said.'

'No you won't. That is one thing you will never do. Admit yourself to be Ramsay's son! Daddy would probably disinherit you. You'd have to go and live with Ramsay. You'd be branded as a bastard, a love-child, a merry-begot –'

'Stop milking the dictionary, and tell me.'

'Okay. I am in a kindly mood, and I won't torture you. Netty killed Mummy.'

I must have looked very queer, for Caroline dropped her Torquemada manner and went on.

'This is deduction, you understand, but deduction of a very superior kind. Consider : the orders were strict against Mummy getting a chill, so we must accept either that Mummy opened those windows herself or somebody else opened them, and the only person around who could have done it was Netty. If Mummy did it, she killed herself knowingly, and that would be suicide, and forgetting all that Netty so rightly calls Anglican guff are you ready to believe Mummy killed herself?'

'But why would Netty do it?'

'Love, dumb-bell. That tempest of passion of which you still know nothing. Netty loves Daddy. Netty has a very fierce, loyal nature. Mummy had deceived Daddy. Listen, do you know what she said to me, after we had left you hogging the wine? We talked a long time about Mummy, and she said, "Everything considered, I think your mother's better out of it."'

'But that isn't admitting she killed anybody.'

'I am not simple. I put the question directly – or as directly as seemed possible in the rather emotional situation. I said, "Netty, tell me truly, who opened the windows? Netty, darling, I'll never breathe it to a soul – did you do it, out of loyalty to Daddy?" She gave me the very queerest look she's ever given me – and there have been some dillies – and said, "Caroline don't you ever breathe or hint any such terrible thing again!"'

'Well, then, there you have it. She said she didn't.'

'She said no such thing! If she didn't, who did? Things make sense, Davey. There is nothing without an explanation. And that is the only explanation possible. She didn't say she hadn't done it. She chose her words carefully.'

'God! What a mess.'

'But fascinating, don't you think? We are children of a fated house.'

'Oh, bullshit! But look – you've jumped to a lot of conclusions. I mean, about us being Ramsay's children –'

'About you being Ramsay's child. I don't come into that part.'

'Why me?'

'Well, look at me; I am unmistakably Boy Staunton's daughter. Everybody says so. I look very much like him. Do you?'

'That doesn't prove anything.'

'I can quite understand you don't want to think so.'

'I think this is all something you've made up to amuse yourself. And I think it's damn nasty – throwing dirt on Mother and making me out to be a bastard. And all this crap about love. What do you know about love? You're just a kid! You haven't even got your monthlies yet!'

'So what, Havelock Ellis? I've got my full quota of intelligence and that's more than you can say.'

'Intelligence! You're just a nasty-minded, mischief-making kid!'

'Oh, go and pee up a tree!' said my sister, who picked up a lot of coarse language at Bishop Cairncross's.

I took my headache, which was now much worse, to my own room. I looked in the mirror. Caroline was crazy. There was nothing in my face to suggest Dunstan Ramsay. Or was there? If you put my beautiful mother and old Buggerlugs together, would you produce anything like me? Caroline had such certainty. Of course she was a greedy novel-reader and romancer, but she was no fool. I didn't look in the least like my father, or the Stauntons, or the Cruikshanks. But –?

I went to bed disheartened but could not sleep. I wanted something, and it took me a long time to admit to myself what I wanted. It was Felix. This was terrible. At my age, wanting a toy bear! It must be the drink. I would never touch a drop of that awful stuff again.

Next day, with elaborate casualness, I asked Netty what had happened to Felix.

'I threw him out years ago,' she said. 'What would you want with an old thing like that? He'd only breed moths.'

DR VON HALLER: Your sister sounds very interesting. Is she still like that?

MYSELF: In an adult way, yes, she is. A great manager. And quite a mischief-maker.

DR VON HALLER: She sounds like a very advanced Feeling Type.

MYSELF: Was it Feeling to sow a doubt in my mind that I have never completely settled since?

DR VON HALLER: Oh, certainly. The Feeling Type understands feeling; that does not mean that such people always share feeling or use it tenderly. They are very good at evoking and managing feeling in others. As your sister did with you.

MYSELF: She caught me off balance.

DR VON HALLER: At fourteen, you were no match for a girl of twelve who was an advanced Feeling Type. You were trying to think your way out of an extremely emotional situation. She was just interested in stirring things up and getting Netty under her thumb. Probably it never occurred to her that you would take seriously what she said about your parentage, and would have laughed at you for being foolish if she knew that you did so.

MYSELF: She planted terrible doubts in my mind.

DR VON HALLER: Yes, but she woke you up. You must be grateful to her for that. She made you think of who you were. And she put your beautiful mother in a different perspective, as somebody over whom men might quarrel, and whom another woman might think it worthwhile to murder.

MYSELF: I don't see the good of that.

DR VON HALLER: Very few sons ever do. But it is hard on women to be looked on as mothers only. You North American men are especially guilty of casting your mothers in a cramping, minor role. It is bad for men to look back toward their mothers without recognizing that they were also people – people who might be loved, or possibly murdered.

MYSELF: My mother knew great unhappiness.

DR VON HALLER: You have said that many times. You have even said it about periods when you were too young to have known anything of the sort. It is a kind of refrain in your story. These refrains are always significant. Suppose you tell me what genuine reasons you have for thinking of your mother as an unhappy woman. Reasons that Mr Justice Staunton would admit as evidence in his strict court.

MYSELF: Direct evidence? Does a woman ever tell her children she is unhappy? A neurotic woman, perhaps, who is trying to get some special response out of them by saying so. My mother was not neurotic. She was a very simple person, really.

DR VON HALLER: What indirect evidence, then?

MYSELF: The way she faded after that terrible Abdication Christmas. She seemed to be more confused than before. She was losing her hold on life.

DR VON HALLER: She had been confused before, then?

MYSELF: She had problems. My father's high expectations. He wanted a brilliant wife, and she tried to be one, but she wasn't cut out for it.

DR VON HALLER: You observed this before her death? Or did you think of it afterward? Or did somebody tell you it was so?

MYSELF: You're worse than Caroline! My father told me so. He gave me some advice one time: Never marry your childhood sweetheart, he said; the reasons that make you choose her will all turn into reasons why you should have rejected her.

DR VON HALLER: He was talking of your mother?

MYSELF: He was really talking about a girl I was in love with. But he mentioned Mother. He said she hadn't grown.

DR VON HALLER: And did you think she had grown?

MYSELF: Why would I care whether she had grown or not? She was my mother.

DR VON HALLER: Until you were fourteen. At that age one is not intellectually demanding. If she were alive now, do you think that you and she would have much to say to one another?

MYSELF: That is not the kind of question that is admitted in Mr Justice Staunton's court.

DR VON HALLER: Was she a woman of any education? Had she any mind?

MYSELF: Does it matter? I suppose not, really.

DR VON HALLER: Were you angry with your father because of what he said?

MYSELF: I thought it was a hell of a thing to say to a boy about his mother, and I thought it was an unforgivable thing to say about the woman who had been his wife.

DR VON HALLER: I see. Suppose we take a short cut. I wish you would take some time during the next few days to sort out why you think your father must always be impeccable in conduct and opinion, but that very much must be forgiven your mother.

MYSELF: She did try to commit suicide, remember. Doesn't that speak of unhappiness? Doesn't that call for pity?

DR VON HALLER: So far we do not know why she made that attempt. Your sister could be right, don't you see? It could have been because of Ramsay.

MYSELF: That's nonsense! You've never seen Ramsay.

DR VON HALLER: Only through your eyes. As I have seen your parents. But I have seen many women with lovers, and it is not always Venus and Adonis, I assure you. But let us leave this theme until we have done more work, and you have had time to do some private investigation of your feelings about your mother. See what you can do to form an opinion of her as a woman – as a person you might meet. ... But now I should like to talk for a moment about Felix. You tell me he has been appearing in your dreams – What does he do there?

MYSELF: He doesn't do anything. He's just there.

DR VON HALLER: Alive?

MYSELF: Alive as he was when I knew him. He seemed to have a personality, you know. Rather puzzled and considering, and I did all the talking. And he usually agreed. Sometimes he was doubtful and said no. But his attention seemed to lend something to whatever I had talked about or decided. Do I make any sense?

DR VON HALLER: Oh, yes; excellent sense. These figures we have in our deep selves, you know, have a way of being both external and internal. That one we talked of – the Shadow – he was inward, wasn't he? And yet as we talked, it appeared that so many of the things you disliked so strongly about him were also to be found in people you knew. You were particularly vehement about Netty's brother, Maitland Quelch –

MYSELF: Yes, but I should have made it clear that I very rarely met him. I just heard about him from Netty. He was so deserving and he had his way to make in the world single-handed, and he would have been so glad of some of the chances I hardly seemed to notice, and all that sort of thing. Matey's struggle to qualify as a Chartered Accountant pretty much paralleled my own studies for the Bar, but of course in Netty's eyes everything had been made easy for me, whereas he did it the hard way. Meritorious Matey! But when I met him, which was as seldom as decency allowed, I always thought he was a loathsome little squirt –

DR VON HALLER: I know. We went into that quite extensively. But in the end we agreed, I think, that you simply read into Matey's character things you disliked, and these proved after some more investigation to be things which were not wholly absent from your own character. Isn't that so?

MYSELF: It's difficult for me to be objective about Matey. When I talk about him I feel myself becoming waspish, and I can't help describing him as if he were some sort of Dickensian freak. But is it my fault he has damp hands and a bad breath and shows his gums when he smiles and calls me Ted, which nobody else on God's green earth does, and exudes democratic forgiveness of my wealth and success –

DR VON HALLER: Yes, yes: we were through all that, and at last you admitted that Matey was your scapegoat – a type of all you disliked and feared might come to the surface in yourself – please, one moment – not in these physical characteristics but in the character of the Deserving Person, ill rewarded and ill understood by a careless world. The Orphan of the Storm: the Battered Baby. You don't have to blush for harbouring something of this in your most secret image of yourself. The important thing is to know what you are doing. That tends to defuse it, you understand. I was not trying during those difficult hours to make you like Matey. I was trying to persuade you to examine a dark corner of yourself.

MYSELF: It was humiliating, but I suppose it must be true.

DR VON HALLER: The truth will grow as we work. That is what we are looking for. The truth, or some part of it.

MYSELF: But although I admit I projected some of the least admirable things in my own character on Matey – you notice how I am picking up words like 'projected' from you – I have a hunch that there is something fishy about him. He's too good to be true.

DR VON HALLER: I am not surprised. Unless one is very naïve, one does not project one's own evil on people who are especially good. As I have said, if psychiatry worked by rules, every policeman would be a psychiatrist. But let us get back to Felix.

MYSELF: Does his appearance now mean some sort of reversion to childhood?

DR VON HALLER: Only to an emotion you felt in childhood, and which does not seem to have been very common with you since. Felix was a friend. He was a loving friend, but because of your own disposition, he was very much a thinking, considering friend. Now just as the Shadow makes his appearance in this sort of personal investigation, so does a figure we call the Friend. And because you have worked well and diligently for the last few weeks, when the going cannot have been very pleasant, I am glad to be able to give you good news. The appearance of the Friend in your inner life and in your dreams is a favourable sign. It means that your analysis is going well.

MYSELF: You're quite right. This probing and recollecting hasn't been pleasant. There have been times when I have been annoyed and disgusted with you. There were moments when I wondered if I were really out of my mind to put myself in the hands of anyone who tormented me and thwarted me as you have done.

DR VON HALLER: Quite so. I was aware of it, of course. But as we go on you will find that I seem to be many things to you. If you understand me, part of my professional task is to be the bearer of your projections. When the Shadow was under investigation, and so much of your inferior self was coming to light, you found the Shadow in me. Now we seem to have awakened the image of the Friend in your mind, your spirit, your soul – these are not scientific terms but I promised not to deluge you with jargon – and perhaps I shall not now be so intolerable.

MYSELF: I'm delighted. I would truly like to know you better.

DR VON HALLER: It is yourself you must truly know better. And I should warn you that I shall appear as the Friend only for a limited time. Yes; I have many other parts to play before we are done. And even the Friend is not always benevolent: sometimes friends are truest when they seem unfriendly. It's funny that your Friend is a bear; I mean, the Friend often appears as an animal, but rarely as a savage animal ... Now, let me see; we have reached your mother's death, and the moment when Caroline, mischievously but perhaps not untruly, made some suggestions that made you see yourself in a new light. It sounds almost like the end of childhood.

5

It was. I was adolescent now. Of course I knew a good deal about what people stupidly call the facts of life, but I had not had much physical experience of what sex meant. Now it began to be very troublesome. I find it odd, now, to read some of the popular books that glorify masturbation; I never thought it would kill me, or anything stupid like that, but I did my best to control it because – well, it seemed such a shabby thing. I suppose I didn't bring much imagination to it.

As I look back now I see that, although I knew a good deal about sex, I had retained an unusual innocence for my age, and I suppose it was my father's money, and the sense of isolation it brought, that made my innocence possible.

I told you what Netty had said about 'Anglican guff'. She was scornful of what she called 'Pancake Christianity' because we ate pancakes at Shrove; she used to snort when my parents had lobster salad on Fridays in Lent and always demanded that meat be sent up to the nursery for herself. She never, I think, quite forgave my parents for leaving the wholesome bosom of evangelistic Protestantism. Church matters – I won't call it religion – played a big part in my growing up. We were attached to St Simon Zelotes, which had the reputation of being a rich people's church. It wasn't the most fashionable Anglican church in the city, but it had a special cachet. The fashionable one, I suppose, was St Paul's, but it was Broad Church. I suppose you are familiar with these distinctions? And the High Church was St Mary Magdalene, but it was poor. St Simon Zelotes was neither so High as Mary Mag, nor so rich as Paul's. The vicar was Canon Woodiwiss – he later became an Archdeacon and finally Bishop – and he was a gifted apostle to the well-to-do. I don't say that sneeringly. There always seems to be a notion that the rich can't be devout and that God doesn't like them as much as He likes the poor. There are lots of Christians who are all pity and charity for the miserable and the outcast, but who think it a spiritual duty to give the rich a good snubbing whenever they can. So Woodiwiss was a real find for a church like Simon Zelotes.

He soaked the rich for money, which was fair enough. At least once a year he preached his famous sermon about 'it is easier for a camel to go through the eye of a needle than for a rich man to enter into the kingdom of God'. He would explain that the Needle's Eye was the name of a gate to Jerusalem which was so narrow that a heavily laden camel had to be relieved of some of its burden to get through, and that custom demanded that whatever was taken from the camel became the property of the Temple. So the obvious course for a rich man was to divest himself of some of his wealth for the church and thereby take a step toward salvation. I believe that in terms of history and theology this is all moonshine and Woodiwiss may even have invented it himself, but it worked like a charm. Because, as he said, following on from his text, 'with God all things are possible'. So he persuaded his rich camels to strip off a few bales of this world's goods and leave the negotiation of the needle's eye in his capable hands.

I didn't see much of the Canon, though I heard many of his wonder-working sermons. He had the gift of the gab as few parsons do. But I came much under the influence of one of his curates, who was named Gervase Knopwood.

Father Knopwood, as he liked us to call him, had an extraordinary way with boys, though on the face of it this seemed unlikely. He was an Englishman with an almost farcically upper-class accent and long front teeth and an appearance of being an elderly schoolboy. He wasn't old; probably he was in his early forties, but his hair was almost white and he had deep furrows in his face. He wasn't a joker or a jolly good fellow, and he played no games, though he was tough enough to have been a missionary in the Canadian West in some very difficult territory. But everybody respected him, and everybody feared him in a special way, for his standards were high, he expected the best from boys, and he had some ideas that to me were original.

For one thing, he didn't pay the usual lip-service to Art, which enjoyed more than sacred status in the kind of society in which we lived. I discovered this one day when I was talking to him in one of the rooms at the back of the church where we met for the Servers' Guild and Confirmation classes and that sort of thing. There was a picture on the wall, a perfectly hideous thing in vivid colours, of a Boy Scout looking the very picture of boyish virtue, and behind him stood the figure of Christ with His hand on the Scout's shoulder. I was making great game of it for the benefit of some other boys when I became aware that Father Knopwood was standing at a little distance, listening carefully.

'You don't think much of it, Davey?'

'Well, Father, could anybody think much of it? I mean, look at the way it's drawn, and the raw colours. And the sentimentality!'

'Tell us about the sentimentality.'

'Well – it's obvious. I mean, Our Lord standing with His hand on the fellow's shoulder, and everything.'

'I seem to have missed something you have seen. Why is it sentimental to suggest that Christ stands near to anyone, whether it is a boy, or a girl, or an old man, or anyone at all?'

'That's not sentimental, of course. But it's the way it's done. I mean, the concept is so crude.'

'Must a concept be sophisticated to be a good one?'

'Well – surely?'

'Must the workmanship always be superior? If something

is to be said, must it always be said with eloquence and taste?'

'That's what they teach us in the Art Club. I mean, if it's not well done it's no good, is it?'

'I don't know. I've never been able to make up my mind. A lot of modern artists are impatient of technical skill. It's one of the great puzzles. Why don't you come and see me after the meeting, and we'll talk about it and see what we can find out.'

This led to seeing a lot of Father Knopwood. He used to ask me to meals in his rooms, as he called a bed-sitter with a gas ring in a cupboard that he had not far from the church. He wasn't poison-poor, but he didn't believe in spending money on himself. He taught me a lot and put some questions I have never been able to answer.

The art thing was one of his pet subjects. He loved art and knew a lot about it, but he was always rather afraid of it as a substitute religion. He was especially down on the idea that art was a thing in itself – that a picture was simply a flat composition of line and pigment, and the fact that it seemed also to be Mona Lisa or The Marriage at Cana was an irrelevance. Every picture, he insisted, was 'of' something or 'about' something. He was interesting about very modern pictures, and once he took me to a good show of some of the best, and talked about them as manifestations of questing, chaos, and sometimes of despair that artists sensed in the world about them and could not express adequately in any other way. 'A real artist never does anything gratuitously or simply to be puzzling,' he would say, 'and if we don't understand it now, we shall understand it later.'

This was not what Mr Pugliesi said in the Art Club at school. We had a lot of clubs, and the Art Club had rather a cachet, as attracting the more intellectual boys; you were elected to it, you didn't simply join. Mr Pugliesi was always warning us not to look for messages and meanings but to take heed of the primary thing – the picture as an object – so many square feet of painted canvas. Messages and meanings were what Father Knopwood chiefly sought, so I had to balance my ideas pretty carefully. That was why he got after me for laughing at the Boy Scout picture. He agreed that it was an awful picture, but he thought the meaning redeemed it. Thousands of boys would understand it who would never notice a Raphael reproduction if we put one in its place.

I have never been convinced that he was right, and was shocked by his idea that not everybody needed art to be educated. He saved me from becoming an art snob, and he could be terribly funny about changes in art taste; the sort of fashionable enthusiasm that admires Tissot for thirty years, kicks him out of the door for forty, and then drags him back through the window as an artist of hitherto unappreciated quality. 'It's simply the immature business of assuming that one's grandfather must necessarily be a fool, and then getting enough sense to realize that the old gentleman was almost as intelligent as oneself,' he said.

This was important to me because another kind of art was coming to the fore at home. Caroline, who had always had lessons on the piano, was beginning to show some talent as a musician. We had both had some musical training and used to go to Mrs Tattersall's Saturday morning classes, where we sang and played rhythm instruments and learned some basic stuff very pleasantly. But I had no special ability, and Caroline had. By the time she was twelve she had fought through a lot of the donkey-work of learning that extraordinarily difficult instrument that all unmusical parents seem to think their children should play, and she was pretty good. She has never become a first-rate pianist, but she is a much better than average amateur.

When she was twelve, though, she was sure that she was going to be another Myra Hess and worked very hard. She played musically, which is really quite rare, even among people who get paid big fees to do it. Like Father Knopwood, she was interested in content as well as technique, and it was always a puzzle to me how she got to be that way, for nothing at home encouraged it. She played the things young pianists play – Schumann's *The Prophet Bird* and his *Scenes from Childhood*, and of course lots of Bach and Scarlatti and Beethoven. She could wallop out Schumann's *Carnaval* with immense authority for a girl of twelve or thirteen. The mischievous little snip she was in her personal life seemed to disappear, and somebody much more important took her place. I think I liked it best when she played some of the easier things she had learned in earlier years and fully commanded. There is one trifle – I don't suppose it has much musical value – by Stephen Heller, called in English *Curious Story*, which is a very misleading translation of *Kuriose Geschichte*; she really succeeded in making it eerie, not by playing in a false, spooky way, but by a refined, Hans Andersen treatment. I loved listening to her, and though she tormented me horribly at other times, we seemed to be able to reach one another when she was playing and I was listening, and Netty was somewhere else.

Caroline was glad to see me at weekends, because the house was even gloomier than before our mother died. It wasn't neglected ; there were still servants, though the staff had been cut down, and they polished and tidied things that never grew dim or untidy because nobody ever touched them ; but the life had gone out of the house, and even though its former life had been unhappy, it had been life of a kind. Caroline lived there, supposedly under the care of Netty, and once a week Father's secretary, an extremely efficient woman from Alpha Corporation, called to see that everything was in good order. But this secretary didn't want to be involved personally, and I don't blame her. Caroline was a day-girl at Bishop Cairncross's, so she had friends and a social life there, as I did at Colborne College.

We rarely asked anybody home, and our first attempt to take over the house as our own soon spent itself. Father wrote letters now and then, and I know he asked Dunstan Ramsay to keep an eye on us, but Ramsay had his hands full at the school during those war years, and he didn't trouble us often. I rather think he disliked Carol, so he confined his supervision to questioning me now and then at school.

You might suppose my sister and I were to be pitied, but

we rather liked our weekend solitude. We could lighten it whenever we pleased by going out with friends, and people were kind about inviting us both to parties and such things, though during the war they were on a very modest scale. But I didn't want to go out much because I had no money and could get into embarrassing positions; I borrowed all I could from Carol but didn't want to be wholly in her clutch.

What we both liked best were the Saturday evenings when we were together, because it had become the custom for Netty to devote that time to her pestilent brother Maitland and his deserving young family. Carol played the piano, and I looked through books about art which I was able to borrow from the school library. I was determined about this because I didn't want her to think that I had no independent artistic interest of my own, but as I looked at pictures and read about them, I was really listening to her. It was the only time the drawing-room showed any hint of life, but the big empty fireplace – the secretary from Alpha and Netty agreed that it was foolish to light it during wartime, when presumably even cord-wood was involved in our total war effort – was a reminder that the room was merely enduring us, and that as soon as we went to bed a weight of inanition would settle on it again.

I remember one night when Ramsay did drop in, and laughed to see us.

'Music and painting,' said he; 'the traditional diversions of the third generation of wealthy families. Let us hope you will both become discriminating patrons. God knows they are rare.'

We didn't like this, and Carol was particularly offended by his assumption that she would never do anything directly as a musician. But time has proved him right, as it does with so many disagreeable people. Carol and Beesty are now generous patrons of music, and I collect pictures. With both of us, as Father Knopwood feared, it has become the only spiritual life we have, and not a very satisfactory one when life is hard.

Knopwood prepared me for Confirmation, and it was a much more important experience than I believe is usually the case. Most curates, you know, take you through the Catechism and bid you to ask them about anything you don't understand. Of course most people don't understand any of it, but they are content to let sleeping dogs lie. Most curates give you a vaguely worded talk about keeping yourself pure, without any real hope that you will.

Knopwood was very different. He expounded the Creed in tough terms, very much in the C. S. Lewis manner. Christianity was serious and demanding, but worth any amount of trouble. God is here, and Christ is now. That was his line. And when it came to the talk about purity, he got down to brass tacks better than anybody I have ever known.

He didn't expect you to chalk up a hundred per cent score, but he expected you to try, and if you sinned, he expected you to know what you had done and why it was sin. If you knew that, you were better armed next time. This appealed to me. I liked dogma, for the same reason that I grew to like law. It made sense, it told you where you stood, and it had been tested by long precedent.

He was very good about sex. It was pleasure: yes. It could be a duty: yes. But it wasn't divorced from the rest of life, and what you did sexually was of a piece with what you did in your friendships and in your duty to other people in your public life. An adulterer and a burglar were bad men for similar reasons. A seducer and a sneak-thief were the same kind of man. Sex was not a toy. The great sin – quite possibly the Sin against the Holy Ghost – was to use yourself or someone else contemptuously, as an object of convenience. I saw the logic of that and agreed.

There were problems. Not everybody fitted all rules. If you found yourself in that situation you had to do the best you could, but you had to bear in mind that the Sin against the Holy Ghost would not be forgiven you, and the retribution would be in this world.

The brighter members of Knoppy's Confirmation classes knew what he was talking about at this point. It was clear enough that he was himself a homosexual and knew it, and that his work with boys was his way of coping with it. But he never played favourites, he was a dear and thoroughly masculine friend, and there was never any monkey-business when he asked you to his rooms. I suppose there are hundreds like me who remember him with lasting affection and count having known him as a great experience. He stood by me during my early love-affair in a way I can never forget and which nothing I could do would possibly repay.

I wish we could have remained friends.

6

People jeer at first love, and in ridiculous people it is certainly ridiculous. But I have seen how hot its flame can be in people of passionate nature, and how selfless it is in people who are inclined to be idealistic. It does not demand to be requited, and it can be a force where it is obviously hopeless. The worst fight I saw in my schooldays was caused when a boy said something derogatory about Loretta Young; another boy, who cherished a passion for the actress, whom he had seen only in films, hit this fellow in the mouth, and in an instant they were on the ground, the lover trying to murder the loudmouth. Our gym master parted them and insisted that they fight it out in the ring, but it was hopeless: the lover ignored all rules, kicked and bit and seemed like a madman. Of course nobody could explain to the master what the trouble was, but all of us supposed it was a fight about love. What I know now was that it was really a fight about honour and idealism – what Dr von Haller calls a projection – and that it was a necessary part of the spiritual development of the lover. It may also have done something for the fellow who was so free with the name of Miss Young.

I fell in love, with a crash and at first sight, on a Friday night in early December of 1944. I had been in love before, but trivially. Many boys, I think, are in love from the time they are able to walk, and I had cherished my hidden fancies and had had my conquests, of whom Toad Wilson was by no means the best example. Those were childish affairs, with shallow roots in Vanity. But now I was sixteen, serious and lonely, and in three hours Judith Wolff became the central, absorbing element in my life.

Caroline's school, named for a Bishop Cairncross who had been a dominant figure in the nineteenth-century life of our Canadian province, had a reputation for its plays and its music. Every school needs to be known for something other than good teaching, and its Christmas play was its speciality. In the year when I was sixteen the school decided to combine music and drama and get up a piece by Walter de la Mare called *Crossings*. I heard a good deal about it because it had a lot of music and four songs in it, and Caroline was to play the piano off stage. She practised at home and talked about the play as if it were the biggest musical show since Verdi wrote *Aida* for the Khedive of Egypt.

I read the playbook she had to work from, and I did not think much of it. It was certainly not in the Plain Style, and I was now much under the influence of Ramsay's enthusiasm for unadorned prose. It was not a Broadway kind of play, and I am not certain it is even a good play, but it is unmistakably a poet's play, and I was the most deeply enchanted of an audience that seemed, in a variety of ways suitable to their age and state of mind and relationship to the players or the school, to be delighted by it.

It is about some children who are left to their own devices because of a legacy. They have an aunt who has strict educational theories and expects them to get into hopeless messes without her guidance; instead they have some fine adventures with strange people, including fairy people. The oldest child is a girl called Sally, and that was Judith Wolff.

Sally is very much a de la Mare girl, and I don't think I ever saw Judith except through de la Mare eyes. The curtain went up (or rather, was drawn apart with a wiry hiss) and there she sat, at a piano, precisely as the poet describes her in the stage directions – slim, dark, of mobile face, speaking in a low clear voice as if out of her thoughts. She had a song almost at once. The illusion that she was playing the piano was not successful, because the sound was plainly coming from Caroline backstage, and her pretence to be playing was no better than it usually is. But her voice made shortcomings of that sort irrelevant. I suppose it was just a charming girl's voice, but I shall never know. It was a voice that seemed to be for me only in all the world. I was engulfed in love, and I suppose I have been in love with Judith ever since. Not as she is now. I see her from time to time, by chance ; a woman of my own age, still gravely beautiful. But she is a Mrs Julius Meyer, whose husband is an admired professor of chemistry, and I know that she has three clever children and is an important figure on the committee of the Jewish hospital. Mrs Julius Meyer is not Judith Wolff to me, but her ghost, and when I see her I get away as fast as possible. The David Staunton who fell in love still lives in me, but Judith Wolff – the girl of the de la Mare play – lives only in my memories.

Judith had two songs in *Crossings*. She acted as she sang, with a grave natural charm, and was much, much, much the best of the girls in the play.

There were people who thought differently. As always at these affairs, there were people who thought the girls who played masculine parts were wildly funny, and I suppose that when they turned their whiskered, carefully made-up faces away, and we saw their girl-shaped bottoms, it was funny if that is where you find your fun. There was much applause for a small blonde who played the Queen of the Fairies ; she acted with a sweetness which I thought painfully overdone. There was a ballet of fairies, very pretty as they danced through a snow-scene, holding little lanterns ; there were plenty of parents with eyes only for a special fairy. But I saw nothing clearly but Judith, and in justice to the audience generally I must say that they thought that she was – always excepting their own child – the best. For the curtain call the stage was filled with the whole cast, and also the inevitable clown assembly of mistresses in sensible shoes who had helped in some way, looking as such helpers always do, too big and too clumsy to have had anything to do with creating an illusion. Judith stood in the centre of the first line, and it seemed to me that she was aware of her popularity and was blushing at it.

I applauded uproariously, and I noticed some parents looking approvingly at me. I suppose they thought I was clapping for Caroline and was a loyal brother. Caroline was on the stage, certainly, holding the score of the music so people would know what she had done, but I had no eyes for her. After the party for the cast and friends – school coffee and school cookies – I took Caroline home and tried to find out something about Judith Wolff. She had been surrounded by some foreign-looking people whom I supposed to be her parents and their friends, and I had not been able to get a good look at her. But Caroline was full of herself, as always, and demanded again and again that I reassure her that the music had been suitably audible, yet not too loud, and had supported the weaker singers without seeming to dominate them, and had really carried the ballet, who were just little girls and had no more sense of rhythm than so many donkeys, and had indeed been fully orchestral in effect. This was egotistical nonsense, but I had to put up with it in order to bring the conversation around to what I wanted to know.

Weren't they lucky to get such a good girl for the part of Sally? Who was she?

Oh – Judy Wolff. Nice voice, but dark. Brought it too much from the back of her throat. Needed some lessons in production.

Perhaps. Good for that part, though.

Possibly. A bit of a cow at rehearsal. Hard to stir her up.

I considered killing Caroline and leaving her battered body on the lawn of one of the houses we were passing.

Caroline knew I wouldn't have noticed, because it was a fine point not many people would get, but in Sally's *Lullaby* in Act Two, at 'Leap fox, hoot owl, wail warbler sweet,' Judy was all over the place, and as Caroline had a very tricky succession of chromatic chords to play there was nothing she could do to drag Judy back, and she just hoped it would be better tomorrow night.

You cannot have a sister like Caroline without picking up a few tricks. I asked if there was any chance that I could see the play again on Saturday night?

'So you can go and moon at Judy again?' she said. In another age Caroline would have been burnt as a witch; she could smell what you were thinking, especially when you wanted to conceal it. I set aside plans for burning her then and there.

'Judy who? Oh, the Sally girl. Don't be silly. No, I just thought it was good, and I'd like to see it again. And I was thinking you didn't really get the recognition you deserved tonight. If I came tomorrow night, I could send you a bouquet, and it could be handed up over the footlights at the end, and people would know what you were worth.'

'Not a bad idea, but where would you get any money to send a bouquet? You're broke.'

'I'd wondered if you could possibly see your way to making me a small loan. As it's really for you, anyhow.'

'What's the need? Why can't I just send myself a bouquet? That would cut out the middleman.'

'Because it's ridiculous and undignified and cheap and generally two-bit and no-account, and if Netty heard of it, as she would from me, she would make your life a burden. Whereas if the bouquet comes from me, nobody need know, and if they find out they'll think what a sweet brother I am. But I'll put a big ticket on it with "Homage to those eloquent fingers, from Arturo Toscanini" if you like.'

It worked. I thought it would be a cheap dollar bouquet, but I had underrated Caroline's vanity, and she handed over a nice, resounding five bucks as a tribute to herself. This was splendid because I had craftily decided to sequester some portion of whatever I got from Caroline, and use it to send another bouquet to Judy Wolff. With five dollars I could do the thing in style.

Florists were more grasping than I had supposed, but after

shopping around on Saturday I managed quite a showy tribute for Caroline, of chrysanthemums with plenty of fern to eke them out, for a dollar seventy-five. With the remaining three twenty-five, to which I added fifty cents I ground out of Netty by pretending I had to get a couple of special pencils for making maps, I bought roses for Judy. Not the best roses; I had no money for those; but indubitable roses.

I was playing a dangerous game. I knew it, yet I could not help myself. Caroline would find out about the two bouquets and would take it out of me in some dreadful way, for she was a terrible skinflint. But I was ready to risk anything, so long as Judy Wolff received the tribute that was her due. The thought of the evening sustained me through a nervous, worrisome Saturday.

It worked out quite differently from anything I could have foreseen. In the first place, Netty wanted to go to *Crossings*, and it was assumed that I should take her. There is a special sort of enraged misery that overcomes a young man who is absorbed in his love for an ideal girl and who is thrust into the company of a distasteful, commonplace older woman. Dr von Haller talks about the concept of the Shadow; how much of my Shadow – of my impatience, my snobbery, my ingratitude – was visited on poor Netty that night! To have to sit beside her, and answer her tomfool questions and listen to her crass assertions, and breathe up her smell of fevered flesh and laundry starch, and be conscious of her garment of state, her sheared mouton coat, among all the minky mothers, was torture to me. Had I been Romeo and she the Nurse, I could have risen above her with aristocratic ease, and everybody would have known she was my retainer; but I was Davey and she was Netty who had washed under my foreskin and threatened to cut my heart out with a whip when I was naughty, and my dread was that the rest of the audience would think she was my mother! But Netty was not sensitive; she was on a spree; she was to witness the triumph of her adored Caroline. I was merely her escort, and she felt kindly toward me and sought to divert me with her Gothic vivacity. How was I to insinuate myself into the

409

moonlight world of Judith Wolff after the play, with this goblin in tow?

Consequently I did not enjoy the play as I had expected to do. I was conscious of faults Caroline had been niggling about all day, and although my worship of Judy was more agonizing than before, it heaved on a sea of irritability and discontentment. And always there was the dread of the moment when the bouquets would be presented.

Here again I had reckoned without Fate, which was disposed to spare me from the consequences of my folly. When the curtain call came, some of the girls who had been serving as ushers rushed to the footlights like Birnam Wood moving to Dunsinane, loaded with bouquets. Judy got my roses and another much finer bunch from another usher. Caroline was handed the measly bundle of chrysanthemums, but also a very grand bunch of yellow roses, which were her favourites; she pretended extreme astonishment, read the card, and gave a little jump of joy! When the applause was over and almost every girl on stage had been given flowers of some sort, I stumbled out of the hall like one who has, at the last minute, been snatched from in front of the firing-squad.

The party in the school's dining-room was larger and gayer than the night before, though the food was the same. There were so many people that they stood in groups, and not in a single mass. Netty made a bee-line for Caroline, demanding to know who had sent her flowers. Caroline was busy displaying the roses and the card that was with them, on which was printed, in bold script, 'From a devoted admirer, who wishes to remain unknown.' The chrysanthemums and their rotten little card, on which I had printed 'Congratulations and Good Luck', she gave to Netty to hold. She was in tearing high spirits and loved all mankind; she seized me by the arm and rushed me over to Judy Wolff and shrieked, 'Judy, I want you to meet my baby brother; he thinks you're the tops,' and left me gangling. But she immediately showed her roses to Judy, and made a great affair of wondering who could have sent them; Judy, like every girl when confronted

with an obvious admirer, ignored me and chattered away to
Caroline and tried to talk about the mystery of her own
roses. My roses. Hopeless. Caroline was not to be distracted.
But in time she did go away, and I was left with Judy, and
had opened my mouth to say my carefully prepared speech –
'You sang awfully well ; you must have a marvellous teacher.' (Oh, was it too daring? Would she think I was a pushy
nuisance? Would she think it was just a line I used with all
the dozens of girls I knew who sang? Would she think I was
trying to move in on her like some football tough who –
Knopwood, stand by me now! – wanted to use her as an
object of convenience?) But near her were the same smiling,
dark-skinned, big-nosed people I had seen last night, and they
took me over as Judy (what manners, what aplomb, she must
be foreign) introduced me as Caroline's brother. My father,
Dr Louis Wolff. My mother. My Aunt Esther. My uncle,
Professor Bruno Schwarz.

They were very kind to me, but they all had X-ray eyes, or
extrasensory perception, because they assumed without asking that it was I who had sent Judy the other bouquet of
roses. And this flummoxed me. There I stood, a declared
lover, a role for which I had no preparation whatever, and
which I had entered on a level of roses, which I was utterly
unable to sustain. But what was most remarkable was that
they took it for granted that I should admire Judy and send
her flowers as an entirely suitable way of getting to know
her. I gathered that being Caroline's brother was, to them, a
sufficient introduction. How little they knew Caroline! They
understood. They sympathized. Of course they said nothing
directly, but their attitude toward me and their conversation
made it plain that they supposed I wanted to be accepted as
a friend, and were willing that it should be so. I didn't know
what to do. The course of true love was, contrary to everything that was right and proper, running smooth, and I was
not ready for it.

Friends of mine at school were in love with girls. The parents of these girls were always hilarious nuisances, eager to
tar and feather Cupid and make a clown of him ; or, if not

that, they were unpleasantly ironic and seemed to have forgotten all about love except as something that ailed puppies
and calves. The Wolffs took me seriously as a human being.
I had hoped for a furtive romance, unknown to anyone else
in the world. But here was Mrs Wolff saying that they were
always at home on Sunday afternoons between four and
six, and if I liked to look in, they would be delighted to see
me. I asked if tomorrow would be too soon. No, tomorrow
would do beautifully. They were delighted to meet me. They
hoped we would meet often.

During all of this, Judy said very little, and when I shook
hands with her at parting – an awful struggle ; was this the
thing to do, or not ; did one shake the hands of girls? – she
cast down her eyes.

This was something I had never seen a girl do. Caroline's
friends always looked you straight in the eye, especially if
they had something disagreeable to say. This dropping of the
gaze almost disembowelled me with its modest beauty.

But the publicity of it all! Can I have been so obvious? On
the way home even Netty remarked that I certainly seemed
to be taken with that dark girl, and when I asked her haugh-
tily what she meant she said she had eyes in her head like
anybody else, and I had been lallygagging so nobody could
miss it.

Netty was in high good humour. Dunstan Ramsay had
been at *Crossings*, invited, I suppose, as Headmaster of a
neighbouring school. He had paid Netty a good deal of attention. That was like Buggerlugs; he never overlooked anybody, and he seemed to put himself out to be gallant to
women nobody else could stand. He had introduced Netty to
Miss Gostling, the Headmistress of Bishop Cairncross's, and
had said she was the mainstay of the Staunton household
while Father had to be away on war business. Miss Gostling
had been quite the lady ; hadn't put on any airs. But it was
a good thing that place was a school and not a hotel, because
their coffee would choke a dog.

As we were going to bed, Caroline came to my room to

thank me for the flowers. 'I must say you did it in style,' said she, 'and you must have shopped around for quite a while to get yellow roses like that for five dollars. I know what these things cost ; this is identical with the bunch Buggerlugs sent Ghastly Gostling, and I'll bet it didn't cost him a cent less than eight.'

I was in a mood to dare much. 'Who sent you the other flowers ?' I asked.

'Scotland Yard suspects Tiger McGregor,' she replied. 'He's been lurking for a couple of months. Cheap creep! It looks like about a dollar seventy-five' – this with a glint of her pawnbroker's eye – 'and he'll probably expect me to go to the Colborne dance with him on the strength of it. Maybe I will, at that. . . . By the way, you and I are invited to tea at Judy Wolff's tomorrow. I worked that for you, so clean yourself up and do me credit.'

So Buggerlugs had sent the roses and saved me from God knows what humiliation and servitude to Carol ! Could he have known anything? Not possibly. He was just doing right by an old friend's daughter and having a little joke on his card. But he was a friend, whether he knew it or not. Was he more than a friend? . . . Damn Carol !

We went to tea with the Wolffs next day. It was not a social occasion I knew anything about, and I was in a frenzy of nerves. But the Wolff apartment was full of people, and Tiger McGregor was there and kept Caroline out of my way. I had a few words with Judy, and once she gave me a plate of sandwiches to hand around, so obviously she thought I was a trustworthy person and not just somebody who regarded her as an object of convenience. Her parents were charming and kind, and although I had experienced kindness, I was a stranger to charm, so I fell in love with all the Wolffs and Schwarzes in properly respectful degrees, and felt that I had suddenly moved into a new sort of world.

Thus began a love which fed my life and expanded my spirit for a year, before it was destroyed by an act of kindness which was in effect an act of shattering cruelty.

Need we go into details about what I said to Judy? I am no poet, and I suppose what I said was very much what everybody always says, and although I remember her as speaking golden words, I cannot recall precisely anything she said. If love is to be watched and listened to without embarrassment, it must be transmuted into art, and I don't know how to do that, and it is not what I have come to Zürich to learn.

DR VON HALLER: We must go into it a little, I think. You told her you loved her?

MYSELF: On New Year's Day. I said I would love her always, and I meant it. She said she couldn't be sure about loving me; she would not say it unless she was sure she meant it, and forever. But she would not withhold it, if ever she were sure, and meanwhile the greatest kindness I could show was not to press her.

DR VON HALLER: And did you?

MYSELF: Yes, quite often. She was always gentle and always said the same thing.

DR VON HALLER: What was she like? Physically, I mean. Was her appearance characteristically feminine? A well-developed bosom? Was she a clean person?

MYSELF: She was dark. Complexion what is called olive, but with wonderful deep red colour in her cheeks when she blushed. Hair dark brown. Not tall, but not short. She laughed at herself about being fat, but of course she wasn't. Curvy. Those uniforms that schools like Bishop Cairncross's insisted on at that time were extraordinarily revealing. If a girl had breasts, they showed up under those middies, and some girls had positive shelves almost under their chins. And those absurd short blue skirts, showing seemingly miles of leg from ankle to thigh. It was supposed to be a modest outfit, to make them look like children, but a pretty girl dressed like that is a quaint, touching miracle. The sloppy ones and the fatties were pretty spooky, but not a girl like Judy.

DR VON HALLER: You felt physical desire for her, then?

MYSELF: I most certainly did! There were times when I nearly fried! But I was heedful of what Knopwood said. Of course I talked to Knopwood about it, and he was wonderful. He said it was a very great experience, but I was the man, and the greater responsibility was mine. So – nothing that would harm Judy. He also gave me a hint about Jewish girls; said they were brought up to be modest and that her parents, being Viennese, were probably pretty strict. So – no casual Canadian ways, and never get the parents against me.

DR VON HALLER: Did you have erotic dreams about her?

MYSELF: Not about her. But wild dreams about women I couldn't recognize, and sometimes frightful hags, who ravished me. Netty began to look askew and hint about my pyjamas. And of course she had some awful piece of lore from Deptford to bring out. It seems there had been some woman there when she was a little girl who had always been 'at it' and eventually been discovered in a gravel pit, 'at it' with a tramp; of course this woman had gone stark, staring mad and had had to be kept in her house, tied up. But I think this tale of lust rebuked was really for Caroline's benefit, because Tiger McGregor was lurking more and more, and Carol was getting silly. I spoke to her about it myself, and she replied with some quotation about showing her the steep and thorny way to heaven, while I was making an ass of myself over Judy Wolff. But I kept my eye on her, just the same.

DR VON HALLER: Yes? A little more, please.

MYSELF: It's not a part of my life I take pride in. Now and then I would gum-shoe around the house when Tiger was there, just to see that everything was on the level.

DR VON HALLER: And was it?

MYSELF: No. There was a lot of prolonged kissing, and once I caught them on the sofa, and Carol's skirt was practically over her head, and Tiger was snorting and puffing, and it was what Netty would call a scene.

DR VON HALLER: Did you intervene?

MYSELF: No. I didn't quite do that, but I was as mad as

415

hell, and went upstairs and walked around over their heads and then took another peep, and they had straightened up.

DR VON HALLER: Were you jealous of your sister?

MYSELF: She was just a kid. She oughtn't to have known about that kind of thing. And I couldn't trust Tiger to understand that the greater responsibility was his. And Carol was as hot as a Quebec heater anyhow.

DR VON HALLER: What did you say to Tiger?

MYSELF: That's where the shame of the thing comes in. I didn't say anything to him. I was pretty strong; I got over all that nonsense about being frail by the time I was twelve; but Tiger was a football tough, and he could have killed me.

DR VON HALLER: Should you not have been prepared to fight for Father Knopwood's principles?

MYSELF: Knopwood prepared Carol for Confirmation; she knew what his principles were as well as I did. But she laughed at him and referred to him as my 'ghostly father'. And Tiger had no principles, and still hasn't. He's ended up as a public-relations man in one of Father's companies.

DR VON HALLER: So what was perfectly all right for you and Judy was not all right for Tiger and Carol?

MYSELF: I loved Judy.

DR VON HALLER: And you had no sofa-scenes?

MYSELF: Yes – but not often. The Wolffs lived in an apartment, you see, and though it was a big one there was always somebody going or coming.

DR VON HALLER: In fact, they kept their daughter on a short string?

MYSELF: Yes, but you wouldn't think of it that way. They were such charming people. A kind of person I'd never met before. Dr Wolff was a surgeon, but you'd never know it from his conversation. Art and music and the theatre were his great interests. And politics. He was the first man I ever met who was interested in politics without being a partisan of some kind. He was even cool about Zionism. He actually had good words for Mackenzie King; he admired King's political astuteness. He weighed the war news as nobody else did, that I knew, and even when the Allies were having

416

setbacks near the end, he was perfectly certain the end was near. He and Professor Schwarz, who was his brother-in-law, had seen things clearly enough to leave Austria in 1932. There was a sophistication in that house that was a continual refreshment to me. Not painted on, you know, but rising from within.

DR VON HALLER: And they kept their daughter on a short string?

MYSELF: I suppose so. But I was never aware of the string.

DR VON HALLER: And there were some tempestuous scenes between you?

MYSELF: Whenever it was possible, I suppose.

DR VON HALLER: To which she consented without being sure that she loved you?

MYSELF: But I loved her. She was being kind to me because I loved her.

DR VON HALLER: Wasn't Carol being kind to Tiger?

MYSELF: Carol was being kind to herself.

DR VON HALLER: But Judy wasn't being kind to herself?

MYSELF: You won't persuade me that the two things were the same.

DR VON HALLER: But what would Mr Justice Staunton say if these two young couples were brought before him? Would he make a distinction? If Father Knopwood were to appear as a special witness, would he make a distinction?

MYSELF: Knopwood was the soul of charity.

DR VON HALLER: Which you are not? Well, don't answer now. Charity is the last lesson we learn. That is why so much of the charity we show people is retrospective. Think it over and we shall talk about it later. Tell me more about your wonderful year.

It was wonderful because the war was ending. Wonderful because Father was able to get home for a weekend now and then. Wonderful because I found my profession. Wonderful because he raised my allowance, because of Judy.

That began badly. One day he told Caroline he wanted to see her in his office. She thought it was about Tiger, and was in a sweat for fear Netty had squealed. Only Supreme Court cases took place in Father's office. But he just wanted to know why she had been spending so much money. Miss Macmanaway, the secretary, advanced Caroline money as she needed it, without question, but of course she kept an account for Father. Caroline had been advancing me the money I needed to take Judy to films and concerts and plays, and to lunch now and then. I think Caroline thought it kept me quiet about Tiger, and I suppose she was right. But when Father wanted to know how she had been getting through about twenty-five dollars a week, apart from her accounts for clothes and oddments, she lost her nerve and said she had been giving money to me. Why? He takes this girl out, and you know what he's like when he can't have his own way. Carol warned me to look out for storms.

There was no storm. Father was amused, after he had scared me for a few minutes. He liked the idea that I had a girl. Raised my allowance to seven dollars and fifty cents a week, which was a fortune after my miserable weekly dollar for so long. Said he had forgotten I was growing up and had particular needs.

I was so relieved and grateful and charmed by him – because he was really the most charming man I have ever known, in a sunny, open way which was quite different from the Wolffs' complex, baroque charm – that I told him a lot about Judy. Oddly enough, like Knopwood, he warned me about Jewish girls; very strictly guarded on the level of people like the Wolffs. Why didn't I look a little lower down? I didn't understand that. Why would I want a girl who was less than Judy, when not only she, but all her family, had such distinction? I knew Father liked distinguished people. But he didn't make any reply to that.

So things were very much easier, and I was out of Carol's financial clutch.

7

Summer came, and the war had ended, in Europe, on May 7.

I went to camp for the last time. Every year Caroline and I were sent to excellent camps, and I liked mine. It was not huge, it had a sensible program instead of one of those fake-Indian nightmares, and we had a fair amount of freedom. I had grown to know a lot of the boys there, and met them from year to year, though not otherwise because few of them were from Colborne College.

There was one fellow who particularly interested me because he was in so many ways unlike myself He seemed to have extraordinary dash. He never looked ahead and never counted the cost. His name was Bill Unsworth.

I went to camp willingly enough because Judy's parents were taking her to California. Professor Schwarz was going there to give some special lectures at Cal Tech and other places, and the Wolffs went along to see what was to be seen. Mrs Wolff said it was time Judy saw something of the world, before she went to Europe to school. I did not grasp the full significance of that, but thought the end of the war must have something to do with it.

Camp was all very well, but I was growing too old for it, and Bill Unsworth was already too old, though he was a little younger than I. When the camp season finished, about the middle of August, he asked me and two other boys to go with him to a summer place his parents owned which was in the same district, for a few days before we returned to Toronto. It was pleasant enough, but we had had all the boating and swimming we wanted for one summer, and we were bored. Bill suggested that we look for some fun.

None of us had any idea what he had in mind, but he was certain we would like it, and enjoyed being mysterious. We drove some distance – twenty miles or so – down country roads, and then he stopped the car and said we would walk the rest of the way.

We struck into some pretty rough country, for this was

Muskoka and it is rocky and covered with scrub which is hard to break through. After about half an hour we came to a pretty summer house on a small lake ; it was a fussy place, with a little rock garden around it – gardens come hard in Muskoka – and a lot of verandah furniture that looked as if it had been kept in good condition by fussy people.

'Who lives here?' asked Jerry Wood.

'I don't know their names,' said Bill. 'But I do know they aren't here. Trip to the Maritimes. I heard it at the store.'

'Well – did they say we could use the place ?'

'No. They didn't say we could use the place.'

'It's locked,' said Don McQuilly, who was the fourth of our group.

'The kind of locks you open by spitting on them,' said Bill Unsworth.

'Are you going to break a lock?'

'Yes, Donny, I am going to break a lock.'

'But what for?'

'To get inside. What else?'

'But wait a minute. What do you want to get inside for?'

'To see what they've got in there, and smash it to bug-gery,' said Bill.

'But why?'

'Because that's the way I feel. Haven't you ever wanted to wreck a house?'

'My grandfather's a judge,' said McQuilly. 'I have to watch my step.'

'I don't see your grandfather anywhere around,' said Bill, sweeping the landscape with eyes shaded by his hand like a pirate in a movie.

We had an argument about it. McQuilly was against going ahead, but Jerry Wood thought it might be fun to get in and turn a few things upside down. I was divided in my opinion, as usual. I was sick of camp discipline ; but I was by nature law-abiding. I had often wondered what it would be like to wreck something ; but on the other hand I had a strong con-viction that if I did anything wrong I would certainly be caught. But no boy likes to lose face in the eyes of a leader, and Bill Unsworth was a leader, of a sort. His sardonic smile as we haggled was worth pages of wordy argument. In the end we decided to go ahead, I for one feeling that I could put on the brakes any time I liked.

The lock needed rather more than spitting on, but Bill had brought some tools, which surprised and rather shocked us. We got in after a few minutes. The house was even more fussy inside than the outside had promised. It was a holiday place, but everything about it suggested elderly people.

'The first move in a job like this,' Bill said, is to see if they've got any booze.'

They had none, and this made them enemies, in Bill's eyes. They must have hidden it, which was sneaky and deserved punishment. He began to turn out cupboards and storage places, pulling everything onto the floor. We others didn't want to seem poor-spirited, so we kicked it around a little. Our lack of zeal angered the leader.

'You make me puke!' he shouted and grabbed a mirror from the wall. It was round, and had a frame made of that plaster stuff twisted into flowers that used to be called barbola. He lifted it high above his head, and smashed it down on the back of a chair. Shattered glass flew everywhere.

'Hey, look out!' shouted Jerry. 'You'll kill somebody.'

'I'll kill you all,' yelled Bill, and swore for three or four minutes, calling us every dirty name he could think of for being so chicken-hearted. When people talk about 'leadership quality' I often think of Bill Unsworth; he had it. And like many people who have it, he could make you do things you didn't want to do by a kind of cunning urgency. We were ashamed before him. Here he was, a bold adventurer, who had put himself out to include us – lily-livered wretches – in a daring, dangerous, highly illegal exploit, and all we could do was worry about being hurt! We plucked up our spirits and swore and shouted filthy words, and set to work to wreck the house.

Our appetite for destruction grew with feeding. I started gingerly, pulling some books out of a case, but soon I was tearing out pages by handfuls and throwing them around. Jerry got a knife and ripped the stuffing out of the mattresses. He threw feathers from sofa cushions. McQuilly, driven by some dark Scottish urge, found a crowbar and reduced wooden things to splinters. And Bill was like a fury, smashing, overturning, and tearing. But I noticed that he kept back some things and put them in a neat heap on the dining-room table, which he forbade us to break. They were photographs.

The old people must have had a large family, and there were pictures of young people and wedding groups and what were clearly grandchildren everywhere. When at last we had done as much damage as we could, the pile on the table was a large one.

'Now for the finishing touch,' said Bill. 'And this is going to be all mine.'

He jumped up on the table, stripped down his trousers, and squatted over the photographs. Clearly he meant to defecate on them, but such things cannot always be commanded, and so for several minutes we stood and stared at him as he grunted and swore and strained and at last managed what he wanted, right on the family photographs.

How long it took I cannot tell, but they were critical moments in my life. For as he struggled, red-faced and pop-eyed, and as he appeared at last with a great stool dangling from his apelike rump, I regained my senses and said to myself, not 'What am I doing here?' but 'Why is he doing that? The destruction was simply a prelude to this. It is a dirty, animal act of defiance and protest against – well, against what? He doesn't even know who these people are. There is no spite in him against individuals who have injured him. Is he protesting against order, against property, against privacy? No; there is nothing intellectual, nothing rooted in principle – even the principle of anarchy – in what he is doing. So far as I can judge – and I must remember that I am his accomplice in all but this, his final outrage – he is simply being as evil as his strong will and deficient imagination will permit. He is possessed, and what possesses him is Evil.'

I was startled out of my reflection by Bill shouting for something with which to wipe himself.

'Wipe on your shirt-tail, your dirty pig,' said McQuilly. 'It'd be like you.'

The room stank, and we left at once, Bill Unsworth last, looking smaller, meaner, and depleted, but certainly not repentant.

We went back to the car in extremely bad temper. Nobody spoke on the way to the Unsworths' place, and the next day Wood, McQuilly, and I took the only train home to Toronto. We did not speak of what we had done, and have never done so since.

On the long Journey from Muskoka back to Toronto I had plenty of time to think, and I made my resolve then to be a lawyer. I was against people like Bill Unsworth, or who were possessed as he was. I was against whatever it was that possessed him, and I thought the law was the best way of making my opposition effective.

8

It was a surprise that brought no pleasure when I discovered that I was in love with Dr von Haller.

For many weeks I had been seeing her on Mondays, Wednesdays, and Fridays and was always aware of changes in my attitude toward her. In the beginning, indifference; she was my physician, and though I was not such a fool as to think she could help me without my cooperation I assumed that there would be limits to that; I would answer questions and provide information to the best of my ability, but I assumed without thinking that some reticences would be left me. Her request for regular reports on my dreams I did not take very seriously, though I did my best to comply and even reached a point where I was likely to wake after a dream and make notes on it before sleeping again. But the idea of dreams as a key to anything very serious in my case or any other was still strange and, I suppose, unwelcome. Netty had set no store by dreams, and the training of a Netty is not quickly set aside.

In time, however, quite a big dossier of dreams accumulated, which the doctor filed, and of which I kept copies. I had taken rooms in Zürich; a small service flat, looking out on a courtyard, did me very well; meals with wine could be taken at the *table d'hôte*, and I found after a time that the wine was enough, with a nightcap of whisky, just so that I should not forget what it tasted like. I was fully occupied, for the doctor gave me plenty of homework. Making up my notes for my next appointment took far more time than I had expected – quite as much as preparing a case for court – because my problem was to get the tone right; with Johanna von Haller I was arguing not for victory, but for truth. It was hard work, and I took to napping after lunch, a thing I had never done before. I walked, and came to know Zürich fairly well – certainly well enough to understand that my knowledge was still that of a visitor and a stranger. I took to the museums; even more, I took to the churches, and sometimes sat for long spells in the Grossmünster, looking at the splendid modern windows. And all the time I was thinking, remembering, reliving; what I was engaged on with Dr von Haller (which I suppose must be called an analysis, though it was nothing like what I had ever imagined an analysis to be) possessed me utterly.

To what extent should I surrender myself, I asked, and as I asked I was aware that the time for turning back had passed and I no longer had any choice in the matter. I even lost my embarrassment about dreams, and would take a good dream to my appointment as happily as a boy who has prepared a good lesson.

(*The dream dossier I kept in another notebook, and only a few references to its contents appear here. This is not wilful concealment. The dreams of someone undergoing such treatment as mine are numbered in tens and hundreds, and extracting meaning from the mass is slow work, for dreams say*

424

their say in series, and only rarely is a single dream revela-
tory. Reading such a record of dreams is comparable to
reading the whole of a business correspondence when pre-
paring a case – dull panning for gold, with a hundredweight
of gravel discarded for every nugget.)

Indifference gave way to distaste. The doctor seemed to
me to be a commonplace person, not as careful about her
appearance as I had at first thought, and sometimes I suspected her of a covert antipathy toward me. She said things
that seemed mild enough until they were pondered, and then
a barb would appear. I began to wonder if she were not like
so many people I have met who can never forgive me for
being a rich and privileged person. Envy of the rich is understandable enough in people whose lives are lived under a sky
always darkened by changing clouds of financial worry and
need. They see people like me as free from the one great
circumstance that conditions their lives, their loves and the
fate of their families – want of cash. They say, glibly
enough, that they do not envy the rich, who must certainly
have many cares; the reality is something very different.
How can they escape envy? They must be especially envious
when they see the rich making fools of themselves, squan-
dering big sums on trivialities. What that fellow has spent
on his yacht, they think, would set me up for life. What
they do not understand is that folly is to a great extent a
question of opportunity, and that fools, rich or poor, are
always as foolish as they can manage. But does money
change the essential man? I have been much envied, and I
know that many people who envy me my money are, if they
only knew it, envying me my brains, my character, my
appetite for work, and a quality of toughness that the wealth
of an emperor cannot buy.
   Did Dr von Haller, sitting all day in her study listening to
other people's troubles, envy me? And perhaps dislike me? I
felt that it was not impossible.
   Our relationship improved after some time. It seemed to
me that the doctor was friendlier, less apt to say things that

needed careful inspection for hidden criticism. I have always liked women, in spite of my somewhat unusual history with them ; I have women friends, and have had a substantial number of women clients whose point of view I pride myself on understanding and setting forward successfully in court.

In this new atmosphere of friendship, I opened up as I had not done before. I lost much of my caution. I felt that I could tell her things that showed me in a poor light without dreading any reprisal. For the first time in my life since I lost Knopwood, I felt the urge to confide. I know what a heavy burden everybody carries of the unconfessed, which sometimes appears to be the unspeakable. Very often such stuff is not disgraceful or criminal ; it is merely a sense of not having behaved well or having done something one knew to be contrary to someone else's good ; of having snatched when one should have waited decently ; of having turned a sharp corner when someone else was thereby left in a difficult situation ; of having talked of the first-rate when one was planning to do the second-rate ; of having fallen below whatever standards one had set oneself. As a lawyer I heard masses of such confessions; a fair amount of what looks like crime has its beginning in some such failure. But I had not myself confided in anybody. For in whom could I confide? And, as a criminal lawyer – comic expression, but the usual one for a man who, like myself, spends much of his time defending people who are, or possibly may be, criminals – I knew how dangerous confession was. The priest, the physician, the lawyer – we all know that their lips are sealed by an oath no torture could compel them to break. Strange, then, how many people's secrets become quite well known. Tell nobody anything, and be closemouthed even about that, had been my watchword for more than twenty of my forty years. Yet was it not urgent need for confession that brought me to Zürich? Here I was, confident that I could confide in this Swiss doctor, and thinking it a luxury to do so.

What happened to my confidences when I had made

them? What did I know about Johanna von Haller? Where was she when she was not in her chair in that room which I now knew very well? Whence came the information about the world that often arose in our talks? I took to reading *Die Neue Zürcher Zeitung* to keep abreast of her, and although at first I thought I had never read such an extraordinary paper in my life, my understanding and my German improved, and I decided that I had indeed never read such an extraordinary paper, meaning that in its most complimentary sense.

Did she go to concerts? Did she go to the theatre? Or to films? I went to all of these entertainments, because I had to do something at night. I had made no friends, and wanted none, for my work on my analysis discouraged it, but I enjoyed my solitary entertainments. I took to arriving early at the theatre and staring about at the audience to see if I could find her. My walks began to lead me near her house, in case I should meet her going or coming. Had she any family? Who were her friends? Did she know any men? Was there a husband somewhere? Was she perhaps a Lesbian? These intellectual women – but no, something told me that was unlikely. I had seen a good many collar-and-tie teams in my professional work, and she was neither a collar nor a tie.

Gradually I realized that I was lurking. This is not precisely spying; it is a kind of meaningful loitering, in hopes. Lurking could only mean one thing, but I couldn't believe it of myself. In love with my analyst? Absurd. But why absurd? Was I too old for love? No, I was going on forty-one, and knew the world. She was mature. Youthful, really, for her probable age. I took her to be about thirty-eight, but I had no way of finding out. Except for the relationship in which we stood to one another, there was nothing in the world against it. And what was that, after all, but doctor and patient? Didn't doctors and patients fall in love? I have been involved in more than one case that made it clear they did.

Everything in me that had kept its reason was dismayed. What could come of such a love? I didn't want to marry; I didn't want an affair. No, but I wanted to tell Johanna von Haller that I loved her. It had to be said. Love and a cough cannot be hid, as Netty told me when I was seventeen.

I dressed with special care for my next appointment, and told Johanna that before we began. I had something of importance to say. I said it. She did not seem to be as dumbfounded as I had expected, but after all, she was not a girl.

'So what is to be done?' I said.

'I think we should continue as before,' said she. But she smiled quite beautifully as she said it. 'I am not ungrateful, or indifferent, you know ; I am complimented. But you must trust me to be honest with you, so I must say at once that I am not surprised. No, no ; you must not imagine you have been showing your feelings and I have been noticing. Better be completely frank : it is part of the course of the analysis, you understand. A very pleasant part. But still well within professional limits.'

'You mean I can't even ask you to dinner ?'

'You may certainly ask me, but I shall have to say no.'

'Do you sit there and tell me it is part of my treatment that I should fall in love with you ?'

'It is one of those things that happens now and then, because I am a woman. But suppose I were a wise old doctor, like our great Dr Jung; you would hardly fall in love with me then, would you? Something quite other would happen ; a strong sense of discipleship. But always there comes this period of special union with the doctor. This feeling you have – which I understand and respect, believe me – is because we have been talking a great deal about Judy Wolff.'

'You are not in the least like Judy Wolff.'

'Certainly not – in one way. In another way – let us see. Have you had any dreams since last time?'

'Last night I dreamed of you.'

'Tell.'

'It was a dream in colour. I found myself in an underground passage, but some light was entering it, because I could see that it was decorated with wall-paintings, in the late Roman manner. The whole atmosphere of the dream was Roman, but the Rome of the decadence ; I don't know how I knew that, but I felt it I was in modern clothes. I was about to walk down the passage when my attention was taken by the first picture on the left-hand side. These pictures, you understand, were large, almost life-size, and in the warm but not reflective colours of Roman frescoes. The first picture – I couldn't see any others – was of you, dressed as a sibyl in a white robe with a blue mantle ; you were smiling. On a chain you held a lion, which was staring out of the picture. The lion had a man's face. My face.'

'Any other details?'

'The lion's tail ended in a kind of spike, or barb.'

'Ah, a manticore!'

'A what?'

'A manticore is a fabulous creature with a lion's body, a man's face, and a sting in his tail.'

'I never heard of it.'

'No, they are not common, even in myths.'

'How can I dream about something I've never heard of?'

'That is a very involved matter, which really belongs to the second part of your analysis. But it is a good sign that this sort of material is making its way into your dreams already. People very often dream of things they don't know. They dream of minotaurs without ever having heard of a minotaur. Thoroughly respectable women who have never heard of Pasiphaë dream that they are a queen who is enjoying sexual congress with a bull. It is because great myths are not invented stories but objectivizations of images and situations that lie very deep in the human spirit ; a poet may make a great embodiment of a myth, but it is the mass of humanity that knows the myth to be a spiritual truth, and that is why they cherish his poem. These myths, you know, are very widespread ; we may hear them as children, dressed in pretty Greek guises, but they are African, Oriental, Red Indian – all sorts of things.'

'I should like to argue that point.'

'Yes, I know, but let us take a short cut. What do you suppose this dream means?'

'That I am your creature, under your subjection, kept on a short string.'

'Why are you so sure that I am the woman in the sibyl's robe?'

'How can it be anyone else? It looked like you. You are a sibyl. I love you. You have me under your control.'

'You must believe me when I tell you that the only person you can be certain of recognizing in a dream is yourself. The woman might be me. Because of what you feel about me – please excuse me if I say what you at present suppose you feel about me – the woman could be me, but if so why do I not appear as myself, in this modern coat and skirt with which I am sure you are becoming wearily familiar.'

'Because dreams are fanciful. They go in for fancy dress.'

'I assure you that dreams are not fanciful. They always mean exactly what they say, but they do not speak the language of every day. So they need interpretation, and we cannot always be sure we have interpreted all, or interpreted correctly. But we can try. You appear in this dream ; you are in two forms, yourself and this creature with your face. What do you make of that?'

'I suppose I am observing my situation. You see, I have learned something about dream interpretation from you. And my situation is that I am under your dominance; willingly so.'

'Women have not appeared in your dreams very prominently, or in a flattering light, until recently. But this sibyl has the face of someone you love. Did you think it was the face of someone who loved you?'

'Yes. Or at any rate someone who cared about me. Who was guiding me, obviously. The smile had extraordinary calm beauty. So who could it be but you?'

'But why are you a manticore?'

'I haven't any idea. And as I never heard of a manticore till now, I have no association with it.'

'But we have met a few animals in your dreams before now. What was Felix?'

'We agreed that Felix was a figure who meant some rather kind impulses and some bewilderment that I was not quite willing to accept as my own. We called him the Friend.'

'Yes. The Animal-Friend, and because an animal, related to the rather undeveloped instinctual side of your nature. He was one of the characters in your inner life. Like the Shadow. Now, as your sister Caroline used to say, you know my methods, Watson. You know that when the Shadow and the Friend appeared, they had a special vividness. I felt the vividness and I bore the character of Shadow and Friend. That was quite usual ; part of my professional task. I told you I should play many roles. This latest dream of yours is vivid, and apparently simple, and clearly important. What about the manticore?'

'Well, as he is an animal, I suppose he is some baser aspect of me. But as he is a lion, he can't be wholly base. And he has a human face, my face, so he can't be wholly animal. Though I must say the expression on the face was fierce and untrustworthy. And there I run out of ideas.'

'What side of your nature have we considered as not being so fully developed as it could be?'

'Oh, my feeling. Though I must say once more that I have plenty of feeling, even if I don't understand and use it well.'

'So might not your undeveloped feeling turn up in a dream as a noble creature, but possibly dangerous and only human in part?'

'This is the fanciful side of this work that always rouses my resistance.'

'We have agreed, have we not, that everything that makes man a great, as opposed to a merely sentient creature, is fanciful when tested by what people call common sense? That common sense often means no more than yesterday's opinions? That every great advance began in the realm of the fanciful? That fantasy is the mother not merely of art, but of science as well? I am sure that when the very first primitives began to think that they were individuals and not creatures of a herd and wholly bound by the ways of the herd, they seemed fanciful to their hairy, low-browed brothers – even though those hairy lowbrows had no concept of fantasy.'

''I know. You think the law has eaten me up. But I have lived by reason, and this is unreason.'

'I think nothing of the kind. I think you do not understand the law. So far as we can discover, anything like a man that has inhabited this earth lived by some kind of law, however crude. Primitives have law of extraordinary complexity. How did they get it? If they worked it out as a way of living tribally, it must once have been fantasy. If they simply knew what to do from the beginning, it must have been instinct, like the nest-building instinct of birds.'

'Very well; if I accept that the lion represents my somewhat undeveloped feeling, what about it?'

'Not a lion; a manticore. Do not forget that stinging tail. The undeveloped feelings are touchy – very defensive. The manticore can be extremely dangerous. Sometimes he is even described as hurling darts from his tail, as people once thought the porcupine did. Not a bad picture of you in court, would you say? Head of a man, brave and dangerous as a lion, capable of wounding with barbs? But not a whole man, or a whole lion, or a merely barbed opponent. A manticore. The Unconscious chooses its symbolism with breath-taking artistic virtuosity.'

'All right. Suppose I am the manticore. Why shouldn't you be the sibyl?'

'Because we have come to a part of our work together where a woman, or a variety of women, are very likely to appear in your dreams in just some such special relationship to you as this. Did you notice the chain?'

'I noticed everything, and I can call it up now. It was a handsome gold chain.'

'Good. That is much better than if it had been an iron chain, or a chain with spikes. Now, what have we: an image that appears on the left-hand side, which means that it comes from the Unconscious –'

'I haven't completely swallowed the idea of the Unconscious, you know.'

'Indeed I do know. "Fanciful . . . fancy dress . . ." all these scornful words come up whenever we discuss it. But we are at a point where you are going to have to face it, because that is where that blue-mantled sibyl resides. She has emerged from the Unconscious and can be of great help to you, but if you banish her you might as well stop this work now and go home.'

'I have never heard you so threatening before.'

'There comes a time when one must be strong with rationalists, for they can reduce anything whatever to dust, if they happen not to like the look of it, or if it threatens their deep-buried negativism. I mean of course rationalists like you, who take some little provincial world of their own as the whole of the universe and the seat of all knowledge.'

'Little, provincial world . . . I see. Well, what is the name of this lady I am compelled to meet?'

'Oho – irony! How well that must sound in court! The lady's name is Anima.'

'Latin for Soul. I gave up the idea of a soul many years ago. Well?'

'She is one of the figures in your psychological make-up, like the Shadow and the Friend, whom you have met and about whom you entertain few doubts. She is not a soul as Christianity conceives it. She is the feminine part of your nature: she is all that you are able to see, and experience, in woman: she is not your mother, or any single one of the women you have loved, but you have seen all of them – at least in part – in terms of her. If you love a woman you project this image upon her, at least at the beginning, and if you hate a woman it is again the Anima at work, because she has a very disagreeable side which is not at all like the smiling sibyl in the blue mantle. She has given rise to some of the world's greatest art and poetry. She is Cleopatra, the enchantress, and she is Faithful Griselda, the patient, enduring woman ; she is Beatrice, who glorifies the life of Dante, and she is Nimue, who imprisons Merlin in a thorn-bush. She is the Maiden who is wooed, the Wife who bears the sons, and she is the Hag who lays out her man for his last rest. She is an angel, and she may also be a witch. She is Woman as she appears to every man, and to every man she appears somewhat differently, though essentially the same.'

'Quite a nicely practised speech. But what do women do about this fabulous creature?'

'Oh, women have their own deep-lying image of Man, the Lover, the Warrior, the Wizard, and the Child – which may be either the child of a few months who is utterly dependent, or the child of ninety years who is utterly dependent. Men often find it very hard to carry the projection of the Warrior or the Wizard that is put upon them by some woman they may not greatly like. And of course women have to bear the projection of the Anima, and although all women like it to some degree, only rather immature women like that and nothing else.'

'Very well. If the Anima is my essential image, or pattern of woman, why does she look like you? Isn't this proof that I love you?'

'No indeed; the Anima must look like somebody. You spoke of dreadful hags who assailed you in sexual dreams when you were a boy. They were the Anima, too. Because your sister and Netty could see you were in love, which I expect was pretty obvious, you projected witchlike aspects of the Anima on their perfectly ordinary heads. But you can never see the Anima pure and simple, because she has no such existence; you will always see her in terms of something or somebody else. Just at present, you see her as me.'

'I am not convinced.'

'Then think about it. You are good at thinking. Didn't you dislike me when the Shadow was being slowly brought to your notice; do you suppose I didn't see your considering looks as you eyed my rather perfunctory attempts at fashionable dress; do you suppose I was unaware of the criticism and often the contempt in your voice? Don't look alarmed or ashamed. It is part of my professional duty to assume these roles; the treatment would be ineffective without these projections, and I am the one who is nearest and best equipped to carry them. And then when we changed to the Friend, I know very well that my features began to have a look, in your eyes, of Felix's charming bear-expression of puzzled goodwill. And now we have reached the Anima, and I am she; I am as satisfactory casting for the role as I was for the Shadow or the Friend. But I must assure you that there is nothing personal about it.

'And now our hour is finished. We shall go on next day talking more about Judy Wolff. I trust it will be delightful.'

'Well, Dr von Haller, I am sorry to inform you, sibyl though you seem to be, that you are about to be disappointed.'

9

The autumn that followed the war was wonderful. The world seemed to breathe again, and all sorts of things that had been taut were unfolding. Women's clothes, which had been so skimped during the war, changed to an altogether more pleasing style. When Judy was not in the Bishop Cairncross uniform she was marvellous in pretty blouses and flaring skirts; it was almost the last time that women were allowed by their epicene masters of fashion to wear anything that was unashamedly flattering. I was happy, for I was on top of my world: I had Judy, I was in my last year at Colborne College, and I was a prefect.

How can I describe my relationship with Judy without looking a fool or a child? Things have changed so startlingly in recent years that the idealism with which I surrounded everything about her would seem absurd to a boy and girl of seventeen now. Or would it? I can't tell. But now, when I see girls who have not yet attained their full growth storming the legislatures for abortion on demand, and adolescents pressing their right to freedom to have intercourse whenever and however they please, and read books advising women that anal intercourse is a jolly lark (provided both partners are 'squeaky clean'), I wonder what has happened to the Davids and Judys and if the type is extinct? I think not; it is merely waiting for another age, different from our supernal autumn but also different from this one. And, as I look back, I do not really wish we had greater freedom than was ours; greater freedom is only another kind of servitude. Physical fulfilment satisfies appetite, but does it sharpen perception? What we had of sex was limited; what we had of love seems, in my recollection, to have been illimitable. Judy was certainly kept on a short string, but the free-ranging creature is not always the best of the breed.

That autumn Bishop Cairncross's was shaken by unreasonable ambition; the success of *Crossings* had been so great that the music staff and all the musical girls like Caroline and Judy were mad to do a real opera. Miss Gostling, after the usual Headmistress's doubts about the effect on schoolwork, gave her consent, and it was rumoured that unheard-of sums of money had been set aside for the project – something in the neighbourhood of five hundred dollars, which was a Metropolitan budget for the school.

What opera? Some of the girls were shrieking for Mozart; a rival band, hateful to Caroline, thought Puccini would be more like it, and with five hundred dollars they could not see why *Turandot* would not be the obvious choice. Of course the mistresses made the decision, and the music mistress resurrected, from somewhere, Mendelssohn's *Son and Stranger*. It was not the greatest opera ever written; it contained dialogue, which to purists made it no opera at all; nevertheless, it was just within the range of what schoolgirls could manage. So *Son and Stranger* it was to be, and quite hard enough, when they got down to it.

I heard all about it. Judy told me of its charms because its gemütlich, nineteenth-century naïveté appealed strongly to her; either she was innocent in her tastes or else sophisticated in seeing in this humble little work delights and possibilities the other girls missed; I rather think her feeling was a combination of both these elements. Caroline was a bore about its difficulties. She and another girl were to play the overture and accompaniments at two pianos, which is trickier than it seems. In full view, too; no hiding behind the scenes this time. Of course, as always with Caroline, nobody but herself knew just how it ought to be done, and the music mistress, and the mistress who directed the production, and the art mistress who arranged the setting, were all idiots, without a notion of how to manage anything. I even had my own area of agitation and knowing-best; if Miss Gostling were not such a lunatic, insisting that everything about the production be kept within the school, I could have mustered a crew of carpenters and scene-shifters and painters and electricians among the boys at Colborne who would have done all the technical work at lightning speed, with masculine thoroughness and craftsmanship, and guaranteed wondrous result. Both Judy and Carol and most of their friends agreed that this was undoubtedly so, but none of them quite saw her way to suggesting it to Miss Gostling, who was, as we all agreed, the last surviving dinosaur.

Not many people know *Son and Stranger*. Mendelssohn wrote it for private performance, indeed for the twenty-fifth wedding anniversary of his parents, and it is deeply, lumberingly domestic in the nineteenth-century German style. 'A nice old bit of Biedermeier,' said Dr Wolff, and lent some useful books to the art mistress for her designs.

The plot is modest; the people of a German village are expecting a recruiting-sergeant who will take their sons away to fight in the Napoleonic wars; a peddler, a handsome charlatan, turns up and pretends to be the sergeant, hoping to win the favours of the Mayor's ward Lisbeth; but he is unmasked by the real sergeant, who proves to be Herrmann, the Mayor's long-lost soldier son, and Lisbeth's true love. The best part is the peddler, and there was the usual wrangle as to whether it should be played by a girl who could act but couldn't sing, or whether a girl who could sing but couldn't act should have it. The acting girl was finally banished to the comic role of the Mayor, who must have been no singer in the original production, for Mendelssohn had given him a part which stayed firmly on one note. Judy was Lisbeth, of course, and had some pretty songs and a bit of acting for which her quiet charm was, or seemed to me to be, exactly right.

At last early December came, *Son and Stranger* was performed for two nights, and of course it was a triumph. What school performance of anything is ever less than a triumph? Judy sang splendidly; Caroline covered herself with honour; even the embarrassing dialogue – rendered from flat-footed German into murderous English, Dr Wolff assured me – was somehow bathed in the romantic light that enveloped the whole affair.

This year my father was in the audience, and cut a figure because everybody knew him from newspaper pictures and admired the great work he had done during the war years. I took Netty on the Friday and went again with Father on Saturday. He asked me if I really wanted to go twice or was I going just to keep him company; not long after Judy appeared on the stage I felt him looking at me with curiosity, so I suppose I was as bad at concealing my adoration as I had always been. Afterward, at the coffee and school-cake debauch in the dining-room, I introduced him to the Wolffs and the Schwarzes, and to my astonishment Judy curtsied to him – one of those almost imperceptible little bobs that girls used to do long ago in Europe and which some girls of Bishop Cairncross's kept for the Bishop, who was the patron of the school. I knew Father was important, but I had never dreamed of him as the kind of person anybody curtsied to. He liked it; he didn't say anything, but I knew he liked it.

If any greater glory could be added to my love for Judy, Father's approval supplied it. I had been going through hell at intervals ever since Mother's death because of Carol's declaration that I was Dunstan Ramsay's son. I had come to the conclusion that whether or not I was Ramsay's son in the flesh, I was Father's son in the spirit. He had not been at home during the period of my life when boys usually are possessed with admiration for their fathers, and I was having, at seventeen, a belated bout of hero-worship. Sometimes I had found Ramsay's saturnine and ironic eye on me at school, and I had wondered if he were reflecting that I was his child. That seemed less significant now because Father's return had diminished Ramsay's importance; after all, Ramsay was the Acting Headmaster of Colborne, filling in for the war years, but Father was the Chairman of the school's Board of Governors and in a sense Ramsay's boss, as he seemed to be the boss of so many other people. He was a natural boss, a natural leader. I know I tried to copy some of his mannerisms, but they fitted me no better than his hats, which I also tried.

Father's return to Toronto caused a lot of chatter, and some of it came to my ears because the boys with whom I was at school were the sons of the chatterers. He had been remarkable as a Minister of Food, a Cabinet position that had made him even more significant in the countries we were supplying during the war than at home. He had been extraordinary in his ability to get along with Mackenzie King without wrangling and without any obvious sacrifice of his own opinions, which were not often those of the P.M. But there was another reputation that came home with him, a reputation spoken of less freely, with an ambiguity I did not understand or even notice for a time. This was a reputation as something called 'a swordsman'.

It is a measure of my innocence that I took this word at its face value. It was new then in the connotation it has since acquired, and I was proud of my father being a swordsman. I assumed it meant a gallant, cavalier-like person, a sort of Prince Rupert of the Rhine as opposed to the Cromwellian austerity of Mackenzie King.

When boys at school talked to me about Father, as they did because he was increasingly a public figure, I sometimes said, 'You can sum him up pretty much in a word – a swordsman.' I now remember with terrible humiliation that I said this to the Wolffs, who received it calmly, though I thought I saw Mr Wolff's nostrils pinch and if I had been more sensitive I would surely have noticed a drop in the social temperature. But the word had such a fine savour in my mouth that I think I repeated it; I knew the Wolffs and Schwarzes liked me, but how much better they would like me if they understood that I was the son of a man who was recognized for aristocratic behaviour and a temperament far above that of the upper-bourgeois world in which we lived and which, in Canada, was generally supposed to be the best world there was. Swordsmen were people of a natural distinction, and I was the son of one of them. Would I ever be a swordsman myself? Oh, speed the day!

The Wolffs, like many Jewish people, were going to a resort for Christmas, so I was not dismayed by the thought of any loss of time with Judy when my father asked me to go with him to Montreal on Boxing Day. He had some business to do there and thought I might like to see the city. So we went, and I greatly enjoyed the day-long journey on the train and putting up at the Ritz when we arrived. Father was a good traveller; everybody heeded him and our progress was princely.

'We're having dinner with Myrrha Martindale,' he said; 'she's an old friend of mine, and I think you'll like her very much.'

She was, it appeared, a singer, and had formerly lived in New York and had been seen – though not in leading roles – in several Broadway musical comedies. A wonderful person. Witty. Belonged to a bigger world. Would have had a remarkable career if she had not sacrificed everything to marriage.

'Was it worth it?' I asked. I was at the age when sacrifice and renunciation were great, terrifying, romantic concepts.

'No, it blew up,' said Father. 'Jack Martindale simply had no idea what a woman like that is, or needs. He wanted to turn her into a Westmount housewife. Talk about Pegasus chained to the plough!'

Oh, indeed I was anxious to talk about Pegasus chained to the plough. That was just the kind of swordsman thing Father could say; he could see the poetry in daily life. But he didn't want to talk about Myrrha Martindale; he wanted me to meet her and form my own opinion. That was like him, too: not dictating or managing, as so many of my friends' fathers seemed to do.

Mrs Martindale had an apartment on Côte des Neiges Road with a splendid view over Montreal; I guessed it was costing the banished Jack Martindale plenty, and I thought it was quite right that it should do so, for Mrs Martindale was indeed a wonderful person. She was beautiful in a mature way, and had a delightful voice, with an actress's way of making things seem much more amusing than they really were. Not that she strove to shine as a wit. She let Father do that, very properly, but her responses to his jokes were witty in themselves – not topping him, but supporting him and setting him off.

'You mustn't expect a real dinner,' she said to me. 'I thought it would be more fun if we were just by ourselves, the three of us, so I sent my maid out. I hope you won't be disappointed.'

Disappointed! It was the most grown-up affair I had ever known. Wonderful food that Myrrha – she insisted I call her Myrrha, because all her friends did – produced herself from under covers and off hot-trays, and splendid wines that were better than anything I had ever tasted. I knew they must be good because they had that real musty aftertaste, like dusty red ink instead of fresh red ink.

'This is terribly good of you, Myrrha,' said Father. 'It's time Davey learned something about wines. About vintage wines, instead of very new stuff.' He raised his glass to Mrs Martindale, and she blushed and looked down as I had so often seen Judy do, only Mrs Martindale seemed more in command of herself. I raised my glass to her, too, and she was delighted and gave me her hand, obviously meaning that I should kiss it. I had kissed Judy often enough, though never while eating and seldom on the hand, but I took it as gallantly as I could – surely I was getting to be a swordsman – and kissed it on the tips of the fingers. Father and Mrs Martindale looked pleased but didn't say anything, and I felt I had done well.

It was a wonderful dinner. It wasn't necessary to be excited, as if I were with people my own age; calmness was the keynote, and I told myself that it was educational in the very best sense and I ought to keep alert and not miss anything. And not drink too much wine. Father talked a lot about wines, and Mrs Martindale and I were fascinated. When we had coffee he produced a huge bottle of brandy, which was very hard to get at that time.

'Your Christmas gift, Myrrha dear,' he said. 'Winston gave it to me last time I saw him, so you can be sure it's good.'

It was. I had tasted whisky, but this was a very different thing. Father showed me how to roll it around in the mouth and get it on the sides of the tongue where the tastebuds are, and I rolled and tasted in adoring imitation of him.

How wonderfully good food and drink lull the spirit and bring out one's hidden qualities! I thought something better than just warm agreement with everything that was said was expected of me, and I raked around in my mind for a comment worthy of the occasion. I found it.

'And much as Wine has played the infidel,
And robbed me of my Robe of Honour – Well,
   I wonder often what the Vintners buy
   One half so precious as the stuff they sell,'

said I, looking reflectively at the candles through my glass of brandy, as I felt a swordsman should. Father seemed nonplussed, though I knew that was an absurd idea. Father? Nonplussed? Never!

'Is that your own, Davey?' he said.

I roared with laughter. What a wit Father was! I said I wished it was and then reflected that perhaps a swordsman ought to have said Would that it were, but by then it was too late to change. Myrrha looked at me with the most marvellous combination of amusement and admiration, and I felt that in a modest way I was making a hit.

At half-past nine Father said he must keep another appointment. But I was not to stir. Myrrha too begged me not to think of going. She had known all along that Father would have to leave early, but then she was so grateful that he had been able to spare her a few hours from a busy life. She would love it if I would stay and talk further. She knew Omar Khayyam too, and would match verses with me. Father kissed her and said to me that we would meet at breakfast.

So Father went, and Myrrha talked about Omar, whom she knew a great deal better than I did, and it seemed to me that she brought a weight of understanding to the poem that was far outside my reach. All that disappointment with Martindale I supposed. She was absolutely splendid about the fleetingness of life and pleasure and the rose that blows where buried Caesar bled, and it seemed to me she was piercing into a world of experience utterly strange to me but which, of course, I respected profoundly.

> 'Yet Ah, that Spring should vanish with the Rose!
> That Youth's sweet-scented manuscript should close!
>   The Nightingale that in the branches sang,
> Ah, whence, and whither flown again, who knows!'

she recited, thrillingly, and talked about what a glorious thing youth was, and how swift its passing, and the terrible sadness of life which pressed on and on, without anybody being able to halt it, and how wise Omar was to urge us to get on with enjoyment when we could. This was all wonderful to me, for I was new to poetry and had just begun reading some because Professor Schwarz said it was his great alternative to chemistry. If a professor of chemistry thought well of poetry, it must be something better than the stuff we worked through so patiently in Eng. Lit. at school. I had just begun to see that poetry was about life, and not ordinary life but the essence and miraculous underside of life. What a leap my understanding took when I heard Myrrha reciting in her beautiful voice; she was near to tears, and so was I. She mastered herself, and with obvious effort not to break down she continued –

> 'Ah Love! could you and I with Him conspire
> To grasp this sorry Scheme of Things entire,
>   Would not we shatter it to bits – and then
> Remold it nearer to the Heart's Desire!'

I could not speak, nor could Myrrha. She rose and left me to myself, and I was full of surging thoughts, recognition of the evanescence of life, and wonder that this glorious under-standing woman should have stirred my mind and spirit so profoundly.

I do not know how much time passed until I heard her voice from another room, calling me. She has been crying, I thought, and wants me to comfort her. And so I should. I must try to tell her how tremendous she is, and how she has opened up a new world to me, and perhaps hint that I know something about the disappointment with Martindale. I went through a little passage into what proved to be her bedroom, very pretty and full of nice things and filled with the smell of really good perfume.

Myrrha came in from the bathroom, wearing what it is a joke to call a diaphanous garment, but I don't know how else to name it. I mean, as she stood against the light, you could see she had nothing under it, and its fullness and the way it swished around only made it seem thinner. I suppose I gaped, for she really was beautiful.

'Come here, angel,' she said, 'and give me a very big kiss.'

I did, without an instant of hesitation. I knew a good deal about kissing, and I took her in my arms and kissed her ten-derly and long. But I had never kissed a woman in a diapha-nous garment before, and it was like Winston Churchill's brandy. I savoured it in the same way.

'Wouldn't you like to take off all those stupid clothes?' she said, and gave me a start by loosening my tie. It is at this point I cease to understand my own actions. I really didn't know where this was going to lead and had no time for thought, because life seemed to be moving so fast, and taking me with it. But I was delighted to be, so to speak, under this life-enlarging authority. I got out of my clothes quickly, dropping them to the floor and kicking them out of the way.

There is a point in a man's undressing when he looks stupid, and nothing in the world can make him into a roman-tic figure. It is at the moment when he stands in his underwear and socks. I suppose a very calculating man would keep his shirt on to the last, getting rid of his socks and shorts as fast as possible, and then cast off the shirt, revealing himself as an Adonis. But I was a schoolboy undresser, and had never stripped to enchant. When I was in the socks-shorts moment, Myrrha laughed. I whipped off the socks, hurling them toward the dressing-table, and trampled the shorts beneath my feet. I seized her, held her firmly, and kissed her again.

'Darling,' said she, breaking away, 'not like a cannibal. Come and lie down with me. Now, there's no hurry whatever. So let us just do nice things for a while, shall we, and see what comes of it.'

So we did that. But I was a virgin bursting with partly gratified desire for Judy Wolff, and had no notion of preliminaries ; nor, in spite of her words, did Myrrha seem greatly interested in them. I was full of poetry and power.

> Now is she in the very lists of love,
> Her champion mounted for the hot encounter –

thought I when, after some discreet stage-management by Myrrha, I was properly placed and out of danger of committing an unnatural act. It was male vanity. I was seventeen, and it was the first time I had done this ; it would have been clear to anyone but me that I was not leading the band. Very quickly it was over, and I was lying by Myrrha, pleased as Punch.

So we did more nice things, and after a while I was conscious that Myrrha was nudging and manoeuvring me back into the position of advantage. Good God! I thought ; do people do it twice at a time? Well, I was ready to learn, and well prepared for my lesson. Myrrha rather firmly gave the time for this movement of the symphony, and it was a finely rhythmic *andante*, as opposed to the lively *vivace* I had set before. She seemed to like it better, and I began to understand that there was more to this business than I had supposed. It seemed to improve her looks, though it had not occurred to me that they needed improvement. She looked younger, dewier, gentler. I had done that. I was pleased with myself in quite a new way.

More nice things. Quite a lot of talk, this time, and some scraps of Omar from Myrrha, who must have had him by heart. Then again the astonishing act, which took much longer, and this time it was Myrrha who decided that the third movement should be a *scherzo*. When it was over, I was ready for more talk. I liked the talking almost as much as the doing, and I was surprised when Myrrha showed a tendency to fall asleep. I don't know how long she slept, but I may have dozed a little myself. Anyhow, I was in a deep reverie about the strangeness of life in general, when I felt her hand on my thigh. Again? I felt like Casanova, but as I had never read Casanova, and haven't to this day, I suppose I should say I felt as a schoolboy might suppose Casanova to feel. But I was perfectly willing to oblige and soon ready. I have read since that the male creature is at the pinnacle of his sexual power at seventeen, and I was a well-set-up lad in excellent health.

If I am to keep up the similitude of the symphony, this movement was an *allegro con spirito*. Myrrha was a little rough, and I wondered who was the cannibal now? I was even slightly alarmed, because she seemed unaware of my presence just when I was most poignantly aware of being myself, and made noises that I thought out of character. She puffed. She grunted. Once or twice I swear she roared. We brought the symphony to a fine Beethovenian finish with a series of crashing chords. Then Myrrha went to sleep again.

So did I. But not before she did, and I was lost in wonderment.

I do not know how long it was until Myrrha woke, snapped on her bedside light, and said, 'Good God, sweetie, it's time you went home.' It was in that instant of sudden light that I saw her differently. I had not observed that her skin did not fit quite so tightly as it once had done, and there were some little puckers at the armpits and between the breasts. When she lay on her side her stomach hung down, slightly but perceptibly. And under the light of the lamp, which was so close, her hair had a metallic sheen. As she turned to kiss me, she drew one of her legs across mine, and it was like a rasp. I knew women shaved their legs, for I had seen Carol do it, but I did not know that this sandpaper effect was the result. I kissed her, but without making a big thing of it, dressed myself, and prepared to leave. What was I to say?

'Thanks for a wonderful evening, and everything,' I said.

'Bless you, darling,' said she, laughing. 'Will you turn out the lights in the sitting-room as you go?' and with that she turned over, dragging most of the bed-clothes with her, and prepared to sleep again.

It was not a great distance back to the Ritz, and I walked through the snowy night, thinking deeply. So that was what sex was! I dropped into a little all-night place and had two bacon-and-egg sandwiches, two slices of their hot mince pie, and two cups of chocolate with whipped cream, for I found I was very hungry.

DR VON HALLER: When did you realize that this ceremony of initiation was arranged between your father and Mrs Martindale?

MYSELF: Father told me as we went back to Toronto in the train; but I didn't realize it until I had a terrible row with Knopwood. What I mean is, Father didn't say in so many words that it was an arranged thing, but I suppose he was proud of what he had done for me, and he gave some broad hints that I was too stupid to take. He said what a wonderful woman she was and what an accomplished amorist – that was a new word to me – and that if there were such a thing as a female swordsman, certainly Myrrha Martindale was one.

DR VON HALLER: How did he bring up the subject?

MYSELF: He remarked that I was looking very pleased with myself, and that I must have enjoyed my evening with Myrrha. Well, I knew that you aren't supposed to blab about these things, and anyhow she was Father's friend and perhaps he felt tenderly toward her and might be hurt if he discovered she had fallen for me so quickly. So I simply said I had, and he said she could teach me a great deal, and I said yes, she was very well read, and he laughed and said that she could teach me a good deal that wasn't to be found in books. Things that would be very helpful to me with my little Jewish piece. I was shocked to hear Judy called a 'piece' because it isn't a word you use about anybody you love or respect, and I tried to set him right about Judy and how marvellous she was and what very nice people her family were. It was then he became serious about never marrying a girl you met when you were very young. 'If you want fruit, take all you want, but don't buy the tree,' he said. It hurt me to hear him talk that way when Judy was obviously in his mind, and then when he went on to talk about swordsmen I began to wonder for the first time if I knew everything there was to know about that word.

DR VON HALLER: But did he say outright that he had arranged your adventure?

MYSELF: Never flatly. Never in so many words. But he talked about the wounding experiences young men often had learning about sex from prostitutes or getting mixed up with virgins, and said that the only good way was with an experienced older woman, and that I would bless Myrrha as long as I lived, and be grateful it had been managed so intelligently and pleasantly. That's the way the French do it, he said.

DR VON HALLER: Was Myrrha Martindale his mistress?

MYSELF: Oh, I don't imagine so for a minute. Though he did leave some money for her in his will, and I know from things that came out later that he helped her with money from time to time. But if he ever had an affair with her, I'm sure it was because he loved her. It couldn't have been a money thing.

DR VON HALLER: Why not?

MYSELF: It would be sordid, and Father always had such style.

DR VON HALLER: Have you ever read Voltaire's *Candide*?

MYSELF: That was what Knopwood asked me. I hadn't, and he explained that Candide was a simpleton who believed everything he was told. Knopwood was furious with Father. But he didn't know Father, you see.

DR VON HALLER: And you did?

MYSELF: I sometimes think I knew him better than anyone. Do you suggest I didn't?

DR VON HALLER: That is one of the things we are working to find out. Tell me about your row with Father Knopwood.

I suppose I brought it on because I went to see Knopwood a few days after returning to Toronto. I was in a confused state of mind. I didn't regret anything about Myrrha; I was grateful to her, just as Father had said, though I thought I had noticed one or two things about her that had escaped him, or that he didn't care about. Really they only meant that she wasn't as young as Judy. But I was worried about my feelings toward Judy. I had gone to see her as soon as I could after returning from Montreal; she was ill – bad headache or something – and her father asked me to chat for a while. He was kind, but he was direct. Said he thought Judy and I should stop seeing each other so much, because we weren't children any longer, and we might become involved in a way we would regret. I knew he meant he was afraid I might seduce her, so I told him I loved her, and would never do anything to hurt her, and respected her too much to get her into any kind of mess. Yes, he said, but there are times when good resolutions weaken, and there are also hurts that are not hurts of the flesh. Then he said something I could hardly believe; he said that he was not sure Judy might not weaken at some time when I was also weak, and then what would our compounded weakness lead to? I had assumed the man always led in these things, and when I said that to Dr Wolff he smiled in what I can only describe as a Viennese way.

'You and Judy have something that is charming and beautiful,' he said, 'and I advise you to cherish it as it is, for then it will always be a delight to you. But if you go on, we shall all change our roles; I shall have to be unpleasant to you, which I have no wish to do, and you will begin to hate me, which would be a pity, and perhaps you and Judy will decide that in order to preserve your self-respect you must deceive me and Judy's mother. That would be painful to us and I assure you it would also be dangerous to you.'

Then he did an extraordinary thing. He quoted Burns to me! Nobody had ever done that except my Cruikshank grandfather, down by the crick in Deptford, and I had always assumed that Burns was a sort of crick person's poet. But here was this Viennese Jew, saying,

> 'The sacred lowe of weel-placed love,
>   Luxuriously indulge it;
> But never tempt th' illicit rove
>   Tho' naething should divulge it;
> I waive the quantum of the sin
>   The hazard of concealing;
> But, och! it hardens a' within,
>   And petrifies the feeling.

'You are a particularly gentle boy,' he said (and I was startled and resented it); 'it would not take many bad experiences to scar your feelings over and make you much less than the man you may otherwise become. If you seduced my daughter, I should be very angry and might hate you; the physical injury is really not very much, if indeed it is anything at all, but the psychological injury – you see I am too much caught up in the modern way of speaking to be quite able to say the spiritual injury – could be serious if we all parted bad friends. There are people, of course, to whom such things are not important, and I fear you have had a bad example, but you and Judy are not such people. So be warned, David, and be our friend always; but you will never be my daughter's husband, and you must understand that now.'

'Why are you so determined I should never be Judy's husband?' I asked.

'I am not determined alone,' said he. 'There are many

hundreds of determining factors on both sides. They are called ancestors, and there are some things in which we are wise not to defy them.'

'You mean, I'm not a Jew,' I said.

'I had begun to wonder if you would get to it,' said Dr Wolff.

'But does that matter in this day and age?' I said.

'You were born in 1928, when it began to matter terribly, and not for the first time in history,' said Dr Wolff. 'But set that aside. There is another way it matters which I do not like to mention because I do not want to hurt you and I like you very much. It is a question of pride.'

We talked further, but I knew the conversation was over. They were planning to send Judy to school abroad in the spring. They would be happy to see me from time to time until then. But I must understand that the Wolffs had talked to Judy, and though Judy felt very badly, she had seen the point. And that was that.

It was that night I went to Knopwood. I was working up a rage against the Wolffs. A question of pride! Did that mean I wasn't good enough for Judy? And what did all this stuff about being Jews mean from people who gave no obvious external evidence of their Jewishness? If they were such great Jews, where were their side-curls and their funny underwear and their queer food? I had heard of these things as belonging to the bearded Jews in velours hats who lived down behind the Art Gallery. I had assumed the Wolffs and the Schwarzes were trying to be like us; instead I had been told I wasn't good enough for them! Affronted Christianity boiled up inside me. Christ had died for me, I was certain, but I wouldn't take any bets on His having died for the Wolffs and the Schwarzes! Off to Knopwood! He would know.

I was with him all evening, and in the course of an involved conversation everything came out. To my astonishment he sided with Louis Wolff. But worst of all, he attacked Father in terms I had never heard from him, and he was amused, and contemptuous and angry about Myrrha.

'You triple-turned jackass!' he said, 'couldn't you see it

was an arranged thing? And you thought it was your own attraction that got you into bed with such a scarred old veteran! I don't blame you for going to bed with her; show an ass a peck of oats and he'll eat it, even if the oats is musty. But it is the provincial vulgarity of the whole thing that turns my stomach – the winesmanship and the tatty gallantries and the candlelit frumpery of it! The "good talk", the imitations of Churchill by your father, the quotations from *The Rubaiyat*. If I could have my way I'd call in every copy of that twenty-fourth-rate rhymed gospel of hedonism and burn it! How it goes to the hearts of trashy people! So Myrrha matched verses with you, did she? Well, did the literary strumpet quote this –

> '"Well," murmured one, "Let whoso make or buy,
> My Clay with long Oblivion is gone dry:
>   But fill me with the old familiar Juice
>   Methinks I might recover by and by."

Did she whisper that in your ear as Absalom went in unto his father's concubine?'

'You don't understand,' I said; 'this is a thing French families do to see that their sons learn about sex in the right way.'

'Yes, I have heard that, but I didn't know they put their cast mistresses to the work, the way you put a child rider on your safe old mare.'

'That's enough, Knoppy,' I said; 'you know a lot about the Church and religion, but I don't think that qualifies you to talk about what it is to be a swordsman.'

That made him really furious. He became cold and courteous.

'Help me then,' he said. 'Tell me what a swordsman is and what lies behind the mystique of the swordsman.'

I talked as well as I could about living with style, and not sticking to dowdy people's ways. I managed to work in the word amorist because I thought he might not know it. I talked about the Cavaliers as opposed to the Roundheads, and I dragged in Mackenzie King as a sort of two-bit Cromwell, who had to be resisted. Mr King had made himself unpopular early in the war by urging the Canadian people to 'buckle on the whole armour of God', which when it was interpreted meant watering and rationing whisky without reducing the price. I said that if that was the armour of God, I would back the skill and panache of the swordsman against it any day. As I talked he seemed to be less angry, and when I had finished he was almost laughing.

'My poor Davey,' he said, 'I have always known you were an innocent boy, but I have hoped your innocence was not just the charming side of a crippling stupidity. And now I am going to try to do something that I had never expected to do, and of which I disapprove, but which I think is necessary if between us we are going to save your soul. I am going to disillusion you about your father.'

He didn't, of course. Not wholly. He talked a lot about Father as a great man of business, but that cut no ice with me. I don't mean he suggested Father was anything but honest, because there were never any grounds for that. But he talked about the corrupting power of great wealth and the illusion it created in its possessor that he could manipulate people, and the dreadful truth that there were a great many people whom he undoubtedly could manipulate, so that the illusion was never seriously challenged. He talked about the illusion wealth creates that its possessor is of a different clay from that of common men. He talked about the adulation great wealth attracts from people to whom worldly success is the only measure of worth. Wealth bred and fostered illusion and illusion brought corruption. That was his theme.

I was ready for all of this because Father had talked a great deal to me since he began to be more at home. Father said that a man you could manipulate had to be watched because other people could manipulate him as well. Father had also said that the rich man differed from the ordinary man only in that he had a wider choice, and that one of his dangerous choices was a lightly disguised slavery to the source of his wealth. I even told Knoppy something he had never guessed. It was about what Father called the Patholo-

453

gical Compassion of Big Business, which seems to demand that above a certain executive level a man's incompetence or loss of quality had to be kept from him so that he would not be destroyed in the eyes of his family, his friends, and himself. Father estimated that Corporation Compassion cost him a few hundred thousand every year, and this was charity of a kind St Paul had never foreseen. Like a lot of people who have no money, Knoppy had some half-baked ideas about people who had it, and the foremost of these was that wealth was achieved, and held, only by people who were essentially base. I accused him of lack of charity, which I knew was a very great matter to him. I accused him of a covert, Christian jealousy, that blinded him to Father's real worth because he could not see beyond his wealth. People strong enough to get wealth are sometimes strong enough to resist illusion. Father was such a man.

'You should do well at the Bar, Davey,' he said. 'You are already an expert at making the worser seem the better cause. To be cynical is not the same as avoiding illusion, for cynicism is just another kind of illusion. All formulas for meeting life – even many philosophies – are illusion. Cynicism is a trashy illusion. But a swordsman – shall I tell you what a swordsman is? It is just what the word implies: a swordsman is an expert at sticking something long and thin, or thick and curved, into other people; and always with intent to wound. You've read a lot lately. You've read some D. H. Lawrence. Do you remember what he says about heartless, cold-blooded fucking? That's what a swordsman is good at, as the word is used nowadays by the kind of people who use it of your father. A swordsman is what the Puritans you despise so romantically would call a whoremaster. Didn't you know that? Of course swordsmen don't use the word that way; they use other terms, like amorist, though that usually means somebody like your Myrrha, who is a great proficient at sex without love. Is that what you want? You've told me a great deal about what you feel for Judy Wolff. Now you have had some skilful instruction in the swordsman-and-amorist game. What is it? Nothing but the cheerful trumpet-and-drum of the act of kind. Simple music for simple souls. Is that what you want with Judy? Because that is what her father fears. He doesn't want his daughter's life to be blighted by a whoremaster's son and, as he very shrewdly suspects, a whoremaster's pupil.'

This was hitting hard, and though I tried to answer him I knew I was squirming. Because – believe it or not, but I swear it is the truth – I had never understood that was what people meant when they talked about a swordsman, and it suddenly accounted for some of the queer responses I had met with when I applied the word so proudly to Father. I remembered with a chill that I had even used this word about him to the Wolffs, and I was sure they were up to every nuance of speech in three languages. I had made a fool of myself, and of course the realization made me both weak and angry. I lashed out at Knoppy.

'All very well for you to be so pernickety about people's sexual tastes,' I said. 'But what cap do you wear? Everybody knows what you are. You're a fairy. You're a fairy who's afraid to do anything about it. So what makes you such an authority about real men and women, who have passions you can't begin to share or understand?'

I had hit home. Or so I thought. He seemed to become smaller in his chair, and all the anger had gone out of him.

'Davey, I want you to listen very carefully,' he said. 'I suppose I am a homosexual, really. Indeed, I know it. I'm a priest, too. By efforts that have not been trivial I have worked for over twenty years to keep myself always in full realization of both facts and to put what I am and the direction in which my nature leads me at the service of my faith and its founder. People wounded much worse than I have been good fighters in that cause. I have not done too badly. I should be stupid and falsely humble if I said otherwise. I have done it gladly, and I shall only say that it has not been easy. But it was my personal sacrifice of what I was to what I loved.

'Now I want you to remember something because I don't think we shall meet again very soon. It is this; however fashionable despair about the world and about people may be at present, and however powerful despair may become in the future, not everybody, or even most people, think and live fashionably; virtue and honour will not be banished from the world, however many popular moralists and panicky journalists say so. Sacrifice will not cease to be because psychiatrists have popularized the idea that there is often some concealed, self-serving element in it; theologians always knew that. Nor do I think love as a high condition of honour will be lost; it is a pattern in the spirit, and people long to make the pattern a reality in their own lives, whatever means they take to do so. In short, Davey, God is not dead. And I can assure you God is not mocked.'

IO

I never saw Knopwood after that. What he meant when he said we would not meet again was soon explained; he had been ordered off to some more missionary work, and he died a few years ago in the West, of tuberculosis, working almost till the end among his Indians. I have never forgiven him for trying to blacken Father. If that is what his Christianity added up to, it wasn't much.

DR VON HALLER: As you report what Father Knopwood said about Mrs Martindale, he was abusive and contemptuous; did he know her, by any chance?

MYSELF: No, he just hated her because she was very much a woman, and I have told you what he was. He made up his mind she was a harlot, and that was that.

DR VON HALLER: You don't think any of it was indignation on your behalf – because she had, so to speak, abused your innocence?

MYSELF: How had she done that? I think that's silly.

DR VON HALLER: She had been party to a plan to manipulate you in a certain direction. I don't mean your virginity, which is simply physical and technical, but the scheme to introduce you to what Knopwood called the cheerful trumpet-and-drum, the simple music.

MYSELF: One has to meet it somehow, I suppose? Better in such circumstances than many we can imagine. I had forgotten the Swiss were so Puritanical.

DR VON HALLER: Ah, now you are talking to me as if I were Father Knopwood. True, everybody has to encounter sex, but usually the choice is left to themselves. They find it; it is not offered to them like a tonic when somebody else thinks it would be good for them. May not the individual know the right time better than someone else? Is it not rather patronizing to arrange a first sexual encounter for one's son?

MYSELF: No more patronizing than to send him to any other school, so far as I can see.

DR VON HALLER: So you are in complete agreement with what was arranged for you. Let me see – did you not say that the last time you had sexual intercourse was on December 26, 1945? – Was Mrs Martindale the first and the last, then? – Why did you hesitate to put this valuable instruction to further use? – Take all the time you please, Mr Staunton. If you would like a glass of water there is a carafe beside you.

MYSELF: It was Judy, I suppose.

DR VON HALLER: Yes. About Judy – do you realize that in what you have been telling me Judy remains very dim? I am getting to know your father, and I have a good idea of Father Knopwood, and you implied much about Mrs Martindale in a very few words. But I see very little of Judy. A well-bred girl, somewhat foreign to your world, Jewish, who sings. Otherwise you say only that she was kind and delightful and vague words like that which give her no individuality at all. Your sister suggested that she was cowlike; I attach quite a lot of significance to that.

MYSELF: Don't. Carol is very sharp.

DR VON HALLER: Indeed she is. You have given a sharp picture of her. She is very perceptive. And she said Judy was cowlike. Do you know why?

457

MYSELF: Spite, obviously. She sensed I loved Judy.

DR VON HALLER: She sensed Judy was an Anima-figure to you. Now we must be technical for a little while. We talked about the Anima as a general term for a man's idea of all a woman is or may be. Women are very much aware of this figure when it is aroused in men. Carol sensed that Judy had suddenly embodied the Anima for you, and she was irritated. You know how women are always saying, 'What does he see in her?' Of course what he sees is the Anima. Furthermore, he is usually only able to describe it in general terms, not in detail. He is in the grip of something that might as well be called an enchantment; the old word is as good as any new one. It is notorious that when one is enchanted, one does not see clearly.

MYSELF: Judy was certainly clear to me.

DR VON HALLER: Even though you do not seem to remember one thing she said that is not a commonplace? Oh, Mr Staunton – a pretty, modest girl, whom you saw for the first time in enchanting circumstances, singing – an Anima, if ever I heard of one.

MYSELF: I thought you people weren't supposed to lead your witnesses?

DR VON HALLER: Not in Mr Justice Staunton's court, perhaps, but this is my court. Now tell me; after your talk with your father, in which he referred to Judy as 'your little Jewish piece', and your talk with her father, when he said you must not think of Judy as a possible partner in your life, and after your talk with that third father, the priest, how did matters stand between you and Judy?

MYSELF: It went sour. Or it lost its gloss. Or anything you like to express a drop in intensity, a loss of power. Of course we met and talked and kissed. But I knew she was an obedient daughter, and when we kissed I knew Louis Wolff was near, though invisible. And try as I would, when we kissed I could hear a voice – it wasn't my father, so don't think it was – saying 'your Jewish piece'. And hateful Knopwood seemed always to be near, like Christ in his sentimental picture, with His hand on the Boy Scout's shoulder. I don't know how it would have worked out because I had rather a miserable illness. It would probably be called mononucleosis now, but they didn't know what it was then, and I was out of school for a long time and confined to the house with Netty as my nurse. When Easter came I was still very weak, and Judy went to Lausanne to a school. She sent me a letter, and I meant to keep it, of course, but I'll bet any money Netty took it and burned it.

DR VON HALLER: But you remember what it said?

MYSELF: I remember some of it. She wrote, 'My father is the wisest and best man I know, and I shall do what he says.' It seemed extraordinary, for a girl of seventeen.

DR VON HALLER: How, extraordinary?

MYSELF: Immature. Wouldn't you say so? Oughtn't she to have had more mind of her own?

DR VON HALLER: But wasn't that precisely your attitude toward your own father?

MYSELF: Not after my illness. Nevertheless, there was a difference. Because my father really was a great man. Dunstan Ramsay once said he was a genius of an unusual, unrecognized kind. Whereas Louis Wolff, though very good of his kind, was just a clever doctor.

DR VON HALLER: A very sophisticated man; sophisticated in a way your father was not, it appears. And what about Knopwood? You seem to have dismissed him because he was a homosexual.

MYSELF: I see a good many of his kind in court. You can't take them seriously.

DR VON HALLER: But you take very few people seriously when you have them in court. There are homosexuals we do well to take seriously and you are not likely to meet them in court. You spoke, I recall, of Christian charity?

MYSELF: I am no longer a Christian, and too often I have uncovered pitiable weakness masquerading as charity. Those who talk about charity and forgiveness usually lack the guts to push anything to a logical conclusion. I've never seen charity bring any unquestionable good in its train.

DR VON HALLER: I see. Very well, let us go on. During

your illness I suppose you did a lot of thinking about your situation. That is what these illnesses are for, you know — these mysterious ailments that take us out of life but do not kill us. They are signals that our life is going the wrong way, and intervals for reflection. You were lucky to be able to keep out of a hospital, even if it did return you to the domination of Netty. Now, what answers did you find? For instance, did you think about why you were so ready to believe your mother had been the lover of your father's best friend, whereas you doubted that Mrs Martindale had been your father's mistress?

MYSELF: I suppose children favour one parent more than the other. I have told you about Mother. And Father used to talk about her sometimes when he visited me when I was ill. Several times he warned me against marrying a boyhood sweetheart.

DR VON HALLER: Yes, I suppose he knew what was wrong with you. People often do, you know, though nothing would persuade them to bring such knowledge to the surface of their thoughts or admit what they so deeply know. He sensed you were sick for Judy. And he gave you very good advice, really.

MYSELF: But I loved Judy. I really did.

DR VON HALLER: You loved a projection of your own Anima. You really did. But did you ever know Judy Wolff? You have told me that when you see her now, as a grown woman with a husband and family, you never speak to her. Why? Because you are protecting your boyhood dream. You don't want to meet this woman who is somebody else. When you go home you had better make an opportunity to meet Mrs Professor Whoever-It-Is, and lay that ghost forever. It will be quite easy, I assure you. You will see her as she is now, and she will see the famous criminal lawyer. It will all be smooth as silk, and you will be delivered forever. So far as possible, lay your ghosts. . . . But you have not answered my question: why adultery for mother but not for father?

MYSELF: Mother was weak.

DR VON HALLER: Mother was your father's Anima-

460

figure, whom he had been so unfortunate, or so unwise, as to marry. No wonder she seemed weak, poor woman, with such a load to carry for such a man. And no wonder he turned against her, as you would probably have turned against poor Judy if she had been so unfortunate as to fall into the clutch of such a clever thinker and such a primitive feeler as you are. Oh, men revenge themselves very thoroughly on women they think have enchanted them, when really these poor devils of women are merely destined to be pretty or sing nicely or laugh at the right time.

MYSELF: Don't you think there is any element of enchantment in love, then?

DR VON HALLER: I know perfectly well that there is, but has anybody ever said that enchantment was a basis for marriage? It will be there at the beginning, probably, but the table must be laid with more solid fare than that if starvation is to be kept at bay for sixty years.

MYSELF: You are unusually dogmatic today.

DR VON HALLER: You have told me you like dogma. . . . But let us get back to an unanswered question: why did you believe your mother capable of adultery but not your father?

MYSELF: Well – adultery in a woman may be a slip, a peccadillo, but in a man, you see – you see, it's an offense against property. I know it doesn't sound very pretty, but the law makes it plain and public opinion makes it plainer. A deceived husband is merely a cuckold, a figure of fun, whereas a deceived wife is someone who has sustained an injury. Don't ask me why; I simply state the fact as society and the courts see it.

DR VON HALLER: But this Mrs Martindale, if I understood you, had left her husband, or he had left her. So what injury could there be?

MYSELF: I am thinking of my mother: Father knew her long before Mother's death. He may have drifted away from Mother, but I can't believe he would do anything that would injure her – that might have played some part in her death. I mean, a swordsman is one thing – a sort of chivalrous concept, which may be romantic but is certainly not squalid. But an adulterer – I've seen a lot of them in court, and none of them was anything but squalid.

DR VON HALLER: And you could not associate your father with anything you considered squalid? So: you emerged from this illness without your beloved, and without your priest, but with your father still firmly in the saddle?

MYSELF: Not even that. I still adored him, but my adoration was flawed with doubts. That was why I determined not to try to be like him, not to permit myself any thought of rivalling him but to try to find some realm where I could show that I was worthy of him.

DR VON HALLER: My God, what a fanatic!

MYSELF: That seems a rather unprofessional outburst.

DR VON HALLER: Not a bit. You are a fanatic. Don't you know what fanaticism is? It is overcompensation for doubt. Well: go on.

Yes, I went on, and what my life lacked in incident it made up for in intensity. I finished school, pretty well but not as well as if I had not had such a long illness, and I was ready for university. Father had always assumed I would go to the University of Toronto, but I wanted to go to Oxford, and he jumped at that. He had never been to a university himself because he was in the First World War – got the D.S.O., too – during what would have been his college years; he had wanted to get on with life and had qualified as a lawyer without taking a degree. You could still do that, then. But he had romantic ideas about universities, and Oxford appealed to him. So I went there, and because Father wanted me to be in a big college, I got into Christ Church.

People are always writing in their memoirs about what Oxford meant to them. I can't pretend the place itself meant extraordinary things to me. Of course it was pleasant, and I liked the interesting buildings; architectural critics are always knocking them, but after Toronto they made my eyes pop. They spoke of an idea of education strange to me; discomfort there was, but no meanness, no hint of edification on the cheap. And I liked the feel of a city of youth, which is what Oxford seems to be, though anybody with eyes in his head can see that it is run by old men. But my Oxford was a post-war Oxford, crammed to the walls and rapidly growing into a big industrial city. And there was much criticism of the privilege it implied, mostly from people who were sitting bang in the middle of the privilege and getting all they could out of it. Oxford was part of my plan to become a special sort of man, and I bent everything that came my way to my single purpose.

I read law, and did well at it. I was very lucky in being assigned Pargetter of Balliol as my tutor. He was a great law don, a blind man who nevertheless managed to be a famous chess-player and such a teacher as I had never known. He was relentless and exacting, which was precisely what I wanted because I was determined to be a first-class lawyer. You see, when I told Father I wanted to be a lawyer, he assumed at once that I wanted law as a preparation for business, which was what he himself had made of it. He was sure I would follow him in Alpha; indeed I don't think any other future for me seemed possible to him. I was perhaps a little bit devious because I did not tell him at once that I had other ideas. I wanted the law because I wanted to master something in which I would know where I stood and which would not be open to the whims and preconceptions of people like Louis Wolff, or Knopwood – or Father. I wanted to be a master of my own craft and I wanted a great craft. Also, I wanted to know a great deal about people, and I wanted a body of knowledge that would go as far as possible to explain people. I wanted to work in a realm that would give me some insight into the spirit that I had seen at work in Bill Unsworth.

I had no notions of being a crusader. One of the things I had arrived at during that wearisome, depleting illness was a determination to be done forever with everything that Father Knopwood stood for. Knoppy, I saw, wanted to manipulate people; he wanted to make them good, and he was sure he knew what was good. For him, God was here and Christ was now. He was prepared to accept himself and impose on others a lot of irrational notions in the interests of his special idea of goodness. He thought God was not mocked. I seemed to see God being mocked, and rewarding the mocker with splendid success, every day of my life.

I wanted to get away from the world of Louis Wolff, who now appeared to me as an extremely shrewd man whose culture was never allowed for an instant to interfere with some age-old ideas that governed him and must also govern his family.

I wanted to get away from Father and save my soul, inso-far as I believed in such a thing. I suppose what I meant by my soul was my self-respect or my manhood. I loved him and feared him, but I had spied tiny chinks in his armour. He too was a manipulator and, remembering his own dictum, I did not mean to be a man who could be manipulated. I knew I would always be known as his son and that I would in some ways have to carry the weight of wealth that I had not gained myself in a society where inherited wealth al-ways implied a stigma. But somehow, in some part of the great world, I would be David Staunton, unreachable by Knopwood or Louis Wolff, or Father, because I had out-stripped them.

The idea of putting sex aside never entered my head. It just happened, and I was not aware that it had become part of my way of living until it was thoroughly established. Par-getter may have had something to do with it. He was un-married, and being blind he was insulated against a great part of the charm of women. He seized on me, as he did on all his students, with an eagle's talons, but I think he knew by the end of my first year that I was his in a way that the others, however admiring, were not. If you hope to master the law, he would say, you are a fool, for it has no single masters ; but if you hope to master some part of it, you had better put your emotions in cold storage at least until you are thirty. I decided to do that, and did it, and by the time I was thirty I liked the chill. It helped to make people afraid of me, and I liked that, too.

Pargetter must have taken to me, though he was not a man to hint at any such thing. He taught me chess, and although I was never up to his standard I grew to play well. His room never had enough light, because he didn't need it and I think he was a little cranky about making people who had their eyesight use it to the full. We would sit by his insufficient fire in a twilight that could have been dismal, but which he contrived somehow to give a legal quality, and play game after game; he sat fatly in his arm-chair, and I sat by the board and made all the moves; he would call his move, I would place the piece as he directed, and then I would tell him my counter-move. When he had beaten me he would go back over the game and tell me precisely the point at which I had gone wrong. I was awed by such a memory and such a spatial sense in a man who lived in darkness; he was contemptuous of me when I could not remember what I had done six or eight moves back, and of sheer necessity I had to develop the memory-trick myself.

He really was alarming: he had three or four boards set up around his room, on which he played chess by post with friends far away. If I arrived for an early tutorial he would say, 'There's a postcard on the table; I expect it's from Johannesburg; read it.' I would read a chess move from it and make the move on a board which he had not touched for perhaps a month. When my tutorial was finished he would dictate a counter-move to me, and I would rearrange the board accordingly. He won a surprising number of these long-distance, tortoise-paced games.

He had never learned Braille. He wrote in longhand on paper he fitted into a frame which had guide-wires to keep him on the lines, and he never seemed to forget anything he had written. He had a prodigious knowledge of law books he had never seen, and when he sent me, with exact directions, to his shelves to hunt up a reference, I often found a slip of paper in the book with a note in his careful, printlike hand. He kept up with books and journals by having them read to him, and I felt myself favoured when he began to ask me to read; he would make invaluable comment as he listened, and it was always a master-lesson in how to absorb, weigh, select, and reject.

This was precisely what I wanted and I came almost to worship Pargetter. Exactitude, calm appraisal, close reasoning applied to problems which so often had their beginning in other people's untidy emotions acted like balm on my hurt mind. It was not ordinary legal instruction and it did not result in ordinary legal practice. Many lawyers are beetle-witted ignoramuses, prey to their own emotions and those of their clients ; some of them work up big practices because they can fling themselves fiercely into other people's fights. Their indignation is for sale. But Pargetter had honed his mind to a shrewd edge, and I wanted to be like Pargetter. I wanted to know, to see, to sift, and not to be moved. I wanted to get as far as possible from that silly boy who had not realized what a swordsman was when everybody else knew, and who mooned over Judy Wolff and was sent away by her father to play with other toys. I wanted to be melted down, purged of dross, and remoulded in a new and better form ; Pargetter was just the man to do it. I had other instructors, of course, and some of them were very good, but Pargetter continues to be my ideal, my father in art.

II

I wrote to Father every week and grew aware that my letters were less and less communicative, for I was entering a world where he could not follow. I visited Canada once a year, for as short a time as I could manage, and it was when I was about to enter my third year at Oxford that he took me to dinner one night, and after some havering which I realize now was shyness about what he was going to say, he made what seemed to me to be an odd request.

'I've been wondering about the Stauntons,' he said. 'Who do you suppose they could have been ? I can't find out anything about Father, though I've wormed out a few facts. He graduated from the medical school here in Toronto in 1887, and the records say he was twenty then, so he must have been born in 1867. They really just gave doctors a lick and a promise then, and I don't suppose he knew much medicine. He was a queer old devil, and as you probably know, we never hit it off. All I know about his background is that he wasn't born in Canada. Mother was, and I've traced her family, and it was easy and dull; farmers culminating in a preacher. But who was Dr Henry Staunton? I want to know. You see, Davey, though it sounds vain, I have a strong hunch that there must be some good blood somewhere in our background. Your grandfather had a lot of ability as a businessman; more than I could ever persuade him to put to work. His plunge into sugar, when nobody else could see its possibilities, took imagination. I mean, when he was a young man, a lot of people were still rasping their sugar off a loaf with a file, and it all came from the Islands. He had drive and foresight. Of course lots of quite ordinary people have done very well for themselves, but I wonder if he was quite ordinary? When I was in England during the war I wanted to look around and find out anything I could, but the time was wrong and I was very busy with immediate things. But I met two people over there at different times who asked me if I were one of the Warwickshire Stauntons. Well, you know how Englishmen like it when Canadians play simple and rough-hewn, so I always answered that so far as I knew I was one of the Pitt County Stauntons. But I tucked it away in the back of my mind, and it might just be so. Who the Warwickshire Stauntons are I haven't the slightest idea, but they appear to be well known to people who are interested in old families. So, when you go back to Oxford, I'd like you to make some enquiries and let me know what you find. We're probably bastards, or something, but I'd like to know for certain.'

I had long known Father was a romantic, and I had once been a romantic myself – two or three years ago – so I said I would do what I could.

How? And what? Go to Warwickshire and find Stauntons, and ask if they had any knowledge of a physician who had been Pitt County's foremost expert on constipation, and to the end of his days a firm believer in *lignum vitae* sap as a treatment for rheumatism? Not for me, thank you. But one day in the Common Room I was looking through the *Times Literary Supplement*, and my eye fell on a modest advertisement. I can see it now:

> GENEALOGIES erected and pedigrees searched by an Oxonian curiously qualified. Strict confidence exacted and extended.

This was what I wanted. I made a note of the box number, and that night I wrote my letter. I wanted a pedigree searched, I said, and if it proved possible to erect a genealogy on it I should like that, too.

I don't know what I expected, but the advertisement suggested a pedant well past youth and of a sharp temper. I was utterly unprepared for the curiously qualified Oxonian when he arrived in my study two days later. He seemed not to be much older than myself, and had a shy, girlish manner and the softest voice that was compatible with being heard at all. The only elderly or pedantic thing about him was a pair of spectacles of a kind nobody wore then – gold-rimmed and with small oval lenses.

'I thought I'd come round instead of writing, because we are near neighbours,' he said, and handed me a cheap visiting card on which was printed –

ADRIAN PLEDGER-BROWN

CORPUS CHRISTI

So this was the curiously qualified Oxonian!

'Sit down,' I said. 'You erect genealogies?'

'Oh, indeed,' he breathed. 'That is to say, I know precisely how it is done. That is to say, I have examined many scores of pedigrees which have already been erected, and I am sure I could do it myself if I were to be entrusted with such a task. It involves research, you see, of a kind I understand quite well and could undertake with a very fair likelihood of success. I know, you see, where to look, and that is everything. Almost everything.'

He smiled such a girlish smile and his eyes swam so unassumingly behind the comic specs that I was tempted to be easy with him. But that was not the Pargetter way. Beware of a witness who appeals to you, he said. Repress any personal response, and if it seems to be gaining the upper hand, go to the other extreme and be severe with the witness. If Ogilvie had remembered that in Cripps-Armstrong vs. Clatterbos & Dudley in 1884 he would have won the case, but he let Clatterbos's difficulty with English arouse his compassion; it's a famous instance. So I sprang upon Pledger-Brown, and rent him.

'Am I right in deducing that you have never erected a genealogy independently before?'

'That would be – well, to put it baldly – yes, you might say that.'

'Never mind what I might say or might not say. I asked a plain question, and I want a plain answer. Is this your first job?'

'My first professional engagement? Working as an independent investigator? If you wish to put it that way, I suppose the answer must be that it is.'

'Aha! You are in a word, a greenhorn.'

'Oh, dear, no. I mean, I have studied the subject, and the method, extensively.'

'But you have never done a job of this kind before, for a fee. Yes or no?'

'To be completely frank, yes; or rather, no.'

'But your advertisement said "curiously qualified". Tell

me, Mr – (business of consulting card) – ah, Pledger-Brown, in precisely what direction does your curious qualification lie?'

'I am the godson of Garter.'

'Godson of –?'

'Garter.'

'I do not understand.'

'Quite possibly not. But that is why you need me, you see. I mean, people who want genealogies erected and pedigrees searched don't usually know these things. Americans in particular. I mean that my godfather is the Garter King of Arms.'

'What's that?'

'He is the principal officer of the College of Heralds. I hope that one day, with luck, I may be a member of the College myself. But I must make a beginning somewhere, you see.'

'Somewhere? What do you imply by somewhere? You regard me as a starting-point, is that it? I would be rough material for your prentice-hand; is that what you mean?'

'Oh, dear me, no. But I must do some independent work before I can hope to get an official appointment, mustn't I?'

'How should I know what you must do? What I want to know is whether there is any chance that you can undertake the job I want done and do it properly.'

'Well, Mr Staunton, I don't think anybody will do it for you if you go on like this.'

'Like this? Like this? I don't understand you. What fault have you to find with the way I have been going on, as you express it?'

Pledger-Brown was all mildness, and his smile was like a Victorian picture of a village maiden.

'Well, I mean playing Serjeant Buzfuz and treating me really quite rudely when I've only come in answer to your letter. You're a law student, of course. I've looked you up, you see. And your father is a prominent Canadian industrialist. I suppose you want some ancestors. Well, perhaps I can find some for you. And I want the work, but not badly enough to be bullied about it. I mean, I am a beginner at genealogy, but I've studied it: you're a beginner at the law, but you've studied it. So why are you being so horrid when we are on an even footing?'

So I stopped being horrid, and in quite a short time he had accepted a glass of sherry and was calling me Staunton and I was calling him Pledger-Brown, and we were discussing what might be done.

He was in his third year at Corpus, which I could almost have hit with a stone from my windows, because I was in Canterbury Quad at the rear of Christ Church. He was mad for genealogy and couldn't wait to get at it, so he had advertised while he was still an undergraduate, and his anxiety for strict confidence was because his college would have been unsympathetic if they thought he was conducting any sort of business within their walls. He was obviously poor, but he had an air of breeding, and there was a strain of toughness in him that lay well below his wispy, maidenly ways. I took to him because he was as keen about his profession as I was about mine, and for anything I knew his diffidence may have been the professional manner of his kind. Soon he was cross-examining me.

'This Dr Henry Staunton who has no known place of birth is a very common figure in genealogical work for people from the New World. But we can usually find the origin of such people, if we sift the parish records, wills, records of Chancery and Exchequer, and Manor Court Rolls. That takes a long time and runs into money. So we start with the obvious, hoping for a lucky hit. Of course, as your father thinks, he may be a Staunton of Longbridge in Warwickshire, but there are also Stauntons of Nottingham, Leicester, Lincolnshire, and Somerset, all of a quality that would please your father. But sometimes we can take a short cut. Was your grandfather an educated man?'

'He was a doctor. I wouldn't call him a man of wide cultivation.'

'Good. That's often a help. I mean, such people often retain some individuality under the professional veneer. Perhaps he said some things that stuck in your mind? Used unusual words that might be county dialect words? Do you recall anything like that?'

I pondered. 'Once he told my sister, Caroline, she had a tongue sharp enough to shave an urchin. I've repeated it to her often.'

'Oh, that's quite helpful. He did use some dialect words then. But urchin as a word for the common hedgehog is very widespread in country districts. Can you think of anything more unusual?'

I was beginning to respect Pledger-Brown. I had always thought an urchin was a boy you didn't like, and could never figure out why Grandfather would want to shave one. I thought further.

'I do just remember that he called some of his old patients who stuck with him, and were valetudinarians, "my old wallowcrops". Is that of any use? Could he have made the word up?'

'Few simple people make up words. "Wallowcrop"; I'll make a note of that and see what I can discover. Meanwhile keep thinking about him, will you? And I'll come again when I have a better idea what to do.'

Think about Grandfather Staunton, powerful but dim in my past. A man, it seemed to me now, with a mind like a morgue in which a variety of defunct ideas lay on slabs, kept cold to defer decay. A man who knew nothing about health, but could identify a number of diseases. A man whose medical knowledge belonged to a time when people talked about The System and had spasms and believed in the efficacy of strong, clean smells, such as oil of peppermint, as charms against infection. A man who never doubted that spankings were good for children, and once soundly walloped both Caroline and me because we had put Eno's Fruit Salts in the bottom of Granny's chamber-pot, hoping she would have a fantod when it foamed. A furious teetotaller, malignantly contemptuous of what he called 'booze-artists' and never fully reconciled to my father when he discovered that Father drank wines and spirits but had contumaciously failed there-

by to become a booze-artist. A man whom I could only recall as gloomy, heavy, and dull, but pleased with his wealth
and unaffectedly scornful of those who had not the wit or
craft to equal it; preachers were excepted as being a class
apart, and sacred, but needing frequent guidance from practical men in the conduct of their churches. In short, a nasty
old village moneybags.

A strange conduit through which to convey the good
blood Father thought we Stauntons must have. But then
Father had never troubled to pretend that he had much regard for Doc Staunton. Which was strange in itself, in a way,
for Father was very strong on the regard children should
have for parents. Not that he ever said so directly, or urged
Caroline and me to honour our father and mother. But I
recall that he was down on H. G. Wells, because in his
Experiment in Autobiography Wells had said frankly that
his parents weren't up to much and that escape from them
was his first step toward a good life. Father was not consistent. But Doc Staunton had been consistent, and what had
consistency made of him?

The hunt was up, and Doc Staunton was the fox.

Notes from Pledger-Brown punctuated the year that followed. He wrote an elegant Italic hand, as became a genealogist, and scraps of intelligence would arrive by the college
messenger service: '*Wallowcrop* Cumberland dialect word.
Am following up this clue. A.P-B.' And, 'Sorry to say nothing
comes of enquiries in Cumberland. Am casting about in Lincoln.' Or, 'Tally-ho! A Henry Staunton born 1866 in Somerset!' followed a week later by, 'False scent; Somerset Henry
died aged 3 mos.' Clearly he was having a wonderful adventure, but I had little time to think about it. I was up to my
eyes in Jurisprudence, that formal science of positive law,
and in addition to formal studies Pargetter was making me
read Kelly's *Famous Advocates and Their Speeches* and
British Forensic Eloquence aloud to him, dissecting the rhetoric of notable counsel and trying to make some progress in
that line myself. Pargetter was determined that I should not

be what he called an ignorant pettifogger, and he made it clear that as a Canadian I started well behind scratch in the journey toward professional literacy and elegance.

'"The law, besides being a profession, is one of the humanities," ' he said to me one day, and I knew from the way he spoke he was quoting. 'Who said that?' I didn't know. 'Then never forget that it was one of your countrymen, your present Prime Minister, Louis St Laurent,' he said, punching me sharply in the side, as he often did when he wanted to make a point. 'It's been said before, but it's never been said better. Be proud it was a Canadian who said it.' And he went on to belabour me, as he had often done before, with Sir Walter Scott's low opinion of lawyers who knew nothing of history or literature; from these studies, said he, I would learn what people were and how they might be expected to behave. 'But wouldn't I learn that from clients?' I asked, to try him. 'Clients!' he said, and I would not have believed anyone could make a two-syllable word stretch out so long; 'you'll learn precious little from clients except folly and duplicity and greed. You've got to stand above that.'

Working as I was under the English system I had to be a member of one of the Inns of Court and go to London at intervals to eat dinners in its Hall; I was enrolled in the Middle Temple, and reverently chewed through the thirty-six obligatory meals. I liked it. I liked the ceremony and solemnity of the law, not only as safeguards against trivializing of the law but as pleasant observances in themselves. I visited the courts, studied the conduct and courtesy of their workings, and venerated judges who seemed able to carry a mass of detail in their heads and boil it down and serve it up in a kind of strong judicial consommé for the jury when all the pleading and testimony were over. I liked the romance of it, the star personalities of the great advocates, the swishing of gowns and flourishing of impractical but traditional blue bags full of papers. I was delighted that although most people seemed to use more modern instruments, everybody had access to quill pens, and could doubtless have called for sand to do their blotting, with full confidence that sand would have been forthcoming. I loved wigs, which established a hierarchy that was palpable and turned unremarkable faces into the faces of priests serving a great purpose. What if all this silk and bombazine and horsehair awed and even frightened the simple people who came to court for justice? It would do them no harm to be a little frightened. Everybody in court, except the occasional accused creature in the dock, seemed calmed, reft from the concerns of everyday; those who were speaking on oath seemed to me, very often, to be revealing an aspect of their best selves. The juries took their duties seriously, like good citizens. It was an arena in which gladiators struggled, but the end for which they struggled was that right, so far as right could be determined, should be done.

I was not naïve. That is how I think of courts still. I am one of the very few lawyers I know who keeps his gown beautifully clean, whose collar and bands and cuffs are almost foppishly starched, whose striped trousers are properly pressed, whose shoes gleam. I am proud that the newspapers often say I cut an elegant figure in court. The law deserves that. The law is elegant. Pargetter took good care that I should not be foolishly romantic about the law, but he knew that there was a measure of romance in my attitude toward it, and if he had thought it should be rooted out, he would have done so. One day he paid me a walloping great compliment.

'I think you'll make an advocate,' said he. 'You have the two necessities, ability and imagination. A good advocate is his client's *alter ego*; his task is to say what his client would say for himself if he had the knowledge and the power. Ability goes hand in hand with the knowledge: the power is dependent on imagination. But when I say imagination I mean capacity to see all sides of a subject and weigh all possibilities; I don't mean fantasy and poetry and moonshine; imagination is a good horse to carry you over the ground, not a flying carpet to set you free from probability.'

I think I grew a foot, spiritually, that day.

DR VON HALLER: So you might. And how lucky you were. Not everybody encounters a Pargetter. He is a very important addition to your cast of characters.

MYSELF: I don't think I follow you. What I am telling you is history, not invention.

DR VON HALLER: Oh, quite. But even history has characters, and a personal history like yours must include a few people whom it would be stupid to call stock characters, even though they appear in almost all complete personal histories. Or let us put it differently. You remember the little poem by Ibsen that I quoted to you during one of our early meetings?

MYSELF: Only vaguely. Something about self-judgement.

DR VON HALLER: No, no; self-judgement comes later. Now pay attention, please:

> To *live* is to battle with trolls
>   in the vaults of heart and brain.
> To *write*: that is to sit
>   in judgement over one's self.

MYSELF: But I have been writing constantly; everything I have told you has been based on careful notes; I have tried to be as clear as possible, to follow Ramsay's Plain Style. I have raked up some stuff I have never told to another living soul. Isn't this self-judgement.

DR VON HALLER: Not at all. This has been the history of your battle with the trolls.

MYSELF: Another of your elaborate metaphors?

DR VON HALLER: If you like. I use metaphor to spare you jargon. Now consider: what figures have we met so far in our exploration of your life? Your Shadow; there was no difficulty about that, I believe, and we shall certainly meet him again. The Friend: Felix was the first to play that part, and you may yet come to recognize Knopwood as a very special friend, though I know you are still bitter against him. The Anima; you are very rich there, for of course there were your mother and Caroline and Netty, who all demonstrate various aspects of the feminine side of life, and finally Judy. This figure has been in eclipse for some years, at least

476

in its positive aspect; I think we must count your step-mother as an Anima-figure, but not a friendly one; we may still find that she is not so black as you paint her. But there are happy signs that the eclipse is almost over, because of your dream – let us be romantic and call it The Maiden and the Manticore – in which you were sure you recognized me. Perfectly in order. I have played all of these roles at various stages of our talks. Necessarily so: an analysis like this is certainly not emotion recollected in tranquillity. You may call these figures many things. You might call them the Comedy Company of the Psyche, but that would be flippant and not do justice to the cruel blows you have had from some of them. In my profession we call them archetypes, which means that they represent and body forth patterns to-ward which human behaviour seems to be disposed; patterns which repeat themselves endlessly, but never in precisely the same way. And you have just been telling me about one of the most powerful of all, which we may call the Magus, or the Wizard, or the Guru, or anything that signifies a power-ful formative influence toward the development of the total personality. Pargetter appears to have been a very fine Magus indeed: a blind genius who accepts you as an apprentice in his art! But he has just turned up, which is unusual though not seriously so. I had expected him earlier. Knop-wood looked rather like a Magus for a time, but we shall have to see if any of his influence lasted. But the other man, the possible father, the man you call Old Buggerlugs – I had expected rather more from him. Have you been keeping any-thing back?

MYSELF: No. And yet . . . there was always something about him that held the imagination. He was an oddity, as I've said. But a man who never seemed to come to anything. He wrote some books, and Father said some of them sold well, but they were queer stuff, about the nature of faith and the necessity of faith – not Christian faith, but some kind of faith, and now and then in classes he would point at us and say, 'Be sure you choose what you believe and know why you believe it, because if you don't choose your beliefs, you

477

may be certain that some belief, and probably not a very creditable one, will choose you.' Then he would go on about people whose belief was in Youth, or Money, or Power, or something like that, and who had found that these things were false gods. We liked to hear him rave, and some of his demonstrations from history were very amusing, but we didn't take it seriously. I have always looked on him as a man who missed his way in life. Father liked him. They came from the same village.

DR VON HALLER: But you never felt any urge to learn from him?

MYSELF: What could he have taught me, except history and the Plain Style?

DR VON HALLER: Yes, I see. It seemed to me for a time that he had something of the quality of a Magus.

MYSELF: In your Comedy Company, or Cabinet of Archetypes, you don't seem to have any figure that might correspond to my father.

DR VON HALLER: Oh, do not be impatient. These are the common figures. You may depend on it that your father will not be forgotten. Indeed, it seems to me that he has been very much present ever since we began. We talk of him all the time. He may prove to be your Great Troll . . .

MYSELF: Why do you talk of trolls? It seems to me that you Jungians sometimes go out of your way to make yourselves absurd.

DR VON HALLER: Trolls are not Jungian; they are just part of my promise not to annoy you with jargon. What is a troll?

MYSELF: A kind of Scandinavian spook, isn't it?

DR VON HALLER: Yes, spook is a very good word for it – another Scandinavian word. Sometimes a troublesome goblin, sometimes a huge, embracing lubberfiend, sometimes an ugly animal creature, sometimes a helper and server, even a lovely enchantress, a true Princess from Far Away: but never a full or complete human being. And the battle with trolls that Ibsen wrote about is a good metaphor to describe the wrestling and wrangling we go through when the archetypes we carry in ourselves seem to be embodied in people we have to deal with in daily life.

MYSELF: But people are people, not trolls or archetypes.

DR VON HALLER: Yes, and our great task is to see people as people and not clouded by archetypes we carry about with us, looking for a peg to hang them on.

MYSELF: Is that the task we are working at here?

DR VON HALLER: Part of it. We take a good look at your life, and we try to lift the archetypes off the pegs and see the people who have been obscured by them.

MYSELF: And what do I get out of that?

DR VON HALLER: That depends on you. For one thing, you will probably learn to recognize a spook when you see one, and keep trolls in good order. And you will recover all these projections which you have visited on other people like a magic lantern projecting a slide on a screen. When you stop doing that you are stronger, more independent. You have more mental energy. Think about it. And now go on about the genealogist.

12

I didn't pay much attention to him, because as I told Dr von Haller, I was greatly taken up with my final year of law studies. Pargetter expected me to get a First, and I wanted it even more than he. The notes kept arriving with reports of nothing achieved in spite of impressive activity. I had written to Father that I had a good man on the job, and had his permission to advance money as it was needed. Pledger-Brown's accounts were a source of great delight to me; I felt like Diogenes, humbled in the presence of an honest man. Sometimes in the vacations he went off hunting Stauntons and sent me bills detailing third-class tickets, sixpenny rides on buses, shillings spent on beer for old men who might know something, and cups of tea and buns for himself. There was never any charge for his time or his knowledge, and when I asked about that he replied that we would agree on a fee when he produced his results. I foresaw that he would starve on that principle, but I cherished him as an innocent. Indeed, I grew to be very fond of him, and we were Adrian and Davey when we talked. His besotted enthusiasm for the practise of heraldry refreshed me; I knew nothing about it, and couldn't see the use of it, and wondered why anybody bothered with it, but in time he brought me to see that it had once been necessary and was still a pleasant personal indulgence, and – this was important – that using somebody else's armorial bearings was no different in spirit from using his name; it was impersonation. It was, in legal terms, no different from imitating a trade-mark, and I knew what that meant. Undoubtedly Pledger-Brown was the best friend I made at Oxford, and I keep up with him still. He got into the College of Heralds, by the way, and is now Clarencieux King of Arms and looks exceedingly peculiar on ceremonial occasions in a tabard and a hat with a feather.

What finally bound us into the kind of friendship that does not fade was complicity in a secret.

Early in the spring term of my third year, when I was deep in work for my Final Schools, a message arrived: 'I have found Henry Staunton. A.P.-B.' I had a mountain of reading to do and had planned to spend all afternoon at the Codrington, but this called for something special, so I got hold of Adrian and took him to lunch. He was as nearly triumphant as his diffident nature would allow.

'I was just about to offer you a non-grandfather,' said he; 'there was a connection of the Stauntons of Warwickshire – not a Longbridge Staunton but a cousin – who cannot be accounted for and might perhaps have gone to Canada at the age of eighteen or so. By a very long shot he might have been your grandfather; without better evidence it would be guesswork to say he was. But then during the Easter vacation I had a flash. You otiose ass, Pledger-Brown, I said to myself, you've never thought of Staunton as a place-name. It is an elementary rule in this work, you know, to check place-names. There is Staunton Harold in Leicestershire and two or three Stantons, and of course I had quite overlooked Staunton in Gloucestershire. So off I went and checked parish records. And there he was in Gloucestershire: Albert Henry Staunton, born April 4, 1866, son of Maria Ann Dymock, and if you can find a better West Country name than Dymock, I'd be glad to hear it.'

'What kind of Staunton is he?' I asked.

'He's an extraordinarily rum Staunton,' said Pledger-Brown, 'but that's the best of it. You get not only a grandfather but a good story as well. You know, so many of these forbears that people ferret out are nothing at all; I mean, perfectly good and reputable, but no personal history of any interest. But Albert Henry is a conversation-piece. Now listen.

'Staunton is a hamlet about ten miles north-west of Gloucester, bearing over toward Herefordshire. In the middle of the last century it had only one public house, called the Angel, and by rights it ought to have been near a church named for the Annunciation, but it isn't. That doesn't matter. What is important is that in the 1860s there was an attractive girl working at the Angel who was called Maria Ann Dymock, and she must have been a local Helen, because she was known as Mary Dymock the Angel.'

'A barmaid?' I asked, wondering how Father was going to take to the idea of a barmaid.

'No, no,' said Adrian; 'barmaids are a bee in the American bonnet. A country pub of that time would be served by its landlord. Maria Ann Dymock was undoubtedly a domestic servant. But she became pregnant, and she said the child's father was George Applesquire, who was the landlord of the Angel. He denied it and said it could have been several other men. Indeed, he said that all Staunton could claim to be the child's father, and he would have nothing to do with it. He or his wife turned Maria Ann out of the Angel.

'Now, the cream of the story is this. Maria Ann Dymock must have been a girl of some character, for she bore the child in the local workhouse and in due time marched off to church to have it christened. "What shall I name the child?"

481

said parson. "Albert Henry," said Maria Ann. So it was done. "And the father's name?" said parson; "shall I say Dymock?" "No," said Maria Ann, "say Staunton, because it's said by landlord the whole place could be his father, and I want him to carry his father's name." I get all this out of the county archaeological society's records, which include quite an interesting diary of the clergyman in question, whose name was the Reverend Theophilus Mynors, by the way. Mynors must have been a sport, and probably he thought the girl had been badly used by Applesquire, because he put down the name as Albert Henry Staunton in the parish record.

'It caused a scandal, of course. But Maria Ann stuck it out, and when Applesquire's cronies threatened to make things too hot for her to stay in the parish, she walked the village street with a collecting bag, saying, "If you want me out of Staunton, give me something for my journey." She must have been a Tartar. She didn't get much, but the Rev. Theophilus admits that he gave her five pounds on the quiet, and there were one or two other contributors who admired her pluck, and soon she had enough to go abroad. You could still get a passage to Quebec for under five pounds in those days if you supplied your own food, and infants travelled free. So off went Maria Ann in late May of 1866, and undoubtedly she was your great-grandmother.'

We were eating in one of those Oxford restaurants that spring up and sink down again because they are run by amateurs, and we had arrived at the stage of eating a charlotte russe made of stale cake, tired jelly, and chemicals; I can still remember its taste because it is associated with my bleak wonder as to what I was going to report to Father. I explained to Pledger-Brown.

'But my dear Davey, you're missing the marvel of it,' he said; 'what a story! Think of Maria Ann's resource and courage! Did she slink away and hide herself in London with her bastard child, gradually sinking to the basest forms of prostitution while little Albert Henry became a thief and a pimp? No! She was of the stuff of which the great New

World has been forged! She stood up on her feet and demanded to be recognized as an individual, with inalienable rights! She braved the vicar, and George Applesquire, and all of public opinion. And then she went off to carve out a glorious life in what were then, my dear chap, still the colonies and not the great self-governing sisterhood of the Commonwealth! She was there when Canada became a Dominion! She may have been among the cheering crowds who hailed that moment in Montreal or Ottawa or wherever it was! You're not grasping the thing at all.'

I was grasping it. I was thinking of Father.

'I confess that I've been meddling,' said Adrian, turning very red; 'Garter would be as mad as hops if he knew I'd been playing with my paint-box like this. But after all, this is my first shot at tracing a forbear independently, and I can't help it. So I beg you, as a friend, to accept this trifle of *anitergium* from me.'

He handed me a cardboard roll, and when I had pried the metal cap off one end, I found a scroll inside it. I folded it out on the table where the medical charlotte russe had given place to some coffee – a Borgia speciality of the place – and it was a coat-of-arms.

'Just a very rough shot at something the College of Heralds would laugh at, but I couldn't help myself,' he said. 'The description in our lingo would be "Gules within a bordure wavy or, the Angel of the Annunciation bearing in her dexter hand a sailing-ship of three masts and in her sinister an apple." In other words, there's Mary the Angel with the ship she went to Canada on, and a good old Gloucester cider apple, on a red background with a wiggly golden border around the shield. Sorry about the wavy border; it means bastardy, but you don't have to tell everybody. Then here's the crest: "a fox statant guardant within his jaws a sugar cane, all proper." It's the Staunton crest, but slightly changed for your purposes, and the sugar cane says where you got your lolly from, which good heraldry often does. The motto, you see, is *De forte egressa est dulcedo* – "Out of the strong came forth sweetness" – from the Book of Judges, and couldn't be neater, really. And look here – you see I've given the fox a rather saucy privy member, just as a hint at your father's prowess in that direction. How do you like it?'

'You called it something,' said I; 'a trifle of something?'

'Oh, *anitergium*,' said Adrian. 'It's just one of those Middle Latin terms I like to use for fun. It means a trifle, a sketch, something disposable. Well, actually the monks used it for the throw-outs from the scriptorium which they used for bum-wipe.'

I hated to hurt his feelings, but Pargetter always said that hard things should be said as briefly as possible.

'It's bum-wipe, all right,' I said. 'Father won't have that.'

'Oh, most certainly not. I never meant that he should. The College of Heralds would have to prepare you legitimate arms, and I don't suppose it would be anything like this.'

'I don't mean the *anitergium*,' I said. 'I mean the whole story.'

'But Davey! You told me yourself your father said you were probably bastards. He must have a sturdy sense of humour.'

'He has,' I said, 'but I doubt if it extends to this. However, I'll try it.'

I did. And I was right. His letter in reply was cold and brief. 'People talk jokingly about being bastards, but the reality is something different. Remember that I am in politics now and you can imagine the fun my opponents would have. Let us drop the whole thing. Pay off Pledger-Brown and tell him to keep his trap shut.'

And that, for a while, was that.

13

I suppose nobody nowadays gets through a university without some flirtation with politics, and quite a few lasting marriages result. I had my spell of socialism, but it was measles rather than scarlet fever, and I soon recovered; as a student of law, I was aware that in our time whatever a man's political convictions may be he lives under a socialist system. Furthermore, I knew that my concern for mankind disposed me toward individuals rather than masses, and as Pargetter was pushing me toward work in the courts, and especially toward criminal law, I was increasingly interested in a class of society for which no political party has any use. There was, Pargetter said, somewhat less than five per cent of society which could fittingly be called the criminal class. That five per cent were my constituents.

I got my First Class in law at Oxford, and was in time called to the Bar in London, but I had always intended to practise in Canada, and this involved me in three more years of work. Canadian law, though rooted in English law, is not precisely the same, and the differences, and a certain amount of professional protectionism, made it necessary for me to qualify all over again. It was not hard. I was already pretty good and was able to do the Canadian work with time to spare for other reading. Like many well-qualified professional men I knew very little but my job, and Pargetter was very severe on that kind of ignorance. '"If practice be the whole that he is taught, practice must also be the whole that he will ever know,"' he would quote from Blackstone. So I read a lot of history, as my schoolwork with Ramsay had given me a turn in that direction, and quite a few great classical works which have formed the minds of men for generations, and of which I retain nothing but a vague sense of how long they were and how clever people must be who liked them. What I really liked was poetry, and I read a lot of it.

It was during this time, too, that I became financially independent of my father. He had been making a man of me, so far as a tight check on my expenditures would do it ; his training was effective, too, for I am a close man with money to this day, and have never come near to spending my income, or that part of it taxation allows me to keep. My personal fortune began quite unexpectedly when I was twenty-one.

Grandfather Staunton had not approved of Father, who

had become what the old man called a 'high-flyer', and although he left him a part of his estate, he left half of it to Caroline, in trust. To me he left what Father regarded as a joke legacy, in the form of five hundred acres of land in Northern Ontario, which he had bought as a speculation when it was rumoured that there was coal up there. Coal there may have been, but as there was no economically sane way of getting it down to places where it could be sold, the land lay idle. Nobody had ever seen it, and it was assumed that it was a wilderness of rock and scrub trees. Grandfather's executor, which was a large trust company, did nothing about this land until my majority, and then suggested that I sell it to a company which had offered to buy it for a hundred dollars an acre; there was fifty thousand dollars to be picked up for nothing, so to speak, and they advised me to take it.

I was stubborn. If the land was worthless, why did anyone want to pay a hundred dollars an acre for it? I had a hunch that I might as well see it before parting with it, so I set off to look at my inheritance. I am no woodsman, and it was a miserable journey from the nearest train-stop to my property, but I did it by canoe, in the company of a morose guide, and was frightened out of my wits by the desolation, the dangers of canoeing in some very rough water, and the apparent untrustworthiness of my companion. But after a couple of days we were on my land, and as I tramped around it I found that there were other people on it, too, and that they were unmistakably drilling for minerals. They were embarrassed, and I became thoughtful, for they had no authority to be doing what they were doing. Back in Toronto I made a fuss with the trust company, who knew nothing about the drillers, and I made something more than a fuss to the mining company. So after some legal huffing and puffing, and giving them the Pargetter treatment, I disposed of my northern land at a thousand dollars an acre, which would have been dirt cheap if there had been a mine. But there was nothing there, or not enough. I emerged from this adventure with half a million dollars. A nice, round sum, surely never foreseen by Grandfather Staunton.

Father was not pleased, because the trust company who had been so casual about my affairs was one of which he was a director, and at one point I had threatened to sue them for mismanagement, which he considered unfilial. But I stuck to my guns, and when it was all over asked him if he would like me to move out of the family house. But he urged me to stay. It was large, and he was lonely when his political career allowed him to be there, and so I stayed where I was and thus came once again under the eye of Netty.

Netty was the survivor of an endless train of servants. She had never been given the title of housekeeper, but she was the Black Pope of the domestic staff, never frankly tattling but always hinting or wearing the unmistakable air of someone who could say a great deal if asked. With no children to look after, she had become almost a valet to Father, cleaning his clothes and washing and ironing his shirts, which she declared nobody else could do to his complete satisfaction.

When I had finished my Canadian legal studies I gave offence to Father once again, for he had always assumed that I would be content to have him find a place for me in the Alpha Corporation. But that was not at all my plan; I wanted to practise as a criminal lawyer. Pargetter, with whom I kept in constant touch (though he never raised me to the level of one of his long-distance chess opponents) urged me to get some general practice first, and preferably in a small place. 'You will see more of human nature, and get a greater variety of experience, in three years in a country town than you will get in five years with a big firm in a city,' he wrote. So once again I returned, not to Deptford, but to the nearby county town, a place of about sixty thousand people, called Pittstown. I easily got a place in the law office of Diarmuid Mahaffey, whose father had once been the lawyer in Deptford and with whom there was a family connection.

Diarmuid was very good to me and saw that I got a little work of every kind, including a few of those mad clients all lawyers seem to have if their practice extends into the country. I don't suggest that city lawyers have no madmen on their books, but I honestly believe the countryside breeds finer examples of the *paranoia querulans*, the connoisseurs of litigation. He bore in mind that I wanted to work in the courts and put me in the way of getting some of those cases on which most young lawyers cut their teeth ; some indignant or incompetent accused person needs a lawyer, and the court appoints a 'lawyer, usually a young man, to act for him.

I learned a valuable lesson from my first case of this kind. A Maltese labourer was charged with indecent assault ; it was not a very serious matter, because the aspiring rapist had trouble with his buttons, and the woman, who was considerably bigger than he, hit him with her handbag and ran away. 'You must tell me honestly,' said I, 'did you do it? I'll do my best to get you off, but I must know the truth.' 'Meester Stown,' said he, with tears in his eyes, 'I swear to you on the grave of my dead mother, I never did no such dirty thing. Spit in my mouth if I even touch this woman !' So I gave the court a fine harangue, and the judge gave my client two years. My client was delighted. 'That judge, he's very clever man,' he said to me afterward; 'he knew all the time I done it.' Then he shook my hand and trotted off with the warder, pleased to have been punished by such an expert in human nature. I decided then that the kind of people with whom I had chosen to associate myself were not to be trusted, or at least not taken literally.

My next serious case was a far bigger thing, nothing less than a murderess. Poor woman, she had shot her husband. He was a farmer, known far and wide to be no good and brutal to her and his livestock, but he was decisively dead ; she had poked a shotgun through the back window of the privy while he was perched on the seat and blown his head off. She made no denial, and was indeed silent and resigned through all the preliminaries. But they still hanged women in those days, and it was my job to save her from the gallows if I could.

I spent a good deal of time with her and thought so much about the case that Diarmuid began to call me Sir Edward, in reference to Marshall Hall. But one night I had a bright idea, and the next day I put a question to my client and got the answer I expected. When at last the case came to trial I spoke of extenuating circumstances, and at the right moment said that the murdered man had repeatedly beaten his wife in order to make her perform *fellatio*.

'Know your judge' was one of Diarmuid's favourite maxims; of course no barrister knows a judge overtly, but most of the Bar know him before he is elevated to the Bench and have some estimate of his temperament. Obviously you don't take a particularly messy divorce before a Catholic judge, or a drunk who has caused an accident before a teetotal judge, if you can help it. I was lucky in this case because our assize judge that season was Orley Mickley, known to be a first-rate man of the law, but in his private life a pillar of rectitude and a great deplorer of sexual sin. As judges often are, he was innocent of things that lesser people know, and the word *fellatio* had not come his way.

'I assume that is a medical term, Mr Staunton,' said he; 'will you be good enough to explain it to the court.'

'May I ask your lordship to order the court cleared?' said I; 'or if your lordship would call a recess I should be glad to explain the term in your chambers. It is not something that any of us would take pleasure in hearing.'

I was playing it up for all it would stand, and I had an intimation – Dr von Haller says I have a good measure of intuition – that I was riding the crest of a wave.

The judge cleared the court and asked me to explain to him and the jury what *fellatio* was. I dragged it out. Oral and lingual caress of the erect male organ until ejaculation is brought about was the way I put it. The jury knew simpler terms for this business, and my delicacy struck them solemn. I did not need to labour the fact that the dead man had been notably dirty: the jury had all seen him. Usually performed by the woman on her knees, I added, and two women jurors straightened up in their chairs. A gross indignity exacted by force ; a perversion for which some American states exacted severe penalties ; a grim servitude no woman with a spark of self-respect could be expected to endure without cracking.

It worked like a charm. The judge's charge to the jury was a marvel of controlled indignation ; they must find the woman guilty but unless they added a recommendation of clemency his faith in mankind would be shattered. And of course they did so, and the judge gave her a sentence which, with good conduct, would not be more than two or three years. I suppose the poor soul ate better and slept better in the penitentiary than she had ever done in her life.

'That was a smart bit of business,' said Diarmuid to me afterward, 'and I don't know how you guessed what the trouble was. But you did, and that's what matters. B'God, I think old Mickley would have hung the corpse, if it'd had a scrap of neck left to put in a rope.'

This case gained me a disproportionate reputation as a brilliant young advocate filled with compassion for the wretched. The result was that a terrible band of scoundrels who thought themselves misunderstood or ill used shouted for my services when they got into well-deserved trouble. And thus I gained my first client to go to the gallows.

Up to this time I had delighted unashamedly in the law. Many lawyers do, and Diarmuid was one of them. 'If lawyers allowed their sense of humour free play, b'God they wouldn't be able to work for laughing,' he once said to me. But the trial and hanging of Jimmy Veale showed me another aspect of the law. What I suppose Dr von Haller would call its Shadow.

Not that Jimmy didn't have a fair trial. Not that I didn't exert myself to the full on his behalf. But his guilt was clear, and all I could do was try to find explanations for what he had done, and try to arouse pity for a man who had no pity for anyone else.

Jimmy had a bad reputation and had twice been in jail for petty thievery. He was only twenty-two, but he was a thorough-going crook of an unsophisticated kind. When I met him the provincial police had run him down, hiding in the woods about thirty miles north of Pittstown, with sixty-five dollars in his pocket. He had entered the house of an old woman who lived alone in a rural area, demanded her money, and when she would not yield he sat her on her own stove to make her talk. Which she did, of course, but when Jimmy found the money and left, she appeared to be dead. However, she was not quite dead, and when a neighbour found her in the morning she lived long enough to describe Jimmy and assure the neighbour that he had repeatedly sworn that he would kill her if she didn't speak up. In this evidence the neighbour was not to be shaken.

Jimmy's mother, who thought him wild but not bad, engaged me to defend him, and I did what I could by pleading insanity. It is a widespread idea that people who are unusually cruel must be insane, though the corollary of that would be that anybody who is unusually compassionate must be insane. But the Crown Attorney applied the McNaghten Rule to Jimmy, and I well recall the moment when he said to the jury, 'Would the prisoner have acted as he did if a policeman had been standing at his elbow?' Jimmy, lounging in the prisoner's dock, laughed and cried out, 'Jeeze, d'you think I'm crazy?' After which it did not take the court long to send him to the gallows.

I decided that I had better be present when Jimmy was hanged. It is a common complaint against the courts that they condemn people to punishments of which the legal profession have no direct knowledge. It is a justifiable reproach when it is true, but it is true less often than tender-hearted people think. There are people who shrink from the whole idea of a court, and there are the There-But-for-the-Grace-of-Godders who seem to think it is only by a narrow squeak that they have kept out of the prisoner's dock themselves; they are bird-brains to whom God's grace and good luck mean the same thing. There are the democrats of justice, who seem to believe that every judge should begin his career as a prisoner at the bar and work his way up to the Bench. Tender-minded people, all of them, but they don't know criminals. I wanted to know criminals, and I made my serious start with Jimmy.

I was sorry for his mother, who was a fool but punished for it with unusual severity ; she had not spoiled Jimmy more than countless mothers spoil boys who turn out to be sources of pride. Jimmy had been exposed to all the supposed benefits of a democratic state; he had the best schooling that could be managed for as long as he cared to take it – which was no longer than the law demanded ; his childhood had been embowered in a complexity of protective laws, and his needs had been guaranteed by Mackenzie King's Baby Bonus. But Jimmy was a foul-mouthed crook who had burned an old woman to death, and never, in all the months I knew him, expressed one single word of regret.

He was proud of being a condemned man. While awaiting trial he acquired from somewhere a jail vocabulary. Within a day of his imprisonment he would greet the trusty who brought him his food with 'Hiya, shit-heel!' that being the term the hardened prisoners used for those who cooperated with the warden. After his trial, when the chaplain tried to talk to him he was derisive, shouting, 'Listen, I'm gonna piss when I can't whistle, and that's all there is to it, so don't give me none of your shit.' He regarded me with some favour, for I qualified as a supporting player in his personal drama ; I was his 'mouthpiece.' He wanted me to arrange for him to sell his story to a newspaper, but I would have nothing to do with that. I saw Jimmy at least twice a week while he was waiting for execution, and I never heard a word from him that did not make me think the world would be better off without him. None of his former friends tried to see him, and when his mother visited him he was sullen and abusive.

When the time for his hanging came, I spent a dismal night with the sheriff and the chaplain in the office of the warden of the jail. None of them had ever managed a hanging, and they were nervous and haggled about details, such as whether a flag should be flown to show that justice had been done upon Jimmy; it was a foolish question, for a flag would have to be flown at seven o'clock anyway, and that was the official hour for Jimmy's execution; in fact he was to be hanged at six, before the other prisoners were awakened. Whether they were sleeping or not I do not know, but certainly there was none of that outcry or beating on cellbars which is such a feature of romantic drama on this subject. The hangman was busy about concerns of his own. I had seen him; a short, stout, unremarkable man who looked like a carpenter dressed for a funeral, which I suppose is what he was. The chaplain went to Jimmy and soon returned. The doctor came at five, and with him two or three newspaper reporters. In all, there were about a dozen of us at last, of whom only the hangman had ever been present at such an affair before.

As we waited, the misery which had been palpable in the small office became almost stifling, and I went out with one of the reporters to walk in the corridor. As six o'clock drew near we moved into the execution chamber, a room like an elevator shaft, though larger, and stuffy from long disuse. There was a platform about nine feet high of unpainted new wood, and under it hung some curtains of unbleached cotton that were crumpled and looked as if they had been used before and travelled far; above the platform, from the roof, was suspended a heavily braced steel beam, painted the usual dirty red, and from this hung the rope, with its foot-long knot which would, if all was well, dislocate Jimmy's cervical vertebrae and break his spinal cord. To my surprise, it was almost white; I do not know what I expected, but certainly not a white rope. The hangman in his tight black suit was bustling about trying the lever that worked the trap. Nobody spoke. When everything was to his liking, the hangman nodded, and two warders brought Jimmy in.

He had been given something by the doctor beforehand, and needed help as he walked. I had seen him the day before, in his cell where the lights always burned and where he had spent so many days without a belt, or braces, or even laces in his shoes – deprivations which seemed to rob him of full humanity, so that he appeared to be ill or insane Now his surly look was gone, and he had to be pushed up the ladder that led to the platform. The hangman, whom he never saw, manoeuvred Jimmy gently to the right spot, then put the noose over his head and adjusted it with great care – in other circumstances one might say with loving care. Then he slid down the ladder – literally, for he put his feet on the out-sides of the supports and slipped down it like a fireman – and immediately pulled the lever. Jimmy dropped out of sight behind the curtains, with a loud thump, as the cord stretched tight.

The silence, which had been so thick before, was now broken as Jimmy swung to and fro and the rope banged against the sides of the trap. Worse than that, we heard gur-gling and gaggling, and the curtains bulged and stirred as Jimmy swung within them. The hanging, as is sometimes the case, had not gone well, and Jimmy was fighting for life.

The doctor had told us that unconsciousness was imme-diate, but that the cessation of Jimmy's heartbeat might take from three to five minutes. If Jimmy were unconscious, why am I sure that I heard him cry out – curses, of course, for these had always been Jimmy's eloquence? But I did hear him, and so did the others, and one of the reporters was violently sick. We looked at one another in terror. What was to be done? The hangman knew. He darted inside the cur-tains, and beneath them we saw a great shuffling of feet, and soon the violent swinging stopped, and the sighs and mur-murings were still. The hangman came out again, flustered and angry, and mopped his brow. None of us met his eye. When five minutes had passed the doctor, not liking his work, went inside the curtains with his stethoscope ready, came out again almost at once, and nodded to the sheriff. And so it was over.

Not quite over for me. I had promised Jimmy's mother that I would see him before he was buried, and I did. He was laid on a table in a neighbouring room, and I looked him right in the face, which took some resolution in the doing.

But I noticed also a damp stain on the front of his prison trousers, and looked enquiringly at the doctor.

'An emission of semen,' he said; 'they say it always happens. I don't know.'

So that was what Jimmy meant when he said he'd piss when he couldn't whistle. Where could he have picked up such a jaunty, ugly, grotesque idea of death by hanging? But that was Jimmy; he had a flair for whatever was brutal and macabre and such knowledge sought him out because he was eager for it.

I had seen a hanging. Worse things happen in wars and in great catastrophes, but they are not directly planned and ordered. This had been the will of Jimmy's fellow-countrymen, as expressed through the legal machinery devised to deal with such people as he. But it was unquestionably a squalid business, an evil deed, and we had all of us, from the hangman down to the reporters, been drawn into it and fouled by it. If Jimmy had to be got rid of – and I fully believe that was all that could have been done with such a man, unless he were to be kept as a caged, expensive nuisance for another fifty years – why did it have to be like this? I do not speak of hanging alone; the executioner's sword, the guillotine, the electric chair are all dreadful and involve the public through its legal surrogates in a revolting act. The Greeks seem to have known a better way than these.

Jimmy's evil had infected us all – had indeed spread far beyond his prison until something of it touched everybody in his country. The law had been tainted by evil, though its great import was for good, or at least for order and just dealing. But it would be absurd to attribute so much power to Jimmy, who was no more than a fool whose folly had become the conduit by which evil had poured into so many lives. When I visited Jimmy in prison I had sometimes seen on his face a look I knew, the look I had seen on the face of Bill Unsworth as he squatted obscenely over a pile of photographs. It was the look of one who has laid himself open to a force that is inimical to man, and whose power to loose that force upon the world is limited only by his imagination, his opportunities, and his daring. And it seemed to me then that it was with such people I had cast my lot, for I was devoting my best abilities to their defence.

I changed my mind about that later. The law gives every accused man his chance, and there must be those who do for him what he cannot do for himself; I was one of these. But I was always aware that I stood very near to the power of evil when I undertook the cases that brought me the greatest part of my reputation. I was a highly skilled, highly paid, and cunning mercenary in a fight which was as old as man and greater than man. I have consciously played the Devil's Advocate and I must say I have enjoyed it. I like the struggle, and I had better admit that I like the moral danger. I am like a man who has built his house on the lip of a volcano. Until the volcano claims me I live, in a sense, heroically.

DR VON HALLER: Good. I was wondering when he would make his appearance.

MYSELF: Whom are we talking about now?

DR VON HALLER: The hero who lives on the lip of the volcano. We have talked of many aspects of your inner life, and we have identified them by such names as Shadow, Anima, and so on. But one has been seen only in a negative aspect, and he is the man you show to the outer world, the man in whose character you appear in court and before your acquaintances. He has a name, too. We call him the Persona, which means, as you know, the actor's mask. This man on the edge of the volcano, this saturnine lawyer-wizard who snatches people out of the jaws of destruction, is your Persona. You must enjoy playing the role very much.

MYSELF: I do.

DR VON HALLER: Good. You would not have admitted that a few months ago, when you first sat in that chair. Then you were all for imposing him on me as your truest self.

MYSELF: I'm not sure that he isn't.

DR VON HALLER: Oh, come. We all create an outward self with which to face the world, and some people come to believe that is what they truly are. So they people the world with doctors who are nothing outside the consulting-room, and judges who are nothing when they are not in court, and businessmen who wither with boredom when they have to retire from business, and teachers who are forever teaching. That is why they are such poor specimens when they are caught without their masks on. They have lived chiefly through the Persona. But you are not such a fool, or you would not be here. Everybody needs his mask, and the only intentional impostors are those whose mask is one of a man with nothing to conceal. We all have much to conceal, and we must conceal it for our soul's good. Even your Wizard, your mighty Pargetter, was not all Wizard. Did you ever find some chink in his armour?

MYSELF: Yes, and it was a shock. He died without a will. A lawyer who dies without a will is one of the jokes of the profession.

DR VON HALLER: Ah, but making a will is not part of a Persona; it is, for most of us, an hour when we look our mortality directly in the face. If he did not want to do that, it is sad, but do you really think it diminishes Pargetter? It lessens him as the perfect lawyer, certainly, but he must have been something more than that, and a portion of that something else had a natural, pathetic fear of death. He had built his Persona so carefully and so handsomely that you took it for the whole man; and it must be said that you might not have learned so much from him if you had seen him more fully; young people love such absolutes. But your own Persona seems to be a very fine one. Surely it was built as a work of art?

MYSELF: Of art, and of necessity. The pressures under which I came to live were such that I needed something to keep people at bay. And so I built what I must say I have always thought of as my public character, my professional manner, but which you want me to call a Persona. I needed armour. You see – this is not an easy thing for me to say, even to someone who listens professionally to what is usually unspeakable – women began to throw out their lures for me. I would have been a good catch. I came of a well-known

497

family; I had money; I was at the start of a career of a kind that some women find as attractive as that of a film actor.

DR VON HALLER: And why were you so unresponsive? Anything to do with Myrrha Martindale?

MYSELF: That wore off, after a time. I had come to hate the fact that I had been initiated into the world of physical sex in something Father had stage-managed. It wasn't sex itself, but Father's proprietorial way with it, and with me. I was young and neither physically cold nor morally austere, but even when the urge and the opportunity were greatest I wanted no more of it. It seemed like following in the swordsman's footsteps, and I wanted none of that. But I might have married if Father had not gone before me, even there.

DR VON HALLER: This was the second marriage, to Denyse?

MYSELF: Yes, when I was twenty-nine. I had passed my third year in Pittstown with Diarmuid, and was thinking it was time to be moving, for one does not become a first-rank criminal lawyer in a town where criminals are few and of modest ambition. One day a letter came from Father; would I meet Caroline for dinner at the family house in Toronto, as he had something of great importance to tell us? Since getting into politics Father had not dwindled in self-esteem, I can assure you, and this was in what painters call his later manner. So up to Toronto I went on the appointed day, and the other guests at dinner were Caroline and Beesty. Caroline had married Beeston Bastable the year before, and it had done her a lot of good; he was no Adonis, running rather to fat, but he was a fellow of what I can only call a sweet disposition, and after Caroline had tormented and jeered at him long enough she discovered she loved him, and that was that. But Father was not there. Only a letter, to be read while we were having coffee. I wondered what it could be, and so did Beesty, but Caroline jumped to it at once, and of course she was right. The letter was rather a floundering and pompous piece of work, but it boiled down to the fact that he was going to marry again and hoped we would approve and love the lady as much as he did, and as much as she

deserved. There was a tribute in it to Mother, rather stiffly
worded. Stuff about how he could never be happy in this
new marriage unless we approved. And, finally, the name of
the lady herself. It was Denyse Hornick. Of course we knew
who she was. She ran a good-sized travel agency of her own,
and was prominent in politics, on the women's side.

DR VON HALLER: A women's liberationist?

MYSELF: Not in any extreme way. An intelligent, moder-
ate, but determined and successful advocate of equality for
women under the law, and in business and professional life.
We knew she had attached herself to Father's personal
group of supporters during his not very fortunate post-war
political career. None of us had ever met her. But we met
her that night because Father brought her home at about
half-past nine to introduce her. It wasn't an easy situation.

DR VON HALLER: He seems to have managed it rather
heavy-handedly.

MYSELF: Yes, and I suppose it was immature of me, but
it galled me to see him so youthful and gallant toward her
when they came in, like a boy bringing his girl home to run
the gauntlet of the family. After all, he was sixty. And she
was modest and sweet and deferential like a girl of seventeen, though she was in fact a hefty forty-one. I don't mean
fat-hefty, but a psychological heavy-weight, a woman of obvious self-confidence and importance in her sphere, so that
these milkmaid airs were a grotesque fancy dress. Of course
we did the decent thing, and Beesty bustled around and prepared drinks with the modesty proper to an in-law at a somewhat tense family affair, and eventually everybody had kissed Denyse and the farce of seeking our approval had been
played out. An hour later Denyse had so far thrown aside
her role as milkmaid that when I showed some signs of getting drunk she said, 'Now only one more tiny one, baa-lamb,
or you'll hate yourself in the morning.' I knew at that moment I couldn't stand Denyse, and that one more very serious
thing had come between me and Father.

DR VON HALLER: You were never reconciled to her?

MYSELF: You doubtless have some family, Doctor. You

must know of the currents that run through families? I'll tell you of one that astonished me. It was Caroline who told Netty about the approaching marriage, and Netty broke into a fit of sobs – she had no tears, apparently – and said, 'And after what I've done for him!' Caroline dropped on that at once, for it could have been proof of her favourite theory that Netty killed Mother, or at least put her in the way of dying. Surely those words couldn't have simply referred to those shirts she'd ironed so beautifully? But with her notion of 'her place' it wouldn't be like Netty to think that years of service gave her a romantic claim on Father. Caroline couldn't get Netty to admit, in so many words, that she had put Mother out of the way because she was an embarrassment to Father. Nevertheless, there was something fishy there. If I could have Netty in the witness-box for half an hour, I bet I could break her down! What do you think of that? This isn't some family in the mythic drama of Greece I'm telling you about; it is a family of the twentieth century, and a Canadian family at that, supposedly the quintessence of everything that is emotionally dowdy and unaware.

DR VON HALLER: Mythic pattern is common enough in contemporary life. But of course few people know the myths, and fewer still can see a pattern under a mass of detail. What was your response to this woman who was so soon proprietorial in her manner toward you?

MYSELF: Derision tending toward hatred; with Caroline it was just derision. Every family knows how to make the newcomer feel uncomfortable, and we did what we dared. And I did more than spar with her when we met. I found out everything I could about her through enquiries from credit agencies and by public records; I also had some enquiries made through underworld characters who had reason to want to please me –

DR VON HALLER: You spied on her?

MYSELF: Yes.

DR VON HALLER: You have no doubts about the propriety of that?

MYSELF: None. After all, she was marrying considerably

over a hundred million dollars. I wanted to know who she was.

DR VON HALLER: And who was she?

MYSELF: There was nothing against her. She had married a serviceman when she was in the W.R.N.S. and divorced him as soon as the war was over. That was where Lorene came from.

DR VON HALLER: The retarded daughter?

MYSELF: An embarrassing nuisance, Denyse's problem. But Denyse liked problems and wanted to add me to her list.

DR VON HALLER: Because of your drinking. When did that begin?

MYSELF: In Pittstown it began to be serious. It is very lonely living in a small town where you are anxious to seem quite ordinary but everybody knows that there is a great fortune, as they put it, 'behind you'. How far behind, or whether you really have anything more than a romantic claim on it, nobody knows or cares. More than once I would hear some Pittstown worthy whisper of me, 'He doesn't have to work, you know; his father's Boy Staunton.' But I did work; I tried to command my profession. I lived in the best hotel in town, which, God knows, was a dismal hole with wretched food; I confined my living to a hundred and twenty-five dollars a week, which was about what a rising young lawyer might be expected to have. I wanted no favours and if it had been practical to take another name I would have done it. Nobody understood, except Diarmuid, and I didn't care whether they understood or not. But it was lonely, and while I was hammering out the character of David Staunton the rising criminal lawyer, I also created the character of David Staunton who drank too much. The two went well together in the eyes of many romantic people, who like a brilliant man to have some large, obvious flaw in his character.

DR VON HALLER: This was the character you took with you to Toronto, where I suppose you embroidered it.

MYSELF: Embroidered it richly. I achieved a certain courtroom notoriety; in a lively case I drew a good many spectators because they wanted to see me win. They also had the occasional thrill of seeing me stagger. There were rumours, too, that I had extensive connections in the underworld, though that was nonsense. Still, it provided a whiff of sulphur for the mob.

DR VON HALLER: In fact, you created a romantic Persona that successfully rivalled that of the rich, sexually adventurous Boy Staunton without ever challenging him on his own ground?

MYSELF: You might equally well say that I established myself as a man of significance in my own right without in any way wearing my father's cut-down clothes.

DR VON HALLER: And when did the clash come?

MYSELF: The –?

DR VON HALLER: The inevitable clash between your father and yourself. The clash that gave so much edge to the guilt and remorse you felt when he died, or was killed, or whichever it was.

MYSELF: I suppose it really came into the light when Denyse made it clear that her ambition was to see Father appointed Lieutenant-Governor of Ontario. She made it very clear to me that what she insisted on calling my 'image' – she had a walletful of smart terms for everything – would not fit very well with my position as son of a man who was the Queen's represent ive.

DR VON HALLER: In effect she wanted to reclaim you and make you into your father's son again.

MYSELF: Yes, and what a father! She is a great maker of images, is Denyse! It disgusted and grieved me to see Father being filed and pumiced down to meet that inordinate woman's idea of a fit candidate for ceremonial office. Before, he had style – his personal style: she made him into what she would have been if she had been born a man. He became an unimaginative woman's creation. Delilah had shorn his locks and assured him he looked much neater and cooler without them. He gave her his soul, and she transformed it into a cabbage. She reopened the whole business of the Staunton arms because he would need something of the sort in an official position and it looked better to take the position with all the necessary trappings than to cobble them up during his first months in office. Father had never told her about Maria Ann Dymock, and she wrote boldly to the College of Arms, and I gather she pretty much demanded that the arms of the Warwickshire Stauntons, with some appropriate differences, be officially granted to Father.

DR VON HALLER: What did your father think about it?

MYSELF: Oh, he laughed it off. Said Denyse would manage it if anyone could. Didn't want to talk about it. But it never happened. The College took a long time answering letters and asked for information that was hard to provide. I knew all about it because by this time my old friend Pledger-Brown was one of the pursuivants, and we had always written to each other at least once a year. One of his letters said, as I remember it, 'This can never be, you know ; not even your stepdame's New World determination can make you Stauntons of Longbridge. My colleague in charge of the matter is trying to persuade her to apply for new arms, which your father might legitimately have, for after all bags of gold are a very fair earnest of gentility, and always have been. But she is resolute, and nothing will do but a long and very respectable descent. It is one of the touching aspects of our work here in the College that so many of you New World people, up to the eyebrows in all the delights of republicanism, hanker after a link with what is ancient and rubbed by time to a fine sheen. It's more than snobbery ; more than romanticism ; it's a desire for an ancestry that somehow postulates a posterity and for an existence in the past that is a covert guarantee of immortality in the future. You talk about individualism ; what you truly want is to be links in a long unbroken chain. But you, with our secret about Maria Ann and the child whose father might have been all Staunton, know of a truth which is every bit as good in its way, even though you use it only as food for your sullen absalonism.'

DR VON HALLER: Absalonism ; I do not know that word. Explain it, please.

MYSELF: It was one of Adrian's revivals of old words. It refers to Absalom, the son of King David, who resisted and revolted against his father.

DR VON HALLER: A good word. I shall remember it.

14

The time was drawing near to Christmas, when I knew that Dr von Haller would make some break in my series of appointments. But I was not prepared for what she said when next we met.

'Well, Mr Staunton, we seem to have come to the end of your *anamnesis*. Now it is necessary to make a decision about what you are going to do next.'

'The end? But I have a sheaf of notes still! I have all sorts of questions to ask.'

'Doubtless. It is possible to go on as we have been doing for several years. But you have been at this work for a little more than one year, and although we could haggle over fine points and probe sore places for at least another year, I think that for you that is unnecessary. Ask your questions of yourself. You are now in a position to answer them.'

'But if I give wrong answers?'

'You will soon know that they are wrong. We have canvassed the main points in the story of your life; you are equipped to attend to details.'

'I don't feel it. I'm not nearly through with what I have to say.'

'Have you anything to say that seems to you extraordinary?'

'But surely I have been having the most remarkable spiritual – well, anyhow, psychological – adventures?'

'By no means, Mr Staunton. Remarkable in your personal experience, which is what counts, but – forgive me – not at all remarkable in mine.'

'Then you mean this is the end of my work with you?'

'Not if you decide otherwise. But it is the end of this work – this reassessment of some personal, profound experience. But what is most personal is not what is most profound. If you want to continue – and you must not be in a hurry to say you will – we shall proceed quite differently. We shall examine the archetypes with which you are already superficially familiar, and we shall go beyond what is personal about them. I assure you that is very close and psychologically demanding work. It cannot be undertaken if you are always craving to be back in Toronto, putting Alpha and Castor and all those things into good order. But you are drinking quite moderately now, aren't you? The symptom you complained of has been corrected. Wasn't that what you wanted?'

'Yes, though I had almost forgotten that was what I came for.'

'Your general health is much improved? You sleep better?'
'Yes.'

'And you will not be surprised or angry when I say you are a much pleasanter, easier person?'

'But if I go on – what then?'

'I cannot tell you, because I don't know, and in this sort of work we give no promises.'

'Yes, but you have experience of other people. What happens to them?'

'They finish their work, or that part of it that can be done here, with a markedly improved understanding of themselves, and that means of much that goes beyond self. They are in better command of their abilities. They are more fully themselves.'

'Happier, in fact.'

'I do not promise happiness, and I don't know what it is. You New World people are, what is the word, hipped on the idea of happiness, as if it were a constant and measurable thing, and settled and excused everything. If it is anything at all it is a by-product of other conditions of life, and some people whose lives do not appear to be at all enviable, or indeed admirable, are happy. Forget about happiness.'

'Then you can't, or won't, tell me what I would be working for?'

'No, because the answer lies in you, not in me. I can help, of course. I can put the questions in such a way as to draw forth your answer, but I do not know what your answer will be. Let me put it this way: the work you have been doing here during the past year has told you *who* you are; further work would aim at showing you *what* you are.'

'More mystification. I thought we had got past all that. For weeks it seems to me that we have been talking nothing but common sense.'

'Oh, my dear Mr Staunton, that is unworthy of you! Are you still scampering back to that primitive state of mind where you suppose psychology must be divorced from common sense? Well – let me see what I can do. Your dreams – We have worked through some dozens of your dreams, and I think you are now convinced that they are not just incomprehensible gases that get into your head during sleep. Recall your dream of the night before you first came to me. What was that enclosed, private place where you commanded such respect, from which you walked out into strange country? Who was the woman you met, who talked in an unknown language? Now don't say it was me, because you had never met me then, and though dreams may reflect deep concerns and thus may hint at the future, they are not second sight. After some exploration, you came to the top of a staircase that led downward, and some commonplace people discouraged you from going down, though you sensed there was treasure there. Your decision now is whether or not you are going to descend the staircase and find the treasure.'

'How do I know it will be a treasure?'

'Because your other recurrent dream, where you are the little prince in the tower, shows you as the guardian of a treasure. And you manage to keep your treasure. But who are all those frightening figures who menace it? We should certainly encounter them. And why are you a prince, and a child? – Tell me, did you dream last night?'

'Yes. A very odd dream. It reminded me of Knopwood because it was Biblical in style. I dreamed I was standing on a plain, talking with my father. I was aware it was Father, though his face was turned away. He was very affectionate and simple in his manner, as I don't think I ever knew him to be in his life. The odd thing was that I couldn't really see his face. He wore an ordinary business suit. Then suddenly he turned from me and flew up into the air, and the astonishing thing was that as he rose, his trousers came down, and I saw his naked backside.'

'And what are your associations?'

'Well, obviously it's the passage in Exodus where God promises Moses that he shall see Him, but must not see His face; and what Moses sees is God's back parts. As a child I always thought it funny for God to show His rump. Funny, but also terribly real and true. Like those extraordinary people in the Bible who swore a solemn oath clutching one another's testicles. But does it mean that I have seen the weakness, the shameful part of my father's nature because he gave so much of himself into the keeping of Denyse and because Denyse was so unworthy to treat him properly? I've done what I can with it, but nothing rings true.'

'Of course not, because you have neglected one of the chief principles of what I have been able to tell you about the significance of dreams. That again is understandable, for when the dream is important and has something new to tell us, we often forget temporarily what we know to be true. But we have always agreed, haven't we, that figures in dreams, whoever or whatever they may look like, are aspects of the dreamer? So who is this father with the obscured face and the naked buttocks?'

'I suppose he is my idea of a father – my own father?'

'He is something we would have to talk about if you decided to go on to a deeper stage in the investigation of yourself. Because your real father, your historical father, the man whom you last saw lying so pitiably on the dock with his face obscured in filth, and then so dishevelled in his coffin with his face destroyed by your stepmother's ambitious meddling, is by no means the same thing as the archetype of fatherhood you carry in the depths of your being, and which comes from – well, for the present we won't attempt to say where. Now tell me, have you had any of those demanding, humiliating sessions in Mr Justice Staunton's court during the past few weeks? You haven't mentioned them.'

'No. They don't seem to have been necessary recently.'

'I thought that might be so. Well, my friend, you know now how very peculiar dreams are, and you know that they are not liars. But I don't believe you have found out yet that they sometimes like a little joke. And this is one. I believe that you have, in a literal sense, seen the end of Mr Justice Staunton. The old Troll King has lost his trappings. No court, no robes, a sense of kindliness and concern, a revelation of that part of his anatomy he keeps nearest to the honoured Bench, and which nobody has ever attempted to invest with awe or dignity, and then – gone! If he should come again, as he well may, at least you have advanced so far that you have seen him with his trousers down ... Our hour is finished. If you wish to arrange further appointments, will you let me know sometime in the week between Christmas and the New Year? I wish you a very happy holiday.'

3

My Sorgenfrei Diary

DEC. 17, Wed.: Wretched letter from Netty this morn. Was feeling particularly well because of Dr Johanna's saying on Monday that I had finished my *anamnesis* so far as she thought it necessary to go; extraordinary flood of energy and cheerfulness. Now this.

Seven pages of her big script, like tangled barbed wire, the upshot of which is that Meritorious Matey has at last done what I always expected him to do – revealed himself as a two-bit crook and opportunist. Has fiddled trust funds which somehow lay in his clutch; she doesn't say how and probably doesn't know. But she is certain he has been wronged. Of course he is her brother and the apple of her eye and Netty is nothing if not loyal, as the Staunton family knows to its cost – and also, I suppose, to its extraordinary benefit. One must be fair.

But how can I be fair to Matey? He has always been the deserving, hard-working fellow with his own way to make, while I have hardly been able to swallow for the weight of the silver spoon in my mouth. Certainly this is how Netty has put it to me, and when Father refused to take Matey into Alpha and wouldn't let Matey's firm handle the audit of Castor, she thought we were bowelless ingrates and oppressors. But Father smelled Matey as no good, and so did I, because of the way he sponged on Netty when he had no need. And now Netty begs me to return to Canada as soon as possible and undertake Matey's defence. 'You have spent your talents on many a scoundrel, and you ought to be ready to see that a wronged honest boy is righted before the world'; that is how she puts it. And: 'I've never asked you or the family for a thing and God knows what I've done for the Stauntons through thick and thin, and some things will never be known, but now I'm begging you on my bended knees.'

There is a simple way of handling this, and I have done the simple thing already. Cabled Huddleston to look into it and let me know: he can do whatever can be done fully as well as I. Do I now write Netty and say I am unwell, and the doctor forbids, etc., and Frederick Huddleston, Q.C., will take over? But Netty doesn't believe there is anything wrong with me. She has let Caroline know that she is sure I am in some fancy European home for booze-artists, having a good time and reading books, which I was always too ready to do anyhow. She will think I am dodging. And in part she will be right.

Dr Johanna has freed me from many a bogey, but she has also sharpened my already razorlike ethical sense. In her terms I have always projected the Shadow onto Matey; I have seen in him the worst of myself. I have been a heel in too many ways to count. Spying on Carol; spying on Denyse; making wisecracks to poor slobbering Lorene that she wasn't able to understand and which would have hurt her if she had understood; being miserable to Knopwood; miserable to Louis Wolff; worst of all, miserable to Father about things where he was vulnerable and I was strong. The account is long and disgusting.

I have accepted all that; it is part of what I am and unless I know it, grasp it, and acknowledge it as my own, there can be no freedom for me and no hope of being less a miserable stinker in future.

Before I came to my present very modest condition of self-recognition I was a clever lad at projecting my own faults onto other people, and I could see them all and many more in Maitland Quelch, C.A. Of course he had his own quiverful of perfectly real faults; one does not project one's Shadow on a man of gleaming virtue. But I detested Matey more than was admissible, for he never put a stone in my way, and in his damp-handed, grinning fashion he tried to be my friend. He was not a very nice fellow, and now I know that it was my covert spiritual kinship with him that made me hate him.

So when I refuse to go back to Canada and try to get Matey off, what is my ethical position? The legal position is perfectly clear; if Matey is in trouble with the Securities Commission there is good reason for it, and the most I could do would be to try to hoodwink the court into thinking he didn't know what he was doing, which would make him look like a fool if slightly less a crook. But if I refuse to budge and hand him over even to such a good man as Huddleston, am I still following a course that I am trying, in the middle of my life, to change?

Oh Matey, you bastard, why couldn't you have kept your nose clean and spared me this problem at a time when I am what I suppose must be called a psychic convalescent?

*

DEC. 18, Thurs.: Must get away. Might have stayed in Zürich over Xmas if it were not for this Matey thing, but Netty will try to get me on the telephone, and if I talk with her I will be lost ... What did she mean by 'some things will never be known'? Could it possibly be that Carol was right? That Netty put Mother in the way of dying (much too steep to say she killed her) because she thought Mother had been unfaithful to Father and Father would be happier without her? If Netty is like that, why hasn't she put rat-poison in Denyse's martinis? She hates Denyse, and it would be just like Netty to think that her opinion in such a matter was completely objective and beyond dispute.

Thinking of Netty puts me in mind of Pargetter's warning about the witnesses, or clients, whose creed is *esse in re*; to such people the world is absolutely clear because they cannot understand that our personal point of view colours what we perceive; they think everything seems exactly the same to everyone as it does to themselves. After all, they say, the world is utterly objective; it is plain before our eyes; therefore what the ordinary intelligent man (this is always themselves) sees is all there is to be seen, and anyone who sees differently is mad, or malign, or just plain stupid. An astonishing number of judges seem to belong in this category ...

Netty was certainly one of those, and I never really knew why I was always at odds with her (while really loving the old girl, I must confess) till Pargetter rebuked me for being an equally wrong-headed, though more complex and amusing creature, whose creed is *esse in intellectu solo*. 'You think the world is your idea,' he said one November day at a tutorial when I had been offering him some fancy theorizing, 'and if you don't understand that and check it now it will make your whole life a gigantic hallucination.' Which, in spite of my success, is pretty much what happened, and my extended experiments as a booze-artist were chiefly directed to checking any incursions of unwelcome truth into my illusion.

But what am I headed for? Where has Dr Johanna been taking me? I suspect toward a new ground of belief that wouldn't have occurred to Pargetter, which might be called *esse in anima*: I am beginning to recognize the objectivity of the world, while knowing also that because I am who and what I am, I both perceive the world in terms of who and what I am and project onto the world a great deal of who and what I am. If I know this, I ought to be able to escape the stupider kinds of illusion. The absolute nature of things is independent of my senses (which are all I have to perceive with), and what I perceive is an image in my own psyche.

All very fine. Not too hard to formulate and accept intellectually. But to *know* it; to bring it into daily life – that's the problem. And it would be real humility, not just the mock-modesty that generally passes for humility. Doubtless that is what Dr Johanna has up her sleeve for me when we begin our sessions after Christmas.

Meanwhile I must go away for Christmas. Netty will get

at me somehow if I stay here . . . Think I shall go to St Gall. Not far off and I could hire ski stuff if I wanted it. It is said to have lots to see besides the scenery.

＊

DEC. 19, Fri.: Arrive St Gall early p.m. Larger than I expected ; about 70,000, which was the size of Pittstown, but this place has an unmistakable atmosphere of consequence. Reputedly the highest city in Europe, and the air is thin and clean. Settle into a good hotel (Walhalla – why?) and walk out to get my bearings. Not much snow, but everything is decorated for Christmas very prettily ; not in our N. American whore-house style. Find the Klosterhof square, and admire it, but leave the Cathedral till tomorrow. Dinner at a very good restaurant (Metropole) and to the Stadtheater. It has been rebuilt in the Brutalist-Modern manner, and everything is rough cement and skew-whiff instead of right-angled or curved, so it is an odd setting for Lehar's *Paganini*, which is tonight's piece. Music prettily Viennese. How simple, loud, and potent love always is in these operettas! If I understood the thing, Napoleon would not permit Pag to have his countess because he was not noble: once I could not have the girl I loved because I was not a Jew. But Pag made a lot of eloquent noise about it, where I merely went sour. . . . Did I love Judy? Or just something of myself in her as Dr Johanna implies? Does it matter, now? Yes, it matters to me.

＊

DEC. 20, Sat.: Always the methodical sight-seer, I am off to the Cathedral by 9:30. Knew it was Baroque, but had not been prepared for something *so* Baroque ; breath-taking enormities of spiritual excess everywhere, but no effect of clutter or gimcrackery. Purposely took no guide-book ; wanted to get a first impression before fussing about detail.

Then to the Abbey library, which is next door, and gape at some very odd old paintings and the wonders of their

Baroque room. Keep my coat on as there is no heating in any serious sense ; the woman who sells tickets directs me to put on huge felt overshoes to protect the parquet. Superb library to look at, and there are two or three men of priestly appearance actually reading and writing in a neighbouring room, so it must also be more than a spectacle. I gape reverently at some splendid MSS, including a venerable *Nibelungenlied* and a *Parsifal*, and wonder what a frowsy old mummy, with what appear to be its own teeth, is doing there. I suppose in an earlier and less specialized time libraries were also repositories for curiosities. Hovered over a drawing of Christ's head, done entirely in calligraphy ; dated 'nach 1650'. Some painstaking penman had found a way of writing the Scripture account of the Passion with such a multitude of eloquent squiggles and crinkum-crankum that he had produced a monument of pious ingenuity, if not a work of art.

At last the cold becomes too much, and I scuttle out into the sunshine, and look for a bookshop where I can buy a guide, and turn myself thereby into a serious tourist. Find a fine shop, get what I want, and am poking about among the shelves when my eye is taken by two figures; a man in an engulfing fur coat over what was obviously one of those thick Harris-tweed suits is talking loudly to a woman who is very smartly and expensively dressed, but who is the nearest thing to an ogress I have ever beheld.

Her skull was immense, and the bones must have been monstrously enlarged, for she had a gigantic jaw, and her eyes peered out of positive caverns. She had made no modest concessions to her ugliness, for her iron-gray hair was fashionably dressed, and she wore a lot of make-up. They spoke in German, but there was something decidedly un-German and un-Swiss about the man and the more I stared (over the top of a book) the more familiar his back appeared. Then he moved, with a limp that could only belong to one man in the world. It was Dunstan Ramsay. Old Buggerlugs, as I live and breathe! But why in St Gall, and who could his dreadful companion be? Someone of consequence, unquestionably, for the manageress of the shop was very attentive . . . Now :

was I to claim acquaintance, or sneak away and preserve the quiet of my holiday? As so often in these cases, the decision was not with me. Buggerlugs had spotted me.

—Davey! How nice to see you.

—Good-morning, sir. A pleasant surprise.

—The last person I would have expected. I haven't seen you since poor Boy's funeral. What brings you here?

—Just a holiday.

—Have you been here long?

—Since yesterday.

—How is everyone at home? Carol well? Denyse is well, undoubtedly. What about Netty? Still your dragon?

—All well, so far as I know.

—Liesl, this is my lifelong friend – his life long, that's to say – David Staunton. David, this is Fraulein Doktor Liselotte Naegeli, whose guest I am.

The ogress gave me a smile which was extraordinarily charming, considering what it had to work against. When she spoke her voice was low and positively beautiful. It seemed to have a faintly familiar ring, but that is impossible. Amazing what distinguished femininity the monster had. More chat, and they asked me to lunch.

The upshot of that was that my St Gall holiday took an entirely new turn. I had counted on being solitary, but like many people who seek solitude I am not quite so fond of it as I imagine, and when Liesl – in no time I was asked to call her Liesl – asked me to join them at her country home for Christmas, I had said yes before I knew what I was doing. The woman is a spellbinder, without seeming to exert much effort, and Buggerlugs has changed amazingly. I have never fully liked him, as I told Dr Johanna, but age and a heart attack he said he had had shortly after Father's death seem to have improved him out of all recognition. He was just as inquisitorial and ironic as ever, but there was a new geniality about him. I gather he has been convalescing with the ogress, whom I suppose to be a medico. She took an odd line with him.

—Wasn't I lucky, Davey, to persuade Ramsay to come to

live with me? Such an amusing companion. Was he an amusing schoolmaster? I don't suppose so. But he is a dear man.

—Liesl, you will make Davey think we are lovers. I am here for Liesl's company, certainly, but almost as much because this climate suits my health.

—Let us hope it suits Davey's health, too. You can see he has been seriously unwell. But is your cure coming along nicely, Davey? Don't pretend you aren't working toward a cure.

—How can you tell that, Liesl? He looks better than when I last saw him, and no wonder. But what makes you think he is taking a cure?

—Well, look at him, Ramsay. Do you think I've lived near Zürich so long and can't recognize the 'analysand look'? He is obviously working with one of the Jungians, probing his soul and remaking himself. Which doctor do you go to, Davey? I know several of them.

—I can't guess how you know, but there's no use pretending, I suppose. I've been a little more than a year with Fraulein Doktor Johanna von Haller.

—Jo von Haller! I have known her since she was a child. Not friends, really, but we know each other. Well, have you fallen in love with her yet? All her male patients do. It's supposed to be part of the cure. But she is very ethical and never encourages them. I suppose with her successful lawyer husband and her two almost grown-up sons it mightn't do. Oh, yes; she is Frau Doktor, you know. But I suppose you spoke in English and it never came up. Well, after a year with Jo, you need something more lively. I wish we could promise you a really gay Christmas at Sorgenfrei, but it is certain to be dull.

—Don't believe it, Davey. Sorgenfrei is an enchanted castle.

—Nothing of the sort, but it should at least be a little more friendly than a hotel in St Gall. Can you come back with us now?

And so it was. An hour after finishing lunch I had picked up my things and was sitting beside Liesl in a beautiful sports car, with Ramsay and his wooden leg crammed into the back with the luggage, dashing eastward from St Gall on the road to Konstanz, and Sorgenfrei – whatever it might be. One of those private clinics, perhaps, that are so frequent in Switzerland? We were mounting all the time, and at last, after half a mile or so through pine woods we emerged onto a shelf on a mountainside, with a breath-taking view – really breath-taking, for the air was very cold and thinner than at St Gall – and Sorgenfrei commanding it.

Sorgenfrei is like Liesl, a fascinating monstrosity. In England it would be called Gothic Revival; I don't know the European equivalent. Turrets, mullioned windows, a squat tower for an entrance and somewhere at the back a much taller, thinner tower like a lead-pencil rising very high. But bearing everywhere the unmistakable double signature of the nineteenth century and a great deal of money. Inside, it is filled with bearskin rugs, gigantic pieces of furniture on which every surface has been carved within an inch of its life with fruits, flowers, birds, hares, and even, on one thing which seems to be an altar to greed but is more probably a sideboard, full-sized hounds; six of them with real bronze chains on their collars. This is the dream castle of some magnate of 150 years ago, conceived in terms of the civilization which has given the world, among a host of better things, the music box and the cuckoo clock.

We arrived at about five p.m., and I was taken to this room, which is as big as the boardroom of Castor, and where I am seizing my chance to bring my diary up to the minute. This is exhilarating. Is it the air, or Liesl's company? I am glad I came.

Later: Am I still glad I came? It is after midnight and I have had the most demanding evening since I left Canada.

This house troubles me and I can't yet say why. Magnificent houses, palaces, beautiful country houses, comfortable houses – I know all these either as a guest or a tourist. But this house, which seems at first appearances to be rather a joke, is positively the damnedest house I have ever entered. One might think the architect had gained all his previous experience illustrating Grimm's fairy stories, for the place is full of fantasy – but spooky, early-nineteenth-century fantasy, not the feeble Disney stuff. Yet, on second glance, it seems all to be meant seriously, and the architect was obviously a man of gifts, for though the house is big, it is still a house for people to live in and not a folly. Nor is it a clinic. It is Liesl's home, I gather.

Sorgenfrei. Free of care. Sans Souci. The sort of name someone of limited imagination might give to a country retreat. But there is something here that utterly contradicts the suggestion of the rich bourgeoisie resting from their money-making.

When I went down to dinner I found Ramsay in the library. That is to say, in an English country-house it would have been the library, comfortable and pleasant, but at Sorgenfrei it is too oppressively literary; bookshelves rise to a high, painted ceiling, on which is written in decorative Gothic script what I can just make out to be the Ten Commandments. There is a huge terrestrial globe, balanced by an equally huge celestial one. A big telescope, not much less than a century old, I judged, is mounted at one of the windows that look out on the mountains. On a low table sits a very modern object, which I discovered was five chess-boards mounted one above another in a brass frame; there are chessmen on each board, arranged as for five different games in progress; the boards are made of transparent lucite or some such material, so that it is possible to look down through them from above and see the position of every man. There was a good fire, and Ramsay was warming his legs, one flesh and one artificial, in front of it. He caught my mood at once.

—Extraordinary house, isn't it?

—Very. Is this where you live now?

—I'm a sort of permanent guest. My position is rather in the eighteenth-century mode. You know – people of intellectual tastes kept a philosopher or a scholar around the place. Liesl likes my conversation. I like hers. Funny way for a Canadian schoolmaster to end up, don't you think?

—You were never an ordinary schoolmaster, sir.

—Don't call me sir, Davey. We're old friends. Your father was my oldest friend; if friends is what we were, which I sometimes doubted. But you're not a lad now. You're a notable criminal lawyer; what used to be called 'an eminent silk'. Of course the problem is that I haven't any name by which all my friends call me. What did you call me at school? Was it Corky? Corky Ramsay? Stupid name, really. Artificial legs haven't been made of cork in a very long time.

—If you really want to know, we called you Buggerlugs. Because of your habit of digging in your ear with your little finger, you know.

—Really? Well, I don't think I like that much. You'd better call me Ramsay, like Liesl.

—I notice she generally calls you 'dear Ramsay'.

—Yes; we're rather close friends. More than that, for a while. Does that surprise you?

—You've just said I'm an experienced criminal lawyer; nothing surprises me.

—Never say that, Davey. Never, never say that. Especially not at Sorgenfrei.

—You yourself just said it was an extraordinary house.

—Oh, quite so. Rather a marvel, in its peculiar style. But that wasn't precisely what I meant.

We were interrupted by Liesl, who appeared through a door which I had not noticed because it is one of those nineteenth-century affairs, fitted close into the bookshelves and covered with false book-backs, so that it can hardly be seen. She was wearing something very like a man's evening suit, made in dark velvet, and looked remarkably elegant. I was beginning not to notice her Gorgon face. Ramsay turned to her rather anxiously, I thought.

—Is himself joining us at dinner tonight?

—I think so. Why do you ask?

—I just wondered when Davey would meet him.

—Don't fuss, dear Ramsay. It's a sign of age, and you are not old. Look, Davey, have you ever seen a chess-board like this?

Liesl began to explain the rules of playing what is, in effect, a single game of chess, but on five boards at once and with five sets of men. The first necessity, it appears, is to dismiss all ideas of the normal game, and to school oneself to think both horizontally and laterally at the same time. I, who could play chess pretty well but had never beaten Pargetter, was baffled – so much so that I did not notice anyone else entering the room, and I started when a voice behind me said:

—When am I to be introduced to Mr Staunton?

The man who spoke was surprising enough in himself, for he was a most elegant little man with a magnificent head of curling silver hair, and the evening dress he wore ended not in trousers, but in satin knee-breeches and silk stockings. But I knew him at once as Eisengrim, the conjuror, the illusionist, whom I had twice seen in Toronto at the Royal Alexandra Theatre, the last time when I was drunk and distraught, and shouted at the Brazen Head, 'Who killed Boy Staunton?' Social custom is ground into our bones, and I put out my hand to shake his. He spoke:

—I see you recognize me. Well, are the police still trying to involve me in the murder of your father? They were very persistent. They even traced me to Copenhagen. But they had nothing to go on. Except that I seemed to know rather more about it than they did, and they put all sorts of fanciful interpretations on some improvised words of Liesl's. How pleasant to meet you. We must talk the whole thing over.

No point in reporting in detail what followed. How right Ramsay was! Never say you can't be surprised. But what was I to do? I was confronted by a man whom I had despised and even hated when last I saw him, and his opening remarks to me were designed to be disconcerting if not downright quarrel-picking. But I was not the same man who shouted his question in the theatre; after a year with Dr Johanna I was a very different fellow. If Eisengrim was cool, I would be cooler. I have delicately slain and devoured many an impudent witness in the courts, and I am not to be bamboozled by a mountebank. I think my behaviour was a credit to Dr Johanna, and to Pargetter; I saw admiration in Ramsay's face, and Liesl made no attempt to conceal her pleasure at a situation that seemed to be entirely to her taste.

We went in to dinner, which was an excellent meal and not at all in the excessive style of the house. There was plenty of good wine, and cognac afterward, but I knew myself well enough to be sparing with it, and once again I could see that Ramsay and Liesl were watching me closely and pleased by what I did. There was none of that English pretence that serious things should not be discussed while eating, and we talked of nothing but by father's murder and what followed it, his will and what sprang from that, and what Denyse, and Carol, and Netty and the world in general – so far as the world in general paid any attention – had thought and said about it.

It was a trial and a triumph for me, because since I came to Zürich I have spoken to nobody of these things except Dr Johanna, and then in the most subjective terms possible. But tonight I found myself able to be comparatively objective, even when Liesl snorted with rude laughter at Denyse's antics with the death-mask. Ramsay was sympathetic, but he laughed when I said that Father had left some money for my non-existent children. His comment was:

—I don't believe you ever knew what a sore touch it was with Boy that you were such a Joseph about women. He felt it put him in the wrong. He always felt that the best possible favour you could do a woman was to push her into bed. He simply could not understand that there are men for whom sex is not the greatest of indoor and outdoor sports, hobbies, arts, sciences, and food for reverie. I always felt that his preoccupation with women was an extension of his miraculous touch with sugar and sweetstuffs. Women were the most delightful confectioneries he knew, and he couldn't understand anybody who hadn't a sweet tooth.

—I wonder what your father would have made of a woman like Jo von Haller?

—Women of that kind never came into Boy's ken, Liesl. Or women like you, for that matter. His notion of an intelligent woman was Denyse.

I found it still pained me to hear Father talked of in this objective strain, so I tried to turn the conversation.

—I suppose all but a tiny part of life lies outside anybody's ken, and we all get shocks and starts, now and then. For instance, who would have supposed that after such a long diversion through Dr von Haller's consulting-room I should meet you three by chance? There's a coincidence, if you like.

But Ramsay wouldn't allow that to pass.

—As an historian, I simply don't believe in coincidence. Only very rigid minds do. Rationalists talk about a pattern they can see and approve as logical; any pattern they can't see and wouldn't approve they dismiss as coincidental. I suppose you had to meet us, for some reason. A good one, I hope.

Eisengrim was interested but supercilious; after dinner he and Liesl played the complex chess game. I watched for a while, but I could make nothing of what they were doing, so I sat by the fire and talked with Ramsay. Of course I was dying to know how he came to be part of this queer household, but Dr von Haller has made me more discreet than I used to be about cross-examining in private life. That suggestion that he and Liesl had once been lovers – could it be? I probed, very, very gently. But I had once been Buggerlugs' pupil, and I still feel he can see right through me. Obviously he did, but he was in a mood to reveal, and like a man throwing crumbs to a bird he let me know:

1. That he had known Eisengrim from childhood.
2. That Eisengrim came from the same village as Father and himself, and Mother – my Deptford.
3. That Eisengrim's mother had been a dominant figure in his own life. He spoke of her as 'saintly', which puzzles me. Wouldn't Netty have mentioned somebody like that?

4. That he met Liesl travelling with Eisengrim in Mexico and that they had discovered an 'affinity' (his funny, old-fashioned word) which existed still.
5. When we veered back to the coincidence of my meeting them in St Gall, he laughed and quoted G. K. Chesterton: 'Coincidences are a spiritual sort of puns.'

He has, it appears, come to Switzerland to recuperate himself after his heart attack, and seems likely to stay here. He is working on another book – something about faith as it relates to myth, which is his old subject – and appears perfectly content. This is not a bad haul, and gives me encouragement for further fishing.

Eisengrim affects royal airs. Everything suggests that this is Liesl's house, but he seems to regard himself as the regulator of manners in it. After they adjourned their game (I gather it takes days to complete), he rose, and I was astonished to see that Liesl and Ramsay rose as well, so I followed suit. He shook us all by the hand, and bade us goodnight with the style of a crowned head taking leave of courtiers. He had an air of You-people-are-welcome-to-sit-up as-long-as you-please-but-We-are-retiring, and it was pretty obvious he thought the tone of the gathering would drop when he left the room.

Not so. We all seemed much easier. The huge library, where the curtains had now been drawn to shut out the night sky and the mountaintops and the few lights that shone far below us, was made almost cosy by his going. Liesl produced whisky, and I thought I might allow myself one good drink. It was she who brought up what was foremost in my mind.

—I assure you, Davey, there is nothing premeditated about this. Of course when we met in the bookshop I knew you must be the son of the man who died so spectacularly when Eisengrim was last in Toronto, but I had no notion of the circumstances.

—Were you in Toronto with him?

—Certainly. We have been business partners and artistic associates for a long time. I am his manager or impresario or whatever you want to call it. On the programs I use another name, but I assure you I am very much present. I am the voice of the Brazen Head.

—Then it was you who gave that extraordinary answer to my question?

—What question are you talking about?

—Don't you recall that Saturday night in the theatre when somebody called out, 'Who killed Boy Staunton?'

—I remember it very clearly. It was a challenge, you may suppose, coming suddenly like that. We usually had warning of the questions the Head might have to answer. But was it you who asked the question?

—Yes, but I didn't hear all of your answer.

—No; there was confusion. Poor Ramsay here was standing at the back of an upstairs box, and that was when he had his heart attack. And I think a great many people were startled when he fell forward into sight. Of course there were others who thought it was part of the show. It was a memorable night.

—But do you remember what you said?

—Perfectly. I said: 'He was killed by the usual cabal: by himself, first of all; by the woman he knew; by the woman he did not know; by the man who granted his inmost wish; and by the inevitable fifth, who was keeper of his conscience and keeper of the stone.'

—I don't suppose it is unreasonable of me to ask for an explanation of that rigmarole?

—Not unreasonable at all, and I hope you get an answer that satisfies you. But not tonight. Dear Ramsay is looking a little pale, and I think I should see him to bed. But there is plenty of time. I know you will take care that we talk of this again.

And with that I have to be contented at least until tomorrow.

*

DEC. 21, Sun.: This morn. Liesl took me on a tour of the house, which was apparently built in 1824 by some forbear who had made money in the watch-and-clock business. The entrance hall is dominated by what I suppose was his masterpiece, for it has dials to show seconds, days of the week, days of the months, the months, the seasons, the signs of the zodiac, the time at Sorgenfrei and the time at Greenwich, and the phases of the moon. It has a chime of thirty-seven bells, which play a variety of tunes, and is ornamented with figures of Day and Night, the Seasons, two heads of Time, and God knows what else, all in fine *verd-antique*. Monstrous but fascinating, like Liesl, and she seems to love it. As we wandered through the house and climbed unexpected staircases and looked at the bewildering views from cunningly placed windows, I did my best to bring the conversation to the strange words of the Brazen Head about Father's death, but Liesl knows every trick of evasion, and in her own house I could not nail her down as I might in court. But she did say one or two things:

—You must not interpret too closely. Remember that I, speaking for the Head, had no time – not even ten seconds – to reflect. So I gave a perfectly ordinary answer, like any experienced fortune-teller. You know there are always things that fit almost any enquirer: you say those things and they will do the interpreting. 'The woman he knew – the woman he did not know.' ... From what I know now, which is only what Ramsay has told me at one time or another, I would have said the woman he knew was your mother, and the woman he did not know was your stepmother. He felt guilty about your mother, and the second time he married a woman who was far stronger than he had understood. But I gather from the terrible fuss your stepmother made that she thought she must be the woman he knew, and was very angry at the idea that she had any part in bringing about his death ... I really can't tell you any more than that about why I spoke as I did. I have a tiny gift in this sort of thing; that was why Eisengrim trusted me to speak for the Head; maybe I sensed something – because one does, you know, if one permits it.

But don't brood on it and try to make too much of it. Let it go.

—My training has not been to let things go.

—But Davey, your training and the way you have used yourself have brought you at last to Zürich for an analysis. I'm sure Jo von Haller, who is really excellent, though not at all my style, has made you see that. Are you going to do more work with her?

—That's a decision I must make.

—Well, don't be in a hurry to say you will.

Went for a long walk alone this afternoon, and thought about Liesl's advice.

This eve. after dinner Eisengrim showed us some home-movies of himself doing things with coins and cards. New illusions, it seems, for a tour they begin early in January. He is superb, and knows it. What an egotist! And only a conjuror, after all. Who gives a damn? Who needs conjurors? Yet I am unpleasantly conscious of a link between Eisengrim and myself. He wants people to be in awe of him, and at a distance: so do I.

*

DEC. 22, Mon.: I suppose Eisengrim sensed my boredom and disgust last night, because he hunted me up after breakfast and took me to see his workrooms, which are the old stables of Sorgenfrei; full of the paraphernalia of his illusions, and with very fine workbenches, at one of which Liesl was busy with a jeweller's magnifying-glass stuck in her eye ... 'You didn't know I had the family knack of clockwork, did you?' she said. But Eisengrim wanted to talk himself:

—You don't think much of me, Staunton? Don't deny it; it is part of my profession to sniff people's thoughts. Well, fair enough. But I like you, and I should like you to like me. I am an egotist, of course. Indeed, I am a great egotist and a very unusual one, because I know what I am and I like it. Why not? If you knew my history, you would understand,

I think. But you see that is just what I don't want, or ask for. So many people twitter through life crying, 'Understand me! Oh, please understand me! To know all is to forgive all!' But you see I don't care about being understood, and I don't ask to be forgiven. Have you read the book about me?

(I have read it, because it is the only book in my bedroom, and so obviously laid out on the bedside table that it seems an obligation of the household to read the thing. I had seen it before; Father bought a copy for Lorene the first time we went to see Eisengrim, on her birthday. *Phantasmata: the Life and Adventures of Magnus Eisengrim*. Shortish; about 120 pages. But what a fairy-tale! Strange birth to distinguished Lithuanian parents, political exiles from Poland; infancy in the Arctic, where father was working on a secret scientific project (for Russia, it was implied, but because of his high lineage the Russians did not want to acknowledge the association); recognition of little Magnus by an Eskimo shaman as a child of strange gifts; little Magnus, between the ages of four and eight, learns arts of divination and hypnosis from the shaman and his colleagues. Father's Arctic work completed and he goes off to do something similar in the dead centre of Australia (because it is implied that father, the Lithuanian genius, is some sort of extremely advanced meteorological expert) and there little Magnus is taught by a tutor who is a great savant, who has to keep away from civilization for a while because he has done something dreadfully naughty. Little Magnus, after puberty, is irresistible to women, but he is obliged to be careful about this as the shaman had warned him women would disagree with his delicately balanced nerves. Nevertheless, great romances are hinted at; a generous gobbet of sadism spiced with pornography here. Having sipped, and rejected with contumely the learning of several great universities, Magnus Eisengrim determines to devote his life to the noble, misunderstood science which he first encountered in the Arctic, and which claimed him for its own ... And this is supposed to explain why he is travelling around with a magic show. A very good magic show, but still – a travelling showman.)

—Is one expected to take it seriously?

—I think it deserves to be taken more seriously than most biographies and autobiographies. You know what they are. The polished surface of a life. What the Zürich analysts call the Persona – the mask. Now, *Phantasmata* says what it is quite frankly in its title ; it is an illusion, a vision. Which is what I am, and because I am such a thoroughly satisfactory illusion, and because I satisfy a hunger that almost everybody has for marvels, the book is a far truer account of me than ordinary biographies, which do not admit that their intent is to deceive and are woefully lacking in poetry. The book is extremely well written, don't you think?

—Yes. I was surprised. Did you write it?

—Ramsay wrote it. He has written so much about saints and marvels, Liesl and I thought he was the ideal man to provide the right sort of life for me.

—But you admit it is a pack of lies?

—It is not a police-court record. But as I have already said, it is truer to the essence of my life than the dowdy facts could ever be. Do you understand? I am what I have made myself – the greatest illusionist since Moses and Aaron. Do the facts suggest or explain what I am? No : but Ramsay's book does. I am truly Magnus Eisengrim. The illusion, the lie, is a Canadian called Paul Dempster. If you want to know his story, ask Ramsay. He knows, and he might tell. Or he might not.

—Thank you for being frank. Are you any more ready than Liesl to throw some light on the answer of the Brazen Head?

—Let me see. Yes, I am certainly 'the man who granted his inmost wish'. You would never guess what it was. But he told me. People do tell me things. When I met him, which was on the night of his death, he offered me a lift back to my hotel in his car. As we drove he said – and as you know this was at one of the peaks of his career, when he was about to realize a dream which he, or your stepmother, had long cherished – he said, 'You know, sometimes I wish I could step on the gas and drive right away from all of this, all the obligations, the jealousies, the nuisances, and the relentlessly demanding people.' I said, 'Do you mean that? I could arrange it.' He said, 'Could you?' I replied, 'Nothing easier.' His face became very soft, like a child's, and he said, 'Very well. I'd be greatly obliged to you.' So I arranged it. You may be sure he knew no pain. Only the realization of his wish.

—But the stone? The stone in his mouth?

—Ah, well, that is not my story. You must ask the keeper of the stone. But I will tell you something Liesl doesn't know, unless Ramsay has told her: 'the woman he did not know' was my mother. Yes, she had some part in it.

With that I had to be contented because Liesl and a workman wanted to talk with him. But somehow I found myself liking him. Even more strange, I found myself believing him. But he was a hypnotist of great powers; I had seen him demonstrate that on the stage. Had he hypnotized Father and sent him to his death? And if so, why?

Later: That was how I put the question to Ramsay when I cornered him this afternoon in the room he uses for his writing. Pargetter's advice: always go to a man in *his* room, for then he has no place to escape to, whereas you may leave when you please. What did he say?

—Davey, you are behaving like the amateur sleuth in a detective story. The reality of your father's death is much more complex than anything you can uncover that way. First, you must understand that nobody – not Eisengrim or anyone – can make a man do something under hypnotism that he has not some genuine inclination to do. So: Who killed Boy Staunton? Didn't the Head say, 'Himself, first of all?' We all do it, you know, unless we are taken off by some unaccountable accident. We determine the time of our death, and perhaps the means. As for the 'usual cabal' I myself think 'the woman he knew and the woman he did not know' were the same person – your mother. He never had any serious appraisal of her weakness or her strength. She had strength, you know, that he never wanted or called on. She was Ben Cruikshank's daughter, and don't suppose that was nothing just because Ben wasn't a village grandee like Doc Staunton. Boy never had any use for your mother as a grown-up woman, and she kept herself childish in the hope of pleasing him. When we have linked our destiny with somebody, we neglect them at our peril. But Boy never knew that. He was so well graced, so gifted, such a genius in his money-spinning way, that he never sensed the reality of other people. Her weakness galled him, but her occasional shows of strength shamed him.

—You loved Mother, didn't you?

—I thought I did when I was a boy. But the women we really love are the women who complete us, who have the qualities we can borrow and so become something nearer to whole men. Just as we complete them, of course; it's not a one-way thing. Leola and I, when romance was stripped away, were too much alike; our strengths and weaknesses were too nearly the same. Together we would have doubled our gains and our losses, but that isn't what love is.

—Did you sleep with her?

—I know times have changed, Davey, but isn't that rather a rum question to put to an old friend about your mother?

—Carol used to insist that you were my father.

—Then Carol is a mischief-making bitch. I'll tell you this, however: your mother once asked me to make love to her, and I refused. In spite of one very great example I had in my life I couldn't rise to love as an act of charity. The failure was mine, and a bitter one. Now I'm not going to say the conventional thing and tell you I wish you were my son. I have plenty of sons – good men I've taught, who will carry something of me into places I would never reach. Listen, Davey, you great clamorous baby-detective, there is something you ought to know at your age: every man who amounts to a damn has several fathers, and the man who begat him in lust or drink or for a bet or even in the sweetness of honest love may not be the most important father. The fathers you choose for yourself are the significant ones. But you didn't choose Boy, and you never knew him. No; no man knows his father. If Hamlet had known his father he would never have made such an almighty fuss about a man who was fool enough to marry Gertrude. Don't you be a two-bit Hamlet, clinging to your father's ghost until you are destroyed. Boy is dead; dead of his own will, if not wholly of his own doing. Take my advice and get on with your own concerns.

—My concerns are my father's concerns and I can't escape that. Alpha is waiting for me. And Castor.

—Not your father's concerns. Your kingdoms. Go and reign, even if he has done a typical Boy trick by leaving you a gavel where he used a golden sceptre.

—I see you won't talk honestly with me. But I must ask one more question; who was 'the inevitable fifth, who was keeper of his conscience and keeper of the stone'?

—I was. And as keeper of his conscience, and as one who has a high regard for you, I will say nothing about it.

—But the stone? The stone that was found in his mouth when they rescued his body from the water? Look, Ramsay, I have it here. Can you look at it and say nothing?

—It was my paperweight for over fifty years. Your father gave it to me, very much in his own way. He threw it at me, wrapped up in a snowball. The rock-in-the-snowball man was part of the father you never knew, or never recognized.

—But why was it in his mouth?

—I suppose he put it there himself. Look at it; a piece of that pink granite we see everywhere in Canada. A geologist who saw it on my desk told me that they now reckon that type of stone to be something like a thousand million years old. Where has it been, before there were any men to throw it, and where will it be when you and I are not even a pinch of dust? Don't cling to it as if you owned it. I did that. I harboured it for sixty years, and perhaps my hope was for revenge. But at last I lost it, and Boy got it back, and he lost it, and certainly you will lose it. None of us counts for much in the long, voiceless, inert history of the stone ... Now I am going to claim the privilege of an invalid and ask you to leave me.

—There's nothing more to be said?

—Oh, volumes more, but what does all this saying amount

to? Boy is dead. What lives is a notion, a fantasy, a whim-wham in your head that you call Father, but which never had anything seriously to do with the man you attached it to.

—Before I go: who was Eisengrim's mother?

—I spent decades trying to answer that. But I never fully knew.

Later: Found out a little more about the super-chess game this eve. Each player plays both black and white. If the player who draws white at the beginning plays white on boards one, three, and five, he must play back on boards two and four. I said to Liesl that this must make the game impossibly complicated, as it is not five games played con-secutively, but one game.

—Not half so complicated as the game we all play for seventy or eighty years. Didn't Jo von Haller show you that you can't play the white pieces on all the boards? Only people who play on one, flat board can do that, and then they are in agonies trying to figure out what black's next move will be. Far better to know what you are doing, and play from both sides.

*

DEC. 23, Tues.: Liesl has the ability to an extraordinary ex-tent to worm things out of me. My temperament and profes-sional training make me a man to whom things are told; somehow she makes me into a teller. I ran into her – better be honest, I sought her out – this morning in her workshop, where she sat with a jeweller's magnifying glass in her eye and tinkered with a tiny bit of mechanism, and in five minu-tes had me caught in a conversation of a kind I don't like but can't resist when Liesl creates it.

—So you must give Jo a decision about more analysis? What is it to be?

—I'm torn about it. I'm seriously needed at home. But the work with Dr von Haller holds out the promise of a kind of satisfaction I've never known before. I suppose I want to have it both ways.

—Well, why not? Jo has set you on your path; do you need her to take you on a tour of your inner labyrinth? Why not go by yourself?

—I've never thought of it – I wouldn't know how.

—Then find out. Finding out is half the value. Jo is very good. I say nothing against her. But these analyses, Davey – they are duets between the analyst and the analysand, and you will never be able to sing louder or higher than your analyst.

—She has certainly done great things for me in the past year.

—Undoubtedly. And she never pushed you too far, or frightened you, did she? Jo is like a boiled egg – a wonder, a miracle, very easy to take – but even with a good sprinkling of salt she is invalid food, don't you find?

—I understand she is one of the best in Zürich.

—Oh, certainly. Analysis with a great analyst is an adventure in self-exploration. But how many analysts are great? Did I ever tell you I knew Freud slightly? A giant, and it would be apocalyptic to talk to such a giant about oneself. I never met Adler, whom everybody forgets, but he was certainly another giant. I once went to a seminar Jung gave in Zürich, and it was unforgettable. But one must remember that they were all men with systems. Freud, monumentally hipped on sex (for which he personally had little use) and almost ignorant of Nature: Adler, reducing almost everything to the will to power: and Jung, certainly the most humane and gentlest of them, and possibly the greatest, but nevertheless the descendant of parsons and professors, and himself a super-parson and a super-professor. All men of extraordinary character, and they devised systems that are forever stamped with that character ... Davey, did you ever think that these three men who were so splendid at understanding others had first to understand themselves? It was from their self-knowledge they spoke. They did not go

533

trustingly to some doctor and follow his lead because they were too lazy or too scared to make the inward journey alone. They dared heroically. And it should never be forgotten that they made the inward journey while they were working like galley-slaves at their daily tasks, considering other people's troubles, raising families, living full lives. They were heroes, in a sense that no space-explorer can be a hero, because they went into the unknown absolutely alone. Was their heroism simply meant to raise a whole new crop of invalids? Why don't you go home and shoulder your yoke, and be a hero too?

—I'm no hero, Liesl.

—Oh, how modest and rueful that sounds! And you expect me to think, isn't he splendid to accept his limitations so manfully. But I don't think that. All that personal modesty is part of the cop-out personality of our time. You don't know whether or not you are a hero, and you're bloody well determined not to find out, because you're scared of the burden if you are and scared of the certainty if you're not.

—Just a minute. Dr von Haller, of whom you think so little, once suggested that I was rather inclined toward heroic measures in dealing with myself.

—Good for Jo! But she didn't encourage you in it, did she? Ramsay says you are very much the hero in court – voice of the mute, hope of the hopeless, last resort of those society has condemned. But of course that's a public personality. Why do you put yourself on this footing with a lot of riff-raff, by the way?

—I told Dr von Haller that I liked living on the lip of a volcano.

—A good, romantic answer. But do you know the name of the volcano? That's what you have to find out.

—What are you suggesting? That I go home and take up my practice and Alpha and Castor and see what I can do to wriggle crooks like Matey Quelch off the hooks on which they have been caught? And at night, sit down quietly and try to think my way out of all my problems, and try to make some sort of sense of my life?

—Think your way out ... Davey, what did Jo say was wrong with you? Obviously you have a screw loose somewhere; everybody has. What did she find at the root of most of your trouble?

—Why should I tell you?

—Because I've asked, and I truly want to know. I'm not just a gossip or a chatterer, and I like you very much. So tell me.

—It's nothing dreadful. She just kept coming back to the point that I am rather strongly developed in Thinking, and seem to be a bit weak in Feeling.

—I guessed that was it.

—But honestly I don't know what's wrong with thinking. Surely it's what everybody is trying to do?

—Oh yes; very fine work, thinking. But it is also the greatest bolt-hole and escape hatch of our time. It's supposed to excuse everything ... 'I think this ... I thought that ... You haven't really thought about it ... Think, for God's sake ... The thinking of the meeting (or the committee, or God help us, the symposium) was that ...' But so much of this thinking is just mental masturbation, not intended to beget anything ... So you are weak in feeling, eh? I wonder why?

—Because of Dr von Haller, I can tell you. In my life feeling has not been very handsomely rewarded. It has hurt like hell.

—Nothing unusual in that. It always does. But you could try. Do you remember the fairy-tale about the boy who couldn't shudder and was so proud of it? Nobody much likes shuddering, but it's better than existing without it, I can assure you.

—I seem to have a natural disposition to think rather than feel, and Dr von Haller has helped me a good deal there. But I am not ambitious to be a great feeler. Wouldn't suit my style of life at all, Liesl.

—If you don't feel, how are you going to discover whether or not you are a hero?

—I don't want to be a hero.

—So? It isn't everybody who is triumphantly the hero of his own romance, and when we meet one he is likely to be a fascinating monster, like my dear Eisengrim. But just because you are not a roaring egotist, you needn't fall for the fashionable modern twaddle of the anti-hero and the mini-soul. That is what we might call the Shadow of democracy; it makes it so laudable, so cosy and right and easy to be a spiritual runt and lean on all the other runts for support and applause in a splendid apotheosis of runtdom. Thinking runts, of course – oh, yes, thinking away as hard as a runt can without getting into danger. But there are heroes, still. The modern hero is the man who conquers in the inner struggle. How do you know you aren't that kind of hero?

—You are as uncomfortable company as an old friend of mine who asked for spiritual heroism in another way. 'God is here and Christ is now,' he would say, and ask you to live as if it were true.

—It is true. But it's equally true to say 'Odin is here and Loki is now.' The heroic world is all around us, waiting to be known.

—But we don't live like that, now.

—Who says so? A few do. Be the hero of your own epic. If others will not, are you to blame? One of the great follies of our time is this belief in some levelling of Destiny, some democracy of *Wyrd*.

—And you think I should go it alone?

—I don't think: I feel that you ought at least to consider the possibility, and not cling to Jo like a sailor clinging to a lifebelt.

—I wouldn't know how to start.

—Perhaps if you felt something powerfully enough it would set you on the path.

—But what?

—Awe is a very unfashionable, powerful feeling. When did you last feel awe in the presence of anything?

—God, I can't remember ever feeling what I suppose you mean by awe.

—Poor Davey! How you have starved! A real little workhouse boy, an Oliver Twist of the spirit! Well, you're rather old to begin.

—Dr von Haller says not. I can begin the second part of this exploration with her, if I choose. But what is it? Do you know, Liesl?

—Yes, but it isn't easily explained. It's a thing one experiences – feels, if you like. It's learning to know oneself as fully human. A kind of rebirth.

—I was told a lot about that in my boyhood days, when I thought I was a Christian. I never understood it.

—Christians seem to have got it mixed up, somehow. It's certainly not crawling back into your mother's womb; it's more a re-entry and return from the womb of mankind. A fuller comprehension of one's humanity.

—That doesn't convey much to me.

—I suppose not. It's not a thinker's thing.

—Yet you suggest I go it alone?

—I don't know. I'm not as sure as I was. You might manage it. Perhaps some large experience, or even a good, sharp shock, might put you on the track. Perhaps you are wrong even to listen to me.

—Then why do you talk so much, and throw out so many dangerous suggestions?

—It's my métier. You thinkers drive me to shake you up. Maddening woman!

*

Dec. 24, Wed. and Christmas Eve: Was this the worst day of my life, or the best? Both.

Liesl insisted this morning that I go on an expedition with her. You will see the mountains at their best, she said; it is too cold for the tourists with their sandwiches, and there is not enough snow for skiers. So we drove for about half an hour, uphill all the way, and at last came to one of those cable-car affairs and swayed and joggled dizzily through the air toward the far-off shoulder of a mountain. When we got out of it at last, I found I was panting.

—We are about seven thousand feet up now. Does it bother you? You'll soon get used to it. Come on. I want to show you something.

—Surely the view elsewhere is the same as it is here?

—Lazy! What I want to show you isn't a view.

It was a cave; large, extremely cold as soon as we penetrated a few yards out of the range of the sun, but not damp. I couldn't see much of it, and although it is the first cave I have ever visited it convinced me that I don't like caves. But Liesl was enthusiastic, because it is apparently quite famous since somebody, whose name I did not catch, proved conclusively in the 'nineties that primitive men had lived here. All the sharpened flints, bits of carbon, and other evidence had been removed, but there were a few scratches on the walls which appear to be very significant, though they looked like nothing more than scratches to me.

—Can't you imagine them, crouching here in the cold as the sun sank, with nothing to warm them but a small fire and a few skins? But enduring, enduring, enduring! They were heroes, Davey.

—I don't suppose they conceived of anything better. They can't have been much more than animals.

—They were our ancestors. They were more like us than they were like any animal.

—Physically, perhaps. But what kind of brains had they? What sort of mind?

—A herd-mind, probably. But they may have known a few things we have lost on the long journey from the cave to – well, to the law-courts.

—I don't see any good in romanticizing savages. They knew how to get a wretched living and hang on to life for twenty-five or thirty years. But surely anything human, any sort of culture or civilized feeling or whatever you want to call it, came ages later?

—No, no; not at all. I can prove it to you now. It's a little bit dangerous, so follow me, and be careful.

She went to the very back of the cave, which may have been two hundred feet deep, and I was not happy to follow

her, because it grew darker at every step, and though she
had a big electric torch it seemed feeble in that blackness.
But when we had gone as far as seemed possible, she turned
to me and said, 'This is where it begins to be difficult; so
follow me very closely, close enough to touch me at all
times, and don't lose your nerve.' Then she stepped behind
an outcropping of rock which looked like solid cave wall
and scrambled up into a hole about four feet above the cave
floor.

I followed, very much alarmed, but too craven to beg off.
In the hole, through which it was just possible to move on
hands and knees, I crept after the torch, which flickered in-
termittently because every time Liesl lifted her back she
obscured its light. And then, after perhaps a dozen yards of
this creeping progress over rough stone, we began what was
to me a horrible descent.

Liesl never spoke or called to me. As the hole grew smaller
she dropped to her knees and crawled on her belly, and
there was nothing for me but to do the same. I was as frightened as I have ever been in my life, but there was nothing
for me to do but follow, because I had no idea of how I
could retreat. Nor did I speak to her; her silence kept me
quiet. I would have loved to hear her speak, and say something in reply, but all I heard was the shuffling as she crawled
and wriggled, and now and then one of her boots kicked
against my head. I have heard of people whose sport it is to
crawl into these mountain holes, and read about some of
them who had stuck and died. I was in terror, but somehow
I kept on wriggling forward. I have not wriggled on my belly
since I was a child, and it hurt; my shoulders and neck began to ache torturingly, and at every hunch forward my
chest, privates, and knees were scraped unpleasantly on the
stone floor. Liesl had outfitted me in some winter clothes she
had borrowed from one of the workmen at Sorgenfrei, and
though they were thick, they were certainly not much protection from the bruises of this sort of work.

How far we wriggled I had no idea. Later Liesl, who had
made the journey several times, said it was just under a

quarter of a mile, but to me it might have been ten miles. At last I heard her say, Here we are, and as I crawled out of the hole and stood up – very gingerly because for some reason she did not use her electric torch and the darkness was complete and I had no idea how high the roof might be – there was the flash of a match, and soon a larger flame that came from a torch she had lit.

—This is a pine-torch ; I think it the most appropriate light for this place. Electricity is a blasphemy here. The first time I came, which was about three years ago, there were remains of pine torches still by the entry, so that was how they must have lit this place.

—Who are you talking about?

—The people of the caves. Our ancestors. Here, hold this torch while I light another. It takes some time for the torches to give much light. Stand where you are and let it unfold before you.

I thought she must mean that we had entered one of those caves, of which I have vaguely heard, which are magnificently decorated with primitive paintings. I asked her if that were it, but all she would say was, 'Very much earlier than that,' and stood with her torch held high.

Slowly, in the flickering light, the cave revealed itself. It was about the size of a modest chapel ; I suppose it might have held fifty people ; and it was high, for the roof was above the reach of the light from our torches. It was bitter cold but there was no ice on the walls ; there must have been lumps of quartz, because they twinkled eerily. Liesl was in a mood that I had never seen in her before ; all her irony and amusement were gone and her eyes were wide with awe.

—I discovered this about three years ago. The outer cave is quite famous, but nobody had noticed the entrance to this one. When I found it I truly believe I was the first person to enter it in – how long would you guess, Davey?

—I can't possibly say. How can you tell?

—By what is here. Haven't you noticed it yet?

—It just seems to be a cave. And brutally cold. Do you suppose somebody used it for something?

—Those people. The ancestors. Look here.

She led me toward the farthest wall from where we had entered, and we came to a little enclosure, formed by a barrier made of heaped up stones; in the cave wall, above the barrier, were seven niches, and I could just make out something of bone in each of these little cupboards; old, dark brown bone, which I gradually made out to be skulls of animals.

—They are bears. The ancestors worshipped bears. Look, in this one bones have been pushed into the eyeholes. And here, you see, the leg-bones have been carefully piled under the chin of the skull.

—Do you suppose the bears lived in here?

—No cave-bear could come through the passage. No; they brought the bones here, and the skins, and set up this place of worship. Perhaps someone pulled on the bear skin, and there was a ceremony of killing.

—That was their culture, was it? Playing bears in here?

—Flippant fool! Yes, that was their culture.

—Well, don't snap at me. I can't pretend it means much to me.

—You don't know enough for it to mean anything to you. Worse for you, you don't feel enough for it to mean anything to you.

—Liesl, are we going to go over all that again in the depths of this mountain? I want to get out. If you want to know, I'm scared. Now look: I'm sorry I haven't been respectful enough about your discovery. I'm sure it means a lot in the world of archaeology, or ethnology, or whatever it may be. The men around here worshipped bears. Good. Now let's go.

—Not just the men around here. The men of a great part of the world. There are such caves as this all over Europe and Asia, and they have found some in America. How far is Hudson Bay from where you live?

—A thousand miles, more or less.

—They worshipped the bear there, between the great ice ages.

—Does it matter, now?

—Yes, I think it matters now. What do we worship today?

—Is this the place or the time to go into that?

—Where better? We share the great mysteries with these people. We stand where men once came to terms with the facts of death and mortality and continuance. How long ago, do you suppose?

—I haven't any idea

—It was certainly not less than seventy-five thousand years ago ; possibly much, much more. They worshipped the bear and felt themselves better and greater because they had done so. Compared with this place the Sistine Chapel is of yesterday. But the purpose of both places is the same. Men sacrificed and ate of the noblest thing they could conceive, hoping to share in its virtue.

—Yes, yes : I read *The Golden Bough* when I was young.

—Yes, yes ; and you misunderstood what you read because you accepted its rationalist tone instead of understanding its facts. Does this place give you no sense of the greatness and indomitability and spiritual splendour of man? Man is a noble animal, Davey. Not a good animal ; a noble animal.

—You distinguish between the two?

—Yes, you – you lawyer, I do.

—Liesl, we mustn't quarrel. Not here. Let's get out and I'll argue all you please. If you want to split morality – some sort of accepted code – off from the highest values we have, I'll promise you a long wrangle. I am, as you say, a lawyer. But for the love of God let's get back to the light.

—For the love of God? Is not God to be found in the darkness? Well, you mighty lover of the light and the law, away we go.

But then, to my astonishment, Liesl flung herself on the ground, face down before the skulls of the bears, and for perhaps three minutes I stood in the discomfort we always feel when somebody nearby is praying and we are not. But what form could her prayers be taking? This was worse – much worse – than Dr Johanna's Comedy Company of the Psyche. What sort of people had I fallen among on this Swiss journey?

When she rose she was grinning and the charm I had learned to see in her terrible face was quite gone.

—Back to the light, my child of light. You must be reborn into the sun you love so much, so let us lose no time. Leave your torch, here, by the way out.

She dowsed her own torch by stubbing it on the ground and I did so too. As the light diminished to a few sparks I heard a mechanical clicking, and I knew she was snapping the switch of her electric torch, but no light came.

—Something is wrong. The batteries or the bulb. It won't light.

—But how are we to get back without light?

—You can't miss the path. Just keep crawling. You'd better go first.

—Liesl, am I to go into that tunnel without a glimmer of light?

—Yes, unless you wish to stay here in the dark. I'm going, certainly. If you are wise you will go first. And don't change your mind on the way, because if anything happens to you, Davey, I can't turn back, or wriggle backward. It's up and out for both of us, or death for both of us . . . Don't think about it any longer. Go on!

She gave me a shove toward the hole of the tunnel, and I hit my head hard against the upper side of it. But I was cowed by the danger and afraid of Liesl, who had become such a demon in the cave, and I felt my way into the entrance and began to wriggle.

What had been horrible coming in, because it was done head downward, was more difficult than anything I have ever attempted until I began the outward journey; but now I had to wriggle upward at an angle that seemed never less than forty-five degrees. It was like climbing a chimney, a matter of knees and elbows, and frequent cracks on the skull. I know I kicked Liesl in the face more than once, but she made no sound except for the grunting and panting without which no progress was possible. I had worn myself out going in; going out I had to find strength from new and unguessed-at sources. I did not think; I endured, and endurance took on a new character, not of passive suffering but of anguished, fearful striving. Was it only yesterday I had been called the boy who could not shudder?

Suddenly, out of the darkness just before me, came a roar so loud, so immediate, so fearful in suggestion that I knew in that instant the sharpness of death. I did not lose consciousness. Instead I knew with a shame that came back in full force from childhood that my bowels had turned to water and gushed out into my pants, and the terrible stench that filled the tunnel was my own. I was at the lowest ebb, frightened, filthy, seemingly powerless, because when I heard Liesl's voice – 'Go on, you dirty brute, go on' – I couldn't go on, dragging with me that mess which, from being hot as porridge, was cooling quickly in the chill of the tunnel.

—It's only a trick of the wind. Did you think it was the bear-god coming to claim you? Go on. You have another two hundred yards at least. Do you think I want to hang about here with your stink? Go on!

—I can't, Liesl. I'm done.

—You must.

—How?

—What gives you strength? Have you no God? No, I suppose not. Your kind have neither God nor Devil. Have you no ancestors?

Ancestors? Why, in this terrible need, would I want such ornaments? Then I thought of Maria Dymock, staunch in the street of Staunton, demanding money from the passers-by to get herself and her bastard to Canada. Maria Dymock, whom Doc Staunton had suppressed, and about whom my father would hear nothing after that first, unhappy letter. (What had Pledger-Brown said? 'Too bad, Davey; he wanted blood and all we could offer was guts.') Would Maria Dymock see me through? In my weakened, terrified, humiliated condition I suppose I must have called upon Maria Dymock and something – but it's absurd to think it could have been she! – gave me the power I needed to wriggle that last two hundred yards, until an air that was sweeter but no less cold told me that the outer cave was near.

Out of the darkness into the gloom. Out of the gloom into sunshine, and the extraordinary realization that it was about three o'clock on a fine Christmas Eve, and that I was seven thousand feet above the sea on a Swiss mountain. An uncomfortable, messy walk back to the cable-railway and the discovery – God bless the Swiss! – that the little station had a good men's toilet with lots of paper towels. A dizzy, light-headed journey downward on one of the swaying cars, during which Liesl said nothing but sulked like some offended shaman from the days of her bear-civilization. We drove home in silence; even when she indicated that she wished me to sit on a copy of the *Neue Zürcher Zeitung* that was in the car, so as not to soil her upholstery, she said nothing. But when we drove into the stable-yard which led to the garages at Sorgenfrei, I spoke.

—Lie.., I am very, very sorry. Not for being afraid, or messing my pants, or any of that. But for falling short of what you expected. You thought me worthy to see the shrine of the bears, and I was too small a person to know what you meant. But I think I have a glimmering of something better, and I beg you not to shut me out of your friendship.

Another woman might have smiled, or taken my hand, or kissed me, but not Liesl. She glared into my eyes.

—Apology is the cheapest coin on earth, and I don't value it. But I think you have learned something, and if that is so, I'll do more than be your friend. I'll love you, Davey. I'll take you into my heart, and you shall take me into yours. I don't mean bed-love, though that might happen, if it seemed the right thing. I mean the love that gives all and takes all and knows no bargains.

I was bathed and in bed by five o'clock, dead beat. But so miraculous is the human spirit, I was up and about and able to eat a good dinner and watch a Christmas broadcast from Lausanne with Ramsay and Eisengrim and Liesl, renewed – yes, and it seemed to me reborn, by the terror of the cave and the great promise she had made to me a few hours before.

*

Dec. 25, Thurs. and Christmas Day: Woke feeling better than I have done in years. To breakfast very hungry (why does happiness make us hungry?) and found Ramsay alone at the table.

—Merry Christmas, Davey. Do you recall once telling me you hated Christmas more than any day in the year?

—That was long ago. Merry Christmas, Dunny. That was what Father used to call you, wasn't it?

—Yes, and I always hated it. I think I'd almost rather be called Buggerlugs.

Eisengrim came in and put a small pouch beside my plate. Obviously he meant me to open it, so I did, and out fell a fine pair of ivory dice. I rolled them a few times, without much luck. Then he took them.

—What would you like to come up?

—Double sixes, surely?

He cast the dice, and sure enough, there they were.

—Loaded?

—Nothing so coarse. They are quite innocent, but inside they have a little secret. I'll show you how it works later.

Ramsay laughed.

—You don't suppose an eminent silk would use such things, Magnus? He'd be thrown out of all his clubs.

—I don't know what an eminent silk might do with dice but I know very well what he does in court. Are you a lucky man? To be lucky is always to play with – well, with dice like these. You might like to keep them in your pocket, Davey, just as a reminder of – well, of what our friend Ramsay calls the variability and mutability and general rumness of things.

Liesl had come in, and now she handed me a watch.

—From the Brazen Head.

It was a handsome piece, and on the back was engraved, 'Time is ... Time was ... Time is past,' which is perfectly reasonable if you like inscribed watches, and of course these were the words she and Eisengrim used to introduce their Brazen Head illusion. I knew that, between us, it meant the mystery and immemorial age of the cave. I was embarrassed.

—I had no idea there was to be an exchange of gifts. I'm terribly sorry, but I haven't anything for anyone.

—Don't think of it. It is just as one feels. You see, dear Ramsay has not worried about gifts either.

—But I have. I have my gifts here. I wanted to wait till everyone was present before giving mine.

Ramsay produced a paper bag from under the table and solemnly handed us each a large gingerbread bear. They were handsome bears, standing on their hindlegs and each holding a log of wood.

—These are the real St Gall bears; the shops are full of them at this time of year.

Eisengrim nibbled at his bear experimentally.

—Yes, they are made like the bear which is the city crest, or totem, aren't they?

—Indeed, they are images of the veritable bear of St Gall himself. You know the legend. Early in the seventh century an Irish monk, Gallus, came to this part of the world to convert the wild mountaineers. They were bear-worshippers, I believe. He made his hermitage in a cave near where the present city stands, and preached and prayed. But he was so very much a holy man, and so far above merely creatural considerations, that he needed a servant or a friend to help him. Where would he find one? Now it so happened that Gallus's cave had another inhabitant, a large bear. And Gallus, who was extremely long-headed, made a deal with the bear. If the bear would bring him wood for his fire, he would give the bear bread to eat. And so it was. And this excellent gingerbread – I hope I may say it is excellent without seeming to praise my own gift – reminds us even today that if we are really wise, we will make a working arrangement with the bear that lives with us, because otherwise we shall starve or perhaps be eaten by the bear. You see, like every tale of a saint it has a moral, and the moral is my Christmas gift to you, Davey, you poor Canadian bear-choker, and to you, Magnus, you enchanting fraud, and to you, my dearest Liesl, though you don't need it: cherish your bear, and your bear will feed your fire.

Later: For a walk with Ramsay. It was not long after three o'clock, but already in the mountains sunset was well advanced. He cannot walk far with his game leg, but he went a few hundred yards, toward a precipice; a low stone wall warned us not to go too near, for the drop was steep toward a valley and some little farmsteads. Talked to him about the decision Liesl wants me to make and asked his advice.

—Liesl likes pushing people to extremes. Are you a man for extremes, Davey? I don't think I can help you. Or can I? You still have that stone . . . You know, the one that was found in Boy's mouth?

I took it out of my pocket and handed it to him.

—I can do this for you, anyhow, Davey.

He raised his arm high, and with a snap of the wrist threw it far down into the valley. In that instant it was possible to see that he had once been a boy. We both watched until the little speck could no longer be seen against the valley dusk.

—There. At least that's that. Pray God it didn't hit anybody.

We turned back toward Sorgenfrei, walking in companionable silence. My thoughts were on the dream I dreamed the night before I first confronted Dr von Haller. It was splendidly clear in my recollection. I had left my enclosed, ordered, respected life. Yes. And I had ventured into unknown country, where archaeological digging was in progress. Yes. I had attempted to go down the circular staircase inside the strange, deceptive hut – so wretched on the outside and so rich within – and my desire had been thwarted by trivial fellows who behaved as if I had no right there. Yes. But as I thought about it, the dream changed; the two young men were no longer at the stairhead, and I was free to go down if I pleased. And I did please, for I sensed that there was treasure down there. I was filled with happiness, and I knew this was what I wanted most.

I was walking with Ramsay, I was fully aware of everything about me, and yet it was the dream that was most real to me. The strange woman, the gypsy who spoke so compellingly, yet incomprehensibly – where was she? In my waking dream I looked out of the door of the hut, and there she was, walking toward me ; to join me, I knew. Who was she ? 'Every country gets the foreigners it deserves.' The words which I had thought so foolish still lingered in my mind. They meant something more important than I could yet understand, and I struggled for an explanation. Was I going down the staircase to a strange land? Was I, then, to be a stranger there? But how could I be foreign in the place where my treasure lay? Surely I was native there, however long I had been absent ?

Across the uneven ground the woman came, with a light step. Nearer and nearer, but still I could not see whether her face was that of Liesl or Johanna.

Then Ramsay spoke, and the dream, or vision or whatever it was, lost its compelling quality. But I know that not later than tomorrow I must know what face the woman wore, and which woman is to be my guide to the treasure that is mine.

WORLD OF WONDERS

Contents

I

A Bottle in the Smoke

I

'Of course he was a charming man. A delightful person. Who has ever questioned it? But not a great magician.'

'By what standard do you judge?'

'Myself. Who else?'

'You consider yourself a greater magician than Robert-Houdin?'

'Certainly. He was a fine illusionist. But what is that? A man who depends on a lot of contraptions – mechanical devices, clockwork, mirrors, and such things. Haven't we been working with that sort of rubbish for almost a week? Who made it? Who reproduced that *Pâtissier du Palais-Royal* we've been fiddling about with all day? I did. I'm the only man in the world who could do it. The more I see of it the more I despise it.'

'But it is delightful! When the little baker brings out his bonbons, his patisseries, his croissants, his glasses of port and Marsala, all at the word of command, I almost weep with pleasure! It is the most moving reminiscence of the spirit of the age of Louis Philippe! And you admit that you have reproduced it precisely as it was first made by Robert-Houdin. If he was not a great magician, what do you call a great magician?'

'A man who can stand stark naked in the midst of a crowd and keep it gaping for an hour while he manipulates a few coins, or cards, or billiard balls. I can do that, and I can do it better than anybody today or anybody who has ever lived. That's why I'm tired of Robert-Houdin and his Wonderful Bakery and his

Inexhaustible Punch Bowl and his Miraculous Orange Tree and all the rest of his wheels and cogs and levers and fancy junk.'

'But you're going to complete the film?'

'Of course. I've signed a contract. I've never broken a contract in my life. I'm a professional. But I'm bored with it. What you're asking me to do is like asking Rubinstein to perform on a player-piano. Given the apparatus anybody could do it.'

'You know of course that we asked you to make this film simply because you are the greatest magician in the world – the greatest magician of all time, if you like – and that gives tremendous added attraction to our film –'

'It's been many years since I was called an added attraction.'

'Let me finish, please. We are presenting a great magician of today doing honour to a great magician of the past. People will love it.'

'It shows me at a disadvantage.'

'Oh, surely not. Consider the audience. After we have shown this on the B.B.C. it will appear on a great American network – the arrangements are almost complete – and then it will go all over the world. Think how it will be received in France alone, where there is still a great cult of Robert-Houdin. The eventual audience will be counted in millions. Can you be indifferent to that?'

'That just shows what you think about magic, and how much you know about it. I've already been seen all over the world. And I mean *I've been seen*, and the unique personal quality of my performance has been felt by audiences with whom I've created a unique relationship. You can't do that on television.'

'That is precisely what I expect to do. I don't want to speak boastfully. Perhaps we have had enough boasting here tonight. But I am not unknown as a film-maker. I can say without immodesty that I'm just as famous in my line as you are in yours. I am a magician too, and not a trivial one –'

'If my work is trivial, why do you want my help? Film – yes, of course it's a commonplace nowadays that it is an art, just as people used to say that Robert-Houdin's complicated automatic toys were art. People are always charmed by clever mechanisms that give an effect of life. But don't you remember what the little actor in Noel Coward's play called film? "A cheesy photograph".'

'Please –'

'Very well, let's not insist on "cheesy". But we can't escape "photograph". Something is missing, and you know what it is: the inexplicable but beautifully controlled sympathy between the artist and his audience. Film isn't even as good as the player-piano; at least you could add something personal to that, make it go fast or slow, loud or soft as you pleased.'

'Film is like painting, which is also unchanging. But each viewer brings his personal sensibility, his unique response to the completed canvas as he does to the film.'

'Who are your television viewers? Ragtag and bobtail; drunk and sober; attentive or in a nose-picking stupor. With the flabby concentration of people who are getting something for nothing. I am used to audiences who come because they want to see *me*, and have paid to do it. In the first five minutes I have made them attentive as they have never been before in their lives. I can't guarantee to do that on TV. I can't see my audience, and what I can't see I can't dominate. And what I can't dominate I can't enchant, and humour, and make partners in their own deception.

'You must understand that that is where my art comes in. I am your audience, and I contain in myself all these millions of whom we speak. You satisfy me and you satisfy them, as well. Because I credit them with my intelligence and sensitivity and raise them to my level. Have I not shown it in more than a dozen acknowledged film masterpieces? This is my gift and my art. Trust me. That is what I am asking you to do. Trust me.'

2

THIS was the first serious quarrel since we had begun filming. Should I say 'we'? As I was living in the house, and extremely curious about everything connected with the film, they let me hang around while they worked, and even gave me a job; as an historian I kept an eye on detail and did not allow the film-makers to stray too far from the period of Louis Philippe and his Paris, or at least no farther than artistic licence and necessity allowed. I had foreseen a quarrel. I was not seventy-two years old for nothing, and I knew Magnus Eisengrim very well. I thought I was beginning to know a little about the great director Jurgen Lind, too.

The project was to make an hour-long film for television about the great French illusionist, Jean-Eugène Robert-Houdin, who died in 1871. It was not simply to mark this centenary; as Lind had said, it would doubtless make the rounds of world television for years. The title was *Un Hommage à Robert-Houdin* – easily translatable – and its form was simple; the first twelve minutes were taken up with the story of his early life, as he told it in his *Confidences d'un prestidigitateur*, and for this actors had been employed; the remainder of the hour was to be an historical reproduction of one of Robert-Houdin's *Soirées Fantastiques* as he gave it in his own theatre in the Palais-Royal. And to play the part of the great conjuror the film-makers and the British Broadcasting Corporation had engaged, at a substantial fee, the greatest of living conjurors, my old friend Magnus Eisengrim.

If they had filmed it in a studio, I do not suppose I should have been involved at all, but the reproduction of Robert-Houdin's performance demanded so much magical apparatus, including several splendid automata which Eisengrim had made particularly for it, that it was decided to shoot this part of the picture in Switzerland, at Sorgenfrei, where Eisengrim's stage equipment was stored in a large disused riding-school on the estate. It was not a difficult matter for the scene designers and artificers to fit Robert-Houdin's tiny theatre, which had never seated more than two hundred spectators, into the space that was available.

This may have been a bad idea, for it mixed professional and domestic matters in a way that could certainly cause trouble. Eisengrim lived at Sorgenfrei, as permanent guest and – in a special sense – the lover of its owner and mistress, Dr Liselotte Naegeli. I also had retired to Sorgenfrei after I had my heart attack, and dwelt there very happily as the permanent guest and – in a special sense – the lover of the same Dr Liselotte, known to us both as Liesl. When I use the word 'lover' to describe our relationship, I do not mean that we were a farcical *ménage à trois*, leaping in and out of bed at all hours and shrieking comic recriminations at one another. We did occasionally share a bed (usually at breakfast, when it was convenient and friendly for us all three to tuck up together and sample things from one another's trays), but the athleticism of love was a thing of the past for me, and I suspect it was becoming an infrequent adventure for Eisengrim. We loved Liesl none the less – indeed rather more, and differently – than in our hot days, and what with loving and arguing and laughing and talking, we fleeted the time carelessly, as they did in the Golden World.

Even the Golden World may have welcomed a change, now and then, and we had been pleased when Magnus received his offer from the B.B.C. Liesl and I, who knew more about the world, or at least the artistic part of it, than Eisengrim, were excited that the film was to be directed by the great Jurgen Lind, the Swedish film-maker whose work we both admired. We wanted to meet him, for though we were neither of us naive people we had not wholly lost our belief that it is delightful to meet artists who have given us pleasure. That was why Liesl proposed that, although the film crew were living at an inn not far down the mountain from Sorgenfrei, Lind and one or two of his immediate entourage should dine with us as often as they pleased, ostensibly so that we could continue discussion of the film as it progressed, but really so that we could become acquainted with Lind.

We should have known better. Had we learned nothing from our experience with Magnus Eisengrim, who had a full share, a share pressed down and overflowing, of the egotism of the theatre artist? Who could not bear the least slight; who expected, as of right, to be served first at table, and to go through all doors first; who made the most unholy rows and fusses if he were not treated virtually as royalty? Lind had not been on the spot a day before we knew that he was just such another as our dear old friend Magnus, and that they were not going to hit it off together.

Not that Lind was like him in external things. He was modest, reticent, dressed like a workman, and soft of speech. He always hung back at doors, cared nothing for the little ceremonials of daily life in a rich woman's house, and conferred with his chief colleagues about every detail. But it was clear that he expected and got his own way, once he had determined what it was.

Moreover, he seemed to me to be formidably intelligent. His long, sad, unsmiling face, with its hanging underlip that showed long, yellow teeth, the tragedy line of his eyelids, which began high on the bridge of his nose and swept miserably downward toward his cheeks, and the soft, bereaved tone of his voice, suggested a man who had seen too much to be amused by life; his great height – he was a little over six feet eight inches – gave him the air of a giant mingling with lesser creatures about whom he knew some unhappy secret which was concealed from themselves; he spoke slowly in an elegant English only slightly marked by that upper-class Swedish accent which suggests a man delicately sucking a lemon. He had been extensively educated – his junior assistants all were careful to speak to him as Dr Lind – and he had as well that theatre artist's quality of seeming to know a great deal, without visible study or effort, about whatever was necessary for his immediate work. He did not know as much about the politics and economics of the reign of Louis Philippe as I did, for after all I had given my life to the study of history; but he seemed to know a great deal about its music, the way its clothes ought to be worn, the demeanour of its people, and its quality of life and spirit, which belonged to a sensibility far beyond mine. When historians meet with this kind of informed, imaginative sympathy with a past era in a non-historian, they are awed. How on earth does he know that, they are forced to ask themselves, and why did I never tumble to that? It takes a while to discover that the knowledge, though impressive and useful, has its limitations, and when the glow of imaginative creation no longer suffuses it, it is not really deeply grounded. But Lind was at work on the era of Louis Philippe, and specifically on the tiny part of it that applied to Robert-Houdin the illusionist, and for the present I was strongly under his spell.

That was the trouble. To put it gaudily but truly, that was where the canker gnawed. Liesl and I were both under Lind's spell, and Eisengrim's nose was out of joint.

That was why he was picking a quarrel with Lind, and Lind, who had been taught to argue logically, though unfairly, was at a disadvantage with a man who simply argued – pouted, rather – to get his own way and be cock of the walk again.

I thought I should do something about it, but I was forestalled by Roland Ingestree.

He was the man from the B.B.C., the executive producer of the film, or whatever the proper term is. He managed all the business, but was not simply a man of business, because he brooded, in a well-bred, don't-think-I'm-interfering-but manner, over the whole venture, including its artistic side. He was a sixtyish, fattish, bald Englishman who always wore gold-rimmed half-glasses, which gave him something of the air of Mr Pickwick. But he was a shrewd fellow, and he had taken in the situation.

'We mustn't delude ourselves, Jurgen,' he said. 'Without Eisengrim this film would be nothing – nothing at all. He is the only man in the world who can reproduce the superlatively complex Robert-Houdin automata. It is quite understandable that he looks down on achievements that baffle lesser beings like ourselves. After all, as he points out, he is a magnificent classical conjuror, and he hasn't much use for mechanical toys. That's understood, of course. But what I think we've missed is that he's an actor of the rarest sort; he can really give us the outward form of Robert-Houdin, with all that refinement of manner and perfection of grace that made Robert-Houdin great. How he can do it, God alone knows, but he can. When I watch him in rehearsal I am utterly convinced that a man of the first half of the nineteenth century stands before me. Where could we have found anyone else who can act as he is acting? John? Too tall, too subjective. Larry? Too flamboyant, too corporeal. Guinness? Too dry. There's nobody else, you see. I hope I'm not being offensive, but I think it's as an actor we must think of Eisengrim. The conjuring might have been faked. But the acting – tell me, frankly, who else is there that could touch him?'

He was not being offensive, and well he knew it. Eisengrim glowed, and all might have been well if Kinghovn had not pushed the thing a little farther. Kinghovn was Lind's cameraman, and I gathered he was a great artist in his own right. But he was a man whose whole world was dominated by what he could see, and make other people see, and words were not his medium.

'Roly is right, Jurgen. This man is just right for looks. He compels belief. He can't go wrong. It is God's good luck, and we mustn't quarrel with it.'

Now Lind's nose was out of joint. He had been trying to placate a prima donna, and his associates seemed to be accusing him of underestimating the situation. He was sure that he never underestimated anything about one of his films. He was accused of flying in the face of good luck, when he was certain that the best possible luck that could happen to any film was that he should be asked to direct it. The heavy lip fell a little lower, the eyes became a little sadder, and the emotional temperature of the room dropped perceptibly.

Ingestree put his considerable talents to the work of restoring Lind's self-esteem, without losing Eisengrim's goodwill.

'I think I sense what troubles Eisengrim about this whole Robert-Houdin business. It's the book. It's that wretched *Confidences d'un prestidigitateur*. We've been using it as a source for the biographical part of the film, and it's certainly a classic of its kind. But did anybody ever read such a book? Vanity is perfectly acceptable in an artist. Personally, I wouldn't give you sixpence for an artist who lacked vanity. But it's honest vanity I respect. The false modesty, the exaggerated humility, the greasy bourgeois assertions of respectability, of good-husband-and-father, of debt-paying worthiness are what make the *Confidences* so hard to swallow. Robert-Houdin was an oddity; he was an artist who wanted to pass as a bourgeois. I'm sure that's what irritates both you men, and sets you against each other. You feel that you are putting your very great, fully realized artistic personalities to the work of exalting a man whose attitude toward life you despise. I don't blame you for being irritable – because you have been, you know; you've been terribly irritable tonight – but that's what art is, as you very well know, much of the time: the transformation and glorification of the commonplace.'

'The revelation of the glory in the commonplace,' said Lind, who had no objection to being told that his vanity was an admirable and honest trait, and was coming around.

'Precisely. The revelation of the glory in the commonplace. And you two very great artists – the great film director and (may I say it) the great actor – are revealing the glory in Robert-Houdin, who perversely sought to conceal his own artistry behind that terrible good-citizen mask. It hampered him, of course, because it was against the grain of his talent. But you two are able to do an extraordinary, a metaphysical thing. You are able to show the world, a century after his death, what Robert-Houdin would have been if he had truly understood himself.'

Eisengrim and Lind were liking this. Magnus positively beamed, and Lind's sad eyes rolled toward him with a glance from which the frost was slowly disappearing. Ingestree was well in the saddle now, and was riding on to victory.

'You are both men of immeasurably larger spirit than he. What was he, after all? The good citizen, the perfection of the bourgeoisie under Louis Philippe that he pretended? Who can believe it? There is in every artist something black, something savouring of the crook, which he may not even understand himself, and which he certainly keeps well out of the eye of his public. What was it in Robert-Houdin?

'He gives us a sniff of it in the very first chapter of his other book, which I have read, and which is certainly familiar to you, Mr Ramsay' – this with a nod to me – ' called *Les Secrets de la prestidigitation et de la magie* –'

'My God, I read it as a boy!' I said.

'Very well. Then you recall the story of his beginnings as a magician? How he was befriended by the Count de l'Escalopier? How this nobleman gave a private show in his house, where Robert-Houdin amused the guests? How his best trick was burning a piece of paper on which the Archbishop of Paris had written a splendid compliment to Robert-Houdin, and the discovery of the piece of paper afterward in the smallest of twelve envelopes which were all sealed, one inside the other? It was a trick he learned from his master, de Grisy. But how did he try to make it up to l'Escalopier for putting him on his feet?'

'The trap for the robber,' I said.

'Exactly. A thief was robbing l'Escalopier blind, and nothing he tried would catch him. So Robert-Houdin offered to help, and what did he do? He worked out a mechanism to be concealed in the Count's desk, so that when the robber opened it a pistol would be discharged, and a claw made of sharp needles would seize the thief's hand and crunch the word 'Voleur' on the back of it. The needles were impregnated with silver nitrate, so that it was in effect tattooing – branding the man for life. A nice fellow, eh? And do you remember what he says? That this nasty thing was a refinement of a little gubbins he had made as a boy, to catch and mark another boy who was pinching things from his school locker. That was the way Robert-Houdin's mind worked; he fancied himself as a thief-catcher. Now, in a man who makes such a parade of his integrity, what does that suggest? Over-compensation, shall we say? A deep, unresting doubt of his own honesty?

'If we had time, and the gift, we could learn a lot about the inner life of Robert-Houdin by analysing his tricks. Why are so many of the best of them concerned with giving things away? He gave away pastries, sweets, ribbons, fans, all sorts of stuff at every performance; yet we know how careful he was with money. What was all that generosity meant to conceal? Because he was concealing something, take my word for it. The whole of the *Confidences* is a gigantic whitewash job, a concealment. Analyse the tricks and you will get a subtext for the autobiography, which seems so delightfully bland and cosy.

'And that's what we need for our film. A subtext. A reality running like a subterranean river under the surface; an enriching, but not necessarily edifying, background to what is seen.

'Where are we to get it? Not from Robert-Houdin. Too much trouble and perhaps not worth the trouble when we got it. No. It must come from the working together of you two great artists : Lind the genius-director and Eisengrim the genius-actor. And you must fish it up out of your own guts.'

'But that is what I always do,' said Lind.

'Of course. But Eisengrim must do it, as well. Now tell me, sir : you can't always have been the greatest conjuror in the world. You learned your art somewhere. If we asked you – invited you – begged you – to make your own experience the subtext for this film about a man, certainly lesser than yourself, but of great and lasting fame in his special line, what would it be?'

I was surprised to see Eisengrim look as if he were considering this question very seriously. He never revealed anything about his past life, or his innermost thoughts, and it was only because I had known him – with very long intervals of losing him – since we had been boys together, that I knew anything about him at all. I had fished – fished cunningly with the subtlest lures I could devise – for more information about him than I had, but he was too clever for me. But here he was, swimming in the flattery of this clever Englishman Ingestree, and he looked as if he might be about to spill the beans. Well, anyhow I would be present when, and if, he did so. After some consideration, he spoke.

'The first thing I would tell you would be that my earliest instructor was the man you see in that chair yonder: Dunstan Ramsay. God knows he was the worst conjuror the world has ever seen, but he introduced me to conjuring, and by a coincidence his textbook was *The Secrets of Stage Conjuring*, by the man we are all talking about and, if you are right in what you say, Mr Ingestree, serving! Robert-Houdin.'

This caused some sensation, as Eisengrim knew it would. Ingestree, having forced the oyster to yield a little, pressed the knife in.

'Wonderful! We would never have taken Ramsay for a conjuror. But there must have been somebody else. If Ramsay was your first master, who was your second?'

'I'm not sure I'm going to tell you,' said Eisengrim. 'I'll have to think about it very carefully. Your idea of a subtext – the term and the idea are both new to me – is interesting. I'll tell you this much. I began to learn conjuring seriously on 30 August 1918. That was the day I descended into hell, and did not rise again for seven years. I'll consider whether I'm going to go farther than that. Now I'm going to bed.'

3

LIESL had said little during the quarrel – or rivalry of egotisms, or whatever you choose to call it – but she caught me the following morning before the film crew arrived, and seemed to be in high spirits.

'So Magnus has come to the confessional moment in his life,' she said. 'It's been impending for several months. Didn't you notice? You didn't! Oh, Ramsay, you are such a dunce about some things. If Magnus were the kind of man who could write an autobiography, this is when he would do it.'

'Magnus has an autobiography already. I should know. I wrote it.'

'A lovely book. *Phantasmata: the Life and Adventures of Magnus Eisengrim*. But that was for sale at his performance; a kind of super-publicity. A splendid Gothic invention from your splendid Gothic imagination.'

'That's not the way he regards it. When people ask he tells them that it is a poetic autobiography, far more true to the man he has become than any merely factual account of his experience could be.'

'I know. I told him to say that. You don't suppose he thought it out himself, do you? You know him. He's marvellously intelligent in his own way – sensitive, aware, and intuitive – but it's not a literary or learned intelligence. Magnus is a truly original creature. They are of the greatest rarity. And as I say, he's reached the confessional time of life. I expect we shall hear some strange things.'

'Not as strange as I could tell about him.'

'I know, I know. You are obsessed with the idea that his mother was a saint. Ramsay, in all your rummaging among the lives of the saints, did you ever encounter one who had a child? What was that child like? Perhaps we shall hear.'

'I'm a little miffed that he considers telling these strangers things he's never told to you and me.'

'Ass! It's always strangers who turn the tap that lets out the truth. Didn't you yourself babble out all the secrets of your life to me within a couple of weeks of our first meeting? Magnus is going to tell.'

'But why, now?'

'Because he wants to impress Lind. He's terribly taken with Lind, and he has his little fancies, like the rest of us. Once he wanted to impress me, but it wasn't the right time in his life to spill the whole bottle.'

'But Ingestree suggested that Lind might do some telling, too. Are we to have a great mutual soul-scrape?'

'Ingestree is very foxy, behind all that fat and twinkling bonhomie. He knows Lind won't tell anything. For one thing, it's not his time; he's only forty-three. And he is inhibited by his education; it makes people cagey. What he tells us he tells through his films, just as Ingestree suggested that Robert-Houdin revealed himself through his tricks. But Magnus is retired – or almost. Also he is not inhibited by education, which is the great modern destroyer of truth and originality. Magnus knows no history. Have you ever seen him read a book? He really thinks that whatever has happened to him is unique. It is an enviable characteristic.'

'Well, every life is unique.'

'To a point. But there are only a limited number of things a human creature can do.'

'So you think he is going to tell all?'

'Not all. Nobody tells that. Indeed, nobody knows everything about themselves. But I'll bet you anything you like he tells a great deal.'

I argued no further. Liesl is very shrewd about such things. The morning was spent in arrangements about lighting. A mobile generator from Zürich had to be put in place, and all the lamps connected and hung; the riding-school was a jungle of pipe-scaffolding and cable. Kinghovn fussed over differences which seemed to me imperceptible, and as a script-girl stood in for Eisengrim while the lighting was being completed, he had time to wander about the riding-school, and as lunchtime approached he steered me off into a corner.

'Tell me about subtext,' he said.

'It's a term modern theatre people are very fond of. It's what a character thinks and knows, as opposed to what the play-wright makes him say. Very psychological.'

'Give me an example.'

'Do you know Ibsen's *Hedda Gabler*?'

He didn't, and it was a foolish question. He didn't know anything about any literature whatever. I waded in.

'It's about a beautiful and attractive woman who has mar-ried, as a last resort, a man she thinks very dull. They have returned from a honeymoon during which she has become greatly disillusioned with him, but she knows she is already pregnant. In the first act she is talking to her husband's adoring aunt, trying to be civil as the old woman prattles on about the joys of domesticity and the achievements of her nephew. But all the time she has, in her mind, the knowledge that he is dull, timid, a tiresome lover, that she is going to have a child by him, and that she fears childbirth. That's the subtext. The awareness of it thickens up the actress's performance, and emphasizes the irony of the situation.'

'I understand. It seems obvious.'

'First-rate actors have always been aware of it, but dramatists like Shakespeare usually brought the subtext up to the surface and gave it to the audience directly. Like Hamlet's soliloquies.'

'I've never seen *Hamlet*.'

'Well – that's subtext.'

'Do you think the circumstances of my own life really form a subtext for this film?'

'God only knows. One thing is certain : unless you choose to tell Lind and his friends about your life, it can't do so.'

'You're quite wrong. I would know, and I suppose whatever I do is rooted in what I am, and have been.'

It was never wise to underestimate Magnus, but I was always doing so. The pomposity of the learned. Because he didn't know *Hamlet* and *Hedda* I tended to think him simpler than he was.

'I'm thinking of telling them a few things, Dunny. I might surprise them. They're all so highly educated, you know. Edu-cation is a great shield against experience. It offers so much, ready-made and all from the best shops, that there's a tempta-tion to miss your own life in pursuing the lives of your betters. It makes you wise in some ways, but it can make you a blindfolded fool in others. I think I'll surprise them. They talk so much about art, but really, education is just as much a barrier between a man and real art as it is in other parts of life. They don't know what a mean old bitch art can be. I think I'll surprise them.'

So Liesl had been right! He was ready to spill.

Well, I was ready to hear. Indeed, I was eager to hear. My reason was deep and professional. As an historian I had all my life been aware of the extraordinary importance of documents. I had handled hundreds of them: letters, reports, memoranda, sometimes diaries; I had always treated them with respect, and had come in time to have an affection for them. They summed up something tnat was becoming increasingly important to me, and that was an earthly form of immortality. Historians come and go, but the document remains, and it has the importance of a thing that cannot be changed or gainsaid. Whoever wrote it continues to speak through it. It might be honest and it might be complete: on the other hand it could be thoroughly crooked or omit something of importance. But there it was, and it was all succeeding ages possessed.

I deeply wanted to create, or record, and leave behind me a document, so that whenever its subject was dealt with in future, the notation 'Ramsay says ...' would have to appear. Thus, so far as this world is concerned, I should not wholly die. Well, here was my chance.

Would anyone care? Indeed they would. I had written an imaginative account of the life of Magnus Eisengrim, the great conjuror and illusionist, at his own request and that of Liesl, who had been the manager and in a very high degree the brains of his great show, the *Soirée of Illusions*. The book was sold in the foyers of any theatre in which he appeared, but it had also had a flattering success on its own account; it sold astonishingly in the places where the really big sales of books are achieved – cigar stores, airports, and bus stops. It had extravagantly outsold all my other books, even my *Hundred Saints for Travellers* and my very popular *Celtic Saints of Britain and Europe*. Why? Because it was a wonderfully good book of its kind. Readable by the educated, but not rebuffing to somebody who simply wanted a lively, spicy tale.

Its authorship was still a secret, for although I received a half-share of the royalties it was ostensibly the work of Magnus Eisengrim. It had done great things for him. People who believed what they read came to see the man who had lived the richly adventurous and macabre life described in it; sophisticates came to see the man who had written such gorgeous, gaudy lies about himself. As Liesl said, it was Gothic, full of enormities bathed in the delusive lights of nineteenth-century romance. But it was modern enough, as well; it touched the sexy, rowdy string so many readers want to hear.

Some day it would be known that I had written it. We had already received at Sorgenfrei a serious film offer and a number of inquiries from earnest Ph.D. students who explained apologetically that they were making investigations, of one kind or another, of what they called 'popular literature'. And when it became known that I had written it, which would probably not be until Eisengrim and I were both dead, then – Aha! then my document would come into its own. For then the carefully tailored life of Magnus Eisengrim, which had given pleasure to so many millions in English, French, German, Danish, Italian, Spanish, and Portuguese, and had been accorded the distinction of a pirated version in Japanese, would be compared with the version I would prepare from Eisengrim's own confessions, and 'Ramsay says . . .' would certainly be heard loud and clear.

Was this a base ambition for an historian and a hagiologist? What had Ingestree said? In every artist there is something black, something savouring of the crook. Was I, in a modest way, an artist? I was beginning to wonder. No, no; unless I falsified the record what could be dishonest, or artistic, about making a few notes?

4

'I HAVE spent a good deal of time since last night wondering whether I should tell you anything about my life,' said Eisengrim, after dinner that evening, 'and I think I shall, on the condition that you regard it as a secret among ourselves. After all, the audience doesn't have to know the subtext, does it? Your film isn't Shakespeare, where everything is revealed; it is Ibsen, where much is implied.'

How quickly he learns, I thought. And how well he knows the power of pretending something is secret which he has every intention of revealing. I turned up my mental, wholly psychological historian's hearing-aid, determined to miss nothing, and to get at least the skeleton of it on paper before I went to sleep.

'Begin with going to hell,' said Ingestree. 'You've given us a date: 30 August 1918. You told us you knew Ramsay when you were a boy, so I suppose you must be a Canadian. If I were going to hell, I don't think I'd start from Canada. What happened?'

'I went to the village fair. Our village, which was called Deptford, had a proud local reputation for its fair. Schoolchildren were admitted free. That helped to swell the attendance, and the Fair Board liked to run up the biggest possible annual figure. You wouldn't imagine there was anything wrong in what I did, but judged by the lights of my home it was sin. We were an unusually religious household, and my father mistrusted the fair. He had promised me that he might, if I could repeat the whole of Psalm 79 without an error, at suppertime, take me to the fair in the evening, to see the animals. This task of memorizing was part of a great undertaking that he had set his heart on: I was to get the whole of the Book of Psalms by heart. He assured me that it would be a bulwark and a stay to me through the whole of my life. He wasn't rushing the job; I was supposed to learn ten verses each day, but as I was working for a treat, he thought I might run to the thirteen verses of Psalm 79 to get to the fair. But the treat was conditional; if I stumbled, the promise about the fair was off.'

'It sounds very much like rural Sweden, when I was a boy,' said Kinghovn. 'How do the children of such people grow up?'

'Ah, but you mustn't misunderstand. My father wasn't a tyrant; he truly wanted to protect me against evil.'

'A fatal desire in a parent,' said Lind, who was known throughout the world – to film-goers at least – as an expert on evil.

'There was a special reason. My mother was an unusual person. If you want to know the best about her, you must apply to

Ramsay. I don't suppose I can tell you my own story without giving you something of the other side of her nature. She was supposed to have some very bad instincts, and our family suffered for it. She had to be kept under confinement. My father, with what I suppose must be described as compassion, wanted to make sure I wouldn't follow in her ways. So, from the age of eight, I was set to work to acquire the bulwark and the stay of the Psalms, and in a year and a half – something like that – I had gnawed my way through them up to Psalm 79.'

'How old were you?' said Ingestree.

'Getting on for ten. I wanted fiercely to go to the fair, so I set to work on the Psalm. Do you know the Psalms? I have never been able to make head or tail of a lot of them, but others strike with a terrible truth on your heart, if you meet them at the right time. I plugged on till I came to *We are become a reproach to our neighbours, a scorn and derision to them that are round about us.* Yes! Yes, there we were! The Dempsters, a reproach to our neighbours, a scorn and derision to the whole village of Deptford. And particularly to the children of Deptford, with whom I had to go to school. School was to begin on the day after Labour Day, less than a week from the day when I sat puzzling over Psalm 79. Tell me, Lind, you know so much about evil, and have explored it in your films, Liesl tells me, like a man with an ordnance map in his hand; have you ever explored the evil of children?'

'Even I have never dared to do that,' said Lind, with the tragic grin which was the nearest he ever came to a laugh.

'If you ever decide to do so, call me in as a special adviser. It's a primal evil, a pure malignance. They really enjoy giving pain. This is described by sentimentalists as innocence. I was tormented by the children of our village from the earliest days I can remember. My mother had done something – I never found out what it was – that made most of the village hate her, and the children knew that, so it was all right to hate me and torture me. They said my mother was a hoor – that was the local pronunciation of whore – and they tormented me with a virtuosity they never showed in anything else they did. When I cried, somebody might say, "Aw, let the kid alone; he can't help it his mother's a hoor." I suppose the philosopher-kings who struggled up to that level have since become the rulers of the place. But I soon determined not to cry.

'Not that I became hard. I simply accepted the wretchedness of my station. Not that I hated them – not then; I learned to hate them later in life. At that time I simply assumed that children must be as they were. I was a misfit in the world, and didn't know why.

'Onward I went with Psalm 79. *O remember not against us former iniquities: let thy tender mercies speedily prevent us: for we are brought very low.* But as soon as I put my nose into the schoolyard they would remember former iniquities against me. God's tender mercies had never reached the Deptford school-yard. And I was unquestionably brought very low, for all that desolation would begin again next Tuesday.

'Having got that far with me, Satan had me well on the path to hell. I knew where some money was kept; it was small change for the baker and the milkman when they called; under my mother's very nose – she was sitting in a chair, staring into space, tied by a rope to a ringbolt my father had set in the wall – I pinched fifteen cents; I held it up so that she could see it, so that she would think I was going to pay one of the delivery-men. Then I ran off to the fair, and my heart was full of terrible joy. I was wicked, but O what a delicious release it was!

'I pieced out the enjoyment of the fair like a gourmet savouring a feast. Begin at the bottom, with what was least amusing. That would be the Women's Institute display of bottled pickles, embalmed fruit, doilies, home-cooking, and "fancy-work". Then the animals, the huge draught-horses, the cows with enormous udders, the prize bull (though I did not go very near to him, for some of my schoolmates were lingering there, to snigger and work themselves up into a horny stew, gaping at his enormous testicles), the pigs so unwontedly clean, and the foolish poultry, White Wyandottes, Buff Orpingtons, and Mrs Forrester's gorgeous Cochin Chinas, and in a corner a man from the Department of Agriculture giving an educational display of egg-candling.

'Pleasure now began to be really intense. I looked with awe and some fear at the display from the nearby Indian Reservation. Men with wrinkled, tobacco-coloured faces sat behind a stand, not really offering slim walking-canes, with ornate whittled handles into which patterns of colour had been worked; their women, as silent and unmoving as they, displayed all sorts of fancy boxes made of sweet-grass, ornamented with beads an^d dyed porcupine quill. But these goods, which had some merit a. craftwork, were not so gorgeous in my eyes as the trash offered by a booth which was not of local origin, in which a man sold whirligigs of gaudy celluloid, kewpie dolls with tinsel skirts riding high over their gross stomachs, alarm-clocks with two bells for determined sleepers, and beautiful red or blue pony-whips. I yearned toward those whips, but they cost a whole quarter apiece, and were thus out of my reach.

'But I was not cut off from all the carnal pleasures of the fair. After a great deal of deliberation I spent five of my ill-gotten cents on a large paper cornet of pink candy floss, a delicacy I had never seen before. It had little substance, and made my mouth sticky and dry, but it was a luxury, and my life had known nothing of luxuries.

'Then, after a full ten minutes of deliberation, I laid out another five cents on a ride on the merry-go-round. I chose my mount with care, a splendid dapple-grey with flaring nostrils, ramping wonderfully up and down on his brass pole; he seemed to me like the horse in Job that saith among the trumpets, Ha, ha; for a hundred and eighty seconds I rode him in ecstasy, and dismounted only when I was chased away by the man who took care of such things and was on the look-out for enchanted riders like myself.

'But even this was only leading up to what I knew to be the crown of the fair. That was Wanless's World of Wonders, the one pleasure which my father would certainly never have permitted me. Shows of all kinds were utterly evil in his sight, and this was a show that turned my bowels to water, even from the outside.

'The tent seemed vast to me, and on a scaffold on its outside were big painted pictures of the wonders within. A Fat Woman, immense and pink, beside whom even the biggest pigs in the agricultural tents were starvelings. A man who ate fire. A Strong Man, who would wrestle with anybody who dared to try it. A Human Marvel, half man and half woman. A Missing

Link, in itself worth more than the price of admission, because it was powerfully educational, illustrating what Man had been before he decided to settle in such places as Deptford. On a raised platform outside the tent a man in fine clothes was shouting to the crowd about everything that was to be seen; it was before the days of microphones, and he roared hoarsely through a megaphone. Beside him stood the Fire Eater, holding a flaming torch in front of his mouth. "See Molza, the man who can always be sure of a hot meal," bellowed the man in the fine clothes, and a few Deptfordians laughed shyly. "See Professor Spencer, born without arms, but he can write a finer hand with his feet than any of your schoolteachers. And within the tent the greatest physiological marvel of the age, Andro, the Italian nobleman so evenly divided between the sexes that you may see him shave the whiskers off the one side of his face, while the other displays the peachy smoothness of a lovely woman. A human miracle, attested to by doctors and men of science at Yale, Harvard, and Columbia. Any local doctor wishing to examine this greatest of marvels may make an appointment to do so, in the presence of myself, after the show tonight."

'But I was not very attentive to the man in the fine clothes, because my eyes were all for another figure on the platform, who was doing wonders with decks of cards; he whirled them out from his hands in what appeared to be ribbons, and then drew them – magically it seemed to me – back into his hands again. He spread them in fans. He made them loop-the-loop from one hand to another. The man in the fine clothes introduced him as Willard the Wizard, positively the greatest artist in sleight-of-hand in the world today, briefly on loan from the Palace Theater in New York.

'Willard was a tall man, and looked even taller because he wore what was then called a garter-snake suit, which had wriggling lines of light and dark fabric running perpendicularly through it. He was crowned by a pearl-grey hard hat – what we called a Derby, and known in Deptford only as part of the Sunday dress of doctors and other grandees. He was the most elegant thing I had ever seen in my life, and his thin, unsmiling face spoke to me of breathtaking secrets. I could not take my eyes off him, nor did I try to still my ravening desire to know

575

those secrets. I too was a conjuror, you see; I had continued, on the sly, to practise the few elementary sleights and passes I had learned from Ramsay, before my father put a stop to it. I longed with my whole soul to know what Willard knew. As the hart pants after the water brooks, even so my blasphemous soul panted after the Wizard. And the unbelievable thing was that, of the fifteen or twenty people gathered in front of the platform, he seemed to look most often at me, and once I could swear I saw him wink!

'I paid my five cents – a special price for schoolchildren until six o'clock – and entered in the full splendour of Wanless's World of Wonders. It is impossible for me to describe the impression it made on me then, because I came to know it so well later on. It was just a fair-sized tent, capable of holding ten or twelve exhibits and the spectators. It was of that discouraged whitey-grey colour that such tents used to be before somebody had the good idea of colouring canvas brown. A few strings of lights hung between the three main poles, but they were not on, because it was assumed that we could see well enough by the light that leaked in from outdoors. The exhibits were on stands the height of a table; indeed, they were like collapsible tables, and each exhibit had his own necessities. Professor Spencer had the blackboard on which he wrote so elegantly with his feet; Molza had his jet of flaming gas, and a rack to hold the swords he swallowed; it was really, I suppose, very tacky and ordinary. But I was under the spell of Willard, and I didn't, at that time, take much heed of anything else, not even of the clamorous Fat Woman, who seemed never to be wholly quiet, even when the other exhibits were having their turn.

'The loud-voiced man had followed us inside, and bellowed about each wonder as we toured round the circle. Even to such an innocent as I, it was plain that the wonders were shown in an ascending order of importance, beginning with the Knife Thrower and Molza, and working upward through Zovene the Midget Juggler and Sonny the Strong Man to Professor Spencer and Zitta the Serpent Woman. She seemed to mark a divide, and after her came Rango the Missing Link, then the Fat Woman, called Happy Hannah, then Willard, and finally Andro the Half-Man Half-Woman.

'Even though my eyes constantly wandered toward Willard, who seemed now and then to meet them with a dark and enchantingly wizard-like gaze, I was too prudent to ignore the lesser attractions. After all, I had invested five ill-gotten cents in this adventure, and I was in no position to throw money away. But we came to Willard at last, and the loud-voiced man did not need to introduce him, because even before Happy Hannah had finished her noisy harangue and had begun to sell pictures of herself, he threw away his cigarette, sprang to his feet, and began to pluck coins out of the air. He snatched them from everywhere – from the backs of his knees, from his elbows, from above his head – and threw them into a metal basin on his little tripod table. You could hear them clink as they fell, and as the number increased the sound from the basin changed. Then, without speaking a word, he seized the basin and hurled its contents into the crowd. People ducked and shielded their faces. But the basin was empty! Willard laughed a mocking laugh. Oh, very Mephistophelian! It sounded like a trumpet call to me, because I had never heard anybody laugh like that before. He was laughing at us, for having been deceived. What power! What glorious command over lesser humanity! Silly people often say that they are enraptured by something which has merely pleased them, but I was truly enraptured. I was utterly unaware of myself, whirled into a new sort of comprehension of life by what I saw.

'You must understand that I had never seen a conjuror before. I knew what conjuring was, and I could do some tricks. But I had never seen anybody else do sleight-of-hand except Ramsay here, who made very heavy weather of getting one poor coin from one of his great red hands to the other, and if he had not explained that the pass was supposed to be invisible you would never have known it was a trick at all. Please don't be hurt, Ramsay. You are a dear fellow and rather a famous writer in your own line, but as a conjuror you were abject. But Willard! For me the Book of Revelation came alive: here was an angel come down from heaven, having great power, and the earth was lightened with his glory; if only I could be like him, surely there would be no more sorrow, nor crying, nor any more pain, and all former things – my dark home, my mad, disgraceful mother, the torment of school – would pass away.'

'So you ran away with the show,' said Kinghovn, who had no tact.

'Ramsay tells me they say in Deptford that I ran away with the show,' said Eisengrim, smiling what I would myself have called a Mephistophelian smile, beneath which he looked like any other man whose story has been interrupted by somebody who doesn't understand the form and art of stories. 'I don't think Deptford would ever comprehend that it was not a matter of choice. But if you have understood what I have said about the way Deptford regarded me, you will realize that I had no choice. I did not run away with the show; the show ran away with me.'

'Because you were so utterly entranced by Willard?' said Ingestree.

'No, I think our friend means something more than that,' said Lind. 'These possessions of the soul are very powerful, but there must have been something else. I smell it. The Bible obsession must somehow have supported the obsession with the conjuror. Not even a great revelation wipes out a childhood's indoctrination; the two must have come together in some way.'

'You are right,' said Eisengrim. 'And I begin to see why people call you a great artist. Your education and sophistication haven't gobbled up your understanding of the realities of life. Let me go on.

'Willard's show had to be short, because there were ten exhibits in the tent, and a full show was not supposed to run over forty-five minutes. As one of the best attractions he was allowed something like five minutes, and after the trick with the coins he did some splendid things with ribbons, pulling them out of his mouth and throwing them into the bowl, from which he produced them neatly braided. Then he did some very flashy things with cards, causing any card chosen by a member of the audience to pop out of a pack that was stuck in a wine-glass as far away from himself as his platform allowed. He finished by eating a spool of thread and a packet of needles, and then producing the thread from his mouth, with all the needles threaded on it at intervals of six inches. During the Oohs and Aahs, he nonchalantly produced the wooden spool from his ear, and threw it into the audience – threw it so that I caught it. I remember being amazed that it wasn't even wet, which shows how very green I was.

'I didn't want to see Andro, whose neatly compartmentalized sexuality meant nothing to me. As the crowd moved on to hear the loud-mouthed man bellow about the medical miracle called hermaphroditism – *only one in four hundred million births, ladies and gentlemen, only six thoroughly proven hermaphrodites in the whole long history of mankind, and one of them stands before you in Deptford today!* – I hung around Willard's table. He leapt down from it and lighted another cigarette. Even the way he did that was magical, for he flicked the pack toward his mouth, and the cigarette leaped between his lips, waiting for the match he was striking with the thumbnail of his other hand. There I was, near enough to the Wizard to touch him. But it was he who touched me. He reached toward my left ear and produced a quarter from it, and flicked it toward me. I snatched it out of the air, and handed it back to him. "No, it's for you, kid," he said. His voice was low and hoarse, and not in keeping with the rest of his elegant presentation, but I didn't care. A quarter! For me! I had never known such riches in my life. My infrequent stealings had never, before this day, aspired beyond a nickel. The man was not only a Wizard; he was princely.

'I was inspired. Inspired by you, Ramsay, you may be surprised to hear. You remember your trick in which you pretended to eat money, though one could always see it in your hand as you took it away from your mouth? I did that. I popped the quarter into my mouth, chewed it up, showed Willard that it was gone, and that I had nothing in my hands. I could do a little magic, too, and I was eager to claim some kinship with this god.

'He did not smile. He put his hand on my shoulder and said, "Come with me, kid. I got sumpn to show ya," and steered me toward a back entry of the tent which I had not noticed.

'We walked perhaps halfway around the fairground, which was not really very far, and we kept behind tents and buildings. I would have been proud to be seen by the crowd with such a hero, but we met very few people, and they were busy with their own affairs in the agricultural tents, so I do not suppose anybody noticed us. We came to the back of the barn where the horses were stabled when they were not being shown; it was one of the two or three permanent buildings of the fair. Behind it was a lean-to with a wall which did not quite reach to the roof, nor fully to the ground. It was the men's urinal, old, dilapidated, and smelly. Willard peeped in, found it empty, and pushed me in ahead of him. I had never been in such a place before, because it was part of my training that one never "went" anywhere except at home, and all arrangements had to be made to accommodate this rule. It was a queer place, as I remember it; just a tin trough nailed to the wall, sloping slightly downward so that it drained into a hole in the ground. A pile of earth was ready to fill in the hole, once the fair was over.

At the end of this shanty was a door which hung partly open, and it was through this that Willard guided me. We were in an earth closet, as old as Deptford fair, I should judge, for a heavy, sweetish, old smell hung over it. Hornets buzzed under the sloping roof. The two holes in the seat were covered by rounds of wood, with crude handles. I think I would know them if I saw them now.

'Willard took a clean white handkerchief out of his pocket, twisted it quickly into a roll, and forced it between my teeth. No: I should not say "forced". I thought this was the beginning of some splendid illusion, and opened my mouth willingly. Then he whirled me round, lifted me up on the seat in a kneeling position, pulled down my pants and sodomized me.

'Quickly said: an eternity in the doing. I struggled and resisted: he struck me such a blow over the ear that I slackened my grip with the pain, and he had gained an entry. It was rough: it was painful, and I suppose it was soon over. But as I say, it seemed an eternity, for it was a kind of feeling I had never guessed at.

'I am anxious you should not misunderstand me. I was no Greek lad, discovering the supposed pleasures of pederastic love in a society that knew it and condoned it. I was a boy not yet quite ten years old, who did not know what sex was in any form. I thought I was being killed, and in a shameful way.

'The innocence of children is very widely misunderstood. Few of them – I suppose only children brought up in wealthy families that desire and can contrive a conspiracy of ignorance – are unknowing about sex. No child brought up so near the country as I was, and among schoolchildren whose ages might reach as high as fifteen or sixteen, can be utterly ignorant of sex. It had touched me, but not intimately. For one thing, I had heard the whole of the Bible read through several times by my father; he had a plan of readings which, pursued morning and evening, worked through the whole of the book in a year. I had heard the sound as an infant, and as a little child, long before I could understand anything of the sense. So I knew about men going in unto women, and people raising up seed of their loins, and I knew that my father's voice took on a special tone of shame and detestation when he read about Lot and his daughters, though I had never followed what it was they did in that cave, and thought their sin was to make their father drunk. I knew these things because I had heard them, but they had no reality for me.

'As for my mother, who was called hoor by my schoolmates, I knew only that hoors – my father used the local pronunciation, and I don't think he knew any other – were always turning up in the Bible, and always in a bad sense which meant nothing to me as a reality. Ezekiel, sixteen, was a riot of whoredoms and abominations, and I shivered to think how terrible they must be: but I did not know what they were, even in the plainest sense of the words. I only knew that there was something filthy and disgraceful that pertained to my mother, and that we all, my father and I, were spattered by her shame, or abomination, or whatever it might be.

'I was aware that there was some difference between boys and girls, but I didn't know, or want to know, what it was, because I connected it somehow with the shame of my mother. You couldn't be a hoor unless you were a woman, and they had something special that made it possible. What I had, as a male, I had most strictly been warned against as an evil and shameful part of my body. "Don't you ever monkey with yourself, down there," was the full extent of the sexual instruction I had from my father. I knew that the boys who were gloating over the bull's testicles were doing something dirty, and my training was such that I was both disgusted and terrified by their sly nastiness. But I didn't know why, and it never would have occurred to me to relate the bull's showy apparatus with those things I possessed, in so slight a degree, and which I wasn't to monkey with. So you can see that without being utterly ignorant, I was innocent, in my way. If I had not been innocent, how could I have lived my life, and even have felt some meagre joy, from time to time?

'Sometimes I felt that joy when I was with you, Ramsay, because you were kind to me, and kindness was a great rarity in my life. You were the only person in my childhood who had treated me as if I were a human creature. I don't say, who loved me, you notice. My father loved me, but his love was a greater burden, almost, than hate might have been. But you treated me as a fellow-being, because I don't suppose it ever occurred to you to do anything else. You never ran with the crowd.

'The rape itself was horrible, because it was painful physically, but worse because it was an outrage on another part of my body which I had been told to fear and be ashamed of. Liesl tells me that Freud has had a great deal to say about the importance of the functions of excretion in deciding and moulding character. I don't know anything about that; don't want to know it, because all that sort of thinking lies outside what I really understand. I have my own notions about psychology, and they have served me well. But this rape – it was something filthy going in where I knew only that filthy things should come out, as secretly as could be managed. In our house there was no word for excretion, only two or three prim locutions, and the word used in the schoolyard seemed to me a horrifying indecency. It's very popular nowadays in literature, I'm told by Liesl. She reads a great deal. I don't know how writers can put it down, though there was a time when I used it often enough in my daily speech. But as I have grown older I have returned to that early primness. We don't get over some things. But what Willard did to me was, in a sense I could understand, a reversal of the order of nature, and I was terrified that it would kill me.

'It didn't, of course. But that, and Willard's heavy breathing, and the flood of filthy language that he whispered as a kind of ecstatic accompaniment to what he was doing, were more horrible to me than anything I have met with since.

'When it was over he pulled my head around so that he could see my face and said. "You O.K., kid?" I can remember the tone now. He had no idea at all of what I was, or what I might feel. He was obviously happy, and the Mephistophelian smile had given place to an expression that was almost boyish. "Go on now," he said. "Pull up your pants and beat it. And if you blat to anybody, by the living Jesus I'll cut your nuts off with a rusty knife."

'Then I fainted, but for how long, or what I looked like when I did it, I of course can't tell you. Perhaps I was out for a few minutes, because when I became aware again Willard was look-ing anxious, and patting my cheeks lightly. He had taken the gag out of my mouth. I was crying, but making no noise. I had learned very early in life not to make a noise when I cried. I was still crumpled up on the horrible seat, and now its stench was too much for me and I vomited. Willard sprang back, anxious for his fine trousers and the high polish on his shoes. But he dared not leave me. Of course I had no idea how frightened he was. He felt he could trust in my shame and his threats up to a point, but I might be one of those terrible children who go beyond the point set for them by adults. He tried to placate me.

' "Hey," he whispered,"you're a pretty smart kid. Where'd you learn that trick with the quarter, eh? Come on now, show it to me again. I never seen a better trick than that, even at the Palace, New York. You're the kid that eats money; that's who you are. A real show-business kid. Now look, I'll give you this, if you'll eat it." He offered me a silver dollar. But I turned my face away, and sobbed, without sound.

' "Aw now, look, it wasn't as bad as that," he said. "Just some fun between us two. Just playing paw and maw, eh? You want to grow up to be smart, don't you? You want to have fun? Take it from me, kid, you can't start too young. The day'll come, you'll thank me. Yes, sir, you'll thank me. Now look here. I show you I've got nothing in my hands, see? Now watch.' He spread his fingers one by one, and magically quarters appeared between them until he held four quarters in each hand. "Magic money, see? All for you; two whole dollars if you'll shut up and get the hell outa here, and never say anything to anybody."

'I fainted again, and this time when I came round Willard was looking deeply worried. "What you need is rest," he said "Rest, and time to think about all that money. I've gotta get back for the next show, but you stay here, and don't let anybody in. Nobody, see? I'll come back as soon as I can and I'll bring you something. Something nice. But don't let anybody in, don't holler, and keep quiet like a mouse."

'He went, and I heard him pause for a moment outside the door. Then I was alone, and I sobbed myself to sleep.

'I did not wake until he came back, I suppose an hour later. He brought me a hot dog, and urged me to eat it. I took one bite – it was my first hot dog – and vomited again. Willard was now very worried indeed. He swore fiercely, but not at me. All he said to me was, "My God you're a crazy kid. Stay here. Now *stay* here, I tell ya. I'll come back as soon as I can."

'That was not very soon. Perhaps two hours. But when he came he had an air of desperation about him, which I picked up at once. Terrible things had happened, and terrible remedies must be found. He had brought a large blanket, and he wrapped me in it, so that not even my head was showing, and lugged me bodily – I was not very heavy – out of the privy; I felt myself dumped into what I suppose was the back of a buggy or a carry-all, or something, and other wraps were thrown over me. Off I went, bumping along in the back of the cart, and it was some time later that I felt myself lifted out again, carried over rough ground, and humped painfully up onto what seemed to be a platform. Then another painful business of being lugged over a floor, some sounds of objects being moved, and at last the blanket was taken off. I was in a dark place, and only vaguely conscious that some distance away a door, like the door of a shed, was open, and I could see the light of dusk through it.

'Willard lost no time. "Get in here," he commanded, and pushed me into a place that was entirely dark, and confined. I had to climb upward, boosted by him, until I came to what seemed to me a shelf, or seat, and on this he pushed me. "Now you'll be all right," he said, in a voice that carried no confidence at all that I would be all right. It was a desperate voice. "Here's something for you to eat." A box was pushed in beside me. Then a door below me was closed, and snapped from the outside, and I was in utter darkness.

'After a while I felt around me. Irregular walls, seeming to be curved everywhere; there was even a small dome over my head. A smell, not clean, but not as disgusting as the privy at the fair. A little fresh air from a point above my head. I fell asleep again.

'When I woke, it was because I heard the whistle of a train, and a train-like thundering near by. But I was not moving. I was wretchedly hungry, and in the darkness I explored Willard's box. Something lumpy and sticky inside it, which I tried to eat, and then greedily ate it all. Sleep again. Terrible fatigue all through my body, and the worst pain of all in my bottom. But I could not move very much in any direction, and I had to sit on my misery. At last, a space of time that seemed like a geological age later, I felt movement. Banging and thumping which went on for some time. A sound of voices. The sound of another whistle, and then trundling, lumbering movement, which increased to a good speed. For the first time in my life I was on a train, but of course I didn't know that.

'And that, my friends, is the first instalment of my subtext to the memoirs of Robert-Houdin, whose childhood, you recall, was such an idyll of family love and care, and whose introduction to magic was so charmingly brought about. Enough, I think, for one evening. Good-night.'

5

WHEN I made my way to bed, some time later, I tapped at Eisengrim's door. As I had expected, he was awake, and lay, looking very fine, against his pillows, wearing a handsome dressing-robe.

'Kind of you to come in and say good-night, Dunny.'

'I expected you'd be waiting up to see what your notices were.'

'A disgusting way of putting it. Well, what were they?'

'About what you'd expect. Kinghovn had a fine sense of the

appearance of everything. I'll bet that as you talked he had that fair all cut up into long shots, close-ups, and atmosphere shots. And of course he's a devil for detail. For one thing, he wondered why nobody wanted to use the privy while you were left in it for so long.'

'Simple enough. Willard wrote a note which said "INFECTION: Closed by Doctor's Order", and pinned it to the door.'

'Also he was anxious to know what it was you ate when you found yourself in the curious prison with the rounded walls.'

'It was a box of Cracker-Jack. I didn't know what it was at the time, and had never eaten it before. Why should I have included those details in my story? I didn't know them then. It would have been a violation of narrative art to tell things I didn't know. Kinghovn ought to have more sense of artistic congruity.'

'He's a cameraman. He wants to get a shot of everything, and edit later.'

'I edit as I go along. What did the others say?'

'Ingestree talked for quite a while about the nature of puritanism. He doesn't know anything about it. It's just a theological whimwham to him. He's talked about puritanism at Oxford to Ronny Knox and Monsignor D'Arcy, but that stuff means nothing in terms of the daily, bred-in-the-bone puritanism we lived in Deptford. North American puritanism and the puritanism the English know are worlds apart. I could have told him a thing or two about that, but my time for instructing people is over. Let 'em wallow in whatever nonsense pleases 'em, say I.'

'Did Lind have anything to say?'

'Not much. But he did say that nothing you told us was incomprehensible to him, or even very strange. "We know of such things in Sweden," he said.'

'I suppose people know of such things everywhere. But every rape is unique for the aggressor and the victim. He talks as if he knew everything.'

'I don't think he means it quite that way. When he talks about Sweden, I think it is a mystical rather than a geographical concept. When he talks of Sweden he means himself, whether he knows it or not. He really does understand a great deal. You remember what Goethe said? No, of course you don't. He said he'd never heard of a crime of which he could not believe himself capable. Same with Lind, I suppose. That's his strength as an artist.'

'He's a great man to work with. I think between us we'll do something extraordinary with this film.'

'I hope so. And by the way, Magnus, I must thank you for the very kind things you said about me tonight. But I assure you I didn't especially mean to be kind to you, when we were boys. I mean, it wasn't anything conscious.'

'I'm sure it wasn't. But that's the point, don't you see? If you'd done it out of duty, or for religious reasons, it would have been different. But it was just decency. You're a very decent man, Dunny.'

'Really? Well – it's nice of you to think so. I've heard dissenting opinions.'

'It's true. That's why I think you ought to know something I didn't see fit to tell them tonight.'

'You suggested you had been editing. What did you leave out?'

'One gets carried away, telling a story. I may have leaned a little too heavily on my character as the wronged child. But would they have understood the whole truth? I don't after fifty years when I have thought it over and over. You believe in the Devil, don't you?'

'In an extremely sophisticated way, which would take several hours to explain, I do.'

'Yes. Well, when the Devil is walking beside you, as he was walking beside me at that fair, it doesn't take a lot of argument to make him seem real.'

'I won't insult you by saying you're a simple man, but you're certainly a man of strong feeling, and your feelings take concrete shapes. What did the Devil do to you that you withheld when you were talking downstairs?'

'The whole nub of the story. When Willard gave me that quarter in the tent, we were standing behind the crowd, which was gaping at Andro who was showing his big right bicep while twitching his sumptuous left breast. Nobody was looking. Willard had slipped his hand down the back of my pants and gently stroked my left buttock. Gave it a meaning squeeze. I remember very well how warm his hand felt.'

'Yes?'

'I smiled up into his face.'

'Yes?'

'Is that all you have to say? Don't you see what I'm getting at? I had never had any knowledge of sex, had never known a sexual caress before, even of the kind parents quite innocently give their children. But at this first sexual approach I yielded. I cosied up to Willard. How could I, without any true understanding of what I was doing, respond in such a way to such a strange act?'

'You were mad to learn his magic. It doesn't seem very strange to me.'

'But it made me an accomplice in what followed.'

'You think that? And you still blame yourself?'

'What did I know of such things? I can only think it was the Devil prompting me, and pushing me on to what looked then, and for years after, like my own destruction.'

'The Devil isn't a popular figure nowadays. The people who take him seriously are few.'

'I know. How he must laugh. I don't suppose God laughs at the people who think He doesn't exist. He's above jokes. But the Devil isn't. That's one of his most endearing qualities. But I still remember that smile. I had never smiled like that before. It was a smile of complicity. Now where would such a child as I was learn such a smile as that?'

'From that other old joker, Nature, do you suppose?'

'I don't take much stock in Nature ... Thanks for coming in. Good-night, decent man.'

'Magnus, are you becoming sentimental in your old age?'

'I'm fully ten years younger than you, you sour Scot. Good-night, kind man.'

I went to my room, and to my bed, but it was a long time before I slept. I lay awake, thinking about the Devil. Many people would have considered my bedroom at Sorgenfrei a first-class place for such reflection, because so many people associate the Devil with a high standard of old-fashioned luxury. Mine was a handsome room in a corner tower, with an area of floor as big as that of a modest modern North American house. Sorgenfrei was an early-nineteenth-century construction, built by a forebear of Liesl's who seemed to have something in common, at least in his architectural taste, with the mad King of Bavaria; it was a powerfully romantic Gothic Revival house, built and furnished with Teutonic thoroughness. Everything was heavy, everything was the best of its kind, everything was carved, and polished, and gilded, and painted to the highest possible degree, and everything would drive a modern interior decorator out of his tasteful mind. But it suited me splendidly.

Not, however, when I wanted to think about the Devil. It was too romantic, too Germanic altogether. As I lay in my big bed, looking out of the windows at the mountains on which moonlight was falling, what could be easier than to accept an operatic Devil, up to every sort of high-class deception, and always defeated at the end of the story by the power of sheer simple-minded goodness? All my life I have been a keen opera-goer and playgoer, and in the theatre I am willing to accept the notion that although the Devil is a very clever fellow, he is no match for some ninny who is merely good. And what is this goodness? A squalid, know-nothing acceptance of things as they are, an operatic version of the dream which, in North America, means Mom and apple pie. My whole life had been a protest against this world, or the smudged, grey version of it into which I had been born in my rural Canada.

No, no; that Devil would never do. But what else is there? Theologians have not been so successful in their definitions of the Devil as they have been in their definitions of God. The words of the Westminster Confession, painstakingly learned by heart as a necessity of Presbyterian boyhood, still seemed, after many wanderings, to have the ring of indisputable authority. God was *infinite in being and perfection, a most pure spirit, invisible, without body, parts or passions, immutable, immense, eternal, incomprehensible, almighty, most wise, most holy, most free, most absolute, working all things according to the counsel of his own immutable and most righteous will, for his own glory*. Excellent, even if one is somewhat seduced by the high quality of the prose of 1648. What else? *Most loving, most gracious, merciful, longsuffering, abundant in goodness and*

*truth, forgiving iniquity, transgression and sin; the rewarder of
those that diligently seek him.* Aha, but where does one seek
God? In Deptford, where Eisengrim and I were born, and might
still be living if, in my case, I had not gone off to the First World
War, and in his case, if he had not been abducted by a mountebank in a travelling show? I had sought God in my lifelong,
unlikely (for a Canadian schoolmaster) preoccupation with that
fantastic collection of wise men, virtuous women, thinkers,
doers, organizers, contemplatives, crack-brained simpletons, and
mad mullahs that are called Saints. But all I had found in that
lifelong study was a complexity that brought God no nearer.
Had Eisengrim sought God at all? How could I know? How can
anybody know what another man does in this most secret part
of his life? What else had I been taught in that profound and
knotty definition? That God was *most just and terrible in his
judgements, hating all sin, one who will by no means clear the
guilty.* Noble words, and (only slightly cloaked by their nobility)
a terrifying concept. And why should it not be terrifying? A
little terror, in my view, is good for the soul, when it is terror
in the face of a noble object.

The Devil, however, seems never to have been so splendidly
mapped and defined. Nor can you spy him simply by turning a
fine definition of God inside out; he is something decidedly
more subtle than just God's opposite.

Is the Devil, then, sin? No, though sin is very useful to him;
anything we may reasonably call sin involves some personal
choice. It is flattering to be asked to make important choices.
The Devil loves the time of indecision.

What about evil, then? Is the Devil the origin and ruler of
that great realm of manifestly dreadful and appalling things
which are not, so far as we can determine, anybody's fault or
the consequences of any sin? Of the cancer wards, and the wards
for children born misshapen and mindless? I have had reason
to visit such places – asylums for the insane in particular – and I
do not think I am fanciful or absurdly sensitive in saying that I
have felt evil to be palpable there, in spite of whatever could be
done to lessen it.

These are evil things within my knowledge: I am certain
there are worse things I have never encountered. And how

constant this evil is! Let mankind laboriously suppress leprosy, and tuberculosis rages: when tuberculosis is chained, cancer rushes to take its place. One might almost conclude that such evils were necessities of our collective life. If the Devil is the inspirer and ruler of evil, he is a serious adversary indeed, and I cannot understand why so many people become jokey and facetious at the mention of his name.

Where is the Devil? Was Eisengrim, whose intuitions and directness of observation in all things concerning himself I had come to respect, right in saying the Devil stood beside him when Willard the Wizard solicited him to an action which, under the circumstances, I should certainly have to call evil? Both God and the Devil wish to intervene in the world, and the Devil chooses his moments shrewdly.

What had Eisengrim told us? That on 30 August 1918, he had descended into hell, and did not rise again for seven years? Allowing for his wish to startle us, and his taste for what a severe critic might call flashy rhetoric, could what he said be discounted?

It was always a mistake, in my experience, to discount Magnus Eisengrim. The only thing to do was to wait for the remainder of his narrative, and hope that it would make it possible for me to reach a conclusion. And that would be my much-desired document.

6

I KNEW nothing about filming, but Lind's subordinates told me that his methods were not ordinary. He was extremely deliberate, and because he liked careful rehearsal and would not work at night he semed to take a lot of time. But as he wasted none of this time, his films were not as devastatingly expensive as impatient people feared they might be. He was a master of his craft. I did not presume to question him about it, but I sensed that he attached more importance to Eisengrim's story than ordinary curiosity would explain, and that the dinners and discussions at Sorgenfrei fed the fire of his creation. Certainly he and Kinghovn and Ingestree were anxious for more as we settled down in the library on the third night. Liesl had seen to it that there was plenty of brandy, for although Eisengrim drank very little, and I was too keen on my document to drink much, Lind loved to tipple as he listened and had a real Scandinavian head; brandy never changed him in the least. Kinghovn was a heavy drinker, and Ingestree, a fatty, could not resist anything that could be put into his mouth, be it food, drink, or cigar.

Magnus knew they were waiting, and after he had toyed with them for a few minutes, and appeared to be leading them into general conversation, he yielded to Lind's strong urging that he go on with his story or – as Ingestree now quite seriously called it – 'the subtext'.

'I told you I was on a train, but didn't know it. I think that is true, but I must have had some notion of what was happening to me, because I had heard the whistle, and felt the motion, and of course I had seen trains. But I was so wretched that I couldn't reason, or be sure of anything, except that I was in close quarters in pitchy darkness. My mind was on a different unhappiness. I knew that when I was in trouble I should pray, and God would surely help me. But I couldn't pray, for two reasons. First, I couldn't kneel, and to me prayer without kneeling was unknown. Second, if I had been able to kneel I could not have dared to do it, because I was horribly aware that what Willard had done to me in that disgusting privy had been done while I was in a kneeling posture. I assure you, however strange it may seem, that I didn't know what he had done, but I felt strongly that it was a blasphemy against kneeling, and if I knew nothing of sex I certainly knew a lot about blasphemy. I guessed I might be on a train, but I knew for a certainty that I had angered God. I had been involved in what was very likely the Sin against the Holy Ghost. Can you imagine what that meant to me? I had never known such desolation. I had wept in the privy and now I could weep no more. Weeping meant sound, and I had a confused idea that although God certainly knew about me, and undoubtedly had terrible plans for me, He might be waiting for me to betray myself by sound before He went to work on me. So I kept painfully still.

'I suppose I was in a state of what would now be called shock.

How long it went on I could not then tell. But I know now that it was from Friday night until the following Sunday morning that I sat in my close prison, without food or water or light. The train had not been travelling all that time. All day Saturday Wanless's World of Wonders had a day's work at a village not many miles from Deptford, and I was conscious of the noises of unloading the train in the morning, and of loading it again very late at night, though I could not interpret them. But Sunday morning brought a kind of release.

'There were more men's voices, and more sounds of heavy things being methodically moved near where I was. Then after a period of silence I heard Willard's voice. "He's in there," it said. Then sounds somewhat below me, and a hand reached up and touched my leg. I made no sound – could not make a sound, I suppose – and was rather roughly hauled out into a dim light, and laid on the floor. Then a strange voice. "Jesus, Willard," it said, "you've killed him. Now we're all up the well-known creek." But then I moved a little. "Christ, he's alive," said the strange voice; "thank God for that." Then Willard's voice: "I'd rather he was dead," it said; "what are we going to do with him now?"

' "We got to get Gus," said the strange voice. "Gus is the one who'll know what to do. Don't talk about him being dead. Haven't you got any sense? We got to get Gus right now." Then Willard spoke. "Yeah, Gus, Gus, Gus; it's always Gus with you. Gus hates me. I'll be outa the show." "Leave Gus to me about you and the show," said the other voice; "but only Gus can deal with this right now. You wait here."

'The other man went away, and as he went I heard the heavy door of the freight-car – for I was in a freight-car in which the World of Wonders took its trappings from town to town – and I was for a second time alone with Willard. Through my eye-lashes I could see him sitting on a box beside me. His Mephisto-phelian air of command was gone; he looked diminished, shabby, and afraid.

'After a time the other man returned with Gus, who proved to be a woman – a real horse's godmother of a woman, a little, hard-faced, tough woman who looked like a jockey. But she inspired confidence, and while it would be false to say that my spirits lightened, I felt a little less desolate. I have always had a quick response to people, and though it is sometimes wrong it is more often right. If I like them on sight they are lucky people for me, and that's really all I care about. Gus was in a furious temper.

' "Willard, you son-of-a-bitch, what the hell have you got us into now? Lemme look at this kid." Gus knelt and hauled me round so that she could see me. Then she sent the other man to open the doors further, to give her a better light.

'Gus had a rough touch, and she hurt me so that I whimpered. "What's your name, kid?" she said. "Paul Dempster." "Who's your Dad?" "Reverend Amasa Dempster." This pushed Gus's rage up a few notches. "A reverend's kid," she shouted; "you had to go and kidnap a reverend's kid. Well, I wash my hands of you, Willard. I hope they hang you, and if they do, by God I'll come and swing on your feet!"

'I can't pretend to remember all their talk, because Gus sent the unknown man, whom she called Charlie, to get water and milk and food for me, and while they wrangled she fed me, first, sugared water from a spoon, and then, when I had plucked up a little, some milk, and finally a few biscuits. I can still remember the pain as my body began to return to its normal state, and the pins-and-needles in my arms and legs. She put me on my feet and walked me up and down but I was wobbly, and couldn't stand much of that.

'Nor can I pretend that I understood much of what was said at that time, though later, from knowledge I picked up over a period of years, I know what it must have been. I was not Gus's chief problem; I was a complication of a problem that was already filling the foreground of her mind. Wanless's World of Wonders belonged to Gus, and her brothers Charlie and Jerry; they were Americans, although their show toured chiefly in Canada, and Charlie ought to have been in the American Army, for the 1917 draft had included him and he had had his call-up. But Charlie had no mind for fighting, and Gus was doing her best to keep him out of harm's way, in hopes that the War would end before his situation became desperate. Charlie was very much her darling, and I judge he must have been at least ten years younger than she; Jerry was the oldest. Therefore, involvements with the law were not to Gus's taste, even though they might bring about the downfall of Willard. She detested him because he was Charlie's best friend, and a bad influence. Willard, in his panic, had abducted me, and it was up to Gus to get me out of the way without calling attention to the Wanless family.

'It is easy now to think of several things they might have done, but none of those three were thinkers. Their obsession was that I must be kept from running to the police and telling my tale of seduction, abduction, and hard usage; it never occurred to them to ask me, or they would have found out that I had no clear idea of who or what the police were, and had no belief in any rights of mine that might have gone contrary to the will of any adult. They assumed that I was aching to return to my loving family, whereas I was frightened of what my father would do when he found out what had happened in the privy, and what the retribution would be for having stolen fifteen cents, a crime of the uttermost seriousness in my father's eyes.

'My father was no brute, and I think he hated beating me, but he knew his duty. "He that spareth his rod hateth his son; but he that loveth him chasteneth him betimes"; this was part of the prayer that always preceded a beating and he laid the rod on hard, while my mother wept or – this was very much worse, and indeed quite horrible – laughed sadly as if at something my father and I did not and could not know. But Gus Wanless was a sentimentalist, American-style, and it never entered her head that a boy in my situation would be prepared to do anything rather than go home.

'There was another thing which seems extraordinary to me now, but which was perfectly in keeping with that period in history and the kind of people into whose hands I had fallen. There was never, at any time, any reference to what had happened in the privy. Gus and Charlie certainly knew that Willard had not stolen a boy, or thought it necessary to conceal a boy, simply as a matter of caprice. As I grew to know these carnival people I discovered that their deepest morality was precisely that of the kind of people they amused; whatever freedom their travelling way of life might give them, it did not cut far into the rock of North American accepted custom and morality. If Willard had despoiled a girl, I think Gus would have known better what to do, but she was unwilling to strike out into the deep and dirty waters that Willard's crime had revealed in the always troubled landscape of Wanless's World of Wonders.

'I think she was right; if Willard had fallen into the hands of the law as we knew it in Deptford, and in the county of which it was a part, the scandal would have wrecked the World of Wonders and Charlie would have been shipped back to the States to face the music. A showman, a magician at that, a stranger, an American, who had ravaged a local child in a fashion of which I am certain half the village had never heard except as something forbidden in the Bible – we didn't go in for lynchings in our part of the world, but I think Willard might have been killed by the other prisoners when he went to jail; jails have their own morality, and Willard would have found himself outside it. So nothing was said about that, then or afterward. This was all the worse for me, as I found out in the years to come. I was part of something shameful and dangerous everybody knew about, but which nobody would have dreamed of bringing into the light.

'What were they to do with me? I am sure Willard had spoken truly when he wished me dead, but he hadn't the courage to kill me when he had his chance. Now that Gus, who was the whole of the law and the prophets in the World of Wonders, knew about me, that moment had passed. As I have said, none of them had any capacity for thought or reasoning, and as they talked on and on Gus's mood turned from rage to fear. Willard was more at home in the air of fear than in that of anger.

' "Honest to God, Gus, nothing would ever have happened, if the kid hadn't shown some talent."

'This was a lucky string to touch. Gus was sure she knew everything there was to know about Talent – a word she always pronounced with the air of one giving it a capital letter. And so it came out that when Willard had given me a quarter, out of pure open-heartedness, I had immediately done a trick with it. As neat a palm-and-pass as Willard had ever seen. Good enough for the Palace Theater in New York.

' "You mean the kid can do tricks?" It was Charlie who spoke.

"Then why can't we fix him up a little with some hair-dye and maybe colour his skin, and use him as a Boy-Conjuror – Bonzo the Boy Wonder, or like that?"

'But this did not sit well with Willard. He wanted no rival conjurors in the show.

' " Jeeze, Willard, I only meant as a kind of assistant to you. Hand you things and like that. Maybe do a funny trick or two when you're not looking. You could plan something."

'Now it was Gus who objected. "Charlie, you ought to know by now that you can't never disguise anybody from somebody that knows him well. The law's going to follow the show; just keep that in mind. The kid's Dad, this reverend, comes into the show, sees a kid this size, and no hair-dye and blackface is going to hide him. Anyway, the kid sees his Dad, this reverend, and he gives him the high-sign. Use whatever head you got, Charlie."

'Now it was Willard's turn to have a bright idea. "Abdullah!" he said.

'Even though I was busy with the biscuits I stopped eating to look at them. They were like people from whose minds a cloud had lifted.

' "But can he handle Abdullah?" said Gus.

' "I betcha he can. I tell you, this kid's Talent. A natural. He's made for Abdullah. Don't you see, Gus? This is the silver lining. I made a little slip, I grant ya. But if Abdullah's back in the show, what does it matter? Abdullah's the big draw. Now look; we put Abdullah back, and I go to the top of the show, and let's not hear any more about Happy Hannah or that gaffed morphodite Andro."

' " Just hold your horses, Willard. I'll believe a kid can handle Abdullah when I've seen it. You got to show me."

' "And I'll show you. Gimme time, just a very little time, and I'll show you. Kid, can you handle a pack of cards?" Nothing could make me admit that I could handle a pack of cards. Ramsay had taught me a few card tricks, but when my father found it out he gave me such a beating as only a thoroughgoing Baptist can give a son who has been handling the Devil's Picture Book. It had been thoroughly slashed into my backside that cards were not for me. I denied all knowledge of cards before I had thought for an instant. Yet, immediately I had spoken, the four suits and the ways in which they could be made to dance began to rise in my memory.

'Willard was not troubled by my lack of knowledge. He had the real showman's enthusiasm for a new scheme. But Gus was dubious.

' "Just give me today, Gus," said Willard. "Only just this one Sunday, to show you what can be done. I'll work him in. You'll see. We can do it right here."

'That was how I became the soul of Abdullah, and entered into a long servitude to the craft and art of magic.

'We began at once. Gus bustled away on some of the endless business she always had in hand, but Charlie remained, and he and Willard began to uncover something at the very back of the car – the only object in it which the handlers had not unloaded for Monday's fair – which was under several tarpaulins. Whatever it was, this was the prison in which I had spent my wretched, starving hours.

'When it was pulled forward and the wraps thrown aside, it was revealed as, I think still, the most hideous and offensive object I have ever seen in my life. You gentlemen know how particular I have always been about the accoutrements of my show. I have spent a great deal of money, which foolish people have thought unnecessary, on the beauty and workmanship of everything I have exhibited. In this I have been like Robert-Houdin, who also thought that the best was none too good for himself and his audiences. Perhaps some of my fastidiousness began with my hatred of the beastly figure that was called Abdullah.

'It was a crude effigy of a Chinese, sitting on top of a chest, with his legs crossed. To begin with, the name was crassly wrong. Why call a Chinese figure Abdullah? But everything about it was equally inartistic and inept. Its robes were of frowsy sateen; its head was vulgarly moulded in papier mâché with an ugly face, sharply slanted eyes, dangling moustaches, and yellow fangs which hung down over the lower lip. The thing was, in itself, reason for a sharp protest from the Chinese Ambassador, if there had been one. It summed up in itself all that spirit combined of jocosity and hatred with which ignorant people approach whatever is foreign and strange.

'The chest on which this monster sat was in the same mode of workmanship. It was lacquered with somebody's stupid notion of a dragon, half hideous and half cute, in gaudy red on a black background. A lot of cheap gold paint had been splashed about.

'Neither Willard nor Charlie explained to me what this thing was, or what relationship I was expected to bear to it. However, I was used to being ignored and rather liked it; being noticed had, in my experience, usually meant trouble. All they told me was that I was to sit in this thing and make it work, and my lesson began as soon as Abdullah was unveiled.

'Once again, but this time in daylight and with some knowledge of what I was doing, I crawled into the chest at the back of the figure, and thence upward, rather like an old-fashioned chimney-sweep climbing a chimney, into the body, where there was a tiny ledge on which I could sit and allow my feet to hang down. But that was not the whole of my duty. When I was in place, Willard opened various doors in front of the chest, then turned the whole figure around on the wheels which supported the chest, and opened a door in the back. These doors revealed to the spectators an impressive array of wheels, cogs, springs, and other mechanical devices, and when Willard touched a lever they moved convincingly. But the secret of these mechanisms was that they were shams, displayed in front of polished steel mirrors, so that they seemed to fill the whole of the chest under the figure of Abdullah, but really left room for a small person to conceal himself when necessary. And that time came after Willard had closed the doors in the chest, and pulled aside Abdullah's robes to show some mechanism, and nothing else, in the figure itself. When that was happening, I had to let myself down into the secret open space in the chest and keep out of the way. Once Abdullah's mechanical innards had been displayed I crept back up into the figure, thrust aside the fake mechanism, which folded out of the way, and prepared to make Abdullah do his work.

'Willard and Charlie both treated me as if I were very stupid, which God knows I was not. However, I thought it best not to be too clever at the beginning. This was intuition; I did not figure it out consciously. They showed me a pack of cards, and painstakingly taught me the suits and the values. What Abdul-

lah had to do was to play cards, on a very simple principle, with
anybody who would volunteer from an audience to try their
luck with him. This spectator – the Rube, as Willard called him
– shuffled and cut a deck which lay on a little tray across
Abdullah's knees. Then the Rube drew a card and laid it face
down on the tray. At this point Willard pulled a lever on the
side of Abdullah's chest, which set up a mechanical sound in the
depths of the figure, which in fact I, the concealed boy, set
going by pumping a pedal with my left foot. While this was
going on it was my job to discover what card the Rube had
drawn – which was easy, because he had put it face downward
on a ground-glass screen, and I could fairly easily make it out –
and to select a higher card from a rack concealed inside Abdullah ready to my hand. Having chosen my card, I set Abdullah's
left arm in motion, slipping my own arm into the light framework in its sleeve; at the far end of this framework was a
device into which I inserted the card that was to confound the
Rube. I then made Abdullah's right arm move slowly to the
deck of cards on the tray, and cut them; this was possible because the fingers had a pincers device in them which could be
worked from inside the arm by squeezing a handle. When
Abdullah had cut the cards his left hand moved to the deck and
took a card from the top. But in fact he did nothing of the sort,
because his sleeve fell forward for a moment and concealed what
was really happening; it was at this instant I pushed the little
slide which shot the card I had chosen from the rack into
Abdullah's fingers, and it seemed to the spectators that this was
the card he picked up from the deck. The Rube was then invited
to turn up his card – a five, let us say; then a spectator was asked
to turn up Abdullah's card. A seven in the same suit! Consterna-
tion of the Rube! Applause of the audience! Great acclaim for
Willard, who had never touched a card at any time and had
merely pulled the lever which set in motion Abdullah, the
Card-Playing Automaton, and Scientific Marvel of the Age!

'We slaved away all of that Sunday. I lost my fright because
Willard and Charlie were so pleased with what I could do, and
although they still talked about me as though I had no ears to
hear them, and no understanding, the atmosphere became cheerful and excited and I was the reason for it. I must not pretend

that I mastered the mechanisms of Abdullah in an instant, and even when I had done so I had to be taught not to be too quick; I thought the essence of the work was to do it as fast as possible. Willard and Charlie knew, though they never bothered to tell me, that a very deliberate, and even slow, pace created a far better effect on the spectators. And I had much to learn. When I sat inside Abdullah my head was at the level of his neck, and here his robes parted a little to allow me to see through a piece of wire mesh that was painted the colour of his gown. It was by observing the actions of the Rube that I timed my own work. I had to learn to pump the little treadle that made the mechanical noise which simulated the finely scientific machinery of the automaton, and it was easy to forget, or to pump too fast and make Abdullah too noisy. The hardest part was ducking my head just enough to see what card the Rube had chosen and laid on the tray; as I said, this was ground glass, and there was a mirror underneath it so that I could see the suit and value of his card, but it was not as easy or as convenient as you might suppose, because the light was dim. And I had to be quick and accurate in choosing a card of greater value. A deck identical with the one used by the Rube was set up in a rack concealed by Abdullah's folded legs; it had eight pigeon-holes, in which each suit was divided into the cards from two to ten, and the Jack, Queen, King, and Ace by themselves. It was dark in Abdullah, and there was not much time for choosing, so I had to develop a good deal of dexterity.

'It was thrilling, and I worked feverishly to make myself perfect. How many times we went through the routine, when once I had mastered the general principle of it, I cannot guess, but I remember well that it was the management of the arms that gave me the most trouble, and any mistiming there made a mess of the whole deception. But we toiled as only people toil who are busy at the delicious work of putting something over on the public. There was a short noonday pause for a picnic, of which my share was milk and a lot of sticky buns; Gus had left instructions that I was not to be starved or overworked, because I was still weak, and I certainly was not starved.

'It was a hot day, and hotter still inside Abdullah. Also, Abdullah had a heavy smell, because of all the papier mâché and glue and size with which it was made. During my thirty-six hours or so of imprisonment I had been compelled to urinate, in spite of my awful thirst, and this had done nothing to freshen the atmosphere of that close confinement. Moreover, although I did not know it then, I learned later that the former operator of Abdullah had been a dwarf who cannot have been fastidious about his person, and there was a strong whiff of hot dwarf as I grew hotter myself. I suppose I became rather feverish, but although I would not describe my emotion as happiness I was possessed by an intensity of interest and ambition that was better than anything I had ever known in my life. When you were teaching me magic, Ramsay, I felt something like it, but not to the same degree, because – please don't be hurt – you were so tooth-achingly rotten at all your simple tricks. But this was the real thing. I didn't know quite what this reality was, but it was wonderful, and I was an important part of it.

'Charlie, who was as good-hearted as he was soft-headed, did all he could to make a game of it. He played the part of the Rube, and he did his best to include every kind of Rube he could think of. He was a terrible ham, but he was funny. He approached Abdullah as Uncle Zeke, the euchre champion of Pumpkin Centre, and as Swifty Dealer, the village tinhorn sport, and as Aunt Samantha, who didn't believe she could be bested by any Chinaman that ever lived, and as a whole gallery of such caricatures. I had to beg him not to be so funny, because I couldn't concentrate on my work when I was laughing so much. But Willard never laughed. He was the taskmaster, demanding the greatest skill I could achieve in the management of the mechanism. Charlie was a hearty praiser; he would gladly tell me that I was a wonderful kid and a gift to the carnival business and the possessor of a golden future. But Willard never praised a good piece of management; he was sharp about mistakes, and demanded more and more refinement of success. I didn't care. I felt that inside Abdullah I had entered into my kingdom.

'Come five o'clock Willard and Charlie thought we were ready to show our work to Gus. I had never been associated with any kind of show folk, and I thought it quite wonderful the way Gus climbed into the freight-car and behaved as if she had never seen any of us before; Willard and Charlie too behaved as if it were a real show and Gus a stranger. Willard gave a speech that I had not heard before, about the wonders of Abdullah, and the countless hours and boundless ingenuity that had gone into his construction; during all of it I kept as still as a mouse, and fully convinced myself that Gus did not know I was anywhere near; perhaps she thought I had run away. Then Gus, at the right time, came forward reluctantly and suspiciously, like a real Rube and not one of Charlie's comic turns, and cut the deck and chose a card : either Gus knew some sleight-of-hand herself or Willard had prepared a sharp test for me, because it was the Ace of Spades; there was no card to top it. And then I had one of those flashes which, I think I may say without boasting, have lifted my work above that of even a very good illusionist. At the bottom of the tray that held the court-cards in spades, there was a Joker, and that was what I caused Abdullah to put down on the tray to top Gus's Ace. Of course it would not do so, but it showed that I was able to meet an unexpected situation, and Charlie gave a whoop that would have drawn a crowd if there had been anybody hanging around the railway siding on a late Sunday afternoon.

'Gus was impressed, but the expression of her jockey's face did not change. "O.K. I guess it'll do," was what she said, and immediately the three began haggling again about some of the questions that had come up in the morning. I did not understand them then, but they concerned Abdullah's place in the show, which Willard insisted should be next to last, the place of honour reserved for the top attraction. It was now held by Andro, against whom Willard harboured a complicated grudge. Gus did not want to be rushed, and insisted that Abdullah should not be shown for a while, until we were far from Deptford.

'Charlie begged very hard that Abdullah should go into the show at once. Business wasn't good; they needed a strong attraction, especially now Hannah was getting out of hand and would have to be sat on; nobody would know the kid was in Abdullah because they would all be convinced Abdullah was a mechanical marvel. Yes, countered Gus, but how was she going to explain to the Talent a kid who turned up without warning and whom they would certainly know was the secret of Abdullah's card-playing genius? Would they just tell her that? A kid out of nowheres! Especially if there was any inquiry by Nosey Parkers and policemen. Could Hannah be trusted not to spill the beans? She was a religious old bitch and would love to do a mean thing for a holy reason. Ah, said Charlie, Gus surely knew how to handle Hannah; if Hannah had to go for as much as eight hours without the assistance of Elephant Gus, where would she be? And here Willard struck in to say that he knew a thing or two about Hannah that would keep her in order. And so on, at length, because they all argued in a circle, enjoying the contention rather than wishing to reach a conclusion. I had had a hard day, and the inside of Abdullah was like a Turkish bath; they had quite forgotten the living reality of the thing they were discussing. So I fell into an exhausted sleep. I did not understand it at the time, but I came to understand it very well later : when I was in Abdullah, I was Nobody. I was an extension and a magnification of Willard; I was an opponent and a baffling mystery to the Rube; I was something to be gawped at, but quickly forgotten, by the spectators. But as Paul Dempster I did not exist. I had found my place in life, and it was as Nobody.'

The film-makers sipped their brandy for a time before Lind spoke. 'It would be interesting to do a film about Nobody,' he said. 'I know I mustn't hurry you, so I won't ask you if you were Nobody for long. But you are going to continue, aren't you?'

'You must,' said Ingestree. 'Now we are getting a true story. Not like Robert-Houdin's faked-up reminiscences. He was never Nobody. He was always triumphantly and self-assuredly Somebody. He was charming, lively little Eugene Robert, the delight of his family and his friends; or he was that deserving young watch- and clock-maker; or he was the interesting young traveller who extracted the most amazing confidences from everybody; or he was the successful Parisian entertainer, drawing the cream of society to his little theatre, but always respectful, always conscious of his place, always the perfect bourgeois, always Somebody. Do you suppose many people are Nobody?'

Eisengrim looked at him with a not very agreeable smile. 'Have you any recollection of being Nobody?' he said.

'Not really. No, I can't say I have.'

'Have you ever met anyone who was Nobody?'

'I don't believe so. No, I'm sure I haven't. But then, if one met Nobody, I don't suppose Nobody would make much of an impression on one.'

'Obviously not,' said Eisengrim.

It was I who saw the film-makers to their car and watched them begin the descent from Sorgenfrei to the village where their inn was. Then I went back to the house as fast as my artificial leg would carry me and caught Eisengrim as he was getting into bed.

'About the Devil,' I said, 'I've been thinking more about what we said.'

'Have you pinned him down, then?'

'Nothing like it. I am simply trying to get a better hold on his attributes. The attributes of God have been very carefully explored. But the Devil's attributes have been left vague. I think I've found one of them. It is he who puts the prices on things.'

'Doesn't God put a price on things?'

'No. One of his attributes is magnanimity. But the Devil is a setter of prices, and a usurer, as well. You buy from him at an agreed price, but the payments are all on time, and the interest is charged on the whole of the principal, right up to the last payment, however much of the principal you think you have paid off in the meantime. Do you suppose the Devil invented numbers? I shouldn't be surprised if the Devil didn't invent Time, with all the subtle terrors that Time comprises. I think you said you spent seven years in hell?'

'I may have underestimated my sentence.'

'That's what I mean.'

'You're developing into a theologian, Dunny.'

'A diabologian, rather. It's a fairly clear field, these days.'

'Do you think you can study evil without living it? How are you going to discover the attributes of the Devil without getting close to him? Are you the man for that? Don't bother your old grey head, Dunny.'

That was Magnus all over. He simply had to be the damnedest man around. What an egotist!

WE were eating sandwiches and drinking beer at a lunch-break the following day. Magnus was not with us, because he had gone off to make some repairs and alterations in his make-up, about which he was extremely particular. Robert-Houdin had been a handsome man, in a French style, with strong features, a large, mobile mouth, and particularly fine eyes: Magnus would make no concession to a likeness, and insisted on playing the role of the great illusionist as his handsome self, and he darted away to touch up his face whenever he could. As soon as he was out of the way, Kinghovn turned the conversation to what we had heard the night before.

'Our friend puzzles me,' he said. 'You remember that he said the image of Abdullah was the ugliest thing he had ever seen? Then he described it, and it sounded like the sort of trash one would expect in such a poor little travelling show, and just what would seem marvellous to a small boy. How much is he colouring his story with opinions he formed later?'

'But inevitably it's all coloured by later opinions,' said Ingestree. 'What can you expect? It's the classic problem of autobiography; it's inevitably life seen and understood backwards. However honest we try to be in our recollections we cannot help falsifying them in terms of later knowledge, and especially in terms of what we have become. Eisengrim is unquestionably the greatest magician of our day, and to hear him tell it, of any day. How is he to make himself into a photographic record of something that happened fifty years ago?'

'Then how can we reconstruct the past?' said Kinghovn. 'Look at it from my point of view — really my point of view, which is through the camera. Suppose I had to make a film of what Eisengrim has told us, how could I be sure of what Abdullah looked like?'

'You couldn't,' said Lind. 'And you know it. But you and I and a good designer would work together, and we would produce an Abdullah that would give the right effect, though it might be far, far away from the real Abdullah of 1918. What would the real Abdullah be? Perhaps not as ugly as Eisengrim says, but certainly a piece of cheap junk. You and I, Harry, would show the world not simply what little Paul Dempster saw, but what he felt. We would even get that whiff of hot dwarf across to the public somehow. That's what we do. That's why we are necessary people.'

'Then the truth of the past can never be recovered?'

'Harry, you should never talk. Your talk is the least useful part of you. You should just stick to your cameras, with which you are a man of genius. The truth of the past is to be seen in museums, and what is it? Dead things, sometimes noble and beautiful, but dead. And cases and cases of coins, and snuff-boxes, and combs, and mirrors that won't reflect any more, and clothes that look as if the wearers had all been midgets, and masses of frowsy tat that tells us nothing at all. Once a man showed me a great treasure of his family; it was a handkerchief which somebody, on 30 January 1649, had dipped in the blood of the executed English King Charles I. It was a disgusting, rusty rag. But if you and I and Roly here had the money and the right people, we could fake up an execution of King Charles that would make people weep. Which is nearer to the truth? The rag, or our picture?'

I thought it was time for me to intervene. 'I wouldn't call either the rag or your picture truth,' I said; 'I am an historian by training and temperament, and I would go to the documents, and there are plenty of them, about the execution of Charles, and when I had read and tested and reflected on them, I would back my truth against yours and win.'

'Ah, but you see, my dear Ramsay, we would not dream of making our picture until we had consulted you or somebody like you, and given the fullest importance to your opinion.'

'Well, would you be content to film the execution on a grey day? Wouldn't you want a shot of the sun rising behind White-hall as the sun of English monarchy was setting on the scaffold?'

Lind looked at me sadly. 'How you scholars underestimate us artists,' he said, with wintry Scandinavian melancholy. 'You think we are children, always beguiled by toys and vulgarities. When have you ever known me to stoop to a sunrise?'

'Besides, you don't understand what we could do with all those wonderful pearly greys,' said Kinghovn.

'You will never persuade me to believe that truth is no more than what some artist, however gifted he may be, thinks is truth,' I said. 'Give me a document, every time.'

'I suppose somebody has to write the document?' said Lind. 'Has he no feeling? Of course he has. But because he is not used to giving full weight to his feelings, he is all the more likely to be deluded into thinking that what he puts into his document is objective truth.'

Ingestree broke in. 'Eisengrim is coming back from tarting himself up for the next few shots,' he said. 'And so far as his story is concerned, we might as well make up our minds that all we are going to get is his feeling. As a literary man, I am just pleased that he has some feelings. So few autobiographers have any feeling except a resolute self-protectiveness.'

'Feeling! Truth! Balls! Let's have a few hundred good feet in the can before our star decides he is tired,' said Kinghovn. And that is what we did.

A good day's filming put Magnus in an expansive mood. Ingestree's flattery about the quality of his acting had also had its effect on him, and that night he gave us a gallery of impersonations.

'Charlie had his way, and I was soon on the show. Charlie was right; Abdullah pulled them in because people cannot resist automata. There is something in humanity that is repelled and entranced by a machine that seems to have more than human powers. People love to frighten themselves. Look at the fuss nowadays about computers; however deft they may be they can't do anything a man isn't doing, through them; but you hear people giving themselves delicious shivers about a computer-dominated world. I've often thought of working up an illusion, using a computer, but it would be prohibitively expensive, and I can do anything the public would find amusing better and cheaper with clockwork and bits of string. But if I invented a computer-illusion I would take care to dress the computer up to look like a living creature of some sort – a Moon Man or a Venusian – because the public cannot resist clever dollies.

Abdullah was a clever dolly of a simple kind, and the Rubes couldn't get enough of him.

'That was where Gus had to use her showman's discretion. Charlie and Willard would have put Abdullah in a separate tent to milk him for twenty shows a day, but Gus knew that would exhaust his appeal. Used sparingly, Abdullah was good for years, and Gus took the long view. It appeared, too, that I was an improvement on the dwarf, who had become unreliable through some personal defect – booze, I would guess – and was apt to make a mess of the illusion, or give way to a fit of temperament and deal a low card when he should have dealt a high one. Willard had had no luck with Abdullah; he had bought the thing, and hired the dwarf, but the dwarf was so unreliable it was risky to put the automaton on the show, and then the dwarf had disappeared. It had been months since Abdullah was in commission, and so far as the show was concerned it was a new attraction.

'I was anxious to succeed as Abdullah, though I had no particular expectation of gaining anything thereby. I had no notion of the world, and for quite a long time I did not understand how powerful I was, or that I might profit by it. Nor did anyone in the World of Wonders seek to enlighten me. So far as I can recall my feelings during those first few months, they were restricted to a desire to do the best I could, lest I should be sent back to my father and inevitable punishment. To begin with, I liked being the hidden agent who helped in the great game of hoodwinking Rubes, and I was happiest when I was out of sight, in the smelly bowels of Abdullah.

'When I was in the open air I was Cass Fletcher. I always hated the name, but Willard liked it because he had invented it in one of his very few flights of fancy. Willard had no imagination, to speak of. I learned as time went on that he had learned his conjuring skill from an old performer, and had never expanded it or altered it by a jot. He had as little curiosity as any man I have ever known. But when we were riding on the train, in my very first week, he found that I must have a name, because the other performers, riding in the car reserved for the World of Wonders, were surprised to see a small boy in their midst, for whom no credentials were offered. Who was I?

'When the question was put directly to him by the wife of Joe Dark the Knife Thrower, Willard hesitated a moment, looked out of the window, and said: "Oh, this is young Cass, a kind of relative of mine; Cass Fletcher." Then he went off into one of his very rare fits of laughter.

'As soon as he could catch Charlie, who wandered up and down the car as it travelled through the flatlands of Western Ontario, and gossiped with everybody, Willard told him his great joke. "Em Dark wanted to know the kid's name, see, and I was thinking who the hell is he, when I looked outa the window at one of these barns with a big sign saying FLETCHER'S CASTORIA, CHILDREN CRY FOR IT; and quick as a wink I says Cass Fletcher, that's his name. Pretty smart way to name a kid, eh?" I was offended at being named from a sign on a barn, but I was not consulted, and a general impression spread that I was Willard's nephew.

'At least, that was the story that was agreed on. As time went on I heard whispers between Molza the Fire Eater and Sonny Sonnenfels the Strong Man that Willard was something they called an arse-bandit – an expression I did not understand – and that the kid was probably more to him than just a nephew and the gaff for Abdullah.

'Gaff. That was a word I had to learn at once, in all its refinements. The gaff was the element of deception in an exhibition, and though all the Talent would have admitted you couldn't manage without it, there was a moral stigma attaching to it. Sonnenfels was not gaffed at all; he really was a strong man who picked up big bar-bells and tore up telephone books with his hands and lifted anybody who would volunteer to sit in a chair, which Sonny then heaved aloft with one hand. There are tricks to being a strong man, but no gaff; anybody was welcome to heft the bar-bells if they wanted to. Frank Molza the Fire Eater and Sword Swallower was partly gaffed, because his swords weren't as sharp as he pretended, and eating fire is a complicated chemical trick which usually proves bad for the health. But Professor Spencer, who had been born without arms – really he had two pathetic little flippers but he did not show them – was wholly free of gaff; he wrote with his feet, on a blackboard and, if you wanted to pay twenty-five cents, in an elegant script on twelve visiting cards, where your name would be handsomely displayed. Joe Dark and his wife Emily were not gaffed at all; Joe threw knives at Emily with such accuracy that he outlined her form on the soft board against which she stood; it was skill, and the only skill poor Joe possessed, for he was certainly the dullest man in the World of Wonders. Nor could you say there was any gaff about Heinie Bayer and his educated monkey Rango; it was an honest monkey, as monkeys go, and its tricks were on the level. The Midget Juggler, Piccino Zovene, was honest as a juggler, but as crooked as a corkscrew in any human dealings; he wasn't much of a juggler, and might have been improved by a little gaff.

'Gaff may have been said to begin with Zitta the Jungle Queen, whose snakes were kept quiet by various means, especially her sluggish old cobra who was over-fed and drugged. Snakes don't live long in the sort of life Zitta gave them; they can't stand constant mauling and dragging about; she was always wiring a supplier in Texas for new rattlers. I judged that a snake lived about a month to six weeks when once Zitta had got hold of it; they were nasty things, and I never felt much sympathy for them. Zitta was a nasty thing, too, but she was too stupid to give her nastiness serious play. Andro the Hermaphrodite was all gaff. He was a man, of a kind, and besottedly in love with himself. The left side of his body was supposed to be the female half, and he spent a lot of time on it with depilatories and skin creams; when he attached a pretty good left breast to it, and combed out the long, curly hair he allowed to grow on one side of his head, he was an interesting sight. His right side he exercised strenuously, so that he had big leg and arm muscles which he touched up with some fancy shadowing. I never became used to finding him using the men's bucket in the donniker – which was the word used on the show for the primitive sanitary conveniences in the small back dressing tent. He was a show-off; in show business you get used to vanity, but Andro was a very special case.

'Of course Abdullah was one hundred per cent gaff. I don't think anybody would have cared greatly, if they had not been stirred up to it by the one very remarkable Talent I haven't yet mentioned. She was Happy Hannah the Fat Lady.

'A Fat Lady, or a Fat Man, is almost a necessity for a show like Wanless's. Just as the public is fascinated by automata, it is unappeasable in its demand for fat people. A Human Skeleton is hardly worth having if he can't do something else – grow hair to his feet, or eat glass or otherwise distinguish himself. But a Fat Lady merely has to be fat. Happy Hannah weighed 487 pounds; all she needed to do was to show herself sitting in a large chair, and her living was assured. But that wasn't her style at all; she was an interferer, a tireless asserter of opinions, and – worst of all – a determined Moral Influence. It was this quality in her which made it a matter of interest whether she was gaffed or not.

'Willard was her enemy, and Willard said she was gaffed. For one thing, she wore a wig, a very youthful chestnut affair, curly and flirtatious; a kiss-curl coiled like a watchspring in front of each rosy ear. The rosy effect was gaffed, too, for Hannah was thickly made up. But these things were simple showmanship. Willard's insistence that the Fat Lady was gaffed rose from an occupational disability of Fat Ladies; this is copious sweating, which results, in a person whose bodily creases may be twelve inches deep, in troublesome chafing. Three or four times a day Hannah had to retire to the women's part of the dressing tent, and there Gus stripped her down and powdered her in these difficult areas with cornstarch. Very early in my experience on the show I peeped through a gap in the lacing of the canvas partition that divided the men's dressing-room from the women's, and was much amazed by what I saw; Hannah, who looked fairly jolly sitting on her platform, in a suit of pink cotton rompers, was a sorry mass of blubber when she was bent forward, her hands on the back of a chair; she had collops of fat on her flanks, like the wicked man in the Book of Job; her monstrous abdomen hung almost to her knees, the smart wig concealed an iron-grey crewcut, and her breasts hung like great half-filled wallets of suet far down on her belly. I have seen nothing like her since, except for an effigy of Smet Smet, the Hippopotamus Goddess, in an exhibition of African art Liesl made me attend a few years ago. The gaffing consisted of two large bath-towels, which were rolled and tucked under her breasts, giving them what was, in comparison with the reality, a buxom contour. These towels were great matters of contention between Hannah and Willard, for she insisted that they were sanitary necessities, and he said they were gross impostures on the public. He cared nothing about gaffing; it was Hannah who made it a moral issue and drew a sharp line between gaffed Talent, like Abdullah, and honest Talent, like Fat Ladies.

'They wrangled about it a good deal. Hannah was voluble and she had a quality of shrewishness that came strangely from one whose professional personality depended on an impression of sunny good nature. She would nag about it for half an hour at a stretch, as we travelled on the train, until at last the usually taciturn Willard would say, in a low, ugly voice: 'Listen, Miz Hannah, you shut your goddam trap or next time we got a big crowd I'm gonna tell 'em about those gaffed tits of yours. See? Now shut up, I tell ya!

'He would never have done it, of course. It would have been unforgivable professional conduct, and even Charlie would not have been able to keep Gus from throwing him off the show. But the menace in his voice would silence Hannah for a few hours.

'I was entranced by the World of Wonders during those early weeks and I had plenty of time to study it, for it was part of the agreement under which I lived that I must never be seen during working hours, except when real necessity demanded a quick journey to the donniker, between tricks. I often ate in the seclusion of Abdullah. The hours of the show were from eleven in the morning until eleven at night, and so I ate as big a breakfast as I could get, and depended on a hot dog or something of the sort being brought to me at noon and toward evening. Willard was supposed to attend to it, but he often forgot, and it was good-hearted Emily Dark who saw that I did not starve. Willard never ate much, and like so many people he could not believe that anyone wanted more than himself. There was an agreement of some sort between Willard and Gus as to what my status was; I know he got extra money for me, but I never saw any of it; I know Gus made him promise he would look after me and treat me well, but I don't think he had any idea of what such words meant, and from time to time Gus would give him a dressing down about the condition I was in;

for years I never had any clothes except those Gus bought me, stopping the money out of Willard's pay, but Gus had no idea of how to dress a child, and always bought everything too big, so that I would have lots of room to grow into it. Not that I needed many clothes; inside Abdullah I wore nothing but cotton shorts. I see now that it was a miserable life, and it is a wonder it didn't kill me; but at the time I accepted it as children must accept the world made for them by their guardians.

'At the beginning I was beglamoured by the show, and peeped at it out of Abdullah's bosom with unresting excitement. There was one full show an hour, and the whole of it was known as a trick. The trick began outside the tent on a platform beside the ticket-seller's box, and this part of it was called the bally. Not ballyhoo, which was an expression I had heard in the carnival world in my time. Gus usually sold the tickets, though there was someone to spell her when she had other business to attend to. Charlie was the outside talker, not a barker, which is another expression I did not hear until a movie or a play made it popular. He roared through a megaphone to tell the crowd about what was to be seen inside the tent. Charlie was a flashy dresser and handsome in a flashy way, and he did his job well, most of the time.

'High outside the tent hung the banners, which were the big painted signs advertising the Talent; each performer had to pay for his own banner, though Gus ordered them from the artist and assured that there would be a pleasing similarity of style. As well as the banners, some of the Talent had to appear on the bally, and this boring job usually fell to the lesser artistes; Molza ate a little fire, Sonny heaved a few weights, the Professor would lie on his back and write "Pumpkin Centre, Agricultural Capital of Pumpkin County" on a huge piece of paper with his feet, and this piece of paper was thrown into the crowd, for whoever could grab it; Zovene the Midget Juggler did a few stunts, and now and then if business was slow Zitta would take out a few snakes, and the Darks would have to show themselves. But the essence of the bally was to create an appetite for what was inside the tent, not to give away entertainment, and Charlie pushed the purchase of tickets as hard as he could.

'After Abdullah was put on the show, which was as soon as

we could get a fine banner sent up from New York, Willard did not have to take a turn on the bally.

'The bally and the sale of tickets took about twenty minutes, after which a lesser outside talker than Charlie did what he could to collect a crowd, and Charlie hurried inside, carrying a little cane he used as a pointer. Once in the tent he took on another role, which was called the lecturer, because everything in the World of Wonders was supposed to be improving and educational; Charlie's style underwent a change, too, for outside he was a great joker, whereas inside he was professorial, as he understood the word.

'I was much impressed by the fact that almost all the Talent spoke two versions of English – whatever was most comfortable when they were off duty, and a gaudy, begemmed, and gilded rhetoric when they were before the public. Charlie was a master of the impressive introduction when he presented the Talent to an audience.

'As spectators bought their tickets they were permitted into the tent, where they walked around and stared until the show began. Sometimes they asked questions, especially of Happy Hannah. "You will assuredly hear everything in due season," she would reply. The show was not supposed to begin without Charlie. When he pranced into the tent – he had an exaggeratedly youthful, high-stepping gait – he would summon the crowd around him and begin by introducing Sonny, *the Strongest Man you have ever seen, ladies and gentlemen, and the best-natured giant in the known world.* Poor old Sonny wasn't allowed to speak, because he had a strong German accent, and Germans were not popular characters in rural Canada in the late summer of 1918. Sonny was not allowed to linger over his demonstration, either, because Charlie was hustling the crowd toward Molza the Human Salamander, who thrust a lighted torch into his mouth, and then blew out a jet of flame which ignited a piece of newspaper Charlie held in his hand; Molza then swallowed swords until he had four of them stuck in his gullet. When I came to know him I got him to show me how to do it, and I can still swallow a paper-knife, or anything not too sharp. But swallowing swords and eating fire are hard ways to get a living, and dangerous after a few years. Then Professor

Spencer wrote with his feet, having first demonstrated with some soap and a safety-razor with no blade in it how he shaved himself every day; the Professor would write the name of anybody who wished it; with his right foot he would write from left to right, and at the same time, underneath it and with his left foot, he would write the name from right to left. He wrote with great speed in a beautiful hand – or foot, I should say. It was quite a showy act, but the Professor never had his full due, I thought, because people were rather embarrassed by him. Then the Darks did their knife-throwing act.

'It was a very good act, and if only Joe had possessed some instinct of showmanship it would have been much better. But Joe was a very simple soul, a decent, honest fellow who ought to have been a workman of some sort. His talent for throwing knives was one of those freakish things that are sometimes found in people who are otherwise utterly unremarkable. His wife, Emily, was ambitious for him; she wanted him to be a veterinary, and when we were on the train she kept him pegging away at a correspondence course which would, when it was completed, bring him a diploma from some cut-rate college deep in the States. But it was obvious to everybody but Emily that it would never be completed, because Joe couldn't get anything into his head from a printed page. He could throw knives, and that was that. They both wore tacky home-made costumes, which bunched unbecomingly in the wrong places, and Emily stood in front of a pine board while Joe outlined her pleasant figure in knives. Nice people : minor Talent.

'By this time the audience had climbed the ladder of marvels to Rango the Missing Link, exhibited by Heinie Bayer. Rango was an orang-outang, who could walk a tightrope carrying a parasol; at the mid-point, he would suddenly swing downward, clinging to the rope with his toes, and reflectively eat bananas; then he would whirl upright, throw away the skin, and complete his journey. After that he sat at a table, and rang a bell, and Heinie, dressed as a clown waiter, served him a meal, which Rango ate with affected elegance, until he was displeased with a badly prepared dish, and pelted Heinie with food. Rango was surefire. Everybody loved him, and I was of their number until I tried to make friends with him and Rango spat some chewed-up nuts in my face. It was part of Heinie's deal with the management that Rango had to share a berth with him in our Pullman; although he was house-trained he was a nuisance because he was a bad sleeper, and likely to stick his hand into your berth in the night and pinch you – a very mean, twisting pinch. It was uncanny to poke your head out of your berth and see Rango swinging along the car, holding on to the tops of the green curtains, as if they were part of his native jungle.

'After Rango came Zitta the Jungle Queen. Snake acts are all the same. She pulled the snakes around her neck, wound them around her arms, and as a topper she knelt down and charmed her cobra *by no other means than that of the unaided human eye, with which she exerts hypnotic dominance over this most dreaded of jungle monsters,* as Charlie said, and ended by kissing it on its ugly snout.

'This was good showmanship. First the sunny side of nature, then the ominous side of nature. The trick, I learned, was that Zitta leaned down to the cobra from above its head; cobras cannot strike upwards. It was a thrill, and Zitta had to know her business. As I grew older and more cynical I sometimes wondered what it would be like if Zitta exercised her hypnotic powers on Rango, and kissed him, for a change. I don't think Rango was a lady's man.

'This left only Willard, Andro the Hermaphrodite, and Happy Hannah to complete the show; Zovene the Midget Juggler was only useful to get the audience out of the tent. On the basis of public attraction it was acknowledged that Willard must have the place of honour once Abdullah was on display. Charlie was in favour of giving Andro the place just before Abdullah but Happy Hannah would have none of it. She was clamorous. If a natural, educational wonder like herself, without any gaff about her, didn't take precedence over a gaffed monsterosity she was prepared to leave carnival life and despair of the human race. She made herself so unpleasant that she won the argument; Andro became very shrewish when he was under attack, but he lacked Hannah's large, embracing, Biblical flow of condemnation. When he had said that Hannah was a fat, loud-mouthed old bitch his store of abuse was exhausted; but she sailed into him with all guns firing.

' "Don't think I hold it against you personally, Andro. No, I know you for what you are. I know the rock from whence ye are hewn – that no-good bunch o' Boston Greek fish-peddlers and small-time thieves; and I likewise know the hole of the Pit whence ye are digged – offering yourself to stand bare-naked in front of artists, some of 'em women, at fifty cents an hour. So I know it isn't really you that's speaking against me; it's the spirit of an unclean devil inside you, crying with a loud voice; and I rebuke it just as our dear Lord did; I'm sitting right here, crying, 'Hold thy peace and come out of him!' "

'This was Hannah's strength. All her immense bulk was crammed with Bible knowledge and quotations and it oozed out of her like currant-juice oozing out of a jelly-bag. She offered herself to the public as a Biblical marvel, a sort of she-Leviathan. She would not allow Charlie to speak for her. As soon as he had given her a lead – *And now, ladies and gentlemen, I present Happy Hannah, four hundred and eighty-seven pounds of good humour and chuckles* – she would burst in, "Yes friends, and I'm the living proof of how fat a person can get and still bear it gladly in the Lord's name. I hope every person here knows his Bible and if they do, they know the comforting message of Proverbs eleven, twenty-five : *The liberal soul shall be made fat.* Yes friends, I am here not as a curiosity and certainly not as a monsterosity but to attest in my daily life and my public career to the Lord's abounding grace. I don't hafta be here; many offers from missionary societies and the biggest evangelists have been turned down in order that I may get around this whole continent and talk to the biggest possible audience of the real people, God's own folks, and attest to the Faith. Portraits of me as you see me now, each one individually autographed by my own hand, may be purchased at twenty-five cents apiece, and for another mere quarter I will include a priceless treasure, this copy of the New Testament which fits in the pocket and in which each and every word uttered by our Lord Jesus Christ during his earthly ministry is printed in RED. No Testament sold except with a portrait. Don't miss this great offer which is made by me at a financial sacrifice in order that the Lord's will may be done more abundantly here in Pumpkin Centre. Don't hang back folks; grab what I'm giving to you, I been made fat and when you possess this portrait of me as you see me now and this New Testament you'll hafta admit that I'm certainly the Liberal Soul. Come on, now, who's gonna be the first?"

'Hannah was able to hawk her pictures and her Testaments because of an arrangement written into every artiste's contract that they should be allowed to sell something at every show. They made their offer, or Charlie made it for them, as the crowd was about to move on to the next Wonder. The price was always twenty-five cents. Sonny had a book on body-building; Molza had only a picture of himself with his throat full of swords – a very slow item in terms of sales; Professor Spencer offered his personally written visiting cards, which were a nuisance because they took quite a while to prepare; Em Dark sold throwing knives Joe made in his spare time out of small files – a throwing knife has no edge, only a point; Heinie sold pictures of Rango; Zitta offered belts and bracelets which she made out of the skins of the snakes she had mauled to death – though Charlie didn't put it quite like that; Andro was another seller of pictures; Willard sold a pamphlet called *Secrets of Gamblers Revealed*, which was offered by Charlie as an infallible protection against dishonest card-players you might meet on trains; a lot of people bought them who didn't look like great travellers, and I judged they wanted to know the secrets of gamblers for some purpose of their own. I read it several times, and it was a stupefyingly uncommunicative little book, written at least thirty years before 1918. The agreement was that each Wonder offered his picture or whatever it might be after he had been exhibited, and that when the show had been completed, except for the Midget Juggler, Charlie would invite the audience once again not to leave without one of *these valuable mementoes of a unique and unforgettable personal experience and educational benefit*.

'From being an extremely innocent little boy it did not take me long to become a very knowing little boy. I picked up a great deal as we travelled from village to village on the train, for our Pullman was an educational benefit and certainly, for me, an unforgettable personal experience. I had an upper berth at the very end of the car, at some distance from Willard, whose importance in the show secured him a lower in the area where the shock of the frequent shuntings and accordion-like contractions of the train were least felt. I came to know who had bottles of liquor, and also who was generous with it and who kept it for his own use. I knew that neither Joe nor Em Dark drank, because it would have been a ruinous indulgence for a knife-thrower. The Darks, however, were young and vigorous, and sometimes the noises from their berth were enough to raise comment from the other Talent. I remember one night when Heinie, who shared his bottle with Rango, put Rango up to opening the curtains of the Darks' upper; Em screamed, and Joe grabbed Rango and threw him down into the aisle so hard that Rango screamed; Heinie offered to fight Joe, and Joe, stark naked and very angry, chased Heinie back to his berth and pummelled him. It took a full hour to soothe Rango; Heinie assured us that Rango was used to love and could not bear rough usage; Rango had to have at least two strong swigs of straight rye before he could sleep. But in the rough-and-tumble I had had a good look at Em Dark naked, and it was very different from Happy Hannah, I can assure you. All sorts of things that I had never heard of began, within a month, to whirl and surge and combine in my mind.

'A weekly event of some significance in our Pullman was Hannah's Saturday-night bath. She lived in continual hope of managing it without attracting attention, but that was ridiculous. First Gus would bustle down the aisle with a large tarpaulin and an armful of towels. Then Hannah, in an orange mobcap and a red dressing-gown, would lurch and stumble down the car; she was too big to fall into anybody's berth, but she sometimes came near to dragging down the green curtains when we were going around a bend. We all knew what happened in the Ladies' Retiring Room; Gus spread the tarpaulin, Hannah stood on it hanging onto the wash-basin, and Gus swabbed her down with a large sponge. It was for this service of Christian charity that she was called Elephant Gus when she was out of earshot. Drying Hannah took a long time, because there were large portions of her that she could not reach herself, and Gus used to towel her down, making a hissing noise between her teeth, like a groom.

'Sometimes Charlie and Heinie and Willard would be sitting

up having a game of poker, and while the bath was in progress they would sing a hymn, "Wash me and I shall be whiter than snow". If they were high they had another version –

> Wash me in the water
>> That you wash the baby in,
> And I shall be whiter
>> Than the whitewash on the wall.

This infuriated Hannah, and on her return trip she would favour them with a few Biblical admonitions; she had a good deal to say about lasciviousness, lusts, excess of wine, revellings, banquetings, games of hazard, and abominable idolatries, out of First Peter. But she hocussed the text. There is no mention of "games of hazard" or gambling anywhere in the Bible. She put that in for her own particular satisfaction. I knew it, and I soon recognized Hannah as my first hypocrite. A boy's first recognition of hypocrisy is, or ought to be, more significant than the onset of puberty. By the time Gus had stowed her into her special lower, which was supported from beneath with a few fence-posts, she was so refreshed by anger that she fell asleep at once, and snored so that she could be heard above the noise of the train.

'Very soon I became aware that the World of Wonders which had been a revelation to me, and I suppose to countless other country village people, was a weary bore to the Talent. This is the gnawing canker of carnival life : it is monstrously boring.

'Consider. We did ten complete shows a day; we had an hour off for midday food and another hour between six and seven; otherwise it was unremitting. We played an average of five days a week, which means fifty shows. We began our season as early as we could, but nothing much was stirring in the outdoor carnival line till mid-May, and after that we traipsed across country playing anywhere and everywhere – I soon stopped trying to know the name of the towns, and called them all Pumpkin Centre, like Willard – until late October. That makes something over a thousand shows. No wonder the Talent was bored. No wonder Charlie's talks began to sound as if he was thinking about something else.

'The only person who wasn't bored was Professor Spencer. He was a decent man, and couldn't give way to boredom, because his affliction meant perpetual improvisation in the details of his life. For instance, he had to get somebody to help him in the donniker, which most of us were ready to do, but wouldn't have done if he had not always been cheerful and fresh. He offered to teach me some lessons, because he said it was a shame for a boy to leave school as early as I had done. So he taught me writing, and arithmetic, and an astonishing amount of geography. He was the one man on the show who had to know where we were, what the population of the town was, the name of the mayor, and other things that he wrote on his blackboard as part of his show. He was a good friend to me, was Professor Spencer. Indeed, it was he who persuaded Willard to teach me magic.

'Willard had not been interested in doing that, or indeed anything, for me. I was necessary, but I was a nuisance. I have never met anyone in my life who was so bleakly and unconsciously selfish as Willard, and for one whose life has been spent in the theatre and carnival world that is a strong statement. But Professor Spencer nagged him into it – you could not shame or bully or cajole Willard into anything, but he was open to nagging – and he began to show me a few things with cards and coins. As my years with the World of Wonders wore on, I think what he taught me saved my reason. Certainly it is at the root of anything I can do now.

'Whoever taught Willard did it very well. He never gave names to the things he taught me, and I am sure he didn't know them. But since that time I have found that he taught me all there is to know about shuffling, forcing, and passing cards, and palming, ruffling, changing, and bridging, and the wonders of the *biseauté* pack, which is really the only trick pack worth having. With coins he taught me all the basic work of palming and passing, the French drop, *La Pincette*, *La Coulée*, and all the other really good ones. His ideal among magicians was Nelson Downs, whose great act, The Miser's Dream, he had seen at the Palace Theater, New York, which was the paradise of his limited imagination. Indeed, it was a very much debased version of The Miser's Dream that he had been doing when I first saw him. He now did little conjuring in the World of Wonders, because of the ease of managing Abdullah.

'Inside Abdullah I was busy for perhaps five minutes in every hour. My movement was greatly restricted; I could not make a noise. What was I to do? I practised my magic, and for hours on end I palmed coins and developed my hands in the dark, and that is how I gained my technique which has earned me the compliment of this film you gentlemen are making. I recommend the method to young magicians; get yourself into a close-fitting prison for ten hours a day, and do nothing but manipulate cards and coins; keep that up for a few years and, unless you are constitutionally incapable, like poor Ramsay here, you should develop some adroitness, and you will at least have no chance to acquire the principal fault of the bad magician, which is looking at your hands as you work. That was how I avoided boredom: constant practice, and entranced observation, through Abdullah's bosom, of the public and the Talent of the World of Wonders.

'Boredom is rich soil for every kind of rancour and ugliness. In my first months on the show this attached almost entirely to the fortunes of the War. I knew nothing about the War, although as a schoolchild I had been urged to bring all my family's peachstones to school, where they were collected for some war-like purpose. Knowing boys said that a terrible poison gas was made from them. Every morning in prayers our teacher mentioned the Allied Forces, and especially the Canadians. Once again knowing boys said you could always tell where her brother Jim was by the prayer, which was likely to contain a special reference to "our boys at the Front", and later, "our boys in the rest camps", and later still, "our boys in the hospitals". The War hung over my life like the clouds in the sky, and I heeded it as little. Once I saw Ramsay in the street, in what I later realized was the uniform of a recruit, but at the time I couldn't understand why he was wearing such queer clothes. I saw men in the streets with black bands on their arms, and asked my father why they wore them, but I can't remember what he answered.

'In the World of Wonders the War seemed likely at times to tear the show to pieces. The only music on the fairgrounds where we appeared came from the merry-go-round; tunes were fed into its calliope by the agency of large steel discs, perforated with rectangular holes; they worked on the same principle as the roll of a player-piano, but were much more durable, and rotated instead of uncoiling. Most of the music was of the variety we associate with merry-go-rounds. Who wrote it? Italians, I suspect, for it always had a gentle, quaintly melodious quality, except for one new tune which Steve, who ran the machine, had bought to give the show a modern air. It was the American war song – by that noisy fellow Cohan, was it? – called "Over There!" It was less than warlike on a calliope, played at merry-go-round tempo, but everybody recognized it, and now and then some Canadian wag would sing loudly, to the final phrase –

> And we won't be over
> Till it's over
> Over there!

If Hannah heard this, she became furious, for she was an inflamed American patriot and the War, for her, had begun when the Americans entered it in 1917. The Darks were Canadians, and not as tactful as Canadians usually are when dealing with their American cousins. I remember Em Dark, who was a most unlikely person to tell a joke, saying one midday, in September of 1918, when the Talent was in the dressing tent, eating its hasty picnic: "I heard a good one yesterday. This fellow says, Say, why are the American troops called Doughboys? And the other fellow says, Gee, I dunno; why? And the first fellow says, It's because they were needed in 1914 but they didn't rise till 1917. Do you get it? Needed, you see, like kneading bread, and –" But Em wasn't able to continue with her explanation of the joke because Hannah threw a sandwich at her and told her to knead that, and she was sick and tired of ingratitude from the folks in a little, two-bit backwoods country where they still had to pay taxes to the English King, and hadn't Em heard about the Argonne and the American blood that was being shed there by the bucketful, and how did Em think they would make the Hun say Uncle anyways with a lot of fat-headed Englishmen and Frenchmen messing it all up, and what they needed over there was American efficiency and American spunk?

'Em didn't have a chance to reply, because Hannah was

immediately in trouble with Sonnenfels and Heinie Bayer, who smouldered under a conviction that Germany was hideously wronged and that everybody was piling on the Fatherland without any cause at all, and though they were just as good Americans as anybody they were damn well sick of it and hoped the German troops would show Pershing something new about efficiency. Charlie tried to quiet them down by saying that everybody knew the War was a put-up job and nobody was getting anything out of it but the Big Interests. This was a mistake, because Sonny and Heinie turned on him and told him that they knew why he was so glad to be in Canada, and if they were younger men they'd be in the scrap and they weren't going to say which side they'd be on, neither, but if they met anything like Charlie on the battlefield they'd just put a chain on him and show him off beside Rango.

'The battle went on for weeks, during which Joe Dark suffered the humiliation of having Em tell everybody that he wasn't in the Canadian Army because he had flat feet, and Hannah replying that you didn't need feet to fly a plane, but you sure needed brains. The only reasonable voice was that of Professor Spencer, who was a great reader of the papers, and an independent thinker; he was all for an immediate armistice and a peace conference. But as nobody wanted to listen to him, he lectured me, instead, so that I still have a very confused idea of the causes of that War, and the way it was fought. Hannah got a Stars and Stripes from somewhere, and stuck it up on her little platform. She said it made her feel good just to have it there.

'It all came about because of boredom. Boredom and stupidity and patriotism, especially when combined, are three of the greatest evils of the world we live in. But a worse and more lasting source of trouble was the final show in each village, which was called the Last Trick.

'It was agreed that the Last Trick ought to be livelier than the other nine shows of the day. The fair was at its end, the serious matters like the judging of animals and fancy-work had been completed, and most of the old folks had gone home, leaving young men and their girls, and the village cutups on the fairground. It was then that the true, age-old Spirit of Carnival descended on Wanless's World of Wonders, but of course it didn't affect everybody in the same way. Outside, the calliope was playing its favourite tune, "The Poor Butterfly Waltz"; supposedly unknown to Gus, the man who ran the cat-rack had slipped in the gaff, so that the eager suitor who was trying to win a kewpie doll for the girl of his heart by throwing baseballs found that the stuffed pussy-cats wouldn't be knocked down. It was a sleazier, crookeder fair altogether than the one the local Fair Board had planned, but there was always a young crowd that liked it that way.

'On the bally, Charlie allowed his wit a freer play. As Zovene juggled with his spangled Indian clubs, Charlie would say, in a pretended undertone which carried well beyond his audience: "Pretty good, eh? He isn't big, but he's good. Anyways, how big would you be if you'd been strained through a silk handkerchief?" The young bloods would guffaw at this, and their girls would clamour to have it explained to them. And when Zitta showed her snakes, she would drag the old cobra suggestively between her legs and up her front, while Charlie whispered, "Boys-oh-boys, who wouldn't be a snake?"

'Inside the tent Charlie urged the young men to model themselves on Sonnenfels, so that all the girls would be after them, and they'd be up to the job. And when he came to Andro he would ogle his hearers and say, "He's the only guy in the world who's glad to wake up in the morning and find he's beside himself." He particularly delighted in tormenting Hannah. She did her own talking, but as she shrieked her devotion to the Lord Jesus, Charlie would lean down low, and say, in a carrying whisper, "She hasn't seen her ace o' spades in twenty years." The burst of laughter made Hannah furious, though she never caught what was said. She knew, however, that it was something dirty. However often she complained to Gus, and however often Gus harangued Charlie, the Spirit of Carnival was always too much for him. Nor was Gus whole-hearted in her complaints; what pleased the crowd was what Gus liked.

'Hannah attempted to fight fire with fire. She often made it known, in the Pullman, that in her opinion these modern kids weren't bad kids, and if you gave them a chance they didn't want this Sex and all like that. Sure, they wanted fun, and she knew how to give 'em fun. She was just as fond of fun as anybody, but she didn't see the fun in all this Smut and Filth. So she gave 'em fun.

' "Lots o' fun in your Bible, boys and girls," she would shout. "Didn't you know that? Didya think the Good Book was all serious? You just haven't read it with the Liberal Heart, that's all. Come on now! Come on now, all of you! Who can tell me why you wouldn't dare to take a drink outa the first river in Eden? Come on, I bet ya know. Sure ya know. You're just too shy to say. Why wouldn't ya take a drink outa the first river in Eden? — Because it was Pison, that's why! If you don't believe me, look in Genesis two, eleven." Then she would go off into a burst of wheezing laughter.

'Or she would point — and with an arm like hers, pointing was no trifling effort — at Zovene, shouting: "You call him small? Say, he's a regular Goliath compared with the shortest man in the Bible. Who was he? Come on, who was he? — He was Bildad the Shu-hite, Job two, eleven. See, the Liberal Heart can even get a laugh outa one of Job's Comforters. I betcha never thought of that, eh?" And again, one of her terrible bursts of laughter.

'Hannah understood nothing of the art of the comedian. It is dangerous to laugh at your own jokes, but if you must, it is a great mistake to laugh first. Fat people, when laughing, are awesome sights, enough to strike gravity into the onlooker. But Hannah was a whole World of Wonders in herself when she laughed. She forced her laughter, for after all, when you have told people for weeks that the only man in the Bible with no parents was Joshua, the son of Nun, the joke loses some of its savour. So she pushed laughter out of herself in wheezing, whooping cries, and her face became unpleasantly marbled with dabs of a darker red under the rouge she wore. Her collops wobbled uncontrollably, her vast belly heaved and trembled as she sucked breath, and sometimes she attempted to slap her thigh, producing a wet splat of sound. Fat Ladies ought not to tell jokes; their mirth is of the flesh, not of the mind. Fat Ladies ought not to laugh; a chuckle is all they can manage without putting a dangerous strain on their breathing and circulatory system. But Hannah would not listen to reason. She was determined to drive Smut back into its loathsome den with assaults of Clean Fun, and if she damaged herself in the battle, her wounds would be honourable.

'Sometimes she had an encouraging measure of success. Quite often there would be in the crowd some young man who was of a serious, religious turn of mind, and usually he was accompanied by a girl who had preacher's daughter written all over her. They had been embarrassed by Charlie's jokes when they understood them. They had been even more embarrassed when Rango, at a secret signal from Heinie, left his pretended restaurant table and urinated in a corner, while Heinie pantomimed a waiter's dismay. But with that camaraderie which exists among religious people just as it does among tinhorns and crooks, they recognized Hannah as a benign influence, and laughed with her, and urged her on to greater flights. She gave them her best. "What eight fellas in the Bible milked a bear? *You* know! You musta read it a dozen times. D'ya give it up? Well, listen carefully: Huz, Buz, Kemuel, Chesed, Hazo, Pildash, Jidlaph, and Bethuel – *these eight did Milcah bear to Nahor, Abraham's brother*. Didya never think of it that way? Eh? Didn't ya? Well, it's in Genesis twenty-two."

'When one of these obviously sanctified couples appeared, it was Hannah's pleasure to single them out and hold them up to the rest of the crowd as great cutups. "Oh, I see ya," she would shout; "it's the garden of Eden all over again; the trouble isn't with the apple in the tree, it's with that pair on the ground." And she would point at them, and they would blush and laugh and be grateful to be given a reputation for wickedness without having to do anything to acquire it.

'All of this cost Hannah dearly. After a big Saturday night, when she had exhausted her store of Bible riddles, she was almost too used up for her ritual bath. But she had worked herself up into a shocking sweat, and sometimes the smell of wet cornstarch from her sopping body spread a smell like a gigantic nursery pudding through the whole of the tent, and bathed she had to be, or there would be trouble with chafing.

'Her performance on these occasions made Willard deeply, cruelly angry. He would stand beside Abdullah and I could hear him swearing, repetitively but with growing menace, as she carried on. The worst of it was, if she secured any sort of success, she was not willing to stop; even when the crowd had passed on to see Abdullah, she would continue, at somewhat lesser pitch, with a few lingerers, who hoped for more Bible fun. In the Last Trick it was Willard's custom to have three people cut the cards for the automaton, instead of the usual one, and he wanted the undivided attention of the crowd. He hated Hannah, and from my advantageous peephole I was not long in coming to the conclusion that Hannah hated him.

'There were plenty of places in southern Ontario at that time where religious young people were numerous, and in these communities Hannah did not scruple to give a short speech in which she looked forward to seeing them next year, and implored them to join her in a parting hymn. "God be with you till we meet again," she would strike up, in her thin, piercing voice, like a violin string played unskilfully and without a vibrato, and there were always those who, from religious zeal or just because they liked to sing, would join her. Nor was one verse enough. Charlie would strike in, as boldly as he could : *And now, ladies and gentlemen, our Master Marvel of the World of Wonders – Willard the Wizard and his Card-Playing Automaton, Abdullah, as soon to be exhibited on the stage of the Palace Theater, New York* – but Hannah would simply put on more steam, and slow down, and nearly everybody in the tent would be wailing –

> God be with you till we meet again!
> Keep love's banner floating o'er you,
> Smite death's threatening wave before you :
> God be with you till we meet again;

And then the whole dismal chorus. It was a hymn of hate, and Willard met it with such hate as I have rarely seen.

'As for me, I was only a child, and my experience of hatred was slight, but so far as I could, and with what intensity of spirit I could muster, I hated them both. Hate and bitterness were becoming the elements in which I lived.'

Eisengrim had a fine feeling for a good exit-line, and at this point he rose to go to bed. We rose, as well, and he went solemnly around the circle, shaking hands with us all in the European manner. Lind and Kinghovn even bowed as they did so, and when Magnus turned at the door to give us a final nod, they bowed again.

'Now why do you suppose we accord these royal courtesies to a man who has declared that he was Nobody for so many years,' said Ingestree, when we had sat down again. 'Because it is so very plain that he is not Nobody now. He is almost oppressively Somebody. Are we rising, and grinning, and even bowing out of pity? Are we trying to make it up to a man who suffered a dreadful denial of personality by assuring him that now we are quite certain he is a real person, just like us? Decidedly not. We defer to him, and hop around like courtiers because we can't help it. Why? Ramsay, do you know why?'

'No,' said I; 'I don't, and it doesn't trouble me much. I rather enjoy Magnus's lordly airs. He can come off his perch when he thinks proper. Perhaps we do it because we know he doesn't take it seriously; it's part of a game. If he insisted, we'd rebel.'

'And when you rebelled, you would see a very different side of his nature,' said Liesl.

'You play the game with him, I observe,' said Ingestree. 'You stand up when His Supreme Self-Assurance leaves the company. Yet you are mistress here, and we are your guests. Now why is that?'

'Because I am not quite sure who he is,' said Liesl.

'You don't believe this story he's telling us?'

'Yes. I think that he has come to the time of his life when he feels the urge to tell. Many people feel it. It is the impulse behind a hundred bad autobiographies every year. I think he is being as honest as he can. I hope that when he finishes his story – if he does finish it – I shall know rather more. But I may not have my answer then.

'I don't follow; you hope to hear his story out, but you don't think it certain that you will know who he is even then, although you think he is being honest. What is this mystery?'

'Who is anybody? For me, he is whatever he is to me. Biographical facts may be of help, but they don't explain that. Are you married, Mr Ingestree?'

'Well, no, actually, I'm not.'

'The way you phrase your reply speaks volumes. But suppose

you were married; do you think that your wife would be to you precisely what she was to her women friends, her men friends, her doctor, lawyer, and hairdresser? Of course not. To you she would be something special, and to you that would be the reality of her. I have not yet found out what Magnus is to me, although we have been business associates and friendly intimates for a long time. If I had been the sort of person who is somebody's mistress, I would have been his mistress, but I've never cared for the mistress role. I am too rich for it. Mistresses have incomes, and valuable possessions, but not fortunes. Nor can I say we have been lovers, because that is a messy expression people use when they are having sexual intercourse on fairly regular terms, without getting married. But I have had many a jolly night with Magnus, and many an exciting day with him. I still have to decide what he is to me. If humouring his foible for royal treatment helps me to come to a conclusion, I have no objection.

'Well, what about you, Ramsay? He keeps referring to you as his first teacher of magic. You knew him from childhood, then? You could surely say who he was?'

'I was almost present at his birth. But does that mean anything? An infant is a seed. Is it an oak seed or a cabbage seed? Who knows? All mothers think their children are oaks, but the world never lacks for cabbages. I would be the last man to pretend that knowing somebody as a child gave any real clue to who he is as a man. I can tell you this: he jokes about the lessons I gave him when he was a child, but he didn't think them funny then; he had a great gift for something I couldn't do at all, or could do with absurd effort. He was deadly serious during our lessons, and for a good reason. I could read the books and he couldn't. I think that may throw some light on what we have been hearing about the World of Wonders, which he presents as a kind of joke. I am perfectly certain it wasn't a joke at the time.'

'I am sure he wasn't joking when he spoke of hatred,' said Lind. 'He was funny, or ironic, or whatever you want to call it, about the World of Wonders. We all know why people talk in that way; if we are amusing about our trials in the past, it is as if we say, "See what I overcame – now I treat it as a joke – see

631

how strong I have been and ask yourself if you could have overcome what I overcame?" But when he spoke of hatred, there was no joking.'

'I don't agree,' said Ingestree. 'I think joking about the past is a way of suggesting that it wasn't really important. A way of veiling its horror, perhaps. We shudder when we hear of yesterday's plane accident, in which seventy people were killed; but we become increasingly philosophical about horrors that are further away. What is the Charge of the Light Brigade now? We remember it as a military blunder and we use it as a stick to beat military commanders, who are all popularly supposed to be blunderers. It has become a poem by Tennyson that embarrasses us by its exaltation of unthinking obedience. We joke about the historical fact and the poetic artifact. But how many people ever think of the young men who charged? Who takes five minutes to summon up in his mind what they felt as they rushed to death? It is the fate of the past to be fuel for humour.'

'Have you put your finger on it?' said Lind. 'Perhaps you have. Jokes dissemble horrors and make them seem unimportant. And why? Is it in order that more horrors may come? In order that we may never learn anything from experience? I have never been very fond of jokes. I begin to wonder if they are not evil.'

'Oh rubbish, Jurgen,' said Ingestree. 'I was only talking about one aspect of humour. It's absolutely vital to life. It's one of the marks of civilization. Mankind wouldn't be mankind without it.'

'I know that the English set a special value on humour,' said Lind. 'They have a very fine sense of humour and sometimes they think theirs the best in the world, like their marmalade. Which reminds me that during the First World War some of the English troops used to go over the top shouting, "Marmalade!" in humorously chivalrous voices, as if it were a heroic battle-cry. The Germans could never get used to it. They puzzled tirelessly to solve the mystery. Because a German cannot conceive that a man in battle would want to be funny, you see. But I think the English were dissembling the horror of their situation so that they would not notice how close they were to Death. Again, humour was essentially evil. If they had thought of the truth of their situation, they might not have gone over the top. And that might have been a good thing.'

'Let's not theorize about humour, Jurgen,' said Ingestree; 'it's utterly fruitless and makes the very dullest kind of conversation.'

'Now it's my turn to disagree,' I said. 'This notion that nobody can explain humour, or even talk sensibly about it, is one of humour's greatest cover-ups. I've been thinking a great deal about the Devil lately, and I have been wondering if humour isn't one of the most brilliant inventions of the Devil. What have you just been saying about it? It diminishes the horrors of the past, and it veils the horrors of the present, and therefore it prevents us from seeing straight, and perhaps from learning things we ought to know. Who profits from that? Not mankind, certainly. Only the Devil could devise such a subtle agency and persuade mankind to value it.'

'No, no, no, Ramsay,' said Liesl. 'You are in one of your theological moods. I've watched you for days, and you have been moping as you do only when you are grinding one of your home-made theological axes. Humour is quite as often the pointer to truth as it is a cloud over truth. Have you never heard the Jewish legend – it's in the Talmud, isn't it? – that at the time of Creation the Creator displayed his masterwork, Man, to the Heavenly Host, and only the Devil was so tactless as to make a joke about it. And that was why he was thrown out of Heaven, with all the angels who had been unable to suppress their laughter. So they set up Hell as a kind of jokers' club, and thereby complicated the universe in a way that must often embarrass God.'

'No,' I said; 'I've never heard that and as legends are my speciality I don't believe it. Talmud my foot! I suspect you made that legend up here and now.'

Liesl laughed loud and long, and pushed the brandy bottle toward me. 'You are almost as clever as I am, and I love you, Dunstan Ramsay,' she said.

'New or old, it's a very good legend,' said Ingestree. 'Because that's always one of the puzzles of religion – no humour. Not a scrap. What is the basis of our faith, when we have a faith? The Bible. The Bible contains precisely one joke, and that is a schoolmasterish pun attributed to Christ when he told Peter that he was the rock on which the Church was founded. Very probably a later interpolation by some Church Father who thought it was a real rib-binder. But monotheism leaves no room for jokes, and I've thought for a long time that is what is wrong with it. Monotheism is too po-faced for the sort of world we find ourselves in. What have we heard tonight? A great deal about how Happy Hannah tried to squeeze jokes out of the Bible in the hope of catching a few young people who were brimming with life. Frightful puns; the kind of bricks you make without straw. Whereas the Devil, when he is represented in literature, is full of excellent jokes, and we can't resist him because he and his jokes make so much sense. To twist an old saying, if the Devil had not existed, we should have had to invent him. He is the only explanation of the appalling ambiguities of life. I give you the Devil!'

He raised his glass, but only he and Liesl drank the toast. Kinghovn, who had been getting into the brandy very heavily, was almost asleep. Lind was musing, and no sign of amusement appeared on his long face. I couldn't possibly have drunk such a toast, offered in such a spirit. Ingestree was annoyed.

'You don't drink,' said he.

'Perhaps I shall do so later, when I have had time to think it over,' said Lind. 'Private toasts are out of fashion in the English-speaking world; you only drink them on formal occasions, as part of the decorum of stupidity. But we Scandinavians have still one foot in Odin's realm, and when we drink a toast we mean something quite serious. When I drink to the Devil I shall want to be quite serious.'

'I hesitate to say so, Roland,' I said, 'but I wish you hadn't done that. I quite agree that the Devil is a great joker, but I don't think it is particularly jolly to be the butt of one of his jokes. You have called his attention to you in what I must call a frivolous way – damned silly, to be really frank. I wish you hadn't done that.'

'You mean he'll do something to me? You mean that from henceforth I'm a Fated Man? You know, I've always fancied the role of Fated Man. What do you think it'll be? Car accident? Loss of job? Even a nasty death?'

'Who am I to probe the mind of a World Spirit?' I said. 'But if I were the Devil – which, God be thanked, I am not – I might throw a joke or two in your direction that would test your sense of humour. I don't suppose you're a Fated Man.

'You mean I'm too small fry for that?' said Ingestree. He was smiling, but he didn't like my serious tone and was inviting me to insult him. Luckily Kinghovn woke up, slightly slurred in speech but full of opinion.

'You're all out of your heads,' he shouted. 'No humour in the Bible. All right. Scrub out the Bible. Use the script Eisengrim has given us. Film the subtext. Then I'll show you some humour: that Fat Woman – let me give you a peep-shot of her groaning in the donniker, or being swilled down by Gus; let me show her shrieking her bloody-awful jokes while the Last Trick gets dirtier and dirtier. Then you'll hear some laughter. You're all mad for words. Words are just farts from a lot of fools who have swallowed too many books. Give me things! Give me the appearance of a thing, and I'll show you the way to photograph it so the reality comes right out in front of your eyes. The Devil? Balls! God? Balls! Get me that Fat Woman and I'll photograph her one way and you'll know the Devil made her, then I'll photograph her another way and you'll swear you see the work of God! Light! That's the whole secret. Light! And who understands it? I do!'

Lind and Ingestree decided it was time to take him to his bed. As they manhandled him down the long entry-steps of Sorgenfrei he was shouting, 'Light! Let there be light! Who said that? I said it!'

8

THE film-makers were drawing near the end of their work. All but a few special scenes of *Un Hommage à Robert-Houdin* were 'in the can'; what remained was to arrange backstage shots of Eisengrim being put into his 'gaffed' conjuror's evening coat by the actor who played the conjuror's son and assistant; of assistants working quietly and deftly while the great magician produced astonishing effects on the stage; of Mme Robert-Houdin putting the special padded covers over the precious and delicate automata; of the son-assistant gently loading a dozen doves, or three rabbits, or even a couple of ducks into a space which seemed incapable of holding them; of all the splendidly efficient organization which was needed to produce the effect of the illogical and incredible. That night, therefore, Eisengrim moved his narrative along a little faster.

'You don't want a chronological account of my seven years as the mechanism of Abdullah,' he said, 'and indeed it would be impossible for me to give you one. Something was happening all the time, but only two or three matters were of any importance. We were continually travelling and seeing new places, but in fact we saw nothing. We brought excitement and perhaps a whisper of magic into thousands of rural Canadian lives, but our own lives were vast unbroken prairies of boredom. We were continually on the alert, sizing up the Rubes and trying to match what we gave to what they wanted, but no serious level of our minds was ever put to work.

'For Sonnenfels, Molza, and poor old Professor Spencer it was the only life they knew or could expect to have; the first two kept themselves going by nursing some elaborate, inexhaustible, ill-defined personal grievance which they shared; Spencer fed himself on complex, unworkable economic theories, and he would jaw you half to death about bimetallism, or Social Credit, if you gave him a chance. The Fat Woman had her untiring crusade against smut and irreligion; she could not reconcile herself to being simply fat, and I suppose this suggests some kind of mental or spiritual life in her. I saw hope dying in poor Em Dark, as Joe proved his incapacity to learn anything that would get them out of carnival life. Zitta was continually on the lookout for somebody to marry; she couldn't make any money, because she had to spend so much on new, doctored snakes; but how do you get a sucker to the altar if you are always on the move? She would have snatched at Charlie, but Charlie liked something fresher, and anyhow Gus was vigilant to save Charlie from designing women. Zovene was locked in the misery of dwarfdom; he wasn't really a midget, because a midget has to be perfectly formed, and he had a small but unmistakable hump; he was a sour little fellow, and deeply unhappy, I'm sure. Heinie Bayer had lived so long with Rango that he was more like Rango than like a man; they did not bring out the best in each other.

'Like a lot of monkeys Rango was a great masturbator, and when Happy Hannah complained about it Heinie would snicker and say, "It's natural, ain't it?" and encourage Rango to do it during the Last Trick, where the young people would see him. Then Hannah would shout across the tent, "Whoso shall offend one of these little ones which believe in me, it were better for him that a millstone were hanged about his neck, and that he were drowned in the depth of the sea." But the youngsters can't have been believers in the sense of the text, for they hung around Rango, some snickering, some ashamedly curious, and some of the girls obviously unable to understand what was happening. Gus tried to put a stop to this, but even Gus had no power over Rango, except to put him off the show, and he was too solid a draw for that. Hannah decided that Rango was a type of natural, unredeemed man, and held forth at length on that theme. She predicted that Rango would go mad, if he had any brains to go mad with. But Rango died unredeemed.

'So far as I was concerned, the whole of Wanless's World of Wonders was unredeemed. Did Christ die for these, I asked myself, hidden in the shell of Abdullah. I decided that He didn't. I now think I was mistaken, but you must remember that I began these reflections when I was ten years old, and deep in misery. I was in a world which seemed to me to be filthy in every way; I had grown up in a world where there was little love, but much concern about goodness. Here I could see no goodness, and felt no goodness.'

Lind intervened. 'Excuse me if I am prying,' he said, 'but you have been very frank with us, and my question is one of deep concern, not simple curiosity. You were swept into the carnival because Willard had raped you; was there any more of that?'

'Yes, much more of it. I cannot pretend to explain Willard, and I think such people must be rare. I know very well that homosexuality includes love of all sorts, but in Willard it was just a perverse drive, untouched by affection or any concern at all, except for himself. At least once every week we repeated that first act. Places had to be found, and when it happened it was quick and usually done in silence except for occasional whimpers from me and – this was very strange – something very like whimpers from Willard.'

'And you never complained, or told anybody?'

'I was a child. I knew in my bones that what Willard did to me was very wrong, and he was careful to let me know that it was my fault. If I said a word to anybody, he told me, I would at once find myself in the hands of the law. And what would the law do to a boy who did what I did? Terrible things. When I dared to ask what the law would do to him, he said the law couldn't touch him; he knew highly placed people everywhere.'

'How can you have continued to believe that?'

'Oh, you people who are so fortunately born, so well placed, so sure the policeman is your friend! Do you remember my home, Ramsay?'

'Very well.'

'An abode of love, was it?'

'Your mother loved you very much.'

'My mother was a madwoman. Why? Ramsay has very fine theories about her; he had a special touch with her. But to me she was a perpetual reproach because I knew that her madness was my fault. My father told me that she had gone mad at the time of my birth, and because of it. I was born in 1908, when all sorts of extraordinary things were still believed about child-birth, especially in places like Deptford. Those were the sunset days of the great legend of motherhood. When your mother bore you, she went down in her anguish to the very gates of Death, in order that you might have life. Nothing that you could do subsequently would work off your birth-debt to her. No degree of obedience, no unfailing love, could put the account straight. Your guilt toward her was a burden you carried all your life. Christ, I can hear Charlie now, standing on the stage of a thousand rotten little vaude houses, giving out that message in a tremulous voice, while the pianist played "In a Monastery Garden" –

M is for the million smiles she gave me;
O means only that she's growing old;
T is for the times she prayed to save me;
H is for her heart, of purest gold;
E is every wrong that she forgave me;
R is right – and Right she'll always be!
    Put them all together, they spell MOTHER –
    A word that means the world to me!

That was the accepted attitude toward mothers, at that time, in the world I belonged to. Well? Imagine what it was like to grow up with a mother who had to be tied up every morning before my father could go off to his work as an accountant at the planing-mill; he was a parson no longer because her disgrace had made it impossible for him to continue his ministry. What was her disgrace? Something that made my schoolmates shout "Hoor!" when they passed our house. Something that made them call out filthy jokes about hoors when they saw me. So there you have it. A disgraced and ruined home, and for what reason? Because I was born into it. That was the reason.

'That wasn't all. I said that when Willard used me he whimpered. Sometimes he spoke in his whimpering, and what he said then was, "You goddam little hoor!" And when it was over, more than once he slapped me mercilessly around the head, saying, "Hoor! You're nothing but a hoor!" It wasn't really condemnation; it seemed to be part of his fulfilment, his ecstasy. Don't you understand? "Hoor" was what my mother was, and what had brought our family down because of my birth. "Hoor" was what I was. I was the filthiest thing alive. And I was Nobody. Now do you ask me why I didn't complain to someone about ill usage? What rights had I? I hadn't even a conception of what "rights" were.'

'Could this go on without anybody knowing, or at least suspecting?' Lind was pale; he was taking this hard; I had not thought of him as having so much compassionate feeling.

'Of course they knew. But Willard was crafty and they had no proof. They'd have had to be very simple not to know that something was going on, and carnival people weren't ignorant about perversion. They hinted, and sometimes they were nasty, especially Sonnenfels and Molza. Heinie and Zovene thought it was a great joke. Em Dark had spells of being sorry for me, but Joe didn't want her to mix herself up in anything that concerned Willard, because Willard was a power in the World of Wonders. He and Charlie were very thick, and if Charlie turned against any of the Talent, there were all kinds of ways he could reduce their importance in the show, and then Gus might get the idea that some new Talent was wanted.

'Furthermore, I was thought to be bad luck by most of the Talent, and show people are greatly involved with the idea of luck. Early in my time on the show I got into awful trouble with Molza because I inadvertently shifted his trunk a few inches in the dressing tent. It was on a bit of board I wanted to use in my writing-lesson with Professor Spencer. Suddenly Molza was on me, storming incomprehensibly, and Spencer had trouble quieting him down. Then Spencer warned me against ever moving a trunk, which is very bad luck indeed; when the handlers bring it in from the baggage wagon they put it where it ought to go, and there it stays until they take it back to the train. I had to go through quite a complicated ceremony to ward off the bad luck, and Molza fussed all day.

'The idea of the Jonah is strong with show people. A bringer of ill luck can blight a show. Some of the Talent were sure I was a Jonah, which was just a way of focussing their detestation of what I represented, and of Willard, whom they all hated.

'Only the Fat Woman ever spoke to me directly about who and what I was. I forget exactly when it was, but it was fairly early in my experience on the show. It might have been during my second or third year, when I was twelve or thereabouts. One morning before the first trick, and even before the calliope began its toot-up, which was the signal that the World of Wonders and its adjuncts were opening for business, she was sitting on her throne and I was doing something to Abdullah, which I checked carefully every day for possible trouble.

' "Come here, kid," she said. "I wanta talk to you. And I wanta talk mouth to mouth, even apparently, and not in dark speeches. Them words mean anything to you?"

' "That's from Numbers," I said.

' "Numbers is right; Numbers twelve, verse eight. How do you know that?"

' "I just know it."

' "No, you don't just know it. You been taught it. And you been taught it by somebody who cared for your soul's salvation. Was it your Ma?"

' "My Pa," I said.

' "Then did he ever teach you Deuteronomy twenty-three, verse ten?"

' "Is that about uncleanness in the night?"

' "That's it. You been well taught. Did he ever teach you Genesis thirteen, verse thirteen? That's one of the unluckiest verses in the Bible."

' "I don't remember."

' "Not that the men of Sodom were wicked and sinners before the Lord exceedingly?"

' "I don't remember."

' "I bet you remember Leviticus twenty, thirteen."

' "I don't remember."

' "You do so remember! If a man also lie with mankind as he lieth with a woman, both of them have committed an abomination; they shall surely be put to death; their blood shall be upon them."

'I said nothing, but I am sure my face gave me away. It was one of Willard's most terrible threats that if I were caught I should certainly be hanged. But I was mute before the Fat Woman.

' "You know what that means, dontcha?"

'Oh, I knew what it meant. In my time on the show I had already learned a great deal about mankind lying with women, because Charlie talked about little else when he sat on the train with Willard. It was a very dark matter, for all I knew about it was the parody of this act which I was compelled to go through with Willard, and I assumed that the two must be equally horrible. But I clung to the child's refuge: silence.

' "You know where that leads, dontcha? Right slap to Hell, where the worm dieth not and the fire is not quenched."

'From me, nothing but silence.

' "You're in a place where no kid ought to be. I don't mean the show, naturally. The show contains a lotta what's good. But that Abdullah! That's an idol, and that Willard and Charlie encourage the good folks that come in here for an honest show to bow down and worship almost before it, and they won't be held guiltless. No sirree! Nor you, neither, because you're the works of an idol and just as guilty as they are."

' "I just do what I'm told," I managed to say.

' "That's what many a sinner's said, right up to the time when it's no good saying it any longer. And those tricks. You're learning tricks, aren't you? What do you want tricks for?"

'I had a happy inspiration. I looked her straight in the eye. "I count them but dung, that I may win Christ," I said.

' "That's the right way to look at it, boy. Put first things first. If that's the way you feel, maybe there's some hope for you still." She sat a little forward in her chair, which was all she could manage, and put her podgy hands on her great knees, which were shown off to advantage by her pink rompers. "I'll tell you what I always say," she continued; "there's two things you got to be ready to do in this world, and that's fight for what's right, and read your Bible every day. I'm a fighter. Always have been. A mighty warrior for the Lord. And you've seen me on the train, reading my old Bible that's so worn and thumbed that people say to me, 'That's a disgrace; why don't you get yourself a decent copy of the Lord's Word?' And I reply, 'I hang on to this old Bible because it's seen me through thick and thin, and what looks like dirt to you is the wear of love and reverence on every page.' A clean sword and a dirty Bible! That's my war-cry in my daily crusade for the Lord: a clean sword and a dirty Bible! Now, you remember that. And you ponder on Leviticus twenty, thirteen, and cut out all that fornication and Sodom abomination before it's too late, if it isn't too late already."

'I got away, and hid myself in Abdullah and thought a lot about what Happy Hannah had said. My thoughts were like those of many a convicted sinner. I was pleased with my cleverness in thinking up that text that had averted her attack. I sniggered that I had even been able to use a forbidden word like "dung" in a sanctified sense. I was frightened by Leviticus twenty, thirteen, and – you see how much a child of the superstitious carnival I had already become – by the double thirteen verse from Genesis. Double thirteen! What could be more

642

ominous! I knew I ought to repent, and I did, but I knew I could not leave off my sin, or Willard might kill me, and not only was I afraid to die, I quite simply didn't want to die. And such is the resilience of childhood that when the first trick advanced as far as Abdullah, I was pleased to defeat a particularly obnoxious Rube.

'After that I had many a conversation with Hannah in which we matched texts. Was I a hypocrite? I don't think so. I had simply acquired the habit of adapting myself to my audience. Anyhow, my readiness with the Bible seemed to convince her that I was not utterly damned. I had no such assurance, but I was getting used to living with damnation.

'I had a Bible. I stole it from a hotel. It was one of those sturdy copies the Gideons spread about so freely in hotel rooms. I snitched one at the first opportunity, and as Professor Spencer was teaching me to read very capably I spent many an hour with it. I felt no compunction about the theft, because theft was part of the life I lived. Willard was as good a pickpocket as I have ever known, and one of the marks of his professionalism was that he was not greedy or slapdash in his methods.

'He had an agreement with Charlie. At a point about the middle of the bally, during one of the night shows, Charlie would interrupt his description of the World of Wonders to say, very seriously, *Ladies and gentlemen, I think I ought to warn you, on behalf of the management, that pickpockets may be at work at this fair. I give you my assurance that nothing is farther from the spirit of amusement and education represented by our exhibition than the utterly indefensible practice of theft. But as you know, we cannot control everything that may happen in the vicinity of our show. And therefore I urge you, as your friend and as a member of the Wanless organization which holds nothing dearer than its reputation for unimpeachable honesty, that you should keep a sharp eye, and perhaps also a hand, on your wallets. And if there should be any loss – which the Wanless organization most sincerely hopes may not be the case – we beg you to report it to us, and to your excellent local police force, so that the thief may be apprehended if that should prove to be possible.* The gaff here was that when he spoke of thieves, Rubes who had a full wallet were likely to put a hand on it. Willard spotted them from the back of the crowd, and during the rest of Charlie's pious spiel he would gently lift one from a promising Rube. It had to be very quick work. Then, when he had taken the money, he substituted a wad of newspaper of the appropriate size, and either during the bally, or when the Rube came into the tent, he would put the wallet back in place. Rubes generally carried their wallets on the left hip, and as their pants were often a tight fit, a light hand was necessary.

'Willard was never caught. If the Rube came to complain that he had been robbed, Charlie put on a show for him, shook his head sadly, and said that this was one of the problems that confronted honest show folks. Willard never pinched more than one bankroll in a town, and never robbed in the same town two years running. Willard liked best to steal from the local cop, but as cops rarely had much money this was a larcenous foppery which he did not often allow himself.

'Gus never caught on. Gus was a strangely innocent woman in everything that pertained to Charlie and his doings. Of course Charlie got a fifty per cent cut of what Willard stole.

'Willard knew I stole the Bible, and he was angry. Theft, he gave me to understand, was serious business and not for kids. Get caught stealing some piece of junk, and how were you to get back to serious theft again? Never steal anything trivial. This was perhaps the only moral precept Willard ever impressed on me.

'Anyhow, I had a hotel Bible, and I read it constantly, in many another hotel. The carnival business is a fair-weather business, and in winter it could not be pursued and the carnival had to be put to bed.

'That did not mean a cessation of work. The brother who never travelled with the carnival, but who did all our booking, was Jerry Wanless, and he handled the other side of the business, which was vaudeville booking. As soon as the carnival season was over, Willard and Abdullah were booked into countless miserable little vaudeville theatres throughout the American and Canadian Middle West.

'It was an era of vaudeville and there were thousands of acts to fill thousands of spots all over the continent. There was a hierarchy of performance, beginning with the Big Time, which was composed of top acts that played in the big theatres of big cities for a week or more at a stretch. After it came the Small Big Time, which was pretty good and played lesser houses in big and middle-sized cities. Then came the Small Time, which played smaller towns in the sticks and was confined to split weeks. Below that was a rabble of acts that nobody wanted very much, which played for rotten pay in the worst vaude houses. Nobody ever gave it a name, and those who belonged to it always referred to it as Small Time, but it was really Very Small Time. That was where Jerry Wanless booked incompetent dog acts, jugglers who were on the booze, dirty comedians, Single Women without charm or wit, singers with nodes on their vocal chords, conjurors who dropped things, quick-change artistes who looked the same in all their impersonations, and a crowd of carnies like Willard and some of the other Talent from the World of Wonders.

'It was the hardest kind of entertainment work, and we did it in theatres that seemed never to have been swept, for audiences that seemed never to have been washed. We did continuous vaudeville: six acts followed by a "feature" movie, round and round and round from one o'clock in the afternoon until midnight. The audience was invited to come when it liked and stay as long as it liked. In fact, it changed completely almost every show, because there was always an act called a "chaser" which was reckoned to be so awful that even the people who came to our theatres couldn't stand it. Quite often during my years in vaudeville Zovene the Midget Juggler filled this ignominious spot. Poor old Zovene wasn't really as awful as he appeared, but he was pretty bad and he was wholly out of fashion. He dressed in a spangled costume that was rather like the outfit worn by Mr Punch – a doublet and tight knee-breeches, with striped stockings and little pumps. He had only one outfit, and he had shed spangles for so long that he looked very shabby. There was still a wistful prettiness about him as he skipped nimbly to "Funiculi funicula" and tossed coloured Indian clubs in the air. But it was a prettiness that would appeal only to an antiquarian of the theatre, and we had no such rarities in our audiences.

'There is rank and precedence everywhere, and here, on the

bottom shelf of vaudeville, Willard was a headliner. He had the place of honour, just before Zovene came on to empty the house. The "professor" at the piano would thump out an Oriental theme from *Chu Chin Chow* and the curtain would rise to reveal Abdullah, bathed in whatever passed for an eerie light in that particular house. Behind Abdullah might be a backdrop representing anything – a room in a palace, a rural glade, or one of those improbable Italian gardens, filled with bulbous balustrades and giant urns, which nobody has ever seen except a scene-painter.

'Willard would enter in evening dress, wearing a cape, which he doffed with an air, and held extended briefly at his right side; when he folded it, a shabby little table with his cards and necessaries had appeared behind it. Applause? Never! The audiences we played to rarely applauded and they expected a magician to be magical. If they were not asleep, or drunk, or pawing the woman in the next seat, they received all Willard's tricks with cards and coins stolidly.

'They liked it better when he did a little hypnotism, asking for members of the audience to come to the stage to form a "committee" which would watch his act at close quarters, and assure the rest of the audience that there was no deception. He did the conventional hypnotist's tricks, making men saw wood that wasn't there, fish in streams that had no existence, and sweat in sunlight that had never penetrated into that dismal theatre. Finally he would cause two of the men to start a fight, which he would stop. The fight always brought applause. Then, when the committee had gone back to their seats, came the topper of his act, Abdullah the Wonder Automaton of the Age. It was the same old business; three members of the audience chose cards, and three times Abdullah chose a higher one. Applause. Real applause, this time. Then the front-drop – the one with advertisements painted on it – came down and poor old Zovene went into his hapless act.

'The only other Talent from the World of Wonders that was booked into the places where we played were Charlie, who did a monologue, and Andro.

'Andro was becoming the worst possible kind of nuisance. He was showing real talent, and to hear Charlie and Willard talk about it you would think he was a traitor to everything that was good and pure in the world of show business. But I was interested in Andro, and watched him rehearse. He never talked to me, and probably regarded me as a company spy. There were such things, and they reported back to Jerry in Chicago what Talent was complaining about money, or slacking on the job, or black-mouthing the management. But Andro was the nearest thing to real Talent I had met with up to that time, and he fascinated me. He was a serious, unrelenting worker and perfectionist.

'Imitators of his act have been common in night-clubs for many years, and I don't suppose he was the first to do it, but certainly he was the best of the lot. He played in the dark, except for a single spotlight, and he waltzed with himself. That is to say, on his female side he wore a red evening gown, cut very low in the back, and showing lots of his female leg in a red stocking; on his masculine side he wore only half a pair of black satin knee-breeches, a black stocking and a pump with a phoney diamond buckle. When he wrapped himself in his own arms, we saw a beautiful woman in the arms of a half-naked muscular man, whirling rhythmically around the stage in a rapturous embrace. He worked up all sorts of illusions, kissing his own hand, pressing closer what looked like two bodies, and finally whirling offstage for what must undoubtedly be further romance. He was a novelty, and even our audiences were roused from their lethargy by him. He improved every week.

'Willard and Charlie couldn't stand it. Charlie wrote to Jerry and I heard what he said, for Charlie liked his own prose and read it aloud to Willard. Charlie deplored "the unseemly eroticism" of the act, he said. It would get Jerry a bad name to book such an act into houses that catered to a family trade. Jerry wrote back telling Charlie to shut up and leave the booking business to him. He suggested that Charlie clean up his own act, of which he had received bad reports. Obviously some stool-pigeon had it in for Charlie.

'As a monologist, Charlie possessed little but the self-assurance necessary for the job. Such fellows used to appear before the audience, flashily dressed, with the air of a relative who has made good in the big city and come home to amuse the folks.

"Friends, just before the show I went into one of your local restaurants and looked down the menoo for something tasty. I said to the waiter, Say, have you got frogs' legs? No sir, says he, I walk like this because I got corns. You know, one of the troubles today is Prohibition. Any disagreement? No. I didn't think there would be. But the other day I stepped into a blind pig not a thousand miles from this spot, and I said to the waiter, Bring me a couple of glasses of beer. So he did. So I drank one. Then I got up to leave, and the waiter comes running. Hey, you didn't pay for those two glasses of beer, he said. That's all right, I said, I drank one and left the other to settle. Then I went to keep a date with a pretty schoolteacher. She's the kind of schoolteacher I like best – lots of class and no principle. I get on better with schoolteachers now than I did when I was a kid. My education was completed early. One day in school I put up my hand and the teacher said, What is it, and I said, Please may I leave the room? No, she says, you stay here and fill the inkwells. So I did, and she screamed, and the principal expelled me ..." And so on, for ten or twelve minutes, and then he would say, "But seriously folks –" and go into a rhapsody about his Irish mother, and a recitation of that tribute to motherhood. Then he would run off the stage quickly, laughing as if he had been enjoying himself too much to hold it in. Sometimes he got a spatter of applause. Now and then there would be dead silence, and some sighing. Vaudeville audiences in those places could give the loudest sighs I have ever heard. Prisoners in the Bastille couldn't have touched them.

'In the monologues of people like Charlie there were endless jokes about minorities – Jews, Dutch, Squareheads, Negroes, Irish, everybody. I never heard of anybody resenting it. The sharpest jokes about Jews and Negroes were the ones we heard from Jewish and Negro comedians. Nowadays I understand that a comedian doesn't dare to make a joke about anyone but himself, and if he does too much of that he is likely to be tagged as a masochist, playing for sympathy because he is so mean to himself. The old vaude jokes were sometimes cruel, but they were fairly funny and they were lightning-rods for the ill-will of audiences like ours, who had a plentiful supply of ill-will. We played to people who had not been generously used by life, and I suppose we reflected their state of mind.

'I spent my winters from 1918 to 1928 in vaudeville houses of the humblest kind. As I sat inside Abdullah and peeped out through the spy-hole in his bosom I learned to love these dreadful theatres. However wretched they were, they appealed to me powerfully. It was not until much later in my life that I learned what it was that spoke to me of something fine, even when the language was garbled. It was Liesl, indeed, who showed me that all theatres of that sort – the proscenium theatres that are out of favour with modern architects – took their essential form and style from the ball-rooms of great palaces, which were the theatres of the seventeenth and eighteenth centuries. All the gold, and stucco ornamentation, the cartouches of pan-pipes and tambourines, the masks of Comedy, and the upholstery in garnet plush were democratic stabs at palatial luxury; these were the palaces of the people. Unless they were Catholics, and spent some time each week in a gaudy church, this was the finest place our audiences could enter. It was heart-breaking that they should be so tasteless and run-down and smelly, but their ancestry was a noble one. And of course the great movie and vaudeville houses where Charlie and Willard would never play, or enter except as paying customers, were real palaces of the people, built in what their owners and customers believed to be a regal mode.

'There was nothing regal about the accommodation for the Talent. The dressing-rooms were few and seemed never to be cleaned; when there were windows they were filthy, and high in the walls, and were protected on the outside by wire mesh which caught paper, leaves, and filth; as I remember them now most of the rooms had a dado of deep brown to a height of about four feet from the floor, above which the walls were painted a horrible green. There were wash-basins in these rooms, but there was never more than one donniker, usually in a pitiful state of exhaustion, sighing and wheezing the hours away at the end of a corridor. But there was always a star painted on the door of one of these dismal holes, and it was in the star dressing-room that Willard, and Charlie (as a relative of the management) changed their clothes, and where I was tolerated as a dresser and helper.

'It was as a dresser that I travelled, officially. Dresser, and assistant to Willard. It was never admitted that I was the effective part of Abdullah, and we carried a screen which was set up to conceal the back of the automaton, so that the stage-hands never saw me climbing into my place. They knew, of course, but they were not supposed to know, and such is the curious loyalty and discipline of even these rotten little theatres that I never heard anyone telling the secret. Everybody back-stage closed ranks against the audience, just as in the carnival we were all in league against the Rubes.

'I spent all day in the theatre, because the only alternative was the room I shared with Willard in some cheap hotel, and he didn't want me there. My way of life could hardly have been more in contradiction of what is thought to be a proper environ-ment for a growing boy. I saw little sunlight, and I breathed an exhausted and dusty air. My food was bad, because Willard kept me on a very small allowance of money, and as there was nobody to make me eat what I should, I ate what I liked, which was cheap pastry, candy, and soft drinks. I was not a fanatical washer, but as I shared a bed with Willard he sometimes in-sisted that I take a bath. By every rule of hygiene I should have died of several terrible diseases complicated with malnutrition, but I didn't. In a special and thoroughly unsuitable way, I was happy. I even contrived to learn one or two things which were invaluable to me.

'Except for his dexterity as a conjuror, pickpocket, and card-sharp, Willard did nothing with his hands. As I told you, Abdullah had some mechanism in his base, and when Willard moved the handle that set it in motion, it was supposed to enable Abdullah to do clever things with cards. The mechanism was a fake only in so far as it related to Abdullah's skill; other-wise it was genuine enough. But it was always breaking down, and this was embarrassing when we were on show. Early in my time with Willard I explored those wheels and springs and cogs, and very soon discovered how to set them right when they stuck. The secret was very simple; Willard never oiled the wheels, and if somebody else oiled them for him, he allowed the oil to grow thick and dirty so that it clogged the works. Quite soon I took over the care of Abdullah's fake mechanism, and though I still did not really understand it I was capable enough at maintaining it.

'I suppose I was thirteen or so when a property man at one of the theatres where we played saw me cleaning and oiling these gaffs, and we struck up a conversation. He was interested in Abdullah, and I was nervous about letting him probe the works, fearing that he would find out that they were fakes, but I need not have worried. He knew that at a glance. "Funny that anybody'd take the trouble to put this class of work into an old piece of junk like this," he said. "D'you know who made it?" I didn't. "Well, I'll bet anything you like a clock-maker made it," said he. "Lookit; I'll show you." And he proceeded to give me a lecture that lasted for almost an hour about the essentials of clockwork, which is a wonderful complexity of mechanism that is, at base, quite simple and founded on a handful of principles. I won't pretend that everybody would have understood him as well as I did, but I am not telling you this story to gain a reputation for modesty. I took to it with all the enthusiasm of a curious boy who had nothing else in the world to occupy his mind. I pestered the property man whenever he had a moment of spare time, demanding more explanation and demonstration. He had been trained as a clock- and watch-maker as a boy – I think he was a Dutchman but I never bothered to learn his name except that it was Henry – and he was a kindly fellow. The third day, which was our last stay in that town, he opened his own watch, took out the movement, and showed me how it could be taken to pieces. I felt as if Heaven had opened. My hands were by this time entirely at my command because of my hundreds of hours of practice in the deeps of Abdullah, and I begged him to let me reassemble the watch. He wouldn't do that; he prized his watch, and though I showed some promise he was not ready to take risks. But that night, after the last show, he called me to him and handed me a watch – a big, old-fashioned turnip with a German-silver case – and told me to try my luck with that. "When you come back this way," he said, "let's see how you've got on."

'I got on wonderfully. During the next year I took that watch apart and reassembled it time after time. I tinkered and cleaned and oiled and fiddled with the old-fashioned regulator until it was as accurate a timepiece as its age and essential character allowed. I longed for greater knowledge, and one day when opportunity served I stole a wrist-watch – they were novelties still at that time – and discovered to my astonishment that it was pretty much the same inside as my old turnip, but not such good workmanship. This was the foundation of my mechanical knowledge. I soon had the gaffed works of Abdullah going like a charm, and even introduced a few improvements and replaced some worn parts. I persuaded Willard that the wheels and springs of Abdullah should be on view at all times, and not merely during his preliminary lecture; I put my own control handle inside where I could reach it and cause Abdullah's wheels to change speed when he was about to do his clever trick. Willard didn't like it. He disapproved of changes, and he didn't want me to get ideas above my station.

'However, that is precisely what I did. I began to understand that Willard had serious limitations, and that perhaps his power over me was not so absolute as he pretended. But I was still much too young and frightened to challenge him in anything serious. Like all great revolutions, mine was a long time preparing. Furthermore, the sexual subjection in which I lived still had more power over me than the occasional moments of happiness I enjoyed, and which even the most miserable slaves enjoy.

'From the example of Willard and Charlie I learned a cynicism about mankind which it would be foolish to call deep, but certainly it was complete. Humanity was divided into two groups, the Wise Guys and the Rubes, the Suckers, the Patsys. The only Wise Guys within my range were Willard and Charlie. It was the law of nature that they should prey on the others.

'Their contempt for everyone else was complete, but whereas Charlie was good-natured and pleased with himself when he got the better of a Sucker, Willard merely hated the Sucker. The sourness of his nature did not display itself in harsh judgements or wisecracks; he possessed no wit at all – not even the borrowed wit with which Charlie decked his act and his private conversation. Willard simply thought that everybody but himself was a fool, and his contempt was absolute.

'Charlie wasted a good deal of time, in Willard's opinion, chasing girls. Charlie fancied himself as a seducer, and waitresses and chambermaids and girls around the theatre were all weighed by him in terms of whether or not he would be able to "slip it to them". That was his term. I don't think he was especially successful, but he worked at his hobby and I suppose he had a measure of success. "Did you notice that kid in the Dancing Hallorans?" he would ask Willard. "She's got round heels. I can always tell. What do you wanta bet I slip it to her before we get outa here?" Willard never wanted to bet about that; he liked to bet on certainties.

'The Rubes who wanted to play cards with Abdullah in the vaude houses were of a different stamp from those we met in the carnival world. The towns were bigger than the villages which supported country fairs, and in every one there were a few gamblers. They would turn up at an evening show, and it was not hard to spot them; a gambler looks like anyone else when he is not gambling, but when he takes the cards or the dice in his hands he reveals himself. They were piqued by their defeat at the hands of an automaton and wanted revenge. It was Charlie who sought them out and suggested a friendly game after the theatre was closed.

'The friendly game always began with another attempt to defeat Abdullah, and sometimes money was laid on it. After a sufficient number of defeats – three was usually enough – Willard would say, "You're not going to get anywhere with the Old Boy here, and I don't want to take your money. But how about a hand or two of Red Dog?" He always started with Red Dog, but in the end they played whatever game the Suckers chose. There they would sit, in a corner of the stage, with a table if they could find one, or else playing on top of a box, and it would be three or four in the morning before they rose, and Willard and Charlie were always the winners.

'Willard was an accomplished card-sharp. He never bothered with any of the mechanical aids some crooks use – hold-outs, sleeve pockets, and such things – because he thought them crude and likely to be discovered, as they often are. He always played with his coat off and his sleeves rolled up, which had an honest look; he depended on his ability as a shuffler and dealer, and of course he used marked cards. Sometimes the Rubes brought their own cards, which he would not allow them to use with Abdullah – he explained that Abdullah used a sensitized deck – but which he was perfectly willing to play with in the game. If they were marked he knew it at once, and after a game or two he would say, in a quiet but firm voice, that he thought a change of deck would be pleasant, and produced a new deck fresh from a sealed package, calling attention to the fact that the cards were not marked and could not be.

'They did not remain unmarked for long, however. Willard had a left thumbnail which soon put the little bumps in the tops and sides of the cards that told him all he needed to know. He let the Rubes win for an hour or so, and then their luck changed, and sometimes big money came into Willard's hands at the end of the game. He was the best marker of cards I have ever known except myself. Some gamblers hack their cards so that you could almost see the marks across a room, but Willard had sensitive hands and he nicked them so cleverly that a man with a magnifying glass might have missed it. Nor was he a flashy dealer; he left that to the Rubes who wanted to show off. He dealt rather slowly, but I never saw him deal from the bottom of the deck, although he certainly did so in every game. He and Charlie would sometimes move out of a town with five or six hundred dollars to split between them, Charlie being paid off as the steerer who brought in the Rubes, and Willard as the expert with the cards. Charlie sometimes appeared to be one of the losers in these games, though never so much so that it looked suspicious. The Rubes had a real Rube conviction that show folks and travelling men ought to be better at cards than the opponents they usually met.

'I watched all of this from the interior of Abdullah, because after the initial trials against the automaton it was impossible for me to escape. I was warned against falling asleep, lest I might make some sound that would give away the secret. So, heavy-eyed, but not unaware, I saw everything that was done, saw the greed on the faces of the Rubes, and saw the quiet way in which Willard dealt with the occasional quarrels. And of course I saw how much money changed hands.

'What happened to all that money? Charlie, I knew, was being paid seventy-five dollars a week for his rotten monologues, which would have been good pay if he had not had to spend so much of it on travel; part of Jerry's arrangement was that all Talent paid for its own tickets from town to town, as well as costs of room and board. Very often we had long hops from one stand to another, and travel was a big expense. And of course Charlie spent a good deal on bootleg liquor and the girls he chased.

'Willard was paid a hundred a week, as a headliner, and because the transport of Abdullah, and myself at half-fare, cost him a good deal. But Willard never showed any sign of having much money, and this puzzled me for two or three years. But then I became aware that Willard had an expensive habit. It was morphine. This of course was before heroin became the vogue.

'Sharing a bedroom with him I could not miss the fact that he gave himself injections of something at least once a day, and he told me that it was a medicine that kept him in trim for his demanding work. Taking dope was a much more secret thing in those days than it has become since, and I had never heard of it, so I paid no attention. But I did notice that Willard was much pleasanter after he had taken his medicine than he was at other times, and it was then that he would sometimes give me a brief lesson in sleight-of-hand.

'Occasionally he would give himself a little extra treat, and then, before he fell asleep, he might talk for a while about what the future held. "I'll be up to Albee," he might say; "he'll have to make his decision. I'll tell him – E.F., you want me at the Palace? Okay, you know my figure. And don't tell me I have to arrange it with Martin Beck. You talk to Beck. You paid that French dame, that Bernhardt, $7,000 a week at the Palace. I'm not going to up the ante on you. That figure'll do for me. So any time you want me, you just have to let me know, and I promise you I'll drop everything else to oblige you –" Even in my ignorant ears this sounded unlikely. Once I asked him if he would take Abdullah to the Palace, and he gave one of his rare, snorting laughs. "When I go to the Palace, I'll go alone," he said; "the day I get the high sign from Albee, you're on your own." But he didn't hear from Albee, or any manager but Jerry Wanless.

'He began to hear fairly often from Jerry, whose stool-pigeons were reporting that Willard was sometimes vague on the stage, mistimed a trick now and then, and even dropped things, which is something a headline magician, even on Jerry's circuit, was not supposed to do. I thought these misadventures came from not eating enough, and used to urge Willard to get himself a square meal, but he had never cared much for food, and as the years wore on he ate less and less. I thought this was why he so rarely needed to go to the donniker, and why he was so angry with me when I was compelled to do so, and it was not until years later that I learned that constipation is a symptom of Willard's indulgence. He was usually better in health and sharper on the job when we were with the carnival, because he was in the open air, even though he worked in a tent, but during the winters he was sometimes so dozy – that was Charlie's word for it – that Charlie was worried.

'Charlie had reason to be worried. He was Willard's source of supply. Charlie was a wonder at discovering a doctor in every town who could be squared, because he was always on the lookout for abortionists. Not that he needed abortionists very often, but he belonged to a class of man who regards such knowledge as one of the hallmarks of the Wise Guy. An abortionist might also provide what Willard wanted, for a price, and if he didn't, he knew someone else who would do so. Thus, without, I think, being malignant or even a very serious drug pusher, Charlie was Willard's supplier, and a large part of Willard's winnings in the night-long card games stuck to Charlie for expenses and recompense for the risks he took. When Willard began to be dozy, Charlie saw danger to his own income, and he tried to keep Willard's habit within reason. But Willard was resistant to Charlie's arguments, and became in time even thinner than he had been when first I saw him, and he was apt to be twitchy if he had not had enough. A twitchy conjuror is useless; his hands tremble, his speech is hard to understand, and he makes disturbing faces. The only way to keep Willard functioning efficiently, both as an entertainer and as a card-sharp, was to see that he had the dose he needed, and if his need increased, that was his business, according to Charlie.

'When Willard felt himself denied, it was I who had to put up with his ill temper and spite. There was only one advantage in the gradual decline of Willard so far as I was concerned, and that was that as morphine became his chief craze, his sexual approaches to me became fewer. Sharing a bed with him when he was restless was nervous work, and I usually preferred to sneak one of his blankets and lie on the floor. If the itching took him, his wriggling and scratching were dreadful, and went on until he was exhausted and fell into a stupor rather than a sleep. Sometimes he had periods of extreme sweating, which were very hard on a man who was already almost a skeleton. More than once I have had to rouse Charlie in the middle of the night, and tell him that Willard had to have some of his medicine, or he might go mad. It was always called "his medicine" by me and by Charlie when he talked to me. For of course I was included in the all-embracing cynicism of these two. They assumed that I was stupid, and this was only one of their serious mistakes.

'I too became cynical, with the whole-hearted, all-inclusive vigour of the very young. Why not? Was I not shut off from mankind and any chance to gain an understanding of the diversity of human temperament by the life I led and the people who dominated me? Yet I saw people, and I saw them very greatly to their disadvantage. As I sat inside Abdullah, I saw them without being seen, while they gaped at the curiosities of the World of Wonders. What I saw in most of those faces was contempt and patronage for the show folks, who got an easy living by exploiting their oddities, or doing tricks with snakes or fire. They wanted us; they needed us to mix a little leaven in their doughy lives, but they did not like us. We were outsiders, holiday people, untrustworthy, and the money they spent to see us was foolish money. But how much they revealed as they stared! When the Pharisees saw us they marvelled, but it seemed to me that their inward parts were full of ravening and wickedness. Day after day, year after year, they believed that somehow they could get the better of Abdullah, and their greed and stupidity and cunning drove them on to try their hands at it. Day after day, year after year, I defeated them, and scorned them because they could not grasp the very simple fact that if Abdullah could be defeated, Abdullah would cease to be. Those who tried their luck I despised rather less than those who hung back and let somebody else try his. The change in their loyalty was always the same; they were on the side of the daring one until he was defeated, and then they laughed at him, and sided with the idol.

'In those years I formed a very low idea of crowds. And of all those who pressed near me the ones I hated most, and wished the worst luck, were the young, the lovers, who were free and happy. Sex to me meant terrible bouts with Willard and the grubby seductions of Charlie. I did not believe in the happiness or the innocence or the goodwill of the couples who came to the fair for a good time. My reasoning was simple, and of a very common kind: if I were a hoor and a crook, were not whoredom and dishonesty the foundations on which humanity rested? If I were at the outs with God – and God never ceased to trouble my mind – was anyone else near Him? If they were, they must be cheating. I very soon came to forget that it was I who was the prisoner: I was the one who saw clearly and saw the truth because I saw without being seen. Abdullah was the face I presented to the world, and I knew that Abdullah, the undefeated, was worth no more than I.

'Suppose that Abdullah were to make a mistake? Suppose when Uncle Zeke or Swifty Dealer turned up a ten of clubs, Abdullah were to reply with a three of hearts? What would Willard say? How would he get out of his predicament? He was not a man of quick wit and as the years wore on I understood that his place in the world was even shakier than my own. I could destroy Willard.

'Of course I didn't do it. The consequences would have been terrible. I was greatly afraid of Willard, afraid of Charlie, of Gus, and most afraid of the world into which such an insubordinate act would certainly throw me. But do we not all play, in our minds, with terrible thoughts which we would never dare to put into action? Could we live without some hidden instincts of revolt, of some protest against our fate in life, however enviable it may seem to those who do not have to bear it? I have been, for twenty years past, admittedly the greatest magician in the world. I have held my place with such style and flourish that I have raised what is really a very pretty achievement to the dignity of art. Do you imagine that in my best moments when I have had very distinguished audiences – crowned heads, as all magicians love to boast – that I have not thought fleetingly of producing a full chamber-pot out of a hat, and throwing it into the royal box, just to show that it can be done? But we all hug our chains. There are no free men.

'As I sat in the belly of Abdullah, I thought often of Jonah in the belly of the great fish. Jonah, it seemed to me, had an easy time of it. "Out of the belly of hell cried I, and thou heardest my voice"; that was what Jonah said. But I cried out of the belly of hell, and nothing whatever happened. Indeed, the belly of hell grew worse and worse, for the stink of the dwarf gave place to the stink of Cass Fletcher, who was not a clean boy and ate a bad diet; we can all stand a good deal of our own stink, and there are some earthy old sayings which prove it, but after a few years Abdullah was a very nasty coffin, even for me. Jonah was a mere three days in his fish. After three years I was just beginning my sentence. What did Jonah say? "When my soul fainted within me I remembered the Lord." So did I. Such was the power of my early training that I never became cynical about the Lord – only about his creation. Sometimes I thought the Lord hated me; sometimes I thought he was punishing me for – for just about everything that had ever happened to me, beginning with my birth; sometimes I thought he had forgotten me, but that thought was blasphemy, and I chased it away as fast as I could. I was an odd boy, I can tell you.

'Odd, but – what is truly remarkable – not consciously unhappy. Unhappiness of the kind that is recognized and examined and brooded over is a spiritual luxury. Certainly it was a luxury beyond my means at that time. The desolation of the spirit in which I lived was in the grain of my life, and to admit its full horror would have destroyed me. Deep in my heart I knew that. Somehow I had to keep from falling into despair. So I seized upon, and treasured, every lightening of the atmosphere, everything that looked like kindness, every joke that interrupted the bleak damnation of the World of Wonders. I was a cynic about the world, but I did not dare to become a cynic about myself. Who else? Certainly not Willard or Charlie. If one becomes a cynic about oneself the next step is the physical suicide which is the other half of that form of self-destruction.

'This was the life I lived, from that ill-fated thirtieth of August in 1918 until ten years had passed. Many things happened, but the pattern was invariable; the World of Wonders from the middle of May until the middle of October, and the rest of the time in the smallest of small-time vaudeville. I ranged over all of central Canada, and just about every town of medium size in the middle of the U.S. west of Chicago. When I say that many things happened I am not talking about events of world consequence; in the carnival and the vaude houses we were isolated from the world, and this was part of the paradox of our existence. We seemed to bring a breath of something larger into country fairs and third-rate theatres, but we were little touched by the changing world. The automobile was linking the villages with towns, and the towns with cities, but we hardly noticed. In the vaude houses we knew about the League of Nations and the changing procession of American Presidents because these things provided the jokes of people like Charlie. The splendour of motherhood was losing some of its gloss, and something called the Jazz Age was upon us. So Charlie dropped mother, and substituted a recitation that was a parody of "Gunga Din", which older vaudevillians were still reciting.

> Though I've belted you and flayed you
> By the Henry Ford that made you
> You're a better car than Packard
> Hunka Tin!

– he concluded, and quite often the audience laughed. As we traipsed around the middle of the Great Republic we hardly noticed that the movies were getting longer and longer, and that Hollywood was planning something that would put us all out of work. Who were the Rubes? I think we were the Rubes.

'My education continued its haphazard progress. I would do almost anything to fight the boredom of my life and the sense of doom that I had to suppress or be destroyed by it. I hung around the property-shops of theatres that possessed such things, and learned a great deal from the old men there who had been compelled, in their day, to produce anything from a workable elephant to a fake diamond ring, against time. I sometimes hunted watch-repair shops, and pestered busy men to know what they were doing; I even picked up their trick of looking through a jeweller's *loupe* with one eye while surveying the world fishily through the other. I learned some not very choice Italian from Zovene, some Munich German from Sonny, and rather a lot of pretty good French from a little man who came on the show when Molza's mouth finally became so painful that he took the extraordinary step of visiting a doctor, and came back to the World of Wonders with a very grey face, and packed up his traps. This Frenchman, whose name was Duparc, was an India Rubber Wonder, a contortionist and an uncommonly cheerful fellow. He became my teacher, so far as I had one; Professor Spencer was becoming queerer and queerer and gave up selling the visiting cards which he wrote with his feet; instead he tried to persuade the public to buy a book he had written and printed at his own expense, about monetary reform. He was, I believe, one of the last of the Single Tax men. In spite of the appearance of Duparc, and the disappearance of Andro, who had left the very small time and was now a top-liner on the Orpheum Circuit, we had all been together in the World of Wonders for too many years. But Gus was too tender-hearted to throw anybody off the show, and Jerry got us cheap, and such is the professional vanity of performers of all kinds that we didn't notice that the little towns were growing tired of us.

'Duparc taught me French, and I knew I was learning, but I had another teacher from whom I learned without knowing. Almost everything of great value I have learned in life has been taught me by women. The woman who taught me the realities of hypnotism was Mrs Constantinescu, a strange old girl who travelled around with our show for a few years, running a mitt-camp.

'It was not part of the World of Wonders; it was a concession which Jerry rented, as he rented the right to run a hot-dog stand, a Wheel of Fortune, the cat-rack and, of course, the merry-go-round. The mitt-camp was a fortune-telling tent, with a gaudy banner outside with the signs of the zodiac on it, and an announcement that inside Zingara would reveal the Secrets of Fate. Mrs Constantinescu was Zingara, and for all I know she may have been a real gypsy, as she claimed; certainly she was a good fortune-teller. Not that she would ever admit such a thing. Fortune-telling is against the law in just about every part of Canada and the U.S. When her customers came in she would sell them a copy of *Zadkiel's Dream Book* for ten cents, and offer a personal interpretation for a further fifteen cents, and a full-scale investigation of your destiny for fifty cents, *Zadkiel* included. Thus it was possible for her to say that she was simply selling a book, if any nosey cop interfered with her. They very rarely did so, because it was the job of our advance man to square the cops with money, bootleg hooch, or whatever their fancy might be. Her customers never complained. Zingara knew how to deliver the goods.

'She liked me, and that was a novelty. She was sorry for me, and except for Professor Spencer, nobody had been sorry for me in a very long time. But what made her really unusual in the World of Wonders was that she was interested in people; the Talent regarded the public as Rubes, to be exploited, and whether it was Willard's kind of exploitation or Happy Hannah's, it came to the same thing. But Zingara never tired of humanity or found it a nuisance. She enjoyed telling fortunes and truly thought that she did good by it.

' "Most people have nobody to talk to," she said to me many times. "Wives and husbands don't talk; friends don't really talk because people don't want to get mixed up in anything that might cost them something in the end. Nobody truly wants to hear anybody else's worries and troubles. But everybody has worries and troubles and they don't cover a big range of subjects. People are much more like one another than they are unlike. Did you ever think of that?

' "Well? So I am somebody to talk to. I'll talk, and I'll be gone in the morning, and everything I know goes away with me. I don't look like the neighbours. I don't look like the doctor or the preacher, always judging, always tired. I've got mystery, and that's what everybody wants. Maybe they're church-goers, the people in these little dumps, but what does the church give them? Just sermons from some poor sap who doesn't understand life any more than they do; they know him, and his salary, and his wife, and they know he's no great magician. They want to talk. and they want the old mystery, and that's what I give 'em. A good bargain."

'Clearly they did want it, for though there was never any

crowd around Zingara's tent she took in twenty to twenty-five dollars a day, and after fifty a week had been paid to Jerry, that left her with more money than most of the Talent in the World of Wonders.

' "You have to learn to look at people. Hardly anybody does that. They stare into people's faces, but you have to look at the whole person. Fat or thin? Where is the fat? What about the feet? Do the feet show vanity or trouble? Does she stick out her breast or curl her shoulders to hide it? Does he stick out his chest or his stomach? Does he lean forward and peer, or backward and sneer? Hardly anybody stands straight. Knees bent, or shoved back? The bum tight or drooping? In men, look at the lump in the crotch; big or small? How tall is he when he sits down? Don't miss hands. The face comes last. Happy? Probably not. What kind of unhappy? Worry? Failure? Where are the wrinkles? You have to look good, and quick. And you have to let them see that you're looking. Most people aren't used to being looked at except by the doctor, and he's looking for something special.

' "You take their hand. Hot or cold? Dry or wet? What rings? Has a woman taken off her wedding-ring before she came in? That's always a sign she's worried about a man, probably not the husband. A man – big Masonic or K. of C. ring? Take your time. Tell them pretty soon that they're worried. Of course they're worried; why else would they come to a mitt-camp at a fair? Feel around, and give them chances to talk; you know as soon as you touch the sore spot. Tell them you have to feel around because you're trying to find the way into their lives, but they're not ordinary and so it takes time.

' "Who are they? A young woman – it's a boy, or two boys, or no boy at all. If she's a good girl – you know by the hair-do – probably her mother is eating her. Or her father is jealous about boys. An older woman – why isn't my husband as romantic as I thought he was; is he tired of me; why haven't I got a husband; is my best friend sincere; when are we going to have more money; my son or daughter is disobedient, or saucy, or wild; have I had all the best that life is going to give me?

' "Suppose it's a man; lots of men come, usually after dark.

He wants money; he's worried about his girl; his mother is eating him; he's two-timing and can't get rid of his mistress; his sex is wearing out and he thinks it's the end; his business is in trouble; is this all life holds for me?

' "It's an old person. They're worried about death; will it come soon and will it hurt? Have I got cancer? Did I invest my money right? Are my grandchildren going to make out? Have I had all life holds for me?

' "Sure you get smart-alecks. Sometimes they tell you most. Flatter them. Laugh at the world with them. Say they can't be deceived. Warn them not to let their cleverness make them hard, because they're really very fine people and will make a big mark in the world. Look to see what they are showing to the world, then tell them they are the exact opposite. That works for almost everybody.

' "Flatter everybody. Is it crooked? Most people are starved to death for a kind word. Warn everybody against something, usually something they will be let in for because they are too honest, or too good-natured. Warn against enemies; everybody's got an enemy. Say things will take a turn for the better soon, because they will; talking to you will make things better because it takes a load off their minds.

' "But not everybody can do it. You have to know how to get people to talk. That's the big secret. That Willard! He calls himself a hypnotist, so what does he do? He stands up a half-dozen Rubes and says, I'm going to hypnotize you! Then he bugs his eyes and waves his hands and after a while they're hypnotized. But the real hypnotism is something very different. It's part kindness and part making them feel they're perfectly safe with you. That you're their friend even though they never saw you until a minute ago. You got to lull them, like you'd lull a child. That's the real art. You mustn't overdo it. No saying, you're safe with me, or anything like that. You have to give it out, and they have to take it in, without a lot of direct talk. Of course you look at them hard, but not domineering-hard like vaude hypnotists. You got to look at them as if they was all you had on your mind at the moment, and you couldn't think of anything you'd rather do. You got to look at them as if it was a long time since you met an equal. But don't push; don't shove it. You got to be wide open to them, or else they won't be wide open to you."

'Of course I wanted to have my fortune told by Mrs Constantinescu, but it was against the etiquette of carnival. We never dreamed of asking Sonnenfels to lift anything heavy, or treated the Fat Woman as if she was inconvenient company. But of course Zingara knew what I thought, and she teased me about it. "You want to know your future, but you don't want to ask me? That's right; don't put your faith in sideshow gypsies. Crooks, the whole lot of them. What do they know about the modern world? They belong to the past. They got no place in North America." But one day, when I suppose I was looking blue, she did tell me a few things.

' "You got an easy fortune to tell, boy. You'll go far. How do I know? Because life is goosing you so hard you'll never stop climbing. You'll rise very high and you'll make people treat you like a king. How do I know? Because you're dirt right now, and it grinds your gizzard to be dirt. What makes me think you've got the stuff to make the world admire you? Because you couldn't have survived the life you're leading if you hadn't got lots of sand. You don't eat right and you got filthy hair and I'll bet you've been lousy more than once. If it hasn't killed you, nothing will."

'Mrs Constantinescu was the only person who had ever talked to me about what Willard was still doing to me. The Fat Woman muttered now and then about "abominations" and Sonny was sometimes very nasty to me, but nobody came right out and said anything unmistakable. But old Zingara said: "You're his bumboy, eh? Well, it's not good, but it could be worse. I've known men who liked goats best. It gives you a notion what women got to put up with. The stories I hear! If he calls you 'hoor' just think what that means. I've known plenty of hoors who made it a ladder to something very good. But if you don't like it, do something about it. Get your hair cut. Keep yourself clean. Stop wiping your nose on your sleeve. If you got no money, here's five dollars. Now you start out with a good Turkish bath. Build yourself up. If you gotta be a hoor, be a clean hoor. If you don't want to be a hoor, don't look like a lousy bum."

'At that time, which was the early twenties, a favourite film star was Jackie Coogan; he played charming waifs, often with Charlie Chaplin. But I was a real waif, and sometimes when a Coogan picture was showing in the vaude houses where Willard and I appeared, I was humiliated by how far I fell short of the Coogan ideal.

'I tried a more thorough style of washing, and I got a haircut, a terrible one from a barber who wanted to make everybody look like Rudolph Valentino. I bought some pomade for my hair from him, and the whole World of Wonders laughed at me. But Mrs Constantinescu encouraged me. Later, when I was with Willard on the vaude circuit, we had three days in a town where there was a Turkish bath, and I spent a dollar and a half on one. The masseur worked on me for half an hour, and then said: "You know what? I never seen a dirtier guy. Jeeze, there's still grey stuff comin' outa you! Look at these towels! What you do for a living, kid? Sweep chimneys?" I developed quite a taste for Turkish baths, and stole money regularly from Willard to pay for them. I'm sure he knew I stole; but he preferred that to having me ask him for money. He was growing very careless about money, anyhow.

'I was emboldened to steal enough, over a period of a few weeks, to buy a suit. It was a dreadful suit, God knows, but I had been wearing Willard's cast-offs, cheaply cut down, and it was a royal robe to me. Willard raised his eyebrows when he saw it, but he said nothing. He was losing his grip on the world, and losing his grip on me, and like many people who are losing their grip, he mistook it for the coming of a new wisdom in himself. But when summer came, and Mrs Constantinescu saw me, she was pleased.

' "You're doing fine," she said. "You got to get yourself ready to make a break. This carnival is running downhill. Gus is getting tired. Charlie is getting too big a boy for her to handle. He's drunk on the show now, and she don't even bawl him out. Bad luck is coming. How do I know? What else could be coming to a stale tent-show like this? Bad luck. You watch out. Their bad luck will be your good luck, if you're smart. Keep your eyes open."

'I mustn't give the impression that Mrs Constantinescu was

always at my elbow uttering gypsy warnings. I didn't understand much of what she said, and I mistrusted some of what I understood. That business about looking at people as if you were interested in nothing else, for instance; when I tried it, I suppose I looked foolish, and Happy Hannah made a loud fuss in the Pullman one day, declaring that I was trying to learn the Evil Eye, and she knew who was teaching me. Mrs Constantinescu was very high on her list of abominations. She urged me to search Deuteronomy to learn what happened to people who had the Evil Eye; plagues wonderful, and plagues of my seed, even great plagues of long continuance, and sore sickness; that was what was in store for me unless I stopped bugging my eyes at folks who had put on the whole armour of God, that they might stand against the wiles of the Devil. Like every young person, I was abashed at the apparent power of older people to see through me. I suppose I was pitifully transparent, and Happy Hannah's inveterate malignancy gave her extraordinary penetration. Indeed, I was inclined to think at that time that Mrs Constantinescu was a nut, but she was an interesting nut, and willing to talk. It wasn't until years later that I realized how much good sense was in what she said.

'Of course she was right about bad luck coming to the show. It happened suddenly.

'Em Dark was a nice woman, and she tried to fight down her growing disappointment with Joe by doing everything she could for him, which included making herself attractive. She was small, and rather plump, and dressed well, making all her clothes. Joe was very proud of her appearance, and I think poor Joe was beginning to be aware that the best thing about him was his wife. So he was completely thrown off base one day, as the Pullman was carrying us from one village to another, to see a horrible caricature of Em walk past him and down the aisle toward Heinie and Sonny, who were laughing their heads off in the door of the smoking-room. It was Rango, dressed in Em's latest and best, with a *cloche* hat on his head, and one of Em's purses in his hairy hand. There is no doubt that Heinie and Sonny meant to get Joe's goat, and to spatter the image of Em, because that was the kind of men they were, and that was what they thought funny. Joe looked like a man who has seen a ghost.

He was working, as he so often was, on one of the throwing knives he sold as part of his act, and I think before he knew what he had done, he threw it, and got Rango right between the shoulders. Rango turned, with a look of dreadful pathos on his face, and fell in the aisle. The whole thing took less than thirty seconds.

'You can imagine the uproar. Heinie rushed to Rango, coddled him in his arms, wept, swore, screamed, and became hysterical. But Rango was dead. Sonny stormed and accused Joe in German; he was the kind of man who jabs with his forefinger when he is angry. Gus and Professor Spencer tried to restore order, but nobody wanted order; the excitement was the most refreshing thing that had happened to the World of Wonders in years. Everybody had a good deal to say on one side or the other, but mostly against Joe. The love between Joe and Em concentrated the malignancy of those unhappy people, but this was the first time they had been given a chance to attack it directly. Happy Hannah was seized with a determination to stop the train. What good that would have done nobody knew, but she felt that a big calamity demanded the uttermost in drama.

'I did not at first understand the full enormity of what Joe had done. To kill Rango was certainly a serious injury to Heinie, whose livelihood he was. To buy and train another orang-outang would be months of work. It was Zovene, busily crossing himself, who put the worst of the horror in words: it is a well-known fact in the carnival and circus world that if anybody kills a monkey, three people will die. Heinie wanted Joe to be first on the list, but Gus held him back; luckily for him, because in a fight Joe could have murdered anybody on the show, not excluding Sonny.

'What do you do with a dead monkey? First of all Rango had to be disentangled from Em Dark's best outfit, which Em quite understandably didn't want and threw off the back of the car with Rango's blood on it. (What do you suppose the finder made of that?) Then the body had to be stowed somewhere, and Heinie would have it nowhere except in his berth, which Rango customarily shared with him. You can't make a dead monkey look dignified, and Rango was not an impressive corpse. His eyes wouldn't shut; one stared and the other eyelid drooped, and soon both eyes took on a bluish film; his yellow teeth showed. The Darks felt miserable, because of what Joe had done, and because their love had been held up to mockery in the naked passion and hatred of the hour after Rango's death. Heinie had not scrupled to say that Rango was a lot more use on the show and a lot better person, even though not human, than a little floozie who just stood up and let a dummkopf of a husband throw knives at her; if Joe was so good at hitting Rango, how come he never hit that bitch of a wife of his? This led to more trouble, and it was Em who had to prevent Joe from battering Heinie. I must say that Heinie took the fullest advantage of the old notion that a man is not responsible for what he does in his misery. He got very drunk that night, and wailed and grieved all up and down the car.

'Indeed, the World of Wonders got drunk. Private bottles appeared from everywhere, and were private no more. Professor Spencer accepted a large drink, and it went a very long way with him, for he was not used to it. Indeed, even Happy Hannah took a drink, and quite shortly everyone wished she hadn't. It had been her custom for some years to drink a lot of cider vinegar; she said it kept her blood from thickening, to the great danger of her life, and she got away with so much vinegar that she always smelled of it. Her unhappy inspiration was to spike her evening slug of vinegar with a considerable shot of bootleg hooch which Gus pressed on her, and it was hardly down before it was up again. A nauseated Fat Woman is a calamity on a monumental scale, and poor Gus had a bad night of it with Happy Hannah. Only Willard kept out of the general saturnalia; he crept into his berth, injected himself with his favourite solace, and was out of that world of sorrow, over which the corpse of Rango spread an increasing influence.

'From time to time the Talent would gather around Heinie's berth, and toast the remains. Professor Spencer made a speech, sitting on the edge of the upper berth opposite the one which had become Rango's bier; in this comfortable position he was able to hold his glass with a device he possessed, attached to one foot. He was drunkenly eloquent, and talked touchingly if incoherently about the link between Man and the Lesser Creation, which was nowhere so strong or so truly understood as in circuses and carnivals; had we not, through the years, come to esteem Rango as one of ourselves, a delightful Child of Nature who spoke not with the tongue of man, but through a thousand merry tricks, which now, alas, had been brought to an untimely end? ("Rango'd of been twenty next April," sobbed Heinie; "twenty-two, more likely, but I always dated him from when I bought him.") Professor Spencer did not want to say that Rango had been struck down by a murderer's hand. No, that wasn't the way he looked at it. He would speak of it more as a Cream Passional, brought on by the infinite complexity of human relationships. The Professor rambled on until he lost his audience, who took affairs into their own hands, and drank toasts to Rango as long as the booze held out, with simple cries of "Good luck and good-bye, Rango old pal."

'At last Rango's wake was over. The Darks had lain unseen in their berth ever since it had been possible to go to bed, but it was half past three when Heinie crawled in beside Rango and wept himself to sleep with the dead monkey in his arms. By now Rango was firmly advanced in *rigor mortis* and his tail stuck from between the curtains of the berth like a poker. But Heinie's devotion was much admired; Gus said it warmed the cuckolds of her heart.

'Next morning, at the fairground, our first business was to bury Rango. "Let him lay where his life was spent for others," was what Heinie said. Professor Spencer, badly hung over, asked God to receive Rango. The Darks came, and brought a few flowers, which Heinie ostentatiously spurned from the grave. All Rango's possessions – his cups and plates, the umbrella with which he coquetted on the tightrope – were buried with him.

'Was Zingara tactless, or mischievous, when she said loudly, as we broke up to go about our work: "Well, how long do we wait to see who's first?" The calliope began the toot-up – it was "The Poor Butterfly Waltz" – and we got ready for the first trick which, without Rango, put extra work on all of us.

'As the days passed we realized just how much extra work the absence of Rango did mean. There was nothing Heinie could do without him, and five minutes of performance time had somehow to be made up at each trick. Sonnenfels volunteered to add a minute to his act, and so did Duparc; Happy Hannah was always glad to extend the time during which she harassed her audience about religion, and it was simple for Willard to extend the doings of Abdullah for another minute; so it seemed easy. But an additional ten minutes every day was not so easy for Sonnenfels as for the others; as Strong Men go, he was growing old. Less than a fortnight after the death of Rango, at the three o'clock trick, he hoisted his heaviest bar-bell to his knee, then level with his shoulders, then dropped it with a crash and fell forward. There was a doctor on the fairground, and it was less than three minutes before he was with Sonny, but even at that he came too late. Sonny was dead.

'It is much easier to dispose of a Strong Man than it is of a monkey. Sonny had no family, but he had quite a lot of money in a belt he wore at all times, and we were able to bury him in style. He had been a stupid, evil-speaking, bad-tempered man – quite the opposite of the genial giant described by Charlie in his introduction – and no one but Heinie regretted him deeply. But he left another hole in the show, and it was only because Duparc could do a few tricks on the tightrope that the gap could be filled without making the World of Wonders seem skimpy. Heinie mourned Sonny as uproariously as he had mourned Rango, but this time his grief was not so well received by the Talent.

'Sonny's death was proof positive that the curse of a dead monkey was a fact. Zingara was not slow to point out how short a time had been needed to set the bad luck to work. The Talent turned against Heinie with just as much extravagance of sentimentality as they had shown in pitying him. They were inclined to blame him for Sonny's death. He was still hanging around the show, and he was still drawing a salary, because he had a contract which said nothing about the loss of his monkey by murder. He was on the booze. Gus and Charlie resented him because he cost money without bringing anything in. His presence was a perpetual reminder of bad luck, and soon he was suffering the cold shoulder that had been my lot when Happy Hannah first decided I was a Jonah. Heinie was a proven Jonah, and to look at him was to be reminded that somebody was next on the list of the three who must atone for Rango. Heinie had ceased to be Talent; his reason for being was buried with Rango.

He was an outsider, and in the carnival world an outsider is very far outside indeed.

'We were near the end of the autumn season, and no more deaths occurred before we broke up for winter, some of us to our vaudeville work, and others, like Happy Hannah, to a quiet time in dime museums and Grand Congresses of Strange People in the holiday grounds of the warm south. Zingara was not the only one to remark that poor Gus was looking very yellow. Happy Hannah thought Gus must be moving into The Change, but Zingara said The Change didn't make you belch a lot, and go off your victuals, like Gus, and whispered a word of fear. When we assembled again the following May, Gus was not with us.

'There the deaths seemed to stop, for those who were less perceptive than Zingara, and myself. But something happened during the winter season that was surely a death of a special kind.

'It was in Dodge City. Willard was fairly reliable during our act, but sometimes during the day he was perceptibly under the influence of morphine, and at other and much worse times he was feeling the want of it. I did not know how prolonged addiction works on the imagination; I was simply glad that his sexual demands on me had dropped almost to nothing. Therefore I did not know what to make of it when he seized me one afternoon in the wings of the vaude house, and accused me violently of sexual unfaithfulness to him. I was "at it", he said, with a member of a Japanese acrobatic troupe on the bill, and he wasn't going to stand for that. I was a hoor right enough, but by God I wasn't going to be anybody else's hoor. He cuffed me, and ordered me to get into Abdullah, and stay there, so he would know where I was; and I wasn't to get out of the automaton any more, ever. He hadn't kept me all these years to be cheated by any such scum as I was.

'All of this was said in a low voice, because although he was irrational, he wasn't so far gone that he wanted the stage manager to drop on him, and perhaps fine him, for making a row in the wings during the show. I was seventeen or eighteen, I suppose – I had long ago forgotten my birthday, which had never been a festival in our house anyhow – and although I was still small I had some spirit, and it all rushed to my head when he struck me over the ear. Abdullah was standing in the wings in the place where the image was stored between shows, and I was beside it. I picked up a stage-brace, and lopped off Abdullah's head with one strong swipe; then I took after Willard. The stage manager was soon upon us, and we scampered off to the dressing-room, where Willard and I had such a quarrel as neither of us had ever known before. It was short, but decisive, and when it ended Willard was whining to me to show him the kind of consideration he deserved, as one who had been more than a father to me, and taught me an art that would be a fortune to me; I had declared that I was going to leave him then and there.

'I did nothing of the kind. These sudden transformations of character belong to fiction, not to fact, and certainly not to the world of dependence and subservience that I had known for so many years. I was quite simply scared to leave Willard. What could I do without him? I found out very quickly.

'The stage manager had told the manager about the brief outburst in the wings, and the manager came to set us right as to what he would allow in his house. But with the manager came Charlie, who carried great weight because he was the brother of Jerry, who booked the Talent for that house. It was agreed that – just this once – the matter would be overlooked.

'Willard could not be overlooked a couple of hours later, when he was so far down in whatever world his drug took him to that it was impossible for him to go on the stage. There was all the excitement and loud talk you might expect, and the upshot was that I was ordered to take Willard's place at the next show, and do his act as well as I could, without Abdullah. And that is what I did. I was in a rattle of nerves, because I had never appeared on a stage before, except when I was safely concealed in the body of the automaton. I didn't know how to address an audience, how to time my tricks, or how to arrange an act. The hypnotism was beyond me, and Abdullah was a wreck. I suppose I must have been dreadful, but somehow I filled in the time, and when I had done all I could the spatter of applause was only a little less encouraging than it had been for Willard for several months past.

'When Willard recovered enough to know what had happened he was furious, but his fury simply persuaded him to seek relief from the pain of a rotten world with the needle. This was what precipitated the crisis that delivered me from Abdullah forever; Jerry was on the long-distance telephone, wrangling with Charlie, and the upshot of Charlie's best persuasion was that Willard could finish his season if Charlie would keep him in condition to appear on the stage, and that if Willard didn't appear, I was to do so, and I was able to be made to perform a proper, well-planned act. I see now that this was very decent of Jerry, who had all the problems of an agent to trouble him. He must have been fond of Charlie. But it seemed a dreadful sentence at the time. Beginners in the entertainment world are all supposed to be panting for a chance to rush before an audience and prove themselves; I was frightened of Willard, frightened of Jerry, and most frightened of all of failure.

'As is usually the case with understudies I neither failed nor succeeded greatly. In a short time I had worked out a version of The Miser's Dream that was certainly better than Willard's, and on Charlie's strong advice I did it as a mute act. I had very little voice, and what I had was a thin, ugly croak; I had no vocabulary of the kind that a magician needs; my conversation was conducted in illiterate carnival slang, varied now and then with some Biblical turn of speech that had clung to me. So I simply appeared on the stage and did my stuff without sound, while the pianist played whatever he thought appropriate. My greatest difficulty was in learning how to perform slowly enough. In my development of a technique while I was concealed in Abdullah I had become so fast and so slick that my work was incomprehensible; the quickness of the hand should certainly deceive the eye, but not so fast the eye doesn't realize that it is being deceived.

'Abdullah simply dropped out of use. We lugged him around for a few weeks, but his transport was costly, and as I would not get inside him now he was useless baggage. So one morning, on a railway siding, Charlie and I burned him, while Willard moaned and grieved that we were destroying the greatest thing in his life, and an irreplaceable source of income.

'That was the end of Abdullah, and the happiest moment of

my life up to then was wnen I saw the flames engulf that ugliest of images.

'In their strange way Charlie and Willard were friends, and Charlie thought the moment had come for him to reform Willard. He set about it with his usual enthusiasm, conditioned by a very simple mind. Willard must break the morphine habit. He was to cut the stuff out, at a stroke, and with no thought of looking back. Of course this meant that in a very few days Willard was a raving lunatic, rolling on the floor, the sweating, shrieking victim of crawling demons. Charlie was frightened out of his wits, brought in one of his ambiguous doctors, bought Willard a syringe to replace the one he had dramatically thrown away, and loaded him up to keep him quiet. There was no more talk of abstinence. Charlie kept assuring me that "somehow we've got to see him through it." But there was no way through it. Willard was a gone goose.

'I speak of this lightly now, but at the time I was just as frightened and puzzled as Charlie. I was alarmed to find how dependent on Willard I had become. I had lived with him in dreadful servitude for almost half my life, and now I didn't know what I should do without him. Furthermore, he had been jolted by his attempt at reform into one of those dramatic changes of character which are so astonishing to people who find themselves responsible for a drug addict. He who had been domineering and ugly became embarrassingly fawning and frightened. His great dread was that Charlie and I would put him in hospital. All he wanted was to be cared for, and supplied with enough morphine to keep him comfortable. A simple demand, wasn't it? But somehow we managed it, and one consequence was that I became involved in the nuisance of finding suppliers of the drug, making approaches to them, and paying the substantial prices they demanded.

'By the time it was the season for rejoining the World of Wonders, I had taken over completely the job of filling Willard's place in the vaude programmes, and Willard was an invalid who had to be dragged from date to date. It was a greatly changed carnival that season. Gus was gone, and the new manager was a tough little carnie who knew how to manage the show, but had none of Gus's pride in it; he took his tone from

Charlie, as the real representative of the owners. Charlie had finally wakened up to the fact that the day of such shows was passing, and that fair dates were harder to get. That was when he decided to add a blow-off to the World of Wonders, and as well to set up in a little business of his own, unknown to Jerry.

'A blow-off is an annex to a carnival show. Sometimes it is well-advertised, if it is a speciality that does not quite fit into the show proper, like Australian stock-whip performers, or a man and a girl who do tricks with lariats, in cowboy costume. But it can also be a part of the show that is very quietly introduced, and that is not necessarily seen during every performance. Charlie's blow-off was of this latter kind, and the only attractions in it were Zitta and Willard.

'Zitta was now too fat and too ugly to hold a place in the main tent, but in the blow-off, which occupied a smaller tent entered through the World of Wonders, she could still do a dirty act with some snakes, a logical development from the stunts she had formerly done during the Last Trick. But it was Willard's role that startled me. Charlie had decided to exhibit him as a Wild Man. Willard sat in ragged shirt and pants, his feet bare, in the dust. After he had gone for a few weeks without shaving he looked convincingly wild. His skin had by this time taken on the bluish tinge of the morphine addict, and his eyes, with their habitually contracted pupils, looked terrifying enough to the rural spectators. Charlie's explanation was that Zitta and Willard came from the Deep South, and were sad evidence of what happened when fine old families, reduced from plantation splendour, became inbred. The suggestion was that Willard was the outcome of a variety of incestuous matings. I doubt if many of the people who came to see Willard believed it, but the appetite for marvels and monsters is insatiable, and he was a good eyeful for the curious. The Shame of the Old South, as the blow-off was called, did pretty good business.

'As for Charlie's enterprise, he had become a morphine-pusher. "Cut out the middle man," he said to me by way of explanation; he now bought the stuff from even bigger pushers, and sold it at a substantial price to those who wanted it. The medical profession, he said to me, was intolerably greedy, and he didn't see why he should always be on the paying end of a profitable trade.

'I am sorry to say that I shared Charlie's opinion at that time, and for a while I was his junior in the business. I offer no excuses. I had become fond of the things money can buy, and keeping Willard stoked with what he wanted was very costly. So I became a supplier, rather than a purchaser, and did pretty well by it. But I never put all my eggs in one basket. I was still primarily a conjuror, and the World of Wonders, even in its reduced circumstances, paid me sixty-five dollars a week to do my version of The Miser's Dream for five minutes an hour, twelve hours a day.

'I am going to ask you to excuse me from a detailed account of what followed during the next couple of years. It was inevitable, I suppose, that a simpleton like Charlie, with a greenhorn like myself as his lieutenant, should be caught in one of the periodic crackdowns on drug trafficking. The F.B.I. in the States and the R.C.M.P. in Canada began to pick up some of the small fry like ourselves, as leads to the bigger fish who were more important in the trade. I do not pretend that I behaved particularly well, and the upshot was that Charlie was nabbed and I was not, and that I made my escape by ship with a passport that cost me a great deal of money; I have it still, and it is a beautiful job, but it is not as official as it looks. My problem when the trouble came was what I was going to do with Willard. My solution still surprises me. When every consideration of good sense and self-preservation said that I should ditch him, and let the police find him, I decided instead to take him with me. Explain it as you will, by saying that my conscience overcame my prudence, or that there had grown up a real affection between us during all those years when I was his slave and the secret source of his professional reputation, but I decided that I must take Willard where I was going. Willard was always reminding me that he had never abandoned me when it would have been convenient to do so. So, one pleasant Friday morning in 1927, Jules LeGrand and his invalid uncle, Aristide LeGrand, sailed from Montreal on a C.P.R. ship bound for Cherbourg, and somewhat later Charlie Wanless stood trial in his native state of New York and received a substantial sentence.

'The passports and the steamship passages just about cleaned me out, but I think Willard saved me from being caught. He made a very convincing invalid in his wheelchair, and although I know the ship was watched we had no trouble. But when we arrived in France, what was to be done? Thanks to Duparc I could speak French pretty well, though I could neither read nor write the language. I was a capable conjuror, but the French theatrical world did not have the kind of third-class variety theatre into which I could make my way. However, there were small circuses, and eventually I got a place in *Le grand Cirque forain de St Vite* after some rough adventures during which I was compelled to exhibit Willard as a geek.

'You know what a geek is, Ramsay, but perhaps these gentlemen are not so well versed in the humbler forms of carnival performance. You let it be known that you have, concealed perhaps in a stable at the back of a village inn, a man who eats strange food. When the crowd comes – and not too much of a crowd, because the police don't like such shows – you lecture for a while on the yearning of the geek for raw flesh and particularly for blood; you explain that it is something the medical profession knows about, but keeps quiet so that the relatives of people thus afflicted will not be put to shame. Then, if you can get a chicken, you give the geek a chicken, and he growls and gives a display of animal passion, and finally bites the chicken in the neck, and seems to drink some of its blood. If you are reduced to the point where you can't afford even a superannuated chicken, you find a grass snake or two, or perhaps a rabbit. I was the lecturer, and Willard was the geek. It raised enough money to keep us from starvation, and to keep Willard supplied with just enough of his fancy to prevent a total breakdown.

'You discovered us under the banner of St Vite, Ramsay, when we were travelling in the Tyrol. I suppose it looked very humble to you, but it was a step on an upward path for us. I appeared, you remember as Faustus LeGrand, the conjuror; I thought Faustus sounded well for a magician; poor old Willard was *Le Solitaire des forêts*, which was certainly an improvement on geeking and sounds much more elegant than Wild Man.'

'I remember it very well,' I said, 'and I remember that you were not at all anxious to recognize me.'

'I wasn't anxious to see anybody from Canada. I hadn't seen you for – surely it must have been fourteen years. How was I to know that you had enlisted in the R.C.M.P. – possibly become the pride of the Narcotics Squad? But let that go. I was in a confused state of mind at the time. Do you know what I mean? Something is taking all your attention – something inward – and the outer world is not very real, and you deal with it hastily and badly. I was still battling in my conscience about Willard. By this time I thoroughly hated him. He was an expensive nuisance, yet I couldn't make up my mind to get rid of him. Besides, he might just have enough energy, prompted by anger, to betray me to the police, even at the cost of his own destruction. Still, his life lay in my power. A smallish extra injection some day would have disposed of him.

'But I couldn't do it. Or rather – I've said so much, and put myself so thoroughly to the bad, that I might just as well go all the way – I didn't really want to do it because I got a special sort of satisfaction from his presence. This confused old wreck had been my master, my oppressor, the man who let me live hungry and dirty, who used my body shamefully and never let me lift my head above the shame. Now he was utterly mine; he was my thing. That was how it was now between me and Willard. I had the upper hand, and I admit frankly that it gave me a delicious satisfaction to have the upper hand. Willard had just enough sense of reality left to understand without any question of a mistake who was master. Not that I stressed it coarsely. No, no. If thine enemy be hungry, give him bread to eat; and if he be thirsty, give him water to drink; for thou shalt heap coals of fire on his head, and the Lord shall reward thee. Indeed so. The Lord rewarded me richly, and it seemed to me the Lord's face was dark and gleeful as he did so.

'This was Revenge, which we have all been told is a very grave sin, and in our time psychologists and sociologists have made it seem rather lower class, and unevolved, as well. Even the State, which retains so many primitive privileges that are denied to its citizens, shrinks from Revenge. If it catches a criminal the State is eager to make it clear that whatever it chooses to do is for the possible reform of that criminal, or at the very most for his restraint. Who would be so crass as to suggest that the criminal might be used as he has used his fellow man? We don't admit the power of the Golden Rule when it seems to be working in reverse gear. Do unto others as society says they should do unto you, even when they have done something quite different. We're all sweetness and light now, in our professions of belief. We have shut our minds against the Christ who cursed the fig-tree. Revenge – horrors! So there it was: I was revenging myself on Willard, and I'm not going to pretend to you that when he crunched into a grass snake to give a thrill to a stable filled with dull peasants, who despised him for doing it, I didn't have a warm sense of satisfaction. The Lord was rewarding me. Under the banner of St Vite, the man who had once been Mephistopheles in my life was now just a tremulous, disgusting Wild Man, and if anybody was playing Mephistopheles, the role was mine. Blessed be the name of the Lord, who forgettest not his servant.

'Don't ask me if I would do it now. I don't suppose for a moment that I would. But I did it then. Now I am famous and rich and have delightful friends like Liesl and Ramsay; charming people like yourselves come from the B.B.C. to ask me to pretend to be Robert-Houdin. But in those days I was Paul Dempster, who had been made to forget it and take a name from the side of a barn, and be the pathic of a perverted drug-taker. Do you think I have forgotten that even now? I have a lifelong reminder. I am a sufferer from a tiresome little complaint called *proctalgia fugax*. Do you know it? It is a cramping pain in the anus that wakes you out of a sound sleep and gives you five minutes or so of great unease. For years I thought that Willard, by this nasty use of me, had somehow injured me irreparably. It took a little courage to go to a doctor and find out that it was quite harmless, though I suppose it has some psychogenic origin. It is useless to ask Magnus Eisengrim if he would exert himself to torment a worm like Willard the Wizard; he has the magnanimity that comes so easily to the rich and powerful. But if you had put the question to Faustus LeGrand in 1929 his answer would have been the one I have just given you.

'Yes, gentlemen, it was Revenge, and it was sweet. If I am to be damned for a sin, I expect that will be the one. Shall I tell you the cream of it – or the worst of it, according to your point of view? There came a time when Willard could stand no more. Jaunting around southern France, and the Tyrol and parts of Switzerland, even when he had absorbed the minimum dose I allowed him, was a weariness that he could no longer endure. He wanted to die, and begged me for death. "Just gimme a little too much, kid," was what he said. He was never eloquent but he managed to put a really heart-breaking yearning into those words. What did I reply? "I couldn't do it, Willard. Really I couldn't. I'd have your life on my conscience. You know we're forbidden by every moral law to take life. If I do what you ask, not only am I a murderer, but you are a suicide. Can you face the world to come with that against you?" Then he would curse and call me every foul name he could think of. And next day it would be the same. I didn't kill him. Instead I withheld death from him, and it was balm to my spirit to be able to do it.

'Of course it came at last. From various evidence I judge that he was between forty and forty-five, but he looked far worse than men I have seen who were ninety. You know how such people die. He had been blue before, but for a few hours before the end he was a leaden colour, and as his mouth was open it was possible to see that it was almost black inside. His teeth were in very bad condition from geeking, and he looked like one of those terrible drawings by Daumier of a pauper corpse. The pupils of his eyes were barely perceptible. His breath was very faint, but what there was of it stank horribly. Till quite near the end he was begging for a shot of his fancy. The only other person with us was a member of the St Vite troupe, a bearded lady – you remember her, don't you, Ramsay? – but as Willard spoke no French she didn't know what he was saying, or if she did she gave no sign. Then a surprising thing happened; a short time before he died his pupils dilated extraordinarily, and that, with his wide-stretched mouth and his colour, gave him the look of a man dying of terror. Indeed, perhaps it was so. Was he aware of the lake which burneth with fire and brimstone, where he would join the unbelieving and the abominable, the whore-mongers, sorcerers, and idolaters? I had seen Abdullah go into the fire. Was it so also with Willard?

'But he was dead, and I was free. Had I not been free for years? Free since I struck the head off Abdullah? No; freedom does not come suddenly. One has to grow into it. But now that Willard was dead, I felt truly free, and I hoped that I might throw off some of the unpleasant characteristics I had taken upon myself but not, I hoped, forever taken within myself.

'I finished my season with *Le grand Cirque* because I did not want to attract attention by leaving as soon as Willard was out of the way. Without his luxury to pay for I was able to give up occasional pocket-picking, and save a little money. I knew what I wanted to do. I wanted to get to England; I knew there were vaude houses or variety shows of some kind in England, and I thought I could get a job there.

'I remember that I took stock of myself, as cold-bloodedly as I could, but not, I think, unjustly. The Deptford parson's son, the madwoman's son, had become a pretty widely experienced young tough; I could pick pockets, I could push dope. I could fight with a broken bottle and I had picked up the French knack of boxing with my feet. I could now speak and read French, and a little German and Italian, and I could speak a terrible patois of English, in which I sounded like the worst of Willard and Charlie combined.

'What was there on the credit side? I was an expert conjuror, and I was beginning to have some inkling of what Mrs Constantinescu meant when she talked about real hypnotism as opposed to the sideshow kind. I was a deft mechanic, could mend anybody's watch, and humour an old calliope. Although I had been the passive partner in countless acts of sodomy I was still, so far as my own sexual activity was concerned, a virgin, and likely to remain one, because I knew nothing about women other than Fat Ladies, Bearded Ladies, Snake Women, and mitt-camp gypsies; on the whole I liked women, but I had no wish to do to anybody I liked what Willard had done to me – and although of course I knew that the two acts differed I supposed they were pretty much the same to the recipient. I had none of Charlie's unresting desire to "slip it" to anybody. As you see, I was a muddle of toughness and innocence.

'Of course I didn't think of myself as innocent. What young man ever does? I thought I was the toughest thing going. A verse from the Book of Psalms kept running through my head that seemed to me to describe my state perfectly. "I am become like a bottle in the smoke." It's a verse that puzzles people who think it means a glass bottle, but my father would never have allowed me to be so ignorant as that. It means one of those old wineskins the Hebrews used; it means a goatskin that has been scraped out, and tanned, and blown up, and hung over the fire till it is as hard as a warrior's boot. That was how I saw myself.

'I was twenty-two, so far as I could reckon, and a bottle that had been thoroughly smoked. What was life going to pour into the bottle? I didn't know, but I was off to England to find out.

'And you are off to England in the morning gentlemen. Forgive me for holding you so long. I'll say good night.'

And for the last time at Sorgenfrei we went through that curious little pageant of bidding our ceremonious good night to Magnus Eisengrim, who said his farewells with unusual geniality.

Of course the film-makers didn't go back to their inn. They poured themselves another round of drinks and made themselves comfortable by the fire.

'What I can't decide,' said Ingestree, 'is how much of what we have heard we are to take as fact. It's the inescapable problem of the autobiography : how much is left out, how much has been genuinely forgotten, how much has been touched up to throw the subject into striking relief? That stuff about Revenge, for instance. Can he have been as horrible as he makes out? He doesn't seem a cruel man now. We must never forget that he's a conjuror by profession; his lifelong pose has been demonic. I think he'd like us to believe he played the demon in reality, as well.'

'I take it seriously,' said Lind. 'You are English, Roly, and the English have a temperamental pull toward cheerfulness; they don't really believe in evil. If the Gulf Stream ever deserted their western coast, they'd think differently. Americans are supposed to be the great optimists, but the English are much more truly optimistic. I think he has done all he says he has done. I think he killed his enemy slowly and cruelly. And I think it happens oftener than is supposed by people who habitually avert their minds from evil.'

'Oh, I'm not afraid of evil,' said Ingestree. 'Glad to look on the dark side any time it seems necessary. But I think people dramatize themselves when they have a chance.'

'Of course you are afraid of evil,' said Lind. 'You'd be a fool if you weren't. People talk about evil frivolously, just as Eisengrim says they do; it's a way of diminishing its power, or seeming to do so. To talk about evil as if it were just waywardness or naughtiness is very stupid and trivial. Evil is the reality of at least half the world.'

'You're always philosophizing,' said Kinghovn; 'and that's the dope of the Northern mind. What's evil? You don't know. But when you want an atmosphere of evil in your films you tell me and I arrange lowering skies and funny light and find a good camera angle; if I took the same thing in blazing sunlight, from another place, it'd look like comedy.'

'You're always playing the tough guy, the realist,' said Lind, 'and that's wonderful. I like you for it, Harry. But you're not an artist except in your limited field, so you leave it to me to decide what's evil and what's comedy on the screen. That's something that goes beyond appearances. Right now we're talking about a man's life.'

Liesl had said very little at any of these evening sessions, and I think the film-makers had made the mistake of supposing she had nothing to say. She struck in now.

'Which man's life are you talking about?' she said. 'That's another of the problems of biography and autobiography, Ingestree, my dear. It can't be managed except by casting one person as the star of the drama, and arranging everybody else as supporting players. Look at what politicians write about themselves! Churchill and Hitler and all the rest of them seem suddenly to be secondary figures surrounding Sir Numskull Poop, who is always in the limelight. Magnus is no stranger to the egotism of the successful performing artist. Time after time he has reminded us that he is the greatest creature of his kind in the world. He does it without shame. He is not held back by any middle-class notion that it would be nicer if we said it instead of himself. He knows we're not going to say it, because nothing so destroys the sense of equality on which all pleasant social life depends as perpetual reminders that one member of the company out-ranks all the rest. When it is so, it is considered good manners for the pre-eminent one to keep quiet about it. Because Magnus has been talking for a couple of hours we have assumed that his emphasis is the only emphasis.

'This business of the death of Willard: if we listen to Magnus we take it for granted that Magnus killed Willard after painfully humiliating him for quite a long time. The tragedy of Willard's death is the spirit in which Faustus LeGrand regarded it. But isn't Willard somebody, too? As Willard lay dying, who did he think was the star of the scene? Not Magnus, I'll bet you. And look at it from God's point of view, or if that strains you uncomfortably, suppose that you have to make a movie of the life and death of Willard. You need Magnus, but he is not the star. He is the necessary agent who brings Willard to the end. Everybody's life is his Passion, you know, and you can't have much of a Passion if you haven't got a good strong Judas. Somebody has to play Judas, and it is generally acknowledged to be a fine, meaty role. There's a pride in being cast for it. You recall the Last Supper? Christ said that he would be betrayed by one of those who sat at the table with him. The disciples called out, Lord, is it I? And when Judas asked, Christ said it was he.

'Has it never occurred to you that there might have been just the tiniest feeling in the bosom of one of the lesser apostles – Lebbaeus, for instance, whom tradition represents as a fat man – that Judas was thrusting himself forward again? Christ died on the Cross, and Judas also had his Passion, but can anybody tell me what became of Lebbaeus? Yet he too was a man, and if he had written an autobiography do you suppose that Christ would have had the central position? There seems to have been a Bearded Lady at the deathbed of Willard, and I would like to know her point of view. Being a woman, she probably had too much intelligence to think that she was the central figure, but would she have awarded that role to Willard or to Magnus?'

'Either would do,' said Kinghovn; 'but you need a point of focus, you know. Otherwise you get this *cinéma vérité* stuff which is sometimes interesting but it damn well isn't *vérité* because it fails utterly to convince. It's like those shots of war you see on TV; you can't believe anything serious is happening. If you want your film to look like truth you need somebody ilke

Jurgen to decide what truth is, and somebody like me to shoot it so it never occurs to you that it could appear any other way. Of course what you get is not truth, but it's probably a lot better in more ways than just the cinematic way. If you want the death of Willard shot from the point of view of the Bearded Lady I can certainly do it. And simply because I can do it to order I don't know how you can pretend it has any special superiority as truth.'

'I suppose it's part of that human condition silly-clever people are always grizzling about,' said Liesl. 'If you want truth, I suppose you must shoot the film from God's point of view and with God's point of focus, whatever it may be. And I'll bet the result won't look much like *cinéma vérité*. But I don't think either you or Jurgen are up to that job, Harry.'

'There is no God,[2] said Kinghovn; 'and I've never felt the least necessity to invent one.'

'Probably that is why you have spent your life as a technician; a very fine one, but a technician,' said Lind. 'It's only by inventing a few gods that we get that uneasy sense that something is laughing at us which is one of the paths to faith.'

'Eisengrim talks a lot about God,' said Ingestree, 'and God seems still to be a tremendous reality to him. But there's no question of God laughing. The bottle in the smoke – that's what he was. I really must read the Bible some time; there are such marvellous goodies in it, just waiting to be picked up. But even these Bibles Designed to be Read as Literature are so bloody thick! I suppose one could browse, but when I browse I never seem to find anything except tiresome stud-book stuff about Aminadab begetting Jonadab and that kind of thing.'

'We've only had part of the story,' I said. 'Magnus has carefully pointed out to us that he is looking backward on his early life as a man who has changed decisively in the last forty years. What's his point of focus?'

'Nobody changes so decisively that they lose all sense of the reality of their youth,' Lind said. 'The days of childhood are always the most vivid. He has let us think that his childhood made him a villain. So I think we must assume that he is a villain now. A quiescent villain, but not an extinct one.'

'I think that's a lot of romantic crap,' said Kinghovn. 'I'm sick of all the twaddle about childhood. You should have seen me as a child; a flaxen-haired little darling playing in my mother's garden in Aalborg. Where is he now? Here I sit, a very well-smoked bottle like our friend who has gone to bed. If I met that flaxen-haired child now I would probably give him a good clout over the ear. I've never much liked kids. Which was the greater use in the world? That child, so sweet and pure, or me, as I am now, not sweet and damned well not pure?'

'That's a dangerous question for a man who doesn't believe in God,' I said, 'because there is no answer to it without God. I could answer it for you, if I thought you were open to anything but drink and photography, Harry, but I'm not going to waste precious argument. What I want is to defend Eisengrim against the charge of being a villain, now or at any other time. You must look at his history in the light of myth –'

'Aha, I thought we should get to myth in time,' said Liesl.

'Well, myth explains much that is otherwise inexplicable, just because myth is a boiling down of universal experience. Eisengrim's story of his childhood and youth is as new to me as it is to you, although I knew him when he was very young –'

'Yes, and you were an influence in making him what he is,' said Liesl.

'Because you taught him conjuring?' said Lind.

'No, no; Ramsay was personally responsible for the premature birth of little Paul Dempster, and responsible also for Paul's mother's madness, which marked him so terribly,' said Liesl.

I gaped at her in astonishment. 'This is what comes of confiding in women! Not only can they not keep a secret; they re-tell it in an utterly false way! I must put this matter right. It is true that Paul Dempster was born prematurely because his mother was hit on the head by a snowball. It is true that the snowball was meant to hit me, and it hit her instead because I dodged it. It is true that the blow on the head and the birth of the child seemed to precipitate an instability that sometimes amounted to madness. And it is true that I felt some responsibility in the matter. But that was long ago and far away, in a country which you would scarcely recognize as modern Canada. Liesl, I blush for you.'

'What a lovely old-fashioned thing to say, dear Ramsay.

Thank you very much for blushing for me, because I long ago lost the trick of blushing for myself. But I didn't spill the beans about you just to make you jump. I wanted to make the point that you are a figure in this story, too. A very strange figure, just as odd as any in your legends. You precipitated, by a single action – and who could think you guilty just because you jumped out of the way of a snowball (who, that is, but a grim Calvinist like yourself, Ramsay) – everything that we have been hearing from Magnus during these nights past. Are you a precipitating figure in Magnus's story, or he in yours? Who could comb it all out? But get on with your myth, dear man. I want to hear what lovely twist you will give to what Magnus has told us.'

'It is not a twist, but an explication. Magnus has made it amply clear that he was brought up in a strict, unrelenting form of puritanism. In consequence he still blames himself whenever he can, and because he knows the dramatic quality of the role, he likes to play the villain. But as for his keeping Willard as a sort of hateful pet, in order to jeer at him, I simply don't believe it was like that at all. What is the mythical element in his story? Simply the very old tale of the man who is in search of his soul, and who must struggle with a monster to secure it. All myth and Christianity – which has never been able to avoid the mythical pull of human experience – are full of similar instances, and people all around us are living out this basic human pattern every day. In the study of hagiography –'

'I knew you'd get to saints before long,' said Liesl.

'In the study of hagiography we have legends and all those splendid pictures of saints who killed dragons, and it doesn't take much penetration to know that the dragons represent not simply evil in the world but their personal evil, as well. Of course, being saints, they are said to have killed their dragons, but we know that dragons are not killed; at best they are tamed, and kept on the chain. In the pictures we see St George, and my special favourite, St Catherine, triumphing over the horrid beast, who lies with his tongue out, looking as if he thoroughly regretted his mistaken course in life. But I am strongly of the opinion that St George and St Catherine did not kill those dragons, for then they would have been wholly good, and in-

688

human, and useless and probably great sources of mischief, as one-sided people always are. No, they kept the dragons as pets. Because they were Christians, and because Christianity enjoins us to seek only the good and to have nothing whatever to do with evil, they doubtless rubbed it into the dragons that it was uncommonly broadminded and decent of them to let the dragons live at all. They may even have given the dragon occasional treats: you may breathe a little fire, they might say, or you may leer desirously at that virgin yonder, but if you make one false move you'll wish you hadn't. You must be a thoroughly submissive dragon, and remember who's boss. That's the Christian way of doing things, and that's what Magnus did with Willard. He didn't kill Willard. The essence of Willard lives with him today. But he got the better of Willard. Didn't you notice how he was laughing as he said good night?'

'I certainly did,' said Ingestree. 'I didn't understand it at all. It wasn't just the genial laughter of a man saying farewell to some guests. And certainly he didn't seem to be laughing at us. I thought perhaps it was relief at having got something off his chest.'

'The laugh troubled me,' said Lind. 'I am not good at humour, and I like to be perfectly sure what people are laughing at. Do you know what it was, Ramsay?'

'Yes,' I said, 'I think I do. That was Merlin's Laugh.'

'I don't know about that,' said Lind.

'If Liesl will allow it, I must be mythological again. The magician Merlin had a strange laugh, and it was heard when nobody else was laughing. He laughed at the beggar who was bewailing his fate as he lay stretched on a dunghill; he laughed at the foppish young man who was making a great fuss about choosing a pair of shoes. He laughed because he knew that deep in the dunghill was a golden cup that would have made the beggar a rich man; he laughed because he knew that the pernickety young man would be stabbed in a quarrel before the soles of his new shoes were soiled. He laughed because he knew what was coming next.'

'And of course our friend knows what is coming next in his own story, said Lind.

'Are we to take it then that there was some striking reversal of fortune awaiting him when he went to England?' said Ingestree.

'I know no more than you,' said I. 'I do not hear Merlin's Laugh very often, though I think I am more sensitive to its sound than most people. But he spoke of finding out what wine would be poured into the well-smoked bottle that he had become. I don't know what it was.'

Ingestree was more excited than the rest. 'But are we never to know? How can we find out?'

'Surely that's up to you,' said Lind. 'Aren't you going to ask Eisengrim to come to London to see the rushes of this film we have been making? Isn't that owing to him? Get him in London and ask him to continue.'

Ingestree looked doubtful. 'Can it be squeezed out of the budget?' he said. 'The corporation doesn't like frivolous expenses. Of course I'd love to ask him, but if we run very much over budget, well, it would be as good as my place is worth, as servants used to say in the day when they knew they were servants.'

'Nonsense, you can rig it,' said Kinghovn. But Ingestree still looked like a worried, rather withered baby.

'I know what is worrying Roly,' said Liesl. 'He thinks that he could squeeze Eisengrim's expenses in London out of the B.B.C., but he knows he can't lug in Ramsay and me, and he's too nice a fellow to suggest that Magnus travel without us. Isn't that it, Roly?'

Ingestree looked at her. 'Bang on the head,' he said.

'Don't worry about it,' said Liesl. 'I'll pay my own way, and even this grinding old miser Ramsay might unchain a few pennies for himself. Just let us know when to come.'

And so, at last, they went. As we came back into the large, gloomy, nineteenth-century Gothic hall of Sorgenfrei, I said to Liesl: 'It was nice of you to think of Lebbaeus, tonight. People don't mention him very often. But you're wrong, you know, saying that there is no record of what he did after the Crucifixion. There is a non-canonical Acts of Thaddaeus – Thaddaeus was his surname, you recall – that tells all about him. It didn't get into the Bible, but it exists.'

'What's it like?'

'A great tale of marvels. Real Arabian Nights stuff. Puts him dead at the centre of affairs.'

'Didn't I say so! Just like a man. I'll bet he wrote it himself.'

2

Merlin's Laugh

I

BECAUSE of Jurgen Lind's slow methods of work, it took longer to get *Un Hommage à Robert-Houdin* into a final form than we had expected, and it was nearly three months later when Eisengrim, Liesl, and I journeyed to London to see what it looked like. The polite invitation suggested that criticism would be welcome. Eisengrim was the star, and Liesl had put up a good deal of the money for the venture, expecting to get it back over the next two or three years, with substantial gains, but I think we all knew that criticism of Lind would not be gratefully received. A decent pretence was to be kept up, all the same.

We three rarely travelled together; when we did there was always a good deal of haggling about where we should stay. I favoured small, modest hotels; Liesl felt a Swiss nationalist pull toward any hotel, anywhere, that was called the Ritz; Eisengrim wanted to stop at the Savoy.

The suite we occupied at the Savoy was precisely to his taste. It had been decorated in the twenties, and not changed since; the rooms were large, and the walls were in that most dismal of decorators' colours, 'off-white'; below the ceiling of the drawing-room was a nine-inch border of looking-glass; there was an Art Moderne fireplace with an electric fire in it which, when in use, gave off a heavy smell of roasted dust and reminiscences of mice; the furniture was big, and clumsy in the twenties mode. The windows looked out on what I called an alley, and what even Liesl called 'a mean street', but to our amazement Magnus came up with the comment that nobody who called himself a gentleman ever looked out of the window. (What did he know about the fine points of upper-class behaviour?) There was a master bedroom of astonishing size, and Magnus grabbed it for himself, saying that Liesl might have the other bed in it. My room, not quite so large but still a big room, was nearer the bathroom. That chamber was gorgeous in a style long forgotten, with what seemed to be Roman tiling, a sunken bath, and a giantess's bidet. The daily rate for this grandeur startled me even when I had divided it by three, but I held my peace, and hoped we would not stay long. I am not a stingy man, but I think a decent prudence becoming even in the very rich, like Liesl. Also, I knew enough about the very rich to understand that I should not be let off with a penny less than my full third of whatever was spent.

Magnus was taking his new position as a film star – even though it was only as the star of a television 'special' – with a seriousness that seemed to me absurd. The very first night he insisted on having Lind and his gang join us for what he called a snack in our drawing-room. Snack! Solomon and the Queen of Sheba would have been happy with such a snack; when I saw it laid out by the waiters I was so oppressed by the thought of what a third of it would come to that I wondered if I should be able to touch a morsel. But the others ate and drank hugely, and almost as soon as they entered the room began hinting that Magnus should continue the story he had begun at Sorgenfrei. That was what I wanted, too, and as it was plain that I was going to pay dear to hear it, I overcame my scruple and made sure of my share of the feast.

The showing of *Hommage* had been arranged for the following afternoon at three o'clock. 'Good,' said Magnus; 'that will allow me the morning to make a little sentimental pilgrimage I have in mind.'

Polite interest from Ingestree, and delicately inquisitive probings as to what this pilgrimage might be.

'Something associated with a turning-point in my life,' said Magnus. 'I feel that one should not be neglectful of such observances.'

Was it anything with which the B.B.C. could be helpful, Ingestree asked.

'No, not at all,' said Magnus. 'I simply want to lay some flowers at the foot of a monument.'

Surely, Ingestree persisted, Magnus would permit somebody from the publicity department, or from a newspaper, to get a picture of this charming moment? It could be so helpful later, when it was necessary to work up enthusiasm for the film.

Magnus was coy. He would prefer not to make public a private act of gratitude and respect. But he was willing to admit, among friends, that what he meant to do was part of the subtext of the film; an act related to his own career; something he did whenever he found himself in London.

He had now gone so far that it was plain he wanted to be coaxed, and Ingestree coaxed him with a mixture of affection and respect that was worthy of admiration. It was plain to be seen how Ingestree had not merely survived, but thriven, in the desperate world of television. It was not long before Magnus yielded, as I suppose he meant to do from the beginning.

'It's nothing in the least extraordinary. I'm going to lay a few yellow roses – I hope I can get yellow ones – at the foot of the monument to Henry Irving behind the National Portrait Gallery. You know it. It's one of the best-known monuments in London. Irving, splendid and gracious, in his academical robes, looking up Charing Cross Road. I promised Milady I'd do that, in her name and my own, if I ever came to the point in life where I could afford such gestures. And I have. And so I shall.'

'Now you really mustn't tease us any more,' said Ingestree. 'We must be told. Who is Milady?'

'Lady Tresize,' said Magnus, and there was no hint of banter in his voice any longer. He was solemn. But Ingestree hooted with laughter.

'My God!' he said, 'You don't mean Old Mother Tresize? Old Nan? You knew her?'

'Better than you apparently did,' said Magnus. 'She was a dear friend of mine, and very good to me when I needed a friend. She was one of Irving's protégées, and in her name I do honour to his memory.'

'Well – I apologize. I apologize profoundly. I never knew her well, though I saw something of her. You'll admit she was rather a joke as an actress.'

'Perhaps. Though I saw her give some remarkable performances. She didn't always get parts that were suited to her.'

'I can't imagine what parts could ever have suited her. It's usually admitted she held the old man back. Dragged him down, in fact. He really may have been good, once. If he'd had a decent leading lady he mightn't have ended up as he did.'

'I didn't know that he had ended up badly. Indeed I know for a fact that he had quite a happy retirement, and was happier because he shared it with her. Are we talking about the same people?'

'I suppose it depends on how one looks at it. I'd better shut up.'

'No, no,' said Lind. 'This is just the time to keep on. Who are these people called Tresize? Theatre people, I suppose?'

'Sir John Tresize was one of the most popular romantic actors of his day,' said Magnus.

'But in an absolutely appalling repertoire,' said Ingestree, who seemed unable to hold his tongue. 'He went on into the twenties acting stuff that was moth-eaten when Irving died. You should have seen it, Jurgen! *The Lyons Mail*, *The Corsican Brothers*, and that interminable *Master of Ballantrae*; seeing him in repertory was a peep into the dark backward and abysm of time, let me tell you!'

'That's not true,' said Magnus, and I knew how hot he was by the coolness with which he spoke. 'He did some fine things, if you would take the trouble to find out. Some admired Shakespearean performances; a notable Hamlet. The money he made on *The Master of Ballantrae* he spent on introducing the work of Maeterlinck to England.'

'Maeterlinck's frightfully old hat,' said Ingestree.

'Now, perhaps. But fashions change. And when Sir John Tresize introduced Maeterlinck to England he was an innovator. Have you no charity toward the past?'

'Not a scrap.'

'I think less of you for it.'

'Oh, come off it! You're an immensely accomplished actor yourself. You know how the theatre is. Of all the arts it has least patience with bygones.'

'You have said several times that I am a good actor, because I

695

can put up a decent show as Robert-Houdin. I'm glad you think
so. Have you ever asked yourself where I learned to do that? One
of the things that has given my work a special flavour is that I
give my audiences something to look at apart from good tricks.
They like the way I act the part of a conjuror. They say it has
romantic flair. What they really mean is that it is projected with
a skilled nineteenth-century technique. And where did I learn
that?'

'Well, obviously you're going to tell me you learned it from
old Tresize. But it isn't the same, you know. I mean, I remember
him. He was lousy.'

'Depends on the point of view, I suppose. Perhaps you had
some reason not to like him.'

'Not at all.'

'You said you knew him.'

'Oh, very slightly.'

'Then you missed a chance to know him better. I had that
chance and I took it. Probably I needed it more than you did. I
took it, and I paid for it, because knowing Sir John didn't come
cheap. And Milady was a great woman. So tomorrow morning
– yellow roses.'

'You'll let us send a photographer?'

'Not after what you've been saying. I don't pretend to an
overwhelming delicacy, but I have some. So keep away, please,
and if you disobey me I won't finish the few shots you still have
to make on *Hommage*. Is that clear?'

It was clear, and after lingering a few minutes, just to show
that they could not be easily dismissed, Ingestree, and Jurgen
Lind, and Kinghovn left us.

2

BOTH Liesl and I went with Magnus the following morning on
his sentimental expedition. Liesl wanted to know who Milady
was; her curiosity was aroused by the tenderness and reverence
with which he spoke of the woman who appeared to Ingestree

to be a figure of fun. I was curious about everything concerning him. After all, I had my document to consider. So we both went with him to buy the roses. Liesl protested when he bought an expensive bunch of two dozen. 'If you leave them in the street, somebody will steal them,' she said; 'the gesture is the same whether it's one rose or a bundle. Don't waste your money.' Once again I had occasion to be surprised at the way very rich people think about money; a costly apartment at the Savoy, and a haggle about a few roses! But Eisengrim was not to be changed from his purpose. 'Nobody will steal them, and you'll find out why,' said he. So off we went on foot along the Strand, because Magnus felt that taking a taxi would lessen the solemnity of his pilgrimage.

The Irving monument stands in quite a large piece of open pavement; near by a pavement artist was chalking busily on the flagstones. Beside the monument itself a street performer was unpacking some ropes and chains, and a woman was helping him to get ready for his performance. Magnus took off his hat, laid the flowers at the foot of the statue, arranged them to suit himself, stepped back, looked up at the statue, smiled, and said something under his breath. Then he said to the street performer: 'Going to do a few escapes, are you?'

'Right you are,' said the man.

'Will you be here long?'

'Long as anybody wants to watch me.'

'I'd like you to keep an eye on those flowers. They're for the Guvnor, you see. Here's a pound. I'll be back before lunch, and if they're still there, and if you're still here, I'll have another pound for you. I want them to stay where they are for at least three hours; after that anybody who wants them can have them. Now let's see your show.'

The busker and the woman went to work. She rattled a tambourine, and he shook the chains and defied the passers-by to tie him up so that he couldn't escape. A few loungers gathered, but none of them seemed anxious to oblige the escape-artist by tying him up. At last Magnus did it himself.

I didn't know what he had in mind, and I wondered if he meant to humiliate the poor fellow by tying him up and leaving him to struggle; after all, Magnus had been a distinguished escape-artist himself in his time, and as he was a man of scornful mind such a trick would not have been outside his range. He made a thorough job of it, and before he had done there was a crowd of fifteen or twenty people gathered to see the fun. It is not every day that one of these shabby street performers has a beautifully dressed and distinguished person as an assistant. I saw a policeman halt at the back of the crowd, and began to worry. My philosophical indifference to human suffering is not as complete as I wish it were. If Magnus tied up the poor wretch and left him, what should I do? Interfere, or run away? Or would I simply hang around and see what happened?

At last Magnus was contented with his work, and stepped away from the busker, who was now a bundle of chains and ropes. The man dropped to the ground, writhed and grovelled for a few seconds, worked himself up on his knees, bent his head and tried to get at one of the ropes with his teeth, and in doing so fell forward and seemed to hurt himself badly The crowd murmured sympathetically, and pressed a bit nearer. Then, suddenly, the busker gave a triumphant cry, and leapt to his feet, as chains and ropes fell in a tangle on the pavement.

Magnus led the applause. The woman passed the tattered cap that served as a collection bag. Some copper and a few silver coins were dropped in it. Liesl contributed a fifty-penny piece, and I found another. It was a good round for the busker; astonishingly good, I imagine, for the first show of the day.

When the crowd had dispersed, the busker said softly to Magnus: 'Pro, ain't yer?'

'Yes, I'm a pro.'

'Knew it. You couldn't of done them ties without bein' a pro. You playin' in town?'

'No, but I have done. Years ago, I used to give a show right where we're standing now.'

'You did! Christ, you've done well.'

'Yes. And I started here under the Guvnor's statue. You'll keep an eye on his flowers, won't you?'

'Too right I will! And thanks!'

We walked away, Magnus smiling and big with mystery. He knew how much we wanted to know what lay behind what we had just seen, and was determined to make us beg. Liesl, who has less pride about such things than I, spoke before we had passed the pornography shops into Leicester Square.

'Come along, Magnus. Enough of this. We want to know and you want to tell. I can feel it. When did you ever perform in the London streets?'

'After I got away from France, and the travelling circus, and the shadow of Willard, I came to London, which was dangerous with the kind of passport I carried, but I managed it. What was I to do? You don't get jobs in variety theatres just by hanging around the stage doors. It's a matter of agents, and having press cuttings, and being known to somebody. And I was down and out. I hadn't a penny. No, that's not quite true; I had forty-two shillings and that was just enough to buy a few old ropes and chains. So I took a look around the West End, and soon found out that the choice position for open-air shows was the place we've just visited. But even that wasn't free; street-artists of long standing had first call on the space. I tried to do my little act when they weren't busy, and three of them took me up an alley and convinced me that I had been tactless. Nevertheless, with a black eye I managed to show them a little magic that persuaded one of them to let me add something to his own show, and for that I got a very small daily sum. Still, I was seen, and it wasn't more than a few days before I was taken to Milady, and after that everything was glorious.'

'Why should Milady want to see you? Really, Magnus, you are intolerable. You are going to tell us, so why don't you do it without making me corkscrew every word out of you?'

'If I tell you now, in the street, don't you think I am being rather unfair to Lind? He wants to know too, you know.'

'Last night you virtually ordered Lind and his friends out of the hotel. Do you mean you are going to change your mind about that?'

'I was annoyed with Ingestree.'

'Yes, I know that. But what's so bad about Ingestree? He doesn't agree with you about Milady. Is the man to have no mind of his own? Must everybody agree with you? Ingestree isn't a bad fellow.'

'Not a bad fellow. A fool perhaps.'

'Since when is it a criminal offence to be a fool? You're rather a fool yourself, especially about women. I insist on knowing whatever there is to know about Milady.'

'And so you shall, my dear Liesl. So you shall. You have only to wait until this evening. I guarantee that when we go back to the Savoy we shall find that Lind has called, that Ingestree is ready to apologize, and that we are all three asked to dinner tonight so that I may very graciously go on with my subtext to *Hommage*. Which I am perfectly willing to do. And Ramsay will be pleased, because the free dinner he gets tonight will somewhat offset the cost of the dinner he had to share in giving last night. You see, all things work together for good to them that love God.'

'Sometimes I wish I were a professing Christian, so that I would have the right to tell you how much your blasphemous quoting of Scripture annoys me. And you mustn't torment Ramsay. He hasn't had your advantages. He's never been really poor, and that is a terrible drawback to a man. – Will you promise to be decent to Ingestree?'

An unwonted sound: Eisengrim laughed aloud: Merlin's Laugh, if ever I heard it.

3

MAGNUS was having one of his tiresome spells, during which he was right about everything. We were indeed asked to dine as Lind's guests after the showing of *Hommage*. What we saw in the pokey little viewing-room was a version of the film that was almost complete; everything that was to be cut out had been removed, but a few shots – close-ups of Magnus – had still to be taken and incorporated. It was a source of astonishment, for I saw nothing that I had not seen while it was being filmed; but the skill of the cutting, and the juxtapositions, and the varieties of pace that had been achieved, were marvels to me. Clearly much of what had been done owed its power to the art of Harry Kinghovn, but the unmistakable impress of Lind's mind was on it, as well. His films possessed a weight of implication – in St Paul's phrase, 'the evidence of things not seen' – that was entirely his own.

The greatest surprise was the way in which Eisengrim emerged. His unique skill as a conjuror was there, of course, but somehow magic is not so impressive on the screen as it is in direct experience, just as he had said himself at Sorgenfrei. No, it was as an actor that he seemed like a new person. I suppose I had grown used to him over the years, and had seen too much of his backstage personality, which was that of the theatre martinet, the watchful, scolding, impatient star of the *Soirée of Illusions*. The distinguished, high-bred, romantic figure I saw on the screen was someone I felt I did not know. The waif I had known when we were boys in Deptford, the carnival charlatan I had seen in Austria as Faustus LeGrand in *Le grand Cirque forain de St Vite*, the successful stage performer, and the amusing but testy and incalculable permanent guest at Sorgenfrei could not be reconciled with this fascinating creature, and it couldn't all be the art of Lind and Kinghovn. I must know more. My document demanded it.

Liesl, too, was impressed, and I am sure she was as curious as I. So far as I knew, she had at some time met Magnus, admired him, befriended him, and financed him. They had toured the world together with their *Soirée of Illusions*, combining his art as a public performer with her skill as a technician, a contriver of magical apparatus, and her artistic taste, which was far beyond his own. If he was indeed the greatest conjuror of his time, or of any time, she was responsible for at least half of whatever had made him so. Moreover, she had educated him, in so far as he was formally educated, and had transformed him from a tough little carnie into someone who could put up a show of cultivation. Or was that the whole truth? She seemed as surprised by his new persona on the screen as I was.

This was clearly one of Magnus's great days. The film people were delighted with him, as entrepreneurs always are with anybody who looks as if he could draw in money, and at dinner he was clearly the guest of honour.

We went to the Café Royal, where a table had been reserved in the old room with the red plush benches against the wall, and the lush girls with naked breasts holding up the ceiling, and the flattering looking-glasses. We ate and drank like people who were darlings of Fortune. Ingestree was on his best behaviour, and it was not until we had arrived at brandy and cigars that he said —

'I passed the Irving statue this afternoon. Quite by chance. Nothing premeditated. But I saw your flowers. And I want to repeat how sorry I am to have spoken slightingly about your old friend Lady Tresize. May we toast her now?'

'Here's to Milady,' said Magnus, and emptied his glass.

'Why was she called that?' said Liesl. 'It sounds terribly pretentious if she was simply the wife of a theatrical knight. Or it sounds frowsily romantic, like a Dumas novel. Or it sounds as if you were making fun of her. Or was she a cult figure in the theatre? The Madonna of the Greasepaint? You might tell us, Magnus.'

'I suppose it was all of those things. Some people thought her pretentious, and some thought the romance that surrounded her was frowsy, and people always made a certain amount of fun of her, and she was a cult figure as well. In addition she was a wonderfully kind, wise, courageous person who was not easy to understand. I've been thinking a lot about her today. I told you that I was a busker beside the Irving statue when I came to London. It was there Holroyd picked me up and took me to Milady. She decided I should have a job, and made Sir John give me one, which he didn't want to do.'

'Magnus, do please, I implore you, stop being mysterious. You know very well you mean to tell us all about it. You want to, and furthermore, you must. Do it to please me.' Liesl was laying herself out to be irresistible, and I have never known a woman who was better at the work.

'Do it for the sake of the subtext,' said Ingestree, who was also making himself charming, like a naughty boy who has been forgiven.

'All right. So I shall. My show under the shadow of Irving was not extensive. The buskers I was working with wouldn't give me much of a chance, but they allowed me to draw a crowd by making some showy passes with cards. It was stuff I had learned long ago with Willard — shooting a deck into the air and making it slide back into my hand like a beautiful waterfall, and that sort of thing. It can be done with a deck that is mounted on a rubber string, but I could do it with any deck. It's simply a matter of hours of practice, and confidence that you can do it. I don't call it conjuring. More like juggling. But it makes people gape.

'One day, a week or two after I had begun in this underpaid, miserable work, I noticed a man hanging around at the back of the crowd, watching me very closely. He wore a long overcoat, though it wasn't a day for such a coat, and he had a pipe stuck in his mouth as if it had grown there. He worried me because, as you know, my passport wasn't all it should have been. I thought he might be a detective. So as soon as I had done my short trick, I made for a near-by alley. He was right behind me. "Hi!" he shouted, "I want a word with you." There was no getting away, so I faced him. "Are you interested in a better job than that?" he asked. I said I was. "Can you do a bit of juggling?" said he. Yes, I could do juggling, though I wouldn't call myself a juggler. "Any experience walking a tightrope?" Because of the work I had done with Duparc I was able to say I could. "Then you come to this address tomorrow morning at twelve," said he, and gave me a card on which was his name – James Holroyd – and he had scribbled a direction on it.

'Of course I was there, next day at noon. The place was a pub called The Crown and Two Chairmen, and when I asked for Mr Holroyd I was directed upstairs to a big room, in which there were a few people. Holroyd was one of them, and he nodded to me to wait.

'Queer room. Just an empty space, with some chairs piled in a corner, and a few odds and ends of pillars, and obelisks and altar-like boxes, which I knew were Masonic paraphernalia, also stacked against a wall. It was one of those rooms common enough in London, where lodges met, and little clubs had their gatherings, and which theatrical people rented by the day for rehearsal space.

'The people who were there were grouped around a man who was plainly the boss. He was short, but by God he had presence; you would have noticed him anywhere. He wore a hat, but not as I had ever seen a hat worn before. Willard and Charlie were hat men, but somehow their hats always looked sharp and dishonest – you know, too much down on one side? Holroyd wore a hat, a hard hat of the kind that Winston Churchill made famous later; a sort of top hat that had lost courage and hadn't grown the last three inches, or acquired any gloss. As I came to know Holroyd I sometimes wondered if he had been born in that hat and overcoat, because I hardly ever saw him without both. But this little man's hat looked as if it should have had a plume in it. It was a perfectly ordinary, expensive felt hat, but he gave it an air of costume, and when he looked from under the brim you felt he was sizing up your costume, too. And that was what he was doing. He took a look at me and said, in a kind of mumble, "That's your find, eh? Doesn't look much, does he, mph? Not quite as if he might pass for your humble, what? Eh, Holroyd? Mph?"

' "That's for you to say, of course," said Holroyd.

' "Then I say no. Must look again. Must be something better than that, eh?"

' "Won't you see him do a few tricks?"

' "Need I? Surely the appearance is everything, mph?"

' "Not everything, Guvnor. The tricks are pretty important. At least the way you've laid it out makes the tricks very important. And the tightrope, too. He'd look quite different dressed up."

' "Of course. But I don't think he'll do. Look again, eh, like a good chap?"

' "Whatever you say, Guvnor. But I'd have bet money on this one. Let him flash a trick or two, just to see."

'The little man wasn't anxious to waste time on me, but I didn't mean to waste time either. I threw a couple of decks in the air, made them do a fancy twirl, and let them slip back into my hands. Then I twirled on my toes, and made the decks do it again, in a spiral, which looks harder than it is. There was clapping from a corner – the kind of soft clapping women produce by clapping in gloves they don't want to split. I bowed toward the corner, and that was the first time I saw Milady.

'It was a time when women's clothes were plain; the line of the silhouette was supposed to be simple. There was nothing plain or simple about Milady's clothes. Drapes and swags and swishes, and scraps of fur everywhere, and the colours and fabrics were more like upholstery than garments. She had a hat, like a witch's, but with more style to it, and some soft stuff wrapped around the crown dangled over the brim to one shoulder. She was heavily made up – really she wore an extraordinary amount of make-up – in colours that were too emphatic for daylight. But neither she nor the little man seemed to be meant for daylight; I didn't realize it at the time, but they always looked as if they were ready to step on the stage. Their clothes, and manner and demeanour all spoke of the stage.'

'The Crummles touch,' said Ingestree. 'They were about the last to have it.'

'I don't know who Crummles was,' said Magnus. 'Ramsay will tell me later. But I must make it clear that these two didn't look in the least funny to me. Odd, certainly, and unlike anything I had ever seen, but not funny. In fact, ten years later I still didn't think them funny, though I know lots of people laughed. But those people didn't know them as I did. And as I've told you I first saw Milady when she was applauding my tricks with the cards, so she looked very good to me.

' "Let him show what he can do, Jack," she said. And then to me, with great politeness, "You do juggling, don't you? Let us see you juggle."

'I had nothing to juggle with, but I didn't mean to be beaten. And I wanted to prove to the lady that I was worth her kindness. So with speed and I hope a reasonable amount of politeness I took her umbrella, and the little man's wonderful hat, and Holroyd's hat and the soft cap I was wearing myself, and balanced the brolly on my nose and juggled the three hats in an arch over it. Not easy, let me tell you, for all the hats were of different sizes and weights, and Holroyd's hefted like iron. But I did it, and the lady clapped again. Then she whispered to the little man she called Jack.

' "I see what you mean, Nan," he said, "but there must be some sort of resemblance. I hope I'm not vain, but I can't persuade myself we can manage a resemblance, mphm?"

'I put on a little more steam. I did some clown juggling, pretending every time the circle went round that I was about to drop Holroyd's hat, and recovering it with a swoop, and at last keeping that one in the air with my right foot. That made the little man laugh, and I knew I had had a lucky inspiration. Obviously Holroyd's hat was rather a joke among them. "Come here, m'boy," said the boss. "Stand back to back with me." So I did, and we were exactly of a height. "Extraordinary," said the boss; "I'd have sworn he was shorter. ‚

' "He's a little shorter, Guvnor," said Holroyd, "but we can put him in lifts."

' "Aha, but what will you do about the face?" said the boss. "Can you get away with the face?"

' "I'll show him what to do about the face," said the lady. "Give him his chance, Jack. I'm sure he's lucky for us and I'm never wrong. After all, where did Holroyd find him?"

'So I got the job, though I hadn't any idea what the job was, and nobody thought to tell me. But the boss said I was to come to rehearsal the following Monday, which was five days away. In the meantime, he said, I was to give up my present job, and keep out of sight. I would have accepted that, but again the lady interfered.

' "You can't ask him to do that, Jack," she said. "What's he to live on in the meantime?"

' "Holroyd will attend to it," said the little man. Then he offered the lady his arm, and put his hat back on his head (after Holroyd had dusted it, quite needlessly) and they swept out of that grubby assembly room in the Crown and Two Chairmen as if it were a palace.

'I said to Holroyd, "What's this about lifts? I'm as tall as he is; perhaps a bit taller."

' "If you want this job, m'boy, you'll be shorter and stay shorter," said Holroyd. Then he gave me thirty shillings, explaining that it was an advance on salary. He also asked for a pledge in return, just so that I wouldn't make off with the thirty shillings; I gave him my old silver watch. I respected Holroyd for that; he belonged to my world. It was clear that it was time for me to go, but I still didn't know what the job was, or what I was letting myself in for. That was obviously the style around there. Nobody explained anything. You were supposed to know.

'So, not being a fool, I set to work to find out. I discovered downstairs in the bar that Sir John Tresize and his company were rehearsing above, which left me not much wiser, except that it was some sort of theatricals. But when I went back to the buskers and told them I was quitting, and why, they were impressed, but not pleased.

' "You gone legit on us," said the boss of the group, who was an escape-man, like the one we saw this morning. "You and your Sir John-bloody-Tresize. Amlet and Oh Thello and the like of them. If you want my opinion, you've got above yourself, and when they find out, don't come whinin' back to me, that's all. Don't come whinin' bloody back here." Then he kicked me pretty hard in the backside, and that was the end of my engagement as an open-air entertainer.

'I didn't bother to resent the kick. I had a feeling something important had happened to me, and I celebrated by taking a vacation. Living for five days on thirty shillings was luxury to me at that time. I thought of augmenting my money by doing a bit of pocket-picking, but I rejected the idea for a reason that will show you what had happened to me; I thought such behaviour would be unsuitable to one who had been given a job because of the interference of a richly-dressed lady with an eye for talent.

'The image of the woman called Nan by Sir John Tresize dominated my mind. Her umbrella, as I balanced it on my nose, gave forth an expensive smell of perfume, and I could recall it even in the petrol stink of London streets. I was like a boy who is in love for the first time. But I wasn't a boy; it was 1930, so I must have been twenty-two, and I was a thorough young tough – side-show performer, vaudeville rat, pick-pocket, dope-pusher, a forger in a modest way, and for a good many years the despised utensil of an arse-bandit. Women, to me, were members of a race who were either old and tougher than the men who work in carnivals, or the flabby, pallid strumpets I had occasionally seen in Charlie's room when I went to rouse him to come to the aid of Willard. But so far as any sexual association with a woman went, I was a virgin. Yes, ladies and gentlemen, I was a hoor from the back and a virgin from the front, and so far as romance was concerned I was as pure as the lily in the dell. And there I was, over my ears in love with Lady Tresize, professionally known as Miss Annette de la Borderie, who cannot have been far off sixty and was, as Ingestree is eager to tell you, not a beauty. But she had been kind to me and said she would show me what to do about my face – whatever that meant – and I loved her.

'What do I mean? That I was constantly aware of her, and what I believed to be her spirit transfigured everything around me. I held wonderful mental conversations with her, and although they didn't make much sense they gave me a new attitude toward myself. I told you I put aside any notion of picking a pocket in order to refresh my exchequer because of her. What was stranger was that I felt in quite a different way about the poor slut that helped the escape-artist who kicked me; he was rough with her, I knew, and I pitied her, though I had taken no notice of her before then. It was the dawn of chivalry in me, coming rather late in life. Most men, unless they are assembled on the lowest, turnip-like principle, have a spell of chivalry at some time in their lives. Usually it comes at about sixteen. I understand boys quite often wish they had a chance to die for the one they love, to show that their devotion stops at nothing. Dying wasn't my line; a good religious start in life had given me too much respect for death to permit any extravagance of that sort. But I wanted to live for Lady Tresize, and I was overjoyed by the notion that, if I could do whatever Holroyd and Sir John wanted, I might be able to manage it.

'It wasn't lunacy. She had that effect, in lesser measure, on a lot of people, as I found out when I joined the Tresize Company. Everybody called Sir John "Guvnor", because that was his style; lots of heads of theatrical companies were called Guvnor. But they called Lady Tresize "Milady". It would have been reasonable enough for her maid to do that, but everybody did it, and it was respectful, and affectionately mocking at the same time. She understood both the affection and the mockery, because Milady was no fool.

'Five days is a long time to be cut off from Paradise, and I had nothing to occupy my time. I suppose I walked close to a hundred miles through the London streets. What else was there to do? I bummed around the Victoria and Albert Museum quite a lot, looking at the clocks and watches, but I wasn't dressed for it and I suppose a young tough who hung around for hours made the guards nervous. I looked like a ruffian, and I suppose I was one, and I held no grudge when I was politely warned away. I saw a few free sights – churches and the like – but they meant little to me. I liked the streets best, so I walked and stared, and slept in a Salvation Army hostel for indigents. But I was no indigent; I was rich in feeling, and that was a luxury I had rarely known.

'As the Monday drew near when I was to present myself again I worried a lot about my clothes. All I owned was what I stood up in, and my very poor things were a good protective covering in the streets, where I looked like a thousand others, but they weren't what I needed for a great step upward in the theatrical world. There was nothing to be done, and with my experience I knew my best plan was to present an appearance of honest poverty, so I spent some money on a bath, and washed the handkerchief I wore around my throat in the bathwater, and got a street shoeshine boy to do what he could with my dreadful shoes, which were almost falling apart.

'When the day came, I was well ahead of time, and had my first taste of a theatrical rehearsal. Milady didn't appear at it, and that was a heavy disappointment, but there was plenty to take in, all the same.

'It was education by observation. Nobody paid any heed to me. Holroyd nodded when I went into the room, and told me to keep out of the way, so I sat on a windowsill and watched. Men and women appeared very promptly to time, and a stage manager set out a few chairs to mark entrances and limits to the stage on the bare floor. Bang on the stroke of ten Sir John came in, and sat down in a chair behind a table, tapped twice with a silver pencil, and they went to work.

'You know what early rehearsals are like. You would never guess they were getting up a play. People wandered on and off the stage area, reading from sheets of paper that were bound up in brown covers; they mumbled and made mistakes as if they had never seen print before. Sir John mumbled worse than anyone. He had a way of talking that I could hardly believe belonged to a human being, because almost everything he said was cast in an interrogative tone, and was muddled up with a lot of "Eh?" and "Mphm?" and a queer noise he made high up in the back of his nose that sounded like "Quonk?" But the actors seemed used to it and amid all the muttering and quonking a good deal of work seemed to be done. Now and then Sir John himself would appear in a scene, and then the muttering sank almost to inaudibility. Very soon I was bored.

'It was not my plan to be bored, so I looked for something to do. I was a handy fellow, and a lot younger than the stage manager, so when the chairs had to be arranged in a different pattern I nipped forward and gave him a hand, which he allowed me to do without comment. Before the rehearsal was finished I was an established chair lifter, and that was how I became an assistant stage manager. My immediate boss was a man called Macgregor, whose feet hurt; he had those solid feet that seem to be all in one piece, encased in heavy boots; he was glad enough to have somebody who would run around for him. It was from him, during a break in the work, that I found out what we were doing.

' "It's the new piece," he explained. "*Scaramouche*. From the novel by Rafael Sabatini. You'll have heard of Rafael Sabatini? You haven't? Well, keep your lugs open and you'll get the drift of it. Verra romantic, of course."

' "What am I to do, Mr Macgregor?" I asked.

' "Nobody's told me," he said. "But from the cut of your jib I'd imagine you were the Double."

' "Double what?"

' "The Double in Two, two," he said, in a very Scotch way. I learned long ago, from you, Ramsay, that it's no use asking questions of a Scot when he speaks like that – dry as an old soda biscuit. So I held my peace.

'I picked up a little information by listening and asking an occasional question when some of the lesser actors went downstairs to the bar for a modest lunch. After three or four days I knew that *Scaramouche* was laid in the period of the French Revolution, though when that was I did not know. I had never heard that the French had a revolution. I knew the Americans had had one, but so far as detail went it could have been because George Washington shot Lincoln. I was pretty strong on the kings of Israel; later history was closed to me. But the story of the play leaked out in dribbles. Sir John was a young Frenchman who was "born with a gift of laughter and a sense that the world was mad"; that was what one of the other actors said about him. The astonishing thing was that nobody thought it strange that Sir John was so far into middle age that he was very near to emerging from the far side of it. This young Frenchman got himself into trouble with the nobility because he had advanced notions. To conceal himself he joined a troupe of travelling actors, but his revolutionary zeal was so great that he could not hold his tongue, and denounced the aristocracy from the stage, to the scandal of everyone. When the Revolution came, which it did right on time when it was needed, he became a revolutionary leader, and was about to revenge himself on the nobleman who had vilely slain his best friend and nabbed his girl, when an elderly noblewoman was forced to declare that she was his mother and then, much against her will, further compelled to tell him that his deadly enemy whom he held at the sword's point was – his father!

'Verra romantic, as Macgregor said, but not so foolish as I have perhaps led you to think. I give it to you as it appeared to me on early acquaintance. I was only interested in what I was supposed to do to earn my salary. Because I now had a salary – or half a salary, because that was the pay for the rehearsal period. Holroyd had presented me with a couple of pages of wretchedly typed stuff, which was my contract. I signed it Jules LeGrand, so that it agreed with my passport. Holroyd looked a little askew at the name, and asked me if I spoke French. I was glad that I could say yes, but he gave me a pretty strong hint that I might consider finding some less foreign name for use on the stage. I couldn't imagine why that should be, but I found out when we reached Act Two, scene two.

'We had approached this critical point – critical for me, that's to say – two or three times during the first week of rehearsal, and Sir John had asked the actors to "walk through" it, without doing more than find their places on the stage. It was a scene in which the young revolutionary lawyer, whose name was André-Louis, was appearing on the stage with the travelling actors. They were a troupe of Italian Comedians, all of whom played strongly marked characters such as Polichinelle the old father, Climene the beautiful leading lady, Rhodomont the braggart, Leandre the lover, Pasquariel, and other figures from the Commedia dell' Arte. I didn't know what that was, but I picked up the general idea, and it wasn't so far away from vaudeville as you might suppose. Indeed, some of it reminded me of poor Zovene, the wretched juggler. André-Louis (that was Sir John) had assumed the role of Scaramouche, a dashing, witty scoundrel.

'In Act Two, scene two, the Italian Comedians were giving a performance, and at the very beginning of it Scaramouche had to do some flashy juggling tricks. Later, he seized his chance to make a revolutionary speech which was not in the play as the Comedians had rehearsed it; when his great enemy and some aristocratic chums stormed the stage to punish him, he escaped by walking across the stage on a tightrope, far above their heads, making jeering gestures as he did so. Very showy. And clearly not for Sir John. So I was to appear in a costume exactly like his, do the tricks, get out of the way so Sir John could make his revolutionary speech, and take over again when it was time to walk the tightrope.

'This would take some neat managing. When Macgregor said, "Curtain up," I leapt onto the stage area from the audience's right, and danced toward the left, juggling some plates; when Polichinelle broke the plates with his stick, causing a lot of clatter and uproar, I pretended to dodge behind his cloak, and Sir John popped into sight immediately afterward. Sounds simple, but as we had to pretend to have the plates, and the cloak, and everything else, I found it confusing. The tightrope trick was "walked" in the same way; Sir John was always talking about "walking" something when we weren't ready to do it in reality. At the critical moment when the aristocrats rushed the stage, Sir John retreated slowly toward the left side, keeping them off with a stick; then he hopped backward onto a chair – which I must say he did with astonishing spryness – and there was a flurry of cloaks, during which he got out of the way and I emerged above on the tightrope, having stepped out on it from the wings. Easy, you would say, for an old carnival hand? But it wasn't easy at all, and after a few days it looked as if I would lose my job. Even when we were "walking", I couldn't satisfy Sir John.

'As usual, nobody said anything to me, but I knew what was up one morning when Holroyd appeared with a fellow who was obviously an acrobat and Sir John talked with him. I hung around, officiously helping Macgregor, and heard what was said, or enough of it. The acrobat seemed to be very set on something he wanted, and it wasn't long before he was on his way, and Sir John was in an exceedingly bad temper. All through the rehearsal he bullied everybody. He bullied Miss Adele Chesterton, the pretty girl who played the second romantic interest; she was new to the stage and a natural focus for temper. He bullied old Frank Moore, who played Polichinelle, and was a very old hand and an extraordinarily nice person. He was crusty with Holroyd and chivvied Macgregor. He didn't shout or swear, but he was impatient and exacting, and his annoyance was so thick it cut down the visibility in the room to about half, like dark smoke. When the time came to rehearse Two, two, he said he would leave it out for that day, and he brought the rehearsal to an early close. Holroyd asked me to wait after the others had gone, but not to hang around. So I kept out of the way near the door while Sir John, Holroyd, and Milady held a summit conference at the farther end of the room.

'I couldn't hear much of what they said, but it was about me, and it was hottish. Holroyd kept saying things like, "You won't get a real pro to agree to leaving his name off the bills," and "It's not as easy to get a fair resemblance as you might suppose – not under the conditions." Milady had a real stage voice, and when she spoke her lowest it was still as clear as a bell at my end of the room, and her talk was all variations on "Give the poor fellow a chance, Jack – everybody must have at least one chance." But of Sir John I could hear nothing. He had a stage voice, too, and knew how far it could be heard, so when he was being confidential he mumbled on purpose and threw in a lot of Eh and Quonk, which seemed to convey meaning to people who knew him.

'After ten minutes Milady said, so loudly that there could be no pretence that I was not to hear, "Trust me, Jack. He's lucky for us. He has a lucky face. I'm never wrong. And if I can't get him right, we'll say no more about it." Then she swept down the room to me, using the umbrella, with more style than you'd think possible, as a walking-stick, and said, "Come with me, my dear boy; we must have a very intimate talk." Then something

713

struck her, and she turned to the two men; "I haven't a penny,"
she said, and from the way both Sir John and Holroyd jumped
forward to press pound notes on her you could tell they were
both devoted to her. That made me feel warmly toward them,
even though they had been talking about sacking me a minute
before.

'Milady led the way, and I tagged behind. We went downstairs, where she poked her head into the Public Bar, which was
just opening and said, in a surprisingly genial voice, considering
that she was Lady Tresize talking to a barman, "Do you think I
could have Rab Noolas for a private talk, for about half an hour,
Joey?", and the barman shouted back, "Whatever you say,
Milady," and she led me into a gloomy pen, surrounded on three
sides by dingy etched glass, with Saloon Bar on the door. When
I closed the door behind us this appeared in reverse and I
understood that we were now in Rab Noolas. The barman came
behind the counter on our fourth side and asked us what it
would be. "A pink gin, Joey," said Milady, and I said I'd have
the same, not knowing what it was. Joey produced them, and
we sat down, and from the way Milady did so I knew it was a
big moment. Fraught, as they say, with consequence.

' "Let us be very frank. And I'll be frank first, because I'm the
oldest. You simply have no notion of the wonderful opportunity
you have in *Scaramouche*. Such a superb little cameo. I say to all
beginners : they aren't tiny parts, they're little cameos, and the
way you carve them is the sign of what your whole career will
be. Show me a young player who can give a superb cameo in a
small part, and I'll show you a star of the future. And yours is
one of the very finest opportunities I have ever seen in my life in
the theatre, because you must be so marvellous that nobody –
not the sharpest-eyed critic or the most adoring fan – can distinguish you from my husband. Suddenly, before their very
eyes, stands Sir John, juggling marvellously, and of course they
adore him. Then, a few minutes later, they see Sir John walking
the tightrope, and they see half a dozen of his little special tricks
of gesture and turns of the head, and they are thunderstruck
because they can't believe that he has learned to walk the tightrope. And the marvel of it, you see, is that it's you, all the time!
You must use your imagination, my dear boy. You must see

714

what a stunning effect it is. And what makes it possible? You do!"

' "Oh I do see all that, Milady," I said. "But Sir John isn't pleased. I wish I knew why. I'm honestly doing the very best I can, considering that we haven't anything to juggle with, or any tightrope. How can I do better?"

' "Ah, but you've put your finger on it, dear boy. I knew from the moment I saw you that you had great, great understanding – not to speak of a lucky face. You have said it yourself. You're doing the best *you* can. But that's not what's wanted, you see. You must do the best Sir John can."

' "But – Sir John can't do anything," I said. "He can't juggle and he can't walk rope. Otherwise why would he want me?"

' "No, no; you haven't understood. Sir John can, and will, do something absolutely extraordinary: he will make the public – the great audiences of people who come to see him in everything – believe he is doing those splendid, skilful things. He can make them want to believe he can do anything. They will quite happily accept you as him, if you can get the right rhythm."

' "But I still don't understand. People aren't as stupid as that. They'll guess it's a trick."

' "A few, perhaps. But most of them will prefer to believe it's a reality. That's what the theatre's about, you see. People want to believe that what they see is true, even if only for the time they're in the playhouse. That's what theatre is, don't you understand? Showing people what they wish were true."

'Then I began to get the idea. I had seen that look in the faces of the people who watched Abdullah, and who saw Willard swallow needles and thread and pull it out of his mouth with the needles all dangling from the thread. I nervously asked Milady if she would like another pink gin. She said she certainly would, and gave me a pound note to pay for it. When I demurred she said, "No, no; you must let me pay. I've got more money than you, and I won't presume on your gallantry – though I value it, my dear, don't imagine I don't value it."

'When the gins came, she continued: "Let us be very, very frank. Your marvellous cameo must be a great secret. If we tell everybody, we stifle some of their pleasure. You saw that young man who came this morning, and argued so tiresomely? He could juggle and he could walk the rope, quite as well as you, I expect, but he was no use whatever, because he had the spirit of a circus person; he wanted his name on the programme, and he wanted featured billing. Wanted his name to come at the bottom of the bills, you see, after all the cast had been listed, 'AND Trebelli'. An absurd request. Everybody would want to know who Trebelli was and they would see at once that he was the juggler and rope-walker. And Romance would fly right up the chimney. Besides which I could see that he would never deceive anyone for an instant that he was Sir John. He had a brassy, horrid personality. Now you, my dear, have the splendid qualification of having very little personality. One hardly notices you. You are almost a *tabula rasa*."

‘ "Excuse me, Milady, but I don't know what that is."

‘ "No? Well, it's a – it's a common expression. I've never really had to define it. It's a sort of charming nothing; a dear, sweet little zero, in which one can paint any face one chooses. An invaluable possession, don't you see? One says it of children when one's going to teach them something perfectly splendid. They're wide open for teaching."

‘ "I want to be taught. What do you want me to learn?"

‘ "I knew you were quite extraordinarily intelligent. More than intelligent, really. Intelligent people are so often thoroughly horrid. You are truly sensitive. I want you to learn to be exactly like Sir John."

‘ "Imitate him, you mean?"

‘ "Imitations are no good. There have been people on the music-halls who have imitated him. No : if the thing is to work as we all want it to work, you must quite simply *be* him."

‘ "How, if I don't imitate him?"

‘ "It's a very deep thing. Of course you must imitate him, but be careful he doesn't catch you at it, because he doesn't like it. Nobody does, do they? What I mean is – oh, dear, it's so dreadfully difficult to say what one really means – you must catch his walk, and his turn of the head, and his gestures and all of that, but the vital thing is that you must catch his rhythm."

‘ "How would I start to do that?"

‘ "Model yourself on him. Make yourself like a marvellously

sensitive telegraph wire that takes messages from him. Or perhaps like wireless, that picks up things out of the air. Do what he did with the Guvnor."

' "I thought he was the Guvnor."

' "He is now, of course. But when we both worked under the dear old Guvnor at the Lyceum Sir John absolutely adored him, and laid himself open to him like Danae to the shower of gold – you know about that, of course? – and became astonishingly like him in a lot of ways. Of course Sir John is not so tall as the Guvnor; but you're not tall either, are you? It was the Guvnor's romantic splendour he caught. Which is what you must do. So that when you dance out before the audience juggling those plates they don't feel as if the electricity had suddenly been cut off. Another pink gin, if you please."

'I didn't greatly like pink gin. In those days I couldn't afford to drink anything, and pink gin is a bad start. But I would have drunk hot fat to prolong this conversation. So we had another one each, and Milady dealt with hers much better than I did. A pink gin later – call it ten minutes – I was thoroughly confused, except that I wanted to please her, and must find out somehow what she was talking about.

'When she wanted to leave I rushed to call her a taxi, but Holroyd was ahead of me, and in much better condition. He must have been in the Public Bar. We both bowed her into the cab – I seem to remember having one foot in the gutter and the other on the pavement and wondering what had happened to my legs – and when she drove off he took me by the arm and steered me back into the Public Bar, where we tucked into a corner with old Frank Moore.

' "She's been giving him advice and pink gin," said Holroyd.

' "Better give him a good honest pint of half-and-half to straighten him out," said Frank, and signalled to the barman.

'They seemed to know what Milady had been up to, and were ready to put it in language that I could understand, which was kind of them. They made it seem very simple: I was to imitate Sir John, but I was to do it with more style than I had been showing. I was supposed to be imitating a great actor who was imitating an eighteenth-century gentleman who was imitating a Commedia dell' Arte comedian – that's how simple it was. And

I was doing everything too bloody fast, and slick and cheap, so I was to drop that and catch Sir John's rhythm.

' "But I don't get it about all this rhythm," I said. "I guess I know about rhythm in juggling; it's getting everything under control so you don't have to worry about dropping things because the things are behaving properly. But what the hell's all this human rhythm? You mean like dancing?"

' "Not like any dancing I suppose you know," said Holroyd. "But yes – a bit like dancing. Not like this Charleston and all that jerky stuff. More a fine kind of complicated – well, rhythm."

' "I don't get it at all," I said. "I've got to get Sir John's rhythm. Sir John got his rhythm from somebody called the Guvnor. What Guvnor? Is the whole theatre full of Guvnors?"

' "Ah, now we're getting to it," said old Frank. "Milady talked about the Guvnor, did she? The Guvnor was Irving, you muggins. You've heard of Irving?"

' "Never," I said.

'Old Frank looked wonderingly at Holroyd. "Never heard of Irving. He's quite a case, isn't he?"

' "Not such a case as you might think, Frank," said Holroyd. "These kids today have never heard of anybody. And I suppose we've got to remember that Irving's been dead for twenty-five years. You remember him. You played with him. I just remember him. But what's he got to do with a lad like this? – Well, now just hold on a minute. Milady thinks there's a connection. You know how she goes on. Like a loony, sometimes. But just when you can't stand it any more she proves to be right, and righter than any of us. You remember where I found you?" he said to me.

' "In the street. I was doing a few passes with the cards."

' "Yes, but don't you remember where? I do. I saw you and I came back to rehearsal and said to Sir John, I think I've got what we want. Found him under the Guvnor's statue, picking up a few pennies as a conjuror. And that was when Milady pricked up her ears. Oh Jack, she said, it's a lucky sign! Let's see him at once. And when Sir John wanted to ask perfectly reasonable questions about whether you would do for height, and whether a resemblance could be contrived between you and him, she kept nattering on about how you must be a lucky find because I saw you, as she put it, working the streets under Irving's protection. You know how the Guvnor stood up for all the little people of the theatre, Jack, she said. I'm sure this boy is a lucky find. Do let's have him. And she's stood up for you ever since, though I don't suppose you'll be surprised to hear that Sir John wants to get rid of you."

'The pint of half-and-half had found its way to the four pink gins, and I was having something like a French Revolution in my innards. I was feeling sorry for myself. "Why does he hate me so," I said, snivelling a bit. "I'm doing everything I know to please him."

' "You'd better have it straight," said Holroyd. "The resemblance is a bit too good. You look too much like him."

' "Just what I said when I first set eyes on you," said old Frank. "My God, I said, what a Double! You might have been spit out of his mouth."

' "Well, isn't that what they want?" I said.

' "You have to look at it reasonable," said Holroyd. "Put it like this: you're a famous actor, getting maybe just the tiniest bit past your prime – though still a top-notcher, mind you – and for thirty years everybody's said how distinguished you are, and what a beautiful expressive face you have, and how Maeterlinck damn near threw up his lunch when you walked on the stage in one of his plays, and said to the papers that you had stolen his soul, you were so good – meaning spiritual, romantic, poetic, and generally gorgeous. You still get lots of fan letters from people who find some kind of ideal in you. You've had all the devotion – a bit cracked some of it, but mostly very real and touching – that a great actor inspires in people, most of whom have had some kind of short-change experience in life. So: you want a Double. And when the Double comes – and such a Double that you can't deny him – he's a seedy little carnie, with the shifty eyes of a pickpocket and the breath of somebody that eats the cheapest food, and you wouldn't trust him with sixpenn'orth of copper, and every time you look at him you heave. He looks like everything inside yourself that you've choked off and shut out in order to be what you are now. And he looks at you all the time – you do this, you know – as if he knew something

719

about you you didn't know yourself. Now: fair's fair. Wouldn't you want to get rid of him? Yet here's your wife, who's stood by you through thick and thin, and held you up when you were ready to sink under debts and bad luck, and whom you love so much everybody can see it, and thinks you're marvellous because of it, and what does she say? She says this nasty mess of a Double is lucky, and has to be given his chance. You follow me? Try to be objective. I don't want to say hard things about you, but truth's truth and must be served. You're not anybody's first pick for a Double, but there you are. Sir John's dead spit, as Frank here says."

'Very soon I was going to have to leave them. My stomach was heaving. But I was still determined to find out whatever I could to keep my job. I wanted it now more desperately than before. "So what do I do?" I asked.

'Holroyd puffed at his pipe, groping for an answer, and it was old Frank who spoke. He spoke very kindly. "You just keep on keeping on," he said. "Try to find the rhythm. Try to get inside Sir John."

'These were fatal words. I rushed out into the street, and threw up noisily and copiously in the gutter. Try to get inside Sir John! Was this to be another Abdullah?

'It was, but in a way I could not have foreseen. Experience never repeats itself in quite the same way. I was beginning another servitude, much more dangerous and potentially ruinous, but far removed from the squalor of my experience with Willard. I had entered upon a long apprenticeship to an egoism.

'Please notice that I say egoism, not egotism, and I am prepared to be pernickety about the distinction. An egotist is a self-absorbed creature, delighted with himself and ready to tell the world about his enthralling love affair. But an egoist, like Sir John, is a much more serious being, who makes himself, his instincts, yearnings, and tastes the touchstone of every experience. The world, truly, is his creation. Outwardly he may be courteous, modest, and charming – and certainly when you knew him Sir John was all of these – but beneath the velvet is the steel; if anything comes along that will not yield to the steel, the steel will retreat from it and ignore its existence. The egotist is all surface; underneath is a pulpy mess and a lot of self-doubt.

But the egoist may be yielding and even deferential in things he doesn't consider important; in anything that touches his core he is remorseless.

'Many of us have some touch of egoism. We who sit at this table are no strangers to it. You, I should think, Jurgen, are a substantial egoist, and so are you, Harry. About Ingestree I can't say. But Liesl is certainly an egoist and you, Ramsay, are a ferocious egoist battling with your demon because you would like to be a saint. But none of you begins to approach the egoism of Sir John. His egoism was fed by the devotion of his wife, and the applause he could call forth in the theatre. I have never known anyone who came near him in the truly absorbing and damning sin of egoism.'

'Damning?' I leapt on the word.

'We were both brought up to believe in damnation, Dunny,' said Eisengrim, and he was deeply serious. 'What does it mean? Does it mean shut off from the promptings of compassion; untouched by the feelings of others except in so far as they can serve us; blind and deaf to anything that is not grist to our mill? If that is what it means, and if that is a form of damnation, I have used the word rightly.

'Don't misunderstand. Sir John wasn't cruel, or dishonourable or overreaching in common ways; but he was all of these things where his own interest as an artist was concerned; within that broad realm he was without bowels. He didn't make Adele Chesterton cry at every rehearsal because he was a brute. He hadn't brought Holroyd – who was a tough nut in every other way – to a condition of total subjection to his will because he liked to domineer over a fellow-being. He hadn't turned Milady into a kind of human oilcan who went about cooling wheels he had worn red-hot because he didn't know that she was a woman of rare spirit and fine sensitivity. He did these things and a thousand others because he was wholly devoted to an ideal of theatrical art that was contained – so far as he was concerned – within himself. I think he knew perfectly well what he did, and he thought it worth the doing. It served his art, and his art demanded a remorseless egoism.

'He was one of the last of a kind that has now vanished. He was an actor-manager. There was no Arts Council to keep him afloat when he failed, or pick up the bill for an artistic experiment or act of daring. He had to find the money for his ventures, and if the money was lost on one production he had to get it back from another, or he would soon appeal to investors in vain. Part of him was a financier. He asked people to invest in his craft and skill and sense of business. Beyond that, he asked people to invest in his personality and charm, and the formidable technique he had acquired to make personality and charm vivid to hundreds of thousands of people who bought theatre seats. In justice it must be said that he had a particular sort of taste and flair that lifted him above the top level of actors to the very small group of stars with an assured following. He wasn't personally greedy, though he liked to live well. He did what he did for art. His egoism lay in his belief that art, as he embodied it, was worth any sacrifice on his part and on the part of people who worked with him.

'When I became part of his company the fight against time had begun. Not simply the fight against the approach of age, because he was not deluded about that. It was the fight against the change in the times, the fight to maintain a nineteenth-century idea of theatre in the twentieth century. He believed devoutly in what he did; he believed in Romance, and he couldn't understand that the concept of Romance was changing.

'Romance changes all the time. His plays, in which a well-graced hero moved through a succession of splendid adventures and came out on top – even when that meant dying for some noble cause – were becoming old hat. Romance at that time meant *Private Lives*, which was brand-new. It didn't look to its audiences like Romance, but that was what it was. Our notion of Romance, which is so often exploration of squalor and degradation, will become old hat, too. Romance is a mode of feeling that puts enormous emphasis – but not quite a tragic emphasis – on individual experience. Tragedy puts something above humanity; so does Comedy; Romance puts humanity first. The people who liked Sir John's kind of Romance were middle-aged, or old. Oh, lots of young people came to see him, but they weren't the most interesting kind of young people. Perhaps they weren't really young. The interesting young people were going to see a different sort of play. They were flocking to *Private*

Lives. You couldn't expect Sir John to understand. His ideal of Romance was far from that, and he had shaped a formidable egoism to serve his ideal.'

'It's the peril of the actor,' said Ingestree. 'Do you remember what Aldous Huxley said? "Acting inflames the ego in a way which few other professions do. For the sake of enjoying regular emotional self-abuse, our societies condemn a considerable class of men and women to a perpetual inability to achieve non-attachment. It seems a high price to pay for our amusements." A profound comment. I used to be deeply influenced by Huxley.'

'I gather you got over it,' said Eisengrim, 'or you wouldn't be talking about non-attachment over the ruins of a tremendous meal and a huge cigar you have been sucking like a child at its mother's breast.'

'I thought you had forgiven me,' said Ingestree, being as winsome as his age and appearance allowed. 'I don't pretend to have set aside the delights of this world; I tried that and it was no good. But I have my intellectual fopperies, and they pop out now and then. Do go on about Sir John and his egoism.'

'So I shall,' said Magnus, 'but at another time. The waiters are hovering and I perceive the delicate fluttering of paper in the hands of the chief bandit yonder.'

I watched with envy as Ingestree signed the bill without batting an eyelash. I suppose it was company money he was spending. We went out into the London rain and called for cabs.

4

IN the days that followed, Magnus was busy filming the last scraps of *Hommage* in a studio near London; these were close-ups, chiefly of his hands, as he did intricate things with cards and coins, but he insisted on wearing full costume and make-up. There was also a time-taking quarrel with a fashionable photographer who was to provide publicity pictures, and who kept assuring Magnus that he wanted to catch 'the real you'. But Magnus didn't want candid pictures of himself, and he was rather personal in his insistence that the photographer, a bearded fanatic who wore sandals, was not likely to capture with his camera something he had taken pains to conceal for more than thirty years. So we went to a very famous photographer who was celebrated for his pictures of royalty, and he and Magnus plotted some portraits, taken in a splendid old theatre, that satisfied both of them. All of this took time, until there was no longer any reason for us to stay in London. But Lind and Ingestree, and to a lesser degree Kinghovn, were determined to hear the remainder of Magnus's story, and after a good deal of teasing and protesting that there was really nothing to it, and that he was tired of talking about himself, it was agreed that they should spend our last day in London with us, and have their way.

'I'm doing it for Ingestree, really,' said Magnus, and I thought it an odd remark, as he and Roly had not been on the best of terms since they first met at Sorgenfrei. Inquisitive, as always, I found a time to mention this to Roly, who was puzzled and flattered. 'Can't imagine why he said that,' was his comment; 'but there's something about him that rouses more than ordinary curiosity in me. He's terribly like someone I've known, but I can't say who it is. And I'm fascinated by his crusty defence of old Tresize and his wife. I know a bit about Sir John that puts him in a very different light from the rosy glow Magnus spreads over his memories. These recollections of old actors, you know – awful old hams, most of them. It's the most perishable of the arts. Have you ever had the experience of seeing a film you saw thirty or even forty years ago and thought wonderful? Avoid it, I urge you. Appallingly disillusioning. One remembers something that never had any reality. No, old actors should be let die.'

'What about old conjurors?' I said; 'why *Hommage*? Why don't you leave Robert-Houdin in his grave?'

'That's precisely where he is. You don't think this film we're making is really anything like the old boy, do you? With every modern technique at our command, and Jurgen Lind sifting every shot through his own marvellously contemporary concept of magic – no, no, if you could be whisked back in time and see Robert-Houdin you'd see something terribly tacky in comparison with what we're offering. He's just a peg on which Jurgen is hanging a fine modern creation. We need all the research and reconstruction and whatnot to produce something inescapably contemporary; a paradox, but that's how it is.'

'Then you believe that there is no time but the present moment, and that everything in the past is diminished by the simple fact that it is irrecoverable? I suppose there's a name for that point of view, but at present I can't put my tongue to it.'

'Yes, that's pretty much what I believe. Eisengrim's raptures about Sir John and Milady interest me as a phenomenon of the present; I'm fascinated that he should think as he does at this moment, and put so much feeling into expressing what he feels. I can't be persuaded for an instant that those two old spooks were anything very special.'

'You realize, of course, that you condemn yourself to the same treatment? You've done some work that people have admired and admire still. Are you agreed that it should be judged as you judge Magnus's idols?'

'Of course. Let it all go! I'll have my whack and that'll be the end of me. I don't expect any yellow roses on my monument. Nor a monument, as a matter of fact. But I'm keenly interested in other monument-worshippers. Magnus loves the past simply because it feeds his present, and that's all there is to it. It's the piety and ancestor-worship of a chap who, as he's told us, had a nasty family and a horrid childhood and has had to dig up a better one. Before he's finished he'll tell us the Tresizes were his real parents, or his parents in art, or something of that sort. Want to bet?'

I never bet, and I wouldn't have risked money on that, because I thought that Ingestree was probably right.

5

OUR last day was a Saturday, and the three film-makers appeared in time for lunch at the Savoy. Liesl had arranged that we should have one of the good tables looking out over the Embankment, and it was a splendid autumn day. The light, as it fell on our table, could not have been improved on by King-hovn himself. Magnus never ate very much, and today he confined himself to some cold beef and a dish of rice pudding. It gave him a perverse pleasure to order these nursery dishes in restaurants where other people gorged on luxuries, and he insisted that the Savoy served the best rice pudding in London. The others ate heartily, Ingestree with naked and rather touching relish, Kinghovn like a man who has not seen food for a week, and Lind with a curious detachment, as though he were eating to oblige somebody else, and did not mean to disappoint them. Liesl was in one of her ogress moods and ordered steak tartare, which seemed to me no better than raw meat. I had the set lunch; excellent value.

'You spoke of Tresize's egoism when last we dealt with the subtext,' said Lind, champing his great jaws on a lamb chop.

'I did, and I may have misled you. Shortly after I had my talk with Milady, we stopped rehearsing at the Crown and Two Chairmen, and moved into the theatre where *Scaramouche* was to appear. It was the Globe. We needed a theatre with plenty of backstage room because it was a pretty elaborate show. Sir John still held to the custom of opening in London with a new piece; no out-of-town tour to get things shaken down. It was an eye-opener to me to walk into a theatre that was better than the decrepit vaudeville houses where I had appeared with Willard; there was a discipline and a formality I had never met with. I was hired as an assistant stage manager (with a proviso that I should act "as cast" if required) and I had everything to learn about the job. Luckily old Macgregor was a patient and thorough teacher. I had lots to do. That was before the time when the stagehands' union was strict about people who were not members moving and arranging things, and some of my work was heavy. I was on good terms with the stage crew at once, and I quickly found out that this put a barrier between me and the actors, although I had to become a member of Actors' Equity. But I was "crew", and although everybody was friendly I was not quite on the level of "company". What was I? I was necessary, and even important, to the play, but I found out that my name was to appear on the programme simply as Macgregor's assistant. I had no place in the list of the cast.

'Yet I was rehearsed carefully, and it seemed to me that I was doing well. I was trying to capture Sir John's rhythm, and now, to my surprise, he was helping me. We spent quite a lot of time on Two, two. I did my juggling with my back to the audience, but as I was to wear a costume identical with Sir John's, the audience would assume that was who I was, if I could bring off another sort of resemblance.

'That was an eye-opener. I was vaudeville trained, and my one idea of stage deportment was to be fast and gaudy. That wasn't Sir John's way at all. "Deliberately: deliberately," he would say, over and over again. "Let them see what you're doing. Don't be flashy and confusing. Do it like this." And then he would caper across the stage, making motions like a man juggling plates, but at a pace I thought impossibly slow. "It's not keeping the plates in the air that's important," he would say. "Of course you can do that. It's being Scaramouche that's important. It's the character you must get across. Eh? You understand the character, don't you? Eh? Have you looked at the Callots?"

'No, I hadn't looked at the Callots, and didn't know what they were. "Here m'boy; look here," he said, showing me some funny little pictures of people dressed as Scaramouche, and Polichinelle and other Commedia characters. "Get it like that! Make that real! You must be a Callot in motion!"

'It was new and hard work for me to catch the idea of making myself like a picture, but I was falling under Sir John's spell and was ready to give it a try. So I capered and pointed my toes, and struck exaggerated postures like the little pictures, and did my best.

' "Hands! Hands!" he would shout, warningly, when I had my work cut out to make the plates dance. "Not like hooks, m'boy, like this! See! Keep 'em like this!" And then he would demonstrate what he wanted, which was a queer trick for a juggler, because he wanted me to hold my hands with the little finger and the forefinger extended, and the two middle fingers held together. It looked fine as he did it, but it wasn't my style at all. And all the time he kept me dancing with my toes stuck out and my heels lifted, and he wanted me to get into positions which even I could see were picturesque, but couldn't copy.

' "Sorry, Sir John," I said one day. "It's just that it feels a bit loony."

' "Aha, you're getting it at last!" he shouted, and for the first time he smiled at me. "That's what I want! I want it a bit loony. Like Scaramouche, you see. Like a charlatan in a travelling show."

'I could have told him a few things about charlatans in travelling shows, and the way their looniness takes them, but it wouldn't have done. I see now that it was Romance he was after, not realism, but it was all a mystery to me then. I don't think I was a slow learner, and in our second rehearsal in the theatre, where we had the plates, and the cloaks, and the tight-rope to walk, I got my first real inkling of what it was all about, and where I was wrong and Sir John – in terms of Romance – was right.

'I told you I had to caper across the tightrope, as Scaramouche escaping from the angry aristocrats. I was high above their heads, and as I had only about thirty feet to go, at the farthest, I had to take quite a while over it while pretending to be quick. Sir John wanted the rope – it was a wire, really – to be slackish, so that it rocked and swayed. Apparently that was the Callot style. For balance I carried a long stick that I was supposed to have snatched from Polichinelle. I was doing it circus-fashion, making it look as hard as possible, but that wouldn't do: I was to rock on the wire, and be very much at ease, and when I was half-way across the stage I was to thumb my nose at the Marquis de la Tour d'Azyr, my chief enemy. I could thumb my nose. Not the least trouble. But the way I did it didn't please Sir John. "Like this," he would say, and put an elegant thumb to his long, elegant nose, and twiddle the fingers. I did it several times, and he shook his head. Then an idea seemed to strike him.

' "M'boy, what does that gesture mean to you?" he asked, fixing me with a lustrous brown eye.

' "Kiss my arse, Sir John," said I, bashfully: I wasn't sure he would know such a rude word. He looked grave, and shook his head slowly from side to side three or four times.

' "You have the essence of it, but only in the sense that the snail on the garden wall is the essence of *Escargots à la Niçoise*. What you convey by that gesture is all too plainly the grossly derisive invitation expressed by your phrase, Kiss my arse; it doesn't even get as far as *Baisez mon cul*. What I want is a Rabelaisian splendour of contempt linked with a Callotesque elegance of grotesquerie. What it boils down to is that you're not thinking it right. You're thinking Kiss my arse with a strong American accent, when what you ought to be thinking is —" and suddenly, though he was standing on the stage, he swayed perilously and confidently as though he were on the wire, and raised one eyebrow and opened his mouth in a grin like a leering wolf, and allowed no more than the tip of a very sharp red tongue to loll out on his lips and there it was! Kiss my arse *with class*, and God knows how many years of actors' technique and a vivid memory of Henry Irving all backing it up.

' "I think I get it," I said, and had a try. He was pleased. Again. Better pleased. "You're getting close," he said; "now, tell me what you're thinking when you do that? Mph? Kiss my arse, quonk? But what kind of Kiss my arse? Quonk? Quonk?"

'I didn't know what to tell him, but I couldn't be silent. "Not Kiss my arse at all," I said.

' "What then? What are you thinking? Eh? You must be thinking something, because you're getting what I want. Tell me what it is?"

'Better be truthful, I thought. He sees right into me and he'll spot a lie at once. I took my courage in my hand. "I was thinking that I must be born again," I said. "Quite right, m'boy; born again and born different, as Mrs Poyser very wisely said," was Sir John's comment. (Who was Mrs Poyser? I suppose it's the kind of thing Ramsay knows.)

'Born again! I'd always thought of it, when I thought about it at all, as a spiritual thing; you went through a conversion, or you found Christ, or whatever it was, and from that time you were different and never looked back. But to get inside Sir John I had to be born again physically, and if the spiritual trick is harder than that, Heaven must be thinly populated. I spent hours capering about in quiet places offstage, whenever Macgregor didn't need me, trying to be like Sir John, trying to get style even into Kiss my arse. What was the result? Next time we rehearsed Two, two, I was awful. I nearly dropped a plate, and for a juggler that's a shattering experience. (Don't laugh! I don't mean it as a joke.) But worse was to come. At the right moment I stepped out on the swaying wire, capered toward middle stage, thumbed my nose at Gordon Barnard, who was playing the Marquis, lost my balance, and fell off; Duparc's training stood by me, and I caught the wire with my hands, swung in mid-air for a couple of seconds, and then heaved myself back up and got my footing, and scampered to the opposite side. The actors who were rehearsing that day applauded, but I was destroyed with shame, and Sir John was grinning exactly like Scaramouche, with an inch of red tongue between his lips.

' "Don't think they'll quite accept you as me if you do that, m'boy," said he. "Eh, Holroyd? Eh, Barnard? Quonk? Try it again."

'I tried it again, and didn't fall, but I knew I was hopeless; I hadn't found Sir John's style and I was losing my own. After another bad try Sir John moved on to another scene, but Milady beckoned me away into a box, from which she was watching the rehearsal. I was full of apologies.

' "Of course you fell," she said. "But it was a good fall. Laudable pus, I call it. You're learning."

'Laudable pus! What in God's name did she mean! I thought I would never get used to Milady's lingo. But she saw the bewilderment in my face, and explained.

' "It's a medical expression. Out of fashion now, I expect. But my grandfather was rather a distinguished physician and he used it often. In those days, you know, when someone had a wound, they couldn't heal it as quickly as they do now; they dressed it and probed it every few days to see how it was getting on. If it was healing well, from the bottom, there was a lot of nasty stuff near the surface, and that was evidence of proper healing. They called it laudable pus. I know you're trying your very best to please Sir John, and it means a sharp wound to your own personality. As the wound heals, you will be nearer what we all want. But meanwhile there's laudable pus, and it shows itself in clumsiness and falls. When you get your new style, you'll understand what I mean."

'Had I time to get a new style before the play opened? I was worried sick, and I suppose it showed, because when he had a chance old Frank Moore had a word with me.

' "You're trying to catch the Guvnor's manner and you aren't making a bad fist of it, but there are one or two things you haven't noticed. You're an acrobat, good enough to walk the slackwire, but you're tight as a drum. Look at the Guvnor: he hasn't a taut muscle in his body, nor a slack one, either. He's in easy control all the time. Have you noticed him standing still? When he listens to another actor, have you seen how still he is? Look at you now, listening to me; you bob about and twist and turn and nod your head with enough energy to turn a windmill. But it's all waste, y'see. If we were in a scene, you'd be killing half the value of what I say with all that movement. Just try to sit still. Yes, there you go; you're not still at all, you're frozen. Stillness isn't looking as if you were full of coiled springs. It's repose. Intelligent repose. That's what the Guvnor has. What I have, too, as a matter of fact. What Barnard has. What Milady has. I suppose you think repose means asleep, or dead.

' "Now look, my lad, and try to see how it's done. It's mostly your back. Got to have a good strong back, and let it do ninety per cent of the work. Forget legs. Look at the Guvnor hopping around when he's being Scaramouche. He's nippier on his pins than you are. Look at me. I'm real old, but I bet I can dance a hornpipe better than you can. Look at this! Can you do a double shuffle like that? That's legs, to look at, but it's back in reality. Strong back. Don't pound down into the floor at every step. Forget legs.

' "How do you get a strong back? Well, it's hard to describe it, but once you get the feel of it you'll see what I'm talking about. The main thing is to trust your back and forget you have a front; don't stick out your chest or your belly; let 'em look after themselves. Trust your back and lead from your back. And just let your head float on top of your neck. You're all made of whipcord and wire. Loosen it up and take it easy. But not slump, mind! Easy."

'Suddenly the old man grabbed me by the neck and seemed about to throttle me. I jerked away, and he laughed. "Just as I said, you're all wire. When I touch your neck you tighten up like a spring. Now you try to strangle me." I seized him by the neck, and I thought his poor old head would come off in my hands; he sank to the floor, moaning, "Nay, spare m' life!" Then he laughed like an old loony, because I suppose I looked horrified. "D'you see? I just let myself go and trusted to my back. You work on that for a while and bob's your uncle; you'll be fit to act with the Guvnor."

' "How long do you think it will take?" I said. "Oh, ten or fifteen years should see you right," said old Frank, and walked away, still chuckling at the trick he had played on me.

'I had no ten or fifteen years. I had a week, and much of that was spent slaving for Macgregor, who kept me busy with lesser jobs while he and Holroyd fussed about the scenery and trappings for *Scaramouche*. I had never seen such scenery as the stage crew began to rig from the theatre grid; the vaudeville junk I was used to didn't belong in the same world with it. The production had all been painted by the Harker Brothers, from designs by a painter who knew exactly what Sir John wanted. It was a revelation to me then, but now I understand that it owed much to prints and paintings of France during the Revolutionary period, and a quality of late-eighteenth-century detail had been used in it, apparently in a careless and half-hidden spirit, but adding up to pictures that supported and explained the play just as did the handsome costumes. People are supposed not to like scenery now, but it could be heart-stirring stuff when it was done with love by real theatre artists.

'The first act setting was in the yard of an inn, and when it was all in place I swear you could smell the horses, and the sweet air from the fields. Nowadays they fuss a lot about light in the theatre, and even stick a lot of lamps in plain sight of the audience, so you won't miss how artistic they are being; but Sir John didn't trouble about light in that way – the subtle effects of light were painted on the scenery, so you knew at once what time of day it was by the way the shadows fell, and what the electricians did was to illuminate the actors, and Sir John in particular.

'During all the years I worked with Sir John there was one standing direction for the electricians that was so well understood Macgregor hardly had to mention it: when the play began all lights were set at two-thirds of their power, and when Sir John was about to make his entrance they were gradually raised to full power, so that as soon as he came on the stage the audience had the sensation of seeing – and therefore understanding – much more clearly than before. Egoism, I suppose, and a little hard on the supporting actors, but Sir John's audiences wanted him to be wonderful and he did whatever was necessary to make sure that he damned well was wonderful.

'Ah, that scenery! In the last act, which was in the salon of a great aristocratic house in Paris, there were large windows at the back, and outside those windows you saw a panorama of Paris at the time of the Revolution that conveyed, by means I don't pretend to understand, the spirit of a great and beautiful city under appalling stress. The Harkers did it with colour; it was mostly in reddish browns highlighted with rose, and shadowed in a grey that was almost black. Busy as I was, I still found time to gape at that scenery as it was assembled.

'Costumes, too. Everybody had been fitted weeks before, but when the clothes were all assembled, and the wig-man had done his work, and the actors began to appear in carefully arranged ensembles in front of that scenery, things became clear that I had missed completely at rehearsals: things like the relation of one character to another, and of one class to another, and the Callot spirit of the travelling actors against the apparently everyday clothes of inn-servants and other minor people, and the superiority and unquestioned rank of the aristocrats. Above all, of the unquestioned supremacy of Sir John, because, though his clothes were not gorgeous, like those of Barnard as the Marquis, they had a quality of style that I did not understand until I had tried them on myself. Because, you see, as his double, I had to have a costume exactly like his when he appeared as the charlatan Scaramouche, and the first time I put it on I thought there must be some mistake, because it didn't seem to fit at all. Sir John showed me what to do about that.

' "Don't try to drag your sleeves down, m'boy; they're intended to be short, to show your hands to advantage, mphm? Keep 'em up, like this, and if you use your hands the way I showed you, everything will fit, eh? And your hat – it's not meant to keep off the rain, m'boy, but to show your face against the inside of the brim, quonk? Your breeches aren't too tight; they're not to sit down in – I don't pay you to sit down in costume – but to stand up in, and show off your legs. Never shown your legs off before, have you? I thought as much. Well, learn to show 'em off now, and not like a bloody chorus-girl, but like a man. Use 'em in masculine postures, but not like a butcher boy either, and if you aren't proud of your legs they're going to look damned stupid, eh, when you're walking across the stage on that rope."

'I was green as grass. Naive, though I didn't know the word at that time. It was very good for me to feel green. I had begun to think I knew all there was about the world, and particularly the performing world, because I had won in the struggle to keep alive in Wanless's World of Wonders, and in *Le grand Cirque forain de St Vite*. I had even dared in my heart to think I knew more about the world of travelling shows than Sir John. Of course I was right, because I knew a scrap of the reality. But he knew something very different, which was what the public wants to think the world of travelling shows is like. I possessed a few hard-won facts, but he had artistic imagination. My job was somehow to find my way into his world, and take a humble, responsible part in it.

'Little by little it dawned on me that I was important to *Scaramouche*; my two short moments, when I juggled the plates, and walked the wire and thumbed my nose at the Marquis, added a cubit to the stature of the character Sir John was creating. I had also to swallow the fact that I was to do that without anybody knowing it. Of course the public would tumble to the fact that Sir John, who was getting on for sixty, had not learned juggling and wire-walking since last they saw him, but they wouldn't understand it until they had been thrilled by the spectacle, apparently, of the great man doing exactly those things. I was anonymous and at the same time conspicuous.

'I had to have a name. Posters with the names of the actors were already in place outside the theatre, but in the programme I must appear as Macgregor's assistant, and I must be called something. Holroyd mentioned it now and again. My name at that time, Jules LeGrand, wouldn't do. Too fancy and, said Holroyd, a too obvious fake.

'Here again I was puzzled. Jules LeGrand an obvious fake? What about the names of some of the other members of the company? What about Eugene Fitzwarren, who had false teeth and a wig and, I would bet any money, a name that he had not been born to? What about C. Pengelly Spickernell, a withered, middle-aged fruit, whose eyes sometimes rested warmly on my legs, when Sir John was talking about them? Had any parents, drunk or sober, with such a surname as Spickernell, ever christened a child Cuthbert Pengelly? And if it came to fancy sounds, what about Milady's stage name? Annette de la Borderie? Macgregor assured me that it was indeed her own, and that she came from the Channel Islands, but why was it credible when Jules LeGrand was not?

'Of course I was too green to know that I did not stand on the same footing as the other actors. I was just a trick, a piece of animated scenery, when I was on the stage. Otherwise I was Macgregor's assistant, and none too experienced at the job, and a grand name did not befit my humble station. What was I to be called?

'The question was brought to a head by Holroyd, who approached, not me, but Macgregor, in a break between an afternoon and evening rehearsal during the final week of preparation. I was at hand, but obviously not important to the discussion. "What are you going to call your assistant, Mac?" said Hoyroyd. "Time's up. He's got to have a name." Macgregor looked solemn. "I've given it careful thought," he said, " and I think I've found the verra word for him. Y'see, what's he to the play? He's Sir John's double. That and no more. A shadow, you might say. But can you call him Shadow? Nunno: absurd! And takes the eye, which is just what we don't want to do. So where do we turn –" Holroyd broke in here, because he was apt to be impatient when Macgregor had one of his explanatory fits. "Why not call him Double? Dick Double! Now there's a good, simple name that nobody's going to notice." "Hut!" said Macgregor; "that's a foolish name. Dick Double! It sounds like some fella in a pantomime!" But Holroyd was not inclined to give up his flight of fancy. "Nothing wrong with Double," he persisted. "There's a Double in Shakespeare. *Henry IV*, Part Two, don't you remember? Is Old Double dead? So there must have been somebody called Double. The more I think of it the better I like it. I'll put him down as Richard Double." But Macgregor wouldn't have it. "Nay, nay, you'll make the lad a figure of fun," he said.

"Now listen to me, because I've worked it out verra carefully. He's a double. And what's a double? Well, in Scotland, when I was a boy, we had a name for such things. If a man met a creature like himself in a lane, or in town, maybe, in the dark, it was a sure sign of ill luck or even death. Not that I suggest anything of that kind here. Nunno; as I've often said Airt has her own rules, and they're not the rules of common life. Now: such an uncanny creature was called a fetch. And this lad's a fetch, and we can do no better than to name him Fetch." By this time old Frank Moore joined the group, and he liked the sound of Fetch. "But what first name will you tack on to it?" he said. "I suppose he's got to be something Fetch? Can't be just naked, unaccommodated Fetch." Macgregor closed his eyes and raised a fat hand. "I've thought of that, also," he said. "Fetch being a Scots name, he'd do well to carry a Scots given name, for added authority. Now I've always had a fancy for the name Mungo. In my ear it has a verra firm sound. Mungo Fetch. Can we do better?" He looked around, for applause. But Holroyd was not inclined to agree; I think he was still hankering after Double. "Sounds barbaric to me. A sort of cannibal-king name, to my way of thinking. If you want a Scotch name why don't you call him Jock?" Macgregor looked disgusted. "Because Jock is not a name, but a diminutive, as everybody knows well. It is the diminutive of John. And John is not a Scots name. The Scots form of that name is Ian. If you want to call him Ian Fetch, I shall say no more. Though I consider Mungo a much superior solution to the problem."

'Holroyd nodded at me, as if he and Macgregor and Frank Moore had been generously expending their time to do me a great favour. "Mungo Fetch it's to be then, is it?" he said, and went about his business before I had time to collect my wits and say anything at all.

'That was my trouble. I was like someone living in a dream. I was active and occupied and heard what was said to me and responded reasonably, but nevertheless I seemed to be in a lowered state of consciousness. Otherwise, how could I have put up with a casual conversation that saddled me with a new name – and a name nobody in his right mind would want to possess? But not since my first days in Wanless's World of Wonders had

I been so little in command of myself, so little aware of what fate was doing to me. It was as if I were being thrust toward something I did not know by something I could not see. Part of it was love, for I was beglamoured by Milady and barely had sense enough to understand that my state was as hopeless as it could possibly be, and that my passion was in every way absurd. Part of it must have been physical, because I was getting a pretty good regular wage, and could eat better than I had done for several months. Part of it was just astonishment at the complex business of getting a play on the stage, which presented me with some new marvel every day.

'As Macgregor's assistant I had to be everywhere and consequently I saw everything. Because of my mechanical bent I took pleasure in all the mechanism of a fine theatre, and wanted to know how the flymen and scene-shifters organized their work, how the electrician contrived his magic, and how Macgregor controlled it all with signal-lights from his little cubby-hole on the left-hand side of the stage, just inside the proscenium. I had to make up the call-lists, so that the call-boy – who was no boy but older than myself – could warn the actors when they were wanted on stage five minutes before each entrance. I watched Macgregor prepare his Prompt Book, which was an interleaved copy of the play, with every cue for light, sound, and action entered into it; he was proud of his books, and marked them in a fine round hand, in inks of different colours, and every night the book was carefully locked in a safe in his little office. I helped the property-man prepare his lists of everything that was needed in the play, so that a mass of materials from snuffboxes to hay-forks could be organized on the property-tables in the wings; my capacity to make or mend fiddling little bits of mechanism made me a favourite with him. Indeed the property-man and I worked up a neat little performance as a flock of hens who were heard clucking in the wings when the curtain rose on the inn scene. It was my job to hand C. Pengelly Spickernell the trumpet on which he sounded a fanfare just before the travelling-cart of the Commedia dell' Arte players made its entrance into the inn-yard; to hand it to him and recover it later, and shake C. Pengelly's spit out of it before putting it back on the property-table. There seemed to be no end to my duties.

'I had also to learn to make up my face for my brief appearance. Vaudevillian that I was, I had been accustomed to colour my face a vivid shade of salmon, and touch up my eyebrows; I had never made up my neck or my hands in my life. I quickly learned that something more subtle was expected by Sir John; his make-up was elaborate, to disguise some signs of age but even more to throw his best features into prominence. Eric Foss, a very decent fellow in the company, showed me what to do, and it was from him I learned that Sir John's hands were always coloured an ivory shade, and that his ears were liberally touched up with carmine. Why red ears, I wanted to know. "The Guvnor thinks it gives an appearance of health," said Foss, "and make sure you touch up the insides of your nostrils with the same colour, because it makes your eyes look bright." I didn't understand it, but I did as I was told.

'Make-up was a subject on which every actor had strong personal opinions. Gordon Barnard took almost an hour to put on his face, transforming himself from a rather ordinary-looking chap into a strikingly handsome man. Reginald Charlton, on the other hand, was of the modern school and used as little make-up as possible, because he said it made the face into a mask, and inexpressive. Grover Paskin, our comedian, put on paint almost with a trowel, and worked like a Royal Academician building up warts and nobbles and tufts of hair on his rubbery old mug. Eugene Fitzwarren strove for youth, and took enormous pains making his eyes big and lustrous, and putting white stuff on his false teeth so that they would flash to his liking.

'Old Frank Moore was the most surprising of the lot, because he had become an actor when water colours were used for make-up instead of the modern greasepaints. He washed his face with care, powdered it dead white, and then applied artist's paints out of a large Reeves' box, with fine brushes, until he had the effect he wanted. In the wings he looked as if his face were made of china, but under the lights the effect was splendid. I particularly marvelled at the way he put shadows where he wanted them by drawing the back of a lead spoon over the hollows of his eyes and cheeks. It wasn't good for his skin, and he had a hide like an alligator in private life, but it was certainly good for the stage, and he was immensely proud of the fact that Irving, who made up in the same way, had once complimented him on his art.

'So, working fourteen hours a day, but nevertheless in a dream, I made my way through the week of the final dress rehearsal, and something happened there that changed my life. I did my stage manager's work in costume, but with a long white coat over it, to keep it clean, and when Two, two came I had to whip it off, pop on my hat, take a final look in the full-length mirror just offstage in the corridor, and dash back to the wings to be ready for my plate-juggling moment. That went as rehearsed, but when it was time for my second appearance, walking the rope, I forgot something. During the scene when André-Louis made his revolutionary speech, he began by taking off his hat, and thrusting his Scaramouche mask up on his forehead. It was a half-mask, coming down to the mouth only; it was coloured a rosy red, and had a very long nose, just as Callot would have drawn it. When Sir John thrust it up on his brow, revealing his handsome, intent revolutionary's face, extremely picturesque, it was a fine accent of colour, and the long nose seemed to add to his height. But when I appeared on the rope I was to have the mask pulled down, and when I made my contemptuous gesture toward the Marquis it was the long red nose of the mask I was to thumb.

'I managed very well till it came to the nose-thumbing bit, when I realized with horror that it was my own nose flesh I was thumbing. I had forgotten the mask! Unforgivable! So as soon as I could get away from Macgregor during the interval for the scene-change, I rushed to find Sir John and make my apologies. He had gone out into the stalls of the theatre, and was surrounded by a group of friends, who were congratulating him in lively tones, and I didn't need to listen for long to find out that it was his performance on the rope they were talking about. So I crept away, and waited till he came backstage again. Then I approached him and said my humble say.

'Milady was with him and she said, "Jack, you'd be mad to throw it away. It's a gift from God. If it fooled Reynolds and Lucy Bellamy it will fool anyone. They've known you for years, and it deceived them completely. You must let him do it." But Sir John was not a man to excuse anything, even a happy accident, and he fixed me with a stern eye. "Do you swear that was by accident? You weren't presuming? Because I won't put up with any presumption from a member of my company." "Sir John, I swear on the soul of my mother it was a mistake," I said. (Odd that I should have said that, but it was a very serious oath of Zovene's, and I needed something serious at that moment; actually, at the time I spoke, my mother was living and whatever Ramsay says to the contrary, her soul was in bad repair.) "Very well," said Sir John, "we'll keep it in. In future, when you walk the rope, wear your mask up on your head, as I do mine. And you'd better come to me for a lesson in make-up. You look like Guy Fawkes. And bear in mind that this is not to be a precedent. Any other clever ideas that come to you you'd be wise to suppress. I don't encourage original thought in my productions." He looked angry as he walked away. I wanted to thank Milady for intervening on my behalf, but she was off to make a costume change.

'When I went back to Macgregor I thought he looked at me very queerly. "You're a lucky laddie, Mungo Fetch," said he, "but don't press your luck too hard. Many a small talent has come to grief that way." I asked him what he meant, but he just made his Scotch noise – "Hut" – and went on with his work.

'I don't think I would have dared to carry the matter any further if Holroyd and Frank Moore had not borne down on Macgregor after the last act. "What do you think of your Mungo now?" said Frank, and once again they began to talk exactly as if I were not standing beside them, busy with a time-sheet. "I think it would have been better to give him another name," said Macgregor; "a fetch is an uncanny thing, and I don't want anything uncanny in any theatre where I am in a place of responsibility." But Holroyd was as near buoyant as I ever saw him. "Uncanny, my eye," he said; "it's the cherry on the top of the cake. The Guvnor's close friends were deceived. *Coup de théâtre*, they called it; that's French for a bloody good wheeze." "You don't need to tell me it's French," said Macgregor. "I've no use for last-minute inspirations and unrehearsed effects. Amateurism, that's what that comes to."

'I couldn't be quiet. "Mr Macgregor, I didn't mean to do it," I said; "I swear it on the soul of my mother." "All right, all right, I believe you without your Papist oaths," said Macgregor, "and I'm just telling you not to presume on the resemblance any further, or you'll be getting a word from me." "What resemblance?" I said. "Don't talk to us as if we're fools, m'boy," said old Frank. "You know damned well you're the living image of the Guvnor in that outfit. Or the living image of him when I first knew him, I'd better say. Don't you hear what's said to you? Didn't I tell you a fortnight ago? You're as like the Guvnor as if you were spit out of his mouth. You're his fetch, right enough." "Dinna say that," shouted Macgregor, becoming very broad in his Scots; "haven't I told you it's uncanny?" But I began to understand, and I was as horrified as Macgregor. The impudence of it! Me, looking like the Guvnor! "What'd I better do?" I said, and Holroyd and old Frank laughed like a couple of loonies. "Just be tactful, that's all," said Holroyd. "It's very useful. You're the best double the Guvnor's ever had, and it'll be a livelihood to you for quite a while, I dare say. But be tactful."

'Easy to tell me to be tactful. When your soul is blasted by a sudden uprush of pride, it's cruel hard work to be tactful. Within an hour my sense of terrible impertinence in daring to look like the Guvnor had given way to a bloating vanity. Sir John was handsome, right enough, but thousands of men are handsome. He was something far beyond that. He had a glowing splendour that made him unlike anybody else – except me, it appeared, when the circumstances were right. I won't say he had distinction, because the word has been chewed to death to describe all kinds of people who simply look frozen. Take almost any politician and put a special cravat on him and stick a monocle in his eye and he becomes the distinguished Sir Nincome Poop, M.P. Sir John wasn't frozen and his air of splendour had nothing to do with oddity. I suppose living and breathing Romance through a long career had a great deal to do with it, but it can't have been the whole thing. And I was his fetch! I hadn't really understood it when Moore and Holroyd had told me in the Crown and Two Chairmen that I looked like him. I knew I was of the same height, and we were built much the same – shorter than anybody wants to be, but with a length of leg that made the difference between being small and being stumpy. In my terrible clothes and with my flash, carnie's ways

– outward evidence of the life I had led and the kind of thinking it begot in me – I never thought the resemblance went beyond a reasonable facsimile. But when Sir John and I were on equal terms – dressed and wigged alike, against the same scenery and under the same lights, and lifted into the high sweet air of Romance – his friends had been deceived by the likeness. That was a stupefying drink for Paul Dempster, alias Cass Fletcher, alias Jules LeGrand – cheap people, every one of them. Ask me to be tactful in the face of that! Ask the Prince of Wales to call you a taxi!

'With the first night at hand my new vanity would not have been noticed, even if I had been free to display it. Our opening was exciting, but orderly. Macgregor, splendid in a dinner jacket, was a perfect field officer and everything happened smartly on cue. Sir John's first entrance brought the expected welcome from the audience, and in my new role as a great gentleman of the theatre I watched carefully while he accepted it. He did it in the old style, though I didn't know that at the time: as he walked swiftly down the steps from the inn, calling for the ostler, he paused as though surprised at the burst of clapping; "My dear friends, is this generosity truly for me?" he seemed to be saying, and then, as the applause reached its peak, he gave the least perceptible bow, not looking toward the house, but keeping within the character of André-Louis Moreau, and began calling once more, which brought silence. Easy to describe, but no small thing to do, as I learned when my time came to do it myself. Only the most accomplished actors know how to manage applause, and I was lucky to learn it from a great master.

'Milady was welcomed in the same way, but her entrance was showy, as his was not – except, of course, for that little vanity of the lighting, which was a great help. She came on with the troupe of strolling players, and it couldn't have failed. There was C. Pengelly Spickernell on the trumpet, to begin with, and a lot of excited shouting from the inn-servants, and then further shouting from the Italian Comedians, as they strutted onstage with their travelling-wagon; Grover Paskin led on the horse that pulled the cart, and it was heaped high with drums and gaudy trunks, baskets and rolls of flags, and on the top of the heap sat Milady, making more racket than anybody as she waved a banner in the air. It would have brought a round from a Presbyterian General Assembly. The horse alone was a sure card, because an animal on the stage gives an air of opulence to a play no audience can resist, and this stage horse was famous Old Betsy, who did not perhaps remember Garrick but who had been in so many shows that she was an admired veteran. My heart grew big inside me at the wonder of it, as I watched from the wings, and my eyes moistened with love.

'They were not too moist to notice one or two things that followed. The other women in the troupe of players walked on foot. How slim they looked, and I saw that Milady, with every aid of costume, was not slim. How fresh and pretty they looked, and Milady, though extraordinary, was not fresh nor pretty. When Eugene Fitzwarren gave her his arm to descend from the cart I could not help seeing that she came down on the stage heavily, with an audible plop that she tried to cover with laughter, and the ankles she showed were undeniably thick. All right, I thought, in my fierce loyalty, what of it? She could act rings around any of them, and did it. But she was not young, and if I had been driven to the last extreme of honesty I should have had to admit that she was like nothing in the heavens above, nor in the earth beneath, nor in the waters under the earth. I only loved her the more, and yearned for her to show how marvellous she was, though – it had to be faced – too old for Climene. She was supposed to be the daughter of old Frank Moore as Polichinelle, but I fear she looked more like his frivolous sister.

'It was not until I read the book, years later, that I found out what sort of woman Sabatini meant Climene to be. She was a child just on the verge of love whose ambition was to find a rich protector and make the best bargain for her beauty. That wasn't in Milady's range, physically or temperamentally, for there was nothing calculating or cheap about her. So, by patient re-writing of the lines during rehearsals, she became a witty, large-hearted actress, as young as the audience would believe her to be, but certainly no child, and no beauty. Or should I say that? She had a beauty all her own, of that rare kind that only great comic actresses have; she had beauty of voice, boundless charm of manner, and she made you feel that merely pretty women were lesser creatures. She had also I cannot tell how many decades of technique behind her, because she had begun her career when she really was a child, in Irving's Lyceum, and she could make even an ordinary line sound like wit.

'I saw all of that, and felt it through and through me like the conviction of religion, but still, alas, I saw that she was old, and eccentric, and there was a courageous pathos about what she was doing.

'I was bursting with loyalty – a new and disturbing emotion for me – and Two, two went just as Sir John wanted it. My reward was that when I appeared on the tightrope there was an audible gasp from the house, and the curtain came down to great applause and even a few cries of Bravo. They were for Sir John; of course I knew that and wished it to be so. But I was aware that without me that climax would have been a lesser achievement.

'The play went on, it seemed to me, from triumph to triumph, and the last act, in Madame de Plougastel's salon, shook me as it had never done in rehearsal. When André-Louis Moreau, now a leader in the Revolution, was told by the tearful Madame de Plougastel that she was his mother and that his evil genius, the Marquis de la Tour d'Azyr, was his father – this revelation drawn from her only when Moreau had his enemy at the sword's point – it seemed to me drama could go no higher. The look that came over Sir John's face of disillusion and defeat, before he burst into Scaramouche's mocking laugh, I thought the perfection of acting. And so it was. It wouldn't do now – quite out of fashion – but if you're going to act that kind of thing, that's the way to do it.

'Lots of curtain calls. Flowers for Milady and some for Adele Chesterton, who had not been very good but who was so pretty you wanted to eat her with a silver spoon. Sir John's speech, which I came to know very well, in which he declared himself and Milady to be the audience's "most obedient, most devoted, and most humble servants". Then the realities of covering the furniture with dust-sheets, covering the tables of properties, checking the time-sheet with Macgregor, and watching him hobble off to put the prompt-copy to bed in the safe. Then taking off my own paint, with a feeling of exaltation and desolation combined, as if I had never been so happy before, and would certainly never be so happy again.

'It was never the custom in that company to sit up and wait to see what the newspapers said; I think that was always more New York's style than London's. But when I went to the theatre the following afternoon to attend to some duties, all the reports were in but those of the great Sunday thunderers, which were very important indeed. Most of the papers said kind things, but even I sensed something about these criticisms that I could have wished otherwise expressed, or not said at all. "Unabashed romanticism ... proof positive that the Old School is still vital ... dear, familiar situations, resolved in the manner hallowed by romance ... Sir John's perfect command shows no sign of diminution with the years ... Lady Tresize brings a wealth of experience to a role which, in younger hands, might have seemed contrived ... Sabatini is a gift to players who require the full-flavoured melodrama of an earlier day ... where do we look today for acting of this scope and authority?"

'Among the notices there had been one, in the *News-Chronicle*, where a clever new young man was on the job, which was downright bad. PITCHER GOES TOO OFTEN TO WELL, it was headed, and it said flatly that the Tresizes were old-fashioned and hammy, and should give way to the newer theatre.

'When the Sunday papers came, the *Observer* took the same line as the dailies, as though they had been looking at something very fine, but through the wrong end of the binoculars; it made *Scaramouche* seem small and very far away. James Agate, in the *Sunday Times*, condemned the play, which he likened to clockwork, and used Sir John and Milady as sticks to beat modern actors who did not know how to speak or move, and were ill bred and brittle.

'"Nothing there to pull 'em in," I heard Holroyd saying to Macgregor.

'Nevertheless, we did pull 'em in for nearly ten weeks. Business was slack at the beginning of each week, and grew from Wednesday onward; matinees were usually sold out, chiefly to women from the suburbs, in town for a look at the shops

745

and a play. But I knew from the gossip that business like that, in a London theatre, was covering running costs at best, and the expenses of production were still on the Guvnor's overdraft. He seemed cheerful, and I soon found out why. He was going to do the old actor-manager's trick and play *Scaramouche* as long as it would last and then replace it "by popular request" with a few weeks of his old war-horse, *The Master of Ballantrae*.'

'Oh my God!' said Ingestree, and it seemed to me that he turned a little white.

'You remember this play?' said Lind.

'Vividly,' said Roly.

'A very bad play?'

'I don't want to hurt the feelings of our friend here, who feels so strong about the Tresizes,' said Ingestree. 'It's just that *The Master of Ballantrae* coincided with rather a low point in my own career. I was finding my feet in the theatre, and it wasn't really the kind of thing I was looking for.'

'Perhaps you would like me to pass over it,' said Magnus, and although he was pretending to be solicitous I knew he was enjoying himself.

'Is it vital to your subtext?' said Ingestree, and he too was half joking.

'It is, really. But I don't want to give pain, my dear fellow.'

'Don't mind me. Worse things have happened since.'

'Perhaps I can be discreet,' said Magnus. 'You may rely on me to be as tactful as possible.'

'For God's sake don't do that,' said Ingestree. 'In my experience tact is usually worse than the brutalities of truth. Anyhow, my recollections of that play can't be the same as yours. My troubles were mostly private.'

'Then I shall go ahead. But please feel free to intervene whenever you feel like it. Put me right on matters of fact. Even on shades of opinion. I make no pretence of being an exact historian.'

'Shoot the works,' said Ingestree. 'I'll be as still as a mouse. I promise.'

'As you wish. Well – *The Master of Ballantrae* was another of the Guvnor's romantic specials. It too was from a novel, by somebody-or-other –'

'By Robert Louis Stevenson,' said Ingestree, in an under-tone, 'though you wouldn't have guessed it from what appeared on the stage. These adaptations! Butcheries would be a better word –'

'Shut up, Roly,' said Kinghovn. 'You said you'd be quiet.'

'I'm no judge of what kind of adaptation it was,' said Magnus, 'because I haven't read the book and I don't suppose I ever will. But it was a good, tight, well-caulked melodrama, and people had been eating it up since the Guvnor first brought it out, which I gathered was something like thirty years before the time I'm talking about. I told you he was an experimenter and an innovator, in his day. Well, whenever he had lost a packet on Maeterlinck, or something new by Stephen Phillips, he would pull *The Master* out of the storehouse and fill up the bank-account again. He could go to Birmingham, and Manchester, and Newcastle, and Glasgow, and Edinburgh or any big pro-vincial town – and those towns had big theatres, not like the little pill-boxes in London – and pack 'em in with *The Master*. Especially Edinburgh, because they seemed to take the play for their own. Macgregor told me, "*The Master*'s been a mighty get-penny for Sir John." When you saw him in it you knew why it was so. It was made for him.'

'It certainly was,' said Ingestree. 'Made for him out of the blood and bones of poor old Stevenson. I have no special affec-tion for Stevenson, but he didn't deserve that.'

'As you can see, it was a play that called forth strong feel-ing,' said Magnus. 'I never read it, myself, because Macgregor always held the prompt-copy and did the prompting himself, if anybody was so absurd as to need prompting. But of course I picked up the story as we rehearsed.

'It had a nice meaty plot. Took place in Scotland around the middle of the eighteenth century. There had been some sort of trouble – I don't know the details – and Scottish noblemen were divided in allegiance between Bonnie Prince Charlie and the King of England. The play was about a family called Durie; the old Lord of Durrisdeer had two sons, the first-born being called the Master of Ballantrae and the younger being simply Mr Henry Durie. The old Lord decided on a sneaky com-promise when the trouble came, and sent the Master off to fight for Bonnie Charlie, while Mr Henry remained at home to be loyal to King George. On those terms, you see, the family couldn't lose, whichever way the cat jumped.

'The Master was a dashing, adventurous fellow, but essentially a crook, and he became a spy in Prince Charlie's camp, leaking information to the English: Mr Henry was a scholarly, poetic sort of chap, and he stayed at home and mooned after Miss Alison Graeme; she was the old Lord's ward, and of course she loved the dashing Master. When news came from the wars that the Master had been killed, she consented to marry Mr Henry as a matter of duty and to provide Durrisdeer with an heir. "But ye ken she never really likit the fella," as Macgregor explained it to me; her heart was always with the Master, alive or dead. But the Master wasn't dead; he wasn't the dying kind: he slipped away from the battle and became a pirate – not one of your low-living dirty-faced pirates, but a very classy privateer and spy. And so, when the troubles had died down and Bonnie Charlie was out of the way, the Master came back to claim Miss Alison, and found that she was Mrs Henry, and the mother of a fine young laird.

'The Master tried to lure Miss Alison away from her husband: Mr Henry was noble about it, and he nobly kept mum about the Master having turned spy during the war. "A verra strong situation," as Macgregor said. Consequence, a lot of taunting talk from the Master, and an equal amount of noble endurance from Mr Henry, and at last a really good scene, of the kind Roly hates, but our audiences loved.

'The Master had picked up in his travels an Indian servant, called Secundra Dass; he knew a lot of those Eastern secrets that Western people believe in so religiously. When Mr Henry could bear things no longer, he had a fight with the Master, and seemed to kill him; but as I told you, the Master wasn't the dying kind. So he allowed himself to be buried, having swallowed his tongue (he'd learned that from Secundra Dass) and, as it said in the play, "so subdued his vital forces that the spark of life, though burning low, was not wholly extinguished". Mr Henry, tortured by guilt, confessed his crime to his wife and the old Lord, and led them to the grove of trees where the body was buried. When the servants dug up the corpse, it was no corpse at all, but the Master, in very bad shape; the tongue-trick hadn't worked quite as he expected – something to do with the chill of the Scottish climate, I expect – and he came to life only to cry, "Murderer, Henry – false, false!" and drop dead, but not before Mr Henry shot himself. Thereupon the curtain came down to universal satisfaction.

'I haven't described it very respectfully. I feel irreverent vibrations coming to me from Roly, the way mediums do when there is an unbeliever at a seance. But I assure you that as the Guvnor acted it, the play compelled belief and shook you up pretty bad. The beauty of the old piece, from the Guvnor's point of view, was that it provided him with what actors used to call "a dual role". He played both the Master and Mr Henry, to the huge delight of his audiences; his fine discrimination between the two characters gave extraordinary interest to the play.

'It also meant some neat work behind the scenes, because there were times when Mr Henry had barely left the stage before the Master came swaggering on through another door. Sir John's dresser was an expert at getting him out of one coat, waistcoat, boots, and wig and into another in a matter of seconds, and his characterization of the two men was so sharply differentiated that it was art of a very special kind.

'Twice, a double was needed, simply for a fleeting moment of illusion, and in the brief last scene the double was of uttermost importance, because it was he who stood with his back to the audience, as Mr Henry, while the Guvnor, as the Master, was being dug up and making his terrible accusation. Then – doubles don't usually get such opportunities – it was the double's job to put the gun to his head, fire it, and fall at the feet of Miss Alison, under the Master's baleful eye. And I say with satisfaction that as I was an unusually successful double – or dead spit, as old Frank Moore insisted on saying – I was allowed to fall so that the audience could see something of my face, instead of dying under suspicion of being somebody else.

'Rehearsals went like silk, because some of the cast were old hands, and simply had to brush up their parts. Frank Moore had played the old Lord of Durrisdeer scores of times, and Eugene Fitzwarren was a seasoned Secundra Dass; Gordon Barnard had played Burke, the Irishman, and built it up into a very good thing; C. Pengelly Spickernell fancied himself as Fond Barnie, a loony Scot who sang scraps of song, and Grover Paskin had a good funny part as a drunken butler; Emilia Pauncefort, who played Madame de Plougastel in *Scaramouche*, loved herself as a Scots witch who uttered the dire Curse of Durrisdeer –

> Twa Duries in Durrisdeer,
>   Ane to bide and ane to ride;
> An ill day for the groom,
>   And a waur day for the bride.

And of course the role of Alison, the unhappy bride of Mr Henry and the pining adorer of the Master, had been played by Milady since the play was new.

'That was where the difficulty lay. Sir John was still great as the Master, and looked surprisingly like himself in his earliest photographs in that part, taken thirty years before; time had been rougher with Milady. Furthermore, she had developed an emphatic style of acting which was not unacceptable in a part like Climene but which could become a little strong as a high-bred Scots lady.

'There were murmurs among the younger members of the company. Why couldn't Milady play Auld Cursin' Jennie instead of Emilia Pauncefort? There was a self-assertive girl in the company named Audrey Sevenhowes who let it be known that she would be ideally cast as Alison. But there were others, Holroyd and Macgregor among them, who would not hear a word against Milady. I would have been one of them too, if anybody had asked my opinion, but nobody did. Indeed, I began to feel that the company thought I was rather more than an actor who doubled for Sir John; I was a double indeed, and a company spy, so that any disloyal conversation stopped as soon as I appeared. Of course there was lots of talk; all theatrical companies chatter incessantly. On the rehearsals went, and as Sir John and Milady didn't bother to rehearse their scenes together, nobody grasped how extreme the problem had become.

'There was another circumstance about those early rehearsals that caused some curiosity and disquiet for a while; a stranger had appeared among us whose purpose nobody seemed to know, but who sat in the stalls making notes busily, and now and then exclaiming audibly in a tone of disapproval. He was sometimes seen talking with Sir John. What could he be up to? He wasn't an actor, certainly. He was young, and had lots of hair, but he wasn't dressed in a way that suggested the stage. His sloppy grey flannels and tweed coat, his dark blue shirt and tie like a piece of old rope – hand-woven, I suppose – and his scuffed suede shoes made him look even younger than he was. "University man," whispered Audrey Sevenhowes, who recognized the uniform. "Cambridge," she whispered, a day later. Then came the great revelation – "Writing a play!" Of course she didn't confide these things to me, but they leaked from her close friends all through the company.

'Writing a play! Rumour was busily at work. It was to be a grand new piece for Sir John's company, and great opportunities might be secured by buttering up the playwright. Reginald Charlton and Leonard Woulds, who hadn't much to do in *Scaramouche* and rather less in *The Master*, began standing the university genius drinks; Audrey Sevenhowes didn't speak to him, but was frequently quite near him, laughing a silvery laugh and making herself fascinating. Old Emilia Pauncefort passed him frequently, and gave him a stately nod every time. Grover Paskin told him jokes. The genius liked it all, and in a few days was on good terms with everybody of any importance, and the secret was out. Sir John wanted a stage version of *Dr Jekyll and Mr Hyde*, and the genius was to write it. But as he had never written a play before, and had never had stage experience except with the Cambridge Marlowe Society, he was attending rehearsals, as he said to "get the feel of the thing".

'The genius was free with his opinions. He thought little of *The Master of Ballantrae*. "Fustian" was the word he used to describe it, and he made it clear that the era of fustian was over. Audiences simply wouldn't stand it any more. A new day had dawned in the theatre, and he was a particularly bright beam from the rising sun.

'He was modest, however. There were brighter beams than he, and the brightest, most blinding beam in the literature of the time was somebody called Aldous Huxley. No, Huxley didn't write plays. It was his outlook – wry, brilliantly witty, rooted in tremendous scholarship, and drenched in the Ironic Spirit – that the genius admired, and was about to transfer to the stage. In no time he had a tiny court, in which Charlton and Woulds and Audrey Sevenhowes were the leaders, and after rehearsals they were always to be seen in the nearest pub, laughing a great deal. With my very long ears it wasn't long before I knew they were laughing at Milady and Frank Moore and Emilia Pauncefort, who were the very warp and woof of fustian, and who couldn't possibly be worked into the kind of play the genius had in mind. No, he hadn't begun writing yet, but he had a Concept, and though he hated the word "metaphysical" he didn't mind using it to give a rough idea of how the Concept would take shape.

'Sir John didn't know about the Concept as yet, but when it was explained to him he would get a surprise. The genius was hanging around *The Master of Ballantrae* because it was from a novel by the same chap that had written *Jekyll and Hyde*. But this chap – Roly says his name was Stevenson, and I'm sure he knows – had never fully shouldered the burden of his own creative gift. This was something the genius would have to do for him. Stevenson, when he had thought of *Jekyll and Hyde*, had seized upon a theme that was Dostoyevskian, but he had worked it out in terms of what some people might call Romance, but the genius regretfully had to use the word fustian. The only thing the genius could do, in order to be true to his Concept, was to re-work the Stevenson material in such a way that its full implications – the ones Stevenson had approached, and run away from in fright – were revealed.

'He thought it could be done with masks. The genius confessed, with a laugh at his own determination, that he would not attempt the thing at all unless he was given a completely free hand to use masks in every possible way. Not only would Jekyll and Hyde wear masks, but the whole company would wear them, and sometimes there would be eight or ten Jekylls on the stage, all wearing masks showing different aspects of that character, and we would see them exchange the masks of Jekyll – because there was to be no nonsense about realism, or pretending to the audience that what they saw had any relationship to what they foolishly thought of as real life – for masks of

Hyde. There would be dialogue, of course, but mostly in the form of soliloquies, and a lot of the action would be carried out in mime – a word which the genius liked to pronounce "meem", to give it the flavour he thought it needed.

'Charlton and Woulds and Audrey Sevenhowes thought this sounded wonderful, though they had some reservations, politely expressed, about the masks. They thought stylized make-up might do just as well. But the genius was rock-like in his insistence that it would be masks or he would throw up the whole project.

'When this news leaked through to the other members of the company they were disgusted. They talked about other versions of *Jekyll and Hyde* they had seen, which did very well without any nonsense about masks. Old Frank Moore had played with Henry Irving's son "H.B." in a Jekyll and Hyde play where H.B. had made the transformation from the humane doctor to the villainous Hyde before the eyes of the audience, simply by ruffling up his hair and distorting his body. Old Frank showed us how he did it: first he assumed the air of a man who is about to be wafted off the ground by his own moral grandeur, then he drank the dreadful potion out of his own pot of old-and-mild, and then, with an extraordinary display of snarling and gnawing the air, he crumpled up into a hideous gnome. He did this one day in the pub and some strangers, who weren't used to actors, left hurriedly and the landlord asked Frank, as a personal favour, not to do it again. Frank had an extraordinarily gripping quality as an actor.

'Nevertheless, as I admired his snorting and chomping depiction of evil, I was conscious that I had seen even more convincing evil in the face of Willard the Wizard, and that there it had been as immovable and calm as stone.

'Suddenly, one day at rehearsal, the genius lost stature. Sir John called to him, "Come along, you may as well fit in here, mphm? Give you practical experience of the stage, quonk?", and before we knew what was happening he had the genius acting the part of one of the menservants in Lord Durrisdeer's household. He wasn't bad at all, and I suppose he had learned a few things in his amateur days at Cambridge. But at a critical moment Sir John said, "Clear away your master's chair, m'boy;

when he comes downstage to Miss Alison you take the chair back to the upstage side of the fireplace." Which the genius did, but not to Sir John's liking; he put one hand under the front of the seat, and the other on the back of the armchair, and hefted it to where he had been told. Sir John said, "Not like that, m'boy; lift it by the arms." But the genius smiled and said, "Oh no, Sir John, that's not the way to handle a chair; you must always put one hand under its apron, so as not to put a strain on its back." Sir John went rather cool, as he did when he was displeased, and said, "That may have been all very well in your father's shop, m'boy, but it won't do on my stage. Lift it as I tell you." And the genius turned exceedingly red, and began to argue. At which Sir John said to the other extra, "You do it, and show him how." And he ignored the genius until the end of the scene.

'Seems a trivial thing, but it rocked the genius to his foundations; after that he never seemed to be able to do anything right. And the people who had been all over him before were much cooler after that slight incident. It was the mention of the word "shop". I don't think actors are particularly snobbish, but I suppose Audrey Sevenhowes and the others had seen him as a gilded undergraduate; all of a sudden he was just a clumsy actor who had come from some sort of shop, and he never quite regained his former lustre. When we dress-rehearsed *The Master* it was apparent that he knew nothing about make-up; he appeared with a horrible red face and a huge pair of false red eyebrows. "Good God, m'boy," Sir John called from the front of the house, when this spook appeared, "what have you been doing to your face?" The genius walked to the footlights – inexcusable, he should have spoken from his place on the stage – and began to explain that as he was playing a Scots servant he thought he should have a very fresh complexion to suggest a peasant ancestry, a childhood spent on the moors, and a good deal more along the same lines. Sir John shut him up, and told Darton Flesher, a good, useful actor, to show the boy how to put on a decent, unobtrusive face, suited to chair-lifting.

'The genius was huffy, backstage, and talked about throwing up the whole business of Jekyll and Hyde and leaving Sir John to stew in his own juice. But Audrey Sevenhowes said, "Oh, don't be so silly; everybody has to learn," and that cooled him down. Audrey also threw him a kind word about how she couldn't spare him because he was going to write a lovely part for her in the new play, and gave him a smile that would have melted – well, I mustn't be extreme – that would have melted a lad down from Cambridge whose self-esteem had been wounded. It wouldn't have melted me; I had taken Miss Sevenhowes' number long before. But then, I was a hard case.

'Not so hard that I hadn't a little sympathy for Adele Chesterton, whose nose was out of joint. She was still playing in *Scaramouche*, but she had not been cast in *The Master*; an actress called Felicity Larcombe had been brought in for the second leading female role in that. She was one of the most beautiful women I have ever seen anywhere: very dark brown hair, splendid eyes, a superb slim figure, and that air of enduring a secret sorrow bravely which so many men find irresistible. What was more, she could act, which poor Adele Chesterton, who was the Persian-kitten type, could only do by fits and starts. But she was a decent kid, and I was sorry for her, because the company, without meaning it unkindly, neglected her. You know how theatre companies are: if you're working with them, you're real, and if you aren't, you have only a half-life in their estimation. Adele was the waning, and Felicity the waxing, moon.

'As usual, Audrey Sevenhowes had a comment. "Nobody to blame but herself," said she; "made a Horlicks – an utter Horlicks – of her part. I could have shown them, but –" Her shrug showed what she thought of the management's taste. "Horlicks" was a word she used a lot; it suggested "ballocks" but avoided a direct indecency. Charlton and Woulds loved to hear her say it; it seemed delightfully daring, and sexy, and knowing. It was my first encounter with this sort of allurement, and I disliked it.

'I mentioned to Macgregor that Miss Larcombe seemed a very good, and probably expensive, actress for her small part in *The Master*. "Ah, she'll have a great deal to do on the tour," he replied, and I pricked up my ears. But there was nothing more to be got out of him about the tour.

'It was all clear before we opened *The Master*, however; Sir John was engaging a company to make a longish winter tour in Canada, with a repertoire of some of his most successful old pieces, and *Scaramouche* as a novelty. Holroyd was asking people to drop into his office and talk about contracts.

'Of course the company buzzed about it. For the established actors a decision had to be made: would they absent themselves from London for the best part of a winter season? All actors under a certain age are hoping for some wonderful chance that will carry them into the front rank of their profession, and a tour in Sir John's repertoire wasn't exactly it. On the other hand, a tour of Canada could be a lark, because Sir John was known to be a great favourite there and they would play to big audiences, and see a new country while they did it.

'For the middle-aged actors it was attractive. Jim Hailey and his wife Gwenda Lewis jumped at it, because they had a boy to educate and it was important to them to keep in work. Frank Moore was an enthusiastic sightseer and traveller, and had toured Australia and South Africa but had not been to Canada since 1924. Grover Paskin and C. Pengelly Spickernell were old standbys of Sir John's, and would cheerfully have toured Hell with him. Emilia Pauncefort wasn't likely to get other offers, because stately old women and picturesque hags were not frequent in West End shows that season, and the Old Vic, where she had staked out quite a little claim in cursing queens, had a new director who didn't fancy her.

'But why Gordon Barnard, who was a very good leading man, or Felicity Larcombe, who was certain to go to the top of the profession? Macgregor explained to me that Barnard hadn't the ambition that should have gone with his talent, and Miss Larcombe, wise girl, wanted to get as much varied experience as she could before descending on the West End and making it hers forever. There was no trouble at all in recruiting a good company, and I was glad to sign my own contract, to be assistant to Mac and play doubles without having my name on the programme. And to everybody's astonishment, the genius was offered a job on the tour, and took it. So eighteen actors were recruited, not counting Sir John and Milady, and with Holroyd and some necessary technical staff, the final number of the company was to be twenty-eight.

'The work was unrelenting. We opened *The Master of Ballantrae*, and although the other critics were not warm about it

Agate gave it a push and we played a successful six weeks in London. God, what audiences! People came out of the woodwork to see it, and it seemed they had all seen it before and couldn't get enough of it. "It's like peeping into the dark backward and abysm of time," the genius said, and even I felt that in some way the theatre had been put back thirty years when we appeared in that powerful, thrilling, but strangely antique piece.

'Every day we were called for rehearsal, in order to get the plays ready for the tour. And what plays they were! *The Lyons Mail* and *The Corsican Brothers*, in both of which I doubled for Sir John, and *Rosemary*, a small play with a minimum of scenery, which was needed to round out a repertoire in which all the other plays were big ones, with cartloads of scenery and dozens of costumes. I liked *Rosemary* especially, because I didn't double in it but I had a showy appearance as a stilt walker. How we sweated! It was rough on the younger people, who had to learn several new parts during days when they were working a full eight hours, but Moore and Spickernell and Paskin and Miss Pauncefort semed to have been playing these melodramas for years, and the lines rolled off their tongues like grave old music. As for Sir John and Milady, they couldn't have been happier, and there is nothing so indestructibly demanding and tireless as a happy actor.

'Did I say we worked eight hours? Holroyd and Macgregor, with me as their slave, worked much longer than that, because the three plays we were adding to *Scaramouche* and *The Master* had to be retrieved from storage and brushed up and made smart for the tour. But it was all done at last, and we closed in London one Saturday night, with everything finished that would make it possible for us to sail for Canada the following Tuesday.

'A small matter must be mentioned. The genius's mother turned up for one of the last performances of *The Master*, and it fell to me to show her to Sir John's dressing-room. She was a nice little woman, but not what one expects of the mother of such a splendid creature, and when I showed her through the great man's door she looked as if she might faint from the marvel of it all. I felt sorry for her; it must be frightening when one mothers such a prodigy, and she had the humble look of somebody who can't believe her luck.'

It was here that Roland Ingestree, who had been decidedly out of sorts for the past half-hour, intervened.

'Magnus, I don't much mind you taking the mickey out of me, if that's how you get your fun, but I think you might leave poor old Mum out of it.'

Magnus pretended astonishment. 'But my dear fellow, I don't see how I can. I've done my best to afford you the decency of obscurity. I'd hoped to finish my narrative without letting the others in on our secret. I could have gone on calling you "the genius", though you had other names in the company. There were some who called you "the Cantab" because of your degree from Cambridge, and there were others who called you "One" because you had that mock-modest trick of referring to yourself as One when in your heart you were crying, "Me, me, glorious ME!" But I can't leave you out, and I don't see how I can leave your Mum out, because she threw so much light on you, and therefore lent a special flavour to the whole story of Sir John's touring company.'

'All right, Magnus; I was a silly young ass, and I freely admit it. But isn't one permitted to be an ass for a year or two, when one is young, and the whole world appears to be open to one, and waiting for one? Because you had a rotten childhood, don't suppose that everybody else who had better luck was utterly a fool. Have you any idea what you looked like in those days?'

'No, I haven't, really, but I see you are dying to tell me. Do please go ahead.'

'I shall. You were disliked and distrusted because everybody thought you were a sneak, as you've said yourself. But you haven't told us that you were a sneak, and blabbed to Mac-gregor about every trivial breach of company discipline – who came into the theatre after the half-hour call, and who might happen to have a friend in the dressing-room during the show, and who watched Sir John from the wings when he had said they weren't to, and anything else you could find out by pussy-footing and snooping. Even that might have passed as your job, if you hadn't had such a nasty personality – always smiling like a pantomime demon – always stinking of some sort of cheap hair oil – always running like a rabbit to open doors for Milady – and vain as a peacock about your tuppenny-ha'penny juggling and wire-walking. You were a thoroughly nasty little piece of work, let me tell you.'

'I suppose I was. But you make the mistake of thinking I was pleased with myself. Not a bit of it. I was trying to learn the ropes of another mode of life –'

'Indeed you were! You were trying to be Sir John off the stage as well as on. And what a caricature you made of it! Walking like Spring-Heeled Jack because Frank Moore had tried to show you something about deportment, and parting your greasy long hair in the middle because Sir John was the last actor on God's earth to do so, and wearing clothes that would make a cat laugh because Sir John wore eccentric duds that looked as if he'd had 'em since Mafeking Night.'

'Do you think I'd have been better off to model myself on you?'

'I was no prize as an actor. Don't think I don't know it. But at least I was living in 1932, and you were aping a man who was still living in 1902, and if there hadn't been a very strong uncanny whiff about you you'd have been a total freak.'

'Ah, but there was an uncanny whiff about me. I was Mungo Fetch, don't forget. We fetches can't help being uncanny.'

Lind intervened. 'Dear friends,' he said, being very much the courtly Swede, 'let us not have a quarrel about these grievances which are so long dead. You are both different men now. Think, Roly, of your achievements as a novelist and broadcaster; One, and the Genius and the Cantab are surely buried under that? And you, my dear Eisengrim, what reason have you to be bitter toward anyone? What have you desired that life has not given you? Including what I now see is a very great achievement; you modelled yourself on a fine actor of the old school, and you have put all you learned at the service of your own art, where it has flourished wonderfully. Roly, you sought to be a literary man, and you are one; Magnus, you wanted to be Sir John, and it looks very much as if you had succeeded, in so far as anyone can succeed –'

'Just a little more than most people succeed,' said Ingestree, who was still hot; 'you ate poor old Sir John. You ate him down to the core. We could see it happening, right from the beginning of that tour.'

'Did I really?' said Magnus, apparently pleased. 'I didn't know it showed so plainly. But now you are being melodramatic, Roly. I simply wanted to be like him. I told you, I apprenticed myself to an egoism, because I saw how invaluable that egoism was. Nobody can steal another man's ego, but he can learn from it, and I learned. You didn't have the wits to learn.'

'I'd have been ashamed to toady as you did, whatever it brought me.'

'Toady? Now that's an unpleasant word. You didn't learn what there was to be learned in that company, Ingestree. You were at every rehearsal and every performance of *The Master of Ballantrae* that I was. Don't you remember the splendid moment when Sir John, as Mr Henry, said to his father: "There are double words for everything: the word that swells and the word that belittles; my brother cannot fight me with a word." Your word for my relationship to Sir John is toadying, but mine is emulation, and I think mine is the better word.'

'Yours is the dishonest word. Your emulation, as you call it, sucked the pith out of that poor old ham, and gobbled it up and made it part of yourself. It was a very nasty process.'

'Roly, I idolized him.'

'Yes, and to be idolized by you, as you were then, was a terrible, vampire-like feeding on his personality and his spirit – because his personality as an actor was all there was of his spirit. You were a double, right enough, and such a double as Poe and Dostoyevsky would have understood. When we first met at Sorgenfrei I thought there was something familiar about you, and the minute you began to act I sensed what it was; you were the fetch of Sir John. But I swear it wasn't until today, as we sat at this table, that I realized you really were Mungo Fetch.'

'Extraordinary! I recognized you the minute I set eyes on you, in spite of the rather Pickwickian guise you have acquired during the past forty years.'

'And you were waiting for a chance to knife me?'

'Knife! Knife! Always these belittling words! Have you no sense of humour, my dear man?'

'Humour is a poisoned dagger in the hands of a man like you. People talk of humour as if it were all jolly, always the lump of sugar in the coffee of life. A man's humour takes its quality from what a man is, and your humour is like the scratch of a rusty nail.'

'Oh, balls,' said Kinghovn. Ingestree turned on him, very white in the face.

'What the hell do you mean by interfering?' he said.

'I mean what I say. Balls! You people who are so clever with words never allow yourselves or anybody else a moment's peace. What is this all about? You two knew each other when you were young and you didn't hit it off. So now we have all this gaudy abuse about vampires and rusty nails from Roly, and Magnus is leading him on to make a fool of himself and cause a fight. I'm enjoying myself. I like this subtext and I want the rest of it. We had just got to where Roly's Mum was paying a visit to Sir John backstage. I want to know about that. I can see it in my mind's eye. Colour, angle of camera, quality of light – the whole thing. Get on with it and let's forget all this subjective stuff; it has no reality except what somebody like me can provide for it, and at the moment I'm not interested in subjective rubbish. I want the story. Enter Roly's Mum; what next?'

'Since Roly's Mum is such a hot potato, perhaps Roly had better tell you,' said Eisengrim.

'So I will. My Mum was a very decent body, though at the time I was silly enough to underrate her; as Magnus has made clear I was a little above myself in those days. University does it, you know. It's such a protected life for a young man, and he so easily loses his frail hold on reality.

'My people weren't grand, at all. My father had an antique shop in Norwich, and he was happy about that because he had risen above his father, who had combined a small furniture shop with an undertaking business. Both my parents had adored Sir John, and ages before the time we are talking about – before the First Great War, in fact – they did rather a queer thing that brought them to his attention. They loved *The Master of Ballantrae*; it was just their meat, full of antiquery and romance; they liked selling antiques because it seemed romantic, I truly believe. They saw *The Master* fully ten times when they were young, and loved it so that they wrote out the whole play from memory – I don't suppose it was very accurate, but they did – and sent it to Sir John with an adoring letter. Sort of tribute from playgoers whose life he had illumined, you know. I could hardly believe it when I was young, but I know better now; fans get up to the queerest things in order to associate themselves with their idols.

'Sir John wrote them a nice letter, and when next he was near Norwich, he came to the shop. He loved antiques, and bought them all over the place, and I honestly think his interest in them was simply romantic, like my parents'. They never tired of telling about how he came into the shop, and inquired about a couple of old chairs, and finally asked if they were the people who had sent him the manuscript. That was a glory-day for them, I can tell you. And afterward, whenever they had anything that was in his line, they wrote to him, and quite often he bought whatever it was. That was why it was so bloody-minded of him to take it out of me about the proper way to handle a chair, and to make that crack about the shop. He knew it would hurt.

'Anyhow, my mother was out of her mind with joy when she wangled me a job with his company; thought he was going to be my great patron, I suppose. My father had died, and the shop could keep her, but certainly not me, and anyhow I was set on being a writer. I admit I was pleased to be asked to do a literary job for him; it wasn't quite as grand as I may have pretended to Audrey Sevenhowes, but who hasn't been a fool in his time? If I'd been shrewd enough to resist a pretty girl I'd have been a sharp little piece of glass like Mungo Fetch, instead of a soft boy who had got a swelled head at Cambridge, and knew nothing about the world.

'When my Mum knew I was going to Canada with the company she came to London to say good-bye – I'm ashamed to say I had told her there was no chance of my going to Norwich, though I suppose I could have made it – and she wanted to see Sir John. She'd brought him a gift, the loveliest little wax portrait relievo of Garrick you ever saw; I don't know where she picked it up, but it was worth eighty pounds if it was worth a ha'penny, and she gave it to him. And she asked him, in terms that made me blush, to take good care of me while I was abroad. I must say the old boy was decent, and said very kindly that he was sure I didn't need supervision, but that he would always be glad to talk with me if anything came up that worried me.'

'Audrey Sevenhowes put it about that your Mum had asked Milady to see that you didn't forget your bedsocks in the Arctic wildernesses of Canada,' said Eisengrim.

'You don't surprise me. Audrey Sevenhowes was a bitch, and she made a fool of me. But I don't care. I'd rather be a fool than a tough any day. But I assure you there was no mention of bedsocks; my Mum was not a complex woman, but she wasn't stupid, either.'

'Ah, there you have the advantage of me,' said Magnus, with a smile of great charm. 'My mother, I fear, was very much more than stupid, as I have already told you. She was mad. So perhaps we can be friends again, Roly?'

He put out his hand across the table. It was not a gesture an Englishman would have made, and I couldn't quite make up my mind whether he was sincere or not. But Ingestree took his hand, and it was perfectly plain that he meant to make up the quarrel.

The waiters were beginning to look at us meaningly, so we adjourned upstairs to our expensive apartment, where everybody had a chance to use the loo. The film-makers were not to be shaken. They wanted the story to the end. So, after the interval – not unlike an interval at the theatre – we reassembled in our large sitting-room, and it now seemed to be understood, without anybody having said so, that Roly and Magnus were going to continue the story as a duet.

I was pleased, as I was pleased by anything that gave me a new light or a new crumb of information about my old friend, who had become Magnus Eisengrim. I was puzzled, however, by the silence of Liesl, who had sat through the narration at the lunch table without saying a word. Her silence was not of the unobtrusive kind; the less she said the more conscious one became of her presence. I knew her well enough to bide my time. Though she said nothing, she was big with feeling, and I knew that she would have something to say when she felt the right moment had come. After all, Magnus was in a very real sense her property : did he not live in her house, treat it as his own, share her bed, and accept the homage of her extraordinary courtesy, yet always understanding who was the real ruler of Sorgenfrei? What did Liesl think about Magnus undressing him-

y inch, in front of the film-makers? Particularly now
clear that there was an old, unsettled hostility bend Roland Ingestree, what did she think?

... did I think, as I carefully wiped my newly scrubbed
dentures on one of the Savoy's plentiful linen hand-towels,
before slipping them back over my gums? I thought I wanted
all I could get of this vicarious life. I wanted to be off to Canada
with Sir John Tresize. I knew what Canada meant to me: what
had it meant to him?

6

WHEN I returned to our drawing-room Roly was already aboard
ship.

'One of my embarrassments – how susceptible the young are
to embarrassment – was that my dear Mum had outfitted me
with a vast woolly steamer-rug in a gaudy design. The company
kept pestering Macgregor to know what tartan it was, and he
thought it looked like Hunting Cohen, so The Hunting Cohen it
was from that time forth. I didn't need it, God knows, because
the C.P.R. ship was fiercely hot inside, and it was too late in the
season for anyone to sit on deck in any sort of comfort.

'My Mum was so solicitous in seeing me off that the company
pretended to think I needed a lot of looking after, and made a
great game of it. Not unkind (except for Charlton and Woulds,
who were bullies) but very jokey and hard to bear, especially
when I wanted to be glorious in the eyes of Audrey Sevenhowes.
But my Mum had also provided me with a *Baedeker's Canada*,
the edition of 1922, which had somehow found its way into the
shop, and although it was certainly out of date a surprising
number of people asked for a loan of it, and informed themselves that the Government of Canada issued a four-dollar bill,
and that the coloured porters on the sleeping-cars expected a
minimum tip of twenty-five cents a day, and that a guard's van
was called a caboose on Canadian railways, and similar useful
facts.

'The Co. may have thought me funny, but they were a quaint

sight themselves when they assembled on deck for a publicity picture before we left Liverpool. There were plenty of these company pictures taken through the whole length of the tour, and in every one of them Emilia Pauncefort's extraordinary travelling coat (called behind her back the Coat of Many Colours) and the fearful man's cap that Gwenda Lewis fastened to her head with a hatpin, so that she would be ready for all New World hardships, and the fur cap C. Pengelly Spickernell wore, assuring everybody that a skin cap with earflaps was absolutely *de rigueur* in the Canadian winter, Grover Paskin's huge pipe, with a bowl about the size of a brandy-glass, and Eugene Fitzwarren's saucy Homburg and coat with velvet collar, in the Edwardian manner – all these strange habiliments figured prominently. Even though the gaudy days of the Victorian mummers had long gone, these actors somehow got themselves up so that they couldn't have been taken for anything else on God's earth but actors.

'It was invariable, too, that when Holroyd had mustered us for one of these obligatory pictures, Sir John and Milady always appeared last, smiling in surprise, as if a picture were the one thing in the world they hadn't expected, and as if they were joining in simply to humour the rest of us. Sir John was an old hand at travelling in Canada, and he wore an overcoat of Raglan cut and reasonable weight, but of an amplitude that spoke of the stage – and, as our friend has told us, the sleeves were always a bit short so that his hands showed to advantage. Milady wore fur, as befitted the consort of an actor-knight; what fur it was nobody knew, but it was very furry indeed, and soft, and smelled like money. She topped herself with one of those *cloche* hats that were fashionable then, in a hairy purple felt; not the happiest choice, because it almost obscured her eyes, and threw her long duck's-bill nose into prominence.

'But never – never, I assure you – in any of these pictures would you find Mungo Fetch. Who can have warned him off? Whose decision was it that a youthful Sir John, in clothes that were always too tight and sharply cut, wouldn't have done in one of these pictures which always appeared in Canadian papers with a caption that read: "Sir John Tresize and his London company, including Miss Annette de la Borderie (Lady Tresize), who are touring Canada after a triumphant season in the West End." '

'It was a decision of common sense,' said Magnus. 'It never worried me. I knew my place, which is more than you did, Roly.'

'Quite right. I fully admit it. I didn't know my place. I was under the impression that a university man was acceptable everywhere, and inferior to no one. I hadn't twigged that in a theatrical company – or any artistic organization, for that matter – the hierarchy is decided by talent, and that art is the most rigorously aristocratic thing in our democratic world. So I always pushed in as close to Audrey Sevenhowes as I could, and I even picked up the trick from Charlton of standing a bit sideways, to show my profile, which I realize now would have been better kept a mystery. I was an ass. Oh, indeed I was a very fine and ostentatious ass, and don't think I haven't blushed for it since.'

'Stop telling us what an ass you were,' said Kinghovn. 'Even I recognize that as an English trick to pull the teeth of our contempt. "Oh, I say, what a jolly good chap : says he's an ass, don't yer know; he couldn't possibly say that if he was really an ass." But I'm a tough-minded European; I think you really were an ass. If I had a time-machine, I'd whisk myself back into 1932 and give you a good boot in the arse for it. But as I can't, tell me why you were included on the tour. Apparently you were a bad actor and an arguing nuisance as a chair-lifter. Why would anybody pay you money, and take you on a jaunt to Canada?'

'You need a drink, Harry. You are speaking from the deep surliness of the deprived boozer. Don't fuss; it'll be the canonical, appointed cocktail hour quite soon, and then you'll regain your temper. I was taken as Sir John's secretary. The idea was that I'd write letters to fans that he could sign, and do general dog's-body work, and also get on with Jekyll-and-Hyde.

'That was where the canker gnawed, to use an appropriately melodramatic expression. I had thought, you see, that I was to write a dramatization of Stevenson's story, and as Magnus has told you I was full of great ideas about Dostoyevsky and masks. I used to quote Stevenson at Sir John : "I hazard the guess that man will be ultimately known for a mere polity of multifarious, incongruous, and independent denizens," I would say, and entreat him to let me put the incongruous denizens on the stage, in masks. He merely shook his head and said, "No good, m'boy; my public wouldn't like it." Then I would have at him with another quotation, in which Jekyll tells of "those appetites I had long secretly indulged, and had of late begun to pamper". Once he asked me what I had in mind. I had lots of Freudian capers in mind: masochism, and sadism, and rough-stuff with girls. That rubbed his Victorianism the wrong way. "Unwholesome rubbish," was all he would say.

'In the very early days of our association I was even so daring as to ask him to scrap Jekyll-and-Hyde and let me do a version of *Dorian Gray* for him. That really tore it! "Don't ever mention that man to me again," he said; "Oscar Wilde dragged his God-given genius in unspeakable mire, and the greatest kindness we can do is to forget his name. Besides, my public wouldn't hear of it." So I was stuck with Jekyll-and-Hyde.

'Stuck even worse than I had at first supposed. Ages and ages before, at the beginning of their career together, Sir John and Milady had concocted *The Master of Ballantrae* themselves, with their own innocent pencils. They made the scenario, down to the last detail, then found some hack to supply dialogue. This, I discovered to my horror, was what they had done again. They had made a scheme for Jekyll-and-Hyde, and they expected me to write some words for it, and he had the gall to say they would *polish*. Those two mountebanks *polish* my stuff! I was no hack; hadn't I got a meritorious second in Eng. Lit. at Cambridge? And it would have been a first, if I had been content to crawl and stick to the party line about everything on the syllabus from Beowulf on down! Don't laugh, you people. I was young and I had pride.'

'But no stage experience,' said Lind.

'Perhaps not, but I wasn't a fool. And you should have seen the scenario Sir John and Milady had cobbled up between them. Stevenson must have turned in his grave. Do you know *The Strange Case of Dr Jekyll and Mr Hyde*? It's tremendously a *written* book. Do you know what I mean? Its quality is so much in the narrative manner; extract the mere story from it and it's just a tale of bugaboo. Chap drinking a frothy liquid that changes from clear to purple and then to green – *green* if you can imagine anything so corny – and he shrinks into his wicked *alter ego*. I set myself to work to discover a way of getting the heart of the literary quality into a stage version.

'Masks would have helped enormously. But those two had seized on what was, for them, the principal defect of the original, which was that there was no part for a woman in it. Well, imagine! What would the fans of Miss Annette de la Borderie say to that? So they had fudged up a tale in which Dr Jekyll had a secret sorrow; it was that a boyhood friend had married the girl he truly loved, who discovered after the marriage that she truly loved Jekyll. So he adored her honourably, while her husband went to the bad through drink. The big Renunciation ploy, you see, which was such a telling card in *The Master*.

'To keep his mind off his thwarted love, Dr Jekyll took to mucking with chemicals, and discovered the Fateful Potion. Then the husband of the True Love died of booze, and Jekyll and she were free to marry. But by that time he was addicted to the Fateful Potion. Had taken so much of it that he was likely to give a shriek and dwindle into Hyde at any inconvenient moment. So he couldn't marry his True Love and couldn't tell her why. Great final scene, where he is locked in his laboratory, changed into Hyde, and quite unable to change back, because he's run out of the ingredients of the F.P.; True Love, suspecting something's up, storms the door with the aid of a butler and footman who break it in; as the blows on the door send him into the trembles, Jekyll, with one last superhuman clutching at his Better Self, realizes that there is only one honourable way out; he takes poison, and hops the twig just as True Love bursts in; she holds the body of Hyde in her arms, weeping piteously, and the power of her love is so great that he turns slowly back into the beautiful Dr Jekyll, redeemed at the very moment of death.'

'A strong curtain,' said I. 'I don't know what you're complaining about. I should like to have seen that play. I remember Tresize well; he could have done it magnificently.'

'You must be pulling my leg,' said Ingestree, looking at me in reproach.

'Not a bit of it. Good, gutsy melodrama. You've described it in larky terms, because you want us to laugh. But I think it would have worked. Didn't you ever try?'

'Oh yes, I tried. I tried all through that Canadian tour. I would slave away whenever I got a chance, and then show my homework to Sir John, and he would mark it up in his own spidery handwriting. Kept saying I had no notion of how to make words effective, and wrote three sentences where one would do.

'I tried everything I knew. I remember saying to myself one night, as I lay in my berth in a stifling hot Canadian train, What would Aldous Huxley do, in my position? And it came to me that Aldous would have used what we call a distancing-technique – you know, he would have written it all apparently straight, but with a choice of vocabulary that gave it all an ironic edge, so that the perceptive listener would realize that the whole play was ambiguous, and could be taken as a hilarious send-up. So I tried a scene or two like that, and I don't believe Sir John even twigged; he just sliced out all the telling adjectives, and there it was, melodrama again. I never met a man with such a deficient literary sense.'

'Did it ever occur to you that perhaps he knew his job?' said Lind. 'I've never found that audiences liked ambiguity very much. I've got all my best effects by straight statement.'

'Dead right,' said Kinghovn. 'When Jurgen wants ambiguity he tips me the wink and I film the scene a bit skew-whiff, or occasionally going out of focus, and that does the trick.'

'You're telling me this now,' said Ingestree, 'and I expect you're right, in your unliterary way. But there was nobody to tell me anything then, except Sir John, and I could see him becoming more and more stagily patient with me, and letting whatever invisible audience he acted to in his offstage moments admire the way in which the well-graced actor endured the imbecilities of the dimwitted boy. But I swear there was something to be said on my side, as well. But as I say I was an ass. Am I never to be forgiven for being an ass?'

'That's a very pretty theological point,' I said. ' "In the law of God there is no statute of limitations." '

'My God! Do you remember that one?' said Ingestree.

'Oh yes; I've read Stevenson too, you know, and that chilly

769

remark comes in *Jekyll and Hyde*, so you are certainly familiar with it. Are we ever forgiven for the follies even of our earliest years? That's something that torments me often.'

'Bugger theology!' said Kinghovn. 'Get on with the story.'

'High time Harry had a drink,' said Liesl. 'I'll call for some things to be sent up. And we might as well have dinner here, don't you think? I'll choose.'

When she had gone into the bedroom to use the telephone Magnus looked calculatingly at Ingestree, as if at some curious creature he had not observed before. 'You describe the Canadian tour simply as a personal Gethsemane, but it was really quite an elaborate affair,' he said. 'I suppose one of your big problems was trying to fit a part into Jekyll-and-Hyde for the chaste and lovely Sevenhowes. Couldn't you have made her a confidential maid to the True Love, with stirring lines like, "Ee, madam, Dr Jekyll 'e do look sadly mazy-like these latter days, madam"? That would have been about her speed. A rotten actress. Do you know what became of her? Neither do I. What becomes of all those pretty girls with a teaspoonful of talent who seem to drift off the stage before they are thirty? But really, my dear Roly, there was a great deal going on. I was working like a galley-slave.'

'I'm sure you were,' said Ingestree; 'toadying to Milady, as I said earlier. I use the word without malice. Your approach was not describable as courtier-like, nor did it quite sink to the level of fawning; therefore I think toadying is the appropriate expression.'

'Call it toadying if it suits your keen literary sense. I have said several times that I loved her, but you choose not to attach any importance to that. Loved her not in the sense of desiring her, which would have been grotesque, and never entered my head, but simply in the sense of wishing to serve her and do anything that was in my power to make her happy. Why I felt that way about a woman old enough to be my mother is for you dabblers in psychology to say, but nothing you can think of will give the real quality of my feeling; there is a pitiful want of resonance in so much psychological explanation of what lies behind things. If you had felt more, Roly, and been less remorselessly literary, you might have seen possibilities in the plan for the Jekyll and Hyde play. A man redeemed and purged of evil by a woman's love – now there's a really unfashionable theme for a play in our time! So unfashionable as to be utterly incredible. Yet Sir John and Milady seemed to know what such themes were all about. They were more devoted than any people I have ever known.'

'Like a couple of old love-birds,' said Ingestree.

'Well, what would you prefer? A couple of old scratching cats? Don't forget that Sir John was a symbol to countless people of romantic love in its most chivalrous expression. You know what Agate wrote about him once – "He touches women as if they were camellias." Can you name an actor on the stage today who makes love like that? But there was never a word of scandal about them, because off the stage they were inseparables.

'I think I penetrated their secret : undoubtedly they began as lovers but they had long been particularly close friends. Is that common? I haven't seen much of it, if it is. They were sillies, of course. Sir John would never hear a word that suggested that Milady was unsuitably cast as a young woman, though I know he was aware of it. And she was a silly because she played up to him, and clung quite pitiably to some mannerisms of youth. I knew them for years, you know; you only knew them on that tour. But I remember much later, when a newspaper interviewer touched the delicate point, Sir John said with great dignity and simplicity, "Ah, but you see, we always felt that our audiences were ready to make allowances if the physical aspect of a character was not ideally satisfied, because they knew that so many other fine things in our performances were made possible thereby."

'He had a good point, you know. Look at some of the leading women in the Comédie Française; crone is not too hard a word when first you see them, but in ten minutes you are delighted with the art, and forget the appearance, which is only a kind of symbol, anyhow. Milady had extraordinary art, but alas, poor dear, she did run to fat. It's better for an actress to become a bag of bones, which can always be equated somehow with elegance. Fat's another thing. But what a gift of comedy she had, and how wonderfully it lit up a play like *Rosemary*, where she insisted on playing a character part instead of the heroine. Charity, Roly, charity.'

'You're a queer one to be talking about charity. You ate Sir John. I've said it once and I'll say it again. You ate that poor old ham.'

'That's one of your belittling words, like "toady". I've said it : I apprenticed myself to an egoism, and if in the course of time, because I was younger and had a career to make, the egoism became more mine than his, what about it? Destiny, m'boy? Inevitable, quonk?'

'Oh, God, don't do that, it's too horribly like him.'

'Thank you. I thought so myself. And, as I tell you, I worked to achieve it!

'You had quite a jolly time on the voyage to Canada, as I recall. But don't you remember those rehearsals we held every day, in such holes and corners of the ship as the Purser could make available to us? Macgregor and I were too busy to be seasick, which was a luxury you didn't deny yourself. You were sick the night of the ship's concert. Those concerts are utterly a thing of the past. The Purser's assistant was busy almost before the ship left Liverpool, ferreting out what possible talent there might be on board – ladies who could sing "The Rosary" or men who imitated Harry Lauder. A theatrical company was a god-send to the poor man. And in the upshot C. Pengelly Spickernell sang "Mélisande in the Wood" and "The Floral Dance" (nicely contrasted material, was what he called it) and Grover Paskin told funny stories (insecurely cemented together with "And that reminds me of the time –") and Sir John recited Clarence's Dream from *Richard III*; Milady made the speech hitting up the audience for money for the Seaman's Charities, and did it with so much charm and spirit that they got a record haul.

'But that's by the way. We worked on the voyage and after we'd docked at Montreal the work was even harder. We landed on a Friday, and opened on Monday at Her Majesty's for two weeks, one given wholly to *Scaramouche* and the second to *The Corsican Brothers* and *Rosemary*. We did first-rate business, and it was the beginning of what the old actors loved to call a triumphal tour. You wouldn't believe how we were welcomed, and how the audiences ate up those romantic plays –'

'I remember some fairly cool notices,' said Roly.

'But not cool audiences. That's what counts. Provincial critics are always cool; they have to show they're not impressed by what comes from the big centres of culture. The audiences thought we were wonderful.'

'Magnus, the audiences thought England was wonderful. The Tresize company came from England, and if the truth is to be told it came from a special England many of the people in those audiences cherished – the England they had left when they were young, or the England they had visited when they were young, and in many cases an England they simply imagined and wished were a reality.

'Even in 1932 all that melodrama was terribly old hat, but every audience had a core of people who were happy just to be listening to English voices repeating noble sentiments. The notion that everybody wants the latest is a delusion of intellectuals; a lot of people want a warm, safe place where Time hardly moves at all, and to a lot of those Canadians that place was England. The theatre was almost the last stronghold of the old colonial Canada. You know very well it was more than twenty years since Sir John had dared to visit New York, because his sort of theatre was dead there. But it did very well in Canada because it wasn't simply theatre there – it was England, and they were sentimental about it.

'Don't you remember the smell of mothballs that used to sweep up onto the stage when the curtain rose, from all the bunny coats and ancient dress suits in the expensive seats? There were still people who dressed for the theatre, though I doubt if they dressed for anything else, except perhaps a regimental ball or something that also reminded them of England. Sir John was exploiting the remnants of colonialism. You liked it because you knew no better.'

'I knew Canada,' said Magnus. 'At least, I knew the part of it that had responded to Wanless's World of Wonders and Happy Hannah's jokes. The Canada that came to see Sir John was different but not wholly different. We didn't tour the villages; we toured the cities with theatres that could accommodate our productions, but we rushed through many a village I knew as we jaunted all those thousands of miles on the trains.

As we travelled, I began to think I knew Canada pretty well. But quite another thing was that I knew what entertains people, what charms the money out of their pockets, and feeds their imagination.

'The theatre to you was a kind of crude extension of Eng. Lit. at Cambridge, but the theatre I knew was the theatre that makes people forget some things and remember others, and refreshes dry places in the spirit. We were both ignorant young men, Roly. You were the kind that is so scared of life that you only know how to despise it, for fear you might be tricked into liking something that wasn't up to the standards of a handful of people you admired. I was the kind that knew very little that wasn't tawdry and tough and ugly, but I hadn't forgotten my Psalms, and I thirsted for something better as the hart pants for the water-brooks. So Sir John's plays, and the decent manners he insisted on in his company, and the regularity and honesty of the Friday treasury, when I got my pay without having to haggle or kick back any part of it to some petty crook, did very well for me.'

'You're idealizing your youth, Magnus. Lots of the company just thought the tour was a lark.'

'Yes, but even more of the company were honest players and did their best in the work they had at hand. You saw too much of Charlton and Woulds, who were no good and never made any mark in the profession. And you were under the thumb of Audrey Sevenhowes, who was another despiser, like yourself. Of course we had our ridiculous side. What theatrical troupe hasn't? But the effect we produced wasn't ridiculous. We had something people wanted, and we didn't give them short weight. Very different from my carnival days, when short weight was the essence of everything.'

'So for you the Canadian tour was a time of spiritual growth,' said Lind.

'It was a time when I was able to admit that honesty and some decency of life were luxuries within my grasp,' said Magnus. 'Can you imagine that? You people all have the flesh and finish of those who grew up feeling reasonably safe in the world. And you grew up as visible people. Don't forget that I had spent most of my serious hours inside Abdullah.'

'Melodrama has eaten into your brain,' said Roly. 'When I knew you, you were inside Sir John, inside his body and inside his manner and voice and everything about him that a clever double could imitate. Was it really different?'

'Immeasurably different.'

'I wish you two would stop clawing one another,' said King-hovn. 'If it was all so different – and I'm quite ready to believe it was – how was it different? If it's possible to find out, of course. You two sound as if you had been on different tours.'

'Not a bit of it. It was the same tour, right enough,' said Magnus; 'but I probably remember more of its details than Roly. I'm a detail man; it's the secret of being a good illusionist. Roly has the big, broad picture, as it would have appeared to someone of his temperament and education. He saw everything it was proper for the Cantab and One to notice; I saw and tried to understand everything that passed before my eyes.

'Do you remember Morton W. Penfold, Roly? No, I didn't think you would. But he was one of the casters on which that tour rolled. He was our Advance.

'The tour was under the management of a syndicate of rich Canadians who wanted to encourage English theatre companies to visit Canada, partly because they wanted to stem what they felt was a too heavy American influence, partly in the hope that they might make a little money, partly because they felt the attraction of the theatre in the ignorant way rich business-men sometimes do. When we arrived in Montreal some of them met the ship and bore Sir John and Milady away, and there was a great deal of wining and dining before we opened on Monday. Morton W. Penfold was their representative, and he went ahead of us like a trumpeter all across the country. Arranged about travel and saw that tickets for everybody were forthcoming whenever we mounted a train. Saw that trains were delayed when necessary, or that an improvised special helped us to make a difficult connection. Arranged that trucks and sometimes huge sleighs were ready to lug the scenery to and from the theatres. Arranged that there were enough stagehands for our heavy shows, and a rough approximation of the number of musicians we needed to play our music, and college boys or other creatures of the right height and bulk who were needed for the supers in *The Master* and *Scaramouche*. Saw that a horse of guaranteed good character and continence was hired to pull Climene's cart. Placed the advertisements in the local papers ahead of our appearance, and also tasty bits of publicity about Sir John and Milady; had a little anecdote ready for every paper that made it clear that the name Tresize was Cornish and that the emphasis came on the second syllable; also provided a little packet of favourable reviews from London, Montreal, and Toronto papers for the newspapers in small towns where there was no regular critic, and such material might prime the pump of a local reporter's invention. He also saw that the information was provided for the programmes, and warned local theatre managers that Madame de Plougastel's Salon was not a misprint for Madame de Plougastel's Saloon, which some of them were apt to think.

'Morton W. Penfold was a living marvel, and I learned a lot from him on the occasions when he was in the same town with us for a few days. He was more theatrical than all but the most theatrical of the actors; had a big square face with a blue jaw, a hypnotist's eyebrows, and a deceptive appearance of dignity and solemnity, because he was a fellow of infinite wry humour. He wore one of those black Homburg hats that politicians used to affect, but he never dinted the top of it, so that he had something of the air of a Mennonite about the head; wore a stiff choker collar and one of those black satin stocks that used to be called a dirty-shirt necktie, because it covered everything within the V of his waistcoat. Always wore a black suit, and had a dazzling ten-cent shoeshine every day of his life. His business office was contained in the pockets of his black overcoat; he could produce anything from them, including eight-by-ten-inch publicity pictures of the company.

'He was pre-eminently a great fixer. He seemed to know everybody, and have influence everywhere. In every town he had arranged for Sir John to address the Rotarians, or the Kiwanians, or whatever club was meeting on an appropriate day. Sir John always gave the same speech, which was about "cementing the bonds of the British Commonwealth"; he could have given it in his sleep, but he was too good an actor not to make it seem tailor-made for every new club.

'If we were going to be in a town that had an Anglican

Cathedral over a weekend it was Morton W. Penfold who persuaded the Dean that it was a God-given opportunity to have Sir John read the Second Lesson at the eleven o'clock service. His great speciality was getting Indian tribes to invest a visiting English actor as a Chief, and he had convinced the Blackfoot that Sir John should be re-christened Soksi-Poyina many years before the tour I am talking about.

'Furthermore, he knew the idiosyncrasies of the liquor laws in every Canadian province we visited, and made sure the company did not run dry; this was particularly important as Sir John and Milady had a taste for champagne, and liked it iced but not frozen, which was not always a simple requirement in that land of plentiful ice. And in every town we visited, Morton W. Penfold had made sure that our advertising sheets, full-size, half-size, and folio, were well displayed and that our little flyers, with pictures of Sir John in some of his most popular roles, were on the reception desks of all the good hotels.

'And speaking of hotels, it was Morton W. Penfold who took particulars of everybody's taste in accommodation on that first day in Montreal, and saw that wherever we went reservations had been made in the grand railway hotels, which were wonderful, or in the dumps where people like James Hailey and Gwenda Lewis stayed, for the sake of economy.

'Oh, those cheap hotels! I stayed in the cheapest, where one electric bulb hung from a string in the middle of the room, where the sheets were like cheesecloth, and where the mattresses – when they were revealed as they usually were after a night's restless sleep – were like maps of strange worlds, the continents being defined by unpleasing stains, doubtless traceable to the incontinent dreams of travelling salesmen, or the rapturous deflowerings of brides from the backwoods.

'Was he well paid for his innumerable labours? I don't know, but I hope so. He said very little that was personal, but Macgregor told me that Morton W. Penfold was born into show business, and that his wife was the granddaughter of the man whom Blondin the Magnificent had carried across Niagara Gorge on his shoulders in 1859. It was under his splendid and unfailing influence that we travelled thousands of miles across Canada and back again, and played a total of 148 performances

777

in forty-one towns, ranging from places of about twenty thousand souls to big cities. I think I could recite the names of the theatres we played in now, though they showed no great daring in what they called themselves; there were innumerable Grands, and occasional Princesses or Victorias, but most of them were just called Somebody's Opera House.'

'Frightful places,' said Ingestree, doing a dramatic shudder.

'I've seen worse since,' said Magnus. 'You should try a tour in Central America, to balance your viewpoint. What was interesting about so many of the Canadian theatres, outside the big cities, was that they seemed to have been built with big ideas, and then abandoned before they were equipped. They had pretty good foyers and auditoriums with plush seats, and invariably eight boxes, four on each side of the stage, from which nobody could see very well. All of them had drop curtains with views of Venice or Rome on them, and a spyhole through which so many actors had peeped that it was ringed with a black stain from their greasepaint. Quite a few had special curtains on which advertisements were printed for local merchants; Sir John didn't like those, and Holroyd had to do what he could to suppress them.

'Every one had a sunken pen for an orchestra, with a fancy balustrade to cut it off from the stalls, and nobody ever seemed to sweep in there. At performance time a handful of assassins would creep into the pen from a low door beneath the stage, and fiddle and thump and toot the music to which they were accustomed. C. Pengelly Spickernell used to say bitterly that these musicians were all recruited from the local manager's poor relations; it was his job to assemble as many of them as could get away from their regular work on a Monday morning and take them through the music that was to accompany our plays. Sir John was fussy about music, and always had a special overture for each of his productions, and usually an entr'acte as well.

'God knows it was not very distinguished music. When we heard it, it was a puzzle to know why "Overture to *Scaramouche*" by Hugh Dunning did any more for the play that followed than if the orchestra had played "Overture to *The Master of Ballantrae*" by Festyn Hughes. But there it was, and to Sir John and Milady these two lengths of mediocre music were as different as daylight and dark, and they used to sigh and raise their eyebrows at one another when they heard the miserable racket coming from the other side of the curtain, as if it were the ravishing of a masterpiece. In addition to this specially written music we carried a substantial body of stuff with such titles as "Minuet d'Amour", "Peasant Dance", and "Gaelic Memories", which did for *Rosemary*; and for *The Corsican Brothers* Sir John insisted on an overture that had been written for Irving's production of *Robespierre* by somebody called Litolff. Another great standby was "Suite: At the Play", by York Bowen. But except in the big towns the orchestra couldn't manage anything unfamiliar, so we generally ended up with "Three Dances from *Henry VIII*", by Edward German, which I suppose is known to every bad orchestra in the world. C. Pengelly Spickernell used to grieve about it whenever anybody would listen, but I honestly think the audiences liked that bad playing, which was familiar and had associations with a good time.

'Backstage there was nothing much to work with. No light, except for a few rows of red, white, and blue bulbs that hardly disturbed the darkness when they were full on. The arrangements for hanging and setting our scenery were primitive, and only in the big towns was there more than one stagehand with anything that could be called experience. The others were jobbed in as they were needed, and during the day they worked in factories or lumber-yards. Consequently we had to carry everything we needed with us, and now and then we had to do some rapid improvising. It wasn't as though these theatres weren't used; most of them were busy for at least a part of each week for seven or eight months every year. It was simply that the local magnate, having put up the shell of a theatre, saw no reason to go further. It made touring adventurous, I can tell you.

'The dressing-rooms were as ill equipped as the stages. I think they were worse than those in the vaude houses I had known, because those at least were in constant use and had a frowsy life to them. In many towns there were only two wash-basins backstage for a whole company, one behind a door marked

779

M and the other behind a door marked F. These doors, through years of use, had ceased to close firmly, which at least meant that you didn't need to knock to find out if they were occupied. Sir John and Milady used small metal basins of their own, to which their dressers carried copper jugs of hot water – when there was any hot water.

'One thing that astonished me then, and still surprises me, is that the stage door, in nine towns out of ten, was up an unpaved alley, so that you had to pick your way through mud, or snow in the cold weather, to reach it. You knew where you were heading because the only light in the alley was one naked electric bulb, stuck laterally into a socket above the door, with a wire guard around it. It was not the placing of the stage door that surprised me, but the fact that, for me, that desolate and dirty entry was always cloaked in romance. I would rather go through one of those doors, even now, than walk up a garden path to be greeted by a queen.'

'You were stage-struck,' said Roly. 'You rhapsodize. I remember those stage doors. Ghastly.'

'I suppose you're right,' said Magnus. 'But I was very, very happy. I'd never been so well placed, or had so much fun in my life. How Macgregor and I used to labour to teach those stage-hands their job! Do you remember how, in the last act of *The Corsican Brothers*, when the Forest of Fontainebleau was supposed to be covered in snow, we used to throw down coarse salt over the stage-cloth, so that when the duel took place Sir John could kick some of it aside to get a firm footing? Can you imagine trying to explain how that salt should be placed to some boob who had laboured all day in a planing-mill, and had no flair for romance? The snow was always a problem, though you'd think that Canadians, of all people, would understand snow. At the beginning of that act the forest is supposed to be seen in that dull but magical light that goes with snowfall. Old Boissec the wood-cutter – Grover Paskin in one of his distinguished cameos – enters singing a little song; he represents the world of everyday, drudging along regardless of the high romance which is shortly to burst upon the scene. Sir John wanted a powdering of snow to be falling as the curtain rose; just a few flakes, falling slowly so that they caught a little of the winter light. Nothing so coarse as bits of paper for us! It had to be fuller's earth, so that it would drift gently, and not be too fiercely white. Do you think we could get one of those stage-hands on the road to grasp the importance of the speed at which that snow fell, and the necessity to get it exactly right? If we left it to them they threw great handfuls of snow bang on the centre of the stage, as if some damned great turkey with diarrhoea were roosting up in a tree. So it was my job to get up on the catwalk, if there was one, and on something that had been improvised and was usually dangerous if there wasn't, and see that the snow was just as Sir John wanted it. I suppose that's being stage-struck, but it was worth every scruple of the effort it took. As I said, I'm a detail man, and without the uttermost organization of detail there is no illusion, and consequently no romance. When I was in charge of the snow the audience was put in the right mood for the duel, and for the Ghost at the end of the play.'

'You really can't blame me for despising it,' said Roly. 'I was one of the New Men; I was committed to a theatre of ideas.'

'I don't suppose I've ever had more than half a dozen ideas in my life, and even those wouldn't have much appeal for a philosopher,' said Magnus. 'Sir John's theatre didn't deal in ideas, but in feelings. Chivalry, and loyalty and selfless love don't rank as ideas, but it was wonderful how they seized on our audiences; they loved such things, even if they had no intention of trying them out in their own lives. No use arguing about it, really. But people used to leave our performances smiling, which isn't always the case with a theatre of ideas.'

'Art as soothing syrup, in fact.'

'Perhaps. But it was very good soothing syrup. We never made the mistake of thinking it was a universal panacea.'

'Soothing syrup in aid of a dying colonialism.'

'I expect you're right. I don't care, really. It's true we thumped the good old English drum pretty loudly, but that was one of the things the syndicate wanted. When we visited Ottawa, Sir John and Milady were the Governor General's guests at Rideau Hall.'

'Yes, and what a bloody nuisance that was! Actors ought never to stay in private houses or official residences. I had to scamper out there every morning with the letters, and get my orders for the day. Run the gamut of snotty aides who never seemed to know where Lady Tresize was to be found.'

'Didn't she ever tell you any stories about that? Probably not. I don't think she liked you much better than you liked her. Certainly she told me that it was like living in a very pretty little court, and that all sorts of interesting people came to call. Don't you remember that the Governor General and his suite came to *Scaramouche* one night when we were playing in the old Russell Theatre? "God Save the King" was played after they came in, and the audience was so frozen with etiquette that nobody dared to clap until the G.G. had been seen to do so. There were people who sucked in their breath when I thumbed my nose while walking the tightrope; they thought I was Sir John, you see, and they couldn't imagine a knight committing such an unspeakable rudery in the presence of an Earl. But Milady told me the Earl was away behind the times; he didn't know what it meant in Canadian terms, and thought it still meant something called "fat bacon", which I suppose was Victorian. He guffawed and thumbed his nose and muttered, "Fat bacon, what?" at the supper party afterward, at which Mr Mackenzie King was a guest; Mr King was so taken aback he could hardly eat his lobster. Apparently he got over it though, and Milady said she had never seen a man set about a lobster with such wholesouled enthusiasm. When he surfaced from the lobster he talked to her very seriously about dogs. Funny business, when you think of it – I mean all those grandees sitting at supper at midnight, after a play. That must have been romantic too, in its way, although there were no young people present – except the aides and one or two ladies-in-waiting, of course. In fact, I thought a lot of Canada was romantic.'

'I didn't. I thought it was the rawest, roughest, crudest place I had ever set eyes on, and in the midst of that, all those viceregal pretensions were ridiculous.'

'I wonder if that's what you really thought, Roly? After all, what were you comparing it with? Norwich, and Cambridge, and a brief sniff at London. And you weren't in a condition to see anything except through the spectacles of a thwarted lover and playwright. You were being put through the mincer by the lovely Sevenhowes; you were her toy for the tour, and your agonies were the sport of her chums Charlton and Woulds. Whenever we were on one of those long train hops from city to city, we all saw it in the dining-car.

'Those dining-cars! There was romance for you! Rushing through the landscape; that fierce country north of Lake Superior, and the marvellous steppes of the prairies, in an elegant, rather too hot, curiously shaped dining-room, full of light, glittering with tablecloths and napkins so white they looked blue, shining silver (or something very close), and all those clean, courteous, friendly black waiters – if that wasn't romance you don't know the real thing when you see it! And the food! Nothing hotted up or melted out in those days, but splendid stuff that came on fresh at every big stop; cooked brilliantly in the galley by a real chef; fresh fish, tremendous meat, real fruit – don't you remember what their baked apples were like? With thick cream! Where does one get thick cream now? I remember every detail. The cube sugar was wrapped in pretty white paper with Castor printed on it, and every time we put it in our coffee I suppose we enriched our dear friend Boy Staunton, so clear in the memory of Dunny and myself, because he came from our town, though I didn't know that at the time ...' (My ears pricked up: I swear my scalp tingled. Magnus had mentioned Boy Staunton, the Canadian tycoon, and also my lifelong friend, whom I was pretty sure Magnus had murdered. Or, if not murdered, had given a good push on a path that looked like suicide. This was what I wanted for my document. Had Magnus, who withheld death cruelly from Willard, given it almost as a benefaction to Boy Staunton? Would his present headlong, confessional mood carry him to the point where he would admit to murder, or at least give a hint that I, who knew so much but not enough, would be able to interpret? ... But I must miss nothing, and Magnus was still rhapsodizing about C.P.R. food as once it was.) '... And the sauces; real sauces, made by the chef – exquisite!

'There were bottled sauces, too. Commercial stuff I learned to hate because at every meal that dreary utility actor Jim Hailey asked for Garton's; then he would wave it about saying, "Anybody want any of the Handkerchief?" because, as he laboriously pointed out, if you spelled Garton's backward it came out Snotrag; poor Hailey was that depressing creature, a man of one joke. Only his wife laughed and blushed because he was being "awful", and she never failed to tell him so. But I suppose you didn't see because you always tried to sit at the table with Sevenhowes and Charlton and Woulds; if she was cruel and asked Eric Foss to sit with them instead, you sat as near as you could and hankered and glowered as they laughed at jokes you couldn't hear.

'Oh, the trains, the trains! I gloried in them because with Wanless's I had done so much train travel and it was wretched. I began my train travel, you remember, in darkness and fear, hungry, with my poor little bum aching desperately. But here I was, unmistakably a first-class passenger, in the full blaze of that piercing, enveloping, cleansing Canadian light. I was quite content to sit at a table with some of the technical staff, or sometimes with old Mac and Holroyd, and now and then with that Scheherazade of the railways, Morton W. Penfold, when he was making a hop with us.

'Penfold knew all the railway staff; I think he knew all the waiters. There was one conductor we sometimes encountered on a transcontinental, who was a special delight to him, a gloomy man who carried a real railway watch – one of those gigantic nickel-plated turnips that kept very accurate time. Penfold would hail him: "Lester, when do you think we'll be in Sault Ste Marie?" Then Lester would pull up the watch out of the well of his waistcoat, and look sadly at it, and say, "Six fifty-two, Mort, *if we're spared*." He was gloomy-religious, and everything was conditional on our being spared; he didn't seem to have much confidence in either God or the C.P.R.

'Penfold knew the men on the locomotives, too, and whenever we came to a long, straight stretch of track, he would say, "I wonder if Fred is dipping his piles." This was because one of the oldest and best of the engineers was a martyr to haemorrhoids, and Penfold swore that whenever we came to an easy piece of track, Fred drew off some warm water from the boiler into a basin, and sat in it for a few minutes, to ease himself. Penfold never laughed; he was a man of deep, private humour, and his solemn, hypnotist's face never softened, but the liquid on his lower eyelid glittered and occasionally spilled over, and his head shook; that was his laugh.

'Now and then, on long hauls, the train carried a private car for Sir John and Milady; these luxuries could not be hired – or only by the very rich – but sometimes a magnate who owned one, or a politician who had the use of one, would put it at the disposal of the Tresizes, who had armies of friends in Canada. Sir John, and Milady especially, were not mingy about their private car, and always asked a few of the company in, and now and then, on very long hauls, they asked us all in and we had a picnic meal from the dining-car. Now surely that was romance, Roly? Or didn't you find it so? All of us perched around one of those splendid old relics, most of which had been built not later than the reign of Edward the Seventh, full of marquetry woodwork (there was usually a little plaque somewhere that told you where all the woods came from) and filigree doodads around the ceiling, and armchairs with a fringe made of velvet bobbles everywhere that fringe could be imagined. In a sort of altar-like affair at one end of the drawing-room area were magazines in thick leather folders – and what magazines! Always the *Sketch* and the *Tatler* and *Punch* and the *Illustrated London News* – it was like a club on wheels. And lashings of drink for everybody – that was Penfold's craft at work – but it wasn't at all the thing for anybody to guzzle and get drunk, because Sir John and Milady didn't like that.'

'He was a great one to talk,' said Ingestree. 'He could drink any amount without showing it, and it was believed everywhere that he drank a bottle of brandy a day just to keep his voice mellow.'

'Believed, but simply not true. It's always believed that star actors drink heavily, or beat their wives, or deflower a virgin starlet every day to slake their lust. But Sir John drank pretty moderately. He had to. Gout. He never spoke about it, but he suffered a lot with it. I remember one of those parties when the train lurched and Felicity Larcombe stumbled and stepped on his gouty foot, and he turned dead white, but all he said was, "Don't speak of it, my dear," when she apologized.'

'Yes, of course you'd have seen that. You saw everything. Obviously, or you couldn't tell us so much about it now. But we saw you seeing everything, you know. You weren't very good at disguising it, even if you tried. Audrey Sevenhowes and Charlton and Woulds had a name for you – the Phantom of the Opera. You were always somewhere with your back against a wall, looking intently at everything and everybody. "There's the Phantom, at it again," Audrey used to say. It wasn't a very nice kind of observation. It had what I can only call a wolfish quality about it, as if you were devouring everything. Especially devouring Sir John. I don't suppose he made a move without you following him with your eyes. No wonder you knew about the gout. None of the rest of us did.'

'None of the rest of you cared, if you mean the little clique you travelled with. But the older members of the company knew, and certainly Morton W. Penfold knew, because it was one of his jobs to see that the same kind of special bottled water was always available for Sir John on every train and in every hotel. Gout's very serious for an actor. Any suggestion that a man who is playing the Master of Ballantrae is hobbling is bad for publicity. It was clear enough that Sir John wasn't young, but it was of the uttermost importance that on the stage he should seem young. To do that he had to be able to walk slowly; it's not too hard to seem youthful when you're leaping about the stage in a duel, but it's a very different thing to walk as slowly as he had to when he appeared as his own ghost at the end of *The Corsican Brothers*. Detail, my dear Roly; without detail there can be no illusion. And one of the odd things about Sir John's kind of illusion (and my own, when later on I became a master illusionist) is that the showiest things are quite simply arranged, but anything that looks like simplicity is extremely difficult.

'The gout wasn't precisely a secret, but it wasn't shouted from the housetops, either. Everybody knew that Sir John and Milady travelled a few fine things with them – a bronze that he particularly liked, and she always had a valuable little picture of the Virgin that she used for her private devotions, and a handsome case containing miniatures of their children – and that these things were set up in every hotel room they occupied, to give it some appearance of personal taste. But not everybody knew about the foot-bath that had to be carried for Sir John's twice-daily treatment of the gouty foot; a bathtub wouldn't do, because it was necessary that all of his body be at the temperature of the room, while the foot was in a very hot mineral solution.

'I've seen him sitting in his dressing-gown with the foot in that thing at six o'clock, and at half-past eight he was ready to step on the stage with the ease of a young man. I never thought it was the mineral bath that did the trick; I think it was more an apparatus for concentrating his will, and determination that the gout shouldn't get the better of him. If his will ever failed, he was a goner, and he knew it.

'I've often had reason to marvel at the heroism and spiritual valour that people put into causes that seem absurd to many observers. After all, would it have mattered if Sir John had thrown in the towel, admitted he was old, and retired to cherish his gout? Who would have been the loser? Who would have regretted *The Master of Ballantrae*? It's easy to say, No one at all, but I don't think that's true. You never know who is gaining strength as a result of your own bitter struggle; you never know who sees *The Master of Ballantrae*, and quite improbably draws something from it that changes his life, or gives him a special bias for a lifetime.

'As I watched Sir John fighting against age – watched him wolfishly, I suppose Roly would say – I learned something without knowing it. Put simply it is this; no action is ever lost – nothing we do is without result. It's obvious, of course, but how many people ever really believe it, or act as if it were so?'

'You sound woefully like my dear old Mum,' said Ingestree. 'No good action is ever wholly lost, she would say.'

'Ah, but I extend your Mum's wisdom,' said Magnus. 'No evil action is ever wholly lost, either.'

'So you pick your way through life like a hog on ice, trying to do nothing but good actions? Oh, Magnus! What balls!'

'No, no, my dear Roly, I am not quite such a fool as that. We can't know the quality or the results of our actions except in the most limited way. All we can do is to try to be as sure as we can of what we are doing so far as it relates to ourselves. In fact, not to flail about and be the deluded victims of our passions. If you're going to do something that looks evil, don't smear it with icing and pretend it's good; just bloody well do it and keep your eyes peeled. That's all.'

'You ought to publish that. *Reflections While Watching an Elderly Actor Bathing His Gouty Foot*. It might start a new vogue in morality.'

'I was watching a little more than Sir John's gouty foot, I assure you. I watched him pumping up courage for Milady, who had special need of it. He wasn't a humorous man; I mean, life didn't appear to him as a succession of splendid jokes, big and small, as it did to Morton W. Penfold. Sir John's mode of perception was romantic, and romance isn't funny except in a gentle, incidental way. But on a tour like that, Sir John had to do things that had their funny side, and one of them was to make that succession of speeches, which Penfold arranged, at service clubs in the towns where we played. It was the heyday of service clubs, and they were hungrily looking for speakers, whose job it was to say something inspirational, in not more than fifteen minutes, at their weekly luncheon meetings. Sir John always cemented the bonds of the Commonwealth for them, and while he was waiting to do it they levied fines on one another for wearing loud neckties, and recited their extraordinary creeds, and sang songs they loved but which were as barbarous to him as the tribal chants of savages. So he would come back to Milady afterward, and teach her the songs, and there they would sit, in the drawing-room of some hotel suite, singing

> Rotary Ann, she went out to get some clams,
> Rotary Ann, she went out to get some clams,
> Rotary Ann, she went out to get some clams,
> But she didn't get a – clam!

– and at the appropriate moments they would clap their hands to substitute for the forbidden words "God-damn", which good Rotarians knew, but wouldn't utter.

'I tell you it was eerie to see those two, so English, so Victorian, so theatrical, singing those utterly uncharacteristic words in their high-bred English accents, until they were laughing like loonies. Then Sir John would say something like "Of course one shouldn't laugh at them, Nan, because they're really splendid fellows at heart, and do marvels for crippled children

788

– or is it tuberculosis? I can never remember." But the important thing was that Milady had been cheered up. She never showed her failing spirits – at least she thought she didn't – but he knew. And I knew.

'It was another of those secrets like Sir John's gout, which Mac and Holroyd and some of the older members of the company were perfectly well aware of but never discussed. Milady had cataracts, and however courageously she disguised it, the visible world was getting away from her. Some of the clumsiness on stage was owing to that, and much of the remarkable lustre of her glance – that bluish lustre I had noticed the first time I saw her – was the slow veiling of her eyes. There were days that were better than others, but as each month passed the account was further on the debit side. I never heard them mention it. Why would I? Certainly I wasn't the kind of person they would have confided in. But I was often present when all three of us knew what was in the air.

'I have you to thank for that, Roly. Ordinarily it would have been the secretary who would have helped Milady when something had to be read, or written, but you were never handily by, and when you were it was so clear that you were far too busy with literary things to be just a useful pair of eyes that it would have been impertinence to interrupt you. So that job fell to me, and Milady and I made a pretence about it that was invaluable to me.

'It was that she was teaching me to speak – to speak for the stage, that's to say. I had several modes of speech; one was the tough-guy language of Willard and Charlie, and another was a half-Cockney lingo I had picked up in London; I could speak French far more correctly than English, but I had a poor voice, with a thin, nasal tone. So Milady had me read to her, and as I read she helped me to place my voice differently, breathe better, and choose words and expressions that did not immediately mark me as an underling. Like so many people of deficient education, when I wanted to speak classy – that was what Charlie called it – I always used as many big words as I could. Big words, said Milady, were a great mistake in ordinary conversation, and she made me read the Bible to her to rid me of the big-word habit. Of course the Bible was familiar ground to me, and she noticed that when I read it I spoke better than otherwise, but as she pointed out, too fervently. That was a recollection of my father's Bible-reading voice. Milady said that with the Bible and Shakespeare it was better to be a little cool, rather than too hot; the meaning emerged more powerfully. "Listen to Sir John," she said, "and you'll find that he never pushes a line as far as it will go." That was how I learned about never doing your damnedest; your next-to-damnedest was far better.

'Sir John was her ideal, so I learned to speak like Sir John, and it was quite a long time before I got over it, if indeed I ever did completely get over it. It was a beautiful voice, and perhaps too beautiful for everybody's taste. He produced it in a special way, which I think he learned from Irving. His lower lip moved a lot, but his upper lip was almost motionless, and he never showed his upper teeth; completely loose lower jaw, lots of nasal resonance, and he usually spoke in his upper register, but sometimes he dropped into deep tones, with extraordinary effect. She insisted on careful phrasing, long breaths, and never accentuating possessive pronouns – she said that made almost anything sound petty.

'So I spent many an hour reading the Bible to her, and refreshing my memory of the Psalms. "Consider and hear me, O Lord my God : lighten mine eyes, lest I sleep the sleep of death. Lest mine enemy say, I have prevailed against him; and those that trouble me rejoice when I am moved." We had that almost every day. That, and "Open thou mine eyes, that I may behold wondrous things out of thy law." It was not long before I understood that Milady was praying, and I was helping her, and after the first surprise – I had been so long away from anybody who prayed, except for Happy Hannah, whose prayers were like curses – I was pleased and honoured to do it. But I didn't intrude upon her privacy; I was content to be a pair of eyes, and to learn to be a friendly voice. May I put in here that this was another side of apprenticeship to Sir John's egoism, and it was not something I had greedily sought. On the contrary it was something to which I seemed to be fated. If I stole something from the old man, the impulse for the theft was not wholly mine; I seemed to be pushed into it.

'One of the things that pushed me was that as Milady's sight grew dimmer, she liked to have somebody near to whom she could speak in French. As I've told you, she came from the Channel Islands, and from her name I judge that French was her cradle-tongue. So, under pretence of correcting my French pronunciation, we had many a long talk, and I read the Bible to her in French, as well as in English. That was a surprise for me! Like so many English-speaking people I could not conceive of the words of Christ in any language but my own, but as we worked through Le Nouveau Testament in her chunky old Geneva Bible, there they were, coloured quite differently. *Je suis le chemin, & la vérité, & la vie; nul ne vient au Père sinon par moi.* Sounded curiously frivolous, but nothing to *Bienheureux sont les débonnaires: cars ils hériteront la terre.* I thought I concealed the surprise in my voice at that one, but Milady heard it (she heard everything) and explained that I must think of *débonnaire* as meaning *clément*, or perhaps *les doux.* But of course we all interpret Holy Writ to suit ourselves as much as we dare; I liked *les débonnaires*, because I was striving as hard as I could to be debonair myself, and I had an eye on at least a good-sized chunk of *la terre* for my inheritance. Learning to speak English and French with an upper-class accent – or at least a stage accent, which was a little more precise than merely upper class – was part of my campaign.

'As well as reading aloud, I listened to her as she rehearsed her lines. The old plays, like *The Master of Ballantrae*, were impressed on her memory forever, but she liked to go over her words for *Rosemary* and *Scaramouche* before every performance, and I read her cues for her. I learned a good deal from that, too, because she had a fine sense of comedy (something Sir John had only in a lesser degree), and I studied her manner of pointing up a line so that something more than just the joke – the juice in which the joke floated – was carried to the audience. She had a charming voice, with a laugh in it, and I noticed that clever Felicity Larcombe was learning that from her, as well as I.

'Indeed, I became a friend of Milady's, and rather less of an adorer. Except for old Zingara, who was a very different pair of shoes, she was the only woman I had ever known who seemed to like me, and think I was of any interest or value. She rubbed it into me about how lucky I was to be working with Sir John, and doing marvellous little cameos which enhanced the value of a whole production, but I had enough common sense to see that she was right, even though she exaggerated.

'One thing about me that she could not understand was that I had no knowledge of Shakespeare. None whatever. When I knew the Bible so well, how was it that I was in darkness about the other great classic of English? Had my parents never introduced me to Shakespeare? Of course Milady could have had no idea of the sort of people my parents were. I suppose my father must have heard of Shakespeare, but I am sure he rejected him as a fellow who had frittered away his time in the theatre, that Devil's domain where lies were made attractive to frivolous people.

'I have often been amazed at how well comfortable and even rich people understand the physical deprivations of the poor, without having any notion of their intellectual squalor, which is one of the things that makes them miserable. It's a squalor that is bred in the bone, and rarely can education do much to root it out if education is simply a matter of schooling. Milady had come of quite rich parents, who had daringly allowed her to go on the stage when she was no more than fourteen. In Sir Henry Irving's company, of course, which wasn't like kicking around from one stage door to another, and snatching for little jobs in pantomime. To be one of the Guvnor's people was to be one of the theatrically well-to-do, not simply in wages but in estate. And at the Lyceum she had taken in a lot of Shakespeare at the pores, and had whole plays by heart. How could anyone like that grasp the meagreness of the household in which I had been a child, and the remoteness of intellectual grace from the Deptford life? So I was a pauper in a part of life where she had always been wrapped in plenty.

'I was on friendly terms, with proper allowance for the disparity in our ages and importance to the company, by the time we had journeyed across Canada and played Vancouver over Christmas. We were playing two weeks at the Imperial; the holiday fell on the middle Sunday of our fortnight that year, and Sir John and Milady entertained the whole company to dinner at their hotel. It was the first time I had ever eaten a Christmas dinner, though during the previous twenty-three years I suppose I must have taken some sort of nourishment on the twenty-fifth of December, and it was the first time I had ever been in a private dining-room in a first-class hotel.

'It seemed elegant and splendid to me, and the surprise of the evening was that there was a Christmas gift for everybody. They were vanity things and manicure sets and scarves and whatnot for the girls, and the men had those big boxes of cigarettes that one never sees any more and notecases and all the range of impersonal but pleasant stuff you would expect. But I had a bulky parcel, and it was a complete Shakespeare – one of those copies illustrated with photographs of actors in their best roles; this one had a coloured frontispiece of Sir John as Hamlet, looking extremely like me, and across it he had written, "A double blessing is a double grace – Christmas Greetings, John Tresize." Everybody wanted to see it, and the company was about equally divided between those who thought Sir John was a darling to have done that for a humble member of his troupe, and those who thought I must be gaining a power that was above my station; the latter group did not say anything, but their feelings could be deduced from the perfection of their silence.

'I was in doubt about what I should do, because it was the first time in my life that anybody had ever given me anything; I had earned things, and stolen things, but I had never been given anything before and I was embarrassed, suspicious, and clumsy in my new role.

'Milady was behind it, of course, and perhaps she expected me to bury myself in the book that night, and emerge, transformed by poetry and drama, a wholly translated Mungo Fetch. The truth is that I had a nibble at it, and read a few pages of the first play in the book, which was *The Tempest*, and couldn't make head nor tail of it. There was a shipwreck, and then an old chap beefing to his daughter about some incomprehensible grievance in the past, and it was not my line at all, and I gave up.

'Milady was too well bred ever to question me about it, and when we were next alone I managed to say some words of gratitude, and I don't know whether she ever knew that Shakespeare and I had not hit it off. But the gift was very far from being a dead loss: in the first place it was a gift, and the first to come my way; in the second it was a sign of something much akin to love, even if the love went no further than the benevolence of two people with a high sense of obligation to their dependants and colleagues, down to the humblest. So the book became something more than an unreadable volume; it was a talisman, and I cherished it and gave it an importance among my belongings that was quite different from what it was meant to be. If it had been a book of spells, and I a sorcerer's apprentice who was afraid to use it, I could not have held it in greater reverence. It contained something that was of immeasurable value to the Tresizes, and I cherished it for that. I never learned anything about Shakespeare, and on the two or three occasions when I have seen Shakespearean plays in my life they have puzzled and bored me as much as *The Tempest*, but my superstitious veneration of that book has never failed, and I have it still.

'There's evidence, if you need it, that I am not really a theatre person. I am an illusionist, which is a different and probably a lesser creature. I proved it that night. After the dinner and the gifts, we had an impromptu entertainment, a very mixed bag. Audrey Sevenhowes danced the Charleston, and did it very well; C. Pengelly Spickernell sang two or three songs, vaguely related to Christmas, and Home, and England. Grover Paskin sang a comic song about an old man who had a fat sow, and we all joined in making pig-noises on cue. I did a few tricks, and was the success of the evening.

'Combined with the special gift, that put me even more to the bad with the members of the company who were always looking for hidden meanings and covert grabs for power. My top trick was when I borrowed Milady's Spanish shawl and produced from beneath it the large bouquet the company had clubbed together to give her; as I did it standing in the middle of the room, with no apparent place to conceal anything at all, not to speak of a thing the size of a rosebush, it was neatly done, but as sometimes happens with illusions, it won almost as much mistrust as applause. I know why. I had not at that time grasped the essential fact that an illusionist must never seem to be pleased with his own cleverness, and I suppose I strutted a bit.

The Cantab and Sevenhowes and Charlton and Woulds sometimes spoke of me as The Outsider, and that is precisely what I was. I don't regret it now. I've lived an Outsider's life, though not in quite the way they meant; I was outside something beyond their comprehension.

'That was an ill-fated evening, as we discovered on the following day. There was champagne, and Morton W. Penfold, who was with us, gained heroic stature for finding it in what the English regarded as a desert. Everybody drank as much as they could get, and there were toasts, and these were Sir John's downfall. The Spartan regime of a gouty man was always a burden to him, and he didn't see why he should drink whisky when everybody else was drinking the wine he loved best. He proposed a toast to The Profession, and told stories about Irving; it called for several glasses, though not really a lot, and before morning he was very ill. A doctor came, and saw that there was more than gout wrong with him. It was an inflamed appendix, and it had to come out at once.

'Not a great calamity for most people, even though such an operation wasn't as simple then as it is now, but it was serious for a star actor, half-way through a long tour. He would be off the stage for not less than three weeks.

'Sir John's illness brought out the best and the worst in his company. All the old hands, and the people with a thoroughly professional attitude, rallied round at once, with all their abilities at top force. Holroyd called a rehearsal for ten o'clock Monday morning, and Gordon Barnard, who was our second lead, sailed through *Scaramouche* brilliantly; he was very different from Sir John, as a six-foot-two actor of the twentieth century must be different from a five-foot-two actor who is still in the nineteenth, but there was no worry whatever about him. Darton Flesher, who had to step into Barnard's part, needed a good deal of help, solid man though he was. But then somebody had to fill in for Flesher, and that was your friend Leonard Woulds, Roly, who proved not to know the lines which, as an understudy, he should have had cold. So it was a busy day.

'Busy for Morton W. Penfold, who had to tell the papers what had happened, and get the news on the Canadian Press wire, and generally turn a misfortune into some semblance of publicity.

Busy for Felicity Larcombe, who showed herself a first-rate person as well as a first-rate actress; she undertook to keep an eye on Milady, so far as anyone could, because Milady was in a state. Busy also for Gwenda Lewis, who was a dull actress and silly about her dull husband, Jim Hailey; but Gwenda had been a nurse before she went on the stage, and she helped Felicity to keep Milady in trim to act that evening. Busy for old Frank Moore and Macgregor, who both spread calm and assurance through the company – you know how easily a company can be rattled – and lent courage where it was wanted.

'The consequence was that that night we played *Scaramouche* very well, to a capacity audience, and did excellent business until it was time for us to leave Vancouver. The only hitch, which both the papers mentioned humorously, was that when Scaramouche walked the tightrope, it looked as if Sir John had mischievously broken out of the hospital and taken the stage. But there was nothing anybody could do about that, though I did what I could by wearing my red mask.

'It seemed as though the public were determined to help us through our troubles, because we played to full houses all week. Whenever Milady made her first entrance, there was warm applause, and this was a change indeed, because usually Morton W. Penfold had to arrange for the local theatre manager to be in the house at that time to start the obligatory round when she came on. Indeed, by the end of the week, Penfold was able to circulate a funny story to the papers that Sir John had announced from his hospital bed that it was obvious that the most profitable thing a visiting star could do was to go to bed and send his understudy on in his place. Dangerous publicity, but it worked.

'So everything appeared to be in good order, except that we had to defer polishing up *The Lyons Mail*, which we had intended to put into the repertory instead of *The Corsican Brothers* for our return journey across Canada.

'Not everything was satisfactory, however, because the Sevenhowes, Charlton, and Woulds faction were making mischief. Not very serious mischief in the theatre, because Holroyd would not have put up with that, but personal mischief in the company was much more difficult to check. They tried sucking up to

Gordon Barnard, who was now the leading man, telling him how much easier it was to act with him than with Sir John. Barnard wouldn't have any of that, because he was a decent fellow, and he knew his own shortcomings. One of these was that in *The Master* and *Scaramouche* we used a certain number of extras, and these inexperienced people tended to look wooden on the stage unless they were jollied, or harried, into more activity than they could generate by themselves; Sir John was an expert jollier and harrier – as I understand Irving also was – and he had his own ways of hissing remarks and encouragement to these inexperienced people that kept them up to the mark; Barnard couldn't manage it, because when he hissed the extras immediately froze in their places, and looked at him in terror. Just a question of personality, but there it was; he was a good actor, but a poor inspirer. When this happened, Charlton and Woulds laughed, sometimes so that the audience could see them, and Macgregor had to speak to them about it.

'They also made life hard for poor old C. Pengelly Spickernell, in ways that only actors understand; when they were on stage with him, they would contrive to be in his way when he had to make a move, and in a few seconds the whole stage picture was a little askew, and it looked as if it were his fault; also, in *Scaramouche*, where he played one of the Commedia dell' Arte figures, and wore a long, dragging cloak, one or other of them would contrive to be standing on the end of it when he had a move to make, pinning him to the spot; it was only necessary for them to do this two or three times to put him in terror lest it should happen every time, and he was a man with no ability to defend himself against such harassment.

'They were ugly to Gwenda Lewis, overrunning her very few cues, but Jim Hailey settled that by going to their dressing-room and talking it over with them in language he had learned when he had been in the Navy. Trivial things, but enough to make needless trouble, because a theatrical production is a mechanism of exquisitely calculated details. On tour it was useless to threaten them with dismissal, because they could not be re-placed, and although there was a tariff of company fines for unprofessional conduct it was hard for Macgregor to catch them red-handed.

'Their great triumph had nothing to do with performance, but with the private life of the company. I fear this will embarrass you, Roly, but I think it has to be told. The great passion the Cantab felt for Audrey Sevenhowes was everybody's business; love and a cough cannot be hid, as the proverb says. I don't think Audrey was really an ill-disposed girl, but her temperament was that of a flirt of a special order; such girls used to be called cock-teasers; she liked to have somebody mad about her, without being obliged to do anything about it. She saw herself, I suppose, as lovely Audrey, who could not be blamed for the consequences of her fatal attraction. I am pretty sure she did not know what was going on, but Charlton and Woulds began a campaign to bring that affair to the boil; they filled the Cantab full of the notion that he must enjoy the favours of Miss Sevenhowes to the fullest – in the expression they used, he must "tear off a branch" with Audrey – or lose all claim to manhood. This put the Cantab into a sad state of self-doubt, because he had never torn off a branch with anybody, and they assured him that he mustn't try to begin with the Sevenhowes, as he might expose himself as a novice, and become an object of ridicule. Might make a Horlicks of it, in fact. They bustled the poor boob into thinking that he must have a crash course in the arts of love, as a preparation for his great conquest; they would help him in this educational venture.

'It would have been nothing more than rather nasty joking and manipulation of a simpleton if they had kept their mouths shut, but of course that was not their way. I disliked them greatly at that time, but since then I have met many people of their kind, and I know them to be much more conceited and stupid than really cruel. They both fancied themselves as lady-killers, and such people are rarely worse than fools.

'They babbled all they were up to around the company; they chattered to Eric Foss, who was about their own age, but a different sort of chap; they let Eugene Fitzwarren in on their plan, because he looked worldly and villainous, and they were too stupid to know that he was a past president of the Anglican Stage Guild and a great worker on behalf of the Actors' Orphanage, and altogether a highly moral character. So very soon everybody in the company knew about it, and thought it a shame, but didn't know precisely what to do to stop the nonsense.

'It was agreed that there was no use talking to the Cantab, who wasn't inclined to take advice from anybody who could have given him advice worth having. It was also pretty widely felt that interfering with a young man's sexual initiation was rather an Old Aunty sort of thing to do, and that they had better let nature take its course. The Cantab must tear off a branch some time; even C. Pengelly Spickernell agreed to that; and if he was fool enough to be manipulated by a couple of cads, whose job was it to protect him?

'It became clear in the end that Mungo Fetch was elected to protect him, though only in a limited sense. – No, Roly, you can't possibly want to go to the loo again. You'd better sit down and hear this out. – The great worriers about the Cantab were Holroyd and Macgregor, and they were worrying on behalf of Sir John and Milady. Not that the Tresizes knew about the great plot to deprive the Cantab of his virginity; Sir John would have dealt with the matter summarily, but he was in hospital in Vancouver, and Milady was much bereft by his absence and telephoned to the hospital wherever we were. But Macgregor and Holroyd felt that this tasteless practical joke somehow reflected on those two, whom they admired wholeheartedly, and whose devotion to each other established a standard of sexual behaviour for the company that must be respected, if not fully maintained.

'Holroyd kept pointing out to Macgregor that the Cantab was in a special way a charge delivered over to Sir John by his Mum, and that it was therefore incumbent on the company as a whole – or the sane part of it, he said – to watch over the Cantab while Sir John and Milady were unable to do so. Macgregor agreed, and added Calvinist embroideries to the theme; he was no great friend to sex, and I think he held it against the Creator that the race could not be continued without some recourse to it; but he felt that such recourse should be infrequent, hallowed by church and law, and divorced as far as possible from pleasure. It seems odd, looking back, that nobody felt any concern about Audrey Sevenhowes; some people assumed that she was in on the joke, and the others were confident she could take care of herself.

'Charlton and Woulds laid their plan with gloating attention to detail. Charlton explained to the Cantab, and to any man who happened to be near, that women are particularly open to seduction in the week just preceding the onset of their menstrual period; during this time, he said, they simply ravened for intercourse. Furthermore, they had to be approached in the right way; nothing coarsely direct, no grabbing at the bosom or anything of that sort, but a psychologically determined application of a particular caress; this was a firm, but not rough, placing of the hand on the waist, on the right side, just below the ribs; the hand should be as warm as possible, and this could easily be achieved by keeping it in the trousers pocket for a few moments before the approach. This was supposed to impart special, irresistible warmth to the female liver; Liesl tells me it is a very old belief.'

'I think Galen mentions it,' said Liesl, 'and like so much of Galen, it is just silly.'

'Charlton considered himself an expert at detecting the menstrual state of women, and he had had his eye on Miss Sevenhowes; she would be ripe and ready to fall when we were in Moose Jaw, and therefore the last place in which the Cantab could achieve full manhood would be Medicine Hat. He approached Morton W. Penfold for information about the altars to Aphrodite in Medicine Hat, and was informed that, so far as the advance agent knew, they were few and of a Spartan simplicity. Penfold advised against the whole plan; if that was the kind of thing they wanted, they had better put it on ice till they got to Toronto. Anyhow he wanted no part of it. But Charlton and Woulds had no inclination to let their great plan rest until after Sir John had rejoined the company, for though they mocked him, they feared him.

'They played on the only discernible weakness in the strong character of Morton W. Penfold. His whole reputation, Charlton pointed out, rested on his known ability to supply anything, arrange anything, and do anything that a visiting theatrical company might want in Canada; here they were, asking simply for an address, and he couldn't supply it. They weren't asking him to take the Cantab to a bawdy-house, wait, and escort him home again; they just wanted to know where a bawdy-house might be found. Penfold was touched in his vanity. He made some inquiries among the locomotive crew, and returned with the address of a Mrs Quiller in Medicine Hat, who was known to have obliging nieces.

'We were playing a split week, of which Thursday, Friday, and Saturday were spent in Medicine Hat. On Thursday, with Charlton and Woulds at his elbow, the Cantab telephoned Mrs Quiller. She had no idea what he was talking about, and anyways she never did business over the phone. Might he drop in on Friday night? It all depended; was he one of them actors? Yes, he was. Well, if he come on Friday night she supposed she'd be t'home but she made no promises. Was he comin' alone? Yes, he would be alone.

'All day Friday the Cantab looked rather green, and Charlton and Woulds stuck to him like a couple of bridesmaids, giving any advice that happened to come into their heads. At half past five Holroyd sent for me in the theatre, and I found him in the tiny stage-manager's office, with Macgregor and Morton W. Penfold. "I suppose you know what's on tonight?" said he. "*Scaramouche*, surely?" I said. "Don't be funny with me, boy," said Holroyd; "you know what I mean." "Yes, I think I do," said I. "Then I want you to watch young Ingestree after the play, and follow him, and stay as close to him as you can without being seen, and don't leave him till he's back in his hotel." "I don't know how I'm going to do that –" I began, but Holroyd wasn't having it. "Yes, you do," he said; "there's nothing green about you, and I want you to do this for the company; nothing is to happen to that boy, do you understand?" "But he's going with the full intention of having something happen to him," I said; "you don't expect me to hold off the girls with a gun, do you?" "I just want you to see that he doesn't get robbed, or beaten up, or anything worse than what he's going for," said Holroyd. "Oh, Nature, Nature, what an auld bitch ye are!" said Macgregor, who was taking all this very heavily.

'I thought I had better get out before I laughed in their faces; Holroyd and Macgregor were like a couple of old maids. But Morton W. Penfold knew what was what. "Here's ten dollars," he said; "I hear it's the only visiting card Old Ma Quiller understands; tell her you're there to keep an eye on young Ingestree, but you mustn't be seen; in her business I suppose she gets used to queer requests and odd provisos." I took it, and left them, and went off for a good laugh by myself. This was my first assignment as guardian angel.

'All things considered, everything went smoothly. After the play I left Macgregor to do some of my tidy-up work himself, and followed the Cantab after he had been given a back-slapping send-off by Charlton and Woulds. He didn't walk very fast, though it was a cold January night, and Medicine Hat is a cold town. After a while he turned in to an unremarkable-looking house, and after some inquiries at the door he vanished inside. I chatted for a few minutes with an old fellow in a tuque and mackinaw who was shovelling away an evening snowfall, then I knocked at the door myself.

'Mrs Quiller answered in person, and though she was not the first madam I had seen – now and then one of the sisterhood would appear in search of Charlie, who had a bad habit of forgetting to settle his bills – she was certainly the least remarkable. I am always amused when madams in plays and films appear as wonderful, salty characters, full of hard-won wisdom and overflowing, compassionate understanding. Damned old twisters, any I've ever seen. Mrs Quiller might have been any suburban housewife, with a dyed perm and bifocal specs. I asked if I could speak to her privately, and waggled the ten-spot, and followed her into her living-room. I explained what I had come for, and the necessity that I was not to be seen; I was just someone who had been sent by friends of Mr Ingestree to see that he got home safely. "I getcha," said Mrs Quiller; "the way that guy carries on, I think he needs a guardeen."

'I settled down in the kitchen with Mrs Quiller, and accepted a cup of tea and some soda crackers – her nightly snack, she explained – and we talked very comfortably about the theatre. After a while we were joined by the old snow-shoveller, who said nothing, and devoted himself to a stinking cigar. She was not a theatre-goer herself, Mrs Quiller said – too busy at night for that; but she liked a good fillum. The last one she seen was *Laugh, Clown, Laugh* with Lon Chaney in it, and this girl Loretta Young. Now there was a sweet fillum, but it give you a terrible idea of the troubles of people in show business, and did I think it was true to life? I said I thought it was as true as anything dared to be, but the trials of people in the theatre were so many and harrowing that the public would never believe them if they were shown as they really were. That touched the spot with Mrs Quiller, and we had a fine discussion about the surprises and vicissitudes life brought to just about everybody, which lasted some time.

'Then Mrs Quiller grew restless. "I wonder what's happened to that friend of yours," she said; "he's takin' an awful long time." I wondered, too, but I thought it better not to make any guesses. It was not long till another woman came into the kitchen; I would have judged her to be in her early hard-living thirties, and she had never been a beauty; she had an unbecoming Japanese kimono clutched around her, and her feet were in slippers to which remnants of maribou still clung. She looked at me with suspicion. "It's okay," said Mrs Quiller, "this fella's the guardeen. Anything wrong, Lil?" "Jeez, I never seen such a guy," said Lil; "nothin' doing yet. He just lays there with the droops, laughin', and talkin'. I never heard such a guy. He keeps sayin' it's all so ridiculous, and would I believe he'd once been a member of some Marlowe Society or something. What are they, anyway? A bunch o' queers? But anyways I'm sick of it. He's ruining my self-confidence. Is Pauline in yet? Maybe she could do something with him."

'Mrs Quiller obviously had great qualities of generalship. She turned to me. "Unless you got any suggestions, I'm goin' to give him the bum's rush," she said. "When he come in I thought, his heart's not in it. What do you say?" I said I thought she had summed up the situation perfectly. "Then you go back up there, Lil, and tell him to come back when he feels better," said Mrs Quiller. "Don't shame him none, but get rid of him. And no refund, you understand."

'So that was how it was. Shortly afterward I crept from Mrs Quiller's back door, and followed the desponding Cantab back to his hotel. I don't know what he told Charlton and Woulds, but they hadn't much to say to him from then on. The odd thing was that Audrey Sevenhowes was quite nice to him for the rest of the tour. Not in a teasing way – or with as little tease as she could manage – but just friendly. A curious story, but not uncommon, would you say, gentlemen?'

'I say it's time we all had a drink, and dinner,' said Liesl. She took the arm of the silent Ingestree and sat him at the table beside herself, and we were all especially pleasant to him, except Magnus who, having trampled his old enemy into the dirt, seemed a happier man and, in some strange way, cleansed. It was as if he were a scorpion, which had discharged its venom, and was frisky and playful in consequence. I taxed him with it as we left the dinner table.

'How could you,' I said. 'Ingestree is a harmless creature, surely? He has done some good work. Many people would call him a distinguished man, and a very nice fellow.'

Magnus patted my arm and laughed. It was a low laugh, and a queer one. Merlin's laugh, if ever I heard it.

7

EISENGRIM was altogether in high spirits, and showed no fatigue from his afternoon's talking. He pretended to be solicitous about the rest of us, however, and particularly about Lind and Kinghovn. Did they really wish to continue with his narrative? Did they truly think what he had to say offered any helpful subtext to the film about Robert-Houdin? Indeed, as the film was now complete, of what possible use could a subtext be?

'Of the utmost possible use when next I make a film,' said Jurgen Lind. 'These divergences between the acceptable romance of life and the clumsily fashioned, disproportioned reality are part of my stock-in-trade. Here you have it, in your tale of Sir John's tour of Canada; he took highly burnished romance to a people whose life was lived on a different plateau, and the discomforts of his own life and the lives of his troupe were on other levels. How reconcile the three?'

'Light,' said Kinghovn. 'You do it with light. The romance of the plays is theatre-light; the different romance of the company is the queer train-light Magnus has described; think what could be done, with that flashing strobe-light effect you get when a train passes another and everything seems to flicker and lose substance. And the light of the Canadians would be that hard, bright light you find in northern lands. Leave it to me to handle

all three lights in such a way that they are a va
theme of light, instead of just three kinds of light, and
trick for you, Jurgen.'

'I doubt if you can do it simply in terms of appearances,' s
Lind.

'I didn't say you could. But you certainly can't do it without
a careful attention to appearances, or you'll have no romance
of any kind. Remember what Magnus says: without attention to
detail you will have no illusion, and illusion's what you're aiming at, isn't it?'

'I had rather thought I was aiming at truth, or some tiny
corner of it,' said Lind.

'Truth!' said Kinghovn. 'What kind of talk is that for a sane
man? What truth have we been getting all afternoon? I don't
suppose Magnus thinks he's been telling us the truth. He's giving
us a mass of detail, and I don't doubt that every word he says is
true in itself, but to call that truth is ridiculous even for a
philosopher of film like you, Jurgen. What's he been doing to
poor old Roly? He's cast him as the clown of the show –
mother's boy, pompous Varsity ass, snob, and sexual non-starter
– and I'm sure it's all true, but what has it to do with our Roly?
The man you and I work with and lean on? The thoroughly
capable administrator, literary man, and smoother-of-the-way?
Eh?'

'Thank you for these few kind words, Harry,' said Ingestree.
'You save me the embarrassment of saying them myself. Don't
suppose I bear any malice. Indeed, if I may make a claim for my
admittedly imperfect character, it is that I have never been a
malicious man. I accept what Magnus says. He has described
me as I no doubt appeared to him. And I haven't scrupled to let
you know that so far as I was concerned he was an obnoxious
little squirt and climber. That's how I would describe him if I
were writing my autobiography, which I may do, one of these
days. But what's an autobiography? Surely it's a romance of
which one is oneself the hero. Otherwise why write the thing?
Perhaps you give yourself a rather shopworn character, like
Rousseau, or H. G. Wells, and it's just another way of making
yourself interesting. But Mungo Fetch and the Cantab belong to
the drama of the past; it's forty years since they trod the boards.

ple now. Magnus is a great illusionist
after time, a great actor : I'm what you
Harry. So let's not fuss about it.'

sfied. 'You don't believe, then,' said he,
and total of all his actions, from birth to
Dunny believes, and he's our Sorgenfrei
s. I think that's what I believe, too. Squirt
d summing-up of whatever you were able
when first we met, Roly. I'm prepared to
stand by it, en your autobiography comes out I shall look
for myself in the Index under S and C: "Squirts I have known,
Mungo Fetch", and "Climbers I have encountered, Fetch, M.".
We must all play as cast, as my contract with Sir John put it. As
for truth, I suppose we have to be content with the constant
revisions of history. Though there is the odd inescapable fact,
and I still have one or two of those to impart, if you want me to
go on.'

They wanted him to go on. The after-dinner cognac was on
the table and I made it my job to see that everyone had enough.
After all, I was paying my share of the costs, and I might as well
cast myself as host, so far as lay in my power. God knows, that
piece of casting would be undisputed when the bill was presented.

'As we made the return journey across Canada, a change took
place in the spirit of the company,' said Magnus; 'going West it
was all adventure and new experiences, and the country embraced us; as soon as we turned round at Vancouver it was going
home, and much that was Canadian was unfavourably compared with the nests in the suburbs of London toward which
many of the company were yearning. The Haileys talked even
more about their son, and their grave worry that if they didn't
get him into a better school he would grow up handicapped by
an undesirable accent. Charlton and Woulds were hankering for
restaurants better than the places, most of them run by Chinese,
we found in the West. Grover Paskin and Frank Moore talked
learnedly of great pubs they knew, and of the foreign fizziness
of Canadian beer. Audrey Sevenhowes, having squeezed the
Cantab, threw him away and devoted herself seriously to subduing Eric Foss. During our journey West we had seen the

dramatic shortening of the days which has such ominous beauty in northern countries, and which I loved; now we saw the daylight lengthen, and it seemed to be part of our homeward journey; we had gone into the darkness and now we were heading back toward the light, and every night, as we went into those queer little stage doors, the naked bulb that shone above them seemed less needful.

'The foreignness of Canada semed to abate a little at every sunset, but it was not wholly gone. When we played Regina for a week there was one memorable night when five Blackfoot Indian chiefs, asserting their right as tribal brothers of Sir John, sat as his guests in the left-hand stage box : it was rum, I can tell you, playing *Scaramouche* with those motionless figures, all of them in blankets, watching everything with unwinking, jetty black eyes. What did they make of it? God knows. Or perhaps Sir John had some inkling, because Morton W. Penfold arranged that he should meet them in an interval, when there was an exchange of gifts, and pictures were taken. But I doubt if the French Revolution figured largely in their scheme of things. Milady said they loved oratory, and perhaps they were proud of Soksi-Poyina as he harangued the aristocrats so eloquently.

'Sir John had rejoined us by that time, and it was a shock when he appeared in our midst, for his hair had turned almost entirely grey during his time in the hospital. Perhaps he had touched it up before then, and the dye had run its course; he never attempted to return it to its original dark brown, and although the grey became him, he looked much older, and in private life he was slower and wearier. Not so on the stage. There he was as graceful and light-footed as ever, but there was something macabre about his youthfulness, in my eyes, at least. With his return the feeling of the company changed; we had supported Gordon Barnard with all our hearts, but now we felt that the ruler had returned to his kingdom; the lamp of romance burned with a different flame – a return, perhaps, to gaslight, after some effective but comparatively charmless electricity.

'I had a feeling, too, that the critics changed their attitude toward us on the homeward journey, and it was particularly evident in Toronto. The important four were in their seats, as usual : the man who looked like Edward VII from *Saturday*

Night; the stout little man, rumoured to be a Theosophist, from the *Globe*; the smiling little fellow in pince-nez from the *Telegram*; and the ravaged Norseman who wrote incomprehensible rhapsodies for the *Star*. They were friendly (except Edward VII, who was jocose about Milady), but they would persist in remembering Irving (whether they had ever actually seen him, or not), and that bothered the younger actors. Bothered Morton W. Penfold, too, who mumbled to Holroyd that perhaps the old man would be wise to think about retirement.

'The audiences came in sufficient numbers, and were warm in their applause, particularly when we played *The Lyons Mail*. It was another of the dual roles in which Sir John delighted, and so did I, because it gave me a new chance to double. If Roly had been looking for it, he would have found the seed of his Jekyll and Hyde play here, for it was a play in which, as the good Leserques, Sir John was all nobility and candour, and then, seconds later, lurched on the stage as the drunken murderer Dubosc, chewing a straw and playing with a knobbed cudgel. There was one moment in that play that never failed to chill me: it was when Dubosc had killed the driver of the mail coach, and leaned over the body, rifling the pockets; as he did it, Sir John whistled the "Marseillaise" through his teeth, not loudly, but with such terrible high spirits that it summoned up, in a few seconds, a world of heartless, demonic criminality. But even I, enchanted as I was, could understand that this sort of thing, in this form, could not last long on the stage that Noel Coward had made his own. It was acting of a high order, but it was out of time. It still had magic here in Canada, not because the people were unsophisticated (on the whole they were as acute as English audiences in the provinces) but because, in a way I cannot explain, it was speaking to a core of loneliness and deprivation in these Canadians of which they were only faintly aware. I think it was loneliness, not just for England, because so many of these people on the prairies were not of English origin, but for some faraway and long-lost Europe. The Canadians knew themselves to be strangers in their own land, without being at home anywhere else.

'So, night by night, Canada relinquished its hold on us, and day by day we became weary, not perhaps of one another, but of our colleagues' unvarying heavy overcoats and too familiar pieces of luggage; what had been the romance of long hops going West – striking the set, seeing the trucks loaded at the theatre and unloaded onto the train, climbing aboard dead tired at three o'clock in the morning, and finding berths in the dimmed, heavily curtained sleeping-car – grew to be tedious. Another kind of excitement, the excitement of going home, possessed us, and although we were much too professional a company to get out of hand, we played with a special gloss during our final two weeks in Montreal. Then aboard ship, a farewell telegram to Sir John and Milady from Mr Mackenzie King (who semed to be a great friend of the theatre, though outwardly a most untheatrical man), and off to England by the first sailing after the ice was out of the harbour.

'I had changed substantially during the tour. I was learning to dress like Sir John, which was eccentric enough in a young man, but at least not vulgar in style. I was beginning to speak like him, and as is common with beginners, I was overdoing it. I was losing, ever so little, my strong sense that every man's hand was against me, and my hand against every man. I had encountered my native land again, and was reconciled to all of it except Deptford. We passed through Deptford during the latter part of our tour, on a hop between Windsor and London : I found out from the conductor of the train that we would stop to take on water for the engine there, and that the pause would be short, but sufficient for my purpose; as we chugged past the gravel pit beside the railway line I was poised on the steps at the back of the train, and as we pulled in to the station, so small and so familiar, I swung down onto the platform and surveyed all that was to be seen of the village.

'I could look down most of the length of our main street. I recognized a few buildings and saw the spires of the five churches – Baptist, Methodist, Presbyterian, Anglican, and Catholic – among the leafless trees. Solemnly, I spat. Then I went behind the train to the siding where, so many years ago, Willard had imprisoned me in Abdullah, and there I spat again. Spitting is not a ceremonious action, but I crowded it with loathing, and when I climbed back on the train I felt immeasurably better. I had not settled any scores, or altered my feelings, but I had done something of importance. Nobody knew it, but Paul Dempster had visited his childhood home. I have never returned.

'Back to England, and another long period of hand-to-mouth life for me. Sir John wanted a rest, and Milady had the long trial of waiting for her eyes to be ready for an operation – they called it "ripening" in cases of cataracts then – and the operation itself, which was successful in that it made it possible for her to see with thick, disfiguring lenses that were a hum____ation for a woman who still thought of herself as a leading actress. Mac-gregor decided to retire, which was reasonable but made a gap in the organization on which Sir John depended. Holroyd was a thoroughgoing pro, and could get a good job anywhere, and I think he saw farther than either Sir John or Milady, because he went to Stratford-on-Avon and stayed at the Memorial Theatre until he too retired. Nothing came of the Jekyll and Hyde play, though I know the Tresizes tinkered with the scenario for years, as an amusement. But they were comfortably off for money – rich, by some standards – and they could settle down happily in their suburban home, which had a big garden, and amuse them-selves with the antiques that gave them so much delight. I visited them there often, because they kept a kind interest in me, and helped me as much as they were able. But their influence in the theatre was not great; indeed, a recommendation from them took on a queer look in the hands of a young man, because to so many of the important employers of actors in the London theatre in the mid-thirties they belonged to a remote past.

'Indeed, they never appeared at the head of a company again. Sir John had one splendid appearance in a play by a writer who had been a great figure in the theatre before and just after the First World War, but his time, too, had passed; his play suffered greatly from his own illness and some justifiable but prolonged caprice on the part of the star players. Sir John was very special in that play, and he was given fine notices by the press, but nothing could conceal the fact that he was not the undoubted star, but "distinguished support in a role which could not have been realized with the same certainty of touch and golden splendour of personality by any other actor of our time" – so James Agate said, and everybody agreed.

'There was one very bad day toward the end of his life which,

I know, opened the way for his death. In the autumn of 1937, when people were thinking of more immediately pressing things, some theatre people were thinking that the centenary of the birth of Henry Irving should not pass unnoticed. They arranged an all-star matinee, in which tribute to the great actor should be paid, and as many as possible of the great theatre folk of the day should appear in scenes selected from the famous plays of his repertoire. It should be given at his old theatre, the Lyceum, as near as possible to his birthday, which was February 6 in the following year.

'Have you ever had anything to do with such an affair? The idea is so splendid, the sentiment so admirable, that it is disillusioning to discover what a weight of tedious and seemingly unnecessary diplomacy must go into its arrangement. Getting the stars to say with certainty that they will appear is only the beginning of it; marshalling the necessary stage-settings, arranging rehearsals, and publicizing the performance, without ruinously disproportionate expense, is the bulk of the work, and I understand that an excellent committee did it with exemplary patience. But inevitably there were muddles, and in the first enthusiasm many more people were asked to appear than could possibly have been crowded on any stage, even if the matinee had been allowed to go on for six or seven hours.

'Quite reasonably, one of the first people to be asked for his services was Sir John, because he was the last actor of first-rate importance still living who had been trained under Irving. He agreed that he would be present, but then, prompted by God knows what evil spirit of vanity, he began to make conditions: he would appear, and he would speak a tribute to Irving if the Poet Laureate would write one. The committee demurred, and the Poet Laureate was not approached. So Sir John, with the bit between his teeth, approached the Poet Laureate himself, and the Poet Laureate said he would have to think about it. He thought for six weeks, and then, in response to another letter from Sir John, said he didn't see his way clear to doing it.

'Sir John communicated this news to the committee, who had meanwhile gone on with other plans, and they did not reply because, I suppose, they were up to their eyes in complicated arrangements which they had to carry through in the spare time of their busy lives. Sir John, meanwhile, urged an ancient poet of his acquaintance, who had been a very minor figure in the literary world before the First World War, to write the poetic tribute. The ancient poet, whose name was Urban Frawley, thought a villanelle would do nicely. Sir John thought something more stately was called for; his passion for playing the literary Meddlesome Mattie was aroused, and he and the ancient poet had many a happy hour, wrangling about the form the tribute should take. There was also the great question about what Sir John should wear, when delivering it. He finally decided on some robes he had worn not less than twenty-five years earlier, in a play by Maeterlinck; like everything else in his wardrobe it had been carefully stored, and when Holroyd had been summoned from Stratford to find it, it was in good condition, and needed only pressing and some loving care to make it very handsome. This valet work became my job, and in all I made three journeys to Richmond, where the Tresizes lived, to attend to it. Everything seemed to be going splendidly, and only I worried about the fact that nothing had been heard from the committee for a long time.

'There was less than a week to go before the matinee when at last I persuaded Sir John that something must be done to make sure that he had been included in the programme. This was tactless, and he gave me a polite dressing-down for supposing that when Irving was being honoured, his colleagues would be so remiss as to forget Irving's unquestioned successor. I was not so confident, because since the tour I had mingled a little with theatre people, and had learned that there were other pretenders to Irving's crown, and that Sir Johnston Forbes-Robertson and Sir Frank Benson had been spoken of in this regard, and Benson was still living. I took my scolding meekly, and went right on urging him not to leave things to chance. So, rather in the spirit of the Master of Ballantrae giving orders to the pirates, he telephoned the secretary of the committee, and talked, not to him, but to his anonymous assistant.

'Sir John told him he was calling simply to say that he would be on hand for the matinee, as he had been invited to do some months before; that he would declaim the tribute to Irving which had been specially written by that favoured child of the

Muses, Urban Frawley; that he would not arrive at the theatre until half past four, and he would arrive in costume, as he knew the backstage resources of the theatre would be crowded, and nothing was further from his mind than to create any difficulty by requiring the star dressing-room. All of this was delivered in the jocular but imperative mode that was his rehearsal speciality, with much "eh" and "quonk" to make it sound friendly. The secretary's secretary apparently gave satisfactory replies, because when Sir John had finished his call he looked at me slyly, as if I were a silly lad who didn't understand how such things were done.

'It was agreed that I should drive him to the theatre, because he might want assistance in arranging his robes, and although he had an old and trusted chauffeur, the man had no skill as a dresser. So, with lots of time to spare, I helped him into the back seat in his heavy outfit of velvet and fur, climbed into the driver's place, and off we went. It was one of those extremely class-conscious old limousines; Sir John, in the back, sat on fine whipcord, and I, in front, sat on leather that was as cold as death; we were separated by a heavy glass partition, but from time to time he spoke to me through the speaking tube, and his mood was triumphal.

'Dear old man! He was going to pay tribute to Irving, and there was nobody else in the world who could do it with a better right, or more reverent affection. It was a glory-day for him, and I was anxious that nothing should go wrong.

'As it did, of course. We pulled up at the stage door of the Lyceum, and I went in and told the attendant that Sir John had arrived. He wasn't one of your proper old stage doormen, but a young fellow who took himself very seriously, and had a sheaf of papers naming the people he was authorized to admit. No Sir John Tresize was on the list. He showed it to me, in support of his downright refusal. I protested. He stuck his head out of the door and looked at our limousine, and made off through the passage that led to the stage, and I stuck close to him. He approached an elegant figure whom I knew to be one of the most eminent of the younger actor-knights and hissed, "There's an old geezer outside dressed as Nero who says he's to appear; will you speak to him, sir?" I intervened; "It's Sir John Tresize,"

I said, "and it was arranged that he was to speak an Epilogue – a tribute to Irving." The eminent actor-knight went rather pale under his make-up (he was rigged out as Hamlet) and asked for details, which I supplied. The eminent actor-knight cursed with brilliant invention for a few seconds, and beckoned me to the corridor. I went, but not before I was able to identify the sounds that were coming from the stage as a passage from *The Lyons Mail*; the rhythm, the tune of what I heard was all wrong, too colloquial, too matter-of-fact.

'We made our way back to the stage door, and the eminent actor-knight darted across the pavement, leapt into the limousine beside Sir John, and began to talk to him urgently. I would have given a great deal to hear what was said, but I could only catch scraps of it from where I sat in the driver's seat. "Dreadful state of confusion ... can't imagine what the organization of such an affair entails ... would not for the world have slighted so great a man of the theatre and the most eminent successor of Irving ... but when the proposal to the Poet Laureate fell through all communication had seemed to stop ... nothing further had been heard ... no, there had been no message during the past week or something would certainly have been done to alter the programme...but as things stand... greatest reluctance ... beg indulgence ... express deepest personal regret but as you know I do not stand alone and cannot act on personal authority so late in the afternoon ..."

'A great deal of this; the eminent actor-knight was sweating and I could see in the rear-vision mirror that his distress was real, and his determination to stick to his guns was equally real. They were a notable study. You could do wonders with them, Harry : the young actor so vivid, the old one so silvery in the splendour of his distinction; both giving the quality of art to a common human blunder. Sir John's face was grave, but at last he reached out and patted the knee in the Hamlet tights and said, "I won't say I understand, because I don't; still, nothing to be done now, eh? Damned embarrassing for us both, quonk? But I think I may say a little more than just embarrassing for me." Then Hamlet, delighted to have been let off the hook, smiled the smile of spiritual radiance for which he was famous, and did an inspired thing : he took the hand Sir John extended to him and raised it to his lips. It seemed under the circumstances precisely the right thing to do.

'Then I drove Sir John back to Richmond, and it was a slow journey, I can tell you. I hardly dared to look in the mirror, but I did twice, and both times tears were running down the old man's face. When we arrived I helped him inside and he leaned very heavily on my arm. I couldn't bear to hang around and hear what he said to Milady. Nor would they have wanted me.

'So that was how you knifed him, Roly. Don't protest. When the stage doorman showed me that list of people who were included in the performance, it was signed by you, on behalf of the eminent actor-knight. You simply didn't let that telephone message go any farther. It's a pity you couldn't have been on hand to see the scene in the limousine.'

Magnus said no more, and nobody else seemed anxious to break the silence. Ingestree appeared to be thinking, and at last it was he who spoke.

'I don't see any reason now for denying what you've said. I think you have coloured it absurdly, but your facts are right. It's true I devilled for the committee about that Irving matinee; I was just getting myself established in the theatre in a serious way and it was a great opportunity for me. All the stars who formed the committee heaped work on me, and that was as it should be. I don't complain. But if you think Sir John Tresize was the only swollen ego I had to deal with, you'd better think again; I had months of tiresome negotiating to do, and because no money was changing hands I had to treat over a hundred people as if they were all stars.

'Yes, I got the call from Tresize, and it came just at the time when I was hardest pressed. Yes, I did drop it, because by that time I had been given a programme for that awful afternoon that we had to stick to or else disturb I can't think how many careful arrangements. You saw one man disappointed; I saw at least twenty. All my life I've had to arrange things, because I'm that uncommon creature, an artist with a good head for administration. One of the lessons I've learned is to give no ground to compassion, because the minute you do that a dozen people descend upon you who treat compassion as weakness, and drive you off your course without the slightest regard for what happens to you. You've told us that you apprenticed yourself to an egoism, Magnus, and so you did, and you've learned the egoism-game splendidly; but in my life I've had to learn how to deal with people like you without becoming your slave, and that's what I've done. I'm sorry if old Tresize felt badly, but on the basis of what you've told us I think everybody else here will admit that it was nobody's fault but his own.'

'I don't think I'm ready to admit that,' said Lind. 'There is a hole in your excellent story: you didn't tell your superior about the telephone call. Surely he was the man to make final decisions?'

'There were innumerable decisions to be made. If you've ever had any experience of an all-star matinee you can guess how many. During the last week everybody was happy if a decision could be made that would stick. I don't remember the details very clearly. I acted for what seemed the best.'

'Without any recollection of being told how to carry a chair, or that unfortunate reference to your father's shop, or the disappointment about Jekyll-and-Hyde in masks and meem?' said Magnus.

'What do you suppose I am? You can't really imagine I would take revenge for petty things of that sort.'

'Oh yes; I can imagine it without the least difficulty.'

'You're ungenerous.'

'Life has made me aware of how far mean minds rely on generosity in others.'

'You've always disliked me.'

'You didn't like the old man.'

'No. I didn't.'

'Well, in my judgement at least, you killed him.'

'Did I? Something had to kill him, I suppose. Something kills everybody. And when you say something you often mean somebody. Eventually something or somebody will kill us all. You're not going to back me into a corner that way.'

'No, I don't think you can quite attribute Sir John's death to Roly,' said Lind. 'But a not very widely understood or recognized element in life – I mean the jealousy youth feels for age – played a part in it. Have you been harbouring ill-will toward Roly all these years because of this incident? Because I really think that what Sir John was played a large part in the way he died, as is usually the case.'

'Very well,' said Magnus; 'I'll reconsider the matter. After all, it doesn't really signify whether I think Roly killed him, or not. But Sir John and Milady were the first two people in my life I really loved, and the list isn't a long one. After the matinee Sir John wasn't himself; in a few weeks he had flu, which turned to pneumonia, and he didn't last long. I went to Richmond every day, and there was one dreadful afternoon toward the end when I went into the room where Milady was sitting; when she heard my footstep she said, "Is that you, Jack?" and I knew she wasn't going to live long, either.

'She was wandering, of course, and as I have told you I had learned so much from Sir John that I even walked like him; it was eerie and desolating to be mistaken for him by the person who knew him best. Roly says I ate him. Rubbish! But I had done something that I don't pretend to explain, and when Milady thought he was well again, and walking as he had not walked for a year, I couldn't speak to her, or say who I was, so I crept away and came back later, making it very clear that it was Mungo Fetch who had come, and would come as long as he was wanted.

'He died, and at that time everybody was deeply concerned about the war that was so near at hand, and there were very few people at the funeral. Not Milady; she wasn't well enough to go. But Agate was there, the only time I ever saw him. And a handful of relatives were there, and I noticed them looking at me with unfriendly, sidelong glances. Then it broke on me that they thought I must be some sort of ghost from the past, and very probably an illegitimate son. I didn't approach them, because I was sure that nothing would ever make it clear to them that I was indeed a ghost, and an illegitimate son, but in a sense they would never understand.

'Milady died a few weeks later, and there were even fewer at her funeral; Macgregor and Holroyd were there, and as I stood with them nobody bothered to look twice at me. Odd: it was not until they died that I learned they were both much older than I had supposed.

'The day after we buried Milady I left England; I had wanted to do so for some time, but I didn't want to go so long as there was a chance that I could do anything for her. There was a war coming, and I had no stomach for war; the circumstances of my life had not inclined me toward patriotism. There was nothing for me to do in England. I had never gained a foothold on the stage because my abilities as an actor were not of the fashionable kind, and I had not been able to do any better with magic. I kept bread in my mouth by taking odd jobs as a magician; at Christmas I gave shows for children in the toy department of one of the big shops, but the work was hateful to me. Children are a miserable audience for magic; everybody thinks they are fond of marvels, but they are generally literal-minded little toughs who want to know how everything is done; they have not yet attained to the sophistication that takes pleasure in being deceived. The very small ones aren't so bad, but they are in a state of life where a rabbit might just as well appear out of a hat as from anywhere else; what really interests them is the rabbit. For a man of my capacities, working for children was degrading; you might just as well confront them with Menuhin playing "Pop Goes the Weasel". But I drew streams of half-crowns from tiny noses, and wrapped up turtles that changed into boxes of sweets in order to collect my weekly wage. Now and then I took a private engagement, but the people who employed me weren't serious about magic. It sounds odd, but I can't put it any other way; I was wasted on them and my new egoism was galled by the humiliation of the work.

'I had to live, and I understood clocks. Here again I was at a disadvantage because I had no certificate of qualification, and anyhow ordinary cleaning and regulating of wrist-watches and mediocre mantel clocks bored me. But I hung around the clock exhibition in the Victoria and Albert Museum, and worked my way into the private room of the curator of that gallery in order to ask questions, and it was not long before I had a rather irregular job there. It is never easy to find people who can be trusted with fine old pieces, because it calls for a kind of sympathy that isn't directly hitched to mechanical knowledge.

'With those old clocks you need to know not only how they work, but why they are built as they are. Every piece is individual, and something of the temperament of the maker is built into them, so the real task is to discern whatever you can of the maker's temperament and work within it, if you hope to humour his clock and persuade it to come to life again.

'In the States and Canada they talk about "fixing" clocks; it's a bad word, because you can't just fix a clock if you hope to bring it to life. I was a reanimator of clocks, and I was particularly good at the *sonnerie* – you know, the bells and striking apparatus – which is especially hard to humour into renewed life. You've all heard old clocks that strike as if they were being managed by very old, arthritic gnomes; the notes tumble along irregularly, without any of the certainty and dignity you want from a true chime. It's a tricky thing to restore dignity to a clock that has been neglected or misused or that simply has grown old. I could do that, because I understood time.

'I mean my own time, as well as the clock's. So many workmen think in terms of their own time, on which they put a value. They will tell you it's no good monkeying with an old timepiece because the cost of the labour would run too close to the value of the clock, even when it was restored. I never cared how long a job took, and I didn't charge for my work by the hour; not because I put no value on my time but because I found that such an attitude led to hurried work, which is fatal to humouring clocks. I don't suppose I was paid as much as I could have demanded if I had charged by the hour, but I made myself invaluable, and in the end that has its price. I had a knack for the work, part of which was the understanding I acquired of old metal (which mustn't be treated as if it were modern metal), and part of which was the boundless patience and the contempt for time I had gained sitting inside Abdullah, when time had no significance.

'I suppose the greatest advantage I have had over other people who have wanted to do what I can do is that I really had no education at all, and am free of the illusions and commonplace values that education brings. I don't speak against education; for most people it is a necessity; but if you're going to be a genius you should try either to avoid education entirely, or else work hard to get rid of any you've been given. Education is for commonplace people and it fortifies their commonplaceness. Makes them useful, of course, in an ordinary sort of way.

'So I became an expert on old clocks, and I know a great many of the finest chamber clocks, and lantern clocks, and astronomical and equation clocks in the finest collections in the world, because I have rebuilt them, and tinkered them, and put infinitesimal new pieces into them (but always fashioned in old metal, or it would be cheating), and brought their chimes back to their original pride, and while I was doing that work I was as anonymous as I had been when I was inside Abdullah. I was a back-room expert who worked on clocks which the Museum undertook, as a special favour, to examine and put in order if it could be done. And when I had become invaluable I had no trouble in getting a very good letter of recommendation, to anybody whom it might concern, from the curator, who was a well-known man in his field.

'With that I set off for Switzerland, because I knew that there ought to be a job for a good clock-man there, and I was certain that when the war came Switzerland would be neutral, though probably not comfortable. I was right; there were shortages, endless problems about spies who wouldn't play their game according to the rules, bombings that were explained as accidental and perhaps were, and the uneasiness rising toward hysteria of being in the middle of a continent at war when other nations use your neutrality on the one hand, and hate you for it on the other. We were lucky to have Henri Guisan to keep us in order.

'I say "we", though I did not become a Swiss and have never done so; theirs is not an easy club to join. I was Jules LeGrand, and a Canadian, and although that was sometimes complicated I managed to make it work.

'I presented my letter at the biggest watch and clock factories, and although I was pleasantly received I could not get a job, because I was not a Swiss, and at that time there were many foreigners who wanted jobs in important industries, and it was probable that some of them were spies. If I were going to place a spy, I would get a man who could pass for a native, and equip him with unexceptionable papers to show that he was a native; but when people are afraid of spies they do not think rationally. Still, after some patient application I wrangled an interview at the Musée d'Art et d'Histoire in Geneva, and after waiting a while Jules LeGrand found himself once more in the back room of a museum. It was there that one of the great strokes of luck in my life occurred, and most uncharacteristically it came through an act of kindness I had undertaken. There must be a soft side to my nature, and perhaps I should have trusted it more than I have done.

'I was living in a pension, the proprietor of which had a small daughter. The daughter had got herself into deep trouble because she had broken her father's walking-stick, and as the stick had been a possession of her grandfather it had something of the character of an heirloom. It was no ordinary walking-stick, but one of those joke sticks that fashionable young men used to carry – a fine Malacca cane, but with a knob on the top that did a trick. The knob of this particular specimen was of ivory, carved prettily like the head of a monkey; but when you pressed a button in its neck the monkey opened its mouth, stuck out a red tongue, and rolled its blue eyes up to heaven. The child had been warned not to play with grandfather's stick, and had predictably done so, and jammed it so that the monkey was frozen in an expression of idiocy, its tongue half out and its eyes half raised.

'The family made a great to-do, and little Rosalie was lectured and hectored and deprived of her allowance for an indefinite period, and the tragedy of the stick was brought up at every meal; everybody at the pension had ideas about either child-rearing or the mending of the stick and I became thoroughly sick of hearing about it, though not as sick as poor Rosalie, who was a nice kid, and felt like a criminal. So I offered to take it to my workroom at the Musée and do what I could. Mending old toys could not be very different from mending old clocks, and Rosalie was growing pale, so clearly something must be done. The family had tried a few watch-repair people, but none of them wanted to be bothered with what looked like a trouble-some job; it is astonishing that in a place like Geneva, which numbers watch mechanics in the thousands, there should be so few who are prepared to tackle anything old. Something new delights them, but what is old seems to clog their works. I suppose it is a matter of sympathetic approach, which was my chief stock-in-trade as a reanimator of old timepieces.

'The monkey was not really difficult, but he took time. Releasing the silver collar that kept the head in position without destroying it; removing the ivory knob without damage; penetrating the innards of the knob in such a way as to discover its secrets without wrecking them : these were troublesome tasks, but what someone has made, someone else can dismantle and make again. It proved to be a matter of an escapement device that needed replacing, and that meant making a tiny part on one of my tiny lathes from metal that would work well, but not too aggressively, with the old metal in the monkey's works. Simple, when you know how and are prepared to take several hours to do it; not simple if you are in a hurry to finish. So I did it, and restored the stick to its owner with a flowery speech in which I begged forgiveness for Rosalie, and Rosalie thought I was a marvellous man (in which she was quite correct) and a very nice man (in which I fear she was mistaken).

'The significant detail is that one evening after the museum's working day was done I was busy with the walking-stick when the curator of my department walked through the passage outside the small workshop, saw my light, and came in, like a good Swiss, to turn it off. He asked what I was doing, and when I explained he showed some interest. It was a year later that he sent for me and asked if I knew much about mechanical toys; I said I didn't, but that it would be odd if a toy were more complex than a clock. Then he said, "Have you ever heard of Jeremias Naegeli?" and I hadn't. "Well," said he, "Jeremias Naegeli is very old, very rich, and very much accustomed to having his own way. He has retired, except for retaining the chairmanship of the board of So-and-So" – and he mentioned the name of one of the biggest clock, watch, and optical equipment manufacturers in Switzerland – "and he has collected a great number of mechanical toys, all of them old and some of them unique. He wants a man to put them in order. Would you be interested in a job like that?"

'I said, "If Jeremias Naegeli commands several thousand expert technicians, why would he want me?" "Because his people are expected to keep on the job during wartime," said my boss; "it would not look well if he took a first-rate man for what might appear to be a frivolous job. He is old and he doesn't want to wait until the war is over. But if he borrows you from the museum, and you are a foreigner not engaged in war production, it's a different thing, do you understand?" I understood, and in a couple of weeks I was on my way to St Gallen to be looked over by the imperious Jeremias Naegeli.

'It proved that he lived at some distance from St Gallen on his estate in the mountains, and a driver was sent to take me there. That was my first sight of Sorgenfrei. As you gentlemen know, it is an impressive sight, but try to imagine how impressive it was to me, who had never been in a rich house before, to say nothing of such a gingerbread castle as that. I was frightened out of my wits. As soon as I arrived I was taken by a secretary to the great man's private room, which was called his study, but was really a huge library, dark, hot, stuffy, and smelling of leather furniture, expensive cigars, and rich man's farts. It was this expensive stench that destroyed the last of my confidence, because it was as if I had entered the den of some fearsome old animal, which was precisely what Jeremias Naegeli was. It had been many years – in Willard's time – since I had been afraid of anyone, but I was afraid of him.

'He played the role of great industrialist, contemptuous of ceremony and without an instant to spare on inferior people. "Have you brought your tools?" was the first thing he said to me; although it was a silly question – why wouldn't I have brought my tools? – he made it sound as if I were just the sort of fellow who would have travelled across the whole of Switzerland without them. He questioned me carefully about clockwork, and that was easy because I knew more about that subject than he did; he understood principles but I don't suppose he could have made a safety-pin. Then he heaved himself out of his chair and gestured to me with his cigar to follow; he was old and very fat, and progress was slow, but we crawled back into the entrance hall, where he showed me the big clock there, which you have all seen; it has dials for everything you can think of – time at Sorgenfrei and at Greenwich, seconds, the day of the week, the date of the month, the seasons, and the signs of the zodiac, the phases of the moon, and a complex *sonnerie*. "What's that?" he said. So I told him what it was, and how it was integrated and what metals were probably used to balance one another off with enough compensation to keep the thing from needing continual readjustment. He didn't say anything, but I knew he was pleased. "That clock was made for my grandfather, who designed it," he said. "He must have been a very great technician," I said, and that pleased him as well, as I meant it to do. Most men are much more partial to their grandfathers than to their fathers, just as they admire their grandsons but rarely their sons. Then he beckoned me to follow again, and this time we went on quite a long journey, down a flight of steps, through a long corridor, and up steps again into what I judged was another building; we had been through a tunnel.

'In a tall, sunny room in this building there was the most extraordinary collection of mechanical toys that anyone has ever seen; there can be no doubt about that, because it is now in one of the museums in Zürich, and its reputation is precisely what I have said – the most extensive and extraordinary in the world. But when I first saw it, the room looked as if all the little princes and princesses and serene highnesses in the world had been having a thoroughly destructive afternoon. Legs and arms lay about the floor, springs burst from little animals like metal guts, paint had been gashed with sharp points. It was a breathtaking scene of destruction, and as I wandered here and there looking at the little marvels and the terrible damage, I was filled with awe, because some of those things were of indisputable beauty and they had been despoiled in a fit of crazy fury.

'It was here that the old man showed the first touch of humanity I had seen in him. There were tears in his eyes. "Can you mend this?" he asked, waving his heavy stick to encompass the room. It was not a time for hesitation. "I don't know that I can mend it all," I said, "but if anybody can do it, I can. But I mustn't be pressed for time." That fetched him. He positively smiled, and it wasn't a bad smile either. "Then you must begin at once," he said, "and nobody shall ever ask you how you are getting on. But you will tell me sometimes, won't you?" And he smiled the charming smile again.

'That was how I began my life at Sorgenfrei. It was odd, and I never became fully accustomed to the routine of the house. There were a good many servants, most of whom were well up in years, as otherwise they would have been called away for war work. There were also two secretaries, both invalidish young men, and the old Direktor – which was what everybody called him – kept them busy, because he either had, or invented, a lot of business to attend to. There was another curious functionary, also unfit for military service, whose job it was to play the organ at breakfast, and play the piano at night if the old man wanted music after dinner. He was a fine musician, but he can't have been driven by ambition, or perhaps he was too ill to care. Every morning of his life, while the Direktor consumed a large breakfast, this fellow sat in the organ loft and worked his way methodically through Bach's chorales. The old man called them his prayers and he heard three a day; he consumed spiced ham and cheese and extraordinary quantities of rolls and hot breads while he was listening to Bach, and when he had finished he hauled himself up and lumbered off to his study. From that time until evening the musician sat in the secretaries' room and read, or looked out of the window and coughed softly, until it was time for him to put on his dress clothes and eat dinner with the Direktor, who would then decide if he wanted any Chopin that evening.

'We all dined with the Direktor, and with a severe lady who was the manager of his household, but we took our midday meal in another room. It was the housekeeper who told me that I must get a dinner suit, and sent me to St Gallen to buy one. There were shortages in Switzerland, and they were reflected in the Direktor's meals, but we ate extraordinarily well, all the same.

'The Direktor was as good as his word; he never harried me about time. We had occasional conferences about things I needed, because I required seasoned metal – not new stuff – that his influence could command from the large factories in the complex of which he was the nominal ruler and undoubted financial head; I also had to have some rather odd materials to repair finishes, and as I wanted to use egg tempera I needed a certain number of eggs, which were not the easiest things to get in wartime, even in Switzerland.

'I had never dealt with an industrialist before, and I was bothered by his demand for accurate figures; when he asked me how much spring-metal of a certain width and weight I wanted

I was apt to say, "Oh, a fair-sized coil," which tried his temper dreadfully. But after he had seen me working with it, and understood that I really knew what I was doing, he regained his calm, and may even have recognized that in the sort of job he had given me accuracy of estimate was not to be achieved in the terms he understood.

'The job was literally a mess. I set to work methodically on the first day to canvass the room, picking up everything and putting the component parts of every toy in a separate box, so far as I could identify them. It took ten days, and when I had done I estimated that of the hundred and fifty toys that had originally been on the shelves, all but twenty-one could be identified and put into some sort of renewed life. What remained looked like what is found after an aircraft disaster; legs, heads, arms, bits of mechanism and unidentifiable rubbish lay there in a jumble that made no sense, sort it how I would.

'It was a queer way to spend the worst years of the war. So far as work and the nurture of my imagination went, I was in the nineteenth century. None of the toys was earlier than 1790, and most of them belonged to the 1830s and '40s, and reflected the outlook on life of that time, and its quality of imagination – the outlook and imagination, that's to say, of the kind of people – French, Russian, Polish, German – who liked mechanical toys and could afford to buy them for themselves or their children. Essentially it was a stuffy, limited imagination.

'If I have been successful in penetrating the character of Robert-Houdin and the sort of performance he gave, it is because my work with those toys gave me the clue to it and his audience. They were people who liked imagination to be circumscribed: you were a wealthy bourgeois papa, and you wanted to give your little Clothilde a surprise on her birthday, so you went to the very best toymaker and spent a lot of money on an effigy of a little bootblack who whistled as he shined the boot he held in his hands. See Clothilde, see! How he nods his head and taps with his foot as he brushes away! How merrily he whistles "Ach, du lieber Augustin"! Open the back of his case – carefully, my darling, better let papa do it for you – and there is the spring, which pumps the little bellows and works the little barrel-and-pin device that releases the air into the pipes that makes the whistle. And these little rods and eccentric wheels make the boy polish the boot and wag his head and tap his toe. Are you not grateful to papa for this lovely surprise? Of course you are, my darling. And now we shall put the little boy on a high shelf, and perhaps on Saturday evenings papa will make it work for you. Because we mustn't risk breaking it, must we? Not after papa spent so much money to buy it. No, we must preserve it with care, so that a century from now Herr Direktor Jeremias Naegeli will include it in his collection.

'But somebody had gone through Herr Direktor Naegeli's collection and smashed it to hell. Who could it be?

'Who could be so disrespectful of all the careful preservation, painstaking assembly, and huge amount of money the collection represented? Who can have lost patience with the bourgeois charm of all these little people – the ballerinas who danced so delightfully to the music of the music-boxes, the little bands of Orientals who banged their cymbals and beat their drums and jingled their little hoops of bells, the little trumpeters (ten of them) who could play three different trumpet tunes, the canary that sang so prettily in its decorative cage, the mermaid who swam in what looked like real water, but was really revolving spindles of twisted glass, the little tightrope walkers, and the big cockatoo that could ruffle its feathers and give a lifelike squawk – who can have missed their charm and seen instead their awful rigidity and slavery to mechanical pattern?

'I found out who this monster was quite early in my long task. After I had sorted the debris of the collection, and set to work, I spent from six to eight hours a day sitting in that large room, with a jeweller's glass stuck in my eye, reassembling mechanisms, humouring them till they worked as they ought, and then touching up the paintwork and bits of velvet, silk, spangles, and feathers that had been damaged on the birds, the fishes, monkeys, and tiny people who gave charm to the ingenious clockwork which was the important part of them.

'I am a concentrated worker, and not easily interrupted, but I began to have a feeling that I was not alone, and that I was being watched by no friendly eye. I could not see anything in the room that would conceal a snooper, but one day I felt a watcher so close to me that I turned suddenly and saw that I was being watched through one of the big windows, and that the watcher was a very odd creature indeed – a sort of monkey, I thought, so I waved to it and grinned, as one does at monkeys. In reply the monkey jabbed a fist through the window and cursed fiercely at me in some Swiss patois that was beyond my understanding. Then it unfastened the window by reaching through the hole it had made in the glass, threw up the sash, and leapt inside.

'Its attitude was threatening, and although I saw that it was human, I continued to behave as if it were a monkey. I had known Rango pretty well in my carnival days, and I knew that with monkeys the first rule is never to show surprise or alarm; but neither can you win monkeys by kindness. The only thing to do is to keep still and quiet and be ready for anything. I spoke to it in conventional German –'

'You spoke in a vulgar Austrian lingo,' said Liesl. 'And you took the patronizing tone of an animal-trainer. Have you any idea what it is like to be spoken to in the way people speak to animals? A fascinating experience. Gives you quite a new feeling about animals. They don't know words, but they understand tones. The tone people usually use to animals is affectionate, but it has an undertone of "What a fool you are!" I suppose an animal has to make up its mind whether it will put up with that nonsense for the food and shelter that goes with it, or show the speaker who's boss. That's what I did. Really Magnus, if you could have seen yourself at that moment! A pretty, self-assured little manikin, watching to see which way I'd jump. And I did jump. Right on top of you, and rolled you on the floor. I didn't mean to do you any harm, but I couldn't resist rumpling you up a bit.'

'You bit me,' said Magnus.

'A nip.'

'How was I to know it was only meant to be a nip?'

'You weren't. But did you have to hit me on the head with the handle of a screwdriver?'

'Yes, I did. Not that it had much effect.'

'You couldn't know that the most ineffective thing you could do to me was to hit me on the head.'

'Liesl, you would have frightened St George *and* his dragon.

If you wanted gallantry you shouldn't have hit me and squeezed me and banged my head on the floor as you did. So far as I knew I was fighting for my life. And don't pretend now that you meant it just as a romp. You were out to kill. I could smell it on your breath.'

'I could certainly have killed you. Who knew or cared that you were at Sorgenfrei, mending those ridiculous toys? In wartime who would have troubled to trace one insignificant little mechanic, travelling on a crooked passport, who happened to vanish? My grandfather would have been angry, but he would have had to hush the thing up somehow. He couldn't hand his granddaughter over to the police. The old man loved me, you know. If he hadn't, he would probably have killed me or banished me after I smashed up his collection of toys.'

'And why did you smash them?' said Lind.

'Pure bloody-mindedness. For which I had good cause. You have heard what Magnus says: I looked like an ape. I still look like an ape, but I have made my apishness serve me and now it doesn't really matter. But it mattered then, more than anything else in the world, to me. It mattered more than the European War, more than anybody's happiness. I was so full of spleen I could have killed Magnus, and enjoyed it, and then told my grandfather to cope with the situation, and enjoyed that. And he would have done it.

'You'd better let me tell you about it, before Magnus rushes on and puts the whole thing in his own particular light. My life was pretty much that of any lucky rich child until I was fourteen. The only thing that was in the least unusual was that my parents – my father was Jeremias Naegeli's only son – were killed in a motor accident when I was eleven. My grandfather took me on, and was as kind to me as he knew how to be. He was like the bourgeois papa that Magnus described giving the mechanical top to little Clothilde; my grandfather belonged to an era when the attitude toward children was that they were all right as long as they were loved and happy, and their happiness was obviously the same as that of their guardians. It works pretty well when nothing disturbs the pattern, but when I was fourteen something very disturbing happened in my pattern.

'It was at the beginning of puberty, and I knew all about that because my grandfather was enlightened and I was given good, if rather Calvinist, instruction by a woman doctor. So when I began to grow rather fast I didn't pay much attention until it seemed that the growth was too much for me and I began to have fainting fits. The woman doctor appeared again and was alarmed. Then began a wretched period of hospitals and tests and consultations and head-shakings and discussions in which I was not included, and after all that a horrible time when I was taken to Zürich three times a week for treatment with a large ray-machine. The treatments were nauseating and depressing, and I was wretched because I supposed I had cancer, and asked the woman doctor about it. No, not cancer. What, then? Some difficulty with the growing process, which the ray treatment was designed to arrest.

'I won't bore you with it all. The disease was a rare one, but not so rare they didn't have some ideas about it, and Grandfather made sure that everything was done that anyone could do. The doctors were delighted. They did indeed control my growth, which made them as happy as could be, because it proved something. They explained to me, as if it were the most wonderful Christmas gift any girl ever had, that if they had not been able to do wonders with their rays and drugs I would have been a giant. Think of it, they said; you might have been eight feet tall, but we have been able to halt you at five foot eleven inches, which is not impossibly tall for a woman. You are a very lucky young lady. Unless, of course, there is a recurrence of the trouble, for which we shall keep the most vigilant watch. You may regard yourself as cured.

'There were, of course, a few side effects. One cannot hope to escape such an experience wholly unscathed. The side effects were that I had huge feet and hands, a disfiguring thickening of the skull and jaw, and surely one of the ugliest faces anyone has ever seen. But wasn't I lucky not to be a giant, as well?

'I was so perverse as not to be grateful for my luck. Not to be a giant, at the cost of looking like an ape, didn't seem to me to be the greatest good luck. Surely Fortune had something in her basket a little better than that? I raved and I raged, and I made everybody as miserable as I could. My grandfather didn't know what to do. Zürich was full of psychiatrists but my grandfather belonged to a pre-psychiatric age. He sent for a bishop, a good Lutheran bishop, who was a very nice man but I demolished him quickly; all his talk about resignation, recognition of the worse fate of scores of poor creatures in the Zürich hospitals, the necessity to humble oneself before the inscrutable mystery of God's will, sounded to me like mockery. There sat the bishop, with his snowy hair smelling of expensive cologne and his lovely white hands moulding invisible loaves of bread in the air before him, and there sat I, hideous and destroyed in mind, listening to him prate about resignation. He suggested that we pray, and knelt with his face in the seat of his chair. I gave him such a kick in the arse that he limped for a week, and rushed off to my own quarters.

'There was worse to come. With the thickening of the bones of my head there had been trouble with my organs of speech, and there seemed to be nothing that could be done about that. My voice became hoarse, and as my tongue thickened I found speech more and more difficult, until I could only utter in a gruff tone that sounded to me like the bark of a dog. That was the worst. To be hideous was humiliating and ruinous to my spirit, but to sound as I did threatened my reason. What was I to do? I was young and very strong, and I could rage and destroy. So that is what I did.

'It had all taken a long time, and when Magnus first saw me at the window of his workroom I was seventeen. I had gone on the rampage one day, and wrecked Grandfather's collection of toys. It was usually kept locked up but I knew how to get to it. Why did I do it? To hurt the old man. Why did I want to hurt the old man? Because he was at hand, and the pity I saw in his eyes when he came to see me – I kept away from the life in the house – made me hate him. Who was he, so old, so near death, so capable of living the life he liked, to pity me? If Fate had a blow, why didn't Fate strike him? He would not have had to endure it long. But I might easily live to be as old as he, trapped in my ugliness for sixty years. So I smashed his toys. Do you know, he never said a word of reproach? In the kind of world the bishop inhabited his forbearance would have melted my heart and brought me to a better frame of mind. But misfortune had scorched all the easy Christianity out of me, and

I despised him all the more for his compassion, and wondered where I could attack him next.

'I knew Grandfather had brought someone to Sorgenfrei to mend the toys, and I wanted to see who it was. There was not much fun to be got out of the secretaries, and I had exhausted the possibilities of tormenting Hofstätter, the musician; he was poor game, and wept easily, the feeble schlemiel. I had spied on Magnus for quite a time before he discovered me; looking in the windows of his workroom meant climbing along a narrow ledge some distance above ground and as I looked like an ape I thought I might as well behave like one. So I used to creep along the ledge, and watch the terribly neat, debonair little fellow bent over his workbench, tinkering endlessly with bits of spring and tiny wires, and filing patiently at the cogs of little wheels. He always had his jeweller's glass stuck in one eye, and a beautifully fresh long white coat, and he never sat down without tugging his trousers gently upward to preserve their crease. He was handsome, too, in a romantic, nineteenth-century way that went beautifully with the little automata he was repairing.

'Before my trouble I had loved to go to the opera, and *Contes d'Hoffmann* was one of my favourites; the scene in Magnus's workroom always reminded me of the mechanical doll, Olympia, in *Hoffmann*, though he was not a bit like the grotesque old man who quarrelled over Olympia. So there it was, Hoffmann inside the window and outside, what? The only person in opera I resembled at all was Kundry the monstrous woman in *Parsifal*, and Kundry always seemed to be striving to do good and be redeemed. I didn't want to do good and had no interest in being redeemed.

'I read a good deal and my favourite book at that time was Spengler's *Der Untergang des Abendlandes* – I was not a stupid girl, you understand – and from it I had drawn a mishmash of notions which tended to support whatever I felt like doing, especially when I wanted to be destructive. Most adolescents are destructive, I suppose, but the worst are certainly those who justify what they do with a half-baked understanding of somebody's philosophy. It was under the banner of Spengler, then, that I decided to surprise Magnus and rough him up a bit. He looked easy. A man who worried so much in private about the crease of his trousers was sure to be a poor fighter.

'The surprise was mine. I was bigger and stronger but I hadn't had his experience in carnival fights and flophouses. He soon found out that hitting me on the head was no good, and hit me a most terrible blow in the diaphragm that knocked out all my breath. Then he bent one of my legs backward and sat on me. That was when we had our first conversation.

'It was long, and I soon discovered that he spoke my language. I don't mean German; I had to teach him proper German later. I mean that he asked intelligent questions and expected sensible answers. He was also extremely rude. I told you I had a hoarse, thick voice, and he had trouble understanding me in French and English. "Can't you speak better than that?" he demanded, and when I said I couldn't he simply said, "You're not trying; you're making the worst of it in order to seem horrible. You're not horrible, you're just stupid. So cut it out."

'Nobody had ever talked to me like that. I was the Naegeli heiress, and I was extremely unfortunate; I was used to deference, and people putting up with whatever I chose to give them. Here was little Herr Trousers-Crease, who spoke elegant English and nice clean French and barnyard German, cheeking me about the way I spoke. And laying down the law and making conditions! "If you want to come here and watch me work you must behave yourself. You should be ashamed, smashing up all these pretty things! Have you no respect for the past? Look at this: a monkey orchestra of twenty pieces and a conductor, and you've reduced it to a boxful of scraps. I've got to mend it, and it won't take less than four to six months of patient, extremely skilled work before the monkeys can play their six little tunes again. And all because of you! Your grandfather ought to tie you to the weathervane and leave you on the roof to die!"

'Well, it was a change from the bishop and my grandfather's tears. Of course I knew it was bluff. He may have hoped to shame me, but I think he was cleverer than that. All he was doing was serving notice on me that he would not put up with any nonsense; he knew I was beyond shame. But it was a change. And I began, just a little, to like him. Little Herr

Trousers-Crease had quality, and an egoism that was a match for my own.

'Now – am I to go on? If there is to be any more of this I think I should be the one to speak. But is this confessional evening to know no bounds?'

'I think you'd better go ahead, Liesl,' said I. 'You've always been a great one to urge other people to tell their most intimate secrets. It's hardly fair if you refuse to do so.'

'Ah, yes, but dear Ramsay, what follows isn't a tale of scandal, and it isn't really a love-story. Will it be of any interest? We must not forget that this is supposed to provide a subtext for Magnus's film about Robert-Houdin. What is the real story of the making of a great conjuror as opposed to Robert-Houdin's memoirs, which we are pretty much agreed are a bourgeois fake? I don't in the least mind telling my side of the story, if it's of any interest to the film-makers. What's the decision?'

'The decision is that you go on,' said Kinghovn. 'You have paused simply to make yourself interesting, as women do. No – that's unjust. Eisengrim has been doing the same thing all day. But go on.'

'Very well, Harry, I shall go on. But there won't be much for you in what I have to tell, because this part of the story could not be realized in visual terms, even by you. What happened was that I came more and more to the workroom where little Herr Trousers-Crease was mending Grandfather's automata, and I fell under the enchantment of what he was able to do. He has told you that he humoured those little creatures back into life, but you would have to see him at work to get any kind of understanding of what it meant, because only part of it was mechanical. I suppose one of Grandfather's master technicians – one of the men who make those marvellous chronometers that are given to millionaires by their wives, and which never vary from strict time by more than a second every year – could have mended all those little figures so that they worked, but only Magnus could have read, in a cardboard box full of parts, the secret of the tiny performance that the completed figure was meant to give. When he had finished one of his repair jobs, the little bootblack did not simply brisk away at his little boot with his miniature brush, and whistle and tap his foot: he seemed to live, to have a true quality of being as though when you had turned your back he would leap up from his box and dance a jig, or run off for a pot of beer. You know what those automata are like: there is something distasteful about their rattling merriment; but Magnus made them *act* – they gave a little performance. I had seen them before I broke them, and I swear that when Magnus had remade them they were better than they had ever been.

'Was little Herr Trousers-Crease a very great watchmaker's mechanic, then? No, something far beyond that. There must have been in him some special quality that made it worth his while to invest these creatures of metal with so much vitality and charm of action. Roly has talked about his wolfishness; that was part of it, because with that wolfishness went an intensity of imagination and vision. The wolfishness meant only that he never questioned the overmastering importance of what he – whoever and whatever he was – might be doing. But the artistry was of a rare kind, and little by little I began to understand what it was. I found it in Spengler.

'You have read Spengler? No: it is not so fashionable as it once was. But Spengler talks a great deal about what he calls the Magian World View, which he says we have lost, but which was part of the *Weltanschauung* – you know, the world outlook – of the Middle Ages. It was a sense of the unfathomable wonder of the invisible world that existed side by side with a hard recognition of the roughness and cruelty and day-to-day demands of the tangible world. It was a readiness to see demons where nowadays we see neuroses, and to see the hand of a guardian angel in what we are apt to shrug off ungratefully as a stroke of luck. It was religion, but a religion with a thousand gods, none of them all-powerful and most of them ambiguous in their attitude toward man. It was poetry and wonder which might reveal themselves in the dunghill, and it was an understanding of the dunghill that lurks in poetry and wonder. It was a sense of living in what Spengler called a quivering cavern-light which is always in danger of being swallowed up in the surrounding, impenetrable darkness.

'This was what Herr Trousers-Crease seemed to have, and what made him ready to spend his time on work that would have maddened a man of modern education and modern sensibility. We have paid a terrible price for our education, such as it is. The Magian World View, in so far as it exists, has taken flight into science, and only the great scientists have it or understand where it leads; the lesser ones are merely clock-makers of a larger growth, just as so many of our humanist scholars are just cud-chewers or system-grinders. We have educated ourselves into a world from which wonder, and the fear and dread and splendour and freedom of wonder have been banished. Of course wonder is costly. You couldn't incorporate it into a modern state, because it is the antithesis of the anxiously worshipped security which is what a modern state is asked to give. Wonder is marvellous but it is also cruel, cruel, cruel. It is undemocratic, discriminatory, and pitiless.

'Yet here it was, in this most unexpected place, and when I had found it I apprenticed myself to it. Literally, for I begged Herr Trousers-Crease to teach me what he knew, and even with my huge hands I gained skill, because I had a great master. And that means very often an exacting, hot-tempered, and impatient master, because whatever my great countrymen Pestalozzi and Froebel may have said about the education of commonplace people, great things are not taught by blancmange methods. What great thing was I learning? The management of clockwork? No; any great craft tends at last toward the condition of a philosophy, and I was moving through clockwork to the Magian World View.

'Of course it took time. My grandfather was delighted, for what he saw was that his intractable, hideous granddaughter was quietly engaged in helping to repair what she had destroyed. He also saw that I improved physically, because my agony over my sickness had been terribly destructive; physically I had become slouching and simian, and as Magnus saw at once, I made my speech trouble far worse than it was, to spite myself and the world. Magnus helped me with that. Re-taught me, indeed, because he would not tolerate my uncouth mutterings, and gave me some sharp and demanding instruction in the manner of speech he had learned from Lady Tresize. And I learned. It was a case of learn to speak properly or get out of the workroom, and I wanted to stay.

'We were an odd pair, certainly. I knew about the Magian World View, and recognized it in my teacher. He knew nothing of it, because he knew nothing else: it was so much in the grain of the life he had lived, so much a part of him, that he didn't understand that everybody else didn't think – no, not think, feel – as he did. I would not for the world have attempted to explain it to him, because that would have endangered it. His kind was not the kind of mind that is happy with explanations and theories. In the common sense of the expression, he had no brains at all, and hasn't to this day. What does it matter? I have brains for him.

'As his pupil, is it strange that I should fall in love with him? I was young and healthy, and hideous though I was, I had my yearnings – perhaps exaggerated by the unlikelihood that they could find satisfaction. How was I to make him love me? Well, I began, as all the beginners in love do, with the crazy notion that if I loved him enough he must necessarily respond. How could he ignore the devotion I offered? Pooh! He didn't notice at all. I worked like a slave, but that was no more than he expected. I made little gestures, gave him little gifts, tried to make myself fascinating – and that was uphill work, let me assure you. Not that he showed distaste for me. After all, he was a carnival man, and had grown used to grotesques. He simply didn't think of me as a woman.

'At least, that is how I explained it to myself, and I made myself thoroughly miserable about it. At last, one day, when he spoke to me impatiently and harshly, I wept. I suppose I looked dreadful, and he became even more rough. So I seized him, and demanded that he treat me as a human creature and not simply as a handy assistant, and blubbered out that I loved him. I did all the youthful things: I told him that I knew it was impossible that he should love me, because I was so ugly, but that I wanted some sort of human feeling from him.

'To my delight he took me quite seriously. We sat down at the workbench, and settled to a tedious task that needed some attention, but not too much, and he told me about Willard, and his childhood, and said that he did not think that love in the usual sense was for him, because he had experienced it as a form of suffering and humiliation – a parody of sex – and he could not persuade himself to do to anyone else what had been done to him in a perverse and terrifying mode.

'This was going too fast for me. Of course I wanted sexual experience, but first of all I wanted tenderness. Under my terrible appearance – I read a lot of old legends and I thought of myself as the Loathly Maiden in the Arthurian stories – I was still an upper-class Swiss girl of gentle breeding, and I thought of sexual intercourse as a splendid goal to be achieved, after a lot of pleasant things along the way. And being a sensible girl, under all the outward trouble and psychological muddle, I said so. That led to an even greater surprise.

'He told me that he had once been in love with a woman, who had died, and that he could not feel for anyone else as he had felt for her. Romance! I rose to it like a trout to a fly. But I wanted to know more, and the more I heard the better it was. Titled lady of extraordinary charm, understanding, and gentleness. All this was to the good. But then the story began to slide sidewise into farce, as it seemed to me. The lady was not young; indeed, as I probed, it came out that she had been over sixty when he first met her. There had been no tender passages between them, because he respected her too much, but he had been privileged to read the Bible to her. It was at this point I laughed.

'Magnus was furious. The more he stormed the more I laughed, and I am sorry to say that the more I laughed the more I jeered at him. I was young, and the young can be horribly coarse about love that is not of their kind. From buggery to selfless, knightly adoration at one splendid leap! I made a lot of it, and hooted with mirth.

'I deserved to be slapped, and I was slapped. I hit back, and we fought, and rolled on the floor and slugged each other. But of course everyone knows that you should never fight with women if you want to punish them; the physical contact leads to other matters, and it did. I was not ready for sexual intercourse so soon, and Magnus did not want it, but it happened all the same. It was the first time for both of us, and it is a wonder we managed at all. It is like painting in water-colours, you know; it looks easy but it isn't. Real command only comes with experience. We were both astonished and cross. I thought I had been raped; Magnus thought he had been unfaithful to his real love. It looked like a deadlock.

'It wasn't, however. We did it lots of times after that – I mean, in the weeks that followed – and the habit is addictive, as you all know, and very agreeable, if not really the be-all and end-all and cure-all that stupid people pretend. It was good for me. I became quite smart, in so far as my appearance allowed, and paid attention to my hair, which as you see is very good. My grandfather was transported, because I began to eat at the family table again, and when he had guests I could be so charming that they almost forgot how I looked. The Herr Direktor's granddaughter Fräulein Orang-Outang, so charming and witty, though it is doubtful if even the old man's money will find her a husband.

'I am sure Grandfather knew I was sleeping with Magnus, and it must have given him severe Calvinist twinges, but he did not become a great industrialist by being a fool; he weighed the circumstances and was pleased by the obvious balance on the credit side. I think he would have consented to marriage if Magnus had mentioned it. But of course he didn't.

'Nor would I have urged it. The more intimate we became, the more I knew that we were destined to be very great friends, and probably frequent bed-mates, but certainly not a happy bourgeois married couple. For a time I called Magnus Tiresias, because like that wonderful old creature he had been for seven years a woman, and had gained strange wisdom and insight thereby. I thought of him sometimes as Galahad, because of his knightly obsession with the woman we now know as Milady, but I never called him that to his face, because I had done with mocking at his chivalry. I have never understood chivalry, but I have learned to keep my mouth shut about it.'

'It's a man's thing,' said I; 'and I think we have seen the last of it for a while on this earth. It can't live in a world of liberated women, and perhaps the liberation of women is worth the price it is certain to cost. But chivalry won't die easily or unnoticed; banish chivalry from the world and you snap the mainspring of many lives.'

'Good, grey old Ramsay,' said Liesl, reaching over to pat my hand; 'always gravely regretting, always looking wistfully backward.'

'You're both wrong,' said Magnus. 'I don't think chivalry belongs to the past; it's part of that World View Liesl talks so much about, and that she thinks I possess but don't understand. What captured my faith and loyalty about Milady had just as much to do with Sir John. He was that rare creature, the Man of One Woman. He loved Milady young and he loved her old and much of her greatness was the creation of his love. To hear people talk and to look at the stuff they read and see in the theatre and the films, you'd think the true man was the man of many women, and the more women, the more masculine the man. Don Juan is the ideal. An unattainable ideal for most men, because of the leisure and money it takes to devote yourself to a life of womanizing – not to speak of the relentless energy, the unappeasable lust, and the sheer woodpecker-like vitality of the sexual organ that such a life demands. Unattainable, yes, but thousands of men have a dab at it, and in their old age they count their handful of successes like rosary beads. But the Man of One Woman is very rare. He needs resources of spirit and psychological virtuosity beyond the common, and he needs luck, too, because the Man of One Woman must find a woman of extraordinary quality. The Man of One Woman was the character Sir John played on the stage, and it was the character he played in life, too.

'I envied him, and I cherished the splendour those two had created. If, by any inconceivable chance, Milady had shown any sexual affection for me, I should have been shocked, and I would have rebuked her. But she didn't, of course, and I simply warmed myself at their fire, and by God I needed warmth. I once had a hope that I might have found something of the sort for myself, with you, Liesl, but my luck was not to run in that direction. I would have been very happy to be a Man of One Woman, but that wasn't your way, nor was it mine. I couldn't forget Milady.'

'No, no; we went our ways,' said Liesl. 'And you know you were never much of a lover, Magnus. What does that matter? You were a great magician, and has any great magician ever been a great lover? Look at Merlin : his only false step was when he fell in love and ended up imprisoned in a tree for his pains. Look at poor old Klingsor: he could create gardens full of desirable women, but he had been castrated with a magic spear. You've been happy with your magic. And when I gained enough confidence to go out into the world again, I was happy in a casual, physical way with quite a few people, and some of the best of them were of my own sex.'

'Yes, indeed,' said Magnus. 'Who snatched the Beautiful Faustina from under my very nose?'

'Oh, Faustina, Faustina, you always bring her up when you feel a grievance. You must understand, gentlemen, that when my grandfather died, and I was heir to a large fortune, Magnus and I realized a great ambition we had in common; we set up a magic show, which developed and gained sophistication and gloss until it became the famous *Soirée of Illusions*. It takes money to get one of those things on its feet, as you well know, but when it is established it can be very profitable.

'You can't have a magic show without a few beautiful girls to be sawn in two, or beheaded, or whisked about in space. Sex has its place in magic, even if it is not the foremost place. As ours was the best show in existence, or sought to become the best, we had to have some girls better than the pretty numskulls who are content to take simple jobs in which they are no more than living stage properties.

'I found one in Peru, a great beauty indeed but not far evolved in the European sense; a lovely animal. I bought her, to be frank. You can still buy people, you know, if you understand how to go about it. You don't go to a peasant father and say, "Sell me your daughter"; you say, "I can open up a splendid future for your daughter, that will make her a rich lady with many pairs of shoes, and as I realize you need her to work at home, I hope you won't be offended if I offer you five hundred American dollars to recompense you for the loss." He isn't offended; not in the least. And you make sure he puts his mark on an official-looking piece of paper that apprentices the girl to you, to learn a trade – in this case the trade of sempstress, because actress has a bad sound if there is any trouble. And there you are. You wash the girl, teach her to stand still on stage and do what she is told, and you clout her over the ear if she is troublesome. Quite soon she thinks she is a great deal more important than she really is, but that can be endured.

'Faustina was a thrill on the stage, because she really was stunningly beautiful, and for a while it seemed to be good business to let curious people think she was Magnus's mistress; only a few rather perceptive people know that great magicians, as opposed to ham conjurors, don't have mistresses. In reality, Faustina was my mistress, but we kept that quiet, in case some clamorous moralist should make a fuss about it. In Latin America, in particular, the clergy are pernickety about such things. You remember Faustina, Ramsay? I recall you had a wintry yearning toward her yourself.'

'Don't be disagreeable, Liesl,' I said. 'You know who destroyed that.'

'Destroyed it, certainly, and greatly enriched you in the process,' said Liesl, and touched me gently with one of her enormous hands.

'So there you have it, gentlemen,' she continued. 'Now you know everything, it seems to me.'

'Not everything,' said Ingestree. 'The name, Magnus Eisengrim – whose inspiration was that?'

'Mine,' said Liesl. 'Did I tell you I took my degree at the University of Zürich? Yes, in the faculty of philosophy where I leaned toward what used to be called philology – quite a Teutonic speciality. So of course I was acquainted with the great beast-legends of Europe, and in Reynard the Fox, you know, there is the great wolf Eisengrim, whom everyone fears, but who is not such a bad fellow, really. Just the name for a magician, don't you think?'

'And your name,' said Lind. 'Liselotte Vitzlipützli? You were always named on the programmes as Theatre Autocrat – Liselotte Vitzlipützli.'

'Ah, yes. Somebody has to be an autocrat in an affair of that kind, and it sounds better and is more frank than simply Manager. Anyhow, I wasn't quite a manager : I was the boss. It was my money, you see. But I knew my place. Manager I might be, but without Magnus Eisengrim I was nothing. Consequently – Vitzlipützli. You understand?'

'No, gnädiges Fräulein, I do not understand,' said Lind, 'and you know I do not understand. What I am beginning to understand is that you are capable of giving your colleagues Eisengrim and Ramsay a thoroughly difficult time when it is your whim. So again – Vitzlipützli?'

'Dear, dear, how ignorant people are in this supposedly brilliant modern world,' said Liesl. 'You surely know *Faust*? Not Goethe's *Faust*, of course; every Teuton has that by heart – both parts of it – but the old German play on which he based his poem. Look among the characters there, and you will find that the least of the demons attending on the great magician is Vitzlipützli. So that was the name I chose. A delicate compliment to Magnus. It takes a little of the sting out of the word Autocrat.

'But an autocrat is what I must be now. Gentlemen, we have talked for a long time, and I hope we have given you your subtext. You have seen what a gulf lies between the reality of a magician with the Magian World View and such a pack of lies as Robert-Houdin's bland, bourgeois memoirs. You have seen, too, what a distance there is between the pack of lies Ramsay wrote so artfully as a commercial life of our dear Eisengrim, and the sad little boy from Deptford. And now, we must travel tomorrow, and I must pack my two old gentlemen off to their beds, or they will not be happy for the plane. So it is time to say good night.'

Profuse thanks for hospitality, for the conversation, for the pleasure of working together on the film *Un Hommage à Robert-Houdin*, from Lind. A rather curious exchange of friendly words and handshakes between Eisengrim and Roland Ingestree. The business of waking Kinghovn from a drunken stupor, of getting him to understand that he must not have another brandy before going home. And then, at last, we three went by ourselves.

'Strange to spend so many hours answering questions,' said Liesl.

'Strange, and disagreeable,' said Eisengrim.

'Strange what questions went unasked and unanswered,' said I.

'Such as –?' said Liesl.

'Such as "Who Killed Boy Staunton?" ' said I.

3

Le Lit
de Justice

I

'You know the police in Toronto are still not satisfied that you told them all you know about Staunton's death?'

'I told them all I thought proper.'

'Which wasn't everything?'

'Certainly not. The police must work with facts, not fancies and suppositions. The facts were simple. I met him, for the first time in my life, when I visited you at your school in Toronto on the night of 3 November 1968; we went to your room and had a talk that lasted less than an hour. I accepted his offer to drive me back to my hotel. We chatted for a time, because we were both Deptford boys. I last saw him as he drove away from the hotel door.'

'Yes. And he was found less than three hours later in the harbour, into which he appeared to have driven in his powerful car, and when the police recovered the body they found a stone in his mouth.'

'So I understand.'

'If that had been all there was to it, would the police still be wondering about you?'

'No indeed.'

'It was my fault,' said Liesl. 'If I had been more discreet, the police would have been satisfied with what Magnus told them. But one has one's pride as an artist, you know, and when I was asked a question I thought I could answer effectively I did so, and then the fat was in the fire.'

Would anyone who saw us at this moment have thought we were talking about murder? I was convinced that Magnus had murdered Staunton, and with reason. Was not Staunton the initiator of most of what we had heard in the subtext of the life of Magnus Eisengrim? If, when both he and I were ten years old, Percy Boyd Staunton had not thrown a snowball at me, which had instead hit Mrs Amasa Dempster, bringing about the premature birth of her son Paul and robbing her of her wits, would I at this moment be in bed with Magnus Eisengrim and Liselotte Vitzlipützli in the Savoy Hotel, discussing Staunton's death?

We had come to this because we were inclined to share a bed when we had anything important to talk about. People who think of beds only in terms of sexual exercise or sleep simply do not understand that a bed is the best of all places for a philosophical discussion, an argument, and if necessary a showdown. It was not by chance that so many kings of old administered justice from their beds, and even today there is something splendidly parliamentary about an assembly of concerned persons in a bed.

Of course it must be a big bed. The Savoy had outfitted Magnus's room with two splendid beds, each of which was easily capable of accommodating three adults without undue snuggling. (The Savoy is above the meanness of 'single' beds.) So there we were, at the end of our long day of confession and revelation, lying back against the ample pillows, Liesl in the middle, Magnus on her left, and I on her right. He wore a handsome dressing-gown and a scarf he twisted around his head when he slept, because he had a European fear of draughts. I am a simple man; a man of blue pyjamas. Liesl liked filmy night-robes, and she was a delightful person to be in bed with because she was so warm. As I grow older I fuss about the cold, and for some reason I feel the cold for an hour or so after I have removed my artificial leg, as of course I had done before climbing in with them. My chilly stump was next to Liesl.

There we lay, nicely tucked up. I had my usual glass of hot milk and rum, Liesl had a balloon glass of cognac, and Magnus, always eccentric, had the glass of warm water and lemon juice without which he thought he could not sleep. I am sure we looked charmingly domestic, but my frame of mind was that of the historian on a strong scent and eager for the kill. If ever I was to get the confession that would complete my document – the document which would in future enable researchers to write 'Ramsay says ...' with authority – it would be before we slept. If Magnus would not tell me what I wanted to know, surely I might get it from Liesl?

'Consider the circumstances,' she said. 'It was the final Saturday night of our two weeks' engagement at the Royal Alexandra Theatre in Toronto; we had never taken the *Soirée of Illusions* there before and we were a huge success. By far our most effective illusion was *The Brazen Head of Friar Bacon*, second to last on the programme.

'Consider how it worked, Ramsay: the big pretend-brass Head hung in the middle of the stage, and after it had identified a number of objects of which nobody but the owners could have had knowledge, it gave three pieces of advice. That was always the thing that took most planning; the Head would say, "I am speaking to Mademoiselle Such-A-One, who is sitting in Row F, number 32." (We always called members of the audience Madame and Monsieur and so forth because it gave a tiny bit of elegance to the occasion in an English-speaking place.) Then I would give Mademoiselle Such-A-One a few words that would make everybody prick up their ears, and might even make Mademoiselle squeal with surprise. Of course we picked up the gossip around town, through an advance agent, or the company manager might get a hint of it in the foyer, or even by doing a little snooping in handbags and pocket-books – he was a very clever old dip we valued for this talent. I was the Voice of the Head, because I have a talent for making a small piece of information go a long way.

'We had, in the beginning, decided never to ask for questions from the audience. Too dangerous. Too hard to answer effectively. But on that Saturday night somebody shouted from the gallery – we know who it was, it was Staunton's son David, who was drunk as a fiddler's bitch and almost out of his mind about his father's death – "Who killed Boy Staunton?"

'Ramsay, what would you have done? What would you expect me to do? You know me; am I one to shy away from a

846

challenge? And there it was: a very great challenge. In an instant I had what seemed to me an inspiration – just right in terms of the Brazen Head, that's to say; just right in terms of the best magic show in the world. Magnus had been talking to me about the Staunton thing all week; he had told me everything Staunton had said to him. Was I to pass up that chance? Ramsay, use your imagination!

'I signalled to the electrician to bring up the warm lights on the Head, to make it glow, and I spoke into the microphone, giving it everything I could of mystery and oracle, and I said – you remember what I said – *He was killed by the usual cabal: by himself, first of all; by the woman he knew; by the woman he did not know; by the man who granted his inmost wish; and by the inevitable fifth, who was keeper of his conscience and keeper of the stone.* You remember how well it went.'

'Went well! Liesl, is that what you call going well?'

'Of course; the audience went wild. There was greater excitement in that theatre than the *Soirée* had ever known. It took a long time to calm them down and finish the evening with *The Vision of Dr Faustus*. Magnus wanted to bring the curtain down then and there. He had cold feet –'

'And with reason,' said Magnus; 'I thought the cops would be down on us at once. I was never so relieved in my life as when we got on the plane to Copenhagen the following morning.'

'You call yourself a showman; It was a triumph!'

'A triumph for you, perhaps. Do you remember what happened to me?'

'Poor Ramsay, you had your heart attack, there in the theatre. Right-hand upper stage box, where you had been lurking. I saw you fall forward through the curtains and sent someone to take care of you at once. But would you grudge that in the light of the triumph for the *Soirée*? It wasn't much of a heart attack, now, was it? Just a wee warning that you should be careful about excitement. And were you the only one? Staunton's son took it very badly. And Staunton's wife! As soon as she heard about it – which she did within an hour – she forgot her role as grieving widow and was after us with all the police support she could muster, which luckily wasn't enthusiastic. After all, what could they charge us with? Not even fortune-telling, which is always the thing one has to keep clear of. But any triumph is bound to bring about a few casualties. Don't be small, Ramsay.'

I took a pull at my rum and milk, and reflected on the consuming vanity of performers: Magnus, a monster of vanity, which he said he had learned from Sir John Tresize; and Liesl, not one whit less vain, to whom a possible murder, a near-riot in a theatre, an outraged family, and my heart attack – *mine* – were mere sparks from the anvil on which she had hammered out her great triumph. How does one cope with such people?

One doesn't; one thanks God they exist. Liesl was right; I mustn't be small. But if I was allowed my own egoism, I must have the answers I wanted. This was by no means the first time the matter of the death of Boy Staunton had come up among the three of us. On earlier occasions Magnus had put me aside with jokes and evasions, and when Liesl was present she stood by him in doing so; they both knew that I was deeply convinced that somehow Magnus had sent Staunton to his death, and they loved to keep me in doubt. Liesl said it was good for me not to have an answer to every question I asked, and my burning historian's desire to gather and record facts she pretended to regard as mere nosiness.

It was now or never. Magnus had opened up to the film-makers as he had never done to anyone – Liesl knew a little, I presume, but certainly her knowledge of his past was far from complete – and I wanted my answers while the confessional mood was still strong in him. Press on, Ramsay: even if they hate you for it now, they'll get cool in the same skins they got hot in.

One way of getting right answers is to venture a few wrong answers yourself. 'Let me have a try at identifying the group you called "the usual cabal",' I said. 'He was killed by himself, because it was he who drove his car off the dock; the woman he did not know, I should say, was his first wife, whom I think I knew quite well, and certainly he did not know her nearly so well; the woman he did know was certainly his second wife; he came to know her uncomfortably well, and if ever a man stuck his foot in a bear-trap when he thought he was putting it into a flower-bed, it was Boy Staunton when he married Denyse Hornick; the man who granted his inmost wish I suppose must have been you, Magnus, and I am sure you know what is in my mind – you hypnotized poor Boy, stuck that stone in his mouth, and headed him for death. How's that?'

'I'm surprised by the crudeness of your suspicions, Dunny. "I am become as a bottle in the smoke: yet do I fear thy statutes." One of those statutes forbids murder. Why would I kill Staunton?'

'Vengeance, Magnus, vengeance!'

'Vengeance for what?'

'For what? Can you ask that after what you have told us about your life? Vengeance for your premature birth and your mother's madness. For your servitude to Willard and Abdullah and all those wretched years with the World of Wonders. Vengeance for the deprivation that made you the shadow of Sir John Tresize. Vengeance for a wrench of fate that cut you off from ordinary love, and made you an oddity. A notable oddity, I admit, but certainly an oddity.'

'Oh, Dunny, what a coarsely melodramatic mind you have! Vengeance! If I had been as big an oddity as you are I would have embraced Boy Staunton and thanked him for what he had done for me. The means may have been a little rough, but the result is entirely to my taste. If he hadn't hit my mother on the head with that snowball – having hidden a rock in it, which was dirty play – I might now be what my father was: a Baptist parson in a small town. I have had my ups and downs, and the downs were very far down indeed, but I am now a celebrity in a limited way, and I am a master of a craft, which is a better thing by far. I am a more complete human being than you are, you old fool. I may not have had a very happy sex-life, but I certainly have love and friendship, and much of the best of that is in bed with me at this moment. I have admiration, which everybody wants and very few people achieve. I get my living by doing what I most enjoy, and that is rare indeed. Who gave me my start? Boy Staunton! Would I murder such a man? It is to his early intervention in my life I owe what Liesl calls the Magian World View.

'Vengeance, you cry. If anybody wanted vengeance, it was you, Dunny. You lived near Staunton all your life, watched him, brooded over him, saw him destroy that silly girl you wanted – or thought you wanted – and ill-wished him a thousand times. You're the man of vengeance. I never wanted vengeance in my life for anything.'

'Magnus! Remember how you withheld death from Willard when he begged for it! What did you do today to poor Roly Ingestree? Don't you call that vengeance?'

'I admit I toyed with Roly. He hurt people I loved. But if he hadn't come back into my life by chance I should never have bothered about him. I didn't harbour evidence of his guilt for sixty years, as you harboured that stone Staunton put in the snowball.'

'Don't twist, Magnus! When you and Staunton left my room at the College to go back to your hotel you took that stone, and when next it was seen the police had to pry it out of poor Staunton's jaws, where it was clenched so tight they had to break his teeth to get at it!'

'I didn't take the stone, Dunny; Staunton took it himself.'

'Did he?'

'Yes. I saw him. You were putting your box back in the bookshelves. The box that contained my mother's ashes. Dunny, what on earth made you keep those ashes? It was ghoulish.'

'I couldn't bear to part with them. Your mother was a very special figure in my life. To me she was a saint. Not just a good woman, but a saint, and the influence she had in my life was miraculous.'

'So you've often told me, but I knew her only as a madwoman. I had stood at the window of our miserable house trying not to cry while Boy Staunton and his gang shouted "Hoor!" as they passed on their way to school.'

'Yes, and you let the police think you had never met him until the night he died.'

'Perfectly true. I knew who he was, when he was fifteen and I was five. He was the Rich Young Ruler in our village, as you well know. But we had never been formally introduced until you brought us together, and I presumed that was what the police were talking about.'

'A quibble.'

'An evasion, possibly. But I was answering questions, not

instructing my questioners. I was working on advice given me long ago by Mrs Constantinescu: don't blat everything you know, especially to cops.'

'You didn't tell them you knew that Boy had been appointed Lieutenant-Governor of the province when nobody else knew it.'

'Everybody knew it was in the air. I knew it the second night he came to the theatre, because he had the letter of appointment in the inner pocket of his handsome dinner jacket. Liesl has told you we had a member of our troupe – our company manager – who welcomed important patrons in the foyer. I suppose our man found out that the rumour had become a fact by means which I always thought it better not to investigate too closely. So I knew. And the Brazen Head could have spilled the beans that evening, from the stage, but Liesl and I thought it might be just a teeny bit indiscreet.'

'That was another thing you didn't tell the police. Boy Staunton came twice to the *Soirée of Illusions*.'

'Lots of people used to come twice. And three and four times. It's a very good show. But you're right; Staunton came to see me. He was interested in me in the way people used to be interested in Sir John. I suppose there was something about my personality, as there was about Sir John's, that had a special attraction for some people. My personality is a valuable part of our bag of tricks, as you very well know.'

Indeed I did. And how it had come pressing off the screen in *Un Hommage à Robert-Houdin*! I had always thought personal attributes lost something in the cinema; it seemed reasonable that a photograph of a man should be less striking than the man himself. But not when the art of Lind and that rumpot of genius Kinghovn lay behind the photograph. I had sat in the little viewing-room at the B.B.C. entranced by what I saw of a Magnus more vivid than ever I had seen him on the stage. True, his performance was a tiny bit stagey, considered as cinematic acting, but it was a staginess of such grace, such distinction and accomplishment, that nobody could have wished it otherwise. As I watched I remembered what used to be said of stage favourites when I was a boy: they were *polished*. They had enviable repose. They did nothing quite the way anyone else did it, and they had an attitude toward their audiences which was,

quite apart from the role they were playing, splendidly courteous, as if a great man were taking friendly notice of us. I had
thought of this when Magnus told us how Sir John accepted
applause when he made his first entrance in *Scaramouche*, and
later gave those curtain-speeches all across Canada, which
seemed to embrace audiences of people who yearned mutely for
such attention. Magnus had this polish in the highest and most
subtle degree, and I could understand how Boy Staunton, who
was a lifelong hero-worshipper and had not got it out of his
system even at the age of seventy, would have responded to it.

Polish! How Boy had honed and yearned after polish! What
idols he had worshipped! And as a Lieutenant-Governor elect I
could imagine how he coveted what Magnus displayed on the
stage. A Lieutenant-Governor with that sort of distinction – that
would astonish the Rubes!

We were silent for a while. But I was full of questions, mad
for certainties even though I understood there were no certainties. I broke the silence.

'If you weren't the man who granted his inmost wish, who
was it? I have swallowed the pill that I was "the inevitable fifth,
who was keeper of his conscience and keeper of the stone" –
though I accept that only as Liesl's oracular phraseology. But
who granted his wish? And what was the wish?'

This time it was Liesl who spoke. 'It could very well have
been his son, Ramsay. Don't forget David Staunton, who represented continuance to his father. Have you no understanding
of how some men crave for continuance? They see it as their
immortality. Boy Staunton who had built up the great fortune,
from a few fields of sugar-beets to a complex of business that
was known all over the world. You must pardon my nationalist
bias, but it is significant that when Staunton died – or killed himself, as it was supposed – his death was reported at some length
in our *Neue Zürcher Zeitung*. That paper, like the London *Times*,
recognizes only the most distinguished achievements of the
Angel of Death. Their obituary columns are almost the Court
Circular of the Kingdom of God. Well, who inherits an important man's earthly glory? People like Staunton hope it will be a
son.

'A son Staunton had, we know. But what a son! Not a disgrace. One might find the spaciousness of tragedy in a disgrace. David Staunton was a success; a notable criminal lawyer, but also a sharp critic of his father's life. A man whose cold eye watched the glorious Boy growing older, and richer, and more powerful, and was not impressed. A man who did not admire or seek to emulate his father's great success with women. A man who understood, by tie of blood and by a child's intuition, the terrible, unappeasable hunger that lies at the bottom of ambition like Boy Staunton's. I don't know whether David ever understood that consciously; but he thwarted his father's terrible craving to be everything, command everything, and possess everything, and he did it in the way that hurt most: he refused to produce a successor to himself. He refused to continue the Staunton line and the Staunton name and the glory that was Staunton. That was pressing the knife into the vital spot. But don't jump to conclusions: the man who granted his inmost wish wasn't David Staunton.'

'Aren't you doing a lot of fancy guessing?'

'No. Staunton told Magnus and Magnus told me.'

'It was one of those situations Liesl is always talking about,' said Eisengrim. 'You know: a man reaches the confessional time in his life. Sometimes he writes an autobiography; sometimes he tells his story to a group of listeners, as I have been doing. Sometimes there is only one listener, and that was how it was with Staunton.

'Surely you remember what it was like-in your room that night of November 3? Staunton and I had clicked, in the way people sometimes do. He wanted to know me: I was more than commonly interested in him because he was from my past, and not at all what one would have predicted for the fattish, purse-proud kid who had shouted "Hoor" at my mother. You understood that we'd clicked, and you didn't like it at all. That was when you decided to spill the beans, and told Staunton who I was, how he had literally brought about my birth, how you knew about the rock in the snowball and had kept it all those years. You even had my mother's ashes in a casket. And through it all Staunton was cool as a cucumber. Denied everything that he had not – quite honestly, I believe – forgotten. Chose to regard the whole affair as something only very remotely connected with himself. Considering the way you went at him, I thought he showed enviable self-possession. But he said some sharp things about you.

'When we were in his car, driving down the long avenue from the school, he expanded on what he'd said. He cursed you very thoroughly, Dunny. Told me that for boyhood friendship he had kept an eye on your money all through the years, and made you secure and even well-off. Befriended you and brought you to the notice of really important people – people in a very big way of business – as a guest in his house. Confided in you when his first marriage was going on the rocks, and was patient when you sided with his wife. Put up with your ironic attitude toward his success, because he knew it had its root in jealousy.

'He was offended that you never mentioned Mary Dempster – he never spoke of her as my mother – and her long years in asylums; he would have been glad to help a Deptford woman who had come to grief. And he was angry and hurt that you kept that damned stone on your desk to remind you of a grudge you had against him. A stone in a snowball! The kind of thing any boy might do, just for devilment. He would never have thought the dark, judgmatical Ramsay blood in you was so bitter with hate – you, who had made money out of saints!

'It was then I began to know him. Oh yes, I came to know him quite well during the next hour. We'd clicked, as I said, but I've always distrusted that kind of thing since I first clicked with Willard. It's unchancy. There was sympathy of character, I suppose. There was a wolfishness in Boy Staunton that he kept very well under, and probably never recognized in himself. But I know that wolfishness. Liesl has told you I have a good measure of it in myself, and that was why she suggested I take the professional name of Eisengrim, the name of the wolf in the old fables; but the name really means the sinister hardness, the cruelty of iron itself. I took the name, and recognized the fact, and thereby got it up out of my depths so that at least I could be aware of it and take a look at it, now and then. I won't say I domesticated the wolf, but I knew where his lair was, and what he might do. Not Boy Staunton. He had lived facing the sun, and he had no real comprehension of the shadow-wolf that loped after him.

854

'We wolves like to possess things, and especially people. We are unappeasably hungry. There is no reason or meaning in the hunger. It just exists, and possesses you. I saw it once, in myself, and though I didn't know what it was at the time, I knew that it was something that was at the very heart of my being. When we played *Scaramouche* through Canada, I had a little meeting with Sir John, every night, just before Two, two; we had to stand in front of a mirror, to make sure every detail of costume and make-up was identical, so that when I appeared as his double the illusion would be as perfect as possible. I always enjoyed that moment, because I am wolfish about perfection.

'There we stood, the night I speak of; it was in Ottawa, in his dressing-room at the old Russell, and we had a good mirror, a full-length one. He looked, and I looked. I saw that he was good. An egoist, as only a leading actor can be, but in his face, which was old under the make-up, there was gentleness and compassion toward me, because I was young, and had so much to learn, and was so likely to make a fool of myself through my driving greed. Compassion for me, and a silvery relish for himself, too, because he knew he was old, and had the mastery of age. But in my face, which was so like his that my doubling gave the play a special excitement, there was a watchful admiration beneath which my wolfishness could be seen – my hunger not just to be like him but to *be* him, whatever that might cost him. I loved him and served him faithfully right up to the end, but in my inmost self I wanted to eat him, to possess him, to make him mine.

'He saw it, too, and he gave me a little flick with his hand as though to say, "You might let me live out my life, m'boy. I've earned it, eh? But you look as if you'd devour my very soul. Not really necessary, quonk?" Not a word was spoken, but I blushed under my make-up. And whatever I did for him afterward, I couldn't keep the wolf quiet. If I was a little sharp with Roly, it was because I was angry that he had seen what I truly thought I had kept hidden.

'That was how it was with Boy Staunton. Oh, not on the surface. He had a lovely glaze. But he was a devourer.

'He set to work to devour me. He went at it with the ease of long custom, and I don't suppose he had an instant's real awareness of what he was doing. He laid himself out to be charming, and to get me on his side. When he had finished damning you, Dunny, he began to excuse you, in a way that was supposed to be complimentary to me: you had lived a narrow, schoolmaster's life, and had won a certain scholarly reputation, but he and I were the glittering successes and breathed a finer air than yours.

'He was extremely good at what he was doing. It is not easy to assume an air of youth successfully, but when it is well done it has extraordinary charm, because it seems to rock Age, and probably Death, back on their heels. He had kept his voice youthful, and his vocabulary was neither stupidly up-to-the-minute nor flawed with betraying fossil slang. I had to keep reminding myself that this man must be seventy. I have to present a professional picture of physical well-being, if not actually of youth, and I know how it is done because I learned it from Sir John. But Boy Staunton – an amateur, really – could teach me things about seeming youthful without resorting to absurdities. I knew he was eager to make me his own, to enchant me, to eat me up and take me into himself. He had just discovered a defeat; he thought he had eaten you, Ramsay, but you were like those fairy-tale figures who cut their way out of the giant's belly.

'So, not at all unlike a man who loses one girl and bounces to another, he tried to eat me.

'We really must talk, he said. We were driving down from your school to my hotel, and as we were rounding Queen's Park Circle he pulled off the road into what I suppose was a private entry beside the Legislature; there was a porte-cochère and a long flight of steps. It won't be long before this is my personal entrance to this building, he said.

'I knew what he was talking about: the appointment that would be announced next morning; he was full of it.'

'I'll bet he was,' I said; 'it was just his thing – top dog in a large area – women curtsying to him – all that. And certainly his wife wanted it, and engineered it.'

'Yes, but wait: having got it, he wasn't so sure. If you are one of the wolfish brotherhood you sometimes find that you have no sooner achieved what you wanted than you begin to despise it.

Boy's excitement was like that of a man who thinks he has walked into a trap.'

'Well, the job isn't all fun. What ceremonial appointment is? You drive to the Legislature in a carriage, with soldiers riding before and behind, and there is a lot of bowing, because you represent the Crown, and then you find you are reading a speech written by somebody else, announcing policies you may not like. If he didn't want to be a State figurehead, he should have choked off Denyse when she set to work to get him the job.'

'Reason, reason, reason! Dunny, you surely know how limited a part reason plays in some of our most important decisions. He coveted the state landau and the soldiers, and he had somehow managed to preserve the silly notion that as Lieutenant-Governor he would really do some governing. But already he knew he was mistaken. He had looked over the schedule of duties for his first month in office, and been dismayed by the places he would have to go, and the things he would have to do. Presenting flags to Boy Scouts; opening a home for old people; eating a hundredweight of ceremonial dinners to raise money to fight diseases he'd rather not hear about. And he couldn't get out of it; his secretary made it clear that there was no choice in the matter; the office demanded these things and he was expected to deliver the goods. But that wasn't what truly got under his skin.

'Such appointments aren't done in a few days, and he had known it was coming for several weeks. During that time he had some business in London and while he was there he had thought it a good idea to take care of the matter of his ceremonial uniform. That was how he put it, but as a fellow-wolf I knew how eager he must have been to explore the possibilities of state finery. So – off to Ede and Ravenscroft to have the job done in the best possible way and no expense spared. They happened to have a uniform of the right sort which he tried on, just to get the general effect. Even though it was obvious that the uniform was for a smaller man, the effect was catastrophic. "Suddenly I didn't look like myself at all," he said; "I looked old. Not shaky old, or fat old, or grim old, but certainly old."

'He expected me to sympathize, but wolf should never turn to wolf for sympathy. "You are old," I said to him. "Very handsome and well preserved, but nobody would take you for a young man." "Yes," he said, "but not old as that uniform suggested; not a figurehead. I tried putting the hat a little on one side, to see if that helped, but the man with the measuring-tape around his neck who was with me said, *Oh no, sir; never like that*, and put it straight again. And I understood that forever after there would always be somebody putting my hat straight, and that I would be no more than the animation of that uniform, or some version of it.

'As one who had spent seven years as the cunning bowels of Abdullah I didn't see that fate quite as he did. Of course, Abdullah wasn't on the level. He was out to trounce the Rubes. A Lieutenant-Governor can't have any fun of that kind. He is the embodiment of everything that is correct, and on the level, and unsurprising. The Rubes have got him and he must do their will.

' "I have lost my freedom of choice," he said, and he seemed to expect me to respond with horror. But I didn't. I was enjoying myself. Boy Staunton was an old story to you, Dunny, but he was new to me, and I was playing the wolf game, too, in my way. I had not forgotten Mrs Constantinescu, and I knew that he was ready to talk, and I was ready to hear. So I remembered old Zingara's advice. Lull 'em. So I lulled him.

' "I can see that you're in a situation you never would have chosen with your eyes open. But there's usually some way out. Is there no way out for you?"

' "Even if I found a way, what would happen if I suddenly bowed out?" he said.

' "I suppose you'd go on living much as you do now," I told him. "There would be criticism of you because you refused an office you had accepted, under the Crown. But I dare say that's been done before."

'I swear I had nothing in particular in mind when I made that comment. But it galvanized him. He looked at me as if I had said something of extraordinary value. Then he said: "Of course it was different for him; he was younger."

' "What do you mean?" I said.

'He looked at me very queerly. "The Prince of Wales," he said; "he was my friend, you know. Or rather, you don't know.

858

But many years ago, when he toured this country, I was his aide, and he had a profound effect on me. I learned a great deal from him. He was special, you know; he was truly a remarkable man. He showed it at the time of the Abdication. That took guts."

' "Called for guts from several of his relatives, too," I said. "Do you think he lived happily ever after?"

' "I hope so," said he. "But he was younger."

' "I've said you were old," said I, "but I didn't mean life had nothing for you. You are in superb condition. You can expect another fifteen years, at least, and think of all the things you can do."

' "And think of all the things I can't do," he said, and in a tone that told me what I had suspected, because with all the fine surface, and bonhomie, and his careful wooing of me I had sensed something like despair in him.

' "I suppose you mean sex," I said.

' "Yes," he said. "Not that I'm through, you know; by no means. But it isn't the same. Now it's more reassurance than pleasure. And young women – they have to be younger and younger – they're flattered because of what I am and who I am, but there's always a look you surprise when they don't think you're watching : He's-amazing-for-his-age-I-wonder-what-I'd-do-if-he-had-a-heart-attack-would-I-have-to-drag-him-out-into-the-hall-and-leave-him-by-the-elevator-and-how-would-I-get-his-clothes-on? However well I perform – and I'm still good, you know – there's an element of humiliation about it."

'Humiliation was much on his mind. The humiliation of age, which you and I mustn't underestimate, Dunny, just because we've grown old and made our age serve us; it's a different matter if you've devoted your best efforts to setting up an image of a wondrous Boy; there comes a time when the pretty girls think of you not as a Boy but as an Old Boy. The humiliation of discovering you've been a mug, and that the gorgeous office you've been given under the Crown is in fact a tyranny of duty, like the Crown itself. And the humiliation of discovering that a man you've thought of as a friend – rather a humble, eccentric friend from your point of view, but nevertheless a friend – has been harbouring evidence of a mean action you did when you were ten, and still sees you, at least in part, as a mean kid.

'That last was a really tough one – disproportionately so – but Boy was the kind of man who truly believes you can wipe out the past simply by forgetting it yourself. I'm sure he'd met humiliations in his life. Who hasn't? But he'd been able to rise above them. These were humiliations nothing could lift from his heart.

' "What are you going to do with the stone?" I asked him.

' "You saw me take it?" he said. "I'll get rid of it. Throw it away."

' "I wouldn't throw it a second time," I said.

' "What else?" said he.

' "If it really bothers you, you must come to terms with it," I said. "In your place I'd do something symbolic: hold it in your hand, re-live the moment when you threw it at Ramsay and hit my mother, and this time *don't* throw it. Give yourself a good sharp knock on the head with it."

' "That's a damned silly game to play," he said. And would you believe it, he was pouting – the glorious Boy was pouting.

' "Not at all. Consider it as a ritual. An admission of wrongdoing and penitence."

' "Oh, balls to that," he said.

'I had become uncomfortable company: I wouldn't be eaten, and I made peculiar and humiliating suggestions. Also, I could tell that something was on his mind, and he wanted to be alone with it. He started the car and very shortly we were at my hotel – the Royal York, you know, which is quite near the docks. He shook hands with the warmth that I suppose had marked him all his life. "Glad to have met you: thanks for the advice," said he.

' "It's only what I would do myself, in the circumstances," I said. "I'd do my best to swallow that stone." Now I swear to you that I only meant what I said symbolically – meaning to come to terms with what the stone signified. And he seemed not to notice.

' "I meant your advice about the Abdication," he said. "It was stupid of me not to have thought of that myself."

'I suddenly realized what he meant. He was going to abdicate, like his hero before him. But unlike his Prince of Wales he didn't mean to live to face the world afterward. There it is, Dunny:

Liesl and I are convinced that the man who truly granted his inmost wish, though only by example, was the man who decided not to live as Edward VIII.

'What should I have done? Insisted that he come to my room, and plied him with hot coffee and sweet reasonableness? Not quite my line, eh? Hardly what one expects of a brother wolf, quonk?'

'You let him leave you in that frame of mind?'

'Liesl likes to talk about what she calls my Magian World View. She makes it sound splendid and like the Arabian Nights, and dolls it up with fine phrases from Spengler –'

'Phantasmagoria and dream-grotto,' said Liesl, taking a swig of her cognac; 'only that's not Spengler – that's Carlyle.'

'Phantasmagoria and dream-grotto if you like,' said Magnus, 'but – and it is a vital *but* – combined with a clear-eyed, undeluded observation of what lies right under your nose. Therefore – no self-deceiving folly and no meddlesome compassion, but a humble awareness of the Great Justice and the Great Mercy whenever they choose to make themselves known. I don't talk about a Magian World View; I've no touch with that sort of thing. In so far as it concerns me, I live it. It's just the way things strike me, after the life I've lived, which looks pretty much like a World of Wonders when I spread it out before me, as I've been doing. Everything has its astonishing, wondrous aspect, if you bring a mind to it that's really your own – a mind that hasn't been smeared and blurred with half-understood muck from schools, or the daily papers, or any other ragbag of reach-me-down notions. I try not to judge people, though when I meet an enemy and he's within arm's length, I'm not above giving him a smart clout, just to larn him. As I did with Roly. But I don't monkey with what I think of as the Great Justice –'

'Poetic justice,' said Liesl.

'What you please. Though it doesn't look poetic in action; it's rough and tough and deeply satisfying. And I don't administer it. Something else – something I don't understand, but feel and serve and fear – does that. It's sometimes horrible to watch, as it was when my poor, dear old master, Sir John, was brought down by his own vanity, and Milady went with him, though I think she knew what the truth was. But part of the glory and terror of our life is that somehow, at some time, we get all that's coming to us. Everybody gets their lumps and their bouquets and it goes on for quite a while after death.

'So – here was a situation when it was clear to me that the Great Justice had called the name of Boy Staunton. Was it for me to hold him back?

'And to be frank why would I? You remember what was said in your room that night, Dunny. You're the historian : surely you remember everything important? What did I say to Boy when he offered me a lift in his car?'

I couldn't remember. That night I had been too overwrought myself by the memories of Mary Dempster to take note of social conversation.

'You don't remember? I do: I said – "What Ramsay tells me puts you in my debt for eighty days in Paradise, if for nothing in this life. We shall call it quits if you will drive me to my hotel.'

'Eighty days in Paradise?'

'I was born eighty days before my time. Poor little Paul. Popular opinion is very rough on foetuses these days. Horrid little nuisances. Rip 'em out and throw them in the trash pail. But who knows what they feel about it? The depth psychologists Liesl is so fond of think they have a very jolly time in the womb. Warm, protected, bouncing gently in their beautiful grotto light. Perhaps it is the best existence we ever know, unless there is something equally splendid for us after death – and why not? That earliest life is what every humanitarian movement and Welfare State seeks to restore, without a hope of success. And Boy Staunton, by a single mean-spirited action, robbed me of eighty days of that princely splendour. Was I the man to fret about the end of his life when he had been so cavalier about the beginning of mine?'

'Oh, Magnus, that's terribly unjust.'

's this world's justice goes, perhaps. But what about the r Justice?'

Yes, I really do see. So you let him dree his weird?'

getting really old, Dunny. You're beginning to dredge ns from your Scotch childhood. But it says it all. dree his weird.'

'I can very well understand,' I said, 'that you wouldn't have got far explaining that to the police.'

Liesl laughed, and threw her empty brandy balloon against the farthest wall. It made a fine costly crash.

2

'RAMSAY.'

'Liesl! How kind of you to come to see me.'

'Magnus has been asleep for hours. But I have been worrying about you. I hope you didn't take it too badly – his suggestion that you played rather a crucial part in Staunton's death.'

'No, no; I faced that, and swallowed it even before I joined you in Switzerland. While I was recovering from my heart attack, indeed. In an old Calvinist like me the voice of conscience has always spoken long before any mortal accuser.'

'I'm glad. Glad that you're not grieving and worrying, that's to say.'

'Boy died as he lived: self-determined and daring, but not really imaginative. Always with a well-disguised streak of petulance that sometimes looked like malice. The stone in the snowball: the stone in the corpse's mouth – always a nasty surprise for somebody.'

'You think he gobbled the stone to spite you?'

'Unquestionably. Magnus thinks I kept the stone for spite, and I suppose there was something of that in it. But I also kept it to be a continual reminder of the consequences that can follow a single action. It might have come out that it was my paperweight, but even if it didn't, he knew I would know what it was, and Boy reckoned on having the last word in our life-long argument that way.'

'What a detestable man!'

'Not really. But it's always a good idea to keep your eye on the genial, smiling ones, and especially on those who seem to be eternally young.'

'Jealousy, Ramsay, you battered antique.'

'A little jealousy, perhaps. But the principle holds.'

'Is that what you are making notes about, on all that excellent Savoy notepaper?'

'Notes for a work I have in mind. But it's about Magnus; he told me, you know, that the Devil once intervened decisively in his life.'

'He likes to talk that way, and I am sure it is true. But life is a succession of decisive interventions. Magnus himself intervened in my life, and illuminated it, at a time when I needed an understanding friend even more than I needed a lover. It wasn't the Devil that sent him.'

'Why should it be? God wants to intervene in the world, and how is he to do it except through man? I think the Devil is in the same predicament. It would be queer, wouldn't it, if the Devil had only made use of Magnus that one time? And God, too: yes, certainly God as well. It's the moment of decision – of will – when those Two nab us, and as they both speak so compellingly it's tricky work to know who's talking. Where there's a will, there are always two ways.'

'That's what you're making notes about? And you hope to untangle it? What vanity!'

'I'm not expecting to untangle anything. But I'm making a record – a document. I've often talked to you about it. When we're all gone – you dear Liesl, though you're much the youngest, and Magnus – there may be a few who will still prove a point with "Ramsay says …"'

'Egoist!'